THE UNDEAD TWENTY-FIVE.
THE HEAT

RR HAYWOOD

1899 INC, LTD

Copyright © 2021 by RR Haywood

All rights reserved.

No part of this book may be reproduced in any form or by any electronic or mechanical means, including information storage and retrieval systems, without written permission from the author, except for the use of brief quotations in a book review.

The Undead and *The Living Army* are trademarks of RR Haywood.

PROLOGUE

The story so far…

Day Twenty-Eight

THEY START CLAMBERING into the Saxon.

Hot bodies in a hot tin can, but it feels like home to most of them.

The smell of it. The acoustics inside.

Howie looks around at Hinchley Point. The clifftop town overlooking the English Channel. A place once famous for its Mediterranean architecture and white-washed walls.

It's not anymore.

It's a place of ruin and death, and those once white houses now lie as broken and busted as the bodies strewn amongst them. Burn marks everywhere from the C4 explosives used by Carmen as she worked with Sergeant Blowers to draw his team back through the town.

Desperately defending the survivors gathered in the mosque at the rear.

They did well too.

They took thousands down and held the line while Lilly decided to make her play in the fort and force Henry to tell her where the Panacea was.

A great sadness fell upon Howie when Lilly did that.

He realised more than ever that he was fighting to protect a species that even at the end of the world still squabbled, lied, and fought one another. His own father being part of it all.

Howard worked with Henry. He was in charge of dealing with informants for The Office of Fiscal Studies. The codename for a clandestine unit working within Her Majesty's Treasury Department. Howie never knew that. He thought his father was an ordinary man that worked an ordinary job. That meant his father lied. His mother too.

They weren't the only lies.

There might be a vaccine, and if Howie was given a vaccine, then he might have passed it to his team. Except, it's not really a vaccine. It's some kind of mutated version of the infection.

Howie's not sure on that either. Howie isn't sure about a great many things, the least of which is why Lilly is being such a dick. She wants the cure. Why push for it like that? Why try and take something that can't be taken?

But then, she's only sixteen.

She's young, and Howie glances back at her at the same second as Mary seems to recover from the shock of seeing her uncle Peter executed by Henry.

'Ye marked, Henry. I swear it! Ye marked! You! And you! And you!' Mary screams out, pointing at them in turn. Her voice loud and filled with rage, making her accent stronger.

Howie stares at her, feeling jarred at the raw emotion, as the tears stream down Mary's face. She screams and fights to break free while a chill runs down his spine from the cold detachment in Lilly's eyes.

She doesn't look sixteen now. She looks ageless.

'And you, Howie,' Mary says. Her voice dropping low. 'My Uncle Pete fought for you. He stood at your side!'

'You held us hostage!' Paula yells, jumping from the back of the Saxon as Clarence rushes out to hold her back.

'Get Mary away,' Kyle orders, motioning at Willie and Elvis, but they don't look so happy either. None of them do. The shock of it is wearing off. The rage is coming back. 'It's just words, Henry,' Kyle adds, turning to his old CO.

Henry remains still. His own eyes fixed on Mary as he calculates the threat and risk with a look that Howie has seen before on Dave. Normally before he starts killing everything. 'I've given my terms,' Henry says. 'George will be taking control of the fort.'

'Ye can't send George back now, Henry,' Kyle says. 'Not after this.'

'Aye. It's fine, Father,' Mary says with tears rolling down her face. 'We'll take the old fella back with us. And we'll bring his fecking head in a box when we come looking for you. An eye for an eye. And his wife is still there, is she not?'

'Don't you fucking dare!' Paula yells as Clarence starts dragging her away while Cookey and the lads bundle out of the Saxon, filling the air with shouts and yells.

Howie opens his mouth, ready to order his team back, but a sudden nag stops him before he can give the order, and he wonders why Henry, a skilled commander of an elite covert team, would order George to the fort in the first place. Henry's no fool. He knows that by killing Peter he'll create a grudge, and the travellers are the type to never let that grudge go. Mary just said it. *An eye for an eye.*

Why expose George to that risk for a fort that has no real strategic value?

He catches Reginald's eye, with both showing they are thinking hard. Maddox at Reginald's back. Ready to protect him, and the sight of him makes that nag in the back of Howie's head scream louder.

Maddox has natural immunity. A glance to Mary. To Willie and Elvis. They have natural immunity too. They can't get infected.

A series of lightbulbs ping one after the other in Howie's head as Reginald makes the same connection.

The immunes, Reginald mouths.

Howie nods. Heather has a list of immune people. She's out there now. Searching for them with orders to take them back to the fort for protection – because it's not the fort Henry wants. It's the immune people, and the realisation forms a split second later that Henry didn't kill Peter for revenge.

That wasn't payback.

That was a fucking coup.

Henry took Peter out to create a power vacuum.

The travellers are patriarchal. And with Peter dead, they won't accept Mary as a leader. It'll be Willie or Elvis. Maybe Patrick or Tyson.

It will be whoever Henry and George choose to be in charge. That's why George is going back with them. He'll negotiate and pacify with skilled diplomacy, while all the time holding the threat of annihilation over their heads.

Henry can come back.

You don't want that.

Henry will kill you all.

Not only that, but George is Paula's uncle.

Marion is her aunt.

Killing them is hurting one of Howie's family and risking his wrath, and every person in that fort knows what Howie is capable of, and they'll all know about the kiss too.

Everyone in the mosque saw Marcy kiss the survivors and turn them. That's why Henry has left some of the travellers alive; so they'll go back and tell the others what they saw.

A feeling inside of Howie. A sense of disgust that he's just been weaponised against his will, and without his knowledge. But then, power corrupts. It always will. Henry wants the fort. Lilly wants the fort. Fuck the fort. Fuck them too.

'That's enough,' he calls out, ordering his team back, but they shout on, giving abuse and threats to Mary and her kin. Faces twisted in rage and anger. Grudges galore being thrown about like grenades. 'I said enough!' he snaps the words out, harsh and angry, and gaining instant compliance from Blowers who double-takes at the look on Howie's face as they start falling silent.

Everyone does, and that surge of anger radiates out from Howie. Touching them all through whatever hive mind they have. Meredith starts to growl. Moving in next to Howie, flicking her lips up to show Henry her teeth. To show Mary and the others. Faces harden. Blowers and Cookey. Nick and Mo Mo. Booker and Danny. Charlie. Tappy. Marcy. Clarence. Roy. Reginald too, and right there, in the middle of them all, stands Dave, with his pistol already drawn and held at his side.

A shift in power. A shift in focus. Mary swallows. Willie and Elvis glance at each other. Seeing the violence Howie has now aiming at them as the dog growls louder and deeper, and Jess kicks the back of the horsebox, shaking the frame.

'This is not our way,' Howie says. His words meant for Henry. For Lilly and for his own team too, at being drawn into their shit.

'Get loaded,' Clarence orders. 'Tappy, get in the back. The boss will drive.'

The big man stands his ground, waiting for the others to load up. Nobody speaks, and the people in the mosque slowly ease out from the shadows to view their once perfect town, now lying in ruins, and the thousands of spent casings glinting in the evening sun amongst the thousands of corpses.

Smoke drifting from fires. Heat, and the stench of chemicals and innards. Shit and death, and blood.

Only Marcy moves. Stepping over to Howie. Placing a hand on his shoulder, turning him away. She watches him head for the front and steps up into the back of the Saxon. Holding the doors open for Meredith to jump in. A last look out to Lilly. To Mary and everyone else.

The engine starts. Deep and throaty. The wheels start moving. Crunching stones. Crunching bones.

Hot bodies in a hot tin can.

They leave Hinchley Point behind. A place once famous for its Mediterranean architecture and white-washed walls.

It's not anymore.

It's another place of ruin and death in this brave new world.

1

Day Twenty-eight

'*Whatever it takes…*' she mimics a voice as she drives the knife in. 'He bloody said that. He said Heather, *you must do whatever it takes.*'

She brings the machete down, slicing deep into the neck. Her top clinging to her body from sweat and blood. Cheeks flushed. Hair stuck to her scalp.

A crunch from nearby as Paco sweeps in with a long scaffolding pole gripped in his hands, battering them away. Crunching bones and breaking limbs.

They came in hard. Driving the Toyota four-wheel drive into the horde outside the community centre, killing many, before they rushed into the fray for hand-to-hand fighting.

They couldn't risk firing rifles or pistols for fear of a bullet going through a door or window and striking someone inside.

Reginald said it had to be done. And so, they do it. One at a time. Hunting them down. Seeking and searching for the people on the list given to her by Reginald.

The list compiled by Dr Neal Barrett. The list of people with natural immunity.

'I think that's it,' she says when the last infected is killed. She sucks air in and walks over to the community centre entrance as Paco forces the door open.

The smells hit.

Stale body odour. Shit and piss. The unique smells of people living on top of each other for nearly a month.

A set of double doors ahead, and the sight that greets her is the exact image she had in her mind. Men and women clutching bats and sticks. Shielding the children and the weak behind them. Sobs heard. Everyone clustered at one end. Bedding all over the floor.

A single glance tells her their food supplies are low, and the people here are already rationing. Heather is seeing that more and more now. People grabbed what they could when it first happened, but now, nearly a month later, those supplies are dwindling, and they are too afraid to go out scavenging.

'I, err…' she breaks off, her voice cracking with nerves from so many people staring at her. 'I'm here for Jane. For Jane Tildren?'

'I'm Jane,' a whisper from the back. A hand lifting.

It takes minutes, but Jane Tildren and her husband, and child finally edge away from the others.

'I have to take you to the fort,' Heather says quietly.

'What? But-.'

'No buts. No anything. I need to tell you something, but you cannot, you will not tell anyone else. Do you understand? There's a list of people with immunity. Jane Tildren is on it. Your husband and kid can come with you, but that's it. Tell everyone else to go to the fort. You have one minute, and then we are going. I *will* leave without you.'

Two minutes later, and Heather leads Jane and her family through the broken door and the scene of carnage.

'Don't touch anything,' Heather says as they get into the Toyota.

'What about us?' a man asks, emerging from the broken door of the community centre.

'Go to the fort. Leave now. Don't wait.'

Heather gets in the car. Paco the other side. Engine on, and she pulls away. Experience has taught her that she can get sucked into dramas if she waits too long. People start thinking. They start arguing. They start demanding information. It ended in violence a couple of days ago when Paco almost killed a guy with a single punch after he grabbed Heather's arm and shouted at her.

Now, they get in, find who they need, and get out.

It has to be that way.

'Where are we going?' Jane's husband asks from the back, leaning forward to touch the back of Paco's seat.

Heather slams the brake on. 'WHAT DID I SAY?' she demands. 'Do it again, and I will shoot you. We're covered in blood. She's immune, but you're not. Switch on and listen.'

He sits back from the ferocity of the woman yelling at him. At the size of the big man glaring at him. At the awful injuries on his throat. He looks familiar. Like that actor. The famous one, but it can't be him.

They drive in silence, moving out of the town and into the countryside. Through a five-bar gate and over a bumpy field. Something ahead, looming in the darkness. A big barn. A coach parked up alongside it.

They follow Heather to a big door in the barn. Yellow light spills out. People inside. At least thirty. Maybe more. Some asleep. Some awake. Men, women, and children. It looks homely and inviting. Clean and organised. The people inside fall silent, looking out at the newcomers.

'Hi,' a woman on her feet, coming forward. Plump and friendly-looking. 'I'm Gemma. You must be Jane, right? Heather doesn't speak much, and well, Paco does speak a lot, but he takes a bit of getting used to. Anyway. I've got it now, Heather. You get yourselves cleaned up.'

Heather walks off. Not saying a word as she leads Paco to the far side and a hose out of sight. They strip naked and use bottles of spray disinfectant on each other.

Minutes later, they sit in their own section of the barn. Away from everyone else. Blankets about them, and she snuggles down to sleep for an hour or two. She's done okay though and found twenty-three immunes. Some of them have kids too. Maybe that immunity was passed on.

'Fort. Tomorrow. Yes?' Paco asks, his voice broken and rasping, but she understands him now.

She nods and snuggles into his side with a deep contended sigh as Paco strokes her hair. His mind still not his own. It probably never will be. Not like he was before, anyway. He has notions, and he can think, but he struggles to vocalise and form what he's thinking into words. He's not stupid. Not stupid at all. He's just not what he was. Heather guesses that some parts of his brain were damaged when he was fully turned. His speech sections for sure. She yawns again. Her eyes growing heavy as she sinks into blessed, sweet slumber.

2

Day Twenty-eight

Camber Airstrip
South Coast

She stands still for a moment. Filtering particles carried on the gentle breeze. The scents of creatures. Foxes and badgers. Rabbits too. Meredith used to love chasing them, but they don't hold the allure they once had. Not after weeks of chomping on infected.

Cats can still fuck off. They make strange noises and arch their backs. They don't respond the same way other creatures do, and they stink something awful.

Cats can definitely fuck off.

Not rabbits though. Meredith spots a few now and turns her head to track the fluffy, white tails bouncing out from the hedgerow. An urge inside to run at them, for the sheer hell of it, but today has been a long day. She fought with her pack and grew exhausted. She killed many and kept the pups safe until the pack leader arrived.

She's full too. Having scoffed several large bowls of pasta, fish, and canned meat. Then, she ate Danny's leftovers. And Mo's. Then Charlie's. Then Nick saw Meredith eating Tappy's leftovers and tried to join in, but Tappy called him a greedy twat and pushed him away.

Eventually, even Meredith ate more than she could handle and decided to head outside, and now, she stares, with a very full belly, at the white-bottomed rabbits. She can smell them. But then, Meredith can smell so much more than she could before. The air has changed. It's cleaner.

But those rabbits. Those white bums. So many of them. She shouldn't run. She can't run. She's too full. She's eaten too much. She starts to turn away with a heavy sigh, then a second later, she's low to the ground and streaking across the grass. The rabbits scatter. Running crazily in circles, but why have a fluffy, white target stuck to your arse if you don't want to be chased?

She comes to a stop. Panting hard. A memory inside. An image of a park. Chasing birds. Her little ones laughing. Her pack. The pack before now. Sadness. Pain. Regret. Loss. Surges of feelings she doesn't understand. She's changed. The way her brain works is different now. The hive mind allows the others to feel her instincts and reactions, but that's a two-way road, and in return, Meredith is gaining insight into the human mind.

Another feeling inside. In her belly. She vomits on the grass. Spewing her huge dinner up with one long, yacking cough. She definitely should not have run. It's made her want to defecate too. She walks off a few steps and craps on the grass, then goes back to her regurgitated dinner, and wolfs it down again, in case Nick smells it.

He'd definitely try and eat it.

Rabbits scattered. Bowels emptied. Dinner re-consumed, and she heads back to the building. Jess lifts her head from a bucket of oats as Meredith draws closer. A look between them. One that suggests the horse should have given assistance to the chasing of rabbits while the other suggests she has oats so why the hell would she chase rabbits?

'Feel better now?' Clarence asks, shaking his head at Meredith. 'You made us all jump.'

'Would she eat a rabbit?' Roy asks. 'I could probably get a few for her.'

'You'd kill a rabbit?' Paula asks. Meredith likes Paula. She's bossy. She tells the pups off. Pups are naughty. Paula should bite them.

'It's fresh meat for her,' Roy says. 'And it'd be a clean kill.'

'Yeah, but still,' Paula says with a strange look on her face like she ate something bad. Meredith wonders what it was. She generally likes the things humans find bad. Like fish guts and tripe. They should definitely get some fish guts and tripe.

'Actually,' Clarence says. 'It's a known fact that rabbits take more nutrients from the body than they give.'

'Do they heck,' Paula says, still looking like she ate something bad.

'No,' Clarence says, speaking over her. 'There's a famous story about some people in the Australian outback that ate rabbits and died of starvation.'

'Get off!' Marcy says, bursting out laughing. Meredith looks at her. She mates with the pack-leader. She has bigger things at the front than the other female pack members have. The pack leader likes them. He stares at them a lot. 'You've spent too much time with Cookey,' Marcy says. Her energy changes sometimes. She's still pack, but she's not quite the same as the others. She's more like a cat.

'Reggie,' Clarence calls out, turning to look at the side of the van and the small man inside at his desk. 'You must have heard about the rabbit thing.'

'I have indeed,' Reginald says.

'Oh god, here we go. Cue lengthy, boring explanation,' Marcy says.

'I'm sure you can occupy yourself with a mirror, my dear,' Reginald says, earning a middle finger from Marcy. They do that a lot. They squabble and fight. Meredith detects that Marcy had her own pack. She was the leader. Reginald was in her pack. Now, he's in this pack.

Reginald doesn't kill the prey with the others, but his energy is still right. Like the pack leader's energy. Determined. Driven. Relentless.

Ruthless. Pack leaders need that. The pack must survive. Survival needs strength.

'And?' Paula asks. 'Was he right or not?'

'Was he hell!' Marcy says with another laugh. 'You can't die of starvation from eating rabbits.'

'You are correct, my dear,' Reginald says, making Marcy adopt that smug, cat-like grin of hers. 'One cannot die of starvation as starvation comes from a lack of food. However, you *can* die of malnourishment. Which is what the people referred to did, indeed, perish from. Seeing that, Clarence was correct, and a diet purely of rabbit will not be enough to sustain life.'

'Oh, fuck off,' Marcy says, flapping a hand like she wasn't bothered anyway. Which is exactly what a cat would do. 'You ever heard about the rabbit thing, Dave?' she asks as the small man walks over.

Meredith drops her ears to show respect, but she doesn't move to Dave's side like she does with the others because he doesn't like contact.

'What rabbit thing?' Dave asks.

'That you die of starvation if you eat them,' Marcy says.

'We never said that,' Clarence says. 'We said malnourishment, and Dave would have done the same survival training as me. Dave? Rabbits. They teach you about them?'

'Teach me what?'

'About the rabbits,' Clarence asks.

'What about the rabbits?'

'That you can't just eat rabbits,' Clarence says.

Dave doesn't reply. Meredith sometimes detects he does it on purpose.

'Dave?' Clarence prompts after a few seconds.

'What?'

'Jesus. I know how the boss feels now,' Clarence says, rubbing his face. 'Did they teach you about the rabbits?'

'What about the rabbits?'

'He's doing it on purpose,' Clarence says. 'You're doing it on purpose.'

'Doing what?' Dave asks. Meredith watches him. Seeing how his face doesn't change the way the others do when they speak. Like now, with Clarence pulling all manner of expressions while Marcy and Paula smile and share looks, and Roy shakes his head and rolls his eyes. Dogs have lots of signals too. Just like people, but Dave doesn't use those signals. His energy is very different. Meredith has never known anything with an energy like his. It's entirely focused. Unwavering. Unrepentant. Unforgiving. Dave doesn't have that same fear of failure the others have either. Dave fears things none of the others ever think about. He fears water and strangers touching him, and groups of people coming in close.

Clarence goes to speak before sagging on the spot. 'I give up,' he announces.

'Give what up?' Howie asks, coming out with a tray of drinks.

'Dave,' Clarence says. 'We were explaining about rabbits.'

'Rabbits?' Howie asks while Meredith tracks his movements. Ready for any sign that the pack leader might look at her. He does it when he turns back. She flattens her ears and lowers her head while pushing into his side. Showing supplication.

I am pack. You are leader.

The horse looks at her with an expression that she might have shit on the end of her nose from shoving her head up his arse, but Meredith ignores her because she didn't chase the rabbits.

'You like rabbits, don't you,' the pack leader says. His eyes are dark. His energy is fury.

Pure fury.

'Anyway. What were you on about?' Howie asks. 'Oh, the rabbits. Yeah, I read that. Australia, wasn't it? They found some bodies or something and figured they'd only been eating rabbit and died of malnourishment.'

'Yup,' Clarence says. 'Now, ask Dave if he ever heard of that?'

'Dave? Did you ever hear of that?'

'Yes,' Dave says as the others burst out laughing.

Meredith heads inside the clubhouse. Already hearing the younger pack talking quietly. Smelling their scents. Hearing their tones. Feeling their essence.

'I still don't get it,' Cookey says. Meredith goes over to him, pushing her nose into his hand to prompt a fuss that he gives willingly. Smiling at her. Showing pleasure at her presence. He makes the others feel good. That's Cookey's thing. His ability to share his energy when the pack struggles. He's fierce too. Solid and dependable. 'Do you understand it?' he asks, looking at Meredith.

'She's smarter than you, that's for sure,' Blowers says, making the others laugh. He has one eye. He lost a finger. The other pack members aren't entirely sure if he can actually be killed. Meredith respects him.

'So, Henry killed Peter for a hoover?' Cookey asks.

'Fuck me,' Blowers groans, shaking his head. 'This is painful.'

'I said vacuum,' Charlie says. 'Henry killed Peter to create a power vacuum to destabilise the travellers. George will go back and probably choose who they want to be in charge.'

Meredith pushed her head into Charlie's shoulder. Charlie was hurt before she cut her hair off, and now, Charlie is trying to heal from that. The pack will protect her until she is healed. The horse will anyway. The horse would definitely chase rabbits if Charlie was doing it. The horse would eat badger shit if Charlie was doing it.

'Yeah, but I still don't get it,' Cookey says. 'Why do they want the fort?'

'It's not the fort they want,' Charlie replies.

'It's the immunes,' Maddox says as Meredith heads over to him, but she doesn't flatten her ears for him because Maddox isn't pack. Maddox had his own pack once. He was a leader. But his pack died. He was weak. He failed. He was too young to lead.

'Well, it confuses the shit out of me,' Cookey announces.

'Shoelaces confuse you,' Booker says, making the others laugh again.

Meredith moves on, doing the rounds from one to the next. Going over to the new pack member Booker who rubs her head while laughing at the jokes. Meredith doesn't know Booker, but the pack has accepted him, and he fought well today.

Meredith heads over to the double bedroll where Tappy lies on her side, with Nick behind her. Tappy has the right energy. She's hurt too. Like Charlie. Like all of them, but her fear is of failing and losing her new pack. That's the right fear in the right place.

'Not again, Nick. Jesus, mate. Have you got worms or something?' Blowers asks as Meredith spots Nick pushing a biscuit in his mouth. She lunges over Tappy and tries shoving her tongue in his gob in the hope he'll spit it out, but Nick is wise to that trick and moves his head away while chewing faster as she diverts the attack to the biscuit in his hand.

'Mine!' Nick says with a mouthful as Tappy dives in to grab at Nick's hand to help the dog. 'Get off! It's mine!' Nick says with everyone else bundling in to wrestle the biscuit from Nick's hand. A mass of bodies rolling and laughing over the floor, with the dog's tail slapping faces and heads until Meredith snaffles the biscuit and makes good her escape. Lying down between Mo Mo and Danny.

'Did she get it?' Danny asks, shifting position to see Meredith crunching away happily. 'She did!' he adds with a laugh.

'So's anyway, yeah, go on. Then, what happened?' Mo asks, his voice low and whispered. 'She was naked, yeah?'

'Yeah,' Danny whispers. 'Like, she took her top off and... And she was like, *Danny, you can do me*. But she didn't say it like that. She was all sexy.'

'Yeah, yeah, I get it,' Mo says. 'In the dream, yeah? Like all sexy.'

'Proper sexy,' Danny says.

'Like a YouTube model sexy?'

'Like a million plus followers on IG sexy,' Danny says.

'Man. No way,' Mo whispers. Shaking his head. 'Yo, listen, right, if you's have that dream again, you ask her to go get more fitness models, then come wake me up, bro. We've got that hive mind going on, so's we can probably, like, share dreams and shit. And if I dream of hot models, I'll come and wake you up. Yeah?' Mo asks, hovering his hand over the dog's head for Danny's fist bump.

Meredith stays put. Happy to eat her biscuit with the pups. They can fight. And they're fast too. But they're young and full of wild energy. They need to eat and play, and train, and eat, and play, and train. Pups need repetition. And love. And support.

And biting.

Paula should definitely bite them.

They like each other too. Meredith can feel that. The whole pack can feel that. It's a good thing. Pups learn better when they have other pups with them. Danny came from a bad place. Mo Mo did too. They didn't have strong pack leaders to guide them. Now, they do.

She finishes the snack, and after licking the pups a few times each to make sure they're clean, she heads to the back of the room and pushes through the door to where the other pack have made a den.

'Size of her,' Frank says from his own bedroll as Meredith walks in. 'You ever seen a dog that big before?'

She stands over him. Staring down at his craggy features and the mop of thick hair. He smiles up. Toothy and cheeky. Offering a hand to fuss her head. 'Showing us who's the boss, aren't you?'

Bashir stares up at her. Unsure and wary, because dogs are not always pets, especially in a country torn apart by war, and especially not massive guard breed dogs like this one.

A click of a tongue draws Meredith away. She walks over to the other bedding. To the older woman reaching up to stroke her head. Meredith knows Joan. She met her at the fort.

One last person to check. Meredith walks to the far end of the room. To the dark shadows and the bedding roll on the floor where the lean man with the bald head lies on his back. His hands clasped neatly over his chest.

A man that has an energy like her own pack leader. Dark and furious, but he's wiser. Older. More experienced. That's a dangerous combination, and so, Meredith moves in a step closer. Telling him to go carefully because she's watching him.

Henry doesn't flinch. If the dog wanted to hurt him, she would have done it.

'I'll head out for a bit,' Carmen says, gathering her rifle as she heads for the door. Meredith goes with her, slipping out through the clubhouse as Carmen makes her way into the corridor and out into the night. 'Hey,' she says quietly to the others. 'Thought you'd be up top,' she adds. Motioning to the tower offering a 360-degree field of vision.

'We did try,' Paula says, giving Clarence a look. 'But the horse tried following us up.'

'Not my fault,' Clarence says.

'Who keeps giving her biscuits?' Paula asks as Meredith jumps into the back of the Saxon and sniffs about until she finds the plastic bag containing the nightly snacks. The sound of which promptly alerts Jess who barges Howie aside and looms her head over Marcy.

'Fuck me,' Howie says, mopping the spilled tea. 'You might as well get them out now.'

'Can't. We've got rules,' Clarence says. 'We're not like your first watch sex club, you know.'

'We don't have sex on the first watch,' Howie says as everyone turns to look at him. Including Reginald who leans over to give Howie a stare while Meredith settles down. Panting quietly and listening to the pack elders talk as the night grows darker.

'I'm heading in,' Paula eventually says, prompting the others to yawn and stretch, to bid each other goodnight. A few moments later, and only the pack-leader and his mate remain. Meredith detects the change in energy between them. The way Marcy looks at him like a cat does when it wants something, and the way Howie keeps glancing at her chest.

They mate quickly. On the floor, in the back of the Saxon. The doors pulled to but not closed.

'I love your boobs... Oh my god, I love your boobs...'

Meredith cocks her head over at the pack-leader's rushed voice. Listening to the grunts and gasps while wishing they'd hurry up so the second watch can start.

Eventually, it does, and the changeover comes in the small hours as the big man comes out. Sleepy and yawning. Brew made. Biscuits opened, and he grunts softly as Jess and Meredith take their positions, and the air fills with the sounds of happy munching.

3

Day Twenty-nine

'Come on, guys! Get loaded…' Gemma calls as she walks out of the big barn. 'Javid? Have you checked the fuel? Heather said we're not stopping once we get going.'

'I've checked everything,' Javid says, patting the front of the coach. 'Fuel, oil, tyres, engine, electrics.'

'Check them again,' Heather says, striding over.

The sight of her bringing forth a sudden quiet. The weapons she carries. The way she dresses. The scars and marks all over her face and arms. A walking poster of the apocalypse. Especially with Paco at her side. Over six foot and packed with muscle. A red, checked scarf tied about his neck hides the ruined flesh where Meredith tried to tear his throat out, but in the daylight, he's still very obviously Paco Maguire.

'Hey,' a woman says while walking by. Heather rolls her eyes and shoots him a look, but what can he do? He's Paco Maguire.

Then, it's done, and the coach stands ready.

'We've told everyone if it goes wrong, then to either get to the fort or back to the barn,' Gemma says.

Heather nods. She has done all she can do. The automatic door closes, and the coach bounces across the field, towards the road.

Nearly thirty days since the world ended. Cleaner air. Cleaner fields. Greener grass. Hedgerows bursting with life. 'Don't go too fast,' she says while staring intently through the front window.

'I've been driving coaches for twenty-seven years, love,' Javid says.

Heather doesn't know what to say to that, so she stays silent. People really aren't her thing.

She remembers the journey from hell she took trying to get Subi, Rajesh, and Amna to the fort, and how everything that could go wrong, did go wrong.

Complacency kills.

'Looks alright to me,' Javid says, turning through a long, gentle corner as Heather checks his speed. 'Nice day again. All this sunshine and rain is making it all grow. Give it a year, and you won't even see this road. You mark my words. Be gone, it will. Thousand years from now, they'll be digging it up like we do with all that Roman stuff. Anyway. So what else we immune to then? Just the zombie thing, is it? What about the flu? I used to get them flu jabs. Is that what they want us for? They gonna take what we've got and like, you know, spread it about to the others.'

'I don't know,' Heather murmurs.

'Antibodies,' someone says from behind. A man Heather tracked a few days ago. 'That's what they need. We'll have antibodies.'

'Better than catching whatever that is,' Javid says to a low agreeable murmur coming from the others. 'Ah, it'll all work out best. Always does. Just gotta keep smiling.'

'Next left,' Heather says, checking the route.

'I know, love. I know these roads, and we haven't seen a soul.'

'There's the junction.'

'I know, Heather. You don't need to keep telling me. We follow this one through Lowton and-.'

'Through Lowton? Why are we going through Lowton?' Heather asks, snatching the map up. 'I said no towns.'

'It's tiny.'

'I said no towns.'

'But the other road floods. This rain and weather, and the storms. The council have to pump it out. We'll whip through. It's hardly a town. Look. It's right there.'

'Fuck's sake! I said no towns. Towns are dangerous. We need to turn back and find another road.'

'Can you stop swearing, please!' one of the mothers in the back says in a tight voice.

'Oh, now, that's a bit of a pickle,' Javid says with a gentle tut as they go through a corner to see the road ahead blocked by storm damage. Wheelie bins and debris picked up in floods and dumped in the road.

'Go through it,' Heather says.

'I can't. We'll rip the sump out or rupture a pipe.'

'I said no towns. I said no fucking towns,' she snaps the words out while pulling her rifle forward to check the magazine. Slotting it back in. Loaded. Made ready. Safety on. 'What part of that was difficult for you to fucking grasp?'

'Hey!' the mother shouts, rising to her feet.

'Stay here and be ready to go, and do not stop until you hit the fort,' Heather says, stepping out while remembering the lessons Blowers taught her.

Silence.

Nothing happens.

'She likes the drama, doesn't she,' Javid mutters in the coach.

'She's got a potty mouth if you ask me,' the mother says. 'Disgusting language, and she's rude. Just rude. There's no need for it. I'll be speaking to whoever is in charge when we get to this fort. They need to replace her. Awful. Just awful.'

Heather reaches the first bin and starts dragging it away. Cursing at the noise it makes.

'She's moving 'em one at a time,' Javid says with a look to Paco standing by the open coach door. 'I'm going out to help.'

'She said to wait here,' Gemma says.

'It's fine! There's nothing here. She's panicking over nothing. We're immune anyway.'

'We're not all immune,' Jane Tildren calls out, glancing at her husband.

'Go back inside!' Heather snaps, hearing motion behind as Javid steps from the coach.

'Two of us'll clear it faster.'

'Inside. Now!'

'Alright, love. You need to watch how you speak to people.'

It happens then.

Something flares inside Paco's head. His face hardens instantly. His frame stiffening. Heather clocks it. 'GET INSIDE NOW!'

The first-floor windows above them explode in a shower of glass. Men and women. Old and young dropping out as they give voice with howls and screeches.

No time to think. No time for thought, and Heather aims her rifle. Splitting the air apart with gunfire as Paco does the same. Sending rounds at the bodies as they fall.

Screams from inside the coach. Instant chaos. Javid staggers away in fright. His stomach flipping over.

'GET INSIDE,' Heather shouts. 'JAVID. INSIDE!'

Javid doesn't hear. He can't think. It's all happening so fast. From so many directions at once. The air filled with guns and screeches. With screams and yells.

Heather empties a magazine within seconds, but the compression from the attack comes too quickly. 'Get him inside!' Heather yells, slinging her rifle to draw her machete as she runs past Paco. Lashing out with the sharp blade.

A hand on Javid's arm. A sense of motion. The world spins by, and he's off his feet, launched into the coach as Paco ditches his empty rifle and grabs his scaffolding pile. He runs out while pulling back for a strike. Rushing past Heather to slam several down at once.

'Paco, go back!' she shouts as the sound of smashing and screams of terror reach them. A glance back to the coach. To the infected driving headfirst into the skylight on the roof. 'THEY'RE INSIDE!'

She vaults the steps. People on their feet, screaming out. She can't get through. She drops the machete and heaves someone away. Kicking and punching people to move as the infected drops to the floor. Howling out. Heather dives for it. Pulling a knife as she barrels into the male's legs. Taking him down to the floor. He fights hard. Thrashing and bucking. Biting at her arms. Clawing her flesh. She stabs once. Getting the blade into his side as another infected drops through the broken skylight. Teeth on her shoulder. She screams, with every vein pushing through her neck and forehead. She stabs into the neck of the one below her, then twists about onto her back, and drives her thumbs into the eyes of the infected on top of her, popping the sockets. Hot goo sprays out. The creature pays no heed and gets wilder. She scrabbles a hand on her tac-vest. Drawing the pistol to fire rounds into his chest and head. The skull blows out. The infected sags dead. She heaves it away. Snatching views while crawling free.

'GO!' Heather shouts out. Aiming her pistol up to fire into the already busted skylight. Getting a shot through a head as the coach jolts forward from Javid stamping his foot down.

The engine roars out. The speed builds, and Heather runs to the front, grabbing at Paco to pull him back from the open door as the coach slams into the remaining debris. Smashing bins and rubbish aside. Things get trapped underneath. Adding more noise and vibration to the chaos. Paco kicks out into bodies trying to dive inside, but the coach gets moving, pulling away, and the roof fills with thuds as the infected roll over the top and drop off the end.

Paco sags back. The door clear. The coach moving. People crying and whimpering in fear.

'Oh god, no... Oh god, no!' a scream from the back. The mother that told Heather off for swearing now on her feet and clutching at her son. A little boy. Brown hair. His face spattered with blood. His hands clutching his belly. His body tensing up as waves of agony spread through him.

'NO!' Heather yells, but it's too late, and the mother presses her face to the boys. Weeping hard. Screaming out in grief and shock. The blood on his face touching her lips. Heather runs for them. Grabbing at the child. Heaving him away from the mother. She screams out with maternal panic as Heather drags the kid along the aisle. His body locking out with spasms as the infection surges through his body. His mother screaming and grabbing at him.

'OPEN THE FUCKING DOOR!' Heather yells as Paco looms past her, grabbing the mother to hold her back. Javid hits the button. The door opens. The world outside spinning by. The mother fights to get free of Paco, watching in horror as her child is lowered to his feet. His back to the open door. Heather drawing a pistol. Aiming.

'NO!' the mother screams. The gun fires. The boy falls out with a spray of blood. Gone forever. Dead. 'NO!' the mother screams the word, stretching it out as she sinks down. The shock rendering her screams to silence. A pain in her gut. A sudden, awful pain that makes her curl up in agony. Paco carries her. Positions her. Heather aims. The gun fires. She falls out of the coach.

'I said no towns,' Heather mutters, blood and gore once more coating her body. 'I said no fucking towns.'

4
―――

Day Twenty-Nine

DIARY OF CHARLOTTE DOYLE

PAULA HAS REQUESTED that we keep records of what we do as it will be important for other people to understand how things happened. She said our personal accounts should reflect our own views, but we should try and stay factual to what we did and what we saw.

I'm not sure many of the others are writing diaries, but I am happy to do it. I agree with Paula, and that it is important to maintain a record.

So, that being the case, I should think it's best to start at the beginning and tell you that it was a rather eventful start to our morning, but when isn't it?

In fact, I should be rather more surprised if one day we awoke from our slumber, and nothing happened at all.

I've just read that back and realised I used the words *awoke* and *slumber,* and have instinctively reverted to a Jane Austen diary style, but obviously, one with zombies. (I think they actually made Pride and Prejudice into a zombie movie. I never saw it, but I recall Blinky saying, and I quote, *that it was the dog's bollocks cos girls look fit as fuck in those old dresses.*)

I miss Blinky.

I miss her so much that it creates a ball of real pain inside when I think about her, so then, I try *not* to think about her. Which then only makes me feel guilty because it's like I am actively avoiding her memory – which, I guess, is the best coping mechanism I have right now.

But anyway, let me explain what happened this morning. As I said, it was a rather eventful start. We'd spent the night back at Camber airstrip, and at early dawn, I was in the clubhouse lounge asleep in my bedding and having the most pleasant dream.

I was laying on my back (in the dream) and watching the clouds going by when Cookey's face loomed over me, and I knew (in the way you know things in dreams) that he was finally going to kiss me, which I was very happy about, but instead of kissing me, he grabbed one of my ankles and started dragging me across the floor like a caveman.

Which was hot, by the way. Especially when he started barging chairs and tables aside just so he could have his way with me.

Then, it got a bit weird because someone else rolled into me and started getting dragged along, and I was thinking, *oh gosh, does Cookey want a threesome? Am I okay with that? And especially in a shoe shop. What would the customers think?*

Mind you, I wasn't entirely against the idea. I was extremely turned on for a start, which then only got worse when the other person started kissing my cheeks and breathing all hot and heavy into my ear. Which totally does it for me. They were wet kisses too and quite rough. But also very nice.

Then, I heard Tappy murmuring, 'You're too wet, Nick.' And I was thinking *Oh gosh this is escalating.* We're not going for a threesome; we're going into an orgy with Nick and Tappy.

Which, you know, was totally weird while also being totally hot. I mean – I've been waiting forever for Cookey to make a move, and now, he was finally doing it. And there is something very sexy about Tappy and all of her tattoos.

Wow. So, yeah. Okay then. I was into it, and there I was. Giving kisses back to Tappy and getting super wet kisses in return while being dragged by the ankle to have an orgy in a shoe shop.

Which is when, I gather, Sergeant Blowers came awake to see me trapped in my bedroll being dragged across the clubhouse by Jess walking backwards. Not only that, but I also had Tappy cuddled into one side of me, and everyone else's boots snagged against my outstretched arm.

Now that, I am sure, was a strange enough sight on its own, but perhaps nothing compared to the sight of Tappy and I trying to kiss each other while Meredith walked behind us licking our faces.

Which is when everyone else seemed to also wake up. Not that I knew that. Although, I am assuming Blowers said something because I suddenly became aware of him in the shoe shop and feared we would either be told off or that the orgy was about to gain another member.

That, thankfully, was enough to give me sufficient alarm to finally wake up. With both Tappy and I opening our eyes while mid-lick of the other, while also getting sloppy morning kisses from Meredith, and while being dragged across the floor by Jess – whom, at that point, tossed her head and sent poor Tappy flying off across the clubhouse.

And with Tappy gone, Jess sped up, and I was positively sailing along while yelling at Jess to stop it and put me down right now. I told her I meant it too. Not that she listened.

The most awful thought then entered my mind because I went past Danny who was still asleep on his back, with his giant willy pushing up under his sheet, and honestly, I was thinking to grab it for something to hold onto. I mean, it is big enough. (For both hands.) But then, I thought perhaps it is not the done thing for a corporal to grab a young man's big willy, even if that corporal is being dragged by a hungry horse. In the end, I decided against grabbing it and told

Danny to roll over. Which he did most promptly with a sleepy apology.

I then reverted to telling Jess to put me down and continued doing so as we entered the corridor and passed the rooms being used by the elders. Which were all opening, with various people coming out, mostly still in underwear, while Sergeant Blowers and everyone else ran behind me, yelling suggestions.

'That horse needs gripping!' Clarence said after coming out of his room with a look of surprise.

'Stop feeding her bloody biscuits then!' I shouted back at him. (Which I shouldn't have done as Clarence *is* a senior in the team.)

'Biscuits don't cause kidnapping,' Clarence said.

'Gateway drug!' Marcy shouted from her room while stretching like a cat on her bedding. She did give me a beaming smile through the door though, and it's always nice to get a smile from Marcy. It really brightens your day.

Mr Howie, of course, was right in the thick of the action. Rushing about with Clarence and the others. All of them with sleepy eyes and sleepy heads, and all shouting at each other. Such is our way when a non-zombie calamity strikes. And I must be honest, I was joining in and trying to berate both Jess for dragging me and Clarence for the whole ongoing biscuits issue.

'Everyone, just calm down,' Clarence then ordered. 'I've got her,' he said and started picking me up. Which, of course, prompted Jess to think someone was trying to take me away, and seeing as Jess views me as her own personal slave, that was never going to be allowed to happen. And so, Jess pulled harder which only made Clarence pull harder, with the two of them playing tug-o-war with me as the rope.

'What the hell!' Paula snapped as the bathroom door flew open. 'I can't even poo in peace!'

'Gross, Paula!' Cookey said.

'Why is it gross?' Paula asked as the lads all made yucky faces. 'Women do shit too, you know.'

'Oh stop!' Booker said.

'You lot are bloody sexist! And this is because of all those bloody biscuits, Clarence,' Paula said, waggling a roll of toilet paper at him.

'Biscuits don't cause kidnapping, Paula.'

'Gateway drug,' Marcy called helpfully before giving me another big smile while I was suspended in the air outside of her door. She then proceeded to open a small compact to check her reflection, which was all rather surreal given the chaos going on. But then, in fairness, Marcy rarely gets in a flap about anything. Unless she chips a nail, of course, at which point we all become very aware it's *the end of the fucking world*.

I digress.

So, there I was. A human Christmas cracker between a horse and a giant, with the horse slowly winning. Which was confirmed by the almighty bang of Jess's rump crashing into the doors and pulling me outside, with Clarence and everyone else spilling out after us.

It was all very chaotic and noisy, but I then spotted Henry stepping out of the clubhouse, looking all smart and dapper in tan trousers and a checked shirt. He took one look and, quick as a flash, darted in with a knife, sliced the bedding, and caught me in his arms as I dropped free. Which, of course, only made Jess, Clarence, Mr Howie, and everyone else all fall away from the sudden release of pressure. While he – Henry – stood with me in his arms, with barely a tremble, I might add (and he smelled amazing).

'Are you hurt?' Henry asked as he lowered me to my feet.

I said I wasn't while everyone else fell rather quiet. I'll admit I was rather caught out, especially with the rather sexually charged dream I'd just had, and I think that showed as I stammered somewhat and, most likely, blushed furiously.

Henry was charming though. He just smiled politely and headed back towards the clubhouse. 'When you are ready, Mr Howie. Perhaps we can discuss our plans. Oh, and are you drilling this morning, Sergeant Blowers? Carmen and Bashir would like to join in, if that is not an intrusion...'

Henry then fell silent and looked up over our heads with an action that prompted us to do the same, which is when we all saw a bright orb streaking high in the sky with a tail like a comet.

'What's that?' Paula asked as several others showed great concern and alarm.

'It's just a satellite,' Henry said in a calm voice. 'Low orbit comms satellite, I should say. They're affected by the Earth's gravitational pull, and without humans to keep them firing and stabilised, they're starting to come back down.'

'Jesus,' Howie said. 'I thought they burnt up in the atmosphere.'

'Not always. The larger ones are brought down into the Pacific Ocean. But I would suggest that in the absence of human intervention they'll come down all over the planet.'

It was actually very interesting listening to Henry. He has a lovely, deep, cultured voice, and it's like listening to an old Pathè news narrator. Very calm and controlled while keeping you entirely focussed on what he's saying. Even Cookey and the lads stayed silent and didn't make any jokes.

'How many are there?' Paula asked when Henry finished explaining.

'Oh, thousands. But I shouldn't worry. The chances of being struck by one are exceptionally low.'

'Oh god,' Mr Howie said with a groan. 'We're going to get hit by a satellite.'

'We are most certainly not going to get struck by a satellite,' Henry said with a smile. 'Anyway. I shall leave you to get prepared.'

'We will,' Mr Howie said as Henry walked off. 'We're like shit magnets. Right. Everyone, watch out for falling satellites. Cos. You know. It's not like we've got enough shit to deal with. Like zombies and the end of the world, and dads that were spies, and best mates that were spies, and more spies than you can shake a stick at.'

'I like pies,' Nick said.

'Spies, not pies,' Blowers said. 'But more to the point. What the actual were you two doing?' he asked while giving Tappy and I a look.

'Nick's turned another girlfriend gay,' Booker said before darting back from the punch sent by Nick.

'Twat,' Nick said. 'Er, but seriously, you're not gay, are you?' he asked Tappy.

'Charlie was kissing me!' Tappy said as I panicked and blurted that I thought she was Nick. Which, granted, wasn't the best response to give, judging by the looks on everyone's faces. 'No! I meant. I thought Tappy thought I was Nick, and Cookey was taking us into the shoe shop.'

'What shoe shop?' Cookey asked. 'What for?'

'For the sex!' I told him. 'Gosh. No. Right. Forget it. And it was the dog kissing you, Tappy. Not me.'

'Er. No. You were kissing me,' Tappy said.

'I was not! And if we're going to point fingers, then you were most definitely licking my ear.'

'I thought you were Nick!'

'Exactly. So did I. No! Whatever. I said forget it,' I said while feeling annoyed that I couldn't articulate myself out of it.

'Do you know what we need?' Cookey asked in a most serious fashion. 'We need a replay to see who did what.'

'Dick,' Tappy said with a laugh as Cookey winked and smiled at me, with his blue eyes all twinkling. I must admit. I did chuckle too. Cookey has that way about him.

'We are just getting weirder by the day,' Paula said. 'But,' she added, leaning over to make sure Henry has gone, 'how suave was Henry!'

'He was like James Bond or something,' Tappy said.

'I thought that,' Marcy said, also still just in underwear and having just woke up, but while the rest of us resembled a collection of river monsters, she was ready for the lingerie catwalk at London Fashion week. 'Honestly. The way he caught Charlie and was like, *are you okay, miss?* That was so 007.'

'Er, and why didn't one of you do that?' Paula asked, giving Clarence and Howie the stink-eye.

'We didn't have a knife,' Howie said.

'What he said,' Clarence said, pointing at Howie.

'Right. Well, it's a good thing Henry was prepared then, isn't it? With his nice trousers and his shirt all tucked in,' Paula said.

'And he smelled nice,' I told them. 'Something musky and manly.'

We then got distracted from discussing the finer points of Henry as Mo and Dave came over from finishing their training.

'Morning,' Mo said. (I love his cheeky smile) You's okay then?'

'You's okay, Mr Howie,' Dave said, which only made the rest of us frown.

'We're fine, Mo,' the boss told him. 'Apart from falling satellites and James Bond Senior.'

'Dave said satellites fall down all the time,' Mo said as we all looked at Dave.

'Satellites fall down all the time,' Dave said.

'I did actually know that,' Clarence said while clearly not wanting to be outdone on the satellite-fallingdown knowledge. 'They come down all the time.'

'Awesome,' Mr Howie said without much enthusiasm. 'It'll definitely be a big one.'

'What will?' Mo asked.

'The one that hits us,' Blowers said. 'Dave, what do we do if a satellite falls on us?'

'Dave wasn't the only one in the army,' Clarence said.

'Did you do the satellite falling down course too?' Mr Howie asked him.

'No. I just mean Dave isn't the only person here with military training.'

'True. But his old boss just made us look like twats,' the boss said. 'Dave, what do we do if a satellite falls on us?'

'Get out of the way.'

'Good advice. Anything to add, Clarence?'

Clarence thought for a second. 'We should track the trajectory,' he said with a satisfied nod.

'How the fuck do we do that?' the boss asked him.

'I've no idea. Do what Dave said and get out of way.'

'Well. This is all very exciting,' Paula then said. 'But I'm going inside to smell Henry.'

And with that, she jotted off quick as anything, with Marcy a step behind her, then Tappy, and yes, okay, I'll admit it, I went too. But honestly. He did smell really nice.

5

The morning came. The morning proper. The morning after the night before, or rather, the morning after the day before, and then, the night that came after that day.

Whatever. I know what I meant. Or at least, I think I know what I meant.

I did actually know that about satellites. I saw a documentary on them. About how we have low, medium, and high orbit satellites. When the medium and high ones break or stop working, they're simply sent off into space, whereas the lower orbit ones are brought back down.

One thought lead to another, and I started thinking about other things humans have built that are no longer under control or being maintained. Gas stations and oil refineries, and what about the hydro-electric places and those giant wind turbines? Do they just keep turning until they fall down? And what about nuclear power plants? Fuck! Nuclear power plants. The UK's got a few of those. We'll be like Chernobyl. I felt a rush of panic inside, then got a sudden image of luring all the infected to a nuclear power plant and making a heroic last stand just as it goes bang and wipes them all out.

But then, we'd all be dead too. But what if we lured them there, then we scarpered and left the infected to play with some exploding plutonium? I went inside, thinking to find Reginald and outline my brilliant new plan.

'I know that's probably a really stupid question,' Cookey said as I rushed into the clubhouse, looking for Reggie. 'But, yeah, I mean, could that happen?'

'It's not a stupid question at all,' Henry said. 'But sadly, no. The use of a modern nuclear power plant as a weapon would not work.'

Arse it. Cookey had already asked. I came to a stop, looking over at Henry, surrounded by underwear clad people clutching their hot drinks. Marcy, Paula, Tappy, and Charlie being the closest. He looked suave too. All tucked in and neat. And his bald head. It really suited him.

'There are safety mechanisms that kick in the event of an HDE,' Henry said.

'What's an HDE?' Tappy asked.

'Human disappearance event,' Henry explained.

'So it won't go bang then?' Cookey said.

'It's unlikely. However, there may be other factors that cause melt-downs. In any event, I would hope the staff on duty when the event hit would have at least managed to start shutdown procedures. They might even have remained on site to continue to manage the situation.'

'Why would you hide in a nuclear power station?' Marcy asked.

'High walls. Strong gates, large canteens and a sizeable armed force guarding them,' Henry said.

'Howie, we need to find a nuclear power station to live in,' Marcy said, turning to look for me.

'Nick would blow it up,' Cookey said, earning a few laughs. 'He likes setting things on fire,' he told Henry.

'A worthwhile skill, I am sure,' Henry said, sharing a smile with Nick. 'Mr Howie, would you be ready to discuss plans now?'

'I would not be ready because I am preparing to have a poo,' I said in a weird voice as the room fell silent, and everyone stared at me for a few seconds.

'I just had one, nipper,' Frank said, walking out of the toilet. 'Might want to give it a few minutes.'

'Whatever. I'm going for a smoke then.'

'No naked flames near that door,' Frank said, waving towards the toilet as he walked into the clubhouse. 'I bet they give you backache,' he said to Marcy, offering a wink and a cheeky grin at her bra. 'If you need a hand, just say. I don't mind carrying one.'

I waited for Marcy to go nuts and tell him to piss off, but she just laughed and rolled her eyes as the world continued on with its strange new ways where old spies flirt and horses kidnap people while satellites fall out of the sky.

I stepped out and glanced up, with a cigarette halfway to my mouth. 'Literally every half an hour,' I muttered, stuffing the smoke back in the pack as I stalked inside. 'We are actual shit magnets. What did I say?' I called out.

'Already?' Clarence asked, looking up from his mug of tea.

'Yup. Right there,' I said, pointing up. 'Satellite coming right at us.'

6

Day Twenty-nine

'Wow. I was not expecting that,' Heather says, blinking through the front window of the coach at the sight of Lilly's wall enclosing the bay. 'There's a guard coming out,' she adds, nodding forward to a guy walking out from the gap between the containers with a rifle held ready.

The door opens, and Heather drops out, shielding her eyes from the bright sun.

'Ach, are ye Heather now?' a young man asks, coming to a stop a few metres away 'Aye. Lilly said to watch out for you. Feck me! She wasn't lying, lads, it's Paco fecking Maguire, it is,' the man calls out, turning to glance up at the guys on the wall.

'Paco! Great movies there, fella,' someone shouts down. 'Can he still have a selfie being a zombie, miss?'

'Ach, wouldn't that be grand. He's famous as shit,' the lad at ground level says, rolling his eyes. 'I'd love a picture with him?'

'Er,' Heather says as the man grabs his radio.

'Lilly, are ye there? Heather just rocked up. She's got that Paco with her and a big coach full of immunes.'

'Is it Paco?' someone cuts in.

'The actual Paco?' someone else asks.

'Are ye fecking joking or what? Did ye get a picture yet?'

'Ach, not yet. I've asked, mind,' the gate guard says.

'Feck that. We need a group photo,' someone else says.

'It's Lilly here,' Lilly's voice cuts in. Instantly recognisable as Heather relaxes slightly. 'Yes. They can come through. Straight down to the beach, please.'

'Hang on a second, will ya,' one of the lads shouts from the wall as they disappear out of sight, then reappear a few seconds later, pulling iPhones and Samsungs from pockets. 'Miss, will ye take a picture for me?'

'Miss, will ye do mine too?' another asks, thrusting his phone at Heather as they start crowding around Paco.

'Peter would love this, he would,' someone says to a chorus of sad tuts and low murmurs.

'What the actual fuck,' Heather says, holding a phone up to a sea of grinning faces and Paco in the middle, striking a pose. 'Er, say cheese then.'

'CHEESE!'

A moment or two later, they head through the gap in the wall until they reach the road coming from the old estate. Now, a vast car park full of vehicles, and Lilly's Great Wall stretching around the whole bay.

'Stop here,' Heather says, noticing Lilly standing with a woman with a mass of red hair, but Lilly looks different. Older somehow. Hardened. Other traveller men with them. All armed. Kyle and another older man with a neat moustache. He seems to be the focus of their attention, with every face seemingly glaring at him. Then, they spot her and turn as Heather feels a rush of nerves from being stared at when she drops out of the coach.

'You okay, Lilly?' Heather asks, guarded and cautious.

'I'm fine. It's good to see you, Heather,' Lilly replies as Heather notices the black armbands and glances over to a rudimentary flagpole, erected with a black flag fluttering at half-mast.

'Heather. My name is George. Pleasure to meet you,' the older man with the neat moustache says. A pistol on his belt. Tan trousers. A dark, checked shirt tucked in. 'I gather you have been busy?'

Heather pauses. Not liking the tension in the air. 'Howie here?' she asks.

'It's fine, Heather,' Lilly says. 'We are just going through a period of readjustment.'

'Ach, that's a posh way of saying some cunt murdered Peter,' one of the armed men says.

'Willie, ease it back,' Kyle says.

'I'll do no such thing, Father,' Willie says, glaring at George. 'That wee fella wants the fort, he does, and after everything Peter did.'

'Feck that,' Elvis says, staring up. 'There won't be a fort when that thing hits us.'

Heather glances up in surprise at the streak of light, high in the early dawn sky. 'What the hell is that?'

'Satellite,' George says.

'Aye, they're all falling back down, apparently,' Willie says. Shooting a look to George.

'I'm telling you,' Elvis says. 'That's heading straight for us, it is.'

'I can assure you it isn't,' George says. 'It just appears that way.'

'Heather, you look worried,' Kyle says, giving her a concerned look. 'George, can you get Howie on comms. I think Heather might appreciate that.'

'Of course,' George says, pulling a radio from his belt.

'I'm saying it,' Elvis says. 'I'm bloody saying it. We need to move. That thing's coming down.'

'It's still coming through the atmosphere,' Lilly says. 'It'll drop fast once it's clear. I should imagine there have been a few.'

'Why haven't we seen any then, Blondie?' Mary asks.

'Because we tend to look down rather than up, and the sky is still dark, so it's more visible. There's another one over there,' Lilly adds, pointing west.

'Feck this,' Elvis says. 'We need to do something. Standing about with a walloping big satellite coming at us.'

'Elvis, for the love of God,' Kyle says. 'It's not coming at us.'

'Henry? George here. I'm with Lilly and a few of her chaps. Got a moment to speak?' George says into the radio in such a way to tell Henry he is with others.

'George. Yes, I can speak. I'm with Mr Howie's team, watching a satellite re-entry.'

'I'm fucking telling you,' Howie's voice says in the background. *'That thing is coming right at us.'*

'See,' Kyle says, looking at Elvis and the others. 'Howie's miles away, looking at the same thing, he is.'

'He fecking needs to stay miles away. Call him a cunt from me,' Willie says.

'Who's calling me a cunt?' Howie asks.

'I AM, YE FECKING CUNT,' Willie shouts.

'Henry. We have Heather here,' George says, taking another step away. *'She has a coach full of people. I gather she has instructions.'*

'Is Heather there?' Howie asks. *'Mind if I talk to her? Heather, it's Howie. You okay?'*

George passes the radio over, showing Heather where to press to talk as she steps away. 'Hey, boss. You okay... Er... Over.'

'You don't have to call me boss, Heather. You at the fort? How's it looking?'

'Different. There's a big wall, and everyone is wearing black armbands.'

'Yeah. That'll be for Peter. Long story. Anyway. Reginald is with me. How did you get on?'

'I found twenty-three immunes. And their families. They're on the coach now.'

'Heather! That's marvellous. Well done,' Reginald calls out. *'Fantastic work. Twenty-three! Really very good.'*

'It is, Heather,' Howie says. 'Is Lilly with you? Can you call her over?'

'Er, sure. Hang on. Lilly?' Heather calls as Lilly walks over. 'The boss wants to talk to us. She's here.'

'Lilly. It's Howie. You okay?'

'Fine,' Lilly replies. Her voice hard and blunt.

'The mission is still the mission, Lilly. No matter what happened between us.'

'I am fully aware of that. The immunes will be protected as we agreed.'

'Okay. So... We good then?' Howie asks.

'As I just said,' Lilly says. 'The immunes will be protected.'

'Good. Okay. You seen that satellite?' Howie asks as a yell comes from both ends of the radio, with everyone staring up to watch it shoot high overhead and disappear out of sight. 'That didn't land on you lot, did it?' Howie asks

'Was there anything else?' Lilly asks.

She hands the radio back and walks off as Heather shares a look to Paco. 'I'll, er, I'll get it sorted this end, boss. Where are you?'

'Place called Camber. Meet us in the town for a coffee. We'll catch up face to face.'

AN HOUR LATER. That's all. Just an hour, and Heather takes the keys from the young traveller lad and climbs into the four-wheel drive with Paco. Engine started, and they pull away. A mixture of feelings inside. Relief at being away from somewhere so crowded, but a sadness at leaving Subi, Rajesh, and Amna.

Subi loved showing Heather their room in the fort. It was nice too. Not just bedding on the floor, but proper little beds with side tables so the children can learn ownership and boundaries.

One thing was very clear. That whatever is going on between Lilly and Howie might be bad, but Lilly runs the fort brilliantly. There's no question about that. The kids looked healthy and clean.

She heads back to the barn, bouncing the borrowed vehicle over the grass to their own four-wheel drive. The one filled with ammunition, weapons, and water. With cleaning gear and spare kit. They swap over and leave the barn behind. Back into the lanes and roads. Back into the ever-changing landscape of a world without people and doing something she never did before the world ended.

Going to meet friends for coffee.

7

Day Twenty-nine

OKAY. So, fair enough. The satellite didn't fall on our heads, but that doesn't mean another one wouldn't.

Seriously.

We're shit magnets.

I'm telling you.

Whatever. Anyway, after Henry the Handsome was proved right about the satellite, I went and had the poo I was planning to take *before* I ran back inside. It was a nice poo too. Frank had left an old newspaper in the stall, and it's always nice to have something to read when you're having a number two. It used to be the back of shampoo bottles pre-mobile phones. Now, we've kinda drifted back to that. I mean. I've still got my phone, but it's worthless now. It's not even charged up. I only keep it as it's got pictures of my family on it and some songs I like. I think we're all the same, and we've only kept them for that reason.

The point is that I actually read a newspaper for the first time since it all happened. It was so weird, but the thing that stood out more than anything was the sheer banality of our lives and the mind-numbingly dull things we got excited about. Politicians. Football players. Models. Reality stars.

Granted, it was a crappy tabloid paper, but there wasn't one single mention of anything related to science. Nothing about space exploration. Arctic research. Disease control or climate change. Oh, no. I'm wrong. There was a nasty, trolling opinion piece about that young, autistic Scandinavian woman trying to educate people about the dangers of climate change, but nothing about the actual dangers of climate change.

The other thing that stood out after everything that has happened was how it was so warped. Like the news stories didn't present facts in a neutral way. It was all geared towards shaping mindsets and telling people how to think. You could see the same themes running through every page. This paper seemed very right wing. Anti-immigration. Anti-EU. Anti-bloody everything while the reporters all jacked off to pictures of the royal family.

But anyway. I had a nice poo and duly shook my head at the state of the world before remembering the actual state of the world now, and then, got dressed. Seeing as everyone else was dressed, and I was still in my boxers. *And* it was also noticeable that everyone was trying to look a bit smarter too. Mind you, the lads always start the day off nice and smart. But then, they don't have a choice with Dave.

Down and twenty, Alan. Then, tuck your shirt in.
Down and twenty then go back and shave properly, Daniel.
Is that gum? We do not chew gum, Natasha. Everyone down and twenty.
What the fuck, Tappy! Cheers then.
Make it thirty for swearing during inspection.
Cookey, you fucking bellend!
Forty, thank you, Nicholas.
Dave, I can't even do fourteen push ups, let alone forty.
Do them on your knees, Natasha.
Lucky bitch!
Fifty, Alex!

That's so unfair!

NOTANOTHERWORD BECAUSEYOUWILLBESCRUBBING TOILETS ANDMAKINGBREWS FORTHERESTOFYOURNATURALLIVES! WHICHWILLENDINTHIRTYSECONDS IFYOUUTTERONEMORESOUND OTHERTHANAGRUNTOFPAIN.

Okay, So Dave doesn't actually shout at them like. He doesn't need to. He just gives them a look, or, when he really means it, he calls them *Mr Cookey, or Mr Hewitt, or Miss Drinkwater.*

That's when everyone else pretends to look away and find something else to do.

Anyway. Eventually, we got into our vehicles and started off to find Camber Town, stopping after literally ten yards so Marcy could run back for a wee. Then the dog decided she needed to take a crap, during which time Nick said he'd also forgotten something and ran off into the kitchen where he was found ten minutes later trying to shove a whole giant Snickers bar in his mouth in one go. Which is after eating another cold tin of baked beans. Some left-over breakfast pasta. Cheese. More cheese. Another Snickers. Some more cheese and another Snickers. Oh, and some raisins cos, you know, fibre is important in the apocalypse.

And then eventually, we got back into our vehicles and once more headed off to find Camber Town. And this time we only stopped once. Which was so Paula could pee behind a tree because she'd been so busy nagging everyone else about going for a pee that she hadn't gone for a pee herself. And during which time the dog took another crap and Nick ate more food and everyone else bickered a lot about the fifty push-ups and the fact Tappy was allowed to do them on her knees.

'I'm a girl!' she said.

'So? Charlie's a girl and she did them,' Nick said.

'Charlie's ripped!' Tappy said. 'She does more push-ups than all of you. You can't use her as an example. Use Marcy. Marcy? Could you do fifty push-ups?'

'Er. What's a push up again?' Marcy asked. 'Is that the one with the bar thing that you dangle from? I can't do those.'

It was like that.

Cos, you know, it's literally always like that.

And while everyone else was bickering in the back, Clarence was telling me about how he was in the army too. Like for ages and he did loads of army stuff, and literally knows loads of army things.

And during all of that I'm moaning about Henry and how it's easy to look awesome and smell nice when you've been hiding under a table for a month.

Then Clarence told me I should totally say that to Henry, and I told Clarence he should totally tell Dave about the army stuff. And we both agreed we totally would, which is when Paula got back in and told everyone to stop moaning and Nick to stop eating and actually it turned out she needed another poo, which of course set everyone off, which in turn set Paula off because apparently, it's okay for men to talk about having a poo but not a woman.

Then we arrived at Camber Town, which is when I turned around to tell them my views on poo discussions and ran over a bench and into the front window of Superdrug. Which made Marcy happy as she said she needed some more nail files.

I backed up, ran over another bench and eventually parked the Saxon outside the café in the High Street. Albeit with two wooden benches jammed underneath the front. Which Henry looked at for a long second before nodding at me politely.

'I thought we might need them,' I said. Which I meant as a joke, but it came out like a serious comment.

Then in desperation to recover my awesome status as a truly dashing awesome guy, I rushed into the café to show off my coffee making skills, and after Nick and Tappy got the power running I set about pressing buttons and flicking switches and twisting dials in the hope something would work.

Which is when Heather turned up. We saw them outside getting out of their SUV and walking over to the lads outside the door chewing the fat and shooting the shit. They looked cool too. Paco's huge and just shredded with massive arms and like the veins all pushing out, and he was walking up behind Cookey who was pretending he hadn't seen them arrive.

'Yeah,' Cookey said. 'And then Blowers was like, Paco Maguire is such a wanker, and if I ever see him again, I'll totally call him a fuck-witted cockmunching thundercunt. Fact.'

Cookey's got brilliant timing because by the time he finished talking Paco Maguire was standing an inch behind him while Danny, Tappy and Booker were just staring up in awe.

'What? Is there something behind me?' Cookey asked, stepping back into Paco. 'What's behind me? What is it? Oh hey! Didn't see you there. Look everyone it's Dwayne Johnson.'

'Oooh,' Blowers and Nick winced with a laugh at Paco got an arm around Cookey's shoulders and started rubbing knuckles on his skull. I then focussed back on the coffee making and the distinct lack of frothing in the milk jug.

'Why isn't it frothing? The milk's not frothing.'

'It needs more froth,' Clarence said.

'Where's the froth?' Frank asked as they all joined in with turning dials and prodding buttons.

'It probably needs to heat up,' Paula said while pushing into the gaggle to prod and poke the coffee machine.

'Heather? Hi, I'm Carmen,' Carmen said, walking over with a friendly smile. 'Let me point the others out. That's Frank. He's old and stinks of piss. Joan said you've met at the fort, and that's Bash. He doesn't speak English.'

Bashir turned on hearing his name to nod and smile before his eyes lit up. 'The Rock!' he called out in a heavy accent, pointing at Paco.

'Not the Rock,' Heather said.

'Why isn't this bloody thing frothing!' I snapped.

'Excuse me, chaps,' Henry the Handsome said while leaning past me to flick a switch that instantly made the steamer come to life with a loud blast. 'That's the fellow,' he added with a wink before sodding off to charm someone else. The worst thing was that I could smell his aftershave. Which was literally amazing.

'She's frothing now look,' Clarence said, nodding eagerly at the metal jug. 'That's done it, Henry!'

Mugs clattered. Coffee poured. Milk frothed. Too many chefs spoil the broth, but eventually we made coffee, of sorts, while Paula bossed the shit out of everyone to get tables dragged together. It was chaos in a sea of chaos.

Then it was done, and we all sat down to enjoy the super nice coffee I made. Cos if there's one thing I can do it's make nice coffee.

'Jesus, Howie. That tastes like shit,' Marcy said after taking a sip while everyone else gagged.

'God, that's awful, Howie,' Paula said.

'I didn't make it!' I said. 'We all made it.'

'Commander, please tell Mr Howie this coffee is the worst I have ever tried,' Bashir said as Henry took a sip while suppressing the impulse to gag. I don't speak his language so I've actually no idea what the hell Bash said, but he'd just taken a sip and had the same look on his face as everyone else so I kinda worked it out.

'That's not too bad at all, Mr Howie. Really,' Henry said.

Honestly. I don't know what was worse. Henry hating the coffee, or Henry pretending to like the coffee.

'Whatever. It's got caffeine in it,' I said, trying to be all heroic and unflappable while taking a glug. 'Fuck me' I said, spitting it out. 'That's seriously shit. Jesus. Henry, don't drink it.'

'It's fine. Honestly. But perhaps you could refrain from ever making it again.'

Hahaha. What a splendid joke that made everyone chuckle.

Wanker.

'Donkey piss does not taste this bad,' Bashir said. 'I have drunk donkey piss. It was better than this.'

I don't know what Bashir said again. But I heard the word donkey and figured the rest out.

'What did he say?' Clarence asked.

'He said a good soldier will take refreshment when he can,' Henry said as everyone smiled at Bashir who just stared at Paco.

'The Rock,' he said in heavy English.

'Not the Rock,' Heather said

'I can't drink it,' Marcy announced. 'Worst coffee ever. Nick's a good coffee guy. Nick, go and make nice coffee.'

'I can do it,' Henry said, waving at Nick to sit down. 'Heather, perhaps you give me a hand.'

'Sorry, what?' Heather asked.

'Tell you what, Heather,' Henry said. 'You heat the milk and I'll get the coffee going. There's a few spouts too, so we can steam a few at once. There's plenty of long life milk. Which is handy. Okay, let's pour it in and get you started. Just watch that little gauge for the temperature. Got it?'

'Er, yeah, I think so,' Heather said, staring down at the little gauges poking out of the milk jugs as they come to life, sputtering away and forcing noisy steam through a spout.

'Beautiful day out there,' Henry continued. 'I'd say we're in for another hot one. Oh, and did you see the satellites?'

'We did,' Heather said, pouring milk into another jug to get it going. 'Your friend, er, George?'

'George. Yes.'

'He said there will be more.'

'Thousands most likely,' Henry said. 'Poured it in? Flick that switch, turn that dial and it should get going. That's it. I'll get the coffee pouring. So yes, I understand you've had some success tracking down the immunes.'

'We got twenty-three,' Heather said. Her hands full. Her mind occupied. Her back to the room.

'That's incredible. Twenty-three you say.'

'I really enjoyed it actually. I mean. I didn't work much before.'

And the rest of us mere mortals just sat and watched and got schooled by Henry the Handsome who just got the most socially awkward person we ever met to chat openly.

'Now that is nice coffee,' Marcy said, taking the first sip a moment later. 'Oh bless, Howie's face. He's all cross cos his coffee tasted like piss.'

'I didn't make it,' I mumbled into my mug of perfect coffee.

'Anyway. Yes. Here we are again,' Henry said while lifting his mug. 'I think the terms of our deal, for us working together, Mr Howie, are that I tell you what I know, and in return you will aid my team getting into London.'

I shared a quick look with Reginald. 'Let's hear it first,' I said.

Henry paused and started buying time by taking a sip of coffee, which made me think the guy was full of shit and was about to start using the same delay tactics again. Except this time, Henry started speaking openly and clearly.

'Howard was our intelligence gatherer. If my team located an asset and secured them into the UK. A defector for instance. Then one of Howard's roles was to remain in contact with them. Defectors don't always tell us everything they know straight away. They often drip feed intelligence in exchange for ongoing security, or better rewards. Bigger houses and so forth. The point is that Howard had good contacts within the international intelligence community, and it was Howard that first started hearing rumours. And really, that's all it was. Just rumours of something happening. Some kind of project, but again we had no knowledge of where it was, or even what it was about. Only that it had some serious funding and was being kept very hidden. We monitored it, as we do with everything. However, it's also important to note that my department was not the only department of our kind in the UK. MI5. MI6. GCHQ and Army intelligence to name just a few. What I mean is that we didn't always have ownership of cases, or informants for that matter. We specialised you see. I dislike the phrase *deniable ops*, but by and large that's what we did. But Howard. Well. He'd got the bit between his teeth about this rumour and he wouldn't let it go.'

'Now we know where you get it from,' Marcy said, giving me a look.

'And then, all of a sudden, Howard seemed to crack the case,' Henry continued. 'We knew there was a big research project being planned and a list of leading scientists were being invited to take part. Specialists in everything from virology to meteorology, which is where Dr Neal Barrett comes in…'

Another pause as he took an A5 hardback writing pad from his bag at his feet and placed it on the table before sliding it over to Reginald.

'That's the diary from Dr Neal Barrett,' Henry said into the silent air. 'I've marked the date you should start from.'

Reginald stared at it for a second. 'Are you asking me to read it out, Henry?'

'I am, Reginald.'

Reggie looked at me. I gave him a nod and he cleared his throat as he opened the diary and found the page Henry had marked. *'Diary entry. September 15th. Today has been most interesting…'*

8

DIARY ENTRY

September 15th

Today has been most interesting. Truly I am at a loss of even where to begin.

I was at work in my offices in central London when my secretary informed me that two men from the United Nations wished to see me.

That in itself was not alarming. I'm one of Europe's leading statisticians. I hold a doctorate, and will soon be a professor, not only that but I am the chief researcher for the UK's leading independent statistical office, so to be visited by governmental, or even official international organisations is not unusual.

They did, however, normally give notice and book an appointment, so I could prepare, and have some idea of the subject.

No matter though. I went down to the small conference room and met with two older gentlemen in dark business suits.

'Dr Neal Barrett?' one of them asked the second I walked in.

We shook hands and exchanged brief pleasantries. They gave me their names and spoke with European accents, but, as embarrassed as I am to admit it, and because of what came next and the speed of events thereafter, I cannot recall what they were called, nor can I remember if they even told me where they were from.

'Do you mind if we get straight to business, Dr Barrett?' one of them asked and duly pulled a sheet of paper from a case.

The sheet held a list of names, and upon closer inspection, I noticed they were the names of leading scientists from all over the world.

'Do you know any of these people, Dr Barrett?'

'Yes, of course,' I said and explained that I had heard of many, and had even met a few personally,

I then noticed my name was also on the list. About two thirds of the way down.

They then said that some of the others had only agreed to sign up on seeing my name. I asked what they meant.

'We cannot tell you,' the second man said, and he too produced a sheet of paper with a small printed paragraph above a dotted line and asked me to sign it in acceptance of the terms and conditions. Of course, I was rather flummoxed and asked them again what was going on. They said they could not tell me, which was in the terms and conditions.

'Terms and conditions?' I asked. 'What terms and conditions?'

'We cannot tell you until you sign, Dr Barrett,' the first man said.

They then said the private jet was waiting and the secondment would be for an expected duration of three months, but that it could be extended at their discretion, as per the terms and conditions, which I was not allowed to see.

'Gentlemen, I think there has been some mistake,' I said, feeling rather confused and somewhat alarmed too. 'May I see some identification, please.' I wanted to verify they were from the United Nations and was almost at the point of calling security.

'Dr Barrett. Five hundred thousand pounds has already been paid into your personal bank account.'

That made me even more alarmed, and I immediately suspected bribery or blackmail.

'Is this bribery or blackmail?' I asked, although, I did wonder why anyone would want to bribe or blackmail a statistician.

They told me to check my bank account. There was something about those two men and such was the situation that I pulled my phone from my pocket and accessed my online banking. And there it was. A single payment paid into my account by, and I quote, THE UNITED NATIONS.

The United Nations had paid me half a million pounds.

'The second payment of five hundred thousand will be paid on completion of the project, Dr Barrett,' one of them said.

'What project?' I asked.

They shared a look again before the first one leaned over the table towards me. 'There is a project, Dr Barrett. It is highly classified, but your expertise is required. Really, we cannot say anything further.'

One million pounds. Even as a leading statistician I was on less than seventy thousand a year, which in London means I am practically destitute.

Not that I would sell out. God no. I have far more integrity than that.

I signed immediately and said they could have my kidneys if they wished. They didn't laugh, but then they did not strike me as the laughing types.

'Check your phone again, Dr Barrett,' one of them said. I frowned and wondered why, having just used it to check my bank account. The thing was dead.

'There will be no communication with the outside world until the project is complete. Your employer will inform any family, friends, colleagues and associates that you are seconded on a confidential research trip for the foreseeable future. Please come with us.'

The director was waiting outside the room. That being the

director of the entire company. (I've only ever met him once before.) He shook my hand and assured me it was sanctioned and safe.

I'll admit I did need those words of assurance, especially when the two men escorted me through the building and out to a big executive car with blacked out windows parked right outside the door. And trust me, that is no small feat in London.

I was driven to an airfield - I'm not even sure where it was – and escorted on board an otherwise empty executive jet, save for the pilot of course, and flown to a destination unknown.

My guess is that I am in central Europe, due to the flight time and the mountains I saw when I transferred from the jet to a helipad and a waiting chopper.

The chopper landed on another helipad next to a sheer rock-face where an armed guard ushered me from the chopper to a door set within the face of the cliff.

We went through into a long corridor hewn from the rock. I asked where we were, but the chap said he could not tell me.

We reached a wide doorway flanked by two more soldiers and went through into what I can only describe as the lobby of a grand hotel. The floor was laid to marble with potted plants, leather chairs and coffee tables all over the place with polished wooden panelling on the walls to cover the natural rock-face. Doors leading off to meeting rooms, offices and a large restaurant too from which the most heavenly scents of freshly baked bread wafted out.

It was a remarkable transition and truly, one would never know this place was inside a mountain, apart from the lack of windows of course.

There was a crowd of people in the lobby, all talking with a hubbub of noise. I was led around to a reception desk behind which stood a very attractive woman.

'Dr Barrett, it is a pleasure to meet you. My name is Camilla. Let's get you booked in shall we.'

Camilla issued me with a swipe card for my room and proceeded to tell me about the restaurant, swimming pool, health suite, offices and IT system. She said the bar was open during the evenings, but drunken behaviour would not be tolerated. I was informed the IT system was restricted to incoming data only, and that any attempts to contact any person outside of the facility would result in immediate detention within a secure unit until completion of the project, at which point the funds paid would be taken back.'

I was just to ask what the project was about when we were interrupted by a loud Scottish brogue shouting across the lobby.

'BARRETT! WHO LET THE BLOODY BEAN COUNTER IN HERE?'

The voice belonged to Professor Donegal, a loud, uncouth, and shockingly outspoken man, but also a good associate of mine. And truth be told, I was rather glad to see a friendly face.

I saw others too. Professors and doctors from all over the world, and all of them looked the same as I did; confused and clueless.

Camilla then showed me the facilities and took me down to the health suite, and said she hoped to see me in there working a sweat up. I blushed and stuttered like a teenage boy at that point. I've never really been that confident around women, especially ones that look like Camilla. She was very professional though with a lovely friendly manner.

Camilla then took me back to the lobby where I mingled and chatted with the other scientists. Nobody had a clue what was going on. Various suggestions and proposals were put forward. But none of us actually knew anything.

Then, without warning, a middle-aged man in a dark suit walked into the lobby while clapping his hands loudly to draw attention.

'Good evening, ladies and gentlemen. May I have your attention please. My name is Alexander. I am your point of contact for this project and you are in what we call the facility. The only information I can tell you at this stage is that the United Nations are funding this research, but it does not exist. It is not happening. We are deniable, as per the terms and conditions. Any attempts to make contact with the outside world will see you removed from the project and placed in secure holding with your payments taken back. My apologies for beginning with such a stern warning, but it is good to be clear from the outset. Now, we are ready to seal the door, but before we do, I must ask if any person wishes to leave. Once the door is sealed it will not open again until the project is complete. Does anyone wish to leave?'

When none did, Alexander gestured to the armed guards who proceeded to seal the door with much clanging of metal on metal.

'Done!' Alexander called out. 'We are now committed until the project is finished.'

'What is the bloody project!?' Professor Donegal shouted with a good natured and well-timed quip that earned a nice round of laughs.

'Of course,' Alexander said. 'The door is now sealed, and so, without further ceremony, please allow me to inform that you have each received a briefing pack detailing all of the information you need for us to begin.' He paused at that point with a faint smile. 'They're in your rooms now,' he added.

Cue an exodus of scientists all rushing off to their rooms to finally establish just what we were all here for. I was one of them and almost jogged with splendid anticipation back to my room. But alas, there was no briefing pack. I thought to contact reception when there was a knock at my door. I opened it to find Camilla smiling at me.

'I have your briefing pack, Dr Barrett,' she said, holding a thick folder.

I stammered a thanks and went to take the folder as she stepped forward to hand it over, which meant I stepped too close and almost walked into her. We both apologised and laughed at our stupidity. Or rather, I did while she smiled with what I took to be gentle pity.

'Here,' she said, holding it out. 'Anything you need, please do ask me personally.'

'Oh gosh, well that is very nice of you,' I said in reply. I think I said that anyway. I may have said I like licking cricket bats for all I know.

'You're very welcome, Dr Barrett.'

'Neal,' I blurted, rather too quickly, then blushed again.

She left at that point. I don't blame her. I would have run off too.

. . .

But yes. There we are. This day has already proven to be a truly unforgettable experience and I haven't even read the folder yet. I needed to calm myself before delving into serious study, and I do find penning my thoughts in this way is very soothing.

It did just occur to me that I might not even be allowed to keep this diary. That said. I'm not communicating with the outside world, and it is only a private and personal account.

Signing off.
NB

*I've just read the folder. Good grief it's not what I thought at all. No wonder they needed me.

October 2nd

I think this is perhaps the longest I have been without making a diary entry. The last two or so weeks have just been an incredible experience. I have never been so happy in my life. We truly are in a magical place.

The briefing packs stated the project is table-top exercise to examine the effects of a hypothetical global event, and what would happen in three distinct situations.

The hypothetical global event is thus:

A contagion has been developed that can spread from person to person by the tiniest microscopic drop of any bodily fluid.

That contagion, if left in its pure state, is a Panacea that can cure all known diseases.

. . .

EVERY HUMAN on the planet can (hypothetically) be cured of every disease. Not only that, but medical administration is not required as the simple transference of any bodily fluid from one person to another will guarantee infection.

THIS CONTAGION CAN ALSO BE GENETICALLY TWEAKED to scour, identify and fix specific diseases or other infections. For instance, it can be used to treat only Malaria.

THIS HYPOTHETICAL CONTAGION can also be genetically altered to energise the host body into an exceptionally violent predator intent only on finding more hosts. (We're told to think of the zombie movies) (which did make me laugh...I mean zombies? Seriously?)

However. We were also told that 1-2% of the global population will be immune to the tweaked violent version.

THE PROJECT, and the reason we are here, is to understand what would happen if:

1. The Panacea was released into a standing global population of over seven billion people.
2. What would happen if one of the tweaked versions of the Panacea were released to target the deadliest diseases (Malaria, Diphtheria etc)
3. The violent version was released.

AND THAT, I am proud to say, is why my recruitment was so vital, because no one can theorise and predict global events like a statistician.

This is what I do! I am the only one here that can take ALL data from ALL fields of study and correlate the lot into a digestible and understandable globally relevant format.

I have no clue about viruses, bacteria, genomes, DNA strands, pathogens, R-rates, or any of those things, but what I can do is extrapolate data from many different events to understand, and accurately predict how fast a thing will spread, and the reactions to world populations.

MOST OF US do suspect that given the secret nature of the project - and the sheer scale of the funding being thrown at it during such a time of global austerity - that the panacea is real.

You wouldn't offer a million pounds, or dollar equivalent, to so many people and then house them in such luxury with unprecedented access to data for a hypothetical table-top exercise.

No.

This is either real, or they are close to finding a real Panacea. Either way, this is an incredibly exciting thing.

ALEXANDER HAS BEEN ASKED countless times if this is real, but he refuses to be drawn. And for his part, he's made it clear he is here to facilitate the project but not to influence or shape our findings.

'I am here to facilitate, not to tell you how to do your jobs.'

IT IS A FASCINATING PROJECT, not just the subject but the setting too. Being able to work, without distraction, alongside some of the most gifted minds on the planet is truly exceptional. The isolation from distraction is a brilliant idea, so yes, I am extremely pleased I was recruited.

I HAVE STARTED a fitness regime too and have been going to the gym every day. The first visit was a bit awkward as I didn't even know how to get the treadmill working, but one of maintenance guys was also in the gym and seemed to take pity on me.

Albert is ex-military and knows a lot about fitness. (I think that's how he got the maintenance contract for this place.)

I did think he would work security, but then he is an older chap, maybe late fifties? Very funny man though.

Camilla also likes the gym and seems to go at the same time as me, which is both great and awful. She is lovely be around and seems to take pleasure in talking to me, despite me being a terrible sweaty mess.

SIGNING OFF.
NB

OCTOBER 22ND

THE RESEARCH IS CONTINUING and a much greater picture of what will happen if A (the complete Panacea) is released into the population.

IT REALLY IS FASCINATING STUFF, but the results are not what one may immediately think, and again I can understand why my presence here is so vital.

THE PANACEA CURES EVERYTHING.

Releasing it means that, barring incident or accident, a person can expect to live a healthy life from birth to death. Not only that, but life expectancy will increase exponentially. (A huge number of elderly deaths are caused by weakened immune systems.)

. . .

THAT SEEMS fantastic doesn't it? Everyone can lead very long, healthy lives. Wonderful!

NOT SO, unfortunately. Which is where my knowledge and experience comes in, and which is causing some upset.

Think of the explosion of population within one generation if A, or even B, were released because within a decade, we could easily double or even triple the number of people on the planet.

Everyone would be cured of everything, only to starve to death or die of thirst because there isn't enough food, water, shelter or infrastructure.

Some of the global medicinal and pharmaceutical companies have GDP's greater than some countries. Their profits and stock values would be wiped out overnight.

The same with every provider of private healthcare, and all the various subsidiary companies such as insurance, equipment and medical service industries.

They would all cease to function almost immediately.

That would cause mass unemployment, and a shift of those companies redirecting their energies into something that does provide profit. (Weapons, recreational drugs, alcohol, war, people trafficking, prostitution etc.)

Many of those conglomerates have politicians and ruling classes on their payroll, but suddenly they are not needed, and therefore their influence will be gone, which in turn, creates power vacuums and instability.

The black-market for medicines will also vanish and again those profits will be sought from other avenues. (Criminal.)

The use of recreational drugs will soar as the risks linked to lifestyle diseases will be gone. The same with alcohol.

Oppressed populations kept in check by the ever-present fear of change, will rise up and overthrow governments. Reactions will be swift and brutal which will escalate world tensions and land-grabs as nations realise they will very soon be needing more fuel, crops and landmass, which in turn leads to global war and the use of WMD's. (This is a very brief outline but then this is my diary and not a report paper.)

As I said, this data is not what most of the scientists wanted to hear. They are truly gifted academics that are highly skilled in their areas, but for the most part they live in bubbles and are incredibly naïve. Some are also (bizarrely) very religious.

I am still having a blast though. I have never felt so needed. I am the expert for once.

Camilla is lovely. We talk every day in the gym, and she invited me to share the jacuzzi with her yesterday.

'Come on, it'll relax you,' she said when I started to stutter and blush. 'I like talking to you.'

I did go and may I say, respectfully of course, that Camilla looks delightful in a two-piece swimsuit.

Signing off.
NB

November 3rd

Professor Hussein is an awful, loud, obstructive, bullying brute of a man, and I am not the only one glad of Professor Donegal being here to stand up to him.

. . .

AFTER PRESENTING my findings on the results of releasing A (the Panacea) I was tasked to move straight on to C (the violent version).

I was rather glad of this because the spectrum of research for evaluating B (the effects of reducing global rates of specific diseases) was simply too broad.

So yes, I was rather relieved, and I duly paid my focus to the version marked as C. The zombie version! (I'm still embarrassed to call it that.)

THE MAIN THRUST of C is that those infected will be driven by a relentless, insatiable, and incredibly violent urge to seek new hosts.

We were told that a person infected with C would feel no pain. They would need less water and they would be incredibly strong too.

Don't forget, C is still the Panacea. It still cures them of everything else. But this version of the virus turns them into rabid beasts.

My predictions for C, based on our population densities, the global travel infrastructure coupled with the aggression & desire etc, determine that it would spread across the planet within a week. Probably less.

We know, from previous pandemics, that the spread of any disease is nearly impossible to prevent without immediate and very strong actions being taken. And that is only when governments are functioning. Something as violent as this could not be contained. It would wipe humanity out within a few days.

THE DESTRUCTION WOULD BE on an epic scale with an expected loss of 98 - 99% to our species. However, that destruction will mostly be limited to our species only.

THAT IS the thing causing so much upset because although 98 - 99% of the population would most likely die, we can expect 1 - 2% to live and make use of the infrastructure left largely in place. (1 to 2% of seven billion is still a significant number)

The roads will still be there, the shops, the vehicles, the houses, airfields, fuels, technologies. The farms. The crops.

The air would be cleaner too. In fact, there would be an enormously positive impact from a 98% reduction in the human species.

However. The contentious point is this:

The release of the Panacea does <u>not</u> guarantee that 2% of the population will be left,

In fact. The data very strongly suggests that nuclear and weapons of mass destruction will be used which leaves a tainted, broken wartorn world decimated to a point we are put into negative evolution. We're talking an extinction level event here. Not just for people. For everything.

Those findings then prompted a discussion:

<u>What would happen if C was released for targeted culling prior to A being released?</u>

It is abhorrent of course, and no sane person in their right mind would ever do it, but, as Alexander says, we must consider all options.

'How can we eliminate that which we do not consider?'

Professor Hussein is refusing to even consider such a thing, he will not discuss it, not for one second, and further, he is disrupting the whole project.

Hussein is quite possibly the world's foremost expert in virology, so from all of us he has perhaps the best scientific grasp of this, but if

Hussein is not careful, I can see him being removed from the entire project for his bullying and aggressive nature.

Prof Donegal's background is in immunology, and next to Hussein, he has the fullest understanding of the scientific nature of the contagion.

That expert knowledge mixed with such strong personalities within such an enclosed environment is certainly creating fireworks and causing a great deal of very heated debate.

THAT ASIDE, I am having a blast and have made some very dear friends. Albert is a breath of fresh air and always ready with a joke, a quip, a comment or timely observation for me when I break from heated discussions to cool off and gain some perspective.

Albert is also a deceptively intelligent man too, and a great sounding board when I really do need to clear my mind and talk things through. He has a grasp of the project and what it's about.

I wanted to start lifting weights to get a bit more muscle. (Albert has very muscular arms) but he said I should focus on my heart and lungs with strength conditioning. He was quite serious about it too. He said fitness and stamina are more important than looking good in a tight top.

It is paying off too. I feel great.

Camilla said my tummy looked flatter and my love handles are reducing, she also said she liked seeing my little love handles and podgy belly.

If anyone else ever referred to my stomach as podgy I would have been mortified but coming from Camilla it was fine. I'm spending a lot of time with Camilla now. We talk for hours.

Surprisingly, she and Albert both really like Hussein, but aren't too fond of Donegal. Strange how we all see people differently, but then neither Albert nor Camilla have to spend hours locked in ever-increasing debate with them.

I think about Camilla a lot. I do wonder if she has any romantic inclination towards me, but then I look at myself in the mirror and realise a woman like Camilla would never lower herself to be with a chap like me.

SIGNING OFF.
   NB

NOVEMBER 15TH

THE LAST COUPLE of weeks have not really progressed very far at all as we seem to be stuck in the same arguments between Professors' Hussein & Donegal.

Alexander really needs to step in now. I, and several other scientists, have said as much to him.

'Really, Alexander. This is becoming tiresome and draining,' I said to him only this morning.

'How we react and how we respond is representative of how the world will react, we must see it through,' he said.

THE GOOD NEWS is the stalemate means I have plenty of time on my hands, which is being increasingly spent with Albert and Camilla, and a great little threesome of friends we have become too.

NB

NOVEMBER 20TH

. . .

STILL NO BLASTED CHANGE. Why on earth are they funding such an extravagant hypothetical research project only to allow it to collapse into vicious bloody debates that is dividing the whole facility?

And why isn't Alexander taking action?

PROFESSOR DONEGAL AND APPROX. 45% of the scientists are on one side with their fervent belief that C should be released to cull the population before the Panacea is released.

Professor Hussein and approx. 40% of the scientists are on the other side with their also fervent belief that we have an absolute moral obligation to release the Panacea.

THE PROBLEM IS THAT HUSSEIN, despite having the moral upper hand, is aggressive and angry, so although his points are valid, and what he says makes sense, he is turning people away because of his character.

Donegal, however, is charismatic and uses great humour to draw people in. Whereas Hussein just glowers and slams his hands on the desks and throws doors open so they bang into walls.

Surprisingly, both sides have equal numbers of scientists that proclaim faith in the major religions, and those scientists of faith have made use of their religious teachings and understandings to add weight to their arguments.

IT'S ALL VERY TIRESOME.

I, however, am falling head over heels in love with Camilla and cannot stop thinking about her, but the thought of making a move terrifies me. What if she rejects me? What if I have read it all wrong?

It's all very confusing.

SIGNING OFF.
NB

THE UNDEAD TWENTY-FIVE. THE HEAT

November 21ˢᵗ

AN INCREDIBLE THING HAS HAPPENED.

AFTER I FINISHED work last night, I sought the company of Albert.

(Albert agrees with me that any form of culling is just disgusting and there is a clear moral responsibility to release the Panacea).

We exercised and then went for a swim, at which point Camilla joined us. She also agrees with me and Albert that culling is out of the question.

'I can't see why they are even considering it,' she said.

We then sat in the jacuzzi for a long time, laughing and joking until I remarked I would miss the evening meal. Albert and Camilla shared a look and a whisper, then Camilla told me to go with Albert to his rooms.

Albert guided me into the service area used by the staff and snuck me into his room. It was very neat too, and exactly what you'd expect from an ex-military type.

I took the chair by the desk while he sat on the bed and we chatted about the whole blasted culling thing again.

'A thing like that should never happen,' Albert said firmly before Camilla came in with a tray of pizzas in one hand and a box of beer bottles in the other.

'You look like a man that needs beer and pizza,' she told me with a smile.

I was genuinely touched. Really and truly. I've never had friends before, not like that anyway.

Albert told jokes and we laughed until my sides hurt. He even told a story about a soldier he once knew that blew a cow up. It was awful of course to think of a poor cow being blown up, but the way Albert told the story did make us cry with laughter.

After a while, Camilla complained that her bottom was getting numb from sitting on the floor and stood up to massage her cheeks with such a mock pained face it made Albert and I roar with laughter.

She tutted, swiped our heads and plonked down on my lap, which made me go silent and stunned and Albert to laugh even harder at my expression. But I must admit we had drunk quite a few bottles of beer by that time.

Camilla then looped her arms around my neck and stretched up to put her feet on Albert's desk to snuggle in and get comfy. It was magical. Then the beer ran out.

'The beer's run out,' Albert said, nodding at Camilla.

'Get some more then,' she retorted.

'I'm old and stink of piss. You're a woman.' He clicked his fingers then ducked and rolled from the shoe thrown at his head while I laughed.

'I'll get some more,' he said with a grumble. 'Don't touch my bed...'

'Quick, get up...' Camilla said once Albert and left. She grabbed my hand and pulled me onto his bed while giggling and laughing.

'He said to leave his bed alone,' I said, or rather I slurred, and probably stammered quite a bit too.

'Pah!' she said and pulled me down a little too hard, so we ended up rolling over each other on his mattress. That's when she kissed me. I froze in shock. It was over within a second then she pulled back and watched me closely before we both burst out laughing at what we just did.

Albert came back to us sitting up on his bed with mock innocent expressions. He tried to glare and said he wasn't sharing the beer, but he did, and we drank more.

Not being used to drinking alcohol, the beer soon took effect and I toddled off to use Albert's bathroom and was very surprised to see an old-fashioned cut-throat razor on the side next to the basin.

'Albert!' I called out. 'What on earth is this?'

'WHAT?' he shouted from the other room.

I carried out it while laughing to show Camilla. 'Bloody old cut-throat razor...'

Camilla's reaction was quite unexpected. 'Albert!' she whispered angrily, giving him a dark look.

'You'd better hand that over, Neal. It's very sharp,' Albert said, moving very swiftly from the chair to pluck the thing from my hand.

'Albert, put it away,' Camilla said, shaking her head at him. They almost seemed sober at that point, but then I was very drunk so I couldn't be sure of anything.

'Not allowed these here,' Albert said, winking at me. 'Mum's the word eh?'

'But... but... You're all beardy,' I told Albert, pointing at his greying whiskers in case he didn't know where his beard was.

'For my neck and cheeks, hair grows all over the place when you get old,' he quipped, laughing as he pocketed the razor. 'Anyway. Stop going through my kit and drink your beer.'

Later, when Albert dozed off and started snoring. Camilla said I had to go back to my rooms and that she would walk me home.

'In case you get lost,' she slurred, nodding at me seriously.

We went quietly, in the way of drunk people crashing into tables and falling over potted plants and it took a good five minutes to get that blasted swipe card through the narrow slot thing on my bedroom door.

It did work eventually, and I turned to bid the lady a good night.

'I shall bid you a good night my lady,' I said deeply, offering a bow.

'Dear me, Dr Barrett, do you need an invitation in writing?'

'For what?' I enquired, somewhat drunkenly.

She tutted, pushed me into my room, closed the door and took her blouse off.

'Oh,' I said, blinking and staring as she reached back to unclasp her bra. 'I say, will this invitation be forthcoming soon?'

'Idiot,' she laughed that wonderful laugh and the rest was truly an amazing experience. I was very drunk I hasten to add and no doubt my love-making skills were perhaps not as developed as some, but Camilla said it was really good and even said she almost orgasmed too, which is very rare for a first time apparently (for a woman that is.) (Not that I would know.)

. . .

A MOST INCREDIBLE THING INDEED. I am in love!!!

SIGNING OFF.
 NB

November 22nd

SO MANY THINGS ARE HAPPENING, and I need to get my thoughts in order.

CAMILLA CAME to my room last night and truth be told I was still feeling hungover from the previous night's excessive drinking, but I was still very pleased to see her. She said she couldn't stay long and seemed somewhat stressed.

'I can't stay long,' she said quietly once the door was closed. 'Albert found something.'

'Found something?' I asked. 'What has he found?'

'I'll tell you, but you have to promise me you won't say anything.'

'Of course, I won't,' I said, then feared this might be an integrity test of sorts, but then figured we had got drunk and had sex already, so any potential integrity test was well and truly blown.

'You look worried, Neal,' she said on seeing my expression.

'Scientists looking worried are par for the course I'm afraid. Now, whatever is going on?'

She did look ravishing in the subdued light of my room and I'll admit I wanted to kiss her but did not quite know how to prompt such a thing into happening.

Camilla went to speak, stopped, saw my expression again,

appeared to work out my concerns, tutted, smiled and kissed me very passionately.

'Better?' she asked.

I couldn't reply, due to my current state of arousal so I stammered and swallowed a few times at which point she pulled her skirt up and her knickers down then pulled me onto the bed while freeing me from my trousers. It was amazing too! If somewhat quick. I think it was quicker than when I was drunk if I am honest, but Camilla said it was wonderful and that she very nearly orgasmed again, and that I just needed to build my staying power up a bit, but then added that I was lovely and she adored me very much, but could I get off now as she really needed to talk to me.

'Albert's found another level,' she said from the bathroom.

'A what now?' I asked, my legs still somewhat rubbery from the passionate sex.

'Come closer,' she whispered.

I went closer, blanching at the sight of her sitting on the toilet with her knickers round her ankles.

'There's another level below us. A whole complex of... Neal? Are you listening?'

'Yes. Yes, of course. Another level eh? Well, we are in a UN facility so it stands to reason there will be other-.'

'No, listen,' she said urgently, standing up to wipe and yank her knickers up while talking. 'Albert said he saw test subjects in laboratories, rats and mice and he said he saw monkeys with red eyes going absolutely nuts. He said some of them were withered, like emaciated and were attacking the bars of their cages so hard their hands and feet were all broken but they appeared ignorant of any pain.'

'What?' I asked, suddenly very alarmed.

Camilla came closer, her voice very hushed. 'Albert said the wild animals were in a section marked C and the healthy animals were in a section marked A. He saw another section marked B but it was empty...'

'Gosh. Right. Well.'

'It's real... The Panacea is real.'

'Ah now, one must not jump to conclusions. As I said, we are in a UN funded complex so what Albert saw could be any manner of thing. Chemicals, disease research, weaponised diseases like Anthrax or…'

'Neal! They have two active sections marked A and C. A were healthy. C were wild. It fits exactly what they said about the contagion. This is not a table-top exercise. This is real.'

'Okay, right, well that's a good thing. Wow! The Panacea exists.'

'So does the other thing.'

'What other thing?'

'The bad thing. C. The violent one. Albert said it was terrible. He said all the animals in that section were going absolutely crazy.'

'Ah now, yes, yes I can see how that would look but sadly, that's how these science chaps do things. They have to test them on animals you see, and I know it's controversial and awful for any creature to suffer.'

'Neal, listen to me! To be at the level of undertaking live subject trials, in the same place and at the same time as pulling in the world's best scientists, and then leaving those scientists to reflect on the reaction of the world to a point of near mutiny tends to suggest they are in a very advanced position…'

I was rather taken aback at Camilla's manner and studied her anew. 'I say Camilla, are you really just a receptionist?'

She smiled, or rather winced. 'Yes, of course. I'm just very concerned… Why are you looking at me like that?'

'Are you a spy?'

'A spy? Neal, have you heard yourself? Do I look like a spy?'

'Well. I don't know. What does a spy look like?'

'Who would I by spying for?'

'The Russians?'

'The Russians are a member state of the United Nations. They joined in 1945 when they were still the USSR…'

'Right. I see.'

'Okay, yes I am a spy.'

'I knew it!'

'You did not know it.'

'You're right. I didn't know it.'

'And I'm not Russian. I'm British. Anyway. We need your help.'

'Did you only have sex with me because you're a spy?'

'What!? No! Of course not. I liked you, like you I mean. I like you. You're so sweet and honestly, I really was this close to orgasming.'

'Right.'

'Anyway, Albert said… Why do you look so offended?'

'I'm not offended.'

'Now you even sound offended.'

'It's fine.'

'Okay, Albert said we have to monitor now but we have to… Okay listen, I did not just have sex with you because of this.'

'Right.'

'I could have picked anyone.'

'Conceited.'

'I meant I could have picked someone like that pig Donegal, but I like you, I like spending time with you. I love spending time with you.'

'Sure.'

'Neal. They have a virus that will kill 98% of the population. They also have a virus that can cure every disease and illness. We need to focus on that right now.'

'Why do I need to focus on that?'

'Because we need your help?'

'We? Who is we? Is Albert a spy too?'

'Of course, he's a spy! He found the secret level.'

'Oh, well that's just great. Everyone is a spy. I'm the only one that isn't a spy. I say are you and Albert… You know.'

'Oh god no, Jesus no, I love Albert but no… He's old enough to be my father…'

'He's very fit though.'

'I told you, I like love handles and podgy bellies.'

'Humph, mine are almost gone.'

'Almost but not quite. I can still feel them.'

'Get off. No, no we're not having spy sex again. I feel used. Really, I do. Really, Camilla… If that's even your name.'

'It's not my name.'

'Get off! I said no… Don't take your top off. No, please put your bra back on and… And er…Right…I see…I shan't respond you know. I shan't get an erection.'

WE HAD SEX AGAIN. Which was the best one yet even if I do say so myself and Camilla even orgasmed this time. Well, she said she did, and she shuddered a lot, and I did ask if she faked it, but she said she didn't.

'It was real,' she said, then asked me to get off as we needed to talk again. 'We'll need your help.'

'What can I do?' I asked, not in the sense of offering but more in the sense of panicking.

'Influence the others. Make them see Professor Hussein is right. They'll listen to you.'

'They won't listen to me! I think it's gone too far for that.'

'Neal. It has to be A. C will kill everyone. Influence them. Make them understand. Please. For me… And for Albert.'

'Who do you work for?'

'I really can't say, Neal.'

'Well how do I know you're not the bad guys?'

'Hmmm, that is a valid point, but in response I would say that no side ever truly considers themselves to be the bad guys, do they? Only the winning side can ever claim that trophy, and I'd rather be on the side that prevented 98% of the population of the planet being murdered by the release of-.'

'Good gosh. You are far more intelligent than I originally thought, but er, well, on that note, I did tell you my research indicates the release of A could be far worse than the release of C.'

'It's not for us to play God. We have a clear moral responsibility. It's up to people how they respond and what they do.'

'Yes, yes you're right of course.'

'Please try, Neal. That's all we want you to do. Just try and influence them to see reason.'

'I'm not sure.'

'I do like your love handles, I really do.'

'I'll have you know I am a man of integrity and wooing me with sexual favours will not win my professional opinion.'

'But you will try? For me?'

I pondered this, while staring into her eyes in a state of post-coital glow and mumbled that I would try. At which point she kissed me again.

Signing off
NB

November 23rd

What have I got myself into?

Having been persuaded by Camilla, who is very persuasive I might add, I spent the day feeling like a damned politician, going from scientist to scientist trying to guide them towards choosing A over C.

My concerns were that if I were too forceful or opinionated it would gain undue attention and seem odd but, in all honesty, it looked like things had gone too far and by lunchtime I expressed such a view to Camilla.

'I really don't think they're listening to me,' I said.

'Try harder,' Camilla urged me.

I did try harder, I really did. But by the afternoon it felt I had made zero progress, so I retired to the gym hoping to converse with Albert and express my concerns directly.

Albert was not there, and Camilla only stopped by briefly. She seemed rather distracted and quiet as she led me into a small room containing cleaning materials where we had sex. (I never thought I would ever be in a secret UN mountain facility, let alone have sex in a cleaning cupboard with a beautiful spy.)

It was just after I had finished, and while still coupled with Camilla that she whispered in my ear.

'I can't tell you everything, Neal, but I need you to trust me. Do you trust me?'

I said I did and that I hoped I could.

'Good,' she whispered and kissed me again. 'Albert is going back down there tonight.'

'Okay,' I said carefully, suddenly feeling very worried.

'He wants you to go with him.'

I was right to feel very worried.

'He doesn't know what to look for.'

'I am a statistician. I don't know to look for.'

'You can read data and you know how data is stored.'

'Right. Did I say I was just a statistician?'

'You did. Just be ready later. Wear sport shoes in case you have to run.'

'Run? I never said I was going. I'm a stati-.'

'I know you'll do the right thing. Sex with you is so good, Neal. Honestly, I can't stop thinking about you. I want us to be together when this is over.'

'Really?'

'This isn't easy for me to say but I... I think I'm falling for you, Neal.'

'Oh.'

'You are so lovely, I'm mad about you. Be ready for Albert and wear sports shoes.'

. . .

THE UNDEAD TWENTY-FIVE. THE HEAT

CAMILLA THEN SAID she had to get back to work and rushed off after giving me another big kiss and telling me how much she is looking forward to being together after this is over.

I fretted, as you do, at the prospect of sneaking about a secret facility with a spy and tottered out of the cleaning cupboard, and thought about going for a swim then decided I should rather keep my energy for whatever awful night-time adventures awaited me

I must admit, although I was terrified, it felt exciting in a surreal way, and besides, Camilla had said she was in love with me, and already my head was filling with dreams of us living in a little snow-covered cottage somewhere remote, by then of course I would be a rugged spy too with a beard like Albert's and muscular arms that bulged in my sleeves.

I HAD those thoughts in mind as I walked back through the lobby only to be stopped by Alexander who asked if I had a moment.

'Dr Barrett, have you got a moment?'

'Of course, how can I help?' I asked, already panicking a little inside.

He came closer, eyeing me with what I took to be great suspicion before speaking in a low voice. 'I want to show you something, Dr Barrett.'

I swallowed, or rather I gulped, when he motioned for me to follow him behind the reception desk.

'It won't take long,' he said while leading me on. We walked by several staff members including Camilla.

Alexander showed me into what I took to be his office. He closed the door, smiled at me and told me not to worry. 'Really don't worry.' He then crossed over to the wood panelled wall, tapped something and smiled again when a section of the wall moved swung silently inward. 'I think you will be pleased to see this, follow me, Dr Barrett.'

The blasted man then showed me the blasted secret level that Albert had blasted well found.

We went down a flight of stairs to a brightly lit complex of laboratories and offices while all the time I was convincing myself he knew about Camilla and Albert and the sex in the cleaning cupboard and would be feeding me to a tank of disease infected zombie piranhas.

'The Panacea is real, Dr Barrett,' Alexander said, sweeping into the room marked A through which we could see another room containing all manner of creatures held in tanks and cages.

'Is it now?' I whimpered while wishing I had sports shoes on as this seemed a good time to do some running.

He then proceeded to tell me that all of the creatures in this section had been given the Panacea, and subsequently had been exposed to all manner of nasty things but were all living healthy lives.

'As you can see, they are alive and well.'

I cannot actually recall exactly what I said in response due to staring about the place looking for the trapdoors that would drop into the piranha tank.

'You are the only one to maintain such a cool head, Dr Barrett.'

'I was what now?' I asked, not having heard what he said before that.

'Neal!'

'Argh what!' I turned quickly on hearing my name being called to see a chap called Andrew Jackson. Andrew and I knew each other from the circuit of conferences.

'I heard you were here,' he said with a big grin, shaking my trembling hand. 'I'm a lab technician on this one.'

'I don't know what this one is,' I told him clearly. 'I don't know anything. No one has told me anything.'

'Right,' he said slowly. 'Anyway, great to see you again.'

'It is a small world indeed, Dr Barrett,' Alexander said. 'The connections we make in life often come back to us.'

Well that comment certainly increased my paranoia substantially. I could tell he knew I had just had sex in the cleaning cupboard, and that any minute now we'd be led into a room with Camilla and Albert tied to chairs while big burly henchmen stood about laughing.

'This way please, Dr Barrett. Just through here and please may I say in advance how sorry I am to show you this but-.'

I almost blurted right then that I had nothing to do with it and Camilla seduced me but then saw we were back in a corridor heading towards a door marked C that was covered in all manner of bio-hazard warnings.

'I'm afraid this is very unpleasant to see, but we won't be close.' He stopped me in an ante-room next to a window through which we could see a sealed and clearly sterile laboratory filled with glass tanks, and cages containing the same types of creatures as before, except these were all rabid looking beasts. Rats with red bloodshot eyes squeaking angrily while trying to run up the sheer sides. Monkeys with the same eyes but with clawed hands and lips pulled back showing their teeth. Some were attacking their habitats to get out while making the most awful of noises, and I did notice one cage where they were all gathered together drooling.

'That is C, Dr Barrett. You must be wondering why I am showing you this?'

'Oh gosh, not really, I'm fine.'

He smiled and gave me a studied look. 'You are a very cool customer indeed, Dr Barrett, and I suspect there is more to you than meets the eye.'

'There really isn't,' I told him.

'You are the only scientist here that has not joined either Professor Donegal or Professor Hussein, yet you from all of them can accurately predict the outcomes for the release of either. Why is that?'

'I'm a statistician.'

'I meant why are you not expressing a view?'

'Oh right, er... Well, I always thought science was about impartiality. I'm very impartial me. Not on any sides. No sides. Not me.'

'Of course. But you must have an opinion.'

What a blasted awful situation I was in with rabid zombie creatures all screaming the place down and a sinister man asking sinister questions. I didn't know what to say and that blasted silence went on while I fretted, and worried, and tried to think.

'As I thought,' Alexander said as though I had just proven something. 'You have an iron core running through you, Dr Barrett, which is why we need you on board.'

'Right,' I gibbered.

'Big shock,' he said, holding his hands out with the palms facing me. 'But then, something about your reaction suggests you already knew.'

'I didn't know.'

'Of course not, but you worked it out, didn't you? Yes, I think that is the case. Our project is real, Dr Barrett and my offer to you is to remain working with us when the upstairs project comes to an end.'

'I er…'

'You need time to think. Of course, you do. Mull it over, Dr Barrett. What an exciting opportunity though. To be here when we change the world. Naturally I know you will not breathe a word.'

'No,' I said weakly.

'Good man!' he patted me manfully on the shoulder. 'I knew the first time we met that you had some wits about you. I can only apologise for leaving you amongst the angry mob upstairs, but we need them to leave here thinking the whole thing was a disorganised overfunded waste of time. Come on, I'll show you back.'

'WAS THAT IT?' Camilla asked me later in my room while Albert took my heater off the wall in case anyone questioned why they were there so late.

I nodded and said that was it. 'That was it,' I said.

'Jesus. It's real,' Camilla said as though to herself, but she looked at Albert as she said it. 'I mean. We kinda guessed, but…'

I nodded sagely. Trying to appear both knowledgeable and comforting at the same time, and I must confess that it was only then that the reality hit me. The Panacea exists. All of us scientists assumed they either had one, or something close to it, or they were nearing completion. But Camilla was right. Having the confirmation was incredible, but what struck me most was how blasé Alexander was about it.

'He was rather casual about the whole thing actually,' I remarked.

'He can be anything he wants,' Albert said. From all three of us he seemed the least surprised. But then he did strike me a very pragmatic man. 'He's got the cure for everything. He could fuck a nun, and nobody would give a shit if he said he has a Panacea.'

'So why all of this then?' Camilla asked. 'Why run this project?'

'Because,' Albert said while putting the heater back on the wall. 'They haven't decided what to do yet. Seems to me they've cobbled something together, realised what they've got and thought oh cock it, now what?'

'Okay. That's good then. Right?' Camilla said, looking to Albert for guidance. 'Then we've still got time.'

Albert grunted while holding the heater in one hand and screwing it in place with the other. 'Maybe.'

'The project is split, Frank. I mean, quite frankly the results are split,' she said, glancing at me quickly then back to Albert as he rolled his eyes. 'It's fifty fifty. Half want A, half want C. That's it! That's why they want Neal. Bloody hell.'

'Bloody hell what?' I asked, not quite liking where this was going.

'You can still influence them,' she said to me. 'Neal, they don't know what to do. That's why Alexander told you. That's why he wants you on board. To help them decide.'

'Right. And again. I'm just a statistician,' I said while that sinking feeling in my belly sunk even further.

'Neal,' she said.

'No,' I said.

'Neal,' Albert said.

'No,' I said again.

'Neal!' they both said.

I didn't bother replying. What's the point? Between Camilla's seduction and Albert's toothy grin and manly shoulder pats and winks I don't stand a bloody chance.

Albert left a few minutes later. Damn him. He's just so likeable.

Camilla stayed back. We had sex and she orgasmed again. She even said it was a multiple orgasm, and that I'm the best lover she's ever had. She whispered into my ear as I got drowsy and told me we'd be together and start a new life after this. Just me and her in a little cottage somewhere. We'd have children and never get sick.

All I had to do was make sure they released the Panacea, and not the other one.

Signing off
NB

November 24th

I have to be quick. Things are happening now, and I need to get this down while my thoughts are fresh.

Professor Hussein sought me out this morning after breakfast when I had isolated myself in a quiet study room.

I was nervous. Downright frightened even. I just wanted some peace. The walls were starting to close in on me. I was feeling trapped and starting to imagine the weight of the mountain above us. There was no way out. No air. No escape.

'Dr Barrett,' Hussein said from the door, startling me from my thoughts. My tea and toast remained untouched on the desk by my side. I wanted to tell him to bloody well sod off. But even that level of confrontation just isn't me. So, I sat quietly and meekly and said nothing at all as he sat down. 'You are well today?' he asked me.

'I'm fine. How can I help you?'

He paused for a moment and checked the door before shuffling to get closer. 'I am worried. I think maybe it is real. The panacea. Why do all of this for hypothetical research?'

'Gosh. I see,' I said while his dark eyes bored into my soul. 'Well. I think we've all had similar thoughts since arriving.'

'What do you know?' he asked me.

'Me? Oh, very little. Haha! I couldn't even find my own bathroom this morning. Gosh no. I don't know anything. Nothing at all. Absolutely nothing.'

He stared at me for a very long time until I thought some wee might come out.

'I am worried,' he finally said. 'If they have it? What will they do? There are only two choices now. A or C. We cannot release C! It is out of the question. You agree with me, don't you, Neal. You agree with me.'

'I'm not here to give opinions, Professor. I'm here to present my findings.'

He made a noise in his throat and sat back with a blast of air from his nose. 'I respect your position, Dr Barrett. But I fear there are other plans at work here. Dark plans, and I want to know who is on my side when the time comes.'

'When the time for what comes?' I asked before my brain could tell my mouth to shut up.

'When the time comes to stop it, Dr Barrett,' he said quietly, fixing me with that look again. 'We must be ready. We cannot let them release such a violent and barbaric disease. We cannot cull the people. We are not gods, Dr Barrett. I will count on you. When the time comes. Yes?' He nodded and leant in. 'When the time comes. You will be ready.'

He patted me on the shoulder and walked out without saying another word. Leaving me and my shoulder wondering why every sod kept patting it.

'Neal!' Camilla whispered a few moments later, rushing in as my heart missed another beat at being startled. 'What did Hussein want?'

'He was babbling on about joining his side, and that I had to be ready.'

'Ready for what?'

I shrugged. Feeling wretched and increasingly strung out.

'Okay,' she said. 'That's good. That means we've got allies. Great work, Neal!' she grabbed me for a hug and planted a kiss on my lips. 'I'll tell Frank.'

'Who's Frank?'

'Did I say Frank? I meant Albert. I had an uncle Frank. Albert reminds me of him. Tell Hussein we're on his side and not to make a move until we can talk more.'

'But-.' I tried to say but she rushed off and I once more sat and pondered the weight of the mountain over my head.

'BARRETT! Caught you hiding.'

'Shit!' I physically flinched from the Scottish voice yelling from the door as Donegal walked in.

'Hiding away? I don't blame you. All this fuss going on. Having some tea and toast, are you?'

'I er.'

'Mind if I grab a slice? So, what do you make of it all then?' he asked as he sat down while munching on my now cold toast. 'I respect your impartiality. I do. I really do. But you'll get splinters up your arse if you stay on that fence much longer. What did Hussein want with you anyway?'

'Hussein?'

'Aye. I saw him coming in. What did he want?'

'Er. Some… Some toast. He had some toast.'

'Neal. Come on now. How long have we known each other? And we're both British. We're on the same side. What did he want?'

I blinked a few times while feeling like a schoolchild being asked to split on his mates by the headteacher.

'Aye. You're a cool one, you are, Neal. Let me say that. I'm guessing he said he thinks it's real. Is that right? Mind you we all think that. But do you know what, Neal? I think it really is real,' he added in a theatrical whisper before laughing heartily. 'Know what I think? I think they're undecided and that's why we're here. To help them choose between A and C. What do you think about that?'

I didn't tell him what I thought about that. Or that Camilla and Albert had beaten him to that conclusion last night.

'But,' Donegal said and fixed me with his piercing blue eyes. 'What side are you on?'

'I'm impartial,' I said, or rather I farted the words out.

'Ach. No, you're not. I know you, Neal. And they're your findings. If they release A then the world ends. I'm thinking they'll choose C. And when they do, they'll need scientists. Do you understand, Neal? The people on their side will have a place at the table. Do you think Hussein is getting a dose of the Panacea? Now listen. I think they'll make a move soon. Whoever is running this show. They'll make some approaches. And when they do. I know you'll be ready. Aye? Sound good?'

I swallowed and watched him bite into another piece of toast. 'I knew I could count on you, Barrett,' he added before patting me on the shoulder and walking off to leave me really wishing the mountain would come down.

'Nipper,' Albert said, walking in a few minutes later. I didn't bother being startled this time. What's the point? I was half expecting Mother Theresa to walk in any moment and start punching my shoulders. 'Having some toast?' he asked, walking over to snag the last slice.

'Help yourself,' I said rather weakly.

'What did Donegal want?'

I sighed and explained it while watching him eat.

'Donegal's angling for a place in the safe zone,' he said.

'Safe zone?' I asked.

'Yeah. Safe zone. Or whatever they call them. The places where they'll hide when the zombies start munching everyone. Anyway. Camilla told me about Hussein. That's good. Find out if he's had any weapons training.'

'What?'

'It'll be fine,' he said at my look of panic. 'But find out. Some of his chums might have done national service. A lot of countries still have that you know. Never should have got rid of it if you ask me. But don't tell him who we are. And act naturally. Stay passive. Nice toast though.'

My shoulder got another groping and he too went off, leaving me with one empty plate and one mug of cold tea.

'Ah, Dr Barrett,' Alexander said a moment or two later when he walked in. But why wouldn't he? I just wish I'd had some toast for him to steal. Or a white cat to stroke. 'And how are you today?'

'Oh, you know. Busy as ever.'

'Of course. Of course. But I couldn't help but notice, not that you are under surveillance, but I did see Professor Hussein and Professor Donegal coming in.'

'Right. Yes. Yes, they did.'

'And I am assuming they are both trying to get on you on side?'

I nodded. Not trusting myself to speak.

'Of course, they are. And tell me, Dr Barrett? I have also noticed one of the reception staff is frequently seen with you. Camilla.'

Oh god. That was it. Cue gibbering wreck.

'She's very attractive, Dr Barrett.'

'Is she? I er, can't say as I noticed.'

'Oh, come now. You know my secrets. I should know yours,' he said as he sat down in the same blasted chair and stared at me in the same blasted way. 'So?' he prompted with a smile. 'Tell me your secrets.'

'We didn't have sex!' I blurted at which point he roared with laughter and clapped his thighs.

'You rogue you,' he said, shaking his head at me. 'We have rules here, Dr Barrett. I shall have to lock you up now.'

'But-.'

'I'm joking! Relax. It's fine. She's an attractive woman, and you're in my inner circle now. Fuck who you want. We have more women if you'd like one?' he asked, leaning in closer. 'We made sure to bring a few extras in, you know, to keep my guards happy. But they're clean. They all wear condoms. I can guarantee that.'

'Oh god. What?'

'Haha! Not that we have to worry about condoms. Not for diseases anyway. Not with what we have,' he added, tapping his nose and winking and laughing away like we were having jolly japes. 'Anyway. I should get back to work. But Neal, do tell me if anyone says anything to you. Anything I should know about. You would tell me, wouldn't you?'

I nodded quickly.

'Good man!' he said and patted my damned shoulder as he stood up, at which point I thought of the questions Camilla and Albert tasked me to find out.

'Have you chosen one?' I asked, rather too quickly.

'One what?' he asked.

'You know, A or C.'

'Oh,' he said, giving me a long appraising look before walking off.

I've come back to my room to hide from them all. But I can't stay here all day. And I'm hungry too. I never did get to eat any of that toast.

Signing off.

NB

November 24th
   (2nd entry)

Damn it!

I tried to sneak out to snaffle some food and was instantly caught by Camilla rushing into my room as I tried to leave.

'We don't have long,' she said quickly.

'For what?' I enquired, perhaps a little sharply as she fixed me a studied look before melting into my arms for a long kiss.

'I need you to speak to Hussein and find out what numbers he has,' she said between kisses.

'Numbers for what?' I asked, while also thinking I've still got to ask Hussein about guns and national service too.

'For if we need them,' she said as she pulled back to look at me again. 'This is very serious, Neal. The fate of the planet is at stake.'

Good lord. What a line. Honestly. It was like something from a movie. I half expected her to lift one leg and swoon.

'I know we can trust you,' she said earnestly and kissed me again while lifting one leg. 'You make me all giddy,' she added. 'You will ask him. Won't you?'

'I er.'

'I know you'll do the right thing,' she said and darned it if she didn't drop to her knees and unzip me right there and then. Of course, I tried to protest. But I haven't really ever had oral sex before. Not like that anyway, and I must say, there is something about it. 'Promise me you'll try,' she said in between mouthfuls.

'Yes,' I stammered. While pulling faces.

'And tell me if you're about to ejaculate.'

'I will. Oh god. Er-.'

'Neal! I said tell me,' she said as someone knocked on the door.

'Dr Barrett?' an accented voice asked.

'It's Hussein,' she said before rushing off into the bathroom.

'Dr Barrett,' Hussein said and pushed his way in as soon I opened the damned door. 'I must speak with you. Are you okay? You look very red.'

'I er. I was exercising?'

'In your room? We have a gym here, Dr Barrett. Never mind. Listen. I saw Donegal and Alexander talking. I think they know something. They're working together. I'm sure of this.'

'I say. Did you do any national service?'

'Sorry. What?'

'Oh. Just asking. If you, you know, ever fired a gun perhaps?'

He stared at me. I stared back all sweaty and trying to smile. At which point he dropped his eyes with a heavy sigh. 'Of course, I did my national service.'

'Great stuff. That's just great.'

'You have mayonnaise on your trousers, Dr Barrett.'

'That's not mayonnaise.'

'What?'

'What?'

'What did you say?'

'I said I had a sandwich. Cheese and mayo. And some... Some pickles.'

'I see. But yes. I am seeking allies now, Dr Barrett. I think it will be soon.'

'Right. What will? I mean...WHY ARE YOU SEEKING ALLIES?' I asked loudly, for the benefit of Camilla in the bathroom who could maybe pop out and talk to the blasted chap. But she didn't, and again he just stared at me.

'I can count on you. I know I can. Tell me, Dr Barrett. Do you have any friends?'

'Friends?'

'Yes.'

'Er. Well. There's some guys at my squash club.'

'Here. Dr Barrett. Do you have friends here? Perhaps secret friends?'

'DO I HAVE ANY SECRET FRIENDS?'

'Why are you repeating what I say? Never mind. I think the time will come soon. Stay alert, my friend. We must be ready. I can count on you. Yes? With clean trousers though. That mayonnaise is soaking in.'

'BARRETT YOU BLOODY BEAN COUNTER,' Donegal then shouted out while banging on my door, which made both Hussein and I flinch like guilty lovers.

'He cannot see me here,' Hussein whispered.

'No!' I whispered as he headed for the bathroom.

'Neal. Will you open the door you daft sod,' Donegal called.

'I must hide!' Hussein whispered.

'Under the bed,' I whispered back as I looked to the small bed and back to his girth and height. There wasn't even a proper wardrobe and damned if he didn't stride towards the bathroom as the door opened with Camilla offering him a bright smile.

'Professor Hussein. How nice to see you,' she said smoothly while he blinked at her then at me.

'Barrett! Are you masturbating in there,' Donegal called.

'Did you need the bathroom, Professor Hussein?' Camilla asked while I tried to tweak my ears and make faces at her.

'Yes,' Hussein said, rushing by.

'Great. Enjoy,' she said. 'I just popped in for a cheese and mayo sandwich.'

'I know. It's on your ear,' Hussein said, closing the bathroom door as the main door swung open.

'Ah. It's bloody open anyway,' Donegal said, looming large as he looked me up and down then over to Camilla.

'Dr Barrett. Do enjoy your sandwich,' Camilla said brightly, still offering that smile.

'Do you do room service?' Donegal asked with a smile as she squeezed by him. 'If I'd known that eh, love.'

'I need to go too!' I said quickly and loudly as Camilla shot me a look while Donegal frowned. 'To the restaurant. For some food. To eat.'

'You just had a sandwich apparently,' Donegal said with a wink. 'But ney bother. I'll come with you.'

'Coming through, gents,' another voice then called as Donegal stepped inside to let Albert walk by. 'Dr Barrett? Everything okay with that heater now is it, sir?'

'It's fine,' I said as the toilet flushed and a second later the bathroom door opened.

'Hussein?' Donegal said.

'Thank you for letting me use your toilet, Neal,' Hussein said, giving Donegal the evil eye.

'Aye. And what's wrong with your toilet then?' Donegal asked while I started to panic.

'It's blocked,' Albert said with a tut and a roll of his eyes. 'Bad plumbing. We're underground. There's no gravity,' he added as two internationally esteemed scientists and I looked at him. 'Anyway gents. Piss off and let me do some work. Camilla. You've got mayo on your ear.'

'It's semen,' I said as they all looked at me. Carmen just sighed and walked off.

I WALKED to the restaurant with Donegal because what choice did I have? Hussein followed us. Glowering from behind while Donegal spoke loudly about the many benefits of culling the population before releasing the cure. It was like he was already a part of the hierarchy. I even felt an urge to warn him, in case Alexander should hear and start to think he is causing more harm than good.

'Aye, Neal. Just think of how perfect it will be. A world of clean air filled with infrastructure and everything we need, and none of the common trash either. I say that respectfully, but it's natural selection is what it is.'

'Natural selection is the order of nature,' Hussein cut in as we entered the restaurant and the same arguments got underway.

'Nobody is talking to you, Saddam,' Donegal muttered, but loudly enough for Hussein to hear.

'You reduce yourself to racism now, Professor Donegal,' Hussein shouted. 'I am not from Iraq. I am Iranian.'

'Aye, but you bloody look like him with that great moustache. And that's what I mean about natural selection, Neal. No more despots like Saddam, or whoever they have in Iran. You want equality. This brings instant equality because we'll all be rich and healthy. How can you not see this, Hussein? Neal even said everyone will die if we don't cull first.'

'I never said that,' I tried to say.

'Because we are not gods!' Hussein bellowed, slamming his hand down on the restaurant service counter as everyone looked over.

'Where are your gods now, Hussein? Where are they? Why didn't they stop the wars in the Middle East? Childhood cancers. Famine. Poverty. Starvation. Slavery. Where are they, Hussein? You think life is perfect now? It's not anywhere near perfect. I've spent my life specialising in immunology to try and save lives. And this, this saves lives.'

'You will kill over seven billion people!'

'Aye. Damn straight I will, but the seventy million left behind won't ever have to worry. And they won't have people like Saddam Hussein or wankers in North Korea threatening the world with nukes. Damn it, Hussein. You know this makes sense. With what we have left, with that new focus we'll have colonies on Mars within a decade. We won't have to worry about anything else! How can you not see this?'

'Science is pure!' Hussein yelled with the veins bulging in his forehead. 'We are scientists. We present our findings to the world. The world chooses. Not us!'

'Ach, be away with you,' Donegal said with a flash of real temper. 'You know what you sound like now, Hussein? Eh? You know what you sound like? Like a fundamentalist. Working for ISIS are you maybe? Ach, don't all be shushing me. The man is an extremist. You're a damned terrorist, Hussein'

Well, that did it. Let me tell you that, and the verbal altercation swiftly turned violent as Hussein lunged at Donegal with a loud yell. Donegal seemed ready for it and charged into Hussein. They're both sturdy chaps too. Big men. But fortunately, neither are fighters so they pretty much slapped at each other's hands, yelling and pushing while more people from both sides ran in to do the same. It was like watching six-year olds fighting. But with less biting.

The strangest thing, however, which I noticed while hiding behind the counter, was Alexander staring in through the door with a wry smile.

NB

November 24th

This is the third entry for today, but I need to be quick. I got back to my room after the fight in the restaurant and made my diary entry.

Then I stopped to think, and after finally gaining a few moments of peace and quiet. I came to a very chilling conclusion.

My thought process was thus:

I was terrified and growing increasingly anxious. The fight in the canteen was jarring and just bloody awful. I even saw Albert and Camilla loitering nearby, watching it all intently. They both look poised. As though they were ready to react.

I feared we'd reached crisis point, and that the project had to end. There was no point to continuing. There was nothing to be gained. The scientists had split so violently there was no hope of ever working together.

I even heard a few of them telling Alexander they'd had enough. They wanted out they told him, and he could keep the damned money too.

'I'm afraid the terms and conditions specify the project will remain until otherwise deemed appropriate to end.'

That's all he said. But it wasn't an answer, and all it did was inflame everyone back up because now they felt like prisoners.

For my own part, I will admit that had there been a way out right then I would have taken it. And I would have willingly given my money back too. Anything to be free of this damned awful place.

I even contemplated trying to make contact with someone outside the project and maybe alert the British authorities. Then I realised Camilla and Albert were already working for the British authorities, and what good would it do anyway? Nobody could get to us. Not inside a secret mountain facility. I couldn't even say where we were.

Of course. Alexander would realise as our computer usage was completely monitored. How would he react if he caught me trying to whistle blow?

And that is the thought that stopped me in my tracks, because I've just realised how much of a risk I am to them.

I know about the project. I have seen the test subjects and the secret labs. This project is too big, and too important to ever let someone like me jeopardise it. Albert even said it. He said Alexander could fuck a nun and nobody would care. A crass statement, but the meaning is clear.

If I thought I was scared before, I'm bloody well terrified now.

There's only one thing I can do:

If I want to live, I have to do what they want. I have to agree to join them. It's the only way.

24ᵗʰ November.

Another quick entry. I was just finishing putting my thoughts to paper when I heard my room door open and Camilla slipped in. She seemed startled to see me.

'I thought you were out,' she said.

'No. I'm here,' I said as I looked from her to the door as though to question why she was letting herself into my room.

'I er, I wanted to surprise you,' she said quickly. 'And leave you a little love note.' She rushed over to kiss me. But it felt wrong. Everything about it felt wrong. 'What's up?' she asked when I didn't respond. 'Are you okay, Neal?'

'I'm fine. Actually, I'm not bloody fine at all.'

'Oh, you poor baby. What can I do to relax you?'

'No. Get off me,' I said when she started to paw at my clothes. 'Camilla! I said no.'

'You've been so brave, Neal.'

'That is enough!' Something in my tone made her stop and she drew back with a sharp look. 'I'm going to see Alexander. I'm going to tell him I'll join them.'

'Why?' she asked, and damned if her voice wasn't entirely different. Harder too. Colder.

'Because I don't want to bloody well die, that's why not!'

She breathed a sigh of relief and softened her gaze. 'You had me worried then, Neal. I thought you agreed with Donegal for a minute.'

'Don't worry. I won't betray your mission.'

'Neal. You're not just a mission to me. I care for you.'

'Sure, and we'll find a cottage and live happily ever after. But tell me, what's your favourite colour? What's your favourite song? Because I don't know anything about you. I don't even know what hobbies you have when you're not… Not sucking willies and seducing men!'

There was hurt in her eyes. Something else too. A flash of anger perhaps, but damned if I know if she wasn't pretending. I had no way of knowing. I don't know her. I don't know anything about her. Only that she is very beautiful, and women like Camilla just don't find men like me attractive.

'I like birds,' she said into the silence.

'Birds?'

'Yes. Birds. I'm a bird watcher. That's what I do in my spare time. I watch birds.'

'Birds.'

'Yes! Birds. I'm obsessed with them.'

'Right,' I said, thinking she'd obviously just plucked that one out of the air. Pun not intended. I half expected her to say she liked nerdy men too.

'And I've got a thing for geeky men,' she added.

I knew she was playing me for a fool then. Women like Camilla, or whatever her name is, don't like bird watching, and they certainly don't like nerds. 'I need to go,' I said coldly. She pretended to be hurt again and nodded as she moved to the door but paused and looked back.

'They can't release C,' she said. 'You have to influence them.'

I didn't reply. I've had enough of being used. My sole intention is to tell Alexander whatever he wants to hear then get the hell away from this place. That's it. To hell with Donegal and Hussein. And to hell with Camilla and Albert too.

Signing off
NB

9

Day Twenty-nine

CAMBER TOWN

'I'm afraid that was his last diary entry,' Henry said into the silent café as Carmen stared down at her hands. Keeping her gaze low. Hiding her expression.

'Holy shit,' I said, shaking my head. 'Talk about a cliff hanger. But hang on, how do you know all this?'

'Jesus, Howie,' Paula said, giving me a look.

'What?'

'Camilla was obviously sneaking in to read his diaries. He bloody caught her,' she said as Carmen swallows.

'Oh! That's why she was… But I thought she was going in to leave the love note. Okay. Got it. But wow. So, Camilla was reading his diary eh? Blimey. I'm guessing this Camilla told you then, Henry?'

'What the fuck,' Paula said, blinking from me to Henry, then back to me. 'Tell me you didn't just ask that.'

'Ask what? Camilla must have told Henry. How else would he know? Shame that was the last entry though. I wonder what happened. Oh, hang on! Reggie, didn't you have Neal's diaries?'

'I did.'

'Do you know what happened next?'

'I do,' Reginald said as he pulled a notebook from his own bag. The hard outer cover nearly destroyed and torn apart, and the papers within singed with burn marks.

'Right. Spit it out then, Reggie me old mucker. I need to hear this. I'm hooked on the whole Camilla thing. She sounds interesting though. And that Albert. I bet you wished you still had them now, Henry.'

'There is something wrong with you, Howie,' Paula said. 'Anyway, Reggie. Keep going.'

10

December 1st

IT'S BEEN one week since my last diary entry, and one week during which my whole life has changed. Nothing will ever be the same again.

It all came about on that last day. November 24th.

I'd just had a rather confrontational chat with Camilla. I'd effectively called her a whore and suggested she sucked men's willies for her job. She looked hurt by that comment, but the whole darned thing was moving too fast. Hussein and Donegal were constantly on at me. Alexander too. I was being seduced and groomed from all sides, and I'd had enough. The fights in the canteen, and the constant arguments had worn me down. There was no escape, and every little emotion was becoming magnified. Every nuance was bigger. The walls seemed closer. The ceiling seemed lower. The air too stale and too thick.

Even now it brings forth a sense of panic and dread. The feel of that place, and what happened.

. . .

I LEFT my room and headed for the reception. Camilla was back behind the desk and I noticed Albert was also in the lobby fiddling with a light socket. The armed guards were on the doors and I could hear shouts coming from the canteen and work rooms as the scientists continued their loud slanging matches.

'I want to go home!' Dr Chirabati screamed out as she marched up to the exit door and started tugging on the handle. 'LET ME OUT! I DEMAND TO BE LET OUT.' She was desperate and wild. Screaming loudly and hammering her fists. I know that woman. Dr Chirabati is one of the world's leading experts in climate change. She was on Donegal's side from the very start and put forth reasoned discussions on the benefits to the planet for a mass cull to humanity. Yet there she was. Demented and wailing to be set free.

The guards didn't do anything. They just watched her until some of her colleagues rushed over to give her comfort.

'YOU'RE THE TERRORISTS!' Another man yelled out. One of Hussein's side. He was screaming in pure fury at another chap. Both in their sixties. Both grey haired wizened academics now reduced to goading the other to fight. It was the same in every direction. In every room and quarter. The whole thing had been whipped up into a frenzy that was ready to blow.

'Dr Barrett,' Camilla said as I approached the counter. She seemed tense, but the violence in the air was making everyone the same. 'How can I help?'

'I just want to bloody talk to him,' I whispered angrily. 'I'm out of it. Do you understand.'

'Shush,' she whispered back and dropped her eyes as though doing something behind the counter. 'You need to calm down, Neal.'

'I want out of this place. Can you get me out? Can you? I thought not. You're as bloody trapped as I am. I'll do what I can for you, but I'm out of this.'

'Dr Barrett,' Albert said, strolling over with that toothy grin of his. 'You up for the gym later? We need to work on those heart and lungs.'

'What the hell is wrong with you?' I asked while he smiled on like nothing was happening. Then he moved in close and fixed me a look of such violence it made a chill run down my spine.

'Watch your step, nipper. You're on our side. Remember that.'

'Alexander? It's Camilla,' Camilla said into the reception phone. 'I have Dr Barrett here. He wishes to speak with you. Certainly. I'll tell him now. Alexander will be with you shortly, Dr Barrett.'

'Thank you,' I said.

'You do the right thing now, Neal,' Albert said quietly. 'Everything will be okay. Just do what he tells you. If you get out, then make contact with a man called Henry at the Office Of Fiscal Studies in the Treasury Department.'

'What?' I asked.

'Good to see you again, Dr Barrett,' he said with a wink. 'See you in the gym later, and stop flirting with our receptionist.'

'What?' I stammered again as I looked back to Camilla and saw Alexander standing behind her.

'I rather think our good doctor is sweet on you, Camilla,' he said.

'I should be so lucky,' she said while giving me a huge smile. But the whole thing was too surreal for me. There were fights breaking out and people screaming to be set free while they joshed and joked like nothing was happening.

'Dr Barrett. Come through,' Alexander said.

I headed after him into his office as he closed the door and took a seat behind his desk while I glanced to the wood panelling, expecting him to open the secret entrance.

'How can I help, Dr Barrett?' he enquired politely.

'I er. I've been thinking,' I said and glanced back to look through the window in his door to another fight breaking out, and the guards watching on passively as Albert waded in and pulled two old men apart.

'Yes?' Alexander asked. I looked back at him. At that blasted smile. At the games being played. Sweat was breaking out on my forehead. I felt sick to the stomach.

'I agree.'

'You agree?' he asked.

'Yes. I agree.'

'I see. And exactly to what are you agreeing, Dr Barrett?'

There it was. I had to make a choice. 'C!' I blurted. 'I agree with C.'

He nodded slowly. Seemingly evaluating me. 'You would release a deadly virus that will kill 98 to 99% of the human race. Is that right?'

'Yes.'

'Nearly seven billion people will die.'

'Yes.'

'Why?'

Damn him for staring at me like that. Like a cat he was. Toying with a mouse. 'It's the right thing to do,' I said without much enthusiasm then immediately panicked that he would see through me. Of course, he would see through me. He knew I was just trying to save my own skin. 'It's bloody abhorrent,' I added, spitting the words out without knowing I was going to say them. 'The whole thing. It's… It's fucking wrong! But damned if it's not needed. Look at them,' I said and turned to watch the highly esteemed academics screaming abuse and throwing things at each other. And seeing it through the window, as detached as I was, was rather like watching primates in a zoo. The noise of them. The way they were all whipped up and forming gangs and tribes. Seeking allies to form sects to start wars because of belief, because of the interpretation of ideals. Because of free will. I didn't need to say anything else. Alexander joined me and together we looked upon the children of men forever ruining the world.

In truth. Right then. I did believe in the release of C. That's how angry I was. If Alexander had given me a vial, I might have walked out and released it myself.

'We found the Panacea,' he said quietly, and when I turned to look at him, I saw a real man with emotion in his eyes. 'We can cure the world.'

But cure what exactly? To what end? For what purpose? For what gain? I didn't say anything. Words felt cheap. The whole thing felt cheap and sordid. I felt cheap and sordid.

'I want to go home,' I said quietly. 'Before you release it. I want to go home.'

He nodded and seemed genuine this time. 'Of course. We have time. Anyway. Come down and meet the team. I know they will be delighted you are on board.'

'Alexander,' I said as he turned away. 'Did you know?'

'Know what, Dr Barrett?'

'Did you know you were going to release C before this project?'

'Come. We'll talk more.'

We descended once more into the underground section. Once more into the abyss. That's what it felt like anyway. I tried to think, but my thoughts were jumbled. I tried to remind myself I was only agreeing to save my own neck. But was I? Was that the truth? I kept thinking about Camilla, but I felt confused and rejected. She said she still wanted me, but I knew that wasn't true. She said she was in love with me, but I knew that could never be true.

'Dr Barrett?' Alexander said, snapping me from my thoughts as I realised he had stopped by a door and was motioning for me to go through. I offered a mumbled thanks and walked through to a large conference room. An oval table dominated the middle. Covered with pastries and snacks. With bowls of fruit and jugs of coffee and juice. The room was busy and filled with chatter and talk. People in groups. Some in white lab coats. Others in normal attire. 'Ladies and gentlemen,' Alexander called out, bringing forth a sudden quiet as they all turned to look at me. 'I am honoured to present Dr Neal Barrett, who has agreed to join us in our brave new world.'

Applause broke out as those gathered rushed forth to clasp my hands and pat me on the bloody shoulder again. I was giddy with it all. Not knowing what to say or do. Not knowing how to be. My stomach was flipping over. My heart was thudding, and I thought I would pass out. Especially when Professor Donegal clasped my hand.

'BARRETT! I knew you'd see sense. Ach. You're not as daft as you look,' he bellowed out, clapping me on the back as I swallowed and turned to the man stood with him.

'Dr Barrett,' professor Hussein said and took my hand in his. 'I've lost the bet, Donegal.'

'Aye. You bloody have,' Donegal said, laughing with joy while he clapped Hussein on the back. 'I told him, Barrett. I told him he'd never persuade you. Ach, don't you all start chiding me now. I said Neal is a canny lad. I said he's smart and he'd see the sense of it. Am I right, Neal?'

More laughs. More grinning faces. But the sight that nearly broke me was seeing Dr Chirabati eating a pastry with some of Hussein's side.

'At least the mayonnaise is gone now,' Hussein said, glancing at my trousers.

'That's not mayonnaise. That's semen,' Donegal called out to a great laugh.

I don't know what happened next. It's a blur if I'm honest. The next thing I was sitting down and eating a pastry while the room slowly emptied, leaving me alone with Hussein, Donegal and Alexander.

'You look white as a sheet, Neal,' Donegal said as they all lowered down into chairs. 'Are you okay?'

'I'm fine. Just surprised.'

'Aye. I bet you bloody are. Hussein deserves an Oscar for his performance,' he said as he lifted a glass towards Hussein.

'It was er... It was something else,' I said. 'Forgive me, Professor Hussein. You believe in the release of C? I'm just-.'

'Believe in it?' Donegal replied. 'The man does more than believe in it. He bloody made it.'

'What?' I asked, while my mind went into a tailspin.

'It was a joint effort,' Hussein said. 'I stumbled across something and reached out to Donegal. He checked my findings and we realised what we'd found.'

'It wasn't the Panacea at that stage, Neal,' Donegal said. 'More like an early prototype. He'd developed a virus that could be changed at will. That's where I came in with my immunology background. It was my tweak that enabled it to be taken into the host body. But this thing, Neal. This thing is perfect. It doesn't just cure diseases. It makes the blood clot faster. Wounds heal quicker. Muscles grow faster. It primes the body. It makes hair thicker and it strips fat. We're not talking about just curing diseases, Neal. We're talking about the evolution of a whole new species. One that is stronger. Faster. Fitter. They need less food. Less sleep.'

'You've tested it on people!?' I cut in.

Donegal paused and pulled a face. 'We're not sanctioned for human trials. But aye. We have. We've tested it. It works.'

I didn't know what to say. 'When?' I asked.

'When what, Neal?' Donegal asked.

'I think Dr Barrett is asking when it will be released,' Alexander said. 'Not for another year at least.'

'Aye. Is that what you worried about?' Donegal asked as I nodded. 'No, it's fine, Neal. We've got time yet. Alexander says another year, but personally, I think we'll be ready in less time than that.'

I tried to think, but still my thoughts wouldn't come. My mind was so very foggy with too many ideas and questions all spinning about. 'Why?' I asked. 'Why do this?'

They all looked at each other, frowning in puzzlement. 'You told us, Neal,' Donegal said. 'We release A and the world ends.'

'Not the blasted virus! This! The project. The scientists. Why do this?'

'Gentlemen,' Alexander said, addressing the other two. 'Perhaps now might be a good time for me to talk with Dr Barrett.'

'Aye. You do that, Alexander,' Donegal said, getting to his feet as he winked at me. 'Glad you're with us though, Neal. We'll need bean counters in the new world, eh?'

'You can make the cheese and mayo sandwiches,' Hussein added as they clapped my shoulders and headed off.

Silence followed as the door closed. Sealing me inside with Alexander.

'We needed a true reaction,' he said after a while.

'Reaction to what? You've already made your minds up.'

Alexander shrugged. 'They're scientists. They like testing things. I said it's pointless, but there we are. They wanted to see the reactions of their peers. And it was meant to be Donegal in favour of A, and Hussein in favour of C, but they swapped over at the last minute.

They thought there might be a racial or religious tone if Hussein said he wanted to kill seven billion people.'

'But it's fine for a Scotsman.'

'Apparently so,' he replied with a smile at the humourless joke.

'And you?' I asked. 'How are you involved in this?'

He shifted and thought for a second. 'Professor Donegal is good friends with a British minister. Alistair Appleton. You have heard of him? I think everyone has heard of him. Donegal reached out to Alistair when they realised what they had. Alistair reached out to me. Neal. May I call you Neal? Neal, this is a very exclusive club, but both Donegal and Hussein wanted you on board very much. Your expertise will literally shape the new world. It will guide our decisions so that we can be a better society. We want to learn from the mistakes of humanity. We need to know how we are best served to protect our immunes and help re-grow our populations once the culling is complete.'

I could hardly believe my ears and I wondered how many times he had given that same speech. But I suddenly stopped and realised what he'd said. 'Immunes?' I asked.

'Yes. The people with immunity. C only targets 98-99% remember. The survivors will be the building blocks for our new world.'

'Building blocks?'

'Well of course. Once we've gathered them all together and commenced an effective breeding programme. That's where your expertise will come in.'

'I'm a statistician!'

'Exactly! You of all people know how to manage populations. For instance. Which country do you favour?'

'What?'

'My view, personally, is that we remain in Europe. Germany for instance. It has a fantastic infrastructure. Should we base our new world there do you think?'

'What?'

'We'd been in reach of France. Spain. Italy and other countries. Ha! But listen to me. Still thinking like the old order. We wouldn't even call it Germany! We could rename the whole of the European landmass to one entity. How about that? Then we decide where to populate. How to populate. And, of course, everything is owned by everyone.'

'You mean communism.'

'No! Our hardest workers will get rewards. And we'll encourage free trade. As long as it is controlled and managed of course. No weapons. None at all. Apart from personal defence. And sanctioned military and law enforcement. But the hospitals. We won't need them will we. Or the drug stores. I say, what do you think about the use of recreational drugs?'

'What?'

'We're split. I think we should allow them. I mean. They can't cause physical harm can they. We'll have the Panacea by then. But perhaps the psychological impact is something to worry about. We'll have to monitor that one. But yes. Yes, you are right, Neal. No drugs within the breeding programme. We only want the best. And the best education too. But then we still need workers. Manual labour will still be needed. Ha! They can't all be geniuses like you and I, Neal.'

'What the fuck.' I rarely swear, but right then that phrase seemed the most fitting. The man was crazy. Deluded even. 'And Donegal? Hussein? They agree with you?'

'Oh, we have great discussions! I can't wait for you to join in. Hey! We could even name a university after you! The Neal Barrett school of excellence! How about that?'

I was wrong. It wasn't just Alexander. They were all deluded.

'How are you going to get them all together?'

'Who? The immunes? We'll gather them up and get them to where they need to be. The infrastructure still remains, don't forget. And we're actively sourcing protected skill sets to be within the safe zones when the culling starts.'

'And what if these immune people don't want to be gathered up?'

'Why wouldn't they? They're the new race in our new world order. They'll be chomping at the bit to get stuck in. They'll all be living in mansions and driving luxury cars. Ah no. Donegal thinks that's a bad idea. He said they'll get lazy and they should earn what they have. No freeloaders in the new order. I know, right,' he said at my expression. 'I can see you are excited, Neal. I can see your brain spinning away with ideas. And between you and I,' he said, leaning in with a wink. I knew what was coming and I prayed that he didn't say it. 'We'll have the pick of the bunch. Our sperm should definitely be involved in the breeding programme. I mean. We're at the top of our food chains already. What do you fancy? Blondes? Brunettes? Oh! You like black women. Camilla. Of course. Say no more. The first ones in from Africa are yours. No. I won't hear any more about it. They're yours. No need to thank me. They'll be ripe too. I've got a thing for Thai girls personally. The slanted eyes and lithe bodies. Thailand is mine haha! But we can swap. It's fine. Swapping is fine.'

I think the greatest fear came upon me at that point right there. Because I'd assumed there was a strong organisation behind it all. But there wasn't. This was a horny Hitler dreaming of boat loads of young Thai women who of course would all welcome his sexual advances. Within the space of a few minutes he'd mentioned slavery. Brutality. Class structures. Forced work camps and assigned compulsory living sections with higher education reserved only for the best. Rewards for the hardest workers and forced manual labour.

This wasn't communism. This was a bizarre totalitarianism, and in a way, the future he painted within those few words was far worse than the one I predicted if A was released. At least A allowed some element of free will. It allowed some hope. This allowed for none of that. They weren't culling for utopia. They were culling to keep the best for themselves.

'You'll like this,' he then said with a click of his fingers. I looked over at him, but my head moved too slowly. Like I was stuck in a dream. He swung a laptop about and flipped the screen up. Delight was on his face. He even hummed as he took a memory stick from a pocket and popped it into the USB port while I watched on. Feeling sick to the core. Feeling more trapped than ever before.

'There,' he announced and proudly spun the computer about for me to see the screen filled with a spreadsheet of sorts. Names on a list.

Hundreds of them. Thousands even. The scroll bar at the side was tiny.

'What is that?' I asked.

'Those,' he said with a grin. 'Are the immunes. And remember. These are immune to C. Not to A. They can still receive the Panacea. We'll break them down eventually into regions and ages and so forth. That will help with the breeding programme. I was even thinking we could attach images eventually. You know. So we can see what they look like in advance. Like a dating site. That sort of thing. But yes. We're accessing medical records to identify those with a certain genetic structure. Our access is unprecedented actually. Hospital records. Prison records. Military records. Pretty good eh? Ha! I knew you'd like that.'

Again, I couldn't speak, and for a moment I wondered how the hell they'd gotten so much access. But they have a cure for all known diseases. You offer that to anyone, and they'll give you anything you want. Access to anything at all, including secret underground mountain facilities.

'I er. I'm feeling a little overwhelmed, actually.'

'You do look a bit pale,' he said and turned the computer back to shut it down and pocket the memory stick. 'But of course. A lot to take in. Dr Chirabati was the same. She took a good few days to get over the shock. We gave her some sleeping pills. I'll ask Camilla to bring some to your room,' he added with a grin and another wink. 'Come on. I'll show you back up. You look ready to pass out.'

'When can I go home?'

'Soon. But not yet. We'll let the project run its course and see if we can't convert a few more to our side. You can help with that actually. Get mingling and talking to people. Once you're up and about again that is. Then, sadly, we'll have to work out the best method of dealing with those that don't agree with us.'

We were walking back when he said that and I stopped to look as he winced while behind him, through the windows, I could see the rabid beasts attacking their cages and tanks in the section marked C.

'I know,' he said heavily. 'But maintaining secrecy is vital. I don't need to tell you that.'

We hit the stairs and started going up, but my legs felt heavy and solid. My chest felt too tight. My whole world had been skewed.

'Give it a week or two I say,' he added.

I couldn't stay here another day, let alone another week.

'But now you're one of us you can come down in the evenings and have a few drinks. and join in with the discussions on how we're going to build our new world. Maybe get stuck into sorting those names out for us. You could start with the African women.'

We reached his office and it all seemed so desperate and cobbled together. The way the secret door was hidden in his wood panelled office, but anyone could see through the windows.

The way he talked about it all too. The way Donegal and Hussein were playing with people to get them to choose. The stress being caused. The arguments. The fights. The plans for slavery and hearing him talking about sorting the names out as though I would be choosing invites for a party.

It was too much. The Panacea existed. The zombie virus existed, and seven billion people were going to die. But the biggest crushing fear was that I had to stay there for another two weeks.

'Get some rest, Neal,' he patted me on the back and walked me to his office door.

I stepped out and saw I was behind the counter. Camilla was there. She turned to look at me and blanched at the expression on my face. Albert was on the other side of the counter. Sweeping up after fixing a light socket. Scientists were still shouting and arguing.

'You agree with me, Hussein! I know you do,' Donegal shouted from somewhere. Back to playing his role. Back to playing games. But it felt so closed in. So very closed in. I thought I would die right there. I thought my heart was going to give out.

'Neal?' Camilla said, staring at me strangely. 'Are you okay?'

'I agree with the science yes!' Hussein shouted back. 'But not with the method. Convince me. Tell me how it is right to kill seven billion people.'

I couldn't go on. I couldn't. My chest. It was so tight. I couldn't breathe.

'Neal!' Camilla said.

'I think perhaps Dr Barrett is somewhat exhausted,' Alexander said.

'It's real,' I whispered.

'Come now, Dr Barrett. Let's get you to your room,' Alexander said, taking my arm but I pulled away.

'It's real,' I said again. Louder this time. 'IT'S BLOODY REAL!'

'Neal!' Camilla said. I saw Albert staring at me. The guards too. Someone else stopped and looked over. One of the other scientists, but I couldn't process that or anything else. My mind was unravelling. My heart was beating too fast. The dread I'd felt building inside was rushing up.

'THE PANACEA IS REAL,' I yelled out. 'I'VE SEEN IT. THEY'RE RELEASING C!' I couldn't cope. I couldn't deal with it. With the manipulation. With the stress. With being played. 'IT'S REAL! THEY WANT TO MAKE EVERYONE SLAVES!'

'Neal,' Alexander said, lunging at me. 'Shut your mouth.'

'Get off me,' I said, pulling away from him, but I moved too hard and fell against the counter, sending papers and stationary flying. 'IT'S REAL! IT'S REAL!' I yelled out, trying to right myself but I floundered into a chair as Camilla tried to help me, but in my mind, she was one of them so again I wrenched free.

'Neal!' Donegal shouted. 'Whatever's wrong with you?'

'YOU!' I screamed out, pointing at him then at Hussein behind him. 'AND YOU! THEY'RE WORKING TOGETHER! HUSSEIN MADE THE VIRUS. AND AND…AND CHIRABATI. SHE KNOWS TOO. THEY ALL KNOW.'

'The wee fella's having a breakdown,' Donegal said.

'DOWN THERE. DOWN THE STAIRS. THEY HAVE TEST SUBJECTS. IT'S REAL. I'VE SEEN IT.'

My mind was gone. The fear and stress had reached breaking point, and, as I said, the foremost issue for me right at that point was not the genocide or the planned slavery. It was simply that I had to get out. Camilla tried to calm me. Donegal shouted for me to get a grip. Hussein even tried to come closer. Alexander too. More guards were running in, but I shouted. Oh, I shouted everything I could think of. 'They have names! Immune people on a list. He wants the Thai women. They're going to make everyone into slaves. It's real! The Panacea is real. And this... This is to make you believe in culling.'

'Alexander,' Donegal said. 'You need to calm him down. Give him a sedative.'

It wouldn't be sedative. I knew that. I'd be killed. Or worse, I'd be one of the human test subjects and turned into a mouth-frothing beast. I think that's when the panic attack really took hold. When Alexander tried to rush at me.

I don't recall exactly what happened. My memory of it is patchy. I do know I threw a chair at Alexander, perhaps some other items too. I also know everyone was shouting my name. However, even in the midst of that breakdown, I observed, with rather surprising lucidity, that several scientists were listening very intently and calling out to let me speak. I also remember seeing Albert watching me with a very strange expression.

Then some of the guards rushed in and gripped my arms. I thrashed wildly and Camilla shouted at them to let me go. She even tried to intervene, but they shoved her away.

'Get your hands off him!' she told them and tried again, but it was to no avail. There were too many of them.

'Take him down,' Alexander ordered.

'Down where?' someone shouted. One of the other scientists.

'IN HIS OFFICE. THE ENTRANCE IS IN HIS OFFICE,' I screamed. Then a great hubbub went up when another guard rushed behind the counter clutching a syringe with a needle exposed at the end. I went wild with panic and fear, but that only made them use more force to keep me still. One of them even punched me in the belly, which made me gag and wheeze as Camilla yelled louder. I was hit again and forced over the counter as the needle jabbed into my backside. Everyone was rushing over. Everyone was screaming out.

'NOW, FRANK!' I remember hearing Camilla's voice and wondered why she was yelling at her uncle.

Then I saw Albert take the cut throat razor from his pocket and walk up behind one of the guards and slit his throat. I saw it happen. I saw Albert simply bring his hand forward and sweep it across the man's neck. Severing the jugular with blood spraying out. The guy gasped and tried to move, but Frank had already gripped the pistol in the guard's holster and yanked it free before shoving the dying guard away. Then he turned and shot the other guard through the head.

A great scream went up at the loud gunshot, then suddenly the weight of those pinning me down was gone and I fell backwards to see Camilla attacking the guards.

She'd grabbed the one trying to inject me and thrust the syringe into his eye then hit the base hard with her palm, driving it into his socket. His eye popped. The man screamed and fell away as she twisted on the spot and kicked into the leg of another and slammed his face down hard on the counter.

It was all so fast. So very fast, but perhaps the half a dose of whatever drug they'd got into me made my mind slow enough to take it all in. Bits of it anyway. Like flashbacks, I guess. I saw Camilla fighting like she was someone from a movie. She's not a big woman at all, but she was dropping men twice her size with apparent ease. Punching them in the throat and driving her knee into their groins. I saw her break an arm and get in position to pull a pistol from a guard's holster.

Alexander lunged at her from behind at that point. He got her into a bear hug, but she threw her head back and broke his nose. He grunted and fell over me, spraying blood over my face while the air filled with screams and gunshots.

I don't know why I did it, but right at that second, with all of that going on, I reached into Alexander's pocket and took the memory stick containing the names of the immunes.

The next thing I know I was being dragged across the lobby floor by Camilla and saw Albert pistol whipping Alexander hard in the head.

'TELL THEM TO OPEN THIS DOOR!' Albert yelled at him. Then he aimed into the mass of terrified scientists and shot Dr Chirabati in the leg before aiming at Alexander again.

I blacked out again. I don't know. Then I recall smelling smoke and hearing the screams growing louder.

'I'LL BURN YOU ALIVE!' Albert shouted.

Then it was cold. So very cold and I was being forced to my feet. 'Neal! You have to run,' Camilla shouted into my face. We were outside in the access corridor. Outside of the facility. I glanced back through the door to see bodies lying here and there and flames licking up behind the reception counter.

A moment later. Maybe an hour. Maybe a day. I have no clue, but we were outside in the biting wind and there were more dead bodies bleeding in the snow.

'You can't stop it!' Alexander shouted. I only realised he was still there at that point. His face was a mess. Bloodied and swollen. 'There's nothing you can do!'

Camilla shot him. Then we were inside the chopper with Frank pointing his gun at the pilot. I blacked out then blinked awake to see mountains below us.

'Neal, come on,' Camilla said. We'd landed somewhere. After that was just blurred, and I finally woke up a day or two later in a motel room.

Albert and Camilla were there. Talking quietly. I pretended to be asleep.

'I'll go out for food and contact the office,' Albert said. I heard him leave. Then I heard the shower running and when I peeked out, I saw Camilla walking naked into the bathroom.

I threw my clothes on, grabbed the memory stick and ran out.

THAT WAS the last time I saw Camilla, and as much as it hurts, I hope I never see her or Albert again. Just the thought that I was used so easily and to such depth kills me inside.

I quickly used every ATM and bank I could find and kept withdrawing money until I was told there were no funds left.

I stayed beneath the radar and finally made my way to the migrant camps in northern France and paid a lorry driver to sneak me through the Channel Tunnel.

Now. A week or so later, and here I am. A fugitive, I guess. I can't go back to my life because I know they will find me. I won't make contact with this Henry either because they can't stop it. Nobody can stop it. And besides. They'll only use me for their own ends. Or kill me. This thing runs too deep.

I have a year before it happens. One year to get ready for the end of the world. But I have the list too. The names of the people with immunity.

I know I'm not a brave man. I'm not a soldier, and I have no real clue what I am doing. But those people need to be protected from what comes after the cull. Maybe I could try and find a few of them. Get them to safety or something.

I'm tired now. I need to rest. I've rented a secluded property. I've got food and everything I need. But I'm exhausted. I still have nightmares too. About that facility. I don't know what happened to it, or to anyone else. I haven't been online for fear of being tracked.

I'll sign off and sleep. But one thing I did realise while I was on the run, is that cars and vehicles won't last for very long once the end comes. Fuel expires. Engines seize up. I'll need another way of moving about. Perhaps a horse. Yes. I shall get a horse and teach myself how to ride. The company would be nice too, and I've heard that horses are gentle, loving creatures.

Signing off.

NB

11

Day Twenty-nine

CAMBER TOWN

THE CAFÉ once again fell silent as I thought back to when we met Neal at the end of the big battle in the square. By the following morning he was dead from drinking contaminated water. We didn't get a chance to speak properly. To hear his tale, or to know him as a man.

The concepts at play became so complex they boggled my mind – especially in that heat, and so I once again wiped the sweat from my forehead while those around me did the same and absorbed what they just heard.

Carmen kept her head lowered, staring at her hands in her lap as Jess, the gentle loving creature that she is, grew bored of being outside and clip clopped into the café, smacking chairs and tables aside until she reached the counter where she picked up a large carton of oat milk, and burst it between her teeth before setting about licking it up.

'Poor sod,' I said quietly to a few agreeable murmurs. 'He got seduced by that Camilla then chose the most violent horse that's ever lived before meeting us and getting killed. Talk about bad luck.'

'Howie,' Paula snapped, giving me a hard look as Marcy slapped my arm.

'Ow! What was that for?' I asked before spotting Carmen staring at her hands as the penny finally dropped. 'Oh shit. Sorry, Carmen.'

'It's okay,' Carmen said quietly.

'I feel awful now. Was Camilla a friend of yours?'

'Oh, my good god!' Paula said, shaking her head at me. 'Have you turned into Cookey?'

'Huh?' Cookey asked. 'What did I do? But yeah, shit. Sorry, Carmen. Was she your mate?'

'You bloody idiots,' Marcy said. 'She *is* Camilla, and that's Albert,' she added, pointing to Frank.

'Eh, what?' Frank asked, blinking awake. 'We having more coffee are we?'

'You can be really insensitive sometimes, Howie,' Marcy said.

'But... No way, were you Camilla?' I asked. 'With the mayonnaise on your ear.'

'Howie!' Paula snapped as Marcy swiped at him again.

'No, I just meant. Like. I didn't mean-.'

'It's fine,' Carmen said again.

'But er, blimey,' I said, nodding slowly as everyone looked at me. 'Syringe in the eye. Best kill ever. Then face-planting the other guy on the counter.'

'That was fucking awesome,' Blowers said.

'While Albert is taking the guards out,' Nick said.

'Yeah, and he's telling 'em all he'll burn them alive,' Cookey added. 'That's what Dave does. He says things like that.'

'Yeah, but the syringe,' Blowers said.

'In the eye,' Howie said, pointing at his own eye as Carmen finally smiled and looked up. 'Straight from one guy's arse to another guy's eye.'

'Sounds like Blowers' day off.'

'Cookey!' Came the many voices as more laughs went around the table.

'Idiots,' Carmen said, rolling her eyes at them, but at least she was smiling.

'Sounds like you quite liked him,' Charlie said.

'I did,' Carmen said. 'Neal was a good man.'

'Yeah, he was alright for a nerd,' Frank said as Jess popped another carton open over the back of Clarence's head. 'Got milk on your head, nipper.'

'What happened after that?' Paula asked. 'This facility and the scientists.'

'The fire was put down to an electrical fault,' Henry said. 'And the scientists who left the facility were all killed within a day or two. All tragic accidents of course. A few car crashes. One was in a light aircraft that went down. Another drowned after falling from a ferry. A few more committed suicide.'

'Fuck,' I said as the others nodded in agreement.

'We assume the rest decided to join them, but it went dark. Even your father couldn't get any intel, Howie. There was no chatter anywhere.'

'He said that name,' I said. 'The politician.'

'Alistair Appleton,' Henry said. 'Who was also on the select committee that allocated our funding.'

'Ouch,' Paula said with a grimace as Henry continued.

'Of course, our funding was cut, and we were told to start making preparations for closure.'

'And?' I asked as Henry gave me a blank look. 'Don't tell me you did nothing.'

'We thought we had time,' Carmen said. 'The release was meant to be a year from the time of the project.'

'Something must have happened,' Paula said.

'It could be that something spurred them to act sooner,' Henry said. 'Or simply it could be the impatience of people like Donegal and Hussein. You heard the diary entries from Neal. Those people were delusional fantasists acting on their own volition. Any one of them could have decided to make it happen and release the virus. And don't forget one drop is all it takes.

One infected person released into any major city and 98-99% of the population are wiped out, and, as you heard, the plan is to round up the survivors and place them into controlled environments.'

'At which point they'll release the Panacea, right?' Paula asked.

'I'm not so sure,' Reginald cut in. 'Alexander told Neal they wanted to control people, which you don't do by giving them perfect health. They'd have no control over their version of utopia without creating reliance on things like healthcare and medicines and security. I should think they would use it as a way of keeping people controlled. While also allowing fear of the outside to build up. *Stay here. We'll keep you safe and if you get sick, we can cure you.*'

'Okay then,' I said. 'So, we've got a mutating virus that was released on purpose. But that virus is now splitting into sections and becoming sentient. Reggie, is that right?'

'Correct,' Reginald said. 'All of the control points were infected with the same virus. They all have the same thing, but the manifestation differs according to the mind of the individual control point. That means there's not one singular enemy, but lots of them all working independently that all *think* they are the one true race.'

I paused to think for a second. 'The next question is, will all of these sects or players start competing with each other, or will they try and find a way to combine into one entity?'

'I think that is the next logical step,' Reginald said. 'If one of those control points realises the same as we are now, then yes, I believe they will try and unite.'

I nodded. 'Whatever we do needs to be before that. Because we'll be fucked if they gang up. Seriously, that'll be some super mega zombie overlord shit that will. Like Darth Vader and Skeletor made a baby with Genghis Khan and gave it to Hitler to raise. With Stalin as an uncle, and Pol Pot giving it lessons on ethics.'

'I think we get the point,' Paula said.

'No, but can you actually imagine it?' I asked, looking around. 'It'll be worse than Paula when she starts making lists.'

'And you'd all be in dirty undies if I didn't make lists. Speaking of which, we need to go shopping. Yes! I know. Supply run. Shopping. Whatever. Anyway, I've got a question. How did we get our version of the virus?'

'Ah now, yes. I've given this some thought,' Reginald said. 'And I think we now have a verified link. Carmen and Frank were at this secret facility where live test subjects were being handled. Perhaps Frank and Carmen picked up a mutated strain and brought it back with them. Which means they could have passed it to Henry and George and of course, to your father, Howie.'

I shifted in my seat at a sudden thought. 'But what about my sister? She wasn't immune, or infected. And we've nearly all seen family members die from it.'

'My mum,' Cookey said quietly as Charlie reached over to touch his shoulder.

'Siblings and relatives are not genetic clones of each other,' Reginald said. 'But it might also explain why Kyle was able to fight so closely to the infected and not become infected himself.'

'We haven't seen Kyle for years,' Carmen said.

'Maybe Howard met up with him for a brew,' Frank said as Henry nodded in agreement.

'Howard did like maintaining contacts,' Henry said. 'But Reginald is correct. Carmen could be immune, or she could have been vaccinated. Perhaps we can circle back to that point. For now, I would like to know how you are defining your mission. What are your key objectives? And how do you plan to achieve them? Have you established an operation order?'

'Right,' I said as I thought back to the managers meetings I used to sit in. 'I guess our main objective has been to er, try and slow the evolution.'

'Excellent. And how precisely have you been achieving that? What's the methodology?'

'Erm, mainly by killing zombies.'

'Right. That's good. And how are you planning for that part of your mission?'

'Well. We look for the zombies. And then we kill them.'

'I see.'

'We did use some maps once,' I added brightly.

'Maps,' Clarence said, clicking his fingers at Henry.

'And Reggie worked a route out,' I said. 'On the maps.'

'Maps,' Clarence said.

'So the zombies wouldn't know which route we were taking,' I said. 'That was our plan. Oh, but then we did it that day when Reggie was telling it about pies.'

'Pi,' Charlie said.

'But that fucked up cos they jumped us after guessing our route,' I said.

'We didn't use the maps,' Clarence said.

'And then we ended up in the cocaine place. But er, yeah, so. It's been very fluid for us really,' I said.

'Fluid,' Clarence said.

'We've had to stay very fluid,' Roy said.

'Hydrate,' Dave said, making everyone turn to see him staring back without any form of expression.

'Understood,' Henry said into the slightly odd silence. 'Was that your sole mission? To stem the evolution?'

'Oh god no. We're also going to find whoever started it and kill them,' I said. 'And then release the panacea.'

'Or we could release the panacea and then kill them,' Paula said. 'I mean, it's not fixed is it. It's not a fixed plan.'

'No. It's fluid,' I said.

'We're remaining fluid,' Roy said

'It's important to hydrate,' Dave said.

'We'll use maps though,' Clarence added.

Henry nodded slowly. 'One more question if I may. What is the reason for killing those, as you describe them, who started it?'

'Cos they started it.' I said.

'I understand that, Howie. But what for? What is the aim?'

'To bloody kill them.'

'Okay. I'm understanding that part. But my question is what purpose will it serve?'

'Oh. Got it. Sorry,' I said as Paula shifted from the energy in me starting to change. 'So, there was these people right. They had this zombie virus and they released it. Which killed everyone.'

'This is revenge for you then? Is that correct?'

'Yes,' I said quietly. 'It's revenge.'

'And what is *your* mission, Henry?' Reginald asked.

'Our mission objective is to first find and release the panacea, and thereafter to disrupt the plans for gathering the survivors into forced camps.'

'That's very altruistic of you,' Reginald said. 'Is that why you made the power grab for the fort.'

'The fort holds no value to me, Reginald. But if the immunes are being sent there then it needs to be held safely.'

'It is being held,' I said.

'Which is why Lilly was not shot yesterday,' Henry said as I realised I was right, and that Henry and George planned that execution in advance.

'Joan. What about you?' I asked, looking over to the older woman sitting ramrod straight.

'I said last night, Howie. I won't hold a rifle for Lilly. Even if she is an asset,' she added with a look to Henry. 'If it's all the same I'll tag along. I can help with the food too.'

'Joan is a good sniper, Mr Howie,' Dave said from behind.

'And Bash?' Howie asked. 'Does he speak any English?'

'A few words only,' Henry said. 'But I speak his language and he said he would rather shoot zombies than build shithouses. His words.'

'Fair enough,' I said with a slow nod. 'Okay, my terms are that we'll work together to find and release the panacea, and in return, you'll help us find the people that did it... And you won't try and stop us from killing them.'

'Agreed,' Henry said. 'The next obvious step would be to start heading into London. I don't know where they are, but I do know where to start looking. However, before we do that, I am interested in this control point theory. To that end, I would suggest that before we go to London, we seek some infected so I can view them in close situ.'

'Do you really want to risk that?' I asked. 'I mean. We know *we're* immune to it.'

'Indeed. Which is why I'm suggesting Frank and I will undertake a simple test to ensure we have immunity. Marcy is contagious, yes? Perhaps, if you don't mind, Marcy, we could use you.'

'Guess I'd better get snogging then,' Frank said, getting to his feet with a wink to Marcy. 'And I brushed my teeth this morning.'

'Lucky me,' Marcy said. 'Paco's infected. Snog him.'

'He's got a beard. It'll chafe.'

'There won't be any kissing,' Henry said, rising to his feet. 'Let's go outside.'

'Henry, are you sure about this?' I asked as they all started heading out into the hot street.

'Frank was in close combat yesterday and didn't succumb. We know Carmen has immunity, so it stands to reason I am. Dave, if I should become infected then double tap please. Carmen, if that happens then pass message to George that he is the CO. He will task Kyle at the fort and assume command.'

'Understood,' Carmen said as Henry came to a stop in the middle of the street. 'And there's really no need for this to be dramatic either. Marcy, would you prick your finger please,' he added, producing a small pin.

'I'm not pricking my finger, Henry. We can just kiss.'

'I'd rather not do that.'

'Eh, but,' I said, still trying to get my head around it as Marcy planted her lips on Henry's then stepped away. 'Jesus, Marcy,' I said.

'Oh, piss off. You're not the jealous type,' she said. 'How are you feeling, Henry?'

'No change,' Henry said, staring at his watch as I turned with a start at the sight of Dave aiming one of his pistols at Henry.

'Jesus,' I said, looking again at Henry. A lean man with a bald head. He must be sixty years old too. Mind you, he'd not batted at eyelid at the prospect of turning into a zombie, or at being kissed by Marcy either.

'Two minutes,' Henry said, looking up. 'I feel no changes. Are there any outward physical signs?'

'Er, no. None at all,' I said.

'Great. Frank?' Henry said as the rest of us shared looks at the clinical nature of them.

'Righto,' Frank said, handing his weapons over to Henry before walking out into the middle of the road. 'Dave, if I turn into a zombie then sod off and don't shoot me. Let me dribble in peace.'

'You do that now, old man,' Carmen said before glancing at Dave aiming both of his pistols at Frank. 'Dave, he's not done it yet.'

'He's Frank McGill,' Dave said as Carmen turned to look at Frank then a second later she drew and aimed her pistol at his head. Then Henry did the same and the rest of us were looking on like *what the fuck! Just how bad is this guy?*

'Come on then,' Frank sad, puckering his lips and pulling a silly face as Marcy smiled while shooting glances at the way the others were aiming at him. She stepped in and kissed him on the lips. She told me later she was half-expecting him to try and slip his tongue in or something, or even try for a grope. But he stayed perfectly still, showing a grace and decency that she wasn't expecting.

'If it does happen then tell Kyle I called him a god-bothering twat and I'm coming back to haunt him.'

'Okay, Frank,' Carmen said, swallowing as the seconds once more ticked by. 'You okay?' she asked when it hits one minute.

'No,' Frank said, making everyone tense from the strain in his voice. 'I can feel something in my gut.'

'Jesus, Frank... You'll be okay,' Carmen said.

'I'm not so sure, love,' he said quietly.

'Frank. Stop being a prick.'

'I'm sorry, Carmen,' he said, rubbing his gut with a grimace while we're all reaching for our rifles. 'This is going to be bad,' he added before letting rip with a fart. 'Cor, that's better.'

'You fucking dick!' Carmen said as the rest of us laughed at the breaking tension.

'Cor, that really smells. Can I move yet?' Frank asked, checking his watch. 'Yeah. That'll do. Great kiss, and next time don't put your tongue in my mouth,' he said to Marcy while winking at me.

'I didn't,' Marcy said as I gave her a look. 'I didn't! He was joking.'

'What a fucking day,' I said. 'Load up I guess. We're moving out. And watch out for falling satellites,' I added with a glance up at the clear sky. Expecting to see one plummeting down.

There wasn't, but I figured it was only a matter of time.

Cos why wouldn't it? We're shit magnets.

12

After Henry gave Heather one of his encrypted military radios we said our goodbyes and clambered back into the Saxon to follow the path of all that is good and right, and most likely blunder into more shitfests.

'Bloody hell it's hot,' Clarence said. I glanced over to see him shifting about in the passenger seat with beads of sweat rolling down his face. He was right though. The air felt charged with heat. Even the steering wheel felt hot in my hands. 'You happy with everything Henry said then?' he asked.

'Fuck knows. Lot to take in really. What about you?'

'Don't know,' he said at length. 'I think he knew.'

'Knew what?'

'Henry. I think he knew he was immune, or infected. I think he knew before he did that test with Marcy.'

I nodded back, realising that I thought the same, but just not on a level to verbalise. 'The pin,' I said.

Clarence nodded at the same time. 'He had it ready for Marcy. So he knew he was going to do that test.'

'Carmen was worried about Frank though.'

'I'm not saying Carmen knew, or Frank either. But Henry. I think he did. And don't forget, these guys are skilled actors. They see what you want them to see.'

I drove on in silence. Thinking it all over. 'Yeah,' I finally said and offered a shrug because what could we do?

Clarence did the same. Lifting his huge shoulders as he leant closer to the open door. Those doors are heavy too, and to hold one open against the wind without any sign of strain shows just how bloody strong he is. 'He's smart too,' Clarence said. 'I didn't meet that many spooks in the military, but Chris did. He always said they're on another level. He said these guys can think in two languages at once.'

'Eh?'

'Try it. Try and think in two languages at the same time.'

'I don't even know two languages.'

'Exactly. These guys do. They know lots of languages, and they can think on lots of levels all at the same time.'

'Fuck off,' I said, casting him another look before I twisted in my seat. 'Charlie? What languages can you speak?'

'English, French, Spanish, and German, and some others.'

'Can you think in two languages at once?'

'I'm sorry, what?'

'Can you think in two languages at once? Hang on, so I'll give you a question right, but you think of the answer in English, French and Spanish at the same time. What colour are Cookey's eyes?'

'Blue. Bleu. Azul,' she replied then pauses, trying to work out if she thought of them at the same time or one after the other. 'Gosh. I don't know. I think one after the other, but it was so fast it felt like it was at the same time.'

I nodded and offered a thumbs up while driving on into the country lanes. Sunlight dappled the windscreen. The wind blew through the open door and the big engine vibrated the chassis as the wheels trundled on. There's something about that noise and motion. Something deeply soothing and homely and it always brings forth a surge of love for the Saxon. That's it become such a place of safety and comfort.

'Yeah, Henry is smart,' Clarence added a good few moments later and that too shows how far we have come. That our conversations can be broken and filled with long gaps but still flow and have meaning.

'We'll see,' I added.

We drank water and we drove on. We listened and we watched, and the seconds of our lives turned into minutes as the world beyond the hot tin can recovered from the blight of humanity.

'Heather said she opens the gates,' Clarence said after a while longer. 'To the fields. She smashes them down.' I glanced over at him. 'For the animals,' he added. 'So they can get out.'

'That's really nice,' I replied and started looking out for gates to smash down. We spotted one further up, but it was already mangled and busted. The same with the one a mile after that. And then the next ones too. 'It's like breadcrumbs,' I said with a smile. 'We can see where she's been.'

'One mile warning to the town ahead, chaps,' Reginald's voice came through the radio.

'Cheers, Reggie,' I transmitted back then frowned at the thought of Henry remaining impassive while inwardly tutting at our crass non-military ways. 'Er, roger that. Confirmed and affirmative. Ten four and… Ten four copy. Over and out,' I added as Clarence just stared at me.

'Ten four?'

'What's wrong with ten four? That's what radio people say.'

He nodded and stared ahead.

'It's what radio people say,' I said again.

He nodded and stared ahead.

'Fuck you,' I added.

He smiled and stared ahead.

We pulled over, and the hot bodies dropped from the hot tin can, but in so doing, we walked into the air of an oven only to gasp and grumble.

All of us red-faced with slick hair and wet clothes while Henry and his team looked fresh and cool. I headed over to Roy's van and found Maddox already pulling the drone from the back as Nick grabbed it like a protective parent. Clearly not wanting anyone else to touch it.

'Ah. I see. Gaining advanced reconnaissance intelligence,' Henry said as though we might have done something worthy for once.

'Okay,' Nick announced. 'And launching in three, two… We have ground clearance,' he added as the drone flew up and we crowded into the side of the van to watch the screen on Reggie's desk.

'May I see?' Henry asked as a path formed. He said thank you lots of times and got inside the van to hunker down on a case of water as the town came into view on the screen. The pastures and fields giving way to amenity land, allotments and gardens. Streets and roads started showing. Avenues and lanes. Rooftops. Shed tops. Greenhouses and back-garden swimming pools. Vehicles left on driveways. Some in the road. No motion. No movement. Nick flew the drone over the main road in and swept along to the town centre. No motion. No movement.

'Nick, go down please,' Paula said, frowning at the screen. 'Yep. Thought so. They've got an outdoors shop. We can stock up, and there's a supermarket too.'

'Fuck's sake. I thought you saw something,' I said.

'I did,' she said. 'Okay, Nick. Bring it back.'

'Roger that.'

'Ten four,' I said to a few strange glances. 'I don't even know what ten four means.'

'It's part of the universal ten codes,' Henry explained. 'Ten four is to acknowledge and say you understand, which means you were correct in your usage.'

I smiled at the reply as Marcy gave me a pitying look and patted me on the shoulder while Nick brought his drone back, and still refused to let anyone touch it, or go near it, or even look at it. Apart from Henry though. Henry could look at it.

'She's certainly a beauty, Nick,' Henry said in his smart tan trousers and tucked in shirt and still smelling nice.

'Thanks,' Nick said, with obvious glee at the attention. 'She's got incredible range.'

'I should imagine she does. And a payload capacity too. What's the MGW?'

'We haven't tested it,' Nick replied while I tried to work out what MGW meant and shared a look with Clarence, who shrugged as we both looked at Roy.

'Maximum Gross Weight,' he said as Marcy gave me another pitying look.

'She carried a bag of cupcakes from the fort to Camber airstrip though. I'd say that was a kilo,' Nick said. 'But I think she could do more.'

'Did the schematics give any indication?' Henry asked.

'Yeah, probably. But I can't read the words in the boxes,' Nick said with an embarrassed wince.

'Are you dyslexic? I see. Well, let me say dyslexia is never a sign of low intellect. Far from it. Some of the most gifted people I worked with suffered from dyslexia. Tell you what. Perhaps we can do it later. Dig them out and find me. I'd be delighted to take a look.'

'Yeah? Wow. Okay, great. Thanks, Mr Henry.'

'It's just Henry,' Henry said as Nick beamed a smile and walked off. Henry went next, dropping lithely from the van with a nod at me and Clarence as he marched back to his air-conditioned vehicle.

'Bless,' Marcy said, staring at me and Clarence. 'You're like a pair of gay dads that just met the cool stepfather.'

'What the fuck?' I scoffed as Clarence adds his own hearty scoffing.

We got back into the hot tin can like a pair of gay dads and listened to Nick in the back telling his friends about the cool stepfather that's going to read drone schematics to him later.

Engine on and we set off for the last mile into town.

'Another one,' Clarence said, pointing to a busted in gate as we drove through a long sweeping bend and met the ex-residents of the aforementioned field now baaing in the middle of the road. All fluffy and cute and chewing grass and hedges and berries and twigs or whatever sheep eat. 'Road's blocked,' Clarence said. 'By sheep,' he added helpfully.

We cracked our doors open to step from the tin can into the oven and strolled out towards the sheep with the clearly held belief they'll flee before our manliness and thereby open the carriageway.

Except they didn't flee, or even blink, or do anything other than just kind of stand around chewing things and making noises while looking all white and fluffy. One of them did have a poo, and another one had a piss, but mostly they just chewed things and made sheep noises.

Clarence and I shared a look then turned at the same time to yell out. 'NICK!'

'What?' he called, dropping out from the back.

'You're good with animals,' I said.

'When did I become good with animals?'

'When did I become good with animals, Mr Howie!' Dave said, also dropping out the back as everyone else also dropped out of the back to come forth in a gaggle that still had no effect on the sheep.

'Go on then,' Clarence said, looking at Nick.

'What?'

'Get rid of them,' Clarence said.

'Go away,' Nick called out as everyone else looks from him to the sheep who remained quite happy and content. 'What about Meredith? Sheep hate dogs. Get the dog. Where's the dog?'

'She's licking that sheep,' Tappy said as we all looked over to Meredith licking a sheep's bum. The one that did the poo too. Dirty dog.

'COME ON. TIME TO GO,' Paula shouted with her organising voice which made everyone else want to run and flee, apart from the sheep. She even clapped her hands which sends shivers down our spines, but the sheep ignored her and remained in situ. All white and fluffy and cute with Meredith still licking bums.

'What about Jess?' Blowers asked.

'You can't do that to them,' I said. 'Poor things.'

'We could kill one and eat it,' Roy suggested.

'What is it with you and killing animals?' Paula asked.

'Sorry, are you a vegetarian?' Roy asked.

'Well, no, but my meat comes from a packet. Not from a fluffy white coat. We don't even know how to butcher them.'

'I could butcher one,' Henry said from behind, making us all turn to see him and his smooth and highly professional team being all smooth and highly professional.

'You can butcher a sheep?' I asked.

'My uncle used to own a farm,' he replied. 'I'd go there for summers as a child.'

'And solve mysteries with Dick and Jane?' I asked.

'Sorry, what?'

'What?'

'Dick and Jane?'

'No idea,' I said, wondering why I said that as I looked at the other gay dad who frowned at me while the sheep made sheep noises and chewed things. 'Um, but I don't think eating one will clear the road.'

'Of course,' Henry said, coming forward to join Clarence and I. 'Sheep are funny creatures. Cute, but they're not blessed with intelligence,' he added before striding out to smack a sheep bottom. Not hard, but enough to make the sheep give a very sheep-like expression of *what the fuck* before it ran off, which in turn made all the other sheep go *what the fuck* and also run off. Which then increased as Henry waded in smacking more sheep bums like he'd spent a whole life doing it. 'GO ON NOW!' he cried out, all deep and manly as the sheep did more poos and legged it down the road. 'Frank, you drive our vehicle and I'll push them on,' he said and sets off after them.

'Why didn't you do that?' Clarence asked, glaring at Nick.

'Yeah, Nick,' I said. 'You're the animal guy.'

'I'm not the animal guy!'

We got back into the hot tin can and listened to Nick in the back telling his friends he's not the animal guy.

Engine on and we pulled way. Albeit slower this time, which was due to the sheep whisperer ahead of us solving the mystery of the missing flock with Dick and Jane.

Eventually the sheep got safely into some allotments and away from the bottom smacking senior spy and set about eating cabbages and home-grown cannabis plants. But Henry, instead of walking back to his own vehicle, hopped up onto the step next to my door and clung onto the frame with a manly nod to keep going. I give him a look then shared an eye roll with Clarence as we drive on into town.

'Like a pair of gay dads,' muttered a female voice behind us, making us both flick middle fingers.

A moment or two later, and after my wishes for a massed attack while Henry clung to the door went unheeded, we came to a stop. Engine off. Doors open and we dropped from the tin can into the oven once more.

'Eyes up and fan out,' Blowers ordered, slipping into his sergeant role.

I dropped down and grunted at the sticky heat as I looked about at another ubiquitous town centre that looked the exact same as every other town centre in the entire country.

Honestly.

How did people remember where they lived? It's all so samey and bloody boring. The parking bays. The road layouts. The churches and pubs. There's always an old hotel too. Normally called *The George*. Or *The Cask and Fuckstick*. *The Wet Twat* or *The Floppy Knob*. But it always looks rundown. Like it's on the verge of going under. Which it probably was due to the thieving shits that run the councils robbing the poor buggers half to death in fees and taxes before whacking in parking bays to make sure nobody could ever actually visit one of the shitty shops.

'Wow. You are on one today,' Marcy said, walking past me.

'Stop reading my head thoughts!'

'You were muttering,' Paula said, also going by.

'I wasn't,' I told anyone that wanted to listen. Which amounted to Dave and the other gay dad, seeing as everyone else was clustering about the new awesome stepfather.

'I do love these towns,' Henry said with a deep breath and his hands on his hips. 'They're all so unique, aren't they? They each got a different vibe about them. As a child I would often travel through these places and I could just feel the character.'

THE UNDEAD TWENTY-FIVE. THE HEAT

'Was that with Dick and Jane?' I muttered as Paula and Marcy shot me some very stern glances.

'Ah and look!' Henry said, turning to stare at the local hotel. '*The Royal George*. I bet she served some fine ales.'

'Are you a real ale man, Henry?' Roy asked.

'I am indeed. I spent many a happy Sunday with a dark ale and the papers next to a roaring fire in the local,' he said as Roy promptly adopted him as a stepfather too. 'Yes. Rural England at its finest. What about you, Howie? I can see you with an ale or two on a Sunday afternoon. That your bag is it?'

'No. I normally watched internet porn. Anywho,' I added into the weird silence that only comes when a joke falls flat. 'Enough chitty chat. What say we gather our supplies eh chaps and chapessess?' I asked, slipping into a strange jovial accent as the tumbleweed blew by and even Meredith stared at me in pity while in the distance some sheep get stoned and shit on the cabbages.

'You alright, nipper?' Frank asked with a frown. 'Heat getting to you is it? Maybe he needs a lie down.'

'He needs something,' Paula said, clapping her hands. 'Right. I'll do the outdoor store first, then the chemist for cleaning kits and wipes. Blowers, can you organise the supermarket? We need water. And tinned food. And pasta. And don't let Nick inside. There won't be anything left. And don't forget the tinned fruit. Actually, I'll do it. You'll just get fifty cans of ravioli.'

'I like ravioli,' Nick said brightly.

'You the quartermaster then?' Frank asked, strolling over to Paula as she fished her notepad out of a pocket and produced a pen seemingly from thin air. 'We're down on food and fluids, and our medkits need a top up. Henry? What's the SP on the refs front? Joint or single action?'

'Combined I'd say,' Henry said, finally turning away from staring lovingly at the shitty old town to stride over to our newly appointed quartermaster. 'Makes sense logistically,' he added while I still try and work out what Frank asked him.

'It does,' Paula said. 'We'll eat together. Okay, let me know what you need.'

'I have a list,' Henry said, producing one from a pocket. 'But perhaps it would be easier for me to assist you. And I believe Joan is willing to help in these matters too. Many hands make light work after all.'

'And the two gay dads watch on with little hearts breaking in their eyes,' Marcy said as Paula, Joan and Henry set off on their shopping trip.

'I don't even know why you'd say that,' I replied with much haughtiness while Clarence just flicked her the middle finger again. 'And that pub looks like a dump.'

'Dump,' Clarence said.

'Roaring fire,' I said with a huff as Clarence tutted. 'I mean, who does that?'

'Better than internet porn,' Marcy said.

'Yeah. Why did you say that?' Clarence asked.

'I have no idea. Anyway. Fuck it, you know what. I'm going shopping too.'

'Howie, don't. You'll upset her,' Marcy said.

'It'll be fine! Clarence and I can do the supermarket.'

'Paula loves doing the supermarket. Seriously, Howie. Don't do it.'

'We're helping, Marcy. Many hands make light work after all... And anyway. Dave and I worked in an actual supermarket. We're literally supermarket experts.'

'WHAT THE SHIT?' Paula asked a good twenty minutes later, coming to a stop to stare at the rows of trolleys and the mounds of stuff stacked in the road.

'Look at that,' I said, stepping back with a proud nod and a very sweaty face from lugging so much stuff about.

'We did the supermarket,' Clarence announced, also red-faced and sweating.

'Got everything we need,' I told her.

'All sorted,' Clarence said. 'And we got the ravioli you asked for.'

'I didn't ask for ravioli,' she said.

'There's a few different types actually,' I said with my professional supermarket insider knowledge. 'So, you've got your basic value ravioli range of course. But you know, ravioli has come a long way these days. I mean, look. You've got beef ravioli.'

'Chicken ravioli,' Clarence said, holding a can up.

'Vegetarian ravioli,' I said.

'Cheese and tomato ravioli,' Clarence added.

'Four cheese ravioli.'

'We even found some crab ravioli,' Clarence said.

'But that's just the tinned section,' I announced. 'Then of course you've got the fresh range, that's still in date too.'

'You two and Nick are the only ones that eats ravioli,' Paula told me.

'Eh?' We both said, taken aback at this news.

'I made it last week. Everybody said they didn't like it. Apart from you and Nick, but Nick would eat the contents of a bin. Jesus. And why the hell have you got an entire trolley filled with tinned hotdog sausages?'

'We thought we'd have a hotdog night,' I said.

'We don't have buns. It would just be a sausage night.'

'Well. We can have a sausage night then,' I said.

'While Nick eats the ravioli,' Clarence added.

'I want the sausages,' Nick said in alarm.

'Tough. You didn't clear the sheep,' Clarence told him.

'Where's the water?' Paula asked, looking from the mounds to us.

'I thought we had water,' Clarence said. 'Nick? Where's the water?'

'Yeah, Nick. You're the team water guy,' I said.

'What the fuck!'

'What the fuck, Mr Howie!' Dave said.

'Well, at least you got the Lucozade,' Paula said. 'Literally *all* of the Lucozade,' she added, taking in the mountain of stacked cases.

'Ah, but look,' I said with the sudden hope of recovering the situation. 'The piece of the resistance!' I announced.

'Ta da,' Clarence said, wagging the many, many packets of hair bands clutched in his enormous hands.

Paula just stared at them before looking up at Clarence then over to me. 'Firstly, it's *pièce de résistance*, and secondly,' she said, pulling a large packet of hair bands from a bag. 'Those are for children. You got them out of the baby section. These are adult sizes. Right. Just piss off. The pair of you. Seriously. I don't know what's got into you two today. No. I do know. And you can pack it in. Go and sit in Reggie's van and watch porn.'

'Duh. There's no internet,' I replied, which I'll admit isn't the greatest of responses, but we got ushered and harangued, cajoled and physically pushed into Roy's van with Clarence almost bent double while we stared about looking for somewhere to sit.

'Do you like ravioli?' Clarence asked Reginald.

'No,' he replied as the sliding door slammed open again.

'Out you get,' Paula said. 'We need the space for the supplies. Go over there. In that shop.'

I looked at the other gay dad as we got ushered from the van and across the street.

Silence ensued with Clarence and I looking about at the inside of the travel agency. 'But seriously. Why did you say internet porn?'

'I have no idea.'

13

Day Twenty-nine

'Ready, big boy?'

'Es.'

'Bloody hell,' Heather says a few seconds later when she climbs out of the vehicle into the wall of heat and opens the boot to take the big wire cutters and sledgehammer from the back.

Boot lid closed and they set off, side by side. Sunglasses on and looking badass.

'Feels like we should be going in slow-motion,' she says, glancing up at him. 'Like this,' she adds, slowing down to take bigger steps in mimicry of slow-motion.

'No,' he says, shaking his head.

'What? That's slow-motion.'

'No. Wait,' he says and walks back to the car to open the boot again then peers around to make sure she's watching.

He gathers himself up and stands tall with his chin thrust out then reaches up to slam the boot in a way that shows his arm muscles then sets off from the car to her. Each step longer than it should be with an imaginary soundtrack playing in both of their heads.

'Okay. Yeah, that's good,' she says. 'Honestly. It's giving me goosebumps. You're just like The Rock… Argh! Fuck off!' she yells out as he lunges in, grinning and poking her tongue out.

They reach the entry point and give thanks for the shade created by the high perimeter fence.

'It was nice seeing them all though,' she says, taking the wire cutters and stepping away as he sizes the doors up. He nods then swings the sledgehammer into the first toughened pane of glass.

Entry made and they head inside to the distinctive musty smell of a place left undisturbed for nearly a month. Dust on the floor. On the counters and shelves.

She sets off towards another set of doors only to find them locked. 'And it was interesting hearing about Neal and how it all started,' she calls as Paco breaks the locks. 'Howie and his lot and me all have B, whereas you had C, but now you've probably also got B. Same with Marcy. She had C, now she's a B. Or more like a double D. Or a double E. Honestly. Her boobs. I get boob envy just looking at her. Mine are okay though, aren't they? I know they're not that big, but they're not like sagging or anything. They're still perky. Are they perky?'

Paco stops smashing the doors in to consider this thought with great aplomb before determining, in his way of determining things, that he needs to check before he can answer such a question.

'Okay,' she says when he reaches out to cup one. Then he drops the sledgehammer and cups the other, but it's still not right. He can't quite tell. Her top will need to come off.

Five minutes later and she's bent forward with her hands braced on the countertop and her trousers around her ankles.

'Oh my god… We're fucking in a zoo…' she gasps the words out, because they are, indeed, fucking in a zoo. 'OH MY GOD. WE'RE FUCKING IN A ZOO!'

THE UNDEAD TWENTY-FIVE. THE HEAT

A few moments later, and they stagger through the freshly broken-down doors leading from the customer entrance into the main central area of the zoo. Red-faced and rubbery of leg with sweat rolling down their faces that gets mopped by the scarfs wrapped about their necks. Paco's to hide his scars. Hers to keep the sun from burning. And also to mop the sweat away after having sex. Which they do rather a lot. In all manner of places. In fact, pretty much anytime they go anywhere new.

'Hang on,' she says, pulling a battered notepad from a pocket. She flips the lid, finds a pencil and writes zoo reception on the **Places We've Had Sex list**. 'Done. Right. Let's get to it.'

Getting to it means finding doors, cages, traps, hatches and anything enclosed, and then making them unenclosed. They start small and head into the furry creatures section.

Noise greets her. A cacophony of squeaks and squeals coming from small furry things with big ears that looked cute enough to lock up so people could gawp and pay money while slurping sugary drinks and banging on cages and glass walls.

But the noise is good. Noise means life and at least a decent water supply was provided.

A few moments later and they leave that section behind as it explodes into motion with furry bodies hopping about while others hunker down and hide from the noise.

Into the reptile house and they do the same again. Heather likes animals, but she doesn't get the attraction to reptiles.

They start lifting lids and sliding hatches to give freedom to the lizards and geckos until they reach the far end. 'Urgh. I can't,' she says, shaking her head as Paco smiles and goes past her to deal with the snakes and spiders. Most of which will probably try and eat each other. In fact, Heather does realise that most of the things they set free will still starve, or die of thirst, or get eaten, or simply perish. But that's the order of things. That's natural, and at least they'll have a fighting chance.

'I can't believe what Henry said about the immunes either,' she calls out as he pops the door open leading to the back corridor that services the tanks. 'All that stuff about them being herded together and held captive. Which is rather apt considering where we are. But do you know what I mean?'

'Es,' he shouts back while spilling trays of food over the floor and opening cupboards and ripping tops from freezers and fridges. Giving access to the food stored within. It stinks something awful. Previously frozen mice and rats now thawed and rotting. He starts on the tanks next. Opening the lids one after the other. Reaching into tanks containing giant spiders to prop logs and debris against the side so they can climb to freedom. He reaches the last tank, pops the lock from the hatch and reaches in before freezing.

'Ether?' he calls.

She winces outside. Knowing what he's found. 'What is it?'

'Cobra.'

'Fuck,' she says, grimacing again. 'I don't know. What do you think? I mean, it's dangerous right. But it's still an animal. 'Just do it. If it's safe. We said that. We said we'll let everything go and it's up to them what they do.'

'Kay.'

'Have you done it.'

'Es.'

'Did it react?'

'Es.'

'Did it bite you?'

'Es.'

'The cobra bit you?'

'Es,' he says, coming into view with a king cobra attached to his arm with the tail dangling down.

'That's gross, Paco! Get it off. No, seriously. Just get rid of it.'

'Kay,' he says and reaches down to prize the mouth open as the cobra stares back and determines, in his cobra way of determining things, that he's pretty sure most prey tend to keel over once they've been bitten. And he put a shit load of venom in too. He's been locked up for years and been waiting to chomp on something since he got here. Now he's plucked off and sent on his way as Paco looks down at the puncture wounds on his arm and the venom being rejected by his body.

'So gross,' Heather says when he rejoins her. She pulls the notepad out and adds Cobra to the **Things That Have Bitten Paco** list. A rattlesnake had him in the last place. Paco wasn't rattled though. He just plucked it free. A spitting cobra also tried to spit, but Paco glared at it and slunk off. Then there was that big python that tried to pick a fight with him while Paco just tapped it on the nose until it got annoyed and went away.

She checks the snakebite, shaking her head at the lack of swelling. No inflamed skin. No nothing. Just one hungry cobra with a sore nose.

Another door opened to a greeting of screeching that's music to Heather's ears. Whoops and shouts. Yells and wails. The follow the path running between the big caged sections and use the wire cutters to snap locks and open doors. Paco rips most of them off too, to prevent them closing by accident after they leave.

Everything gets freed. Gibbons and lemurs. Capuchins and marmosets. Sloths and macaques. Chimps and orangutans.

Some of the primates inside scatter and run. Some panic and fling shit. Some lie dead. Too weak and too old to have survived the lack of food and water. Most of those have been eaten. It's disturbing to see, but it's what life is, and if Heather died right now, she'd have no issue with these things eating her if it meant they survived. Likewise, she'd eat them if it meant her own survival.

The final act, before they leave the park, is to find the food stores and shred every bag of grain and feed they can find.

It's not enough. Heather knows that. But it's about all they can do, and eventually they head back to the SUV. Grunting and gasping as they sink into the hot seats then sighing in relief when the air-con kicks in.

They drink water and mop faces as she pulls a map out and starts inspecting the roads. 'Do you know what?' she asks, staring over as he glugs from a bottle of Lucozade. 'Stuff the immunes today. Let's do another zoo.'

'Kay,' he says before belching.

A smile shared and they leave the carpark behind to delve once more into the deserted country lanes.

14

D iary of Maddox Doku

I HAVE no idea why I'm doing this. It feels stupid.

I did keep a diary in prison once, but that was only to pass a course about accepting personal responsibility and get a month off my sentence.

Whatever.

It still feels stupid, but I like Paula, and she said we should write things down. It came about from that place we stopped in when Howie and Clarence got all the ravioli cans. I was helping Paula get it all sorted when she stopped and looked at me.

I asked her if she was okay, then she grabbed my arm and pulled a face. Like the face she does when she's thinking. She's cool like that. She does it a lot. She'll put her hand on your arm or your shoulder and lift one eyebrow and cock her head over as though having that physical contact with you is helping her think.

I don't like being touched normally. We didn't grow up all touchy feely where Mo and I come from. You touch people the wrong way on our estate and you either get stabbed up, or your house catches fire. But Paula's got that way about her. She even does it to Dave sometimes. He used to look terrified, but he's used to it now.

Anyway. Paula's got her hand on my arm then she smiles. *Come with me* she said, and she started pulling me over to this shop and telling me to open the door. I was like. *What for.* But she's all eager and nodding so I give the door a kick then grab her to stop her charging in because she didn't have a rifle. I went in first, but it was all dusty and stale. *What did you need anyway?* I asked and she started grabbing all these books. Like diary books. All with nice covers. *What do you think?* She asked me. *About what?* I asked her. *Keeping diaries,* she said then she's stacking them in my arms, and we go outside, and Paula gets everyone together and starts handing the books out.

What're these for? Blowers asked. *I thought it might be nice* she said. *You know, after hearing Neal's diary.* Then Tappy was like *fuck yes! I'll do one.* Danny and Mo got one each and they're like looking at each other then at Paula. *Don't be like that!* she said. *I just thought that what we're doing is pretty important and maybe one day people might want to know about it.*

I'll do one Charlie said. Then Nick looked all smug and smiled at Paula. *Ah man, I'd love to, Paula! But I can't read or write.*

Don't worry she said. *We'll get you a Dictaphone.*

Hey, talking of dicks. I think this is Blowers' diary, Cookey said and he's holding his up with a picture of a drooping dick drawn in it with a sad face on the end. I didn't want to laugh cos I don't think dick jokes are funny, but it was *kinda* funny.

Anyway. Then we set off to find a control point to show Henry what they're like and I was wondering if I already have it. I'm not infected like Howie is. But I'm full of energy all the time. I get hurt like they do when we fight, and I heal up quick too. But then I always did so it's hard to tell.

It was weird having Henry there. The dynamics were all different. I liked the way his team all dressed though. They've had that look. That *don't fuck with us* look but without being dressed like soldiers. Like in the movies when the SF guys are pretending to be civilians.

THE UNDEAD TWENTY-FIVE. THE HEAT

They're calm too, and smart. Bash was like early or mid-twenties. Joan was old. Carmen looked about thirty. She's really attractive. I smiled a few times and made eye contact, but it wasn't returned. That's cool though. I'm like ten years younger than her and she said she doesn't date fit guys either. She likes nerds and smart guys. I mean. I am smart, but I'm fit too. Like – I'm not boasting. I just am.

I was in the front of the van with Roy. I like Roy. He's dull AF and constantly thinks he's sick, but he's calm and smart, and I was glad I wasn't in the Saxon. It was always hot and you're literally always touching someone else. I don't like that. I like my own space.

Tappy is good though. And Danny. They weren't there before with all that bad shit that happened with Lani and the fort, so they don't care about it. And it was cool seeing Mo with a mate. He was different after Jagger died. You could see it affected him.

Booker wasn't there for the bad shit, but he was like the lads. Blowers, Cookey and Nick. He was literally one of them. But I don't know. Like. I mean. I used to get this thing on the estate when I was dealing. Now and then some new guy would pop up and try and score and I'd be like *no way. This guy is five-o. He's a narc. Fuck that.*

It was like a sixth sense. Like a vibe. Even if they weren't five-o, I could just tell if they weren't right. Like maybe from another gang sniffing for new territory or whatever.

I was getting that with Booker. He wasn't a cop. I don't mean that. I just mean something wasn't right.

It was like in the café when Reginald was reading the diaries out, and he got to the part about Camilla having semen on her ear from giving Neal a blowjob. Booker looked shifty AF. Then he was looking at Marcy's chest all the time. She was kind of sat side on so we could see the shape of her boobs. She has got amazing breasts, but it was like Booker just kept staring at them, then he'd clear his throat and look away.

I kept telling myself I was reading too much into it, but then they reached the end when Howie realised Carmen was Camilla. I could tell a few of the others hadn't made the connection either. Danny and Mo looked surprised, and Booker definitely only realised at that point, and it was like he was suddenly uncomfortable. He kept looking away, and blinking.

Then I figured I was wrong, and it was just me getting bored. Guarding Reggie was great. And spending all day in here Roy was better than the Saxon. But yeah. I was seriously bored.

You'd think it would be exciting. It is, and it was. I mean it is full on fucking insane sometimes. But in-between those times is the exact opposite, and that's what I was struggling with.

I kept telling myself I'd go off soon and do my own thing. But I didn't know where to go, and I didn't really want to be alone either.

I didn't know what I wanted.

15

Diary of Paula

HOW DO YOU START A DIARY?

I guess I should introduce myself. So, hello! My name is Paula. But I guess I already know that haha! (Cookey would call that a mum joke.)

I kept a diary when I was a teenager, but that was full of boys, and music, and spots. Oh god I had terrible spots when I was a teenager. I bet Marcy didn't.

I just asked her. She said everyone gets pimples. Pimples? Only pretty girls get pimples. The rest of us get moon-map faces. I'm not jealous though. I love Marcy to bits. No. I am a bit jealous, but Marylyn Monroe would be jealous next to Marcy. You can't help it. She's flawless. I'm not exaggerating either.

But the diaries! Yes. I just thought it would be a nice way of keeping a record of what we do because the awful reality is not all of us will make it.

Honestly. If you are reading this in a year or five years or whenever then you need to know you're probably only alive because of the men and women in that stinking sweat box on wheels. They spend all day fighting and running and getting hurt and they don't ever moan.

No. They do moan. Jesus. They moan non-stop, but never about what we do. They moan about each other (Cookey and Blowers) and being hungry (Nick) and the heat (Me) and breaking nails (Marcy) and handsome older man in tan trousers and checked shirts (Clarence and Howie). They moan about those things, but never about the constant threat of dying, or the killing we do.

But this diary is also about keeping track of what we do *other* than killing – and also how bloody hopeless it is sometimes. (Or how bloody hopeless *we* are more like.)

To give you an idea of what it's like we stopped somewhere. (I need to get a map really so I can record placenames) so we could put the drone up to get a view of the town ahead.

Howie wouldn't normally put the drone up in an area like that. We know the towns and villages are small. (He'd normally just go in and smash them all down.)

But Henry was with us, and I can see H & C (Howie and Clarence) were trying to step their game up, so we did stop and launch the drone.

'Okay guys. Clear the launch area please,' Nick said once we'd stopped. (He does love his drone.) 'And launching in three, two… We're clear. Drone is flying. I repeat, the drone is flying.'

Then Henry told Nick he'd done a good job, which made H & C also tell Nick how great he was, while Marcy and I shared another eye roll. (We do that a lot at H & C).

But anyway. There was nothing to see on the drone. Reginald said the town had been hit badly judging from the debris and signs of disturbance, but there was nothing there now.

He was right too. I saw it when we drove in. A few bloated bodies here and there. Smashed in windows. Cars ditched at angles. Old blood stains on walls. The normal things we see all the time now. But nothing else, and no reaction from Meredith either.

Then Mo saw a big bird on a roof and asked Carmen what it was. I was with H & C and Henry, waiting to see if we'd get a contact but I could hear the lads. (I can *ALWAYS* hear the lads).

'It's a Herring gull,' Carmen said.

'Does it have one of the Italian names?' Danny asked.

'Italian?' Carmen asked. 'Oh Latin! Yes, it does. Larus Argentatus.'

'How do you know that?' Danny asks.

'You learn things when you're interested in them, Danny. What do you like?'

'Danny likes boobs,' Cookey said from the other side of the road. 'Biggus boobus.'

'Smallus boobus,' Nick said.

'Anyeth boobyus,' Tappy said. (I did laugh too. It's hard not to sometimes. But it is nice seeing Danny and Mo take an interest in things.)

Then we got back into the vehicles and did it again before the next town. (Stopped to launch the drone.) But we didn't see any infected, so we got back in and drove into the town and got out again to see if any were hiding in the buildings.

That sounds boring. But it's important to know a lot of our time was spent looking for the infected and seeing where they were. Especially as we were searching for a control point to show Henry.

But when we saw the next empty village Howie told Maddox to go in the Saxon so we (H & C and Marcy and I) could jump in the van with Reggie and plan a route. It was obvious H & C felt under pressure to deliver something to Henry, because right then it looked like we were driving about aimlessly.

16

D iary of Maddox Doku

ME AND MY BIG MOUTH.

I was boasting that I was in the van with AC and not in the sweatbox… and then I was back in the sweatbox because Howie was getting worried that they couldn't find a control point so he jumped in the van and put me back in remedial class.

Nah. I don't mean that. It was okay. It was just hot. Like seriously hot. It was over forty degrees in there. The back doors were open, but it just made it noisier.

Tappy was driving. She's a good driver. *Did you miss me baby?* She said to the steering wheel when she got in the front. It's cute really.

We stopped a few minutes later to snoop about in another town. Man. It was baking though!

Then Danny saw another bird. Him and Mo kept asking about them. I thought they were trying to flirt with Carmen at first, but I then I realised they actually liked learning things.

THE UNDEAD TWENTY-FIVE. THE HEAT

That's a blackbird Carmen said. *But how can you tell?* Mo asked her. *Can you see its willy?*

Carmen laughed and said male blackbirds are black with orange beaks and they have the eye rings, and females are brown.

What's the other name? Danny asked her. *Turdus Merula* she told him.

Turdus Booker said with a laugh. But his joke fell flat, and Carmen just gave him a look.

You's in the sun too much, bro, Mo told him. *Laughing at your own jokes.* Booker told him to fuck off like he was joking, but I could see he was pissed off.

Then we got back into the Saxon and set off again towards another town twenty miles away. (Sturbridge I think it was called.)

Bit different from your nice cool van, mate? Cookey asked me, (but he was just trying to be friendly.)

Roughing it with the losers, Booker said.

Speak for yourself, fatty, Cookey told him.

I'm not fucking fat! Booker said.

I know. That's why it's funny Cookey said.

Yeah, except it's not funny, Booker said.

Neither was your turd joke, bro, Mo said.

What was that? Cookey asked.

Booker giving it large in front of Carmen, Mo said.

Was I fuck. I just made a joke Booker said.

I was studying Booker the whole time. You know. Like scrutinising all the nuances on his face and in his body language and trying to find reasons not to like the guy.

Where you from? I asked him.

Why? We on a date or something? Eh, buy me a drink first.

Before what? I asked. He just blinked at me. *What?* He said.

You said buy me a drink first. First before what?

I don't know. I was just fucking about. Heat's getting to you too is it?

Nah. I'm always cool, bro. You get me? I gave him the look I used to give people when I was enforcing for the bossman. But then I heard Mo Mo clearing his throat and looked over to him giving *me* a look.

Like saying *back it up bro*. He must have heard my tone or something. But yeah. That's fair enough. I backed off after that.

It was that heat. I'm telling you. Even Charlie started fanning her face. I said she could take my place in the van if she needed a break. I've got a lot of time for Charlie.

That's very kind of you, Maddox. Thank you. I'm glad you're here though. I wanted to ask what you thought of this morning?

It was cool that I had someone to talk with who didn't just make dick jokes and fuck about all the time. She's smart and calm. She's very pretty too, but she's nuts about Cookey (go figure that one out).

I thought it was quite cute really, Tappy shouted from the front. *That story about Carmen and Neal. I think she really liked him.*

I got that impression, Charlie said.

The mayonnaise thing was funny though, Cookey said. Then I looked to Booker again and saw him doing the same thing and shifting in his seat and clearing his throat. Like he needed air.

God. Hurry up, Tappy! Charlie shouted. *I need some air.*

Like I said. I was bored and looking for reasons not to like the guy, but I was convinced something wasn't right.

17

D iary of Paula

WE AIMED for a bigger town twenty miles away then did the same as before with Nick launching his drone and the rest of us gathering by Reggie's van to watch the monitor on his desk.

'Okay, there's the town centre,' Howie said. 'Nick, go closer. That's it. There we go!'

(You should have seen the look of relief on Howie's face at finally finding some infected. Mind you, it *was* starting to look like we'd made up the whole zombie thing and it hadn't actually happened.)

'Okay, so, we can only see four infected, Henry,' Howie said. 'But the chances are there will be a load more of them in the houses and flats. We're seeing that a lot now.'

'Understood, Howie. What's the SOP from here? Sorry, forgive me. What's the standard operating procedure from here?'

'I know what SOP means. We used it in Tesco,' Howie said, (while clearly wishing he hadn't.) 'We go in, take those four out then wait for the rest.'

'Understood. And what is the method of attack?' Henry asked.

'I just said it. We go in and take those four and, you know, wait for the rest.'

'Sorry, Howie. My mistake. I meant the actual operational attack method.'

'Oh, I see what you mean. Sorry. Yeah, okay, so I think we'll probably just shoot them. I mean, we could strangle them I guess, but it's quite hot, and Dave's only just cleaned his knife.'

'The method of attack is a frontal charge then. Yes? You wouldn't consider a remote attack, or the use of a sniper, or the deployment of a scout for recon. But straight in and straight to the attack.'

Howie looked at the screen then back to Henry. 'Yes,' Howie said.

'Great stuff. Give me two minutes and we'll be ready to deploy. My team gather in for a hot brief,' Henry said, hopping down from the van. 'This is a verbalised operation order. Joan, I'm sure it will be clear to you, but questions are held until the end. The briefing will also be slower as I need to translate for Bashir as we go.'

Henry was unfolding a map to spread across the front of their SUV while he was talking. During which time the rest of us were watching on like *oh, this is how you do it!*

'The situation is that aerial reconnaissance has identified enemy combatants within the town of Sturbridge.' Henry then stopped and repeated the whole thing in Arabic for Bashir.

'Is that Dari?' Maddox asked.

'Nipper, we're briefing. Wait till the end,' Frank told him.

'Mo speaks Dari,' Maddox said.

'I see,' Henry said. 'Mr Howie? Would that be in order?'

'Er, yeah, I mean, if he's happy to do it. Mo? Henry's asking if you can translate for him.'

'For Bashir, yeah? I can try. I ain't spoken it for a few years though. *Yo, bro, as-salaam alaykum.*'

Honestly! I was so proud of Mo. He just reeled this language off, and Bash seemed to light up at someone else talking to him. Then Bash, Henry and Mo were chatting away for ages. Laughing and joking with Mo doing his impish grin. Which is while H & C shared another look. (Like two gay dads as Marcy keeps calling them).

'Then I shall continue,' Henry announced in English. 'Our mission is to attack and negate the enemy forces within the town of Sturbridge. To that end, we will follow this road into the town centre, where, upon arrival we will move to strike with immediate effect, unless fluidity of the operation dictates otherwise. Once the operation commences, we should expect immediate and heavy counterattack from all sides at once. The overall mission objective is to negate any and all infected persons. Friendly forces will be present in the form of Mr Howie and his team so be aware of troop positions when firing. We will also be in an urban environment. On that note I cannot stress enough how dangerous a broken glass environment is - Mo, you're doing a brilliant job.

'Admin and logistics. Joan and Bashir, your immunity is not known. Therefore, you will travel with Reginald within the secure armoured van. If the situation escalates then you are to locate positions of height and add firepower from a distance. Bashir will carry the GPMG. Joan will act as sniper. Mr Howie's nominated medic is Roy. We will be using assault rifles as primary weapons. Carry your ammunition and ensure you are hydrated prior to moving out. I'm CO on the ground for our team. Mr Howie is CO for his team with Clarence deputising and Sergeant Blowers providing NCO support. Questions? Great stuff. Thank you, Mo. Wonderful work. Return to your unit, please. Mr Howie. My briefing has finished. Do you wish to do yours?'

(Howie looked like a rabbit caught in headlamps bless him and rather than just say something simple he went for one of those awful jokes he does.) 'Right er, yeah. You all heard Henry. We'll be driving in and shooting the zombies.'

Nobody laughed. I mean. *Nobody* laughed.

'And watch out for er, for broken glass. Cos, you know, it can cut you,' Howie added.

'I think we all know what we're doing by now,' I said with a hand clap. (You can't beat a hand clap sometimes.) 'Everyone ready?'

. . .

'You two just need to chill out,' I told H & C in the Saxon. 'Honestly. Stop panicking about him.'

'Who's panicking?' Clarence asked.

'Yeah. Who are we even talking about?' Howie asked. 'But maybe we should do proper briefings from now on.'

'We'll need a briefing guy,' Clarence said as they turned to look at Nick.

'I'm not the briefing guy,' Nick said.

'Anyway. We're here so switch on and everyone stay sharp,' Howie called out. 'That's my actual briefing by the way.'

'Great briefing,' Clarence said. 'Succinct and to the point.'

'Succinct means to the point you bloody idiot,' I told him before dropping back and feeling guilty that I'd snapped at him. 'That was mean of me, sorry,' I said while rubbing the spot I hit. 'You're still lovely. And when I say lovely, I don't mean anything sexual.'

I was trying to be nice but that just made Clarence blush, which in turn made me panic so I kept on rubbing his shoulder while my mouth went blah blah blah. 'Not that you're *not* sexually lovely though. Which I wouldn't know because we haven't had sex yet. Ever! I meant ever. Right. Good. Goooooood. Good chat.'

I couldn't stop myself. Honestly, and Clarence was going redder and Marcy was just staring at me with her mouth hanging open and even Howie was glancing over, and of course, during all that time I'm still groping his bloody shoulder! (He has got beautiful shoulders though). 'I'll er, I'll get ready then. Right, everyone focus now. We're almost there.'

Good grief. I was glad when we finally did arrive. Let me tell you that. The Saxon stopped and I could see Henry watching us all work and how Cookey and Tappy ran with Charlie to give cover while Charlie got mounted on Jess.

'Overwatch on,' Roy said from on top of the van with his longbow all ready. 'They're charging!' he called, and I just turned as he let the first arrow go and watched as it hit one of the four infected in the head. Then the dog jumped in and took another one down as H & C finally lifted their rifles to do something constructive, but they were too late because Dave shot them both.

'What the!' Clarence shouted in surprise then turned to see Dave still aiming his rifle. 'Was that you?'

'Yes.'

'But we had them.'

'So did I,' Dave said, already turning away as Howie walked over to the one that Roy shot and stared down at the arrow sticking out of the eye.

'Well. Glad we kept one alive, guys,' Howie said.

'Is he still alive?' Roy asked.

'I was being sarcastic,' Howie said

'Oh,' Roy said. 'Can you get my arrow back though.'

'Right. I'll just pull it out of his head, then shall I?' Howie muttered.

'Why did you want one alive?' Clarence asked.

'To ask it about the control point thing,' Howie said while tugging at the arrow which just made the dead guy sit up. 'Fuck's sake,' he pushed it back down then pressed a foot into the face and tried again. 'Blimey. It's wedged right in there.'

'Give it a tug,' Roy shouted.

'I am giving it a tug! Clarence, pull this arrow out.'

'I'm not the arrow guy,' Clarence said.

'Oh god, no,' Nick said.

'Nick! Pull this arrow out,' Howie called. 'Are the rest of them attacking yet?'

'Not yet,' Blowers calls.

'Fuckers. Where are they?' Howie asked as Nick ran over and started tugging at the arrow. 'Anyone seeing them yet? Charlie?'

'Nothing yet, Mr Howie,' Charlie called as Jess skittered about.

'Go on, Nick. Give it a tug,' Roy called.

'Seriously. Where are they?' Howie asked as Jess ran past with Charlie trying to guide her back the other way while Meredith gripped the body she took down. Making back-lunges with her arse up and her head low. 'Honestly, Henry. Any minute now,' Howie called. 'And boom, all the windows will explode and they'll leap out.

Actually, Nick, add that to your briefing thing: To watch out for exploding glass.'

'I'm not the briefing guy!' Nick grunted while pulling at the arrow.

'Have you got it out yet, Nick?' Roy called.

'I'm not the arrow guy either,' Nick added as the horse ran back the other way.

'You okay, Charlie?' I asked her.

'Fine thank you! She's a bit headstrong today.'

'Honestly. Just wait,' Howie said, nodding at Henry. 'I bet they're watching us right now. Like tens of them.'

'Dozens probably,' Clarence said

'Hundreds,' Howie added.

'Thousands sometimes,' Clarence said with fading hope as the horse ran past again.

'You sure you're okay, Charlie?' I asked.

'FINE!'

'Have you got it yet, Nick?'

'Does it look like I've got it yet, Roy?'

'That's it guys, stay sharp,' Howie said.

'This fucking arrow,' Nick shouted, losing his temper as he stepped back and pulled his axe free.

'HONESTLY. I'M FINE,' Charlie yelled as Jess turned on the spot having clearly locked onto whatever smell she was scenting in the air and aimed for a shopfront. 'Whoa,' Charlie called, tugging on the reins. 'Jess. JESS! BLOODY STOP!' she yelled as Nick chopped the head off and Meredith finally wrenched the arm free from the body she was attacking and started running back to the Saxon with it.

'There's your fucking arrow,' Nick said, throwing the severed head onto the top of Roy's van as Jess barged through a shop door, smacking chairs and tables aside to reach the cafe counter to snort a few lines of chocolate powder before popping a carton of oatmilk.

'Yeah, I don't think they're coming,' Clarence said.

'Damn,' Howie said. 'Charlie! Is that a café?'

'Yes, Mr Howie,' she shouted with milk dripping from her head.

'Blimey. Best brew up then,' Howie said. 'Where's the coffee guy?'

'Fuck me,' Nick said as he started towards the cafe. 'I'll fucking do it shall I.'

'I actually meant Cookey,' Howie said. 'But whatever. Henry, fancy a coffee? We're not getting in the Saxon for half hour at least. Not until Nick sorts his dog out anyway.'

'She's not my dog!'

18

Day Twenty-nine

A LARGE CAR park shimmering with heat hazes. A lone SUV parked up with the doors open as the air fills with grunts and gasps.

'OH MY GOD WE'RE FUCKING IN A SAFARI CAR PARK!'

A few moments later and once more bathed in sweat while rubbery of leg, Heather and Paco head towards the large entrance area for Stickleton Safari Park. Dozens of sprawling acres set deep within the southern home counties.

'That's going to be interesting,' Heather says, using her scarf to mop the sweat from her face as they pass one of the display boards showcasing the BIG CAT DRIVE THRU.

Images of Landrovers painted in black and white stripes to look like zebras against a backdrop of a savannah complete with pictures of lions and other animals.

They reach the entrance kiosks and head through onto a long winding lane leading to the reception building, and that blistering sun glares down as Paco sets to work on getting inside to the reception area.

'FUCK OFF!'

'HELP!'

'That's a kid!' Heather says, feeling a jolt inside as she clambers through the busted doors and runs towards the Jungle Restaurant. Following the cries for help, and hearing more noises coming from inside. Howls and screeches. Bangs and smashes.

She slams through the doors. Sights and smells hit. Too many all at once as a flash of red flies at them. A huge wingspan and a large beak set in a white face that screams out as it flutters by. *'HELP! FUCK OFF!'*

'Ether!' Paco shouts a warning and grabs her tac-vest to pull her from the path of an ocelot running towards them with its eyes fixed on the macaw flying overhead.

A meowling snarl as it speeds up to leap at the wall, using it to bounce off to launch through the air, just missing the tail feathers as Heather backs into Paco with both looking around at the large open-plan room.

A high vaulted ceiling filled with beams and struts. Plants everywhere. Waterfall features and small bridges over intersecting pools filled with shimmering carp and goldfish. Tables and chairs in the restaurant area. Nearly all of them tipped over and scattered about. A scene of absolute carnage. It stinks too. The smell of dung and urine mixed with foods and earthy plant smells. The heat and humidity only making it worse.

'What the hell?' Heather murmurs, thinking it looks like a troop of wild monkeys have taken refuge and trashed the place.

Which is exactly what's happened, and she blinks at the troop of eighty rhesus monkeys that have taken refuge and trashed the place as the whole room seems to freeze in silence for one second before exploding into noise and motion.

They come from every direction at once. Dozens of monkeys letting rip with wails and yells. Bouncing about all over the place in excitement at seeing people, because people mean food. They pour over the tables and chairs. Over the counter, and from the gift shop. Swinging on plastic ferns and leaping from beam to beam.

'Oh shit,' Heather says, catching sight of a big iguana taking cover under a bridge as an otter peeks through a waterfall with a coy carp flapping in its mouth. 'RUN!'

They turn to flee but the swarm comes with little monkey bodies launching from many places at once.

'I think they want food!' Heather says as Paco prises a primate from his face. She swats at another one clawing at her neck and tries to pull it free. 'God, they're really vicious. Ow! Shit, one bit me. Are they biting you?'

'ES!' Paco shouts, circling his arms wildly as several monkeys fly off, but that just gives space for more to clamber up and scratch and bite as they hunt for food.

'FUCK OFF!' the macaw yells.

'You fuck off,' Heather yells back. 'They need food. Where's the food?'

'THEY NEED FOOD,' the macaw says, in near perfect mimicry as Heather spots Paco starting towards the counter.

She sets off after him, but their motion only seems to elicit an even greater response as the monkeys bounce, and screech, and start grabbing things to throw.

'What the shit!' Heather says as a spoon hits her forehead. 'Who threw that?'

'WHO THREW THAT?' the macaw calls out.

'Piss off! I do not sound like that. Just open the door!' Heather yells as Paco lifts a leg and shakes it free of monkeys before getting donked on the back of the head by a metal pot.

'HAHA!' the macaw says, dancing on an overhead beam and watching the fun below.

'They're worse than bloody zombies,' Heather says as Paco boots the door.

A thud as it slams open and the monkeys, as one, all cease their naughty monkeying about, and turn to look in monkey awe at the door to the secret room of forbidden mystery now standing open.

THE UNDEAD TWENTY-FIVE. THE HEAT

The one they couldn't get through because it was locked, but they could smell the things inside that storeroom. The jars of pickles and jams. The cartons of creams and milks. The packets of bread and boxed cakes.

'Bloody hell,' Heather says, and a second later the ground grows thick with furry brown bodies running through. All whooping and chattering with glee.

'Haha!' the macaw says. 'Bear.'

'What?' Heather asks, scowling up at it.

'Bear!' The macaw shouts, hopping from foot to foot.

'What bear? Oh shit. That Bear… RUN PACO!'

With nowhere to go they dive over the counter to avoid the path of the very hungry three hundred kilo North American black bear charging towards the secret room of forbidden mystery. Which thereby prompts an even greater screech as the eighty or so rhesus monkeys try and fling pots and pans and poop at it.

Heather and Paco hit the ground hard then dart away again from the meowling growl as the ocelot impacts on Paco's chest, using him as a springboard to try and reach the macaw still hopping on the beam overhead.

'HAHA! FUCK OFF!' the bird yells as the bear roars, and the monkeys screech.

'We need to go,' Heather says, clambering to her feet. They set off towards the closest exit point, and out into a scene from the cover of a religious pamphlet.

Zebras and antelopes grazing on the enormous expanse of a grassed area used for outside dining. More water features dotted here and there. Willow trees, and thick green bushes growing all over the place, forming a lush, almost tropical environment baking under the scorching sun.

Asses and donkeys grazing with them. Llamas and goats. A scene of paradise, and tranquillity. Meerkats running about, and a family of capybara drink from a pond as a few shy gazelle glance over to Heather and Paco, while behind them, the fight for the secret room of forbidden mystery intensifies as the rhesus monkeys try and stop the fat bear from eating everything.

'This is mental. Who the hell set them all free?' Heather asks, turning to look at Paco. She spots movement beyond him and smiles in delight at the sight of a baby white rhino waddling into view. 'Oh my god. Look! how cute is that?'

Paco turns as the bushes shake and part from the heads of the mummy and daddy rhinos pushing through to find their calf.

'Oh shit,' Heather says. 'They're really protective, aren't they?'

'Es,' Paco says as the mummy rhino determines, in her rhinoceros' way of determining things, that she is, in fact, extremely protective. As is the daddy rhino who snorts and sniffs the air with both of them detecting the newcomers but unable to pinpoint the exact direction.

'Just stay still,' Heather whispers. 'They've got really poor eyesight.'

'Bear!' The macaw yells out, flying from the restaurant behind them as the rhinos snap their heads over.

'What Bear?' Heather asks. 'Oh shit! That Bear. RUN PACO!' she grabs his arm and sets off as the three-hundred kilo angry bear runs from the restaurant with a face full of jam, and several dozen screeching rhesus monkeys running after it. Which only seems to send a shockwave of panic through the rhinos who burst to motion with such speed they startle the herd of zebra from their contented grazing, which, in turn, startle the gazelles who give fright to the donkeys and asses. Thereby commencing a chain reaction as the flight instinct of those animals - that by their very nature know they like to be eaten – kicks in, and they all commence one huge stampede.

Luckily the ground slopes downhill which aids the speed gained by Heather and Paco. Unluckily, that same downward slope also helps everything else too, most of which are faster, and bigger than Heather and Paco who get swept along within that great press.

Heather spots a gap and tries to get free but bounces off a zebra and slews into an ass then off again to see an antelope springing past. Or it could be a gazelle. Heather isn't quite sure, only that's it leaping. Which is what the kangaroo bounding next to her are also doing. 'They've got kangaroos! I love kangaroos.'

'RUFFALO!' Paco shouts.

'What a fo?' Heather asks, amidst the mayhem. 'Gruffalo?'

'NO. RUFFALO!'

'Oh! Buffalo. FUCK! RUN, PACO!'

Paco thinks maybe Heather needs to stop telling him to run when he is, in fact, already running. But he saves his breath and focuses instead on veering left, which is what the entire stampede does to absorb the Gruffalo Ruffalo Buffalo joining the great flow.

'IT'S LIKE JUMANJI!' Heather yells as Paco then thinks to tell her to fuck off because he was meant to be in Jumanji, but the part was given to The Rock instead.

Wanker.

A flamboyance of flamingos and a party of peacocks run across the path ahead, fleeing from the flock of ostrich coming behind them and the mighty stampede flows on as the energy seems to change with a great surge of fear and panic making the creatures roll eyes as they run. Snorting and huffing. Some wailing and screeching.

Still neither Heather nor Paco can do anything other than keep running while snatching glances to the vast savannah style grounds ahead. Heather tries to think why they're all going that way.

She starts to feel the first real pulse of fear too. She isn't like Paco. She can't run at this speed for more than a few seconds, especially in this heat. Her lungs are already bursting.

The stampede veers again. Like a school of fish reacting to a threat, but fish only move like that when they're reacting to external forces.

That thought brings another jolt of fear as she catches glimpse of something fast and low running just beyond the stampede. Images rush into her mind and she remembers the sign on the way in. THE BIG CAT DRIVE THRU. The pictures on the board. The images of Lions.

'Bear!' The macaw shouts as Heather thinks the sodding bear is the least of their worries right now. She even risks a glance back to see the bear and the rhinos are gone from sight. But then again, they're not exactly on the menu for the pride of lions driving them into the wide-open grounds, and just waiting for something weak to falter.

A scream from the side. Heather spots a young zebra veering away from a lioness lunging at it. The stampeding herd veers again. A glimpse of water somewhere ahead.

The only thing Heather can do is keep running, except she can't. She's running out of energy. Her legs are burning like crazy, and her lungs can't get enough oxygen.

A great compression then comes as the lions close in from all sides. Driving the animals together.

The whole of the thing speeds up, but in so doing they bash and barge into each other. Slamming Heather about as she staggers and tries to keep going.

They come fast. A rush of brown bodies packed with muscle. One leaps past her, aiming for the rear end of the young zebra. The paws connect as the lioness opens her mouth to bite, but the zebra bucks and kicks, making the lion slide off as it runs free.

Fear in its eyes. The noise it makes. A horrible pain-filled cry for help. A cry from a baby to a mother. A cry from a youngling. The lion lunges again as Heather spots more coming in. They've chosen the one they want, and now they're closing it down. Using positioning to isolate the foal away from the bigger animals.

The foal cries again and starts to falter. Growing panicked and skittish. A flash of black and white as an adult zebra tries to flank the foal, but it's not enough, and the foal cries out as the lions close in.

Images of Subi come to Heather's mind. Rajesh and Amna too. The children she got to the fort. That same protective energy flaring up. The same need to defend those too weak to defend themselves, and without thought, Heather draws the pistol from her tac-vest and fires a shot at the lion. The round misses. The sound almost unheard. She starts to slow. Aiming the gun to fire again as Paco hits her from the side, taking her up and over the back of a buffalo. A hand to the backside and the huge animal speeds up with Heather on top.

She grips one of the curved horns while the beast runs on. A snatched look to the side. To Paco diving to get on the back of another Buffalo.

Dust and heat. Motion and noise. She bounces hard, almost shaken free as a rhesus monkey lands on her shoulder and starts to slip off. Squealing out in panic as Heather clocks the baby monkey clinging to his mother. She grabs at the animals and swings hard to get them up onto the head of the buffalo where they can grip the horns, but the motion sends her sliding off. She fights to get back up, and screams out when a lion leaps at her, and her vision fills with a mouth full of huge teeth opening for the bite before missing and dropping away.

A second's worth of view then comes as she hangs upside down, nearly being dragged. A view of the stampeding animals and the monkeys riding heads and backs. The macaw still in the air.

Commotion behind and she cries out in fear as the lions rush in and pounce on the zebra foal. Taking it down in a flurry of dust and screams. An awful thing to see. A most terrible sight that makes Heather try and fling herself off. Thinking to go back and fight. Thinking she must save it.

Then they hit the lake and she drops hard. Bouncing over the surface with arms and legs spinning before she sinks down. Water fills her mouth, and for a second she loses all notion of where is up, and where is down.

She flails wildly until her legs hit mud. She pushes up, breaking the surface to gag and spew. Gasping for air as another buffalo goes by, smacking her aside as the edge of the lake fills with creatures trying to flee the lions.

'GET OFF IT,' she screams out, coughing hard, and trying to wade free. The rifle on the sling now coming forward. Getting in her way. Her tac-vest soaked. Her clothes heavy and clinging. The pistol still in her hand. She fires into the air while trying to get free of the water. While trying to get back to save the foal. Trying to fight through the animals going by. Noise and motion in every direction. A gap ahead. She goes faster. Gasping for air and tripping over a big log. The foal. The lions. She has to reach it. She saw its eyes. She saw the fear. She cannot let it die like that.

'ETHER!' a huge shout from Paco. A surge of water. A rush of motion as the log she was clambering over comes to life and whips about. The great tail slamming her aside as the crocodile spins and comes at her. It's mouth opening. It's belly empty. A month without food for creatures used to regular feeds. Predatory instincts are kicking in. Instincts born from thousands of years, millions for the Crocodile, and it lunges fast, ready to take Heather down for a death roll in the depths.

Heather tries to veer away then screams out when Paco rushes past and dives onto the Crocodile. The beast reacts instantly. Whipping about in a frenzy as Paco wraps his arms about the head and gets ragged like a doll. The tail hits Heather again, sending her staggering back.

She rises again. Spewing and gagging while flailing about with the gun as the Crocodile and Paco breach the surface with plumes of water spraying up. The power of the animal so great that Paco is sent flying off. Landing hard and sinking down as Heather aims the gun and fires rounds that hit the water as the croc sinks down.

Paco pushes up, coughing and heaving for air. Grabbing at Heather as she casts a horror filled glance to the lions and the zebra foal.

'NO!' she screams, holstering the pistol to pull her rifle to the front. Blowers said rifles can still work when they're wet. He said that. It has to work. A bellow from behind. An impact from something hitting their legs with enough power to lift them both like they're made from twigs, sending them up and off. Flying head over arse. Both of them crying out before they plummet down. Hitting the water and mud. Motion in every direction. Things moving too fast with too much noise. The lions roaring and snarling. The stampeding creatures still making sounds. The adult zebras braying. The awful noise from the foal that cuts off as Heather spins to see what threw them. Seeing a wave being pushed ahead from something moving fast through the lake. Displacing the water. A head appears. Grey and smooth. Two small ears. Two protruding eyes. The mouth opening, showing the tusks. The body so impossibly huge for the speed the bull hippo moves at.

The equilibrium of life within the safari has been disturbed. The creatures were all released but left unfed. They roamed and gathered.

THE UNDEAD TWENTY-FIVE. THE HEAT

They grazed and waited, but time rolls on and so does life, and life will always find its own balance. Its own equilibrium, and now the hippo charges. Not to attack Heather and Paco, but to keep the croc away from its own cubs.

Paco grabs her arm, wrenching her away. Both of them falling down as they turn and try to run. Both of them knowing everything else here is faster and bigger than they are.

They hit hard ground and stagger free. Both of them pulling rifles to aim. Both of them ready to fire, for what good it will do. The hippo is enormous, but it's also hot and has no inclination to leave the water. It slows to a stop with one final bellow, and as that noise abates, so they hear the snarls coming from the lions as they feast on the foal. The crack of bones. The sound of meat tearing.

'Go,' Paco says, pulling her away. Paco can see one foal won't feed so many lions. They have to leave. They have to get out.

A cackle sounds out. An awful, harsh laughing sound that make both twist in fright to see the pack of hyenas charging towards the fresh kill. The smell of meat and blood and fear so strong in the air. They are hungry too. Desperately hungry, and those primeval instincts kick in as they charge on mass to try and intimidate the lions from their kill.

The air fills with roars. With snarls and noises. With feet pounding the ground. A larger roar. An almighty noise, and a fully gown adult lion with a thick mane charges from the killed foal towards the hyenas. Sending them scattering as they laugh and cackle with alarm.

Heather and Paco run with everything they have. Coughing from the thick dust in the air with heavy wet clothes slowing them down. A flurry from the side as a hyena runs from the lion into Paco. Snagging his legs and taking him down. The animal cackles again in fear and stress, snapping out with its powerful jaws as Paco scrabbles away. Shots sound out. Heather firing the gun into the air. Trying to scare it away. The hyena bucks and kicks out to get free but another comes in from behind. Snapping at Heather's backside. She screams out and aims the rifle, but the creatures move too fast to shoot.

The ground starts sloping up. A gentle incline at first but growing steeper. Hyenas lunging from behind and starting to position to flank.

'BEAR!' The macaw screeches, making Heather snap her head up then over to see a large hyena running towards her. Intent in its eyes. The teeth showing. She reacts on instinct and fires the rifle. Sending rounds into the animal that slews off with a pained yelp. Guilt floods inside of her. Instant regret at harming an animal, and she cries out as the hyena staggers off and slows. Yelping loudly with blood pouring from its body. The other hyenas all cackling louder.

'Kill it!' Paco shouts, his voice as ruined as ever but she gets what he means. She has to kill it. She can't leave it to suffer. She brings the rifle up. Aiming for the head.

'BEAR!' the macaw says again. Another roar. Deep and terrible and the male lion charges in to grip the injured hyena in its mouth. Ragging it side to side before sinking down with paws the size of plates to start tearing at it.

'GO!' Paco says, dragging Heather on as the hyenas screech and lunge at the back end of the lion while more of the pride run in. Drawn to the blood and that awful frenzy in the air.

'Fence,' Heather gasps, seeing the chainlink fence ahead has been busted down. They aim for it with Paco striding on with one hand clamped on Heather's wrist to keep her going.

They stagger through, tripping over churned up ground made from wheel marks. Gasping and desperate to stop and breathe. Another fence. Another hole. A four-wheel drive vehicle on the other side. Abandoned for weeks. The sides all busted in. Claws marks in the panels. The windows broken. Another roar. Another alarm sounding as a troop of barbary apes scream out to defend the vehicle they've taken refuge in.

Heather and Paco get clear and run on to see a lusher, greener pasture of land. An old weather-beaten shack stands alone in the middle. Rubber car tyres here and there, but thankfully no animals. No anything in fact. Just a silence that sounds weird after the noises and carnage.

'Shit,' she says, veering away sharply from the body on the ground.

THE UNDEAD TWENTY-FIVE. THE HEAT

An adult silverback Gorilla lying dead. The body torn open. The rib cage exposed. The flesh bitten away. Flies in the air. A rancid stench too. They go wide then falter again at seeing the lion. A once majestic, powerful creature with a gloriously thick mane. Now dead from a broken back. The bones also exposed from being eaten. Blood stains on the ground. Smaller bones in the grass. They run on, desperate to be away.

'Ether,' Paco says a few minutes later, pointing at old tyre tracks carved in the mud. They follow them towards the perimeter fence until it comes into view; another busted in section. A way out. They take it without hesitation, getting free of the park.

The edge of a housing estate meets them. The sight of streets and normal urbanity so jarring after what they just saw. Both of them cut and bleeding from scratches and bites. Caked in mud already drying from the heat.

'We'll find a car,' Heather says, her voice rough and low. Paco nods, knowing she means to find a car to go around the park to get their own back. They rush through the grass to the road with that same jarring feeling inside at such a sudden transition.

It feels wrong inside. What they just did. What they just saw. That somehow, they caused it. That their presence affected those changes that caused that stampede that killed the foal.

But then all things have to eat. Heather eats meat. She eats things that lived. Paco does too. Too many thoughts come at once as she tries to process what she just saw and what they just did.

A flutter of wings overhead as the macaw sinks down to land on the roof of a car. Heather comes to a stop. Staring at it. Paco the same. Both of them just staring at the bird and seeing the wings aren't just red but streaked with blues and yellows. It stares back at them. Cocking its head over from one side to the next. 'Fuck off,' it says. No aggression. No malice. Just making sounds.

'I need water,' Heather says, setting off for the end of the street ahead and the rows of houses stretching off. Debris scattered about. Clothes strewn across the ground. Cars smashed up and fences battered down. The same as everywhere else. The same signs of ruin and carnage. Doors busted. Windows busted. Everything busted and dying, or dead, or suffering. This heat. It's too hot. She needs water. She needs to cool down. That poor foal. The look in its eyes. The sound of the screams.

'Bear,' the macaw says, bringing both to a dead stop. The tension rising again.

'Don't fuck about,' Heather says without turning to look at it.

'Bear!' the macaw screeches, bursting up into the air as they both turn fast with rifles up. Looking for whatever threat is coming. Seeing nothing. 'BEAR!'

'Where?' Heather shouts, as though expecting a response. As though expecting it to converse and explain. 'There's nothing here,' she says again, quieter this time. Looking about. 'You see anything?'

'No,' Paco says. Staring this way and that. The old Paco would have died of fright in the safari park, and if he had got free, he would have collapsed and wept in self-pity. This Paco still feels the horror of it, perhaps more than he would have a few days ago. Either way, there's no obvious threat here. Just the bird making sounds.

'Come on,' Heather says. The rifle held ready. 'Blowers said they still work if they get wet,' she whispers across to Paco. 'But he said they need to be dried and cleaned quickly. He said saltwater is worst. That was fresh water wasn't it.'

'Es.'

'The pistols too. He said they're the same...'

'Ether.'

'What?' she stops to see him nodding over to a human body at the side of the road. An adult male, or rather, the remains of one. The limbs torn to shreds. Bones poking through. One of the arms gone. 'Looks recent,' she remarks.

Paco nods and kneels down to peer at the remains before slowly turning the skull so they can see the face. The eyes still open. Staring lifelessly. Not red. Not bloodshot.

Heather swallows at what it means. The dead person wasn't an infected. But if someone gets bitten, they always turn. Unless they're immune. 'Must be an immune,' she says.

'No,' Paco says, pointing to the ruined flesh. 'Not them.'

'Not them?' she murmurs before the realisation hits; that the man wasn't killed by infected hosts, but by something else. 'Oh shit.'

'Bear!' the macaw cries out, circling overhead as Heather turns a full circle with the rifle up and braced. Paco the same. Still nothing. No sounds. No movements.

'Go,' Paco whispers, moving deeper into the street because the only alternative is to go back to the safari park.

They walk on. Senses straining. Expecting an attack any second, but nothing happens. Just the sun glares down. Making heat shimmers that hang over the road. Drying their clothes too fast so they become stiff and matted. The fluids lost in the frenzy need to be replaced. Plus, stupidly, they had sex in the car park just before too. And neither of them thought to bring water.

'Complacency kills,' she whispers, remembering the things Blowers and Clarence taught her. To always be watchful. To always be prepared.

Another body ahead. A large dog, but the flesh is too ruined to see the breed. Just grey fur matted with blood. But it means that the killer is big enough to take a fully-grown man down, and aggressive enough to kill a big dog.

They start picking speed up. Treading faster. Working along the street towards the junction at the end. Reaching it without incident. A four-way split. Signs of carnage in all directions. They stay ahead, aiming away from the safari park.

'BEAR!' the macaw calls out, bringing them to a stop, but still, there's nothing to see or hear.

'Maybe it's just saying the word,' Heather whispers as they hear a soft crashing noise coming from somewhere. Something being knocked over. Ceramic breaking on concrete. Distinctive and clear. 'That's a plant pot,' Heather whispers.

Paco stays silent, and the tension ramps as they realise they're being stalked.

They go deeper into the next street, staying in the middle of the road. Blinking often to rid the sweat from their eyes. Aiming at houses. At windows and doors. Another body in the middle of the road. The remains of one anyway. Half a torso and a leg. Blood stains everywhere.

'Look,' she says, spotting more remains a bit further up. Another dog, or maybe more of the other one they saw. Some of the back end with part of the tail. An awful sight. Bloodied and fresh too.

'Ether,' Paco whispers, motioning ahead to the end of the street that feeds into a park used for dog walking and picnics. A play area for children and huge oak trees giving shade from the heat.

They look for another way around, but that means either going through one of the buildings or going back the way they came. Neither of those options are good. 'Come on,' Heather whispers, making her way along the path into the park area. Passing the swings and slide. Delving into the outer edges of the shade given from the oak tree branches. Something in the grass, and it takes a moment for them to realise its more remains. Bones and limbs. Torsos and heads. Humans faces. Canine skulls.

'What the fuck,' she mouths, seeing more as they get closer to the trees. Men and women. Old and young amongst the grey matted fur. Bits of bodies eaten and feasted upon. The grass stained with blood. White bones stark in the dried-out grass. A head facing them. A young woman. Pretty save for half of her face eaten away. The one remaining eye clear and blue. Not red. Not bloodshot.

She turns to Paco as he gently kicks a head attached to a spinal column. Turning it to show the red eyes of an infected man. Whatever is killing them doesn't care if it's a person, an infected, or a dog.

'BEAR!' the macaw cries out as the sound of another plant pot being knocked over reaches them. Coming from the left side of the street they just left.

They back away, heading deeper into the park. A soft thud. The creak of a fence. The noise of hinges as a gate is pushed open. All of those sounds coming closer.

'BEAR!'

'Shut up!' Heather whispers, feeling the tension ramp. An urge to

THE UNDEAD TWENTY-FIVE. THE HEAT

run. An urge to turn and sprint. Adrenaline dumping in her body. Priming her for flight or fight.

A rustle in the thick bushes between them and the nearest garden. Something low and edging forward. Motion within the shadows. She thinks to fire at it but holds off and keeps backing away through the remains of the kills.

A head emerges. A long nose. Eyes. Ears. A broad head coming slowly into view. Parting the bushes. Another motion a few feet over. Another one pushing through. Another one next to it. Each one dark grey. Each one with shining eyes glinting yellow in the sunshine.

'Wolves,' Heather whispers. 'It's a fucking wolf pack.'

The first one creeps out, the head and body low down. The ears pricked. The eyes fixed on Heather and Paco. The second comes. The third after it. Each of them edging closer, placing one foot after the other. Sniffing the air. Staring without blinking.

'Just keep backing away,' Heather whispers. 'We're in their den. Maybe if we just go,' she scuffs the skull of a woman as she says it, wincing both at the sound and the image of her own skull soon to be forming part of this macabre display. They back away, placing one foot after the other as the three wolves advance into the park.

A great silence between them. The heat bearing down. Hearts thudding. Fingers on triggers.

'BEAR!' the macaw cries out.

'Shut up!' Heather whispers, thinking the sound of the voice could spark the wolves to charge, but the bird comes in low. Flying just inches over their heads.

'BEARBEARBEAR!' It swoops at Paco's head, making him flick a hand up to push it away as the first growls sound out from the wolves. Deep and low and growing louder and closer as the wolves slowly advance.

'DON'T!' Heather shouts out. 'JUST GO... PLEASE!'

The wolves pay no heed but keep coming. Lips pulling back showing huge teeth. Broad shoulders and long flanks. Bigger than dogs. Bigger than Meredith, and Heather has seen what she can do. Plus, there's three of them working together and they've already killed people. A flurry of thoughts rush through her head as the macaw clumps the back of her head while crying out.

'BEAR!'

'WE KNOW!' she risks a glance at it, half turning her head and the realisation dawns with a gut-wrenching jolt of horror as she realises the wolves aren't looking at her or Paco, but at what's behind them.

'SHIT!' she spins around to a snatched view of a Siberian tiger in the branches of the oak tree. The striped face almost lost in the shadows. The eyes glowing red and bloodshot. It drops as she spins. Landing deftly on the grass amongst its kills. Three and a half metres long. Over three hundred kilos in weight. A perfect killing machine.

Then his brother drops from the tree to land next to him and the world erupts as both Paco and Heather pull the triggers on their rifles. Paco to shoot the wolves. Heather to shoot the tigers, but Blowers said rifles will work if they get wet *only* if they're cleaned quickly. And that lake had too much crap in it. Too much silt that now dries and hampers the moving parts, and the dull clicks sound in the air. The misfires from both as Paco shouts out and moves left.

Heather screams. Diving right. The bird cries out and the wolves impact into the first tiger. Heather lands hard, rolling through the grass and remains. Coming to a stop inches from the ruined carcass of a dog. Not a dog. A wolf. Heather realises in that second it's not dogs the tigers have been eating. It's wolves. They must have come from the safari park. That's why there's only three left. That's why the wolves were coming towards them. To seek help. To seek people. To seek refuge.

A yelp from behind. The sound of pain. The sound of fear. On her feet and she draws the pistol from her tac-vest as the first tiger launches up onto its rear legs and swipes a huge front paw at a wolf, sending it flying off with a yelp. The other two wolves go at it. Lunging in to bite as the second tiger runs at the one knocked away. She aims and fires the pistol. Nothing. She curses, shakes the gun, slides the top back and tries again. The gun fires. The round hits the tiger. No reaction. Not a thing.

She fires again. Hitting it once more as it veers from going for the wolf and aims at her. Paco shouts out, his rifle not firing. He casts it aside and draws his pistol. No fire. Heather shoots again. Another misfire. She ditches that gun and snatches the one from her hip as the tiger closes in and the bird drops fast. Screeching out with claws aiming at the tiger's eyes.

A second of time bought for Heather to roll away and come up to fire. She gets another round into it, but the tiger keeps coming. The eyes red and bloodshot. The wolf that got knocked surges up and runs in hard. Slamming into the tiger just before it launches at Heather. The tiger spins. Grabbing the wolf in its mouth. Ragging it side to side. Yelps sound out as Heather tries to aim and find a spot to shoot.

A roar from Paco diving onto the tiger with fists hammering into the sides. Beating so hard it would kill a man within seconds, but the tiger throws him with ease and drops the wolf to turn on the man. Launching at him as Heather fires into the centre of mass.

Still the beast shows no reaction, lunging at Paco as he rolls away. It snags his leg in a claw and yanks him off the ground. Heather fires again until the gun clicks empty.

The third wolf bleeding but getting up to fight on. The other two wolves savaging at the other tiger.

Snarls and growls filling the air as Paco gets launched with ease. The tiger lunges for the bite. The wolf and Heather charge at it. Heather drawing her knife, diving in. The wolf going for the tiger's tail. Heather lands on the back and stabs into the side. Driving the blade deep. The tiger roars out and bucks. She clings on. Kicking and stabbing and biting into the thing with her own teeth. Savaged and wild. An awful yelp as one of the other wolves gets taken in the other tiger's mouth and torn apart.

Heather stabs again. Paco lashes out. The wolf on the tail. Tugging and tugging. The tiger detonates into a ball of pure fury. The strength of it as it shakes her free and rags Paco to the side before twisting with impossible speed to swat the wolf away.

Yelps and howls of pain. Blood spraying out. Two wolves dead and two tigers still very much alive. Heather, Paco and the last wolf fighting with everything they have. To make the thing bleed. To make it hurt. To kill at least one of them before they're all torn apart.

Blood spraying out. Rage and fury. A fight to the death but by fuck they'll go down fighting. All three of them. Heather. Paco. The wolf. Even the bird does what it can until it too gets swatted hard and sent into the tree.

The second tiger roars out and starts to run. The mouth opening. The teeth so big. The muzzle stained and dripping blood. Heather sees it coming. Paco too. The wolf clings on. He could turn and run. He could leave the people to fight and save himself, but he fights because his pack is dead. Because these things have hunted them down one by one and so he has nothing left to live for. He has nothing but the pain he can give back and to die in the fight.

'FUCK YOU!' Heather roars out, stabbing and stabbing at the tiger to no heed. To no response. The thing is infected. It feels no pain. The second one impacts. A shot rings out. Deep and solid. Another one. Something embeds next to Heather's head. Another shot. An arrow hits the tiger she's attacking in the eye. The tiger roars out and flares up on its back legs. Shots taken. Fast and quick. A glance within the chaos to Dave aiming his assault rifle. Taking shots where he can. Roy on top of the Saxon. Firing arrows and Joan with the sniper rifle braced in her shoulder. Meredith streaking across the grass. A face full of rage. Teeth pulled back because if there's one thing worse than infected or cats, it's infected cats.

She hits the one launching up. Slamming into it hard and sinking teeth into the neck, but the fight isn't over and both tigers lash out. Sending Meredith, the wolf, Paco and Heather all flying off.

'STAY CLEAR,' Dave roars but the fight is on. The need to do battle and as one, those four go back in. Diving in with blades and teeth. 'GPMG THAT ONE.'

The dull roar of the machine gun. The second tiger roars out. Struck by rounds. Assault rifles letting rip. Still it stays up. Still it roars. Arrows poking from its body. Both eyes gone. Joan breathes. Joan aims. Joan fires and the subsonic round finally gets through a ruined eye into the brain. Killing it dead.

THE UNDEAD TWENTY-FIVE. THE HEAT

'FUCK YOU!' Heather screams out. Stabbing into the beast they fight with. Images of the zebra foal in her mind. Images of Subi, Rajesh and Amna. That dark place she goes to when she needs this. When she needs this rage to kill. Stabbing relentlessly. Paco the same. The dog and wolf tearing at it. She screams out as Joan breathes. Joan aims. Joan fires and the subsonic round goes through into the tiger's brain, killing it dead.

'IT'S DONE. OVER,' Dave shouts.

'FUCK YOU!' Heather screams out, stabbing at the beast until someone yanks her away, she spins free, dripping with blood, eyes wild with fury. Seeing Howie and the others all looking shocked.

'We saw you on the drone,' Howie says. 'Nick saw the park. The safari park. We were there. Before.'

'You,' Heather gasps, staring at him then looking at the remains on the ground. The people killed. The young and old. The dead wolves. The zebra foal. 'YOU FUCKING CUNT!' she runs at Howie, ready to fight him. Ready to hurt him. 'YOU LET THEM OUT!' she pulls an arm back, thinking to punch him, but Dave wasn't warned. Marcy always tells him when she's going to hit Mr Howie, and he moves in fast, taking Heather's legs out and bringing the pistol up to aim at her head. A roar from Paco. He runs at Dave. Everyone else shouts. Everyone running in.

'She's safe, Dave!' Mo shouts as Paco swings at Dave who dodges back and sends a punch into his side. 'SAFE DAVE!' Mo shouts again.

'HEY!' Clarence yells, rushing in to block Paco who lashes out and punches him hard in the face. A lightning reaction from Clarence, and he throws a punch back, smacking Paco hard on the nose. An instant eruption of violence. The two huge men going at it with punches slamming into heads and faces as Mo runs in to block Dave. Carmen with him. Howie reeling back then yelling out at Paco hitting Clarence. He runs to pull him back but gets smashed aside and sent spinning off as Clarence and Paco go at each other with punches hard enough to kill most men.

It's the women that react. An instinct inside that if one of the guys gets between Paco and Clarence they could get killed. Charlie goes first. Pushing between them. Tappy a split second after. Paula and Marcy with them. All four shouting at the men to stop. Pushing them away. Noses bleeding. Eyes swelling up.

'You colossal fucking prick,' Heather says, spitting the words out. 'You set them free!'

'Then why the fuck were you there?' Howie asks as Heather goes to reply but blinks in confusion. Remembering the foal. The baby zebra. The hyena she shot. The whole of it.

'Fuck you,' she says, furious at him, at herself, at all of it. Sickened and shaken from running and fighting. 'Oh god, no,' she scrabbles up and runs to the two wolves killed by the tigers. 'They were hunting them. The fucking tigers. They were hunting the wolves down... And there was a baby zebra. The lions got it then I shot a hyena.'

'Jesus,' Howie says, the realisation of their actions showing on his face. 'We were there with Milly. Like two weeks ago. I'm so sorry.'

'They came out for help,' Heather says, turning away as she remembers the third one. She spins about, seeing it lying down, gasping for air. She runs to the side, dropping low. 'It needs help!'

'Roy!' Paula shouts.

'I'm a medic, not a vet,' Roy says, rushing over to peer at the wolf. 'Is it friendly?'

'Roy!' Paula says.

'Okay okay,' he says, dropping down to try and examine it. 'It needs water. Nick!'

'I'm not the water guy,' Nick says, flapping his hands as he goes off and runs back with a bottle of water. Working with Roy. Pouring water over the head. Into the mouth.

'Just a few cuts I think,' Roy says. 'Unless it's hurt inside.'

'He's drinking,' Nick says as the wolf starts lapping at the water. Gently at first. Tentatively almost. Then greedily. Gulping it down as fast as he can. Meredith comes close. Sniffing at the head. The wolf stops drinking, growling softly. 'Go away,' Nick says, pushing the dog. She backs up, watching the wolf closely as Paco and Clarence glare at each other. Ready to go again.

'Heather. I'm sorry,' Howie says. 'We couldn't just leave them.'

'I know,' she cuts him off, shaking her head before taking a bottle of water to drink deep. Pouring it over her face. Paco does the same. 'We don't know what we're doing,' she says after a minute. 'I'm running around with a fucking list and setting animals free. Look! Those tigers you let out got into this town. These people aren't infected. They're people.'

'I didn't know,' Howie says.

'You were doing the same thing,' Paula says.

'That's my point!' Heather shouts back. 'I've been going from zoo to zoo just opening cages. Snakes. Spiders. Cats. Wolves. Bears. I don't know what I'm doing. Neither do you. We're not experts in this, Howie. We shouldn't be doing this. We don't know what we're doing!'

'Heather,' Paula says.

'No! We shouldn't be doing this. Any of it. We're not soldiers. He's a fucking actor. I was on disability because of my anxiety. Howie worked in a fucking supermarket!' she shouts the words out, as angry at herself as anyone else. 'Leave it to him,' she says, pointing to Henry staring on with almost benign interest. Like he's viewing another drama in the lives of the misfits.

'He was a spy,' Howie says. 'How would he know what to do with a zoo.'

'A phased release using different exit points,' Henry says without hesitation. 'Or find a vet from the fort and ask them.'

'Oh, fuck off, Henry,' Howie snaps.

'See!' Heather shouts. 'He's right. We shouldn't be doing this. Any of it. Maybe we should just leave it to the experts...' She trails off. Confused. Angry, and not quite sure what her point is. Only that she needed to vent the emotion inside. It's so hot too. A crippling heat pressing down. 'How's the wolf?'

'He's okay I think,' Nick replies as the wolf finally stops drinking and slowly gets up as they all see just how big it is. Taller than Meredith. Longer too. Dark grey with shining yellow eyes and he looks about before seeing his fallen pack members. A low whine as he goes closer and sniffs at their bodies. Pawing at them. Whining harder. Whining longer. Pawing and pawing. Faces grow hard. Knowing what it means. Seeing the grief as the wolf lowers down and lifts his head to howl. A long awful sound of pain and loss. It sends a pang through Howie as he remembers the little girl from the square on the eighteenth day. Her screams and howls. That was the day Neal joined them. He died the next day. They failed to protect him too. Maybe Heather is right. That they don't know what they are doing.

Howie caused this. He told his team to open the cages and enclosures in the safari park. His actions made this happen, and the wolf howls on.

A thing done for thousands of years and as domesticated as Meredith is, she still lifts her head to add her voice to low mournful cry. Filling the air. Filling the park. Those long howls travelling far as the wolf cries for the loss of his pack. Victory has been taken. The tigers are dead, but his pack are gone, and he is alone. He would die right now if he could.

'Heather,' Howie says as she sets about collecting her weapons.

'Please don't,' she says.

'Why didn't you call us?' Paula asks. 'You've got a radio.'

Heather stops and shakes her head. 'I didn't think about it,' she admits with a bitter snort. 'We're not soldiers, Paula. We're just fucking idiots. Paco, we're going.'

'We'll drive you back to your car,' Marcy says.

'We'll walk,' Heather says, cutting over her.

'Heather. It's over forty degrees,' Paula says.

She doesn't reply but holsters her pistols then stops and frowns before rushing over to the base of the tree. 'Are you okay?'

'Who the hell is that?' Paula asks as Heather bends down to pick a bundle of brightly coloured rags up.

'They need food!' The macaw says quietly, mimicking Heather as it shakes its wings out, making everyone else gasp.

'You're a dumb shit,' Heather tells it. 'But thank you, go on then. Fly away,' she throws it up, expecting a dramatic flurry of wings, but it just drops with a squawk and a thud.

'Haha,' the bird says weakly as Heather picks it back up and walks over to Nick. 'Look after it, please.'

'Why you giving it to me? I'm not the bird guy!'

She walks off with Paco at her side. Leaving a heart-broken wolf crying over his lost pack, and Nick holding a macaw while Howie spots the look on Henry's face. The one that suggests that maybe Heather is right, and he should be leaving it to the professionals.

19

Diary of Paula

THAT WAS INCREDIBLY UPSETTING! We do some horrific things sometimes, but that was right up there.

We were in Sturbridge having a coffee. Nick started making it then Henry took over. (Henry does make very good coffee btw.)

Anyway. So then the lads went outside to have a smoke, and Henry told Howie we cannot keep stopping like this and perhaps some better planning might be in order.

Howie was starting to bite (Howie wears his emotions on his sleeve – it's actually one of the most endearing things about him.) But I could see it was really starting to get to him. Clarence was the same. I think it's more personal to Clarence because he was in the same army regiment as Frank and Henry.

Either way. We only had a few sips when Nick put the shout up. Apparently, the lads were outside and one of them realised we weren't far from the safari park they'd been through with Howie a few weeks ago. So they put the drone up to find it – and ended up seeing Heather and Paco almost being eaten by a hippo.

I could see Henry was annoyed at another diversion, but what could we do? We couldn't leave poor Heather on her own!

And thank god we didn't. God it was horrible. Just really horrible. We got there and the two infected tigers had already killed two wolves and we're trying to tear Heather, Paco and another wolf to pieces. And the noise! Those snarls and the whimper from one of the wolves just before it died. You could hear the thumps too from Paco giving one of the tigers a bloody good beating. Not that it noticed. And those three were mincemeat. Let me tell you that. If we'd been thirty seconds later, they would be dead.

Then after that Heather went for Howie, then Dave went for Heather and Paco steamed in and him and Clarence started slugging it out. The whole thing was a bloody mess.

Dead tigers. Dead wolves. And that heat and humidity. I know the tigers were infected, but still. They were so majestic. What an awful rotten thing to do. Not one of us took pleasure in killing them. Not one of us.

Anyway. Then Heather and Paco left and there was this awful silence until the poor wolf started crying. The thing was pawing at the other two dead wolves. It was heartbreaking. I had tears in my eyes, and I know a few more did. Then I caught sight of Howie's face – like I said, he can't hide his emotions. He looked heartbroken too. Staring from Heather and Paco to the wolf then over to the tigers.

I could see what he was thinking. I know he would have been connecting his actions from a few weeks ago to what happened now and assuming responsibility for it.

Truthfully though. I didn't have the energy to get into it. Not right then after all of that. 'I think Heather was more upset than anything,' I said to Howie. It didn't help much but it was all I had.

'I would suggest the tigers killed a host and became infected,' Reginald said, looking at the remains. 'Which then sparked this feeding frenzy. They've certainly killed more than they need to eat.'

I said that was bad. I mean, there's a lot of big cats in this country. What if they all get infected? We wouldn't stand a chance.

'There's about thirty lions just in that safari park,' Nick said.

'Can lions even get infected?' Blowers asked.

'They share 95% DNA with tigers,' Carmen said. 'If a tiger can get it then it's most likely a lion can.'

'Not at all,' Reginald said. 'Mr Doku and I share 99.9% of the same DNA, yet he has natural immunity and I do not. The virus is not species specific, or even sub-species specific.'

'By that argument then one pride of lions could be susceptible whereas another isn't,' Charlie said. (She's a clever sod is our Charlie.)

'Absolutely,' Reginald said.

'But lions are one species,' I said.

'One species, two sub-species,' Carmen says. 'Asiatic lion and the African lion.'

'Humans are one species,' Reginald says. 'But we're all genetically different. Maddox and Carmen are black. Charlie and Booker are mixed race. Mo and Bashir are Arabic. Clarence is nearly seven feet tall. Dave is autistic.'

'Blowers is gay,' Cookey says.

'Not now, Alex!' I snapped at him. (I love Cookey to bits, but those bloody jokes are too much sometimes.) 'And stop it with the gay jokes. I've told you already.'

'Sorry,' Cookey said with a crestfallen look.

'We should still check the lions though. What if they can be infected? We can't risk that,' I said.

'But that means we'd have to kill them,' Marcy said to me.

'And if you do kill the lions then what next?' Henry asked, as we all turned to look at him. 'Are you going to test every other creature too?'

I could see him looking about with distaste at the violence surrounding us and the poor wolf still crying. 'Perhaps we should focus on our mission instead of becoming side-tracked with minor issues. The sooner we accomplish what we need to do, the better for everyone. And our mission, as per our agreement, is to locate and examine the behaviours of the control point theory prior to going into London. Attacking lions only pulls us away from that. I suggest we keep moving.'

It's not very nice to say it, but I could feel the shift in power from the way he spoke. The words he used and the way he projected his voice. Henry is <u>very</u> skilled at speaking. And add to that the fact he still looked fresh. He didn't even have wet patches under his armpits.

And the raw truth is that he was right. We *were* getting bogged down discussing lions. In fact, if left unchecked, we probably would have wasted the day throwing infected meat at different animals and waiting to see if they turned. But that's not the job now. The job is to let Henry study the enemy so we can get into London for the Panacea. I could see it. So could Marcy. But most importantly, so could H & C.

'Okay,' Clarence said, nodding at Howie.

'What about them?' Marcy asked. She meant the parrot and the wolf, but it was another point raised that stopped us moving and I could see the first real show of frustration on Henry's face.

'Just let the bird go,' Carmen said and took the parrot from Nick and seemed to lose herself in staring at the bird with this look of absolute pleasure on her face until Henry called her name. But he didn't say it nicely. It was too sharp, and I could see Carmen almost flinch at being spoken to like that. Anyway. Then she opened her hands and helped the bird get flying. Then she was off and walking back to Henry.

'We can't just leave it,' Nick said as the rest of us hesitated. We all felt it and none of us wanted to leave the poor thing on his own. 'Hey boy! You wanna come with us? Come on. Good boy!' Nick clicked his tongue and patted his leg and tried urging it on. But it's not a dog. It's not a domestic creature like Meredith, and it didn't even look at him.

'How about the fort?' Tappy asked. 'Could they look after it?'

'Chaps,' Henry called. 'I admire your concern, but you cannot place an unpredictable animal like a wolf within the fort. There are too many children. The best thing is to leave it here. Let it fend for itself.'

He was right again. When isn't Henry right? And so, with an awful sinking feeling, we slowly went back to our vehicles. If the wolf noticed we were going, it didn't show it. It just carried on howling over his dead pack.

God. Don't. It's making me cry again.

20

Diary of Dave

TODAY IS SUNDAY. The time is 11:13hrs.

Paula said we should keep diaries so that people will know what we did. She said to write who you are and tell people your background.

My name is Dave. I do not like to be called David. Officers used to call me David in the army. The training corporal told me that officers can call you what they like.

I joined an infantry regiment in the army because I did not do very well on the entry tests. My score was high in maths and English, but not in reasoning. I did not know I was autistic then. Now, I do know because Mr Henry and Mr George had tests done on me. I have high functioning autism which means I can do some things very well, but there are some things I cannot do.

I liked the army. I liked making my bed and running. I liked eating at specific times. I liked that our uniforms looked the same. I liked being told what to do.

I left the infantry to work for Mr Henry, but Mr Henry and Mr George said I am not allowed to talk about that. I am allowed to say I trained with the SAS. But I did not pass the whole course. I excelled at fitness. Weapons handling and unarmed combat. But I failed interrogation and torture training and other reasoning skills. Not because I told them any secrets, but because I did not tell them anything at all.

They teach recruits to reveal secrets or false secrets at certain times, but I cannot read people or understand that they mean something different to what they say. For this reason, I could not understand what I was meant to do during those phases of training.

I was also not allowed to drive in the army. I am a danger to other road users because not all of the other drivers will follow the laws, and a safe driver needs to know when other drivers will break the laws. Or when they should break the laws.

Things like that confuse me.

I am not in the army now. I left the army to work for Tesco.

I do not work for Tesco now. Mr Howie said Tesco has gone. But I can still see the stores in the towns we visit. Marcy said Mr Howie means that Tesco are not operating as a business anymore because of the global pandemic.

Now, I work for Mr Howie. Although, he does not pay me, and I do not have a contract.

Mr Howie sometimes tells me I do not work for him, and I can stay or leave, or do what I want. It confuses me when Mr Howie says that. Marcy heard him say it, and she told me later that Mr Howie has to say that to everyone else, but he doesn't mean me. Marcy said I do work for Mr Howie. She said I can stop when I want, but I should speak with her first.

I do not want to stop working for Mr Howie.

Paula said we should explain what we are doing in our diaries.

I am making a diary entry in my diary now.

She said we can be honest about everything and that our diaries are sacred, and we are not to touch each other's diaries. Paula told the others I will be cross if anyone is caught touching anyone else's diary.

I don't know why I would be cross. I saw Alex drawing testicles in Simon's diary. I told him to stop, but I was not cross.

Paula said we should explain about what we did just before the diary entry. Or if anything unusual happened, and what we feel about it.

Today is very hot, and something did just happen.

I don't feel anything about it.

We have stopped now, and Paula told everyone to take a break and said we could write it down if we wanted.

We were in the Saxon. The others were all very quiet. Some of them were crying.

I think it was because we killed the tigers, or the tigers killed the wolves, and one wolf was left without his pack.

I heard Charlotte say, 'That poor wolf.'

I heard Nicholas say, 'Jesus. Those poor f*cking tigers.'

I heard Alan say, 'I didn't come back to gimpy a f*cking tiger to bits.'

I heard Alex say, 'Did we make that happen? I mean. We let all the animals out.'

Then, I heard Marcy telling them all not to overthink it. She said what's done is done, and Heather was just upset, and that the wolf would be fine. It went very silent, then Marcy said she meant it. 'Seriously. Don't let it take root.'

I wondered what was taking root. I couldn't see any roots.

Then, some minutes later, Mr Howie said, 'Sh*t, look.' And he pointed out the windscreen to a fence ahead of us, 'That's where she went over.'

Paula asked him who, and I saw Clarence smile and say, 'Milly.'

Then, we stopped, and everyone in the back was trying to see out the front.

'That's where we climbed over. Clarence couldn't cos he is too fat,' Alex said that and some of the others smiled. They did not laugh as I think they were still sad. Clarence called him a cheeky sh*t.

Then, we stopped and got out, and Mr Howie asked me if I

remembered this. He was pointing to the fence Milly climbed over to get into the safari park.

I said yes.

'Little sod,' Marcy said. She was smiling. 'She's from here then? I can imagine her running off and playing silly buggers.'

'You have no idea,' Alex said. He was smiling too. 'How far did we run?'

'F*cking miles,' Simon said.

That is not a precise unit of measurement, but I know it is a slang expression used to say it was a long distance.

'I've got polos!' Mr Howie said. He was smiling at me. 'That's what Dave said when we were chasing her. I'VE GOT POLOS!'

I did not have polos when we were chasing Milly. I do not like polos. They have a hole in the middle. I don't know why they have a hole. Other confectionary does not have a hole in the middle.

I had fruit pastilles when we were chasing Milly. I like fruit pastilles. They are made with real fruit. It says that on the packet. Fruit is good for you. But they also have lots of sugar. Sugar is bad for you.

I still like them.

I told Mr Howie I had fruit pastilles.

Nicholas asked me if I had any fruit pastilles now. I said no. Alex laughed and said he'd been Nicholas'd. The lads say that when I use their name sometimes.

Marcy then said, 'Where's her house then?'

I did not know what she meant because we were talking about fruit pastilles.

Mr Howie said he didn't know. He said he thought we had come through a house over the street. But Clarence said it was another house further up.

'No, it was the other side,' Simon said. 'That one.'

'What difference does it make?' Paula said. 'It's too hot to stand around in the sun.'

Marcy said it was because Milly was an orphan at the fort, and it would be nice to get some stuff for her. Then Mr Henry held his hands up and said, 'Chaps?'

Marcy asked him, 'What?' Her voice was hard, and she lifted one eyebrow at him. 'We're not on your schedule, Henry.'

'Ooh. Henry just got Marcy'd,' Alex whispered as Henry looked at Marcy for a second, then got back into his car.

'Right. Operation "Find Milly's House",' Marcy said. 'That's our objective! And don't panic, Henry. It'll be like ten minutes. Right, Howie. Find it then.'

Mr Howie said, 'What the f*ck. Erm. Lads? Any idea?'

'We came through that one,' Clarence said, but Alex said they didn't go in any houses on this street and had run down the road while Simon pointed to a house over the road, and Mr Howie pulled lots of faces as he listened to them all.

'That idea's f*cked then,' Marcy said. 'Seriously? You can't remember between you?'

'It was two weeks ago!' Mr Howie said. Then he asked me if I had any ideas.

I didn't know what ideas I should be having. 'About what, Mr Howie?'

'About the price of fish. Milly's house. Any ideas?'

I told him I did not know the price of fish.

Mr Howie then said, 'F*ck's sake.' Ahe also looked up at the sky.

Then, Marcy told him to be quiet and said she speaks Dave.

'When did you start speaking Dave?' Mr Howie asked, but she hit his arm, and he stopped talking. Then, Marcy looked at me in my eyes and said. 'Dave, can you retrace the route to where you saw Milly?'

I said yes.

She smiled at me and said, 'Great! Lead the way.' She nodded at the same time. I know that someone nodding and smiling is sometimes called a positive instruction. I started walking off. Paula asked how Marcy can speak Dave. I do not know what that means.

Dave is my name. Dave is not a language.

21

Diary of Carmen Eze.

OKAY. So. I guess I'll just jump in. My name is Carmen Eze. I am a sanctioned operative working under the umbrella of covert operations within the United Kingdom Security Services. That is a broad overtitle, but I am not actually sure what the hell I can put in this thing.

And get this. It took less than a minute from me starting to write in this thing to Frank asking, 'what the bloody hell are you doing? Is that a diary?'

I said it was. He looked at me and just laughed.

I said Paula was right. And that maybe we should be keeping records of what we are doing.

'We're deniable ops you daft cow,' Frank said. I told him he was old and stinks of piss and he couldn't keep a diary because he can't read without bifocals rammed up his backside. 'We're still accountable,' I told them him.

'To whom?' Frank asked.

'I don't know! We just are,' I said. 'We kept records before.'

'No. We maintained encrypted mission records held in a secure server,' he said. 'Which Henry vetted before they were submitted.'

That was also a good point. We did keep mission records, and they were very heavily redacted.

'It's fine. Just be careful what you put in it. And give me a code name,' Frank said.

'Double O Twat?' I asked.

So yeah. We'd just been through that whole thing with the tigers and the wolves. Which was brutal and awful.

Then we set off and had only been driving for a few minutes when Howie stopped and got out. Then Marcy told Henry they were going to gather some belongings for a little orphan girl at the fort. I could see Henry was getting angry because when he got back in the car he asked if Howard ever mentioned if Howie was bipolar.

'Not to me,' I said. Frank said the same. 'Why?' I asked Henry.

Henry said it was because Howie looked ready to hang himself five minutes ago. Now he was laughing and collecting nightdresses.

I could kind of see what Henry meant because Howie had gone from near on suicidal to laughing while running after Dave.

'They're all bloody doing it,' Frank said.

'Then maybe they're all bipolar because they can't focus on anything for more than five minutes,' Henry said.

I told Henry that a lack of focus didn't have any connection to being bipolar. That's ADD or ADHD.

'4K 5G whatever then,' Henry said. 'Listen. I get it. He's Howard's lad, and he's done well, but there's a big difference between being brave and being capable. We might have to re-consider our agreement of working together.'

Henry then asked me that if I could cherry pick from Howie's team who would I take?

I said there was no chance they would ever split up. But I guess from all of them, maybe Maddox and Roy would go with us.

'Is Maddox any good?' Henry asked me.

I said he was very good, but he had a chip the size of a planet on his shoulder.

'Peer pressure is a powerful force,' Henry said. 'We shall see. In the meantime, we'll bring Maddox over to our side. Carmen? Can I leave that with you?'

I knew what Henry was asking. I'm black. Maddox is black. I'm a woman. Maddox is a guy. *The right operative for the right task.*

'I'll do him,' Frank said.

'I don't think he'll respond to you as well as he would to Carmen,' Henry said.

'He will,' Frank said with his big toothy grin. 'I can be very persuasive.'

Henry then said Frank would work on Maddox and that at least we had a plan of sorts. He then asked Joan for her discretion in relation to our tactical discussion.

'It's fine, Henry. Just don't ask me to seduce anyone for you either,' she said. 'Unless it's Cary Grant. I always had a thing for Cary Grant. Damn fine specimen of a man.'

'Understood,' Henry said. 'And agreed. Cary Grant was a damn fine specimen of a man.'

Frank raised a good point though. And it's still in my mind now. Especially after the day we had and all the things we did.

Especially now when we're all mangled and hurt I'm thinking back to it.

Who are we accountable to?

22

Diary of Dave

MY NAME IS DAVE.

My last diary entry was detailing what happened in Stickleton. Marcy had asked me to retrace our steps to find the position we had first seen Milly.

I started crossing the road when Mr Howie asked me if I was sure this was the right way.

I said yes and walked through a broken front door.

'How do you know which way?' Mr Howie asked me. 'It was two weeks ago.'

'Blue kettle,' I said, and I pointed at the blue kettle.

'Eh? What's that got to do with anything?' Mr Howie asked.

'Garden gnome,' I said, and I pointed to the garden gnome urinating in the pond in the back garden. 'Greenhouse. Third pane broken. Low wall. Red bricks.' We went past the broken greenhouse and climbed over the low wall. 'Brown fence. White front door. Dead body in the dining room with green socks.'

We all stopped to look at the dead man and his green socks.

'How the sh*tting hell do you remember this stuff?' Mr Howie asked, but Marcy told him to shut up and not break my focus.

We went through another house and out the front door, into the street, and past Mr Henry's vehicle. 'We won't be long,' Mr Howie said.

'Wooden front door. Pictures of a fat man on the wall,' I said. They all stopped to look at the pictures of the fat man.

'He looks happy though,' Marcy said, and the others all agreed that the fat man looked very happy.

'Cannabis shed,' I said and walked into the garden. Mohammed went over to the shed and broke the door open. He said it was full of weed. Weed is a slang term. It means cannabis. Weeds are also plants that grow in gardens that are unwelcome.

'How did he know?' Nicholas asked. 'He's like a Jedi.'

I didn't know if Nicholas meant the person who owned the shed was a Jedi or if I was a Jedi.

I am not a Jedi.

Then, Natasha said she really wanted a joint.

'What you doing here?' Alex asked her. 'I thought you were driving.'

'Driving where? We've been in the same street for ten minutes.'

'We should take one,' Paula said. The others all looked at her. 'What? Just grab one, and let's go. Or two, grab two. Two of the big ones.'

'Paula!' Marcy said. Then, she told the lads to grab three or four cannabis plants. I wanted to tell them cannabis is unlawful, but then, I remembered the next thing in my head.

'What about Henry?' Natasha asked.

'F*ck Henry!' Paula said. But I had seen the sofa in the next garden and went into the house.

'Classy,' Marcy said when she saw the sofa in the garden. 'And Jesus! Look at the size of that TV,' she said when she saw inside the house, and a very big flat screen television parcel taped to the wall.

I saw the yellow clock in the kitchen and was walking through when I saw the body. But the body was not there before. 'That body wasn't here before,' I told Mr Howie.

I thought he should know.

He looked at me, then said, 'It's the apocalypse, Dave.'

I said, 'Okay, Mr Howie.' And I kept going into the next house that Milly went through.

'Stop!' Marcy said in the kitchen. We all stopped, and she took a packet from the side counter. 'Look! Lemon drizzle cake mix. I make the best lemon cake ever. I can beef it up with some extra flour.' She was taking mixing bowls and baking trays from the cupboards. 'Yes! They've got eggs.'

She broke one in the sink and sniffed it. 'Yeah. They're fine. Ish. Kind of. Whatever. It's not like we can get sick, is it. Anyway. Stop messing about,' she told Mr Howie in a very stern voice. 'Dave needs to focus.'

I don't know why she said that. Mr Howie hadn't said anything.

I went outside, and we saw Roy standing next to Mr Henry's open window.

'I mean, a compound bow has manoeuvrability and needs far less power for the pull and hold, but in my opinion, the longbow is the best,' Roy said as Frank pulled a face at everyone going past.

'Honestly. You'll love my sticky drizzle,' Marcy shouted at them.

'I mean. The longbow did the job at Agincourt, didn't it,' Roy said. 'Interesting story actually, did you know that's where doing the V sign with your fingers comes from?'

Mr Henry, Frank, Carmen, and Joan all said YES very loudly while Bashir rubbed his nose. Then, Mr Howie used the radio to ask for the Saxon to be brought around to the next street, and Maddox got out of Roy's van and said he would do it, but Natasha ran over while holding a big cannabis plant and shouted, 'GET OUT OF MY SAXON.'

The Saxon is not owned by Natasha. It is owned by the British Army as a training vehicle deployed to Salisbury Plains.

Then, I saw Mr Henry shaking his head, 'Dear god. They're using Dave like a bloody sniffer dog.'

I am not a sniffer dog.

I cannot smell the way Milly went. My nose is not powerful enough.

I saw the fence Milly climbed over to get into the safari park, and Marcy asked me if I could retrace her steps. That's when the tree on the corner of the street started glowing in my mind, and I knew we had gone past it on that side of the street.

Then, when I saw the tree with my eyes, I saw a white gate glowing in my mind, and I knew we had gone through that gate. Then, when I saw it with my eyes, I saw a door glowing in my mind with a sequential transition from one to the next. The blue kettle. The gnome urinating in the pond. The broken greenhouse. The solar panels on the shed, and the smell of cannabis in the air.

That's what happens when I fight. I can see the next steps in my mind.

Reginald said the neural pathways in my brain are structured differently. Which is how I am able to process vast quantities of data in micro-seconds.

Reginald is right. I can do that. I can look at a group of infected and know the numbers and individual trajectories of each one. I can gauge distance, motion, and risk and prioritise all of those things in order of threat.

But my brain does not work in social situations. I do not understand facial expressions. It is easier the more I know someone. Like with Mr Howie and Marcy, and the others, but it takes me time, and strangers are objects of mystery to me.

I am not a sniffer dog, and I don't like that Mr Henry called me that.

It's just that certain things work well for me. Especially when they are factual and clear. Like when we saw the tigers attacking Heather and Paco. I didn't feel any surprise at seeing that. It was happening. It was fact, and I knew I couldn't fire into them because of the speed they were all moving at. That meant I had to select my shots. Which I did when the tiger reared up, and the only reason I didn't go for the head was because I was firing an assault rifle with a 5.56 round. Tigers have solid bone density, and I couldn't be sure the bullet would not bounce off and hit someone else. That's why I left the headshot for Joan who was armed with a higher calibre weapon while I used multiple shots to try and weaken, and distract the enemy to enable those headshots to be made.

Things like that work well for me. They are factual and clear.

Other things are not always clear.

Like after the tiger was killed, and Heather attacked Mr Howie. I saw the threat and reacted, and had it been a few weeks ago, I would have killed Heather, but now, I understand things a little bit better, and so I swept her legs out to buy a second of time to see what the others would do. Mo said she was safe, and so Heather was allowed to live.

Mr Howie and Paula, and Marcy all said I cannot just kill people. They said I have to be sure.

Sometimes those steps break down, and it's hard for me to find them again. When I was tracking Milly, I saw a blue car glowing in my mind, and then, I saw the blue car in the street. That made me remember a metal watering can behind the wall. But it was not there, and without seeing the watering can, I could not see the next thing, and so I had to stop.

'What's up?' Marcy asked.

'There's no metal watering can,' I told her.

'Right. Everyone, look for a watering can,' Marcy said. 'Watering can? Can anyone see a watering can? Danny? Anything over there? Booker? Watering can? It's metal. A metal watering can.'

'What's up?' Natasha asked from the Saxon that is owned by the British Army.

'Dave's lost his watering can,' Alex said.

'Oh, I saw one! Was it metal?' Natasha said.

I said yes.

She jumped from the Saxon and ran down the street. I told her to go back and fetch her rifle. She ran back to get her rifle, then ran down the street to grab a watering can from another garden. 'Is this it?' she asked.

'Yes,' I said, and everyone looked at me. 'Green toaster,' I said and walked off.

'Dave! Hang on,' Mr Howie said. 'How do you know the watering can was here? I mean. Could it be that house down there is the one we need?'

I said no and walked off.

'But if you knew the watering can was here, then why didn't we just go in this house? I mean. It was this house, right?'

'Yes, Mr Howie.'

'So?'

'So what?'

'Why not just go inside?'

'Because there was no watering can, Mr Howie.'

'No. But you knew the watering can was here.'

'Yes.'

'So why not just keep going?'

'Because it wasn't here.'

'No. But it *was* here. Like before. But just not now.'

'Yes.'

'Right. Was that a yes, it was here, or a yes, that we could have kept going?'

'No.'

'Eh? What the f*ck. No, hang on.'

'Howie, it's hot!' Paula shouted at him.

'No, but something else could be missing. Like… Like a brown bench! What if the brown bench is missing?' Mr Howie said.

I told him there wasn't a brown bench.

'F*ck me. Okay. Then what if the green toaster is missing?'

I told him it wasn't because I could see it.

'But what if it was! What if the green toaster wasn't here? What then?'

I told him they wouldn't have a toaster.

'F*ck me backwards! You're doing it on purpose. He's doing it on purpose. Okay. Fine. What's after the green toaster?'

I said it was the black bin in the garden.

'Okay. The black bin isn't there.'

'Howie! It's hot as shit.'

'Hang on, Paula. The black bin isn't there, Dave. It's gone. What now?'

'What?' I asked him.

'No. I'm asking you. What now? Cos the black bin has gone.'

I asked him where it went.

He said, 'I don't know.'

I asked him then how does he know it's not there?

'Cos the f*cking bin pixies took it away. I don't know. The wind. The wind took it.'

I told him the bin had rocks in it.

'F*ck my ears! The rocks fell out, then the wind took the bin away. The f*cking bin ran off and got married to another bin, and they had bin babies.'

I said okay.

'Okay what?'

I said, 'Okay, Mr Howie.'

'No. No! Everyone, shut up. F*ck me, this cannabis plant stinks. Why are we even carrying them? Put them in the Saxon. Or in the van. Put them in Reggie's van.'

'They're not putting them in my van,' Roy said.

'Roy said you're not putting them in his van,' Tappy shouted over.

'The Saxon then. Put them in the Saxon. Booker, take mine. Right, Dave. Okay. The bin is gone. There is no bin.'

'Howie!' Marcy said. 'Dave, just keep going.'

'What the f*ck!' Mr Howie said. 'But I want to know how it works.'

Marcy said I probably don't know how it works. She said that's the thing with autism, 'Things either work, or they don't work. And not all the time either because it's a spectrum. Like blindness. You can be a bit blind or a lot blind.'

'I know what a spectrum is,' Mr Howie said. I then saw the black bin in the garden and looked at Mr Howie. 'They got divorced,' he said.

I said, 'Sprinkler.' And walked off.

'Don't!' Marcy said and pointed at Howie.

I carried on and found the sprinkler and the next object after that. But Mr Howie was right with what he said because sometimes I do tease him on purpose.

The team all call each other tw*t and c*ck, and d*ck. That's called banter. It strengthens the bond between people within a fighting unit. Just because I am autistic, it doesn't mean I don't want to bond. I do want to bond, and when Mr Howie questions me sometimes, it's my way of calling him a tw*t. But I don't smile on the outside when I do it. That does not mean I don't find things funny. I do find things funny. But I laugh on the inside.

Marcy was also right because I could not explain right at that moment what I would have done if the toaster was not there because the toaster was there.

I would not have been able to verbalise my thoughts. But now, I can. I don't know why that happens. But it is very important to me that Mr Howie cared enough to ask and try, and find out. Nobody ever did that before.

It was the same when we worked at Tesco.

Mr Howard said I had to leave the team and start a new life in a supermarket. I did what I was told. But it was lonely. And because I am autistic, and I don't know how to talk to people, other people thought I wanted to be left alone.

But Mr Howie didn't do that.

Mr Howie spoke to me on every shift. He always asked me how I was. He spoke about the weather and the things going on, and he always made a point of finding me at break times so I was never left on my own. He invited me to sit at his table. He asked what food I had, and he always said goodbye.

I liked the way Mr Howie was a bit sarcastic sometimes too. He'd say things like *great chat, Dave*. But he smiled when he said it. Like banter. Like joking. I was in the army for a long time. I was used to it. It was familiar without being insulting, and Mr Howie never patronised me. Even when he gets cross if we talk and I tease him, I don't think he actually means it. It's like a game because I can't feel his anger.

I can feel Mr Howie's anger when he is really angry. Like at the fort when Mr Howie found out I knew Mr Howard and Mr Henry, and Paula's Uncle George. I felt his anger, and I was sorry I had not told Mr Howie.

I tried to tell Mr Howie why, but the thoughts would not get right in my head. I was scared and upset.

That means that I could tell Mr Howie was not really angry with me for not telling him how I was retracing our steps. This was our banter, and I liked it.

I said the next thing was a pink flamingo.

'I remember that,' Mr Howie said when we found the plastic, pink flamingo in a garden. 'Okay. Let me try one.'

I said okay and waited for him.

'Right. Pink flamingo. Pink flamingo,' Mr Howie said. 'What comes after the pink flamingo?'

'That's like a Blowers' sex line,' Alex said.

Simon called him a tw*t, and I smiled on the inside.

'Leather sofa!' Howie said and clicked his fingers. 'Is there a leather sofa?'

I said I didn't know.

'Jesus. Okay. So what's the next thing for you?' Mr Howie asked me.

I said Wellington boots.

'Green wellies!' Alex said. 'I remember them.'

'By the front door,' Simon said.

I said the Wellington boots were blue, and they were next to the understairs cupboard.

'Burned!' Marcy said. She pulled a face at the others. She did not mean something was burning. She meant I had played a trick. Then, she smiled and winked at me when we saw the Wellington boots. 'And there's no leather sofa either,' she told Mr Howie.

'There's a leather sofa somewhere,' Mr Howie said.

'I've got FOMO going on right now,' Natasha shouted from the Saxon.

'What's FOMO?' Howie asked.

'Fear of missing out,' Marcy said.

I did not know that FOMO means Fear of missing out.

'Ask Maddox to drive then,' Nicholas said.

'Er, f*ck off. She's my Saxon,' Natasha said. (The Saxon is definitely owned by the British Army.)

'Bread bin!' Mr Howie shouted. 'In the kitchen. With a moving lid thing.'

'Painting of a horse,' I said as we walked into a hallway.

'Ooh, I wanna see it,' Charlotte said. They all stopped to stare at the painting. 'That is a really sh*t painting of a horse,' Charlotte said.

'FOMO!' Natasha shouted from outside. (That means fear of missing out.)

'It's a sh*t painting of a horse,' Nicholas told her.

'Ha! No bread bin,' Marcy said.

'F*ck. Okay, you do one,' Mr Howie said.

'How? I wasn't here, you tw*t,' Marcy said.

'Oh, yeah. Ha, oops. Okay. Pond. Dave, there's a pond,' Mr Howie said.

I said there was a Barbie bicycle, and they all came outside to see it.

'I'm telling you. There is a pond somewhere,' Mr Howie said.

'Yeah? Is the leather sofa in it?' Marcy asked. Then, I remembered the dead woman and went to the next garden to see the corpse in the garden, and the next thing came into my mind.

'Leather sofa,' I said.

'No way,' Mr Howie said when he saw the leather sofa in the front room.

'Bread bin,' I said in the kitchen.

'Get in!' Howie yelled. I don't know why because I would never fit in a bread bin that size. 'Come on, three for three. Please let there be a pond,' Mr Howie said.

Then I pointed to the pond in the garden.

'F*CK, YES!' Howie said. He was smiling and laughing.

THE UNDEAD TWENTY-FIVE. THE HEAT

'You lucky sh*t,' Marcy said.

'Luck, my *rse. Skill. Eh, Dave? We're on the same wavelength. We're like brothers,' Mr Howie said. He pushed into my shoulder, and I smiled on the inside.

'What's next?' Alex asked.

'Okay, er, what's next?' Howie asked.

I asked him what next one.

'The next thing,' Mr Howie said. 'Which way?'

I didn't know what he meant. 'What way?' I asked him.

'Howie, stop,' Marcy said and pushed him away to stand in front of me so she could see my eyes. 'Dave, why don't you know?'

I said this was where we first saw Milly.

Mr Howie said blimey and started looking around at the street; then, Paula called out and pointed over the road to a house.

The ground floor windows were all boarded up with planks, and the small garden looked dirty and full of litter and long weeds. (The unwelcome garden plants. Not cannabis plants.)

Then, Paula pointed up, and I saw a piece of paper with torn corners sellotaped to the inside of the window, and the name MILLY written in pink crayon across the front.

'Good spot, Paula,' Mr Howie said.

'Not just a pretty face, eh?' Clarence said; then, he went very red which he does a lot when he talks to Paula. 'Right. Stop p*ssing about, Cookey. You need to focus.'

'Eh? I didn't do anything,' Alex said. He was right. He hadn't done anything.

'And stop the backchat,' Clarence said. He was right too because younger people should not talk back to elders.

'Wow. That's some weird energy right there,' Howie whispered to Marcy.

'Isn't it,' Marcy whispered. 'Even Dave's picking it up.'

I looked at the ground and wondered what I should be picking up, but there was nothing there apart from litter. I thought they meant I should be picking the litter up and looked around to see if anyone else was picking it up.

'Right. Let's get inside then,' Mr Howie said. 'Dave? You coming?'

'What about the litter?' I asked him.

'Eh? What litter?'

'That litter,' I said and pointed to an old can of Pepsi.

Mr Howie tutted. 'Bad, isn't it. People are just lazy. Anyway, let's get this done. I think Henry's having kittens.'

I forgot about the litter and followed Mr Howie across the road to see Mr Henry's kittens. I hadn't seen any cats though. Unless Mr Henry picked up some tiger kittens. But they're called cubs. Not kittens.

'Paula, let Dave,' Mr Howie said as Paula reached the front door. 'Just in case.'

'Fair enough,' she said and moved away.

'Found it then?' Mr Henry asked, but I couldn't see the kittens. I wondered where they are and then thought maybe I should go back and clean that old can up.

'You never switch off, do you, Dave,' Paula said.

I didn't know what that meant either. I definitely don't have an on and off switch though. I would have seen it.

I told Mohammed to come over and said we would do house clearance, and I would be on point. Then, I turned back and waited for his readiness signal when Carmen asked if we wanted a third and ran over to stand behind Mohammed.

'Er, so's, what do I do now?' Mohammed asked.

'What?' Carmen asked.

'What?' I asked.

'We's only drilled with two people entry. Do I keep my hand on Dave?'

'Yes,' Carmen and I said at the same time. 'I'm rear point,' Carmen explained. 'I touch you, you touch Dave, and he knows we're good to go.'

'Got it,' Mohammed said. 'So's, would that work with like four people entry?'

'Yes,' Carmen and I said at the same time.

'Got it,' Mohammed said. 'So's, would that work with like five people entry?'

'All the people entry,' Carmen said.

'What if you got like twelve people entry?' Mohammed asked. 'That'd be like a big conga line or something.'

'You wouldn't have a twelve-person entry,' Carmen said. 'Not for a property this size. Well, no. There's actually lots of different methods of entry. I mean, you could put twelve into a house this size, but only if you were expecting serious opposition.'

'If you were expecting that level of opposition, you'd use another tactic,' Frank said.

'Like what?' Mohammed asked.

'Like a blo*dy missile,' he said as the others laughed.

'You'd split into squads, Mo,' Mr Henry said. 'And stack up either side of the door. Say Team Alpha, and then Team Bravo. But you'd designate the entry flow. Team Alpha to go right for instance, Team Bravo to go left or ahead. But it would be covered in the brief.'

'Ah, okay. Got it,' Mohammed said. 'But like, so's what if you don't got time for a brief?'

'That's a good question, actually,' Carmen said.

'That *is* a very good question,' Henry said. 'And it does happen. In which case, you'd use basic cover and manoeuvre tactics. Point stays on point. The second covers the first point of danger. The third covers the next etc. That's if you are clearing as you go. But if you need rapid entry for, say, an imminent terrorist threat or to detain someone, then, you go in and sweep through at speed. That's when you'd put more operatives in than a normal pre-planned operation.'

'Cool, cool,' Mohammed said.

'You need to tell Dave you're good to go again,' Carmen said.

'I's got my hand on his shoulder.'

'Yes, but we just stopped to have a conversation, so now, Dave needs a signal that we're ready.'

'Got it. Er, Dave, I'm good to go.'

'We're good to go,' Carmen said.

'Dave? Carmen is good to go too. We's all good to go. Ah, man. I feel stupid now. Like you's pros wouldn't say that.'

'We would,' Carmen said. 'It's fine. As long as the comms are clear, and everyone understands, it's fine. Okay, try again. Mo, I'm ready.'

'Dave, I'm ready,' Mohammed said and patted my shoulder as a bolt behind the door slid back and the door opened, with a woman inside smiling at me.

She did not have any weapons or show sign of threat, so I did not kill her.

23

Diary of Carmen Eze

BY THEN IT was already hot as hell. I think Roy had said it was in the mid 30's, but the humidity was the thing though. It felt like a weight was pushing down on my shoulders.

Anyway. I was describing what just happened.

Dave had re-traced their steps from two weeks ago to find Milly's house. (Orphan at the fort). We'd done that then Paula spotted a sign in the window (good spot too).

So Dave was gearing up for a house entry with Mo. I was bored and offered to jump in which sparked an MOE debate. (Method of Entry). Good discussion though.

After that I gave the 'go' signal to Mo. Mo gave the 'go' to Dave, and Dave's readying to put the door in when it opens. And oh my god. I thought this day couldn't get any more surreal. I mean. Tigers? Wolves? A talking parrot? (Who was gorgeous BTW. Green Winged Macaw – *ara chloroptera*)

But yes. What a day. Then the door to that house opened and this woman was just standing there. But she was only wearing a skimpy bra and knickers and everyone fell silent. I mean you could have heard a pin drop because she was stunning. She even made Marcy look plain. Blonde hair and these piercing blue eyes! Big boobs and long legs and a tiny waist. (I've dealt with a lot of Russian honey traps. Some of those women are like supermodels and even my mouth dropped open.) I wasn't the only one either. But she was just standing there smiling at Dave and then the weirdest conversation I ever heard took place.

'Hello,' the woman said. 'I'm Molly.'

'I'm Dave.'

'It's hot today, Dave.'

'Hydrate.'

'What does hydrate mean?'

'Drink water.'

'I like water,' Molly said. 'Do you like water?'

'I like water,' Dave said.

'I like kittens and puppies. Do you like kittens and puppies?'

'Henry has kittens.'

'Can I see the kittens?'

'Henry has the kittens.'

'Which man is Henry?'

'That man is Henry.'

'Hello, Henry. Can I see your kittens?'

And the rest of us were just staring on and listening while Dave and this Playboy looking woman were yacking on about kittens. (No idea why Dave thought Henry had kittens either).

So then eventually Howie blinked and he was like. 'What the shit. Are you okay, love?'

And then Marcy said, 'Oh no you don't!' and she was barging him away as though to stop him staring at Molly (Which we were ALL doing).

Then Paula was demanding to know what Molly thought she was doing.

'I was going to see the kittens. Henry has them,' Molly said. 'Do you like kittens?'

'Jesus. That bloody bra is see-through,' Marcy said.

'The knickers aren't much better,' Paula said.

'Dave said we have to himate,' Molly told them both.

'Hydrate,' Dave said.

'Hydrate,' Molly said and she was smiling at Dave. Then Dave was staring at her mouth and he was literally widening his own mouth to show her his teeth. So then she was doing the same and they're both just showing each other their teeth.

'Seriously! What the fuck are you doing?' Paula asked. 'Put some bloody clothes on!'

'Giles said I shouldn't put clothes on. He said it's hot and I should stay cool.'

'Fucking world's gone mad,' Paula said, and she was shaking her head but then Howie took a step closer and said, 'Hello, Molly. My name is Howie,' but his voice was really soft. Like how you'd speak to a kid. Which is at the same time as Henry asked if the girl was retarded. (Total diversity fail BTW.)

'Hi, Howie. I'm Molly. Do you like water?' Molly asked, then I realised she wasn't showing one bit of surprise at a whole crowd of armed people at her door. Which is when the lightbulbs went on for the rest of us mere mortals not equipped with brains like Howie and Henry.

'I do like water,' Howie said. 'Molly. Are you related to Milly?'

'Milly!' Molly said with the biggest smile you ever saw. 'She's my sister but she went away. I made that so she could remember our house.' She pointed up at the sign in the window as the smile faded to a look of absolute pain. Like how a kid would lurch from emotion to emotion. Like that. Which is exactly what Molly was being:

A child in an adult's body.

And the rest of us are murmuring, *oh god,* and sharing looks.

'Milly's okay. We know where she is,' Howie said. 'But Molly, listen, who else is here with you?'

'Giles. He's my half of a brother. But his friends live here now. Pete and John. And Terry and Adam and Dekkie. He has bad breath.' She said that in a whisper with a grossed-out expression. 'I don't like it when he kisses me.'

'Oh god,' Marcy said. 'Look at her body.'

I leant round Mo to see properly and saw the bruises all over her. Grip marks mostly. Handprints on her breasts and thighs. Another one around her neck. She's fair-skinned and no doubt bruises easily, but still. The placement of them was obvious.

Not that Molly seemed to care. She just burst out laughing when Meredith pushed to the front and asked if she could stroke the doggy.

She then dropped down into a low squat which is when we saw the love bites on her shoulders and back. Like these vivid red welts all over her.

Jesus Christ. I've never felt anything like it. It was like the air was charging. It sounds stupid now. But that's what it was like. There was this energy or whatever pouring from Howie. And his eyes! They were so dark.

'Molly, I need to ask you a question?' Howie asked. His voice had dropped too but he was trying to keep it light. 'Is that okay?'

Molly nodded and said she likes questions. 'But not hard ones though. Giles and his friends ask me hard questions. They said I'm stupid. They said I have to do things if I get them wrong.'

'What things?' Paula asked.

'They make me wash the dishes,' Molly said, like all sulky. 'And I have to clean the toilet.'

'Oh, thank god,' Paula said.

'And I have to put their willies in my mouth and foo-foo until the yucky stuff comes out. Urgh! I hate that.'

Then this guy shouted inside and this guy appeared. 'Molly! You opened that bloody door? I said don't open it you daft bitch! The zombie things will… Oh shit. Who are you lot? Are you the army? No way. Is it over?'

'Are you Giles?' Howie asked.

'Eh? What?'

'I said are you Giles?'

'Giles? No, I'm Pete. Giles is asleep. Hang on. GILES! The army's here. It's over. Fuck me. Is it done?'

'That's Pete,' Molly said.

'Did Pete put his willy in your mouth too?' Howie asked and that energy I said Howie had? Well. It went into overdrive. I can't even explain it. It's like time slowed down or something stupid. He just had this aura. And that guy Pete was blinking at him, and the fear was crawling all over his face.

'Eh? What? What the... No, hang on a sec-.'

'He did,' Molly said with a gag.

Then BANG! Holy shit. Howie moved so fast. Let me say that right now. He had Pete off his feet and pinned to the stairs inside the house faster than the rest of us could blink and he was driving these punches into the guy's head and Dave was sweeping in past him to another subject male grabbing a sawn-off shotgun in the front room.

'GUN!' Dave shouted, but the perp still tried to draw the weapon before Dave put one through his head.

I mean. We train for this and even I was caught out. Only for a second though. Then I'm pushing Mo out of the way and going inside with Frank behind me.

'Me and Carmen sweep. Dave hold,' Frank said while Howie was calling Pete a fucking cunt and punching him in the head.

Frank went ahead towards the kitchen and a subject male coming out of the toilet pulling his trousers up and trying to grab a police rifle and getting the McGill double tap for his troubles. 'Kitchen. One down,' Frank said.

By then I was in the other front room to a subject male coming awake on a sofa. The guy was bathed in sweat and the room was dark and filthy and stank like a crack den with empty cans of beer and bottles of vodka everywhere. I clocked the pistol on the table as the perp looked at it and told him to stay still. 'DO NOT MOVE.' But he went for it. I double tapped his COM and got one through his head. 'Living room. One down.'

'Ground floor clear,' Frank said then I got back to Howie just as another subject male appeared at the top of the stairs.

'What the hell!' the guy was shouting. 'Pete? Giles?'

'ADAM!' Pete shouted as Howie landed another sickening punch into his head, slamming his skull back into the edge of the stairs. Then he ripped the guy off the floor and threw him outside into Clarence.

Then Adam was at the top of the stairs in this pair of filthy white underpants and a look of horror. 'Oh fuck. No, listen… Hey! Listen to me! No… Hang on. Whatever she said… We didn't do it! I didn't do it. Stop it. STOP IT!'

And that perp – Adam – he was screaming out and trying to drop and supplicate but Howie was up the stairs and battering him down with punches to his head. Then a bedroom door opens and another subject male stared out with the blood draining from his face.

'Giles!' Adam shouted, but he was spraying blood and teeth, and Howie literally dropped Adam and charged at Giles. Lifting the guy off his feet to launch across the room with the pair of them falling over this single bed. I was behind Howie and saw the room was filthy. The bedsheets were all stained with shit and piss and blood and there was sexy underwear all over the floor. Like crotchless knickers and PVC bras and sex toys and dildos and used condoms and tissues. But Howie just went at Giles. Driving him over the bed then he pinned him against the wall with a hand to his throat.

'What did you do?' Howie's asked. 'Your own sister. WHAT DID YOU DO?'

I couldn't help it. We're trained to stay cool. But that heat. The humidity. Everything we'd been through. Hearing the diaries that morning and seeing that poor girl Molly in the doorway. I just snapped and kicked a huge dildo at the guy and I was screaming at him and calling him a sick fucker while Frank is pulling me back.

And that Giles? Trust me. It was written all over his face. The sick fuck couldn't think fast enough to lie. Then Howie drew his knife and stuck it in the perp's gut and started twisting it while holding the guy by the throat. The guy wriggled and coughed blood over Howie's face and I thought Jesus, I do not want to die staring into Howie's eyes when he's like that.

Giles though? Fuck him. He had that coming, and if Howie hadn't of done it I would.

Then it was done and Giles just slid down to the floor and I turned around on hearing something and saw Adam still on the floor at the top of the stairs being held by Henry with a handful of his hair.

And so Howie walked out past me. Past Dave and Frank and he took Adam from Henry and pushed his pistol to Adam's head as the guy pissed himself in fear while making these animal noises.

Howie shot him and I heard the guy outside being held by Clarence screaming out and looked down the stairs just as Clarence lifted the guy off his feet and snapped his neck.

And truthfully? The whole thing was probably less than a minute. Then Henry was just staring at Howie and everyone was silent.

I'm telling you. This is a new world. A very strange new world.

24

Diary of Paula

THEN, Howie was inside, and I think he stabbed Molly's brother in the stomach just before he shot Adam in the head. Then Marcy and I turned Molly away just before Clarence killed the guy who opened the door and threw him back inside like he was trash. (Which he totally was.)

Molly though? She didn't blink an eye throughout the whole thing. She didn't even flinch at the gunshots. She was crouching down hugging the dog.

Anyway. I got inside and went upstairs to find Howie in the bedroom surrounded by sex toys and used condoms and dead bodies. (But then when aren't we surrounded by dead bodies now?)

I think the worst thing (for me anyway) was seeing Molly's handwritten sign on the bedroom door.

MOLLYS ROOM: KEEP OUT!

No Mens!

It was just so sad. The thought of her making that sign while those filthy men took turns.

Then I looked at the sign on the door again and realised it said Molly's Room. And not Molly *and* Milly's room.

We worked out that Milly must have been taken into care by social services and Molly was left behind because she was an adult. (Poor sod.) Then H remembered Milly saying she lived with someone called Carly and he asked Dave if he remembers that, but Dave did that thing and said, 'remember what?' to set Howie off. I swear Dave does it on purpose. But it seemed to work though because it stopped Howie from looking like he was going to murder everyone.

Then Marcy (ever the patient one) was shouting up the stairs and asking what was going on.

'Milly didn't live here,' Howie called down.

'Er. Don't tell me we just killed the wrong people.'

'Eh? No! We think Milly was taken into care,' Howie said.

'Thank god for that,' Marcy said. 'Hang on. Charlie? Ask Molly if Milly was taken into care. Charlie's asking her, Howie.'

'Okay,' Howie said. 'And we need to get her to the fort.'

'How?' Marcy asked. 'None of us can take her. And Carmen can't do it either.'

'What about Heather?' I asked.

'Heather was a bit upset,' Howie said.

'Fuck being upset!' Marcy shouted from downstairs. 'She'll have to get on with it like the rest of us.'

'Just radio Lilly and get her to send someone. Tell her it's Milly's sister,' Howie said.

'Why can't Heather just do it?' Marcy asked.

'Cos she got attacked by lions and tigers, Marcy!' Howie shouted as Cookey started doing the *lions and tigers and bears oh my!* song outside. (Which did make me smile, and I could hear Molly laughing her head off too).

Marcy didn't find it very funny. 'Don't you *she got attacked by lions and a tiger, Marcy* me, Howie,' she shouted up the stairs. 'You know what. I'm too hot to argue. Fine. Whatever. Call the princess then.'

'Who's the princess?' Howie asked giving me a look.

'LILLY!' Marcy shouted.

'Okay okay, no need to shout,' Howie said while pulling his radio off his belt. *'Er, hi, it's Howie. Is Lilly there please?'*

'Wrong radio you gimp!' Marcy shouted as Howie's voice came out of our cheap radio sets.

At which point Howie started swearing a lot and Frank was rolling his eyes and no doubt Marcy was getting ready to shout more.

Fortunately, Henry stepped in and said he would do it while Marcy clumped up the stairs. 'Done,' Henry said a moment later. 'Lilly will arrange collection from the town centre.'

'That's nice of the princess,' Marcy said.

'Is Molly okay?' Carmen asked.

'She seems fine on the surface, but she said her foo foo hurts and her back-bottom keeps bleeding, so I'm guessing they raped her anally.'

That poor girl. I don't know what to say. Honestly. But I guess at least we can get her to safety.

'Let's hope she's not pregnant,' Marcy said. 'Anyway. We'll grab some clothes for her, oh and she wants a blue folder. She said it's Milly's. It's got her drawings in.'

We found it on the floor under a set of drawers. Howie grabbed it and we saw the front said MILLY'S FOLDER. But the words were completely different to how Molly had done her sign. They were all flowing and neat. Then we opened the folder to a hand drawn picture of a German Shepherd. 'Bloody hell. That's Meredith!' Howie said.

'Get off. It's just a dog,' Marcy said. 'Milly never saw Meredith before all this.'

'All dogs look the same in pictures,' Carmen said. But then even she agreed the drawing looked a lot like Meredith.

Then Frank found a photo on the floor and asked if Molly would want it. It was a photo of three people in some kind of social services family centre by the looks of it.

Milly, Molly and a young boy about the same age as Milly with the same blonde hair and blue eyes and rosy cheeks.

'He looks familiar,' Carmen said.

'We've seen him before,' Henry said. 'In the canteen in the fort. George commented on the pictures on the wall. One was of that young boy.'

'This photo was a few years ago though,' Marcy said.

'Maybe it's when they got separated,' Howie said, then we spotted the photo had names below each face. Milly, Molly and Mikey. We figured Mikey was the brother and probably got taken into care too.'

Anyway. It was awful. I mean truly upsetting, but the whole day was like that. Everywhere we went was upsetting, and it just got worse by the hour.

25

Diary of Carmen Eze

HONESTLY. That day just got more surreal by the minute.

We'd just stopped for another coffee because things were getting worse between Henry and Howie. Much worse.

But that's not the surreal part. Well, no, it was the surreal part. But it was *all* surreal. And to top it all off by then I was starting to develop a crush.

I know right.

We were still in Stickleton gearing up to meet Princess Lilly (loving her new nickname btw) but Molly needed somewhere to get changed and so Marcy bundled her into Roy's van, but Reggie was still in the back working at his desk.

'Why is she coming in here?' he asked. (You could tell he wasn't happy.) 'Good lord! You can see her bosoms. Get the poor woman covered up. Honestly. It's enough to put me off my book.'

'That's why she's in here,' Marcy told him.

'I like books,' Molly said. 'Is it a book about fairies?'

'No. Sadly it is not,' Reginald said. 'It is a book about the principles of virology and molecular biology.'

Molly then looked all thoughtful for a second and asked him to read to her, and Reggie put on this show of flicking through the pages. 'Okay then. Here we are. This is an interesting one… Are you ready?'

'Oh god, this is going be painful,' Marcy said.

'Indeed. Thank you,' Reginald said. 'Now, young Molly, is that your name? Oh my. Well, I never. The girl in this story is also called Molly. But alas, this Molly is a fairy you see, and one day, Molly was talking to Big Bob, he's a goblin by the way.

Oh, Big Bob. Wherever shall we find some new clothes to wear! The grand party is happening soon, Molly the fairy said.

Donchaworry, Molly, Big Bob replied. *We'll find yer some new clothes quick smart…*'

And Paula's mouthing 'what the fuck,' at me and literally everyone went silent so they could listen to Reginald telling this story. (He was even doing the voices!)

'*Donchaworry, Molly. We're gonna find you a dress. Wot about this one then?*

Oh no! Big Bob. That one is red. I shan't wear that either.

Well. We've only got one left, Moll. And it's blue, and ladies they don't like to wear blue do they.

Oh no! Big Bob! Blue is my most favourite colour and I shall wear it forever… And Molly wore the blue dress to the fairy party and all the other goblins and fairies said she was the prettiest fairy of them all. The end!'

By then Molly was wearing her own pretty blue dress and everyone was smiling because it was just bloody adorable. (Especially after what we'd just seen in the house.)

Well. Not everyone. Henry wasn't happy. He 'suggested' we hurry up. Which only sparked Marcy off (she doesn't hold back, let me tell you that.) And she was leaning out of the van shouting at Henry to sod off. Then slamming the door closed, then opening it again and yelling 'are we bloody going then or what?' (I actually love it that Marcy stands up to Henry. That said. I get the feeling Marcy would do it to anyone. She *really* doesn't suffer fools.)

Diary of Maddox Doku

...So then we finally get going and I was back in the Saxon because Marcy, Charlie and Paula were still playing dress up with Molly. That sounds mean. I don't mean that. Molly was really cute. Not sexually. Well, no, she's hot. Like we all thought that soon as she opened that door. But I was already thinking something wasn't right before Howie started talking to her like she was a kid. It was the make-up she had on. It was all blue and green around the eyes like how a kid would do it.

But that was all weird and even now I'm conflicted because I don't like Howie being judge, jury and executioner. I know I was a criminal and served time, but due process is important. The concept of law has to remain otherwise people become savages.

But I felt conflicted because I agreed with what Howie did. I mean those guys were heroin junkie scum, right? But how do we know Molly didn't just say they raped her? How do we know she won't get to the fort and say Mr Howie or Maddox put their willies in her mouth until the yucky stuff came out?

But when I put myself in Howie's position and imagine it was me at that door when Molly answered it. Honestly? I think I would have done the same thing. I think we all would. (Lynch mob anyone?)

Yeah. So I was back in the Saxon and it was hotter than hell and Booker was shifting about like he couldn't sit still. He was even worse when Molly opened the door at her house. I thought his eyes were going to pop out. But then we ALL had that reaction.

So we were driving for less than ten minutes when we pull into this long narrow street and Howie stops because there's some people ahead blocking the road. Like two groups on either side of the street

THE UNDEAD TWENTY-FIVE. THE HEAT

and they're all armed with sticks and knives, and some guy has a sword, and another one has got some rusty old shotgun.

And Clarence is like *you are joking me.* But we've got no choice but to stop. Then Howie groans and he's telling Clarence to look at the buildings behind the group.

One group was outside of a mosque. And Clarence asked what the other building was. *Synagogue* Howie tells him, but it gets worse because the doors to a church open a bit further up and this third group come out and they're all tooled up and marching towards the first two groups.

This is all we need. Getting dragged into a twatty religious shitstorm Howie said. Clarence suggested we could just drive off, (but you could tell he didn't mean it.)

How? Howie asks him. *We'd never turn around and we can't back up. Henry would tut at us.*

So then, we're all piling out, and Marcy and Paula were asking what was going on. *That's a bit shit then* Marcy said. *We could just go.* But Howie said we'd never turn around. *And Henry would tut at us again.*

By then, Henry is out of his vehicle and walking up. *What's the hold up now?* He asked. And he was pissy. You could see he was pissy.

That is Howie said, and he pointed ahead to the three sides all shouting at each other.

And Henry's like, *I see. A mosque and a synagogue. Understood. Oh, and yes, a church. Hmmm, perhaps we could just leave them to it?*

We'd never turn around, Clarence said. *And you'd tut at us* Howie said.

But Henry just gives him this steely look and says, *right. Well, we'd best get it sorted then. Which ones do you want? How about I take the Muslims. Howie, you do the Jews. Paula, perhaps you and Carmen can do the Christians. I'll take Mo and Bash with me. Do we have any Jews? And are any of you Christian?*

Then Howie was like, *what the fuck?* (I was thinking it too)

But Henry said *always helps to have one of their team on your team so to speak. Bridges gaps like nothing else. You okay if I borrow Mo then?*

And Howie says, *I don't think Mo's a Muslim.*

He's from Afghanistan. Henry says.

No. He's from a council estate and you can't assume someone is a Muslim because of what they look like. Howie says.

I don't. But they will, Henry says and he's pointing down the street. *Trust me, Howie. I've been doing this job for a long time and dealing with religious types is always hard.*

DIARY OF CARMEN EZE

...AND WE'RE ALL OUT in the street by this time listening to Howie detonate at Henry.

'No wonder the world was going to rat shit if you do bollocks like that. What the actual fuck, Henry! Right. *I'm* doing the Christians and *you* can take Bash to the Jews and *Marcy* can do the Muslims.'

Henry was acting cool, but I could see he was starting to get rattled and he then tells Howie there might be an issue with Muslims talking to someone like Marcy.

'What the shit does that mean?' Howie asks him.

'I just mean we need to resolve whatever this is, and get on with what we need to do, which isn't this. Whatever *this* is. Therefore, I am suggesting the most common-sense approach to achieve the best outcome,' Henry said.

'You mean a racist approach,' Howie said.

'It is not racist.'

'It is bloody racist. Fuck me. Right. Tell you what. We're just going to walk into the middle, and they can come and talk to us. How about that?'

Frank then points out that idea isn't tactically sound. But Howie's not having any of it. 'Fuck tactically sound. And I'm not bloody Jewish either. Not that being Jewish is bad, but I'm not. And Mo doesn't look like a Muslim. He looks like a fucking kid! Jesus wept.'

Then someone in the church group shouts PRAISE JESUS and Howie shouts, 'Fuck off!'

'Please don't yell fuck off if someone shouts praise Allah,' Henry warned him quickly.

'Why? Would that be racist?' Howie asked him with a smug nod. Which is fair enough because Henry used the word retarded a minute ago but now he was trying to show sensitivity just to piss Howie off. Which was clearly working as Howie was almost frothing at the mouth by then. 'And why aren't you sweating? It's like forty degrees!' Howie asked him.

'Indeed. A fascinating subject. But shall we resolve this and move on?' Henry said.

'Hang on a second,' Howie said. 'REGGIE! I NEED YOU!' he shouts, but Reginald calls back that he's telling Molly another story.

'It's the fairy sports day and Molly the fairy hasn't got anyone to do the sack race with,' Reginald says.

'Why can't Big Bob do it?' Frank asks.

'Duh. He's Big Bob. He's too big,' I tell him as the lads all go *ah!* Like they were thinking the same as Frank.

'He's too big,' Reginald called from the van. (I was right)

'And why do we need Reginald?' Henry asked.

'Cos he's the smarterest man I know,' Howie said. 'And yes. I know I said smarterest. I meant cleverest.'

'Or maybe just smartest?' Frank suggested.

'Jesus fucking Christ!' Howie said.

'Praise Jesus!' one of the Christians yelled.

'FUCK OFF!' Howie yelled back.

Then Reginald is walking over with Molly but he's still telling her the story. *'Oh no! Big Bob. You are too big to help in the sack race. Whatever shall I do?*

Ere' donchaworry, Moll. How's about we ask Gobby the Goblin?

Oh no, Big Bob! Gobby the Goblin is too slow to help me with the sack race. I want to win. Said Molly the Fairy.

Ha! I got it, Moll. We'll ask Pickle the Pixie!

Oh yes! Big Bob. Pickle the Pixie will be perfect. Well done, Big Bob. And

Pickle the Pixie and Molly the Fairy won the sack race at the fairy sports day…Now. How can I help?' Reginald asked.

Diary of Maddox Doku

So then Howie was like, *Right. We've got Muslims. Jews and Christians all arguing.*

And Reginald said it sounded like the start to a bad Cookey joke.

No. We've got actual religious people. Howe tells him.

And apparently you're the smarterest, Frank said.

Fuck's sake. I meant cleverest. Smartest! Whatever. Ready?

Ready for what? Reginald asked.

To go and sort it out, Howie said.

Sort what out?

Whatever they're arguing about?

Why would we do that? Reginald asked him. *We should just turn around.*

There isn't room, Frank said.

And I would tut apparently, Henry said. *I do, however, still suggest we use Mo and Bash.*

But Howie was like, *you're not using Mo! That's racist. Reggie, tell him it's racist.*

What's racist? Reginald asked.

Saying Mo looks like a Muslim.

And then Reginald says, *is that racism? Or is it perhaps stereotyping? I mean one would assume an element of racism contains a derogatory aspect, whereas the assumption of a religious leaning might not be construed as derogatory at all. In this instance, one could hazard a guess that Mo is, indeed, of Arabic descent, therefore one could assume his religion is that of Islam.*

Then Henry was like, *thank you, Reginald.* But Howie was getting angrier. *What the fuck! No! You can't say Mo looks like he's Muslim just cos he's bloody Arabic.*

Of course, we shouldn't say that, Reginald says. *But the question is of racism, not of the level of right or wrong in the assumption. For instance, would you be offended if I were to assume you identified as Church of England?*

What? Well, no, but that's not the point. Howie said.

Then what is the point? Reginald asked.

And Henry's like. *We're getting off the point.*

But Howie's shouting back. *No! We're nailing this fucking point. The point is I could be offended so therefore the assumption should never be made.*

Then Frank coughed into his hand and said *snowflake*. (Which didn't help but it was funny.)

But Reginald is staying calm, *yes. You are right. The point is that one should never assume. I would suggest that what offence the assumption is causing is the crux of the matter. If you were to assume say a young male from London had a criminal record simply because he was black then yes, that would be racist. But hazarding a guess as to the religious origins of someone may perhaps be a negative stereotype without being racism per se.*

(I've got a LOT of views on this and I really wanted to join in, but Frank beat me to it and said *Bloody hell, Reginald is the smarterest.*

Mr Howie, I understand your views, Henry said. *However, the point is not whether we assume he is Muslim, but if those Muslims assume him to be Muslim, which will then aid our resolution of whatever issue they have.*

Then Howie was telling him to stop speaking like a bloody lawyer. And Henry was telling Howie he is a bloody lawyer.

But Howie was like, *You said you were a spy!*

I said agent. Not spy. And before that I had many roles, one of which was working as an army lawyer, which means I know the best way to resolve issues like this.

Yeah? Well, Tesco gave me two days of diversity training which said, and I quote, that you can fuck off. We're not using Mo. End of.

I did snort a laugh when Howie said that and even Frank smiled, but Henry was getting really cross. *It will help!* he shouted at Howie.

It's the wrong type of help!

How on earth will that be the wrong type of help?

Cos it's the old world type of help that breeds dodgy deals and corruption by tricking people to get what you need. That's why! We're not like that, and I won't do it.

Okay, Howie, Henry said, he was trying to be polite and cool, but he was getting really wound up. *You need to start listening to people with more experience than you. We wouldn't be saying Mo or Bash are Muslims. The perception and assumption will be made by them.*

Okay. So we gonna use Maddox then if we meet some black people? Howie asked him. (And I'm trying to jump in and give my views, but these two are literally not listening to anyone else.)

No. That is completely different. However, given the right circumstances, at the right time, then yes, using the right person to get done what we need to do is absolutely fine.

That's so fucking racist! Howie said.

Diary of Carmen Eze

And by this point Howie and Henry were still tearing chunks out of each other when Paula tapped me on the arm and nodded for me to follow her with Charlie.

I figured I should stay put, but Paula was the XO for Howie's team and I don't know. I just thought what the hell and so I followed her and Charlie over to the three groups down the street. (I did get a quick nod from Frank and clocked him taking a positional step out to get a clear line of fire.)

'Hi! I'm Paula,' Paula said, and she was smiling and so Charlie and I are smiling, and Charlie clocked the way I was holding my rifle low so as not to look threatening and she did the same. 'Is everything okay?' Paula asked while behind us Howie and Henry were still going for it.

'It's not racist!' Henry was shouting. 'Carmen has done it lots of times.'

'That's even worse!' Howie yelled. 'Paula! Tell him that's racist. She'll fucking tell you. She's the most PC person ever. Paula? Paula!?'

And get this.

Seriously. Get this.

Turns out those three groups were fine with each other. It was nothing to do with religion. They were arguing over the best way to go and kill the zombie tigers. But by then Paula was marching back with a face like thunder at Howie and Henry.

Diary of Maddox Doku

And Paula just yelled at them both to pack it in and grow up. Well. She didn't yell, but she meant it. You know when Paula means it.

So we get back into the Saxon and Howie was in the driving seat with Tappy wincing at him slamming the door and grinding the gears.

Did you fucking hear him? Howie asked. *Of all the fucking cheek. That was literally the most racist thing ever. Literally racist. Is Charlie in here?*

She swapped with Mads, Blowers said.

Mads is in here? Mads, you in here? Howie asked. *Was that racist?*

So then I was like, *are you asking me because I'm black?*

Oh shit! He said. *Now I'm being racist. Henry's turned us all racist. Okay, er. Nick! Was that racist?*

But Nick was like, *I'm not the diversity guy.*

And then Clarence said, *actually, diversity stuff is normally covered in the briefing. Nick, make sure you cover diversity stuff in the briefings.*

And I'm not the briefing guy either! Nick said. By which point I was starting to feel a bit stoned from the cannabis plants in the back.

Diary of Carmen Eze

So we get back into our vehicle and the air-con was trying to kick in, but it was weak and it was getting hotter by the minute, and Henry was fuming by that point.

'Did you hear him?' Henry asked as soon as he slammed the door. 'Racist! Me! I am not racist, and I won't be blasted well told that by a Tesco shelf-stacker either. I have never been racist. Carmen. You need to tell Howie I am not racist.'

'Why should I tell him?' I asked.

'Because you're black.'

'But-.'

'Tell him I am not racist and that I was merely pointing out the perception of others when dealing with issues of complex sensitivity. And it wasn't a religious thing either. I have no issues with Muslims.' Then Henry was saying something to Bash in Dari (Probably telling him he doesn't have issue with Muslims.)

But then, I was thinking I hadn't actually seen Bashir praying, and I mentioned that to Henry who said something to Bash. Then, Henry said, 'Bash asked if you are a Christian.'

I said, 'Well. I guess I identify as a Christian, yeah.'

Then Bash said, 'Why aren't *you* praying?' and I said, 'because not all Christians pray.' Then I realised his point, but I was hot and getting annoyed. 'Whatever,' I said. 'Is that air-con on or what?'

'It's on. And I am not racist,' Henry said as we got moving. 'This is rapidly turning into a shower of shit.'

Then I was looking at Frank via the rear-view because Henry <u>never</u> swears, and only when someone <u>really</u> gets under his skin.

Weird day.

Anyway. I am totally not anti-Muslim. I tried telling Bash but he just grinned at me. Whatever. It's fine. I'll get Mo to do it. It's probably better coming from him anyway.

Diary of Paula

. . .

THE UNDEAD TWENTY-FIVE. THE HEAT

DEAR GOD I wanted to throttle the pair of them! Just stood there going at it in the street without even asking what the people wanted. 'Pair of bloody idiots,' I said to Marcy. (Marcy, Charlie, Molly and I were in Roy's van)

'You go sister,' Marcy said to me.

'Honestly!' I said. 'It's just a pissing contest. They might as well get their dicks out and measure them to see who wins.' (Charlie was holding her hands over Molly's ears bless her. Not that Molly seemed to mind. She was staring at Reginald with little hearts in her eyes the whole time.)

'I think Howie's probably got a bigger willy than Henry,' Marcy said. 'Mind you, Henry might be packing a pocket rocket for all we know.'

'Marcy!' Reginald said.

'Oh, sod off, Reggie. Molly can't hear us.'

'But unfortunately, I can. Why aren't you in the Saxon anyway?'

'Cos it stinks of cannabis,' I said.

'From the plants *you* put in there,' Roy said from the front. 'What have you even got them for anyway?'

'To smoke, duh! And this is a woman only chat,' I said before slamming the hatch door closed.

'What about me?' Reginald asked.

'You don't count,' Marcy told him. 'You're like those nerdy alphabet people.'

'Alphabet?' Charlie asked.

'She means A-sexual,' Reginald said as Marcy clicked her fingers.

'Are you A-Sexual, Reggie?' I asked. (I'll be honest. I'd never really given it any thought.)

'And how is that possibly relevant to anything we are doing?' Reginald asked.

'That cannabis really does smell in the Saxon though,' Charlie said.

'Which is why we're in here,' I told her with a wink.

Diary of Maddox Doku

Then Blowers was like, *man, these plants stink!* And we're all agreeing with him.

Why have we even got them? Howie asked from the front. And Clarence said, *Paula wants them, but by all means feel free to tell her to get rid.*

I'm not that bloody stupid, Howie said. *Anyway. Any sign of the princess?* He asked.

Look for a darker patch of sky filled with crows, Tappy said out as Howie and Clarence leant forward to stare up. *She'll be under that... Probably with a strong smell of sulphur and some spooky music.*

Then Howie laughed and called her an idiot but said he was actually looking up. Then he said we should get out and asked Nick for a smoke.

You should give that up. It bloody stinks, Clarence said.

Yeah, cos we smell so nice otherwise, Howie said. Then Paula was coming over with the others and asking to bum a smoke.

You should give that up, Roy told them, and Clarence was like, *that's what I said.*

But Paula said they've got the Panacea in them so fuck it. But Roy said, *it's not just the possible side effects to your health. It's anti-social for a start.*

It's the fucking apocalypse, Howie said. *There is no social.*

Diary of Carmen Eze

So then we were back out of our SUV before the air-con had even kicked in and it was baking! No grass. No trees. No greenery to soak the rays up. Just harsh concrete and glass and heat shimmers.

THE UNDEAD TWENTY-FIVE. THE HEAT

'Any sign of Lilly?' Henry called out as we walked over, and he was back to being cool and calm – or at least trying to be cool and calm.

'Look for the crows,' Tappy said as we all started looking at the sky. 'I'm telling you. Crows. And spooky music.'

Then Bash was bumming a smoke from Nick and lighting up and Roy started moaning.

'Honestly. They're disgusting,' Roy said while pointing at the cigarette in Bashir's hand. 'BAD. MAKE SICK.'

'What the fuck are you doing?' Howie asked while Roy was miming and shouting at Bashir.

'I'm telling him cigarettes are bad.'

'I think he probably knows, mate,' Howie said.

'Maybe he doesn't. Did they even have health warnings in Afghanistan?'

'Yes,' come the replies from those of us that have served in Afghanistan.

'Well. Even so. THEY. ARE. STILL. BAD.'

'What?' Bashir asked in broken English.

'SMOKING. BAD.'

'What?' Bashir asked again, trying to keep a straight face as the others start cracking up.

'He gets it, Roy!' Marcy said. 'You are right though. They do bloody stink. I hate kissing you after you've smoked, Howie.'

'I'll carry a toothbrush.'

'Twat. Just stop smoking. And what if we have babies one day?'

'Eh?'

'Smoking damages sperm.'

'Does it really?' Cookey asked while staring at his lit cigarette.

'Yep. Known fact. Smoking damages the little sperms in your balls. So you carry on gentlemen. Smoke away. I bet Henry's never smoked. Have you ever smoked, Henry?'

'I have not,' Henry said as Howie rolled his eyes.

'Fuck that then,' Cookey said and stubbed his cigarette out. 'Do they get addicted or something?'

'What?' Blowers asked him.

'The sperm. Marcy just said it's bad for their lungs.'

'Sperm don't have lungs you twat.'

'How do they swim then?'

'What!?'

'And it's alright if you've got a small winkle like mine. Imagine the sperm in Danny's balls. They've got to swim miles to get up his willy.'

Then Paula was trying to tell Cookey off, but it was funny and even Frank and Joan were laughing. Henry wasn't though. He was blowing air out through his nose to show displeasure. 'And once again perhaps we can focus on our mission,' he said. 'These constant interruptions are becoming increasingly frustrating. We're not getting anywhere.'

'It's been an organic transition of events,' Clarence said.

'What he said,' Howie said while nodding at Clarence.

'I told you that would catch on, Frank,' I said.

'I didn't get it from Frank,' Clarence said to me. 'Big Chris used to say it.'

'Who do you think told it to Big Chris?' Henry asked.

'Oh, fuck off,' Howie said. 'Did your lot invent farting too? How about air? Was that yours?'

Luckily, that's when another SUV came into view with the Princess and Mary driving. They stopped at the far end of the precinct. (They had to because of the concrete bollards) then they were out and walking towards us.

'Eyes on now, lads,' Henry called out. 'We took a few of Mary's family out yesterday, and this is ripe for an ambush. Sergeant Blowers, I'd ask you to direct your team to watch the first floor and above. My team keep eyes on the ground level. Fan out and stay alert.'

That was awkward because Henry had no right to give orders to Howie's team, but I got the feeling he was getting back at them because I'd gone with Paula. Whatever. It was just awkward. Everyone felt it and I clocked Howie and Clarence sharing a look.

'Just do it,' Howie said. You could see he felt undermined. 'Reggie! Lilly's here.' He shouted then Tappy said she forgot something and ran back to the Saxon just as Reggie and Molly came out of the van.

'All set, my dear? You have Milly's drawings? And your bag? Do come along then. Let's get you to Lilly shall we.'

'Can't I stay with you, Reggie?' Molly asked. It was very sweet with her holding onto his arm and Reggie all smart in his shirt and tie with his sleeves neatly rolled up.

'Oh, come now,' Reginald said. 'You shall see Milly and have a grand old time. And remember what I said. Do you remember, Molly? Tell me what I said.'

'You said no mens can touch me.'

'That's right. No man, or mens, are allowed to touch you. And what do you say if any men do and try and touch you?'

'That Mr Howie is my very good friend, and he will be cross.'

'That's right, Molly. You tell them exactly that. Come along then. And gosh, this heat. I fear we're building towards another storm.'

That guy is something else. Reginald I mean. He's operating on another level than the rest of us anyway. And it was smart too. Molly's only got to mention the name of Howie in the fort and nobody will touch her. But Reginald wasn't just saying it for Molly's benefit. He was telling Henry too.

It was starting to feel like every move was becoming tactical. (Plus he was also right about the weather. There will be one hell of a storm soon.)

Anyway. So the street was silent. And hot. And because of what Henry said about revenge there was this sudden ominous feeling, which wasn't helped by the fact Lilly and Mary had to park way off and walk. And so they were walking. And everything else was silent. Like totally silent.

And right then.

Right at that second when a few of them we're getting the heeby geebies, the whole street filled with the sound of drums. Like orchestral drums all beating slowly with these haunting strings and choir voices, and I was thinking, *that's the music from The Omen*. And we're all turning to the Saxon and Tappy nodding behind the windscreen with the microphone by her mouth. 'Can you smell sulphur yet?'

Of course that set Marcy off, especially at the sight of the Princess and Mary walking in time to the music. Then Charlie snorted a laugh, and the chain reaction kicked in and we were all laughing as Mary did a Howie and detonated. 'YE FECKING TWATS!'

Honestly though. That only made it worse and even I was having to turn away from laughing while Cookey was bent double. 'That's fucking epic,' he said while wiping his eyes.

But the Princess? Now that is one cold cookie. She didn't show a reaction. Nothing. Zero. She didn't look angry or anything. Just cold. (There's a lot of misconceptions about psychopaths. They're not always driven by violence. That's a psychotic episode. A psychopath can also be classed as someone who simply doesn't have remorse. That's the Princess. That's what you see in her eyes.)

Anyway. Then the music cut out. 'Sorry, boss. But that was so worth the bollocking,' Tappy said through the speakers. 'But seriously. Crows. I'm telling you.'

'Tappy!' Paula shouted, but you could tell she was trying not to smile. 'Right. Just some high jinks. No harm, no foul.'

'No foul my fecking arse,' Mary said, and she looked ready to go off on one, but Lilly just said her name and Mary backed down instantly.

Then I clocked the look on Howie's face. He was looking at Mary and it's like he wanted to apologise or something. I'm learning that about Howie. He doesn't hide his emotions. Whatever is on his mind shows on his face. It's endearing and honest and the more time I spend with him, the more I can see why the others follow him.

In the end he didn't say anything. But maybe Mary clocked his expression too because she stayed silent.

Then Reginald was there as polite as ever. 'Is it just you two?' Reginald asked. I could see he'd positioned himself in front of Howie and Paula to take the lead.

'It is,' Lilly said. 'We were told Molly had been subjected to some serious issues.'

'Indeed. That is correct. I would suggest a thorough medical exam, particularly with regard to injuries sustained by repeated penetration of the vagina and anus.'

'Jesus,' Mary said. 'Did ye kill the lads that did it?' she asked Howie. 'Aye. And her own brother was it now?'

'Giles was my half a brother,' Molly said. 'But Milly and Mikey are my whole sister and brother.'

'Mikey?' Lilly asked.

'We think another boy got taken into care,' Howie said. 'Molly? Was Mikey taken into care?'

Molly just nodded and looked sad before telling Mary she liked her hair.

'Aye. Do you now? It's very red is it not? Well anyway. We'll get you home with us. Milly will be chuffed as anything to see you she will.'

'Listen,' Howie said. 'If either of them say where Mikey is give me a shout. We'll try and find him.'

'If we have time,' Henry said as Lilly looked from him to Howie.

'Time for what?' Lilly asked.

'We'll have time,' Howie said.

'Indeed. But perhaps if they do find a location for the other child, they can arrange recovery themselves,' Henry said.

'He's not a car, Henry,' Howie said.

'I am aware he's not a car, Howie. The term is used in reference to collection.'

And Lilly was listening to them and reading the dynamics then bang – she was on Howie like a flash. 'Sure!' she said with a big smile at him. 'If we hear anything, I will let you know, Mr Howie.'

'Thanks. I think,' he said.

'Great. Well. We'll get Molly back. We don't want to keep you from your mission.'

'We're doing that perfectly well on our own,' Henry said.

'What the fuck, mate!' Howie snapped. 'We'll find one.'

'Find one what?' Lilly asked.

'Why are you being nice?' Paula asked Lilly.

'My apologies, Paula. Is this not what you wanted? For us to be cordial and work together?'

'Not like that though you weirdo,' Marcy said. (Love Marcy!)

'Who ye calling a fucking weirdo?' Mary said.

'Fuck me. Okay. Stop,' Howie said. 'This heat. We're all going nuts. We're looking for a control point to-.'

'I'd rather you did not explain our mission objectives, *Mr* Howie,' Henry said.

'What difference does it make? What's she going to do? Run and find one and get them ready? We don't even know where they are.'

'You're looking for a control point, I assume,' Lilly asked.

'See!' Howie said. 'She's a dick, but she's switched on. Yes, Lilly. That's what we're looking for. Which we'd better do before Henry has more kittens.'

'Has Henry got more kittens?' Molly asked. 'I like kittens. Do you like kittens?'

'We have lots of kittens at the fort,' Mary said. 'Seeing as somebody let the cats all free.'

'Anyway. We should return,' Lilly said. 'Tensions are high at the moment. But perhaps what you are looking for is no longer here.'

'Eh?' Howie asked. 'Speak English, Lilly. I'm not as smart as you.'

'You are, Mr Howie. You're one of the smartest men I have ever met,' (what did I say!? Fucking psychotic. And she was holding his eye contact when she said it.) 'But I meant it's very likely there aren't any hordes left around here. I'd suggest you try a new area.'

You could see it on Howie's face that he was struggling with Lilly's change of behaviour. Then a second later he must have realised. 'Oh, fuck off,' he said with a groan. 'Not doing it, Lilly.'

'What?' Paula asked.

'What?' Lilly asked.

'You bloody know what. Pack it in,' Howie said, pointing a finger at her. 'Jesus Christ. She'll run the world one day. I'm telling you. Lilly will run this sodding world. Hopefully not with me in it though. Right, let's bug out.'

'Good seeing you again, Mr Howie. I'm at the end of the radio if you ever need assistance.'

Then Howie stopped and for a second I thought he was going to start frothing at the mouth again, but he just snorted a laugh and shook his head at her. 'You're a dick. Whatever. Bye, Lilly.'

'What's going on?' Paula asked.

'Yeah. What the fuck?' Marcy asked.

'Bye then!' Lilly said before she walked off with Mary and Molly. (It was well-played though. Seriously well-played)

'Honestly. Fucking world's gone mad. Where's Nick?' Howie said as Nick threw the packet of cigarettes over. (I can't work out if it's the same packet or if Nick has lots of packets that all look exactly the same.)

'Er, can someone explain what just happened please,' Marcy asked. 'Why was she being so nice? She just switched like that. Talk about bipolar.'

'I don't think she's the only one,' Henry said. 'And the enemy of my enemy is my friend.'

'That's why,' Howie said nodding at Henry.

Then Paula was like, 'oh Wow. She saw the shit between you and Henry and tried to play you off... What a crafty little bitch.'

'Oh, thank god for that,' Marcy said. 'I thought she was flirting. I was about to poke her eyes out.'

'Get off. She's sixteen,' Howie said.

'So? That young lady has no moral compass whatsoever,' Marcy said before kissing Reggie on the side of his head.

'Good grief. What's that for?'

'For being so good with Molly you weird little nerd. Oh god, he's coming back,' she said as Henry walked over holding a map.

'Howie, do you think there's any validity in what Lilly said?' Henry asked.

'Yeah, probably. It does make sense.'

'Aye. It does,' Clarence said. (He looked seriously undermined too. Like the pair of them were getting slowly worn down.)

'I rather fear it was my responsibility to work that out,' Reginald said. 'My apologies. I have been somewhat pre-occupied, but yes, I would say there is validity in her suggestion.'

'Good. That at least gives us a clear way forward,' Henry said as he tapped the closed map book against his thigh. 'Right. Well, there's a café. We'll set up for a strategy meeting. Troops! Take ten. Nick, Tappy? Can you rig the power supply up please? Sergeant Blowers, I'd suggest you keep your team in the shade wherever possible. That okay with you, Howie?'

It was another step on Howie's toes, but what could Howie do? He'd have looked petty as hell if he'd argued that point.

'And shall I make the coffee again?' Henry asked with a wink at Howie. 'Yours didn't quite turn out so good did it.'

'Sure,' Howie said.

'I'd better get Jess out,' Charlie said into the awkward air.

'Or, perhaps leave her in the air-conditioned trailer,' Henry 'suggested' in that way of his. 'I'd rather like to drink my coffee without getting covered in chocolate powder. If that's okay, of course,' he added with a smile. He's good at it too and Charlie couldn't help but smile back.

She still glanced to Howie. But he just nodded and sagged like he knew he was being outplayed and outclassed. I mean. He could laugh at Lilly, but from Henry it was different.

Seriously. The tension was horrible. I mean it was nasty, and it really did feel like everything was becoming tactical and weird, and unpleasant, and I didn't know how it would end. One thing was very clear though – Howie hated any form of manipulation.

And, like I said, while ALL of that shit was going on, I was starting to get a crush.

I couldn't help it. There was just something about him.

Damn!

26

Reginald's diary

Now I am sure that if you are reading all these accounts from some comfortable position in the future, you will no doubt be also reading the diary entries from some of the others in our team. I have most definitely seen Maddox, Carmen, Charlie and Paula all scribbling away. And, most surprisingly, Dave too. A few more will, I am sure, write their views and accounts out now the day is over, but that will be when they recover. Which may take some time after what we have been through.

The point I am making is thus: as a diary purist, the challenge is to present the events that took place without biased inflection. A diarist can of course, make comment, but the events themselves, the things that happen, they should be accurate and not warped through the lens of the viewer.

That is important to note because as our day wore on the events we experienced became increasingly drastic, and one could be given to think embellishment, or indeed, exaggeration is taking place.

Let me assure that no amount of exaggeration would even begin to describe what we went through. Even if you read the diary entries from the others and think, because of the language, that surely this is made up, I promise you it was not.

But that will be covered in due course. At that stage we still hadn't gained any real traction on the day at all. And by then we were still in Stickleton town centre about to have another coffee. Molly had just been handed over to Lilly and Mary, and Henry was increasing his application of pressure on Howie by the second.

And don't forget, this was still morning. By which time, of course, we'd already travelled through several villages, killed only four infected but also dealt with some truly awful situations. *Viz*; infected tigers, the poor wolf, then of course the incident in the house with Molly.

Howie was just outside the front door puffing on another cigarette while Clarence was sprawled out on a bench nearby, and both of them looked as miserable as the other. Which was very understandable because by then Henry was giving orders to Howie's team and tasking them with jobs, and they, in turn, were responding to him because Henry *is* a natural leader.

That being the problem.

Because so is Howie.

It was inevitable that any suggestion of us working together would cause this exact situation to take place, and that Henry and Howie would butt heads and feel threatened by the other while seeking to take lead.

To put it crudely, a pack can only be led by one wolf – and they are both alpha males.

However, what I didn't bloody well account for was the compression of time and how everything was happening that much faster.

I figured those problems would show out over a period of days, or perhaps weeks, but that bizarre time effect of this new world accelerated and magnified the causal issues to propel the always inevitable confrontation to a head within a matter of hours.

And let me be clear – Henry was winning. Howie could feel it. So could Clarence. As could Paula and I and everyone else.

But also let me be clear that by and large, most of the others were simply not too bothered by the Howie / Henry issue. They figured things would settle down and besides, everyone else really liked both of them.

As I said. By then Howie was outside. Clarence was sweating profusely on a bench, and Henry was in the cafe charming the metaphorical pants off Nick and Tappy by thanking them for getting power into the coffee machine.

'Go and get some fresh air,' Henry told them. 'I'll call you when your drinks are ready, but great work.'

'Cheers, boss!' Nick said while turning away and spotting Howie by the door with a guilty start. 'I meant Henry,' Nick added quickly.

'Awkward,' Tappy murmured, leading Nick across the street to the lads sheltering from the sun and chatting quietly. Shooting the proverbial shit. Chewing the fat. Netflix and chill without the Netflix, or the chill.

Howie stayed where he was. Clarence too. Henry made the drinks. His team sat waiting and Marcy and Paula came out of the toilet. Both with freshly washed faces.

'Need a hand?' Paula asked Henry.

'Tell you what, Paula. Keep an eye on that dial and tell me when she's up to pressure,' Henry said while unfolding the mapbook across a table. 'Howie? Want to take a look?'

'Sure,' Howie said and headed inside with a gentle kick to Clarence's feet.

'Okay, have a look and get your bearings,' Henry said. 'I'll make the coffees then we'll go over where you've been, and where we should try next.'

Henry then walked back to the counter to make more of his perfectly delicious coffee. But that's the kind of man Henry is. A perfectionist. A gifted leader and tactician. An expert in arms. In warfare. In espionage. In law. In many things.

'Do you know where we are by the way?' Henry called over. 'On the map I mean.'

'We know where we are, Henry,' Howie said while most likely without any clue as to where we were. I discreetly tapped our location as Clarence slumped down on a cushioned bench with a long blast of air.

A moment or two later and Henry had the first round made with the lads all bundling inside on being called. Their energy was high too, like I said, they just weren't getting drawn into the Henry / Howie situation. Well, not yet anyway.

'Should have seen her face though,' Cookey said. 'When that music started, and they were both walking. Fucking classic!'

'Totally worth it if I get brew duty,' Tappy said.

'You were very naughty, Natasha,' Henry said, giving her a mock stern look with a quick wink, and again, the skill was effortless as he made the lads all laugh while Tappy blushed lightly from the gently charming rebuke. Even that was awkward though because he'd stepped in and dealt with it like he was their CO, when Tappy wasn't in his team. That was for Paula and Howie to deal with, or Clarence.

But again. What could Howie do? He was being outplayed all along and the more Henry did it, the worse it got.

'Right, my lot. Outside,' Sergeant Blowers ordered.

The second lot of drinks were made and ferried over to the map table. White ceramic mugs topped with thick frothy long-life milk and gently covered with chocolate powder.

But the lack of horse dung on the floor was also noticeable. As was the lack of penises dusted in chocolate powder on the coffees. There was no squabbling or bickering or milk being sprayed all over the show. We'd suddenly gained structure and order – which, perversely, is something I had always wished we'd had, but then when we had it, I found myself missing the chaos of our former ways.

'Right. Where are we then?' Henry asked. He formed it like a question, but again, the implied suggestion was also one of a test.

'We're here,' I said as a big dollop of sweat dripped from Howie's nose.

'Sorry,' he said while smearing it over the map.

Paula passed him a napkin and asked, 'So what do you reckon, Howie?'

'About what?' he asked.

'About what the princess said,' Paula said. 'I mean, it's possible. We have been active in one area for nearly a month.'

'Which area is that specifically?' Henry asked.

'I don't know. I can't read a map,' Howie said.

I know Howie meant it as a quip, but it fell flat. It was too hot, and the energy was weird and wrong.

'Didn't you get the map reading badge at scouts, nipper?' Frank asked into the awkward silence.

'I didn't go to scouts. I worked at Tesco,' Howie said.

'I've been keeping track,' I said quickly.

'Do you know what?' Marcy said, standing up from the table. 'This is all very exciting but I'm going.'

'Going where?' Paula asked.

'To loot the posh department store over the road and avoid whatever weird shit this is turning into,' Marcy replied, waving a hand at Henry and Howie.

I've said it before, but while I detest many of Marcy's qualities, she is also highly complex. Defined as it were by her beauty and in a way accepting that's what people see when they look at her, and not her often profound intelligence. Marcy is also a highly accurate barometer for social situations and reading people. An empath if you like, but also very direct, and I admire her bravery and being strong enough to openly confront the issues, while also tapping into the mood of the day and what most of the others were feeling – that this was a Howie and Henry thing. <u>Not a group thing</u>. I'm stressing that point because of what came shortly after.

'Paula? You coming?' Marcy asked.

'No, you carry on. I'll sort this out with Howie.'

'Fair enough. Carmen? Fancy it?' Marcy asked.

'Me?' Carmen asked. 'Er, I guess,' she said, getting a nod from Henry.

'Joanie?' Marcy asked.

'No, thank you. I'm quite content in here.'

'I'll head out for some air too,' Frank said, following the others towards the door.

Diary of Maddox Doku

Man. It was hot. I am talking hot. I was outside on a bench drinking water while the others were all drinking the strong coffees Henry made. Having a coffee first thing is great. It gets you going. But after that, and in this heat, I'm all about the water. Trust me. I drink bottles of the stuff. Dave is right. Hydration *is* essential.

Yeah. So we're all outside avoiding the Howie / Henry vibe going on, which was getting awkward AF, when Marcy comes out with Carmen.

They finished already? Blowers asked her.

God no. They haven't even started yet, Marcy says.

Where you going then? Cookey asked.

To loot that, Marcy said, pointing at the department store. *Coming ladies?*

That's sexist, Cookey said as Charlie and Tappy rushed after Marcy and Carmen.

Yep, Marcy said.

But then Booker was like, *I might go and have a mooch actually,* and he sets off after them and I'm watching him go by thinking there is something seriously off with this guy. I can just feel it. So then I'm all casual and acting like I need to get out of the sun.

I need some shade, I said to the lads. They just grunted and sipped hot coffee on a hot day. Whatever. I followed Booker in and clocked Frank coming out of the café minding his own business.

Which is because Frank is trained to follow people, and I wasn't.

THE UNDEAD TWENTY-FIVE. THE HEAT

Reginald's Diary

In fairness, it was blisteringly hot in that damned café so you can't blame poor Howie, but he was dripping sweat all over the map, which was only making him more embarrassed as he tried to clean it up.

I carried on showing Henry the geographical boundaries of where we had been focussing thus far. 'So I would say this area within the south east has been our predominant area of operations, Henry.'

'Understood,' Henry said. 'Have you been as far east as Crawley?'

I said we had not, and we were not a big enough team to take on towns of that size. That said, I explained I was confident that the sheer volume of numbers we had faced meant a large number of hosts must have been drawn from those cities.

'But without checking we cannot be sure on that. So let's stick to what we know for fact,' Henry said – his tone had changed by then. Only subtly. But the charm had gone because the lads were all outside and so he felt safe in starting to push buttons again. 'In summary then. This rural, unpopulated area has been mostly cleared to the best of your knowledge. However, some pockets may remain, and we cannot be sure the enemy hasn't back-flooded once you've moved on.'

'There would be no reason for it do so,' I said. 'This isn't an invading army. They're driven to seek more hosts, not to take ground.'

'I understand that, Reginald. But only fools make assumptions in warfare.'

'Reggie isn't a fool,' Howie said.

'I never said he was, Howie. Don't bridle so easily. I didn't think you were this sensitive.'

'I'm not fucking sensitive!'

'Guys,' Paula said, exhaling a blast of air. 'Please. It's getting draining.'

'Of course, Paula. My apologies. I shall monitor my tone around Howie for fear of upsetting him.'

'Fuck you!' Howie said.

'Howie!' Paula said.

'He's doing it on fucking purpose,' Howie said. 'Fine. Okay. Whatever. Let's just look at the map. And yes, we've cleared most of that area I'd say. Clarence?'

'Yep,' Clarence said, staring over from his seat.

'But it hasn't been systematic or anything,' Howie added. 'We've been mostly reactive and dealing with what we find.'

'Such as today. Yes?' Henry asked. 'So, you're saying that you've been reacting to situations arising from the constant stops and interruptions which has largely dictated your haphazard route throughout this area.'

'Yes,' Howie said with forced patience.

'Henry. Don't goad the situation,' Paula said.

'I'm not goading anyone, and not every word I say is aimed as a criticism.'

'Why does it feel like it then?' Paula asked. 'You've come in a month after us. We've been through hell.'

'I am aware of that. But I cannot keep stopping to say well done, and how brave you've all been.'

'Fuck me,' Paula said, 'I'm sorry, Howie. I need some air. This bloody heat.'

I stayed silent, but I was monitoring the situation very closely, and I could see that Henry *was* doing it on purpose. He was steering that situation how he wanted it steered to bring it to a head and make his play.

Paula stormed off and slammed a chair out of her way. But credit to her. She stopped within a few steps, took a breath and came back to the table. 'You know what? I'm not going to flounce. We just need to work together and get this done.'

She could sense it happening. Henry's play I mean. And she was desperately trying to avoid the trap he was leading them into.

I was expecting Henry to push it harder, and no doubt he would have done. Except even he didn't factor for Joan.

'We *all* need to work together,' Joan said before Henry or anyone else could speak. 'Howie, go and rinse your head off. And you, Clarence. And Henry, please watch your tone. It's becoming inflammatory.'

It was a much needed intervention, and it worked as we all complied with her instructions.

But sadly, even Joan couldn't hold off the inevitable for more than a few moments.

Diary of Carmen Eze

It was nice to be away from the Howie and Henry thing, and I don't know, I guess I felt a need to do some normal woman things and mooch through stores and look at stuff. I didn't have female friends in my world, and the more I got to know Marcy, Charlie, Tappy and Paula the more I really liked them.

So yeah. I was happy to get out of the café and go *loot some shit* as Marcy called it. I even broke the lock on the main door for them so we could get inside without smashing through the plate glass doors.

'That was hot,' Marcy said, giving me a wink when I pushed the doors open. I laughed at her jokey flirt, remembering the kiss we'd shared, and we headed inside to the only ever so slightly cooler shade.

Marcy then stopped in the main corridor and stared at all the glass walls with a big sigh. 'Heaven,' she said. 'Honestly. I couldn't sit there listening to Howie and Henry arguing again.'

I knew what she meant. It was becoming draining, and in truth, I didn't want to try and split Howie's team up for Henry. I just wanted the two idiots to get along. We all did.

Anyway. So we headed further inside and I clocked Booker coming in behind us giving our backsides a good look. But, without sounding cocky or arrogant, you kinda get that a lot as a woman, and he is a young man, plus it was so hot outside so you can't blame him seeking shade.

Not that Marcy noticed. Or if she did, she didn't show it. She just made a beeline for the jewellery section.

'Is that a cock ring?' Tappy asked, peering into a case. 'It is. That's a cock ring.'

'How can you tell?' Charlie asked.

'They're normally bigger than a finger ring. My ex had one. He was a tattoo artist. And also a cock.'

'A cock with a cock ring,' Charlie said.

'Trust me. They're not always bigger than a finger,' Marcy said to a few snorts of laughter. 'But anyway. So what was Neal like, Carmen?'

'I like how you went from cock rings to my dead ex-lover,' I said.

'I know, right. Smooth or what,' Marcy said while offering a smile to show she meant no offence. 'Sorry. I can be really blunt sometimes.'

'It's fine. Neal was a nice guy,' I said, but in truth I was confused. I even said that to them, which is very rare for me to ever discuss something personal. I said it was complicated and that I liked him a lot, but hearing it retold from Neal's point of view like that. You know, this morning in the café. That was really hard. I guess I did use him, but I liked him too. I don't know. Like I said, it's complicated. What I didn't tell them about was the crush I was getting because even I couldn't give voice to that yet.

'Shit,' Tappy said into the silence that followed. 'He must have a lot of mayonnaise though to get it on your ear.'

I smiled at the joke as Marcy gave that big smile she does. 'Hey,' she said. 'You know what? Let's go and look at make-up. Charlie, you coming?'

Charlie nodded but paused as she looked at herself in a glass window then walked out after us as we passed Maddox and Frank sitting on a bench in the middle, and you know what? I felt guilty because I knew what Frank would be doing.

Diary of Maddox Doku

. . .

THE UNDEAD TWENTY-FIVE. THE HEAT

So then Frank comes over and sits down next to me on the bench in the central aisle of the department store. I figured he just wanted somewhere cool to sit, but it was good actually cos it made it look like we were chatting while I was secretly spying on Booker.

You don't get on with the others then, Frank said, as though making idle conversation.

What makes you say that? I asked.

You never hang out with them, and what's with that other lad?

Who?

Him, Frank said, nodding over to Booker. *You either fancy him, or you've got a bee stuck up your arse by the way you're staring at him all the time.*

Like I said. Frank was trained. I wasn't, and apparently that showed. I mean. Like really showed.

Don't know what you're on about. I said, cos rule number 1 is deny everything.

Fair enough, Frank said. *Just making conversation.*

Sure.

But if I'm noticing then he will too.

Got it. Thanks for the advice. Cos rule number 2 is don't invite small talk. Keep people at a distance.

Don't do that lad. Being surly plays into the stereotypical view of an angry young black man with a chip on his shoulder. Mind you. What the hell do I know? I'm old and I stink of piss apparently.

I stayed silent, cos rule number 3 – see rule number 2. Anyway, I was trying to see where Booker had gone.

Jesus. Make it more obvious, nipper.

What? I asked, too absorbed in trying to watch Booker to listen properly.

This is painful, Frank said with a tut as he got to his feet. *Come on. I'll show you how it's done.*

How what's done? I asked.

How to follow someone.

Diary of Reginald

A few moments later Howie and Clarence came out of the toilet after rinsing their heads off. Not that you'd notice with the poor chaps still sweating so much. I'd just explained to Henry that Hinchley Point was not in *our* area so to speak, and we cleared a good 20k. So yes. Lilly *was* right. Finding a new control point meant moving out of this area.

Henry nodded while studying the map. 'I see. Well, our options are heading east towards Crawley. Or north. But once we hit the Guildford line, we're into urban warfare territory. That said, didn't you tell me you'd been into London?'

'Howie and Clarence have. I wasn't with them then,' I said. 'Neither was Paula, and I'm not convinced the infection hadn't separated into the factions it has now. In fact. I'd suggest that Darren was the first step in that evolution.'

'Let's keep on topic shall we,' Henry said, tapping the map. 'It's easy to go off on tangents.'

'It's not a tangent, Henry. You asked if we'd been into London,' I said.

'And we've covered it now so we can move on. No offence but today has shown me how easy it is for you chaps to get side-tracked,' Henry said.

And right there I knew what I had to do. Because the silly man was not only trying to outplay Howie, he was trying to do it to me.

Which was never going to work.

And so, having picked my time, I decided to make my own play, and in so doing I adopted an air of confused hurt, as though Henry's words had caused personal offence. Which I knew would provoke Howie into defending me. Which is what I wanted, because like I said, I had just taken control of the situation.

'Dude. Do not speak to Reggie like that,' Howie said firmly.

'My name isn't dude,' Henry said with distaste. 'We need to focus please. North is ruled out. South is the coastline. Yes, there are some cities, but as you pointed out, getting drawn into an urban combat

THE UNDEAD TWENTY-FIVE. THE HEAT

situation should be avoided wherever possible. That leaves east or west. And after a professional assessment I have concluded that proceeding in a westerly direction is the correct course of action.'

'Right. Great work,' Howie said with some energy back into his voice. 'Wish we'd thought of that. Which part of the west do you want to try? The whole west? Some of the west?'

'Listen, Howie,' Henry said, his tone becoming tight again as he peered up while leaning over the map. 'If you carry on like this then our agreement will not be a viable option.'

'Don't put this all on me, Henry. You keep dropping little bombs and being a dick.'

'Do not call me a dick!'

'Stop acting like one then. And stop undermining me so you can cherry pick some of my team. What? Did you think I hadn't noticed?'

'Trust me. They'd stand a better chance with me in charge.'

'But you're not in charge, Henry. You fucking hid for a month while we got busy.'

'Not this again you insufferable idiot.'

'Fuck you!'

'Jesus Christ. I give up,' Paula said, flopping down next to Clarence as Howie and Henry started going at each other again.

Which is exactly what I wanted, because it meant Howie would keep Henry busy while I scarpered back to my van to show Henry what manipulation really looked like.

(Don't _ever_ try and patronise me.)

DIARY OF CHARLOTTE DOYLE

AFTER LEAVING the jewellery section I was starting to feel an insecurity I had never experienced before.

We then headed into the cosmetics department and started walking slowly past the shelves filled with the most weird and wonderful colours and products all used to promote beauty, and that feeling was coming on stronger. There were mirrors everywhere, and with each one we passed I was looking to my own flaws while seeing the outward beauty of the people I was with.

'I've always wondered actually,' Marcy said, coming to a stop as she viewed the foundations and concealers. 'Is it hard to match up for black skin? These are all shaded towards white people, aren't they?'

'It's a bloody nightmare,' Carmen said. 'It has got better, and London has a huge black population, so the stores are more geared up, but it's still nothing like the range for white girls. Do you struggle, Charlie?'

'I'm mixed race so it's not so bad for me,' I said.

'And you don't need make-up,' Marcy told me. 'Your skin is flawless.'

I said thank you and took the compliment in good grace while staring at the scars and my shaved head while wondering why Cookey hadn't even tried to kiss me yet. His signals were so strong sometimes, but nothing ever came of it – and I was perhaps now understanding why.

'What did you do before this, Carmen?' Marcy asked. 'I don't mean now. I mean, you know, before Henry or whatever.'

'I was a prostitute,' Carmen said as something clanged at the end of the aisle, and we all turned to see Booker hopping by with a strange look.

'Tripped,' he called out. 'Soz.'

'Whatever,' Marcy said, looking back at Carmen. 'But what the what now? Were you being serious?'

'Yup,' she said, smiling at our stunned expressions. 'I say prostitute. I was an escort.'

'I… But… Fuck, really?' Marcy said. 'I've got so many questions right now.'

'Let me guess. Why did I do it? Did I make good money, and why did I stop?' Carmen asked as we all nodded in unison. 'I was young, broke, and I thought it was something I could control. Yes, I did make good money, but I spent it on partying. And I stopped when I realised

I wasn't in control and almost got raped by a group of men. Which, incidentally, is how I met Frank. The men were Russian gangsters under observation and Frank came in and shot them all. Then Kyle came in and shouted at Frank. Then I met Henry who told them both off, then a week later Henry recruited me.'

'Wow. That is the best story ever,' Marcy said, in obvious awe. 'Honestly, I did think about it once. You know. Escorting. But...'

'You didn't want be a slut?' Carmen asked.

'No! I wasn't going to say that. I meant, I'm actually not that sexually experienced. Howie's like the fourth guy I've been with, urgh, five including Darren but we're totally discounting him as I was brainwashed at the time – but yeah, the idea just kinda frightened me. I know, right. The way I act you'd think it was dozens. What about you?' she asked Tappy.

'Er. Maybe four? Definitely three. There was one when I was very drunk, which was naughty as I don't remember saying yes. And then Nick. So four. Charlie?'

'Just one,' I said. 'My ex-boyfriend.'

'What about Cookey?' Carmen asked. 'I thought you two were...'

'Er, yeah. Not sure on that front,'

Diary of Maddox Doku

So then Frank literally delivered the fundamentals of foot surveillance within a few minutes while we're walking about the department store following Booker.

And you know what? I loved it. I mean. I seriously loved it.

Frank was telling me that foot surveillance is best done by at least two people, or better with a whole team. One person stays close to the target, and the others all hang back, then they swap over at key points, like at junctions. That way, if the target looks back, they won't see the same person twice.

Frank was then telling me that a smaller team will carry disguises such as reversible jackets, or baseball caps, or other things to change their profile. But you have to be careful not to stand out or say for instance carry a bag that isn't from a store in that area. He said you never look directly at the target, so that any given point, if the target suddenly turns you won't feel the need to react and look away or act innocent.

What really helped was telling me what to look for if I thought I was being followed. I knew some of these from dealing. But Frank said to stop abruptly and look back. Reversing your course. Stopping quickly after turning a corner. Watching reflections in windows. Entering a building then leaving quickly from another exit. Dropping a bit of trash paper to see if anyone picks it up. And cos he said those are things to do when you think someone is following you, it then makes you think what to do when you're following someone else.

And all this time, we're doing that exact same thing as we mooch on behind Booker. We're looking at crap in display cases. Stopping to gawp at clothes in window displays. Leaning against shelves. Then Frank is going off to look through menswear while I get in a bit closer until Booker passed the junction between cosmetics and clothes at which point I veered off into clothing and Frank went closer.

I loved it! Then I was meeting up with Frank who had found a point next to a wall of glass fronted cases.

What's he doing? I asked as Booker stopped with his mouth hanging open, then he jolted forward into a shelf and hopped past the aisle that the ladies were in.

Rubbing his knee by the looks of it. Why are you bothered anyway, nipper? Frank said.

Don't know. Just something about him.

Anyway. It's not about hiding, Frank said, and he was giving me this weird look. *People look guilty when they hide. But then I reckon you won't struggle with that, eh, Mr Doku. Guilt's not on your radar is it. What did you do before this?*

Then I got all defensive, cos see rule 1 and 2. *This and that,* I said.

What? Like dealing drugs and enforcing debts for the bossman? That kind of thing?

I was like, *how the fuck?*

I've got that way about me, lad. People like to tell me things. Like how you blew a kid's head off with a shotgun in your compound, and how you tried to take Mr Howie on. Don't glare at me, nipper. I don't like angry eyes.

I was fronting up when he said that. Then I remembered Carmen saying how dangerous Frank McGill was so I backed off.

Anyway, nipper. Let's find another spot cos your mate's on the move.

I said Booker wasn't my mate.

And there's your problem. Try being nice. Booker might open up like all the people in the fort did who told me about you.

So then I'm trying to front up again, but I'm also annoyed that I didn't think of it myself. Then I'm thinking it's a good idea, so I'll go and be nice and I set off towards Booker. But Frank grabbed my arm.

Not now you bloody idiot!

Why not?

Because you'll go over with a big smile and ask him why he's perving. That's henchman tactics. It unnerves people. You need to play the long game.

I asked how but he just winked and walked off.

First lesson was for free, lad. After that you need to pay.

Diary of Paula

Honestly. It was just awful, but the mistake Henry made was making a nasty remark to Reginald, because by then Howie looked drained and ready to concede, but the merest mention of someone having a go at Reginald set Howie off and bang! There we were with H & H going at it again, only this time it was a thousand times worse.

'You fucking hid!'

'We didn't hide, Howie. We had a strategy. Which is what comes from having experience and training.'

'Okay. Well, while you hid, we were out here gripping it and getting experience.'

'Gripping what? What exactly have you gripped?'

'IT!'

'You fought back and killed a few. Well done, but that's it. That is the sum total of your achievement. And forgive me saying it but you also failed to run the fort and left it to a sixteen year old girl.'

'It wasn't like that,' Howie said through gritted teeth.

'I'm sorry, Howie. But the only reason you are alive is because Howard told Dave to keep an eye on you. Which has enabled you to get out of control-.'

'We are not out of control!'

'You, Howie. Not your team. There is a distinction. You are out of control and if you keep leading these people you will get them killed.'

The strangest thing is that Reginald wasn't getting involved. He was being all passive, whereas before whenever Henry got pushy Reggie wiped the floor with him. Except he wasn't doing it – but then I figured it was the heat. I can't begin to describe what heat like that does to someone.

Then Reggie was pulling back from the table with an apologetic wince like it was all too much for him. 'Would you excuse me, chaps. I might step outside for a few moments. Getting a bit warm.'

And he toddled off, but then a second later I was back to watching H & H tearing chunks out of each other.

Diary of Carmen Eze

By then we'd found our way into the perfume store area because they wanted to find the aftershave Henry uses. Marcy kept asking me, but I said I don't know. I said Henry was a very private man and we just don't ever talk about things like that.

Anyway. So then we get inside with Marcy grabbing at some

THE UNDEAD TWENTY-FIVE. THE HEAT

bottles to spray about with Charlie, Tappy and I all sniffing the air trying to see if it's Henry's. But we all got carried away and we're all spraying aftershaves all over the place. On our wrists. In the air. Over each other. It sounds childish and stupid now, but it was funny. Tappy's got an infectious laugh. Marcy's just a hoot and has zero fear. Charlie was very quiet, but she started to giggle along. It was just nice. And it stands out in my mind - especially with what came after.

The thing that really got us laughing though was how we all started sneezing, but we just carried on spraying bottles to sniff and sneeze and the more we did it the more we laughed and got carried away.

Diary of Maddox Doku

So Frank just walks off, which is a good thing because there was like a cloud of perfumed gas rolling out of the fragrance section. I did take a quick peek as I went after Frank and saw Charlie, Marcy, Tappy and Carmen all pissing themselves with laughter. Spraying aftershaves or whatever on each other's heads while sneezing and rubbing at their eyes.

Then I'm running after Frank asking what he meant by that as he reaches the bench outside and sits down to stare up at the sun like all chilled and calm.

You said the first one was for free. What did that mean? I asked him.

You're blocking the sun, he said. *Just sit down and relax.*

I sat down. But only because I wanted to. Not because he told me.

You've got to learn to let it go, nipper.

Let what go?

It.

Then I was sucking air in and biting down the urge to tell Frank to stop fucking about. It was so hot too.

A good agent needs to know when to relax, Frank said a moment later.

You can't do what we do and get tense about it. You'll blow your own brains out. Or someone else's.

What does that mean? 'Do what we do.' Are you offering me a job?

Henry said you'd be a fast learner, Frank said. *I wasn't so sure. I thought you'd be a cocky cunt. Arrogant too. You're a big lad and probably used to getting your own way. And winning too probably. Apart from the almighty fuck ups with your crews that got killed. And picking a fight with Howie and his lot that is. How did that work out for you by the way?*

I thought about what he said and rule #1 which was to deny everything. Then I'm figuring maybe I could break that rule. *Badly*, I said.

Why?

I looked at him while thinking about rule 1 again. *That I fucked up.*

We all fuck up, lad. I'll tell you about Mogadishu one day. The point is a good agent learns from those mistakes, which means you need humility. And I'm not sure you have any.

I told him *humility is a weakness where I'm from.*

And teatime is dinner time where I'm from. We're all from somewhere, nipper.

Then I'm trying to extrapolate the situation and think what it all means, then I'm thinking I should show humility with words. But then I'm thinking maybe I should shut the fuck up and say nothing at all. Which I think was the right thing to do as Frank just gave me this nod – but then Reggie was running out of the café looking all flappy.

Good gosh. Oh my, oh my, he said. *They're at it again, lads. Having a right old barney as Marcy would say.*

Yeah, Blowers said while staring over to the cafe. *Reggie, I'm not speaking out of turn, but is this a good idea us all working together?*

Nobody could ever accuse you of speaking out of turn, Simon, Reginald said, booting his desk monitor up. *Nick, grab the drone, would you. And in answer to your question, sergeant. Yes. It is a good idea us working together.*

Launching in three, two.... One, Nick said as Booker came out from the department store sneezing hard and wafting the air under his nose.

Fuck me. It's like mustard gas in there. It's worse than your arse, Cookey.

THE UNDEAD TWENTY-FIVE. THE HEAT

So then I'm thinking about what Frank said about being nice and I'm like, *Hey bro!* to Booker and giving him a smile. But he just gives me this look. *What's up with you?* He asked.

Nothing. Just saying hello. They still spraying perfumes then..

Yes. Anyway. I'm going over there, Booker said before walking off.

Smooth as silk, Frank said quietly. *Just get on your knees next time and offer him a blowjob.*

I can't stand not getting things right and so I was smarting a bit and feeling stupid.

Don't beat yourself up, Frank said. *Just go over and join them but be you.*

It'll be awkward, I told him.

Only if you make it awkward. It's about energy, nipper. People give off an energy when they want something. Go over but get it in your head that you don't want anything from them. You're just hanging out. That's it.

Why you telling me this? You offering me a job?

Haven't you heard? It's the end of the world. Money is worthless and there are no jobs.

I'm not spying on Howie for you.

Good for you. Now piss off because I need to fart, Frank said before lifting an arse cheek and farting noisily as the lads turned to look. *Now you've got an excuse*, he whispered.

Fuck me! I said and I was up and moving off with a look of distaste.

Has he shit himself? Cookey called over. *You followed through, Frank?*

I might have done, nipper.

I need some refuge, I said and walked over into the middle of the lads and did what Frank said. I changed my energy so I didn't want anything. It worked too. I just stood there and none of them even looked twice at me. Not even Booker - but that also might be because the shouting in the café got worse

---

DIARY OF PAULA

. . .

AND IT JUST KEPT GETTING WORSE. THE pair of them were really going for it with an escalation that was only going up. The weird thing is that we've all seen Howie get angry. Jesus. His rage pretty much drives us on, and he was angry then, but it wasn't the rage he has inside to kill the infected. This was like a normal anger. It probably doesn't make sense, but it wasn't the violent Howie shouting. It was an infuriated pissed off hot Howie. And there's a big difference, because if Howie had detonated properly then I wouldn't be writing this now.

We'd all be dead.

But my worry right then was that it was heading towards that level of escalation, and I had no idea what to do. I was as drained as Clarence. Exhausted with sweat pouring my face.

'You do not have the experience, training, or understanding of what you are doing,' Henry said while bracing his hands and leaning over the table. 'That is painfully obvious just from today.'

'You can fuck right off,' Howie said. He told me later he was just as furious at himself for not being able to formulate better responses and sound eloquent like Henry.

'The only reason you are still alive is because of that man,' Henry said, pointing at Dave. 'Make no mistake about it, and you need to seriously consider continually leading your people into harm with no viable exit strategy.'

'What fucking exit strategy? It's not politics, Henry. We're killing the zombies so they don't get smart and kill everyone else.'

'Just calling them zombies makes you an imbecile!'

'Don't even think about picking me up on my choice of words you racist throwback fuck!'

DIARY OF REGINALD

NICK THEN LAUNCHED THE DRONE, by which time Maddox had come over to escape the foul gases emitted by Frank. Although I will say at this point that Maddox had been acting strangely all day. I did wonder if Henry was trying to get him on his side. (It's what I would do.) Maddox isn't one of our direct team. He's not *one of Howie's* so to speak.

However, I didn't have time to deal with that as my concern was focussed on the increasing volume of Howie and Henry inside the café. Not just the loudness but the rising anger within their tones. There were by now exchanging open accusations.

Whatever the causal reasons, the situation was upon us, and, as I mentioned, I was taking control before either Henry or anyone else could stop me doing what we needed to do.

'We're up, Reggie,' Nick said to me, and I could see on the monitor that the drone was already rising. 'Which way?' Nick asked.

That was the pickle for me. Because I knew which way to go. But I also knew that once we started on that route there would be no turning back – and I wasn't entirely sure we were ready for it.

But I had to make a decision, and judging by the voices from the café, we weren't that far from reaching the point of detonation. And if left unchecked it would force everyone else to take sides. That's where the danger lies, because they're all armed and ready to fight. Idealistic people are always like that. They like drawing a line in the sand and puffing their chests out.

That's how wars start, and if that war started then the game would finish right there.

'YOU KNOW WHAT, HENRY. THIS WAS A FUCKING MISTAKE,' Howie's voice sailed out as I looked down at my map, trying to determine if this was really what I wanted to do.

'I couldn't agree more!' Henry shouted back.

'WE'LL FIND IT ON OUR OWN,' Howie yelled.

'We blasted well won't, Howie,' I said to myself.

'Which way, Reggie?' Nick asked as the shouting went up a notch in the café.

'Jesus, they're gonna start brawling in a minute,' Blowers said.

The other thing of course, and the reason I didn't give an instant direction, is that I needed it to look like I was choosing it right then, because Frank was watching me closely.

And so I nodded, pursed my lips, exhaled a few times and finally looked up. 'Go east. And Nick? Give it some welly would you, there's a good chap.'

Diary of Carmen Eze

I felt so bad about it. I still do. But we just got carried away.

'One more!' Marcy said with tears streaming down her cheeks as she sprayed from another bottle.

We were all laughing and crying and sneezing at the same time. It was so stupid, but in our defence, it was just meant to be innocent fun.

'Don't spray another one, Marcy,' Tappy said as Marcy tried another one.

'That's it!' Marcy said. 'That's the one. Just sniff it. Come on, just sniff it. Here, I'll spray it on you.'

'Get off!' Charlie said when Marcy started spraying her. 'Oh god that's so strong. I can't stop sneezing.'

'I can't even see,' I said. That's when we heard it. A voice at the door saying, 'er, excuse me.'

But it was nerdy and male, and we tried to turn and look, but we just set off laughing again because we knew it was one of the lads being stupid – but we couldn't actually see anything because of the amount of perfume in the air.

Diary of Maddox Doku

Then Howie was like, *YOU CAN FUCK OFF!* And he was getting seriously pissed.

We'll have to get Marcy to calm him down, Blowers said. *Danny, run and grab and her. Tell her the boss is about to kick off.*

Which would be a very silly thing to do, Frank said from the bench, making them all look over to see him staring back as calm as ever, but with his rifle resting across his knees.

DIARY OF CARMEN EZE,

WE WERE LAUGHING TOO MUCH, and because of the aftershaves we couldn't see clearly, and so Tappy said, 'Don't come in!' to whoever was at the door. But she meant it funny. As in *it stinks in here.*

'Yeah, sorry. I er, I thought you might be soldiers,' the voice said, which is when we *all* realised it wasn't one of the lads and there was a middle aged man standing in the doorway looking nervous as anything.

'Oh shit,' Marcy said. 'Where did you come from?' she asked as the rest of us commenced another fit of sneezing.

'I er, I worked here,' the man said. 'I've been staying out the back…' he trailed off, staring at our guns and looking worried at us all sneezing and laughing.

'God, I'm so sorry. Hang on. Let us get out. Where's my radio? I can't even see my radio,' I said in a way that set the other three off laughing again. 'My bloody eyes. Whose idea was this?'

'Marcy's,' Tappy and Charlie said together.

'Snitches get stitches,' Marcy said, before sneezing and laughing again. 'Sorry, we were looking for some aftershave,' she said as we walked out.

'Sure,' the man said as Danny ran in through the main door.

'Marcy! Blowers said the boss is kicking off with Henry.'

'That's nothing new, Danny.'

'No, but Henry's telling the boss he has to quit and stand down and Reggie's got the drone up and Frank said-.'

'Danny. Slow down. Howie's not the type to start brawling,' Marcy said as she turned back to the man. 'You just hang on here for a sec... Oh god... Oh god...' then she lets rip with this huge sneeze, but she turned away and covered her mouth. I saw it. 'Way too many perfumes,' she told the guy. 'Anyway. Well done ladies! Be right back.'

But then I don't know. I'm guessing the air displaced when Danny pushed the door open caused a draft that swept through and caught the moisture particles expunged from Marcy. I mean – it couldn't have been anything more than a quick soft breeze, but it was enough to get a few of those droplets directly into the face of the man standing well over two metres away from her.

I'm guessing he didn't even feel it, because he didn't wipe his mouth or face, and the only thing we knew was when he takes a sudden lurch back.

'Hey, you okay?' Tappy asked him as he slumped back again with a grunt of pain. 'Oh shit, is he having a heart attack?'

'Eh?' Marcy said, spinning back around as the guy dropped to the floor.

'Get Roy!' Tappy shouted, trying to tug at her radio.

'Oh god no,' Marcy said, and she was already running back to the man. 'Please no... He's turning.'

'Is he bit?' I asked, drawing my pistol because I hadn't connected the dots right then.

'No! I sneezed.'

'What!?'

'I sneezed on him. Oh god. Oh shit. Howie's gonna go mental,' Marcy said as the guy starting writhing in agony. 'Er, hi, listen, I am so sorry,' she yelled at him, looking all panicked and worried. Then she grabbed her radio. 'Howie! I need you here!'

DIARY OF PAULA

. . .

THEN RIGHT WHEN they were almost chest to chest, Marcy's screaming through the radio that she needs Howie.

We're all up and running and out of the café into the street to see Blowers and the rest already sprinting across the road into the department store. Even Nick shoved his beloved drone controller at Reggie and started running – because honestly, none of us have ever heard Marcy sound so panicked.

We get inside the department store, and it took a second or two to adjust from the sunlight outside to the darkness inside, but we're all running up the corridor to see Carmen, Tappy, Charlie and Marcy all gathered about a man clutching his stomach in way we all knew.

'Who bit him?' Howie demanded. 'Where are they? Everyone spread out. Eyes up. Dave, take point. Get into the store,' he ordered while drawing his pistol as Marcy rushed to block him. 'What the hell are you doing? Move out the way, Marcy! They must be in here.'

'Howie, listen. He didn't get bit. I sneezed.'

'What!?'

'I sneezed on him.'

'What the shit,' Howie said, blinking as the others stopped running past.

'Jesus, Marcy,' I said.

'We were spraying perfumes and I sneezed on him,' Marcy says with tears running down her cheeks.

'Fucking hell,' Howie said dropping to the guy's side.

'Hurts,' the guy said.

'It's okay. You're going to be okay,' Howie said, taking his hand. 'Listen to me. It's going to be fine. Roy! Do something.'

'Like what?' Roy asked. 'Take his bloody temperature?'

'Give him morphine or something.'

'Might be a bit late for that,' Roy said as the man gave one final grunt then fell still.

'Fuck me,' Howie groaned, leaning over him. 'Are you sure, Marcy?'

'I...I... I don't know! I covered my mouth.'

'He wasn't even close,' Tappy said. 'Honestly, he was like five metres away.'

'Maybe it's not that,' Howie said. 'I mean. He's a bit fat isn't he. Maybe it's a heart-attack or something. Holy shit!' he cried out as the guy sat up and opened his red bloodshot eyes. 'Okay. Definitely not a heart-attack.'

'Shit, Marcy,' I said. 'You just made a zombie.'

'Paula, don't. I'm so sorry,' Marcy said trying to beg forgiveness while also clearly feeling that rush from the connection that comes when she takes her own hosts.

'You don't look bloody sorry,' Roy said.

'I am! It's the thing,' Marcy said, flapping her hands. 'Honestly. I'm so sorry. Oh god.'

'You just made a zombie,' I said again, looking from the guy to Marcy.

'Stop saying that!'

'But you did.'

'I sneezed. It wasn't my fault. No, it was my fault. But I didn't mean it.'

'It was an accident,' Tappy said. 'Marcy wasn't even close to him.'

'Try telling that to him,' Howie said

'Okay, sure. Er, sir, it was an accident,' Tappy told the zombie.

'What the fuck! I didn't mean actually tell him' Howie said.

'It was just a sneeze,' Marcy said, wincing as she looked from Howie to Paula and everyone else all staring in stunned silence. 'But you know. He's not like, dead or anything.'

'Marcy!' I said.

'Well, he's not. He's just, you know. A zombie. But not a bitey zombie. So that's something, right? I'm not helping am I?'

'No!' Howie said, shaking his head.

'Why didn't you turn away?' I asked.

'I thought I did! It just came out and must have gone in his mouth.'

'Said Blowers to the judge,' Cookey quips.

'Not now, Alex!'

'Sorry, Paula.'

'I don't even know what to think,' Howie said. 'Where's Reggie?'

'He's flying the drone,' Blowers said

'My drone!' Nick yelled before running off. 'REGGIE! DON'T CRASH IT.'

'It was an accident,' Carmen said. 'I was stood right there. She didn't mean it.'

'Okay. Listen. I am so so sorry,' Marcy said. 'I'll do brew duty for like a whole week.'

'What the fuck!' Howie said.

'Okay. Whatever. A month then.'

'Yes!' Cookey said. 'Tell her she has to make cakes as well.'

'Dave, Mo, go and see if anyone else is here,' I said. 'Charlie, go with them and make sure they don't kill anyone. Well. We need a plan now.'

'How are we going to plan for this?' Howie asked.

'I don't bloody know,' I said. 'Get Reggie in here. Danny, go and tell him to come in.'

'Oh god no,' Howie said with a sudden groan. 'Henry's going to love this. I bet he's standing right behind me with this shirt all tucked in and looking seriously pissed off.'

Diary of Carmen Eze

Henry *was* standing right behind Howie, and Henry *was* looking seriously pissed off. That's why I said it was an accident.

'Yes. I am standing right behind you,' Henry said. 'And I think my point has just been made. Because that,' he added while pointing at the infected man. 'Is murder.'

'I'm not a murderer!' Marcy said. 'No, okay. I used to be a murderer, but that was like weeks ago.'

'And he's not dead either,' Roy said. 'I think you need an actual dead body to be a murderer. Although, having said that. The infection does stop the heart, so yes, there *was* a body, albeit he's now come back to life.'

'The measure of human life is free will,' Henry said.

'No, it's not,' Roy said. 'What about people in comas? They don't have free will, but they're still deemed as human.'

'All clear,' Charlie said, running back with Dave and Mo. 'He was living here alone.'

'Thank fuck for that,' Howie said, getting to his feet and drawing his sidearm.

'Howie, don't,' Marcy said.

'What do you want me to do, Marcy? We can't exactly take him with us.'

'*You* won't be taking him anywhere,' Henry said, making everyone turn to look at him. 'And regardless as to the intent, this incident only serves to show your complete lack of competence. The leaders of this team have no clue what they are doing. No briefings. No debriefs. No tactical awareness. No strategy. You can't even read a damned map! You're playing at soldiers, Howie and you will get them all killed.'

'Stop asking us to stand down!' Paula said.

'I'm no longer asking. The fate of the world rests on our ability to fulfil our mission, and you do not have that ability. Therefore, as an agent for the British Government authorised to take such action as deemed appropriate in defence of this country, I am ordering you to-.'

'What fucking planet are you on?' Howie asked. 'What country?'

'This country.'

'Jesus. We're in the twilight zone,' Howie said, sharing a stunned look with Paula and Clarence. 'Henry, there's nothing left, mate. What part of that is hard for you to understand? Clarence isn't a soldier. Frank isn't an operative. Paula's not an accountant. None of those things mean anything anymore. It's all gone, Henry!'

'It has not gone!' Henry said with that tension spiking again. We could all feel it. 'In times of such crisis the government will remain in stasis until such time as control and order can be re-instated.'

'You are fucking delusional,' Howie said.

'Easy with that tongue, nipper,' Frank said.

'Fuck you!' Howie shouted back. His eyes were getting all dark again. Like just before he went into Molly's house, Frank must have clocked it too because his right hand started dropping towards the trigger guard on his rifle strapped to his chest.

'Are you stupid or something?' Marcy asked, looking from Henry to Frank. 'What the hell are you doing? Frank! Take your hand off your gun.'

'This has gone far enough!' Paula said.

'You're right, Paula. It has,' Henry said. 'Mr Howie will stand down. I will be assuming command of his team.'

'We work for the boss,' Blowers said, and all of this is fast. Like bang bang bang. You know when something just gathers instant momentum and won't stop. It was like that, and I could see Frank getting that look in his eyes, and Dave's hands are on his guns, and everyone is starting to get twitchy.

'Howie isn't a commanding officer, Sergeant. He is a supermarket manager. Paula is an accountant. I appreciate your loyalty to them. It's commendable. Which is exactly why you should continue to provide your services.'

DIARY OF REGINALD.

BY THAT TIME I gather things were becoming very heated again as young Danny was shouting updates from the department store doors to Nick and I operating the drone.

'It's going nuts,' Danny said. 'Frank is touching his gun and Marcy's zombie thingy is growling and the dog's getting shitty and-.'

'Zombie thing?' I asked.

'Marcy sneezed on a guy living in there,' Nick said, which seemed a perfectly logical explanation to me. 'I'll bring the drone back,' Nick said.

'No! Keep going,' I told him while willing the drone to move faster before it all went horribly wrong, because once again I hadn't factored for the acceleration of time and how everything bloody well happens that much faster now.

DIARY OF CARMEN EZE,

IT WAS ugly and getting uglier by the second.

'Henry,' Howie said. 'Mate, there's nothing left to serve. It's all gone. The only thing we can do now is get the Panacea out and kill as many infected as we can. That's it. That's all we can do.'

'As I said, Howie. You are neither trained nor experienced to know how these things are done.'

'Nobody is!'

'I am!'

'You fucked up worse than I did! You had the people that released it but you failed. You lost.'

'I did not lose! I told you that. I did everything I could, but it ran too deep!'

'IT WASN'T ENOUGH! You knew it existed. You fucking knew. What did you do? Tell me. What did you do?'

'I do not answer to you, Howie. You have no idea the things we did to keep this country safe.'

'And you failed! All of you. Frank. Carmen. George. My dad. You all failed because they released it, and now you don't get to pop back up and tell everyone else what to do.'

'You will stand down!'

'You didn't see it!' Howie shouted over him, nearly chest to chest with Henry.

I was trying to give Frank a look to say *back off*. But Frank will always back Henry, no matter what the play is. Bashir was tooled up. Everyone was tooled up. And there it was. The tribalism of humanity. The need to belong to one or the other and nearly every face was bathed in sweat from that awful pressing heat feeding the bad energy as the tension got closer to detonation.

'You didn't see what we saw,' Howie said, as Meredith stood at his side. Growling with her hackles up. Head low. Teeth showing. Then I spotted Bash shifting his aim to the dog which only set Tappy off.

'Do not aim at our fucking dog,' she said while bringing her own rifle up to aim at him.

'Tappy!' I shouted, waving a hand at her. 'Mo, tell Bash to stop. Henry, please! We need to stand down before this goes off.'

'Mr Howie will stand down,' Henry said.

'You didn't see it,' Howie said again. 'Walls twenty feet high made from bodies. Children's heads thrown at us. Seeing our families die. Killing them with our own hands. *We* saw that. WE FUCKING SAW THAT! Where were you? Where was the government? Where was the order and structure?'

'I've heard enough of this. Your behaviour today demonstrates you are unfit to lead a team.'

'Jesus, Henry,' Marcy said, shaking her head in shock at him. 'I thought you were so cool this morning.'

'You're acting like a banana republic paramilitary giving out justice as you see fit. Trashing cafes and letting your dog desecrate human remains. Decapitating people to get an arrow back. Arguing over tigers and wolves and safari parks then chasing after Dave to find cannabis plants. What's next? Are you going to start breaking into houses to feed goldfish?'

'They'll be dead by now,' I said, earning a sharp look from Henry.

'There is a cure, Howie,' Henry said. 'There is a cure for all known diseases that will prevent anyone else from becoming infected, but you are too busy looking at drawings of dogs to deal with it. Which is fine. Go and do that. Go and find that… that blonde haired boy if you want but transfer your team to me and let me get the job done.'

DIARY OF CHARLOTTE DOYLE

. . .

Howie's expression when Henry said that was awful. Howie doesn't hide his emotions. What he feels is what you see. It's very endearing. Cookey is the same, and the aura they give off is one of absolute honesty. But right then, it wasn't nice to observe.

Howie looked wretched and confused because, in a way, everything Henry had said made sense, but it was all skewed and wrong – Henry had shifted the perspective on purpose to achieve his own aims, and poor Mr Howie was becoming overwhelmed. So were Clarence and Paula.

Nor could I understand why Reginald wasn't with us. He'd normally be front and centre at anyone daring to attack Howie with an intellectual argument, but he was still outside.

'Howie! See sense. You cannot finish this,' Henry said.

'And you think you can?' Paula asked.

'I know I can!'

'Why?'

'Because I am a professional,' Henry said, but I kept my eyes on Howie and saw him staring at the infected man, then he looked beyond to the glass walls and caught sight of us all in the reflection. I could see what he saw. I could see the difference that stood out so stark and clear.

There was Howie. Dark, sweating, filthy, bruised and scuffed alongside Henry looking spick and span. Tidy and clean. Upright, straight-backed, and professional.

An amateur next to a professional.

And the fact that Henry *is* both highly trained and highly experienced is beyond question, but then I saw the tick in Howie's eye when he's trying to think of something. He narrows his eyes a little, and he was doing it then.

'Howie,' Henry said, but his voice was softer as though he sensed he was close to getting what he wanted. 'Please order your team to work under my command.'

'Why under your command?' Howie asked, staring at Henry. And

Howie's voice was softer too, but inquisitive, like he didn't understand it at all.

'I'm sorry?' Henry asked with a frown. 'I just explained it all.'

'Why under your command?'

'Roy, perhaps you can take Howie and get him hydrated. I think he's burning up. Everyone else muster up outside for a briefing,' Henry ordered, turning away as Blowers and the others stayed still. Looking to Howie and Paula and Clarence for direction.

'Jesus. This heat,' Howie said, wiping the sweat from his face. 'I can't think straight.'

'It's okay, Howie. I've got it from here,' Henry said.

Oh gosh. The air was charged. Let me say that. We were all just glued in place, watching these two men and Howie narrowing his eyes like he was still trying to think.

'Charlie, you're smart,' Howie said to me. 'What did Henry say earlier about being an agent?'

'I'm sorry?' I asked, unsure of what he meant, or what the play was.

'Howie. Go and cool off,' Henry ordered. 'We'll chat again before the team moves out.'

'Sure,' Howie said, smiling in a way that made even Carmen frown before he turned back to me. 'Charlie, what did Henry say about being an agent?' he asked as I spotted the glint in his eyes. It made the hairs on my neck stand up.

'Henry said he is an agent for the British government, Mr Howie,' I said.

'Right. Come along, chaps,' Henry called while waving at them to move. 'Everyone outside please.'

'Specifically, Charlie,' Howie said, cutting over him. 'What did Mr Henry say specifically?'

I looked to Paula and Clarence but could see they were as confused as everyone else. 'Mr Henry said he is an agent for the British Government authorised to take such action as deemed appropriate in defence of this country.'

'What else, Charlie?' Howie asked.

'Howie!' Henry snapped.

'What else, Charlie?'

'Mr Henry said in times of such crisis-.'

'This is absurd!' Henry shouted.

'Keep going. What did Mr Henry say?' Howie asked.

'Mr Henry said in times of such crisis the government will remain in stasis until such time as control can be re-instated,' I said.

'Is that right?' Howie asked, eyeballing Henry.

'Yes!'

'The government will remain in stasis. You said that. I said the government is gone. You said just because I can't see it doesn't mean it's not there. You said that.'

'That's enough, Howie.'

'And Neal's diaries said they will set up safe zones, which means this thing was organised, right?'

'You will stand down!'

'And you said it ran too deep for you to stop it. You said it was too connected. You did say that, didn't you, Henry,' Howie asked as everyone looked to Henry.

'Did Mr Henry say all of those things?' Howie asked, looking around at the nods and murmurs while Henry protested.

'Yes, Mr Howie,' I said. 'Mr Henry said all of those things.'

'Aye. He fucking did,' Howie growled. 'So, tell me, Henry. If you're the professional expert in these things, why didn't they invite you? And how the fuck are you still an agent for a government that doesn't want you anymore?'

Henry remained silent without a flicker of reaction, but the energy hardened, and we could all see that Howie's words just hit a nerve. 'This isn't about policy or procedure, Henry,' Howie continued. 'This is as much about revenge for you as it is for me.'

Diary of Reginald.

. . .

THE UNDEAD TWENTY-FIVE. THE HEAT

OF COURSE, in such a still day we could hear every word coming out of the department store, and I for one certainly smiled at Howie scoring a very good point against Henry. But the danger was far from over, and I knew Henry would not back down until he had what he wanted.

'There!' Nick said outside in the street staring into the small screen on his drone controller.

I looked at my monitor, and right there, on the screen on my desk, was a nice town filled with infected.

I knew the infected would be there, and I knew the route to give to Nick, but I was still worried you see. I was worried because this was a very big undertaking, and I wasn't entirely sure we were ready. My god I wasn't sure at all.

But then without risk there can be no reward, and the thing we needed more than ever right at that point was to just get stuck in and let Howie do what Howie does best.

And so I took a second to exhale and ready my mind before flinging my hands into the air.

'Oh my! Look! Children at risk. Lots of little ones all being chased.'

'Shit. Where?' Nick asked, peering closer at his controller screen

'Somewhere,' I muttered, jumping from the van. 'I SAY, MR HOWIE!' I shouted with a voice full of panic and worry. 'MR HOWIE!' I yelled. Running into the department store to a charged atmosphere waiting to ignite. 'MR HOWIE! Children, Mr Howie!'

'Eh, what?' Howie asked, snapping his head over.

'Huge horde, Mr Howie. All chasing some tiny tots in their little shoes and Barbie dolls... BARBIE DOLLS, MR HOWIE!'

'Fuck. Where?' Howie said as that energy instantly changed from the angered tribalism into the thing I needed it to be.

'Er, that way!' I said, pointing vaguely east. 'CHILDREN, MR HOWIE! IN GRAVE DANGER!'

'Load up. GO!' Howie ordered as he barged past Henry.

'Howie!' Henry said.

'CHILDREN, MR HOWIE,' I shouted over him. 'Come on, team!

We need to get there. That's it. Attaboy! Sergeant Blowers. Come on, Booker. You too, Tappy!'

'What children?' Nick muttered, still peering into his screen. 'Reggie, I can't see any kids.'

'Get your bloody eyes tested then,' I said as the team ran from the department store.

'What about him?' Marcy asked, pointing at the infected.

'Tell him to stay there!' Howie yelled back. 'We'll come back later.'

'Right. Er, sit!' Marcy said as the infected plopped down on his backside. 'And no biting anyone. Got it? Good boy.'

'Howie!' Henry yelled again.

'CHILDREN!' I shouted over him as I plucked the controller from a confused Nick and shoved him towards the Saxon. 'Get in! Quickly now! Children are in peril.'

'But my drone!'

'We'll collect it there. CHILDREN, NICHOLAS!'

'You're not the police, Howie!' Henry yelled out as Howie and Clarence reached the front of the Saxon. 'You might save a few kids but then what?' Henry asked. 'What about the rest of the world that needs the Panacea?'

Of course I bloody cursed under my breath because I could see the stubborn sod wasn't giving up easily. I could see the hesitation in Howie and Clarence and Paula too. All of them pausing to look back. Everyone else doing the same.

'You have to think, Howie,' Henry said. 'You're not a strategist. None of you are. Stop getting sucked into small issues and let me do what I need to do.'

'There are survivors in that town that need our help,' I said firmly as Howie looked at me.

'The whole world needs our help!' Henry said.

Howie held still. Knowing within his heart that everything Henry just said was right. That they do keep getting sucked into petty dramas, and they had to break that cycle. They had to focus on the bigger picture.

THE UNDEAD TWENTY-FIVE. THE HEAT

But I also knew Howie would be thinking of something else because of the words I'd just used to trigger the images in his mind.

The little girl.

That day in the square.

The little girl who screamed for her mummy as the infected fell silent. As the whole place fell silent.

The little boy too. Early on. Howie told me he saw a little boy in teddy bear pyjamas on the second day. He was infected. Howie said the image haunts him.

I knew it was those things that drove Howie. The sense of hopelessness he and the rest of us felt. The sense of confusion and of being weak, and unable to stop it from happening.

'Howie,' Henry urged. 'Please. See sense.'

Howie looked to Clarence, then over to Paula, and I could see all three were feeling the same torn conflict inside.

'Okay,' Howie finally said, nodding at Henry. 'We'll do it your way.'

'Thank you,' Henry said with a long sigh.

'After this one,' Howie added with a wink before diving into the Saxon and slamming the door.

'HOWIE!'

'I'd take that victory if I were you, Henry,' Frank said from behind as Henry fell silent. Watching the lads bundle into the back of the Saxon.

I observed something else too. I observed the way Henry watched the lads and everyone else making ready. The way they were checking rifles over. Ejecting magazines to tap against the sides to rid any grit and prevent stoppages. Pistols being loaded. Rifles bolts being pulled back. The thrill in the air. The pulse of action.

The call to arms.

Henry was many things, but he was also a soldier. I saw him turn to watch Joan yanking the bolt back on her sniper rifle and how Carmen slung her rifle and checked her sidearm. Magazine out. Magazine in. Slide the top back. Loaded. Made ready.

I could see it in his eyes, and that was good, because it meant I could lure him into the game.

'Boss?' Carmen asked, and I saw Henry frown at her. I assumed it was because she'd called him boss, which was wording *we* used, which suggested our teams were already starting to merge. Then I saw the way she glanced to the Saxon almost in fear that it will go, and they'll miss the action.

'You wanted to see a control point,' Frank said, pushing a magazine into his rifle to make ready. He tilted his head over. Not needing to say anything more.

'Fine,' Henry said, about turning as his small team rushed for their vehicle. 'We get this done then we split with whoever we can take. My team, move out!'

I paused a second longer, smiling inwardly at the fact that not once did Henry even glance in my direction.

The ego of men and the belief that warriors rule this world.

They don't of course.

We just let them think they do.

But anyway. It wasn't over yet. Not by a long degree, and in many ways, the day was only just beginning.

27

Diary of Paula

AND THEN LITERALLY FIVE minutes after Howie totally called Henry out with his *they didn't want you in their club* bombshell and we're back in the vehicles.

Mind you. Reginald running in shouting *kiddies, Mr Howie! Kiddies with barbie dolls* was overegging it, but whatever, it did the trick and got that bad energy diverted.

It was all so fast too. It was just one thing after another and on days like that all you can do is hold on for dear life.

Not that it was over. Not by a long way, and at that point we all figured the day couldn't get any harder after the morning we'd had.

How wrong were we.

The morning was the warm-up. After that was just - I don't even know how to describe it. I still can't quite process it. What we saw. What we did. How it all happened.

But anyway. We'd jumped into the Saxon. Howie was up front

driving with Clarence next to him, and the vibe was bad. Like seriously bad.

'Fuck just happened?' Howie asked, looking over at Clarence.

'Let's focus on this,' Clarence said, grabbing the radio. '*Reggie, where are we going?*'

'*We're going east.*'

'*East is a point on the compass. We need directions,*' Clarence snapped before twisting around to shout into the back. 'And those sodding plants stink. Throw them out. We look like bloody idiots.'

'*Er. Some warning would be nice!*' Roy transmitted as a huge cannabis plant smacked into his windscreen.

'Nick. What town?' Clarence asked.

'I don't know.'

'How can you not know?' Clarence asked, twisting about to glare at him.

'I couldn't read the signs! I'm sorry.'

'Jesus,' Clarence said. 'No wonder we look like a shower of shit. *Reginald! Directions.*' (It's worrying when Clarence swears. None of us like it.)

'*Ah yes. Of course. Get on The Street and aim for the A272.*'

'What street?' Howie asked, shooting a look at Clarence.

'*Reggie. Confirm what street,*' Clarence transmitted.

'*The Street.*'

'*What bloody street! Specify, Reginald.*'

'*Chaps. Cutting in,*' Henry transmitted. '*The road we are on is called The Street. It feeds onto the A272.*'

Clarence grunted in pure frustration and gripped the handset so hard it started to creak. '*Reginald? Confirm the last.*'

'*Er, roger that! Wilco. Over and out,*' Reginald said.

'*The A272 runs to Petworth,*' Frank's voice then cut in again. '*Are we aiming for Petworth?*'

'*Hello, Frank. Yes. Petworth it is,*' Reginald said.

'*Fuck me, Reggie!*' Howie said. '*Why not just say that?*'

'*Because we previously agreed not to use location names over the radio,*' Reginald said.

'*Excuse me for being pedantic,*' Roy cut in. '*But saying to stay on The Street then head onto the A272 does in fact give away our location and our destination, in which case stating the name wouldn't make a difference.*'

'Roy, it's Marcy. Can you maybe shut the fuck up cos Howie and Clarence are kinda frothing at the mouth right now.'

'*I was only explaining why saying Petworth doesn't matter.*'

'Roy!' Blowers shouted into the radio.

'*Do not shout at me, Simon!*'

'Everyone stop fucking shouting!' I shouted as the Saxon powered on with a sudden application of thrust. Barrelling along the narrow road bordered by high hedges and a canopy of trees that dappled the sun on the windscreen behind which Howie and Clarence frothed at the mouth with wild eyes and knuckles turning white.

Allotments on the right. A row of houses on the left. A former bakery converted into a plush house and Howie built the speed. Steaming into corners and snapping overhanging branches as the wide vehicle went through.

Another corner ahead. Howie steered into it but clipped a stone wall. Tearing chunks of rubble out as Tappy grimaced. Clearly wanting to drive but not daring to speak out. Everyone else was the same. All of them silent and hanging on to anything they can reach.

A pub on the right. *The Hollist Arms.* The entrance barricaded. A man inside was running at the inner gate waving his arms in the air as he shouted for us to stop, but Howie didn't stop. He couldn't stop. He was too angry.

'Fuck me,' Marcy said when he clipped another wall. 'Howie, slow down or let Tappy drive!'

'I know how to fucking drive!' Howie yelled, overcompensating to avoid another wall as everyone in the back leant one way then the next. 'I bet Henry knows how to fucking drive. I bet I was right. I bet this is revenge for him.'

'Focus on the mission,' Clarence said.

'I am focussed on the mission! I've been focussed since day one!'

'Then focus on the road as well then!' Clarence said.

'Stop telling me to focus!' Howie said, too furious to see the road properly and the junction ahead.

'HOWIE!' Marcy and I yelled from behind as Howie tried to anchor the brakes on. Then Clarence was yelling out and we're all bracing as Howie drove over the junction and smashed through the hedge on the other side with everyone in the back yelping in alarm.

'Bloody hell. Are you alright in there?' Roy asked through the radio.

'We're fine!' Howie shouted back while Marcy was leaning over the front seats swiping at his head.

'I said to bloody slow down you idiot! Tappy. Take over driving.'

'I said I'm fine!' Howie said

'You're not bloody fine. You're too angry. Let Tappy drive,' Marcy shouted, leaning over the back of the seats to grab at the wheel at the same time as Clarence also leant over to help turn the wheel, which is also at the same time as Howie tried to turn it, all of which meant the Saxon swerved about the field. Spewing dust and crap up.

'Hedge!' I shouted on seeing another wall of green coming at us. Honestly. It was a bloody mess. And right after Howie had finally scored a big point against Henry. And bang, straight through the next hedge we went. Throwing up bloody twigs and branches and clouds of dust everywhere. To make it worse, the field was ploughed too, which meant we were bouncing about like tic-tacs inside.

'Tappy! Get up front,' I ordered while grabbing at her wrist to start pushing her forward. 'Tappy's taking over!'

'How? I can't bloody get there!' Tappy said, trying to squeeze through.

'You bloody idiots!' Marcy yelled, now bent double over the seats, with her arse in the air from the motion of going through the hedge. 'I'm stuck! Get me up.' She groped about with a hand swiping at Howie's head while I'm pushing Tappy at the seats while everyone else was getting thrown about.

'I can't get through!' Tappy said.

'I need to get out first,' Marcy said.

'I'm fine to drive!' Howie yelled.

'I said Tappy is taking over,' I said from the back.

'Marcy, get your arse out of my face,' Clarence said.

'Pull me up then!'

'HEDGE!' Tappy yelled as another wall of green came at us with a bang and a scrape as the Saxon slammed into a field full of sheep running off.

'Quick! Get Henry and Dick and Jane,' Howie said, which, to be fair, was very funny and helped break the tension a little, apart from Marcy though. She was seriously pissed off.

'Wasn't funny the first time you twat,' Marcy yelled. 'AND PULL ME OUT!'

'I'm pulling,' Clarence said, gripping her arm to heave while I carried on shoving Tappy over the seats with a mass of arms and legs and boobs and bums and sweaty yelling faces all colliding.

Maddox

And so we're still on the road. Me in Roy's van with Reggie and Henry's SUV behind us, and we're all watching the Saxon driving through hedges and over fields with clouds of dust going up. It was just nuts.

Why don't they just stop? Roy asked, shaking his head while listening to the voices yelling from someone pressing their radio button down in the Saxon.

Carmen

AND WE'RE RIGHT behind the van watching the Saxon driving in the fields after Howie overshot the junction.

'Why don't they just stop?' Henry asked while shaking his head. But that wasn't the crazy part. The worst thing was someone had a radio button pressed down in the Saxon, which meant we could hear every bloody word they were saying.

'OUCH! That's my tit!'
'Get your foot out of my groin!'
'Howie! Let Tappy drive!'
'I'm bloody trying! Someone's got a foot in my face.'
'My poor boobs!'
'TESTICLES!'
'Why is the dog trying to get up here?!'
'She always comes up front with me.'
'Nick! Get your dog back.'
'She's not my dog!'

Maddox

I mean. I've been with them long enough to know how those things start, but hearing it from a distance was just weird.

Wow, Roy said. Do you know what? *Maybe Henry has a point,* he said while we shared a nod.

Henry does not have a point! Reginald said before grabbing his radio. CHILDREN, MR HOWIE!

Paula

Then bloody Reginald is still trying to whip Howie up and yelling through the radio, 'Kiddies, Mr Howie! Kiddies with their barbie dolls!'

'Tell him to stop bloody saying that!' Marcy yelled amidst the mass of limbs and twisting hot bodies. I don't know how but we got them disentangled enough for Tappy to get in over Howie and use her backside to push him out of the way and gain the seat of victory.

'Got it!' she shouted out, giving Howie another hip shove for good measure while Clarence, Marcy, Howie and the dog all squabbled and wrestled about next to her.

Not that Tappy seemed to care. She'd got her Saxon back and was jacking the seat up and sliding it forward as she cricked her neck and grinned like a demon. 'Hold on to yer britches bitches!' she yelled. 'She's gonna get wild.'

'What does that mean?' Marcy asked, risking a peek between Howie's legs as the Saxon seems to settle for a second before speeding up with a vicious punch of thrust.

'SHIT!' Howie yelled. The G force sending him and Marcy over the seats into me, then all of us three into everyone else in the back. Leaving only Clarence and the dog left to argue over the front seat.

'OW! She bloody nipped me,' Clarence said, feeling teeth on his bum.

'It's all those biscuits!' Charlie called from somewhere.

'Gateway drug!' Marcy said.

Carmen

And they still had the radio button pressed, so we're listening to every word and honestly? It sounded terrible. Really terrible. But then Tappy got the driver's seat and the Saxon just seemed to settle for a second before shooting off. It was being handled differently too. Less skittish and holding her own course while building power to where the last few feet of hedgerow meets a solid brick wall that marked the edge of the fields.

'She's never,' Henry said.

Maddox

Roy and me we're staring at the wall and that tiny last bit of hedge and we're both thinking the same.

She can't, I said.

She wont, Roy said.

Charlotte

'I bloody will!' Tappy said, winking at the dog now in the front passenger seat with Clarence sliding into the back while rubbing his sore bottom – and a second later Tappy drives at the last few feet of hedge.

I rather think the rest of us were bracing for a collision, because I wouldn't have driven at it. There was no way we could fit through. We were going to hit the wall. It was so obvious.

But we didn't. We didn't even touch the wall and then a second later we're bouncing back onto the road ahead of the van and the SUV.

'Fuck yes!' Tappy called with a whoop. 'The Saxon on the blacktop speeding through the backdrop. Boom!'

'See! I said she should bloody drive!' Marcy said amidst the chaos in the back of the Saxon.

'Fine. Well obviously, I'm useless then,' Howie muttered, squishing a hand over Cookey's face as he tried to get up.

'Shnor not ushless bosh,' Cookey said, mid face-squish. 'But can I have my face back?'

'Er, sorry to ask. But why didn't we just pull over and swap?' I asked.

'Shut up, Charlie,' Marcy said. 'Go and snog Tappy again.'

'I was snogging the dog!'

'What?' Cookey asked, still mid face-squish.

'It's not like you're interested,' I muttered to myself while offering him a sarcastic smile. Not that Cookey noticed due to the boss still squishing his face while Marcy rubbed her sore boobs and Clarence rubbed his sore bottom.

'We're almost there!' Tappy then called from the front. 'What's the plan?'

'Fuck me! Why does everyone need a plan all of a sudden?' Howie said. 'Nick! Where's the briefing?'

'I'm not the briefing guy! I don't bloody know. Just drive in and kill the cunts.'

'Love it,' Howie shouted, pushing off from Cookey's face to fall on Nick. 'Good plan, Nick!'

'Best plan ever!' Clarence shouted, still sprawled over Paula and Booker and pretty much everyone else.

'And watch out for broken glass,' Nick added to a chorus of squished and muffled laughs.

'Right. Tappy!' Howie called. 'Drive in and kill the cunts.'

'Got it,' Tappy said. *'Reggie! Where are they?'*

'In Petworth.'

'She means where in Petworth you dick?' Marcy asked.

Carmen

Then Marcy's asking where in Petworth and calling Reggie a dick. But I think they have history. (In fact – I think Marcy infected Reginald.)

Anyway. So then Reginald was reeling off directions. *'Oh. Yes. Roger that. Er, first left, then first right, then follow the road.'*

And Henry was up front in our vehicle staring at the radio in his hand and waiting for the rest of the briefing and the essential information that any attacking force should know.

The numbers of opposition.

The entry and egress points.

The fall-back point.

The RVP or maybe even an FCP, or at the very least a muster point.

The objective. The plan of attack. The method. The system. The strategy. The tactics.

Anything.

Something.

But nothing.

'They're not going straight in are they?' he asked, seeing the town ahead and the junction looming at them.

'I think they are,' Frank said.

'Oh, and chaps!' Reginald says. *'Don't shoot the big building in the middle. That's where the survivors are hiding.'*

'What building?' Henry asked, looking at Frank. 'The middle of what?' he asked as Frank shrugged.

Reginald

Ah! It was just what we needed. A jolly good ruck to get stuck into. Huzzah!

And I could hear all the goings on in the Saxon and I knew I was whipping Howie up, but sometimes things have to be pushed along otherwise they never get done. And what was the alternative? A gunfight at the O.K Corral between Sheriff Henry and Sheriff Howie?

No thank you.

Trust me. This is what they needed. And not just Howie, but blasted Henry too. He needed to see it. And not just from the top of a hill like he did at Hinchley Point but down in the guts of it with the blood and bullets. So yes. I was doing my damn best to whip them all up. That's when they're at their best. That's when the magic happens.

'Yes!' I shouted into the radio. 'Go on, Tappy! Get in there!'

I'd kept the drone up and could see the Saxon gain the centre of the road and could imagine Howie inside clambering over everyone else to get up through the hole in the roof. His face growing darker from the filthy violence bursting inside that needed to vent.

I could hear Maddox getting his rifle ready and glimpsed through to see Roy gripping the steering wheel a bit harder, because the adrenaline was flowing you see. The pre-fight energy was rising.

Then Tappy got onto a narrow olde-world road leading into the town centre.

I was watching it on the drone. Seeing the Saxon pass quaint shops

THE UNDEAD TWENTY-FIVE. THE HEAT

and quaint stores constructed in quaint buildings. Old railings. Old windows and old doors. Black and white Tudor. Victorian and Edwardian. A place of history and prestige. A quiet village nestled in the southern English countryside. A place now filling with the roar of a mighty engine and the squeal of mighty tyres as Tappy took the first right into Saddlers Row.

Antique shops filled with old model sailing boats and spinning globes and the trinkets and things of a species now on the verge of extinction. Gifts shops. Coffee shops. The places of the living that are no more.

A few infected ahead. Late comers to the party hobbling, lurching and running along the street towards the centre.

'GET 'EM, TAPPY!' Howie shouted from the top, clambering up and out onto the roof. A second passed. A second and no more as Tappy snarled and ran over an infected. Taking the first kill of Petworth.

The body rode up high into the windscreen then off to the side. Smashing through the window into the antique model yachts and the antique spinning globes.

More infected ahead. More taken down. Rammed aside. Driven over. Pulverised, crushed and killed.

A bend in the road to the left. A curve that led to the centre and the big building made from dark grey concrete in the middle. The windows boarded with thick planks. The infected gathered outside. Throwing themselves at the doors and starting to body-pile so they can climb up to the first-floor windows.

People were leaning out. The people that I knew were there. Screaming in horror. Firing farmer's shotguns. Throwing pots and pans and furniture. Doing what they could as they snapped their heads up to the Saxon driving at them. Their faces showing the shock of seeing such a thing. At seeing Howie riding the top of the Saxon. His dark curly hair blowing in the wind. His face etched with pure fury as he spotted the horde and detonated the hive mind.

'GO ON!' I screamed and slammed my battle swatter on the desk as I was hit by the connection. Roy was the same. Grunting from the surge of power inside - and in that instant, we could feel each other. Blowers and Cookey. Booker and Mo Mo. Danny. Paula. Clarence. Marcy. Charlie. Tappy. Meredith. Roy, and even Jess hooving. All of their energies. All of them at once and above all else we could feel the staggering dark violence coming from Howie.

The Saxon mounted the steps outside the middle building. Tilting over as the solid front battered into the body-piling infected. Smashing the base out as the rest tumbled and dropped. Spinning through the air as they landed on each other and Tappy drove on. Powering along the building line to the corner. Clearing space and gaining ground.

'BRAKE HARD TAPPY!' Howie shouted. Tappy stamped down. Sending Howie flying off the top into the horde ahead. And what a thing to see! What a glorious idea and I have no doubt Howie was enjoying every second of it as he got amongst them to start bashing and boshing, or more likely, biting. Howie does bite them a lot.

But a split-second later and the back doors opened with the rest spilling out. Dave first and fastest. Dropping to turn and run towards Howie at the front. Drawing his pistol to shoot the infected going for Howie's back.

Dave has told me how he thinks, and how he has glowing blooms of light showing in his mind as he tracks targets and feels the sway and tide of the horde. The way they move. The size of them. The numbers they have.

It's what makes him such a devastating opponent, and in less than a second, three had already dropped from his pistol and he was drawing a blade to run in deep.

I should imagine the chaos of life was gone from his mind. The confusion of what people mean now simply not there as he gained a sense of completion inside. A sense of calm as he danced and moved as Howie swung out with his axe and started chopping them down.

The rest fought out too, and within that hive mind they knew Roy was releasing Jess, and we all felt that presence of pure strength as Jess ran into the fray. Aiming at Charlie who ran out to vault up. Landing in the saddle with her axe already spinning and the heads already popping.

The building in the middle was not a big building, but then, it wasn't a big town and with everyone else fighting, Tappy drove the Saxon on. Scooping the infected away from the building line as the others hacked and cleaved the infected down. Firing rifles when they could aim away from the mock fortress in the centre.

Make no mistake about it. Because for all the bickering, arguing, chaos and constant messing about – this is where they excelled. At this. At these few moments of absolute pure savage violence where human forms were ripped apart.

Where bones showed white through bloodied limbs and innards fell to glisten in the sun. Where they attacked with such force the blood of the infected rained down upon them and ran into streams and puddles that steamed in the heat, and the air filled with the tang of iron and shit. With piss and death.

It was only a short fight in truth. And it ended as quickly as it began, and that building in the middle soon stood like an island in a sea of bodies – but the team needed it. Howie needed it.

I could see him dripping with blood. His face darker than ever. His eyes blazing with energy. All of them were the same. Flushed and sweating and still filled with the lust for blood. The jokes gone. The humour not there and of their normal foolishness there was no trace.

Henry stood by the open door of the SUV. His team behind him. Not a shot fired from them. Not an action taken, and they stared out to the violence. Carmen and Frank saw it the day before at Hinchley Point. Joan saw it in the fort, and Bashir had seen death and violence in all forms, and Henry had done more than all of them.

But even so.

It brought them to silence as Roy lowered his bow from the top of the van. His feet planted apart and Jess turned with a snort. Popping skulls while the dog dropped from the Saxon and savaged the neck of an infected still clinging to life. Tearing the throat out.

That's when I made my exit from the van. Dropping out into heat with my battle swatter in my hand. 'Where is it?' I asked.

'Where's what?' Howie replied. His voice was low and rasping.

'The CP?' I asked, holding my swatter out. 'We were here for the control point. Remember?' Of course, I knew there was no CP there. I'm not stupid. You have to tell Howie and the others a million times if you want anything left alive, and even then there's only a slight chance they'll remember. But I needed Henry to hear me asking. That was the point.

'Oh,' Howie said, his eyes losing the fury. 'Right. Er. Did anyone see the control point?'

'Hello?' someone called from a window above them.

'Hi!' Howie said. 'Er. Don't suppose you saw a talking zombie by any chance, did you?'

'I er, I don't think we did, sorry,' the man said with an apologetic wince. 'We didn't know to look for one though,' he added as Howie and the others all looked about at the very dead infected in case any of them might look like a CP. 'Are you Mr Howie?' the man asked after a quick whispered conflab with other people inside.

'I am,' Howie said as Frank and Carmen shared a look while Joan smiled wryly at Henry's expression.

'Thank god. We kept hoping you'd come,' the man said from the window. 'They've been going past for a few days. We stayed quiet but they must have heard us and started trying to get in. We were about to... You know... Get some morphine into the kiddies,' he added in a whisper. 'Stop 'em turning.'

'Be careful giving morphine to kids,' Roy called up. 'They can OD very easily on something that strong.'

'I think that was the point,' Paula said quietly as Roy realised what the man meant and nodded.

'Is anyone hurt?' Roy asked. 'Do you need medical aid?'

'Have you got food?' Paula asks. 'We've got some supplies we can leave you.'

'We're okay,' the man said, his voice choking off with a quiet sob. 'But thank you. We didn't believe. I mean. I didn't believe... I said you were made up or...' he fell silent again, wiping his eyes as people crowded into the windows to look down. Pale and drawn. Haunted even. But alive, and within that spark of life there is always hope. Hope that shines anew at the sight of the armed men and women below them. The people they'd heard about spoken in whispers from survivors passing through. I couldn't have asked for a better start for Henry to see the impact and to hear people responding.

'There's the horse,' someone said.

'And the dog,' someone else said.

'Which one is Dave?'

'I am Dave,' Dave said, answering the question without boast as the people looked and pointed.

'Are you Paula?' the man asked, looking at Paula as she blinked in shock at people knowing her name. She nodded once. Caught out in the surreal moment.

'You said they were going past?' I asked them.

'Look! It's the smart one with the tie!' someone whispered while looking at me.

I smiled politely. 'May I ask what you mean by them going past?' I asked again.

'For a few days,' the man that seemed to be in charge said. 'Like going through the village but not stopping.'

'There was a lot of them,' a woman added from the next window along. 'Probably hundreds. Did you tell them about, Storrington, Alan?' she asked the man in charge.

'Storrington?' I asked

'South-east of here,' she said

'I know Storrington,' Henry called as the people in the windows look over at him. 'What's happening there?'

'Same as us,' the woman said. 'They got surrounded in the supermarket.'

'By the bank just off the High Street,' Alan said.

'Look for The Anchor Inn,' the woman said. 'Opposite that. Not the first bank though. You need the big one where the supermarket is and the coffee shop.'

'Coffee shop?' Howie asked with sudden hope. 'Starbucks?'

'Costa,' the woman said as Howie tutted.

'How do you know that?' Paula asked.

'I used to go there,' the woman said.

'Not the coffee shop. How do you know there's people trapped there?'

'Oh, sorry love,' the woman said. 'Some of the landlines were still working. They said they couldn't get out.'

'They were calling numbers from an old phone book they found,' Alan added. 'They've got a woman in labour but no nurses or doctors.'

'Oh shit,' Paula said already turning as Blowers ordered his team to fall back to the Saxon.

'They've got loads of kiddies there an' all,' the woman said. 'Shall I phone 'em back and say you're coming?'

'Yes!' Paula says.

'And tell them to get away from the windows and doors and stay low,' Clarence called.

'Oh, and ask them if they've seen a talking zombie,' Howie called. 'And tell them they should get a Starbucks instead of a Costa. What? Starbucks is much nicer than Costa,' he said to Paula giving him an eye-roll.

'Howie!' Henry called. 'We had a deal. We agreed.'

'Are you fucking joking?' Howie asked, already flaring back up.

'No, Howie,' I said quickly, holding my swatter up before he could protest as Clarence and the others listened in. 'We did agree. We must abide by that. Henry is right. We should follow this horde to the CP and then do as he requests.'

'Right,' Henry said, caught off guard.

'Agreed?' I asked, giving Howie a stern look. 'We find the CP we agreed to find back at the department store then we let Henry take over. Yes? Paula? Clarence?'

I could see in Howie that he knew I was making a play, although I would suggest he didn't have a clue what it was. But we had trust. We had deep trust, and so he went with it.

'No, okay, yeah, that's fair enough,' Howie said with a reluctant sigh.

'Fine. Agreed,' Paula said with the same tone, no doubt also without a clue but trusting Howie and I enough to go with it.

'Concurred,' Clarence said.

'This is the right thing to do, Howie,' Henry said. 'We need to find this CP, gather what intel we can, then you let me take the reins.'

'Absolutely' I said. 'Right chaps. Let's get into Storrington and get it done. Load up. We're moving out!'

(Seriously. Don't ever patronise me.)

28

Diary of Charlotte Doyle

AS GHOULISH AS IT SOUNDS, I really think we needed that fight in Petworth. It reset the bad energy, and, of course, we then heard straight away that more survivors were in peril in Storrington, which enabled the energy to stay high as we rushed back to our vehicles

'Fuck just happened,' Howie asked. (Now wedged in the back with everyone else.)

'Reggie's up to something,' Clarence said.

'Reggie's always up to something,' Paula said.

'Just let him work,' Marcy said. 'He'll have some nerdy grand master plan going on. Clarence, you're sweating on me! Move back.'

'Where to?' Clarence asked in protest, stooped over Howie, Marcy and Paula in the back of the Saxon as they twisted around to see Meredith sitting happily in the spacious front seat.

'It's those bloody biscuits,' Paula said as Tappy veered over to run an infected down with a jolt and a bang that made us all lean and sway.

'Soz!' Tappy yelled.

'It's fine,' Paula called. 'And no more dicks either.'

'What, me?' Tappy asked while twisting to look back.

'Not you! The dog. Henry's right. We've slipped into some bad habits the last couple of weeks.'

'Oh god, we're trapped in a lecture,' Howie said as Tappy veered the other way to a much louder bang and much bigger jolt.

'Soz. That one was a fatty,' Tappy called.

'Try warning us *before* next time,' Marcy said.

'And don't say fatty,' Paula said.

'What's wrong with fatty?' Howie asked.

'I just said we need to smarten up and be more professional,' Paula said.

'Advanced obesity infected person warning!' Tappy called as the Saxon jolted and made us all lean and sway again.

'Er. Why didn't we just get in the van?' Marcy asked.

'Yeah, Clarence. Why didn't we get in the van?' Howie asked.

'Just pull over. We'll jump out,' Paula said.

'And have Henry make some smug comment about our lack of planning?' Howie asked as Paula thought for a second.

'Fine. Just bloody get there then!' she said as the Saxon broke free from the narrow twists and turns of Petworth onto the wider main road.

It was so hot too. I am sorry to keep mentioning it, but Paula said we must tell people in the future what it was like, and you need to know how brutal that heat was. The air was thick and listless, and the humidity was crushing.

'This has to be the hottest one yet,' Paula said, gasping for air as the others nodded in agreement. 'Jesus, Clarence. Your head. Someone pass me a towel. Let me soak it, right, lean down.'

'I'll sweat on you.'

'It doesn't bother me,' she said, pulling his head down as the sweat ran from his scalp onto her arms and hands. It was really sweet actually. The way she poured a bottle of water over his head and used the wet rag to wipe his cheeks and skull. Around his eyes and the back of his neck. 'Think cool thoughts,' she told him. 'I'll find a freezer truck for you later. You can sit in that and eat biscuits.'

'I'll sleep in it,' he said with his eyes closed.

She snorted a laugh. 'I might join you,' she said as his eyes opened to stare into hers while Marcy smiled and nudged Howie.

Like I said – it was super sweet, and why on earth they don't get together is beyond anybody's guess. They are a perfect match, and they clearly adore each other.

But it also made me think about Cookey, and how I thought we were a perfect match, and how I thought he adored me, but he still hadn't done anything.

The signals were so weird. He flirted with me constantly, but the second we were alone he'd start making jokes, and while he does make me laugh – well, I don't know. I was more than ready for the next step. He, however, clearly wasn't interested.

I fingered the scars on my face, then felt my mangled ear, and ran a hand over my shaved head, and wondered again if it was because of how I look, while all the time I was staring at him.

He seemed to sense my gaze and smiled at me, and I could see how his blue eyes lit up whenever he looked at me which is why it was all so bloody confusing.

'Are you okay?' he mouthed. I nodded back. Confused and unsure while also turned on by him at the same time as feeling guilty about being horny – which is when Tappy shouted that a tree was blocking the road and we started to slow down.

'Go around it,' Howie said. 'We can go off road.'

'Yeah, but the van can't,' Tappy said. Bringing the Saxon to a halt as we all popped out to see a huge tree blocking the road. Too big for even the Saxon to move.

'Fuck's sake,' Howie said. Seeing that Tappy was right and there was no way the van would get over the ground on either side. 'Right. Axes then. We'll cut it up.'

'Chaps?' Henry called, stepping out of his vehicle.

'This isn't our fault, Henry, so unless you've got any smart ideas,'

THE UNDEAD TWENTY-FIVE. THE HEAT

Howie said, giving him a look as he hefted his axe and tried to figure where to start chopping.

'I do actually,' Henry said. Taking a small black bag from the back of his SUV and heading over to the tree. 'The application of force can be delivered in many ways, Mr Howie,' he said while pushing something into the side of the trunk then stretching it round before wrapping it in gaffer tape. 'Establish the objective. Determine the method and find the path of least resistance,' he finished off with a grunt as he secured the tape. 'Because the true victor must be both strong *and* smart,' he said with a nod while striding back to his SUV. 'Oh, and do take cover. Fire in the hole,' he said mildly, holding a detonator up as the rest of us dove for cover.

There was a flash of pure light following instantly by a sharp bang and a searing noise as the C4 severed the tree in half with the two sections rolling off and sagging down from the loss of structure and strength - I must say it was very impressive, especially with Henry back as James Bond Senior.

'I'd say we'll get through easy enough now, Tappy. Load up then chaps. Let's get moving shall we,' Henry said with a bright smile.

'And Henry's back to cool AF again,' Marcy said. 'What is that? One all boys?' she asked as Clarence and Howie got back in the Saxon.

And again, I did wonder why they didn't get in the van.

'Fuck's sake! Why are we in here again?' Howie asked thirty seconds later as Clarence stooped and loomed and sweated and everyone else swayed to the motion of Tappy driving.

'Tell me more about this freezer truck,' Clarence said as Paula smiled at him.

'Get through today and I promise I'll find you one,' she said as Tappy gave a warning before mowing a few more infected down.

'We're seeing a lot of them. Where are they heading?' Howie asked as we went through Fittleworth. A tiny village. The houses with smashed in doors and broken windows. Cars left in the road. The doors open. A body hanging out of one of them. Old and decaying in the awful heat.

'This got hit bad,' Howie said.

A few seconds later and the signs of destruction were gone as we once more delved into the deep rolling countryside. To an open road and the green hedges and towering trees.

I'm detailing the scenery, as I am sure some of the others are, because it's become such a strong defining backdrop to this event. The countryside, aside from the heat, was blooming in every direction. The air was clearer. The colours seemed more vibrant. The wildlife was already more abundant, and yet, when we went into towns and villages all we saw was death.

'Got a few more,' Tappy said aiming for the infected at the side of the road. 'Hang on. They've disappeared. Where'd they go?' she asked while easing the speed off as the rest of us tried to see out the front.

'Where are they?' Howie asked.

'I don't know. They sodded off. There!'

An opening on the left side. A large sign welcoming visitors to **Pulborough Garden Centre.** A long road leading in with the backs of infected seen running towards the buildings within the large grounds.

'Must be people up there,' Howie said.

'What do you want me to do?' Tappy asked as Howie grimaced. I could see his dilemma in that we couldn't keep stopping, but then we couldn't drive by and leave people to suffer either.

'Fuck's sake,' Howie said, grabbing his radio. *'Quick detour. Two minutes,'* he transmitted. 'Right. We're in and out,' he said as Tappy powered along the access road that into the long car park bordering the garden centre.

'Fuck! Look at this lot,' Tappy said, seeing the horde charging into the doors and fronts of the buildings.

'Go to the end,' Howie ordered. 'Everyone make ready - and someone get on the GPMG. Who's closest to it?'

'I'll do it,' I said and wriggled past Clarence to get up through the hole as Tappy battered a path to the end with the thuds banging on the hard metal sides and the vehicle rocking on the chassis.

'Roy! Don't come in. We're firing along the car park,' Howie transmitted. *'Hold on the road. Repeat. Hold on the road.'*

'Got it. Holding on the road,' Maddox transmitted back.

THE UNDEAD TWENTY-FIVE. THE HEAT

Then, a second later, I opened up with the gimpy and started strafing them in burst shots. We're strictly not allowed to fire the GPMG on sustained fire because the barrel overheats. But it's a good weapon, and when it's in the fixed position it has brilliant aim and coverage. It's still classed as small arms, but for our purposes against unarmed foe it does a brilliant job. Dave and Clarence also taught us some good tactics. Like how to take the legs out on the first few ranks of a charging horde to make the ones behind them stumble and trip. Which buys time and hampers their advance.

Carmen

We got out of the SUV just ahead of the van. I could see Roy was already on the roof of his vehicle with his longbow, and Maddox was outside Reggie's sliding door. Then Charlie got to work with burst firing the gimpy and a second or two later everyone else from the Saxon was letting rip with assault rifles.

I then heard Bashir saying something. I didn't know exactly what, but I could tell he was asking Henry why we weren't engaging the enemy.

Joan was also looking tense and tapping her fingers on the side of her sniper rifle.

'Boss?' I asked as Henry just watched the infected get hosed down in droves.

'I think they've done it,' Frank said as the guns fell silent. Then we heard another roar as more infected poured into view from the back of the garden centre, and the weapons once again started firing.

'Commander?' Bashir asked again. This time in heavy English. 'We fight. Yes?' He looked confused and more than a bit annoyed. He'd left his family in the fort to get stuck in and we were just bloody watching. I couldn't blame him either.

'Just hold on,' Henry said in English.

'I think they're done,' Frank said as the guns once more fell silent.

We watched on as a door opened in one of the big outbuildings with a few people edging out.

'Oh god! Thank you! Thank you!' a woman shouted. Her voice drifting over on the hot still air. 'Mr Howie! Paula! Thank you! All of you. Thank you!'

'We can't stop,' Howie called out to them. 'Use a digger or something to scoop the bodies away then burn them. The blood is still dangerous. We have to go. Is everyone okay in there?'

'We're okay. Just hungry. We're almost out of food.'

'We'll leave you what we have,' Paula said as Blowers and his team grabbed what they had in the Saxon and stacked it into a pile.

We could hear the shouts of thank you with people crying and looking the same as those before in Petworth as they squinted up at the sunshine and looked around at the bodies.

A moment later and the Saxon battered through the already broken fence back onto the road.

'*Sorry about that!*' Howie transmitted through the radio. We got back in the SUV and set off, but I know me, Joan and Bash all twisted in our seats to watch the garden centre as it faded from view.

Reginald

The garden centre was a good stop, but we had to maintain the momentum. The situation between Howie and Henry was still too fragile - as evidenced by the brief stop to deal with a fallen tree. Which, I might add, was dealt with brilliantly by Henry, although he didn't need to be quite such a crowing cockerel about it.

We then hit Pulborough. Another small village, but clearly an area of affluence. Large houses and swimming pools in the gardens, and of course lots of signs for tennis clubs.

However, despite its apparent wealth, Pulborough had also suffered badly with obvious signs of destruction and carnage. Blood stains old and new. Bodies old and new. Storm damage and fires the same. Old and new.

The same glimpses everywhere we go. The same thing seen by all of us. The old world giving way to the new, but silent.

So very silent.

No traffic. No people. No jams. No queues. No traffic lights and no roadworks. Downed telegraph poles get shoved aside. The trailing wires tangling and snapping in the Saxon's big wheels.

We reached the town centre, which was surprisingly rundown. It was small too. Blink and you miss it.

A pizza shop next to a barbers. A convenience store further up with a small gathering of infected outside throwing themselves at the boards nailed across the windows.

The Saxon swept them away from the side of the building then stopped as the team piled out and shot the rest down while the survivors upstairs rushed to the windows. What I saw were several large Asian families surviving together. About twenty-five I'd estimate, all in all.

We took but a moment for Paula to share a few words.

'We can't stop. Head to the fort. Don't touch the bodies.'

Carmen

We set off again from Pulborough town centre. Not that you could call it a town centre.

I saw a wine merchants on one side. Then an Olde Worlde pub on the other. The sort of place Henry would stop for a real ale on a Sunday afternoon while Howie was at home watching internet porn. The thought made me snort a sudden laugh in the silent SUV, earning frowns from the others and an odd look from Frank.

Anyway. So our small fleet travelled on past the housing estates where people lived and died with tiny houses and tiny gardens. Trapped in cycles of life that never changed. Waiting to live and waiting to die and then regretting it all when the end came.

On we went. Past more houses that looked the same as all the others. Past more bodies and more blood.

Into the countryside once more where the hedges hung limp and hot, and the trees stood silent and drooping. The ground parched. The air laden with moisture, but not of the right kind. The kind that sapped the energy from your body and supercharged the breath coming from your mouth.

The kind that kept the sweat coming, despite however much water you drink. And you do drink. You drink until your belly feels bloated, while knowing you'll be thirsty as hell again within half an hour.

We left Pulborough onto the long sweeping curve of Mare Hill Road. Farms on one side. Fields on the other. A few infected here and there heading in the same direction.

I could imagine Reggie in his van reading his maps and books. I'd love to be intelligent like that. Don't get me wrong. I'm certainly smart, but not anywhere in the league of someone like Reginald. I loved that he wore a tie and rolled his sleeves up neatly - then I thought back to when he ran inside the department store waving his arms and shouting, *Kiddies, Mr Howie! Little ones carrying their barbie dolls!* It stood out a little, because Reggie didn't strike me as the panicking kind, but the truth is, I didn't care. I was glad he did it. I was glad he stopped Henry and Howie drawing down on each other because it would have been a bloodbath. The thought horrifies me, because I know Dave, and I can see his loyalty is now 100% Howie, which meant he wouldn't hesitate. My guess is that Frank would have tried to feint one side while going another way and use Dave's own team as a shield. But that wouldn't stop Dave. He'd kill his own people to protect Howie. That's how Dave operates.

Urgh. I didn't even want to think about it. I just had to hope that whatever Reggie had done to prevent disaster he would keep doing.

Then I immediately stopped thinking about everything else because I saw a bird of prey hovering on the thermals in the field alongside of us. It looked so majestic! So perfect and poised, and so effortlessly still. It held me rapt with this feeling inside I cannot ever explain. The sight of birds. Any birds, not just birds of prey, always captures my heart. The feeling of freedom they must have. To be able to fly up and see the world from above and not be bound by stupid rules and stupid regulations.

'More infected,' Frank said as I reluctantly turned my attention back to the road and looked ahead to see more infected being mown down by the Saxon. 'The princess was right,' Frank said.

I heard Henry blast air in response and figured he didn't like the way Frank and I were adopting some of the terminologies from Howie's team.

We hit the outskirts of Storrington. The same styles of houses. The same things seen here as ever before. Tiny houses and tiny gardens where the people were trapped in cycles of life that never changed. Waiting to live and waiting to die and then regretting it all when the end came.

'*Reggie. What was the name of that pub the woman said?*' Howie asked over the radio.

'*The Anchor, Mr Howie,*' Reginald said as Henry rolled his eyes at the lack of planning.

'Fools rush in,' he murmured.

'Yeah, but in fairness they did say a woman is in labour,' I said. 'That kind of warrants a fast response, boss.'

'On the contrary. It warrants no response at all. One more child born into this mess doesn't help anybody. And my name is Henry, not boss,' he said, earning a look from Frank, but then Frank is old and stinks of piss, and he's earned the right to give his CO a sharp look now and then if he wants.

Not that Henry seemed to notice or show any concern if he did. He just grabbed his radio. '*Henry here. The mission objective is to the locate and observe the CP. Please remember that.*'

'*Of course, Henry. That is exactly why we are here,*' Reginald replied. '*But surely you will not deny the rendering of aid to a woman in need while we search for it.*'

'*As long as the mission remains primary,*' Henry said.

'*Agreed,*' Howie said bluntly, and once more I couldn't help but think if Reggie had something up his sleeve. Not that I was bothered. In fact – I kind of hoped he did.

29

Reggie definitely had something up his sleeve, but I figured to let him crack on with it and focus on what was in front of me. Which is when I finally realised we'd been doing that same thing for ages.

Reggie steers us in the direction we're needed to go, while I deal with what's in front of us. What is that? What's that called? I figured a strategy like that must have a name that I could ram up Henry's bum and be like, Ha! Fuck you. We do have a tactic. It's called the

Two-stranded

Warfare

And

Targeting

Strategy.

Then I was trying to think of one that spelled *cunt* but Reggie piped up over the radio.

'*End of this road chaps. The mini-roundabout should be outside of The Anchor. Our target location is directly opposite.*'

At which point I then thought I should stop trying to think of ways to get back at Henry and focus on the job.

'Take a dump in his coffee cup,' Clarence said.

'Clarence!' Paula said in shock while I pulled a face and once more delved into the surreal notion of people reading my head thoughts.

'Fuck's sake. You said it,' Marcy said. 'You're a mutterer. You mutter like literally all day long, *I'm gonna fucking fuck Henry up and take a shit in his coffee cup,*' she said while mimicking me.

'Er. Clarence is the one taking a dump in his coffee cup,' I pointed out.

'No. You were looking for revenge suggestions,' Clarence said as he clocked the disgusted look on Paula's face. 'It's a military thing,' he said while clearly trying to back up.

'Dave. Did anyone ever shit in your coffee cup?' I asked.

'No, Mr Howie.'

'I never said anyone shat in *my* coffee cup!' Clarence said. 'I meant it's one method squaddies use to let an officer know they're not welcome.'

'By pooping in their mug,' Paula says.

'Yes!' Clarence said. 'Nick?'

'Fuck that! I am not the pooping guy.'

'No, you daft idiot. You must have heard of it. Cookey? Blowers! You were in the marines.'

'Yeah, marines don't do that,' Blowers said. 'Must be a special para thing.'

'The para pooping initiation,' Cookey said. 'Where they all have to squat and aim into cups.'

'Jesus. That's way too complicated for a para,' Blowers said, earning a few laughs. 'Unless they were colour coded cups,' Blowers added. '*Now boys, these are the cups you don't try and eat. And these are the ones you go potty in.* I'm joking!' he said, leaning back from Clarence trying to swipe at him.

'Almost there, boss!' Tappy called from the front. I twisted around to see we were already in the town. Passing smashed in windows and looted stores. Bodies here and there and lots of infected all heading in the same direction with Tappy trying to clip as many as she could.

I got up close to the seats and grabbed my radio. '*Okay. You guys hold back,*' I transmitted to the other vehicles. '*We'll punch through and* see how it looks. Roy, be ready to jump in with us if we can't get the van through.'

'Standing by,' Roy said. 'There won't be overwatch on this one guys. Watch your backs. I won't have you covered.'

'Got it, Roy,' I said as the energy started charging. The jokes gone. This was business now. This was work.

'There it is!' Tappy said, spotting the mini roundabout ahead. The last stretch of road. The last few metres and the last few seconds before it started, and the carnage began.

Infected thick in number aiming off to the left. Charging across the road from alleys and junctions.

We saw the *Anchor Inn* on the right side then looked left to the target location and a small bank presenting flush to the road – then some signs giving direction to the supermarket and the coffee shop beyond. 'There! That road,' I said, feeling the Saxon surge as Tappy gave it some power.

We reached a roundabout ahead and a low wall bordering a car park to one side. The building line behind it. 'It's a ring road,' I said. 'Roy! The road loops around the building. There's lots of infected here. More than we expected. We'll come back and get you into the car park, but we'll have to reduce the numbers before we get you inside the building.'

Tappy gave it some welly and smashed through the low wall into the car park while Nick got on the GPMG and got a few kills as we went through and got clear on the other side. Aiming back on the ring road towards the other two vehicles still on the main carriageway.

What we could also see was that the buildings in the middle – the ones we needed to get into – were surrounded by thick lines of infected going for the doors and boarded up windows.

The windows on the upper level were barred and sealed. But we could see people behind the gaps waving at the sight of the Saxon.

Maddox

THE UNDEAD TWENTY-FIVE. THE HEAT

I was in the driver's seat by then as Roy was getting his medical bag ready to help the woman in labour inside the buildings.

Then the Saxon drove at us and I held off, waiting for the very last second until it started turning back into the ring road.

Now! Tappy said over the radio. I got the van going. Driving it hard to tuck up close behind the Saxon like I'd seen Roy do before - riding the wake.

Carmen

So then Mads shot off hot on the tail of the Saxon, and Frank got our SUV right on the end of the van and the horsebox. It was the only way we'd get through.

'Where are you debussing?' Frank asked over the radio.

'Car park,' Howie said as Bashir and Joan stirred in their seats next to me. Their hearts no doubt thumping as much as everyone else's.

It was nuts too. I've seen combat, but it still gets you going. And it was a sight to see. Becoming instantly surrounded by infected wild beasts howling with hunger that were once human beings.

'Frank, give Jess room to get out when we get in car park,' I said as Frank nodded. Calm as ever. I doubt his heart was anything above normal.

We saw the roundabout ahead then the car park beyond it. The Saxon was carving a path. Aiming for the building line, and it was like time slowed. That last second before it goes off. Before the action begins.

It's hard to describe. But every colour becomes more vibrant. Every sound becomes clearer. Your senses prime and you become aware of everything.

'NOW!' Howie shouted through the radio. The Saxon stopped. The van stopped. The SUV stopped.

The sliding door in the van opened and Roy was out with his assault rifle up and braced. The medical bag on his back as he slammed the door closed and started moving towards the rear.

'I've got it,' Frank called. Already out of the SUV in the aim position and striding smoothly to the back of the horse box. He kicked the bolt and turned clear with his rifle up.

'JESS!' Charlie shouted, running to vault and grip the saddle with the axe already spinning in her hand. A war cry given. A war cry from old and Jess burst out to run into the ranks.

'Charlie! Go around. Find a way in,' Howie said into the radio. 'EVERYONE ELSE CUT THEM DOWN!'

Nick was up top, firing the gimpy as the others fired their assault rifles away from the direction of the building line. Then Howie was banging on the Saxon and giving Tappy the signal to set off and use the vehicle as a weapon to start reducing the numbers.

Maddox

We literally just arrived and got into the car park when Reginald told me to launch the drone and then go join Mr Howie. I did as he wanted and got the drone up - but I could see Nick on the gimpy going all wide-eyed at me touching his drone – then it was up and flying and I'm just about to ask Blowers where he wants me when I hear Booker shouting magazine, and I'm remembering what Frank told me about being nice and playing the long game. So then I was like, *covering!* And running over to get into Booker's side and making a show of covering him while he changed mag.

Cheers, he shouted as Reggie slammed the door open on his van and started yelling, *HOWIE! THEY'RE ON THE BLASTED ROOF.*

I figured he tried to use the radio, but it's hard to hear sometimes when we're all bunched up with all of us firing. Especially with the infected all howling and going nuts.

So then Howie was like, *WHAT!?*

They're on the blasted roof trying to get into the skylights. They'll be inside in a jiffy! Reginald's yelled.

BOSS! WINDOW. ONE O'CLOCK! Blowers then shouted as we all looked to where Blowers was pointing to a guy inside the building tearing boards away from the window. But he was panicking and frantic. Then someone else joined him trying to get the boards down as the first guy grabbed a fire extinguisher to smash the last board down before using it to break the glass. Then he's leaning out and shouting in panic. *MR HOWIE MR HOWIE MR HOWIE!*

But Howie's cursing cos the idiot just gave the infected a way in. But the boss's voice isn't that loud so then Dave is shouting at them to go back inside. *WE WILL GET TO YOU. GO BACK INSIDE!*

But she's bleeding, the guy yelled with his hands cupped around his mouth. *What do we do? She's bleeding and the baby's stuck. We can't get it out! What do we do?*

Reginald

The blasted radios we use are cheap and awful and with all the guns firing and the damned infected all howling away there was no way Howie could hear me. So then I've shouted they're on the roof when that chap has smashed the window open and was yelling that the baby was stuck.

Let me tell you one thing for a fact. Children in peril will always be the number one motivator for warrior types, but a birthing mother in distress? Gosh. That's a close second and by jove! The pulse it sent through everyone – because there we were you see, already in the thick of it and surrounded by a sizable horde with two sudden dilemmas, both of which demanded instant reaction.

The first being that the infected were already on the flat roof going for the skylights, and once they breached, we'd lose the entire building within minutes.

The second was that the birthing mother was, by all accounts, bleeding out with the tiny tot stuck inside of her.

Good lord. That got the blood pumping, but Howie didn't blink. He didn't even hesitate.

'TAPPY! GET BACK HERE,' Howie ordered into the radio. '*Blowers,* take over ground command. Clarence and Dave with me. We're taking that fucking roof to get Roy inside. MAKE READY!'

'Boss! It's Charlie. I've got a lower flat roof on my side. It's where they're going up. Ride the top of the Saxon to me. I'll start clearing.'

'Tappy here. Coming in hot, boss, get ready.'

It was all happening so incredibly fast, but that's the speed a battle moves at, while also feeling like it lasts forever. It's a bizarre thing.

The Saxon then came in fast with Howie getting up first to detach the machine gun to pass down to Clarence who shoved it at Maddox and Booker. 'You two! Get this set up,' he ordered.

If that wasn't enough. I then heard Henry yelling at Joan who was already striding towards the Saxon with her pistol out, firing into the infected to clear a path. She's an excellent markswoman, and even while moving she was dropping them like flies.

'Fuck me. She is!' Cookey said as she walked calmly by. 'She's Dave's mum!'

I could see Bashir was firing next to their SUV. As were Carmen and Frank, and I gather Henry was displaying irritation at Joan rushing off.

Not that Joan paid him any attention. 'Wait!' she called as Clarence paused then stepped back as she arrived and simply wrapped an arm around her legs to lift her up for Howie and Dave to grab her wrists.

There was no chat or discussion about why she was going with them. There simply wasn't time. And just as Clarence gripped the back to climb up the Saxon was pulling away.

I took to my desk – my battle desk as I called it– and flew the drone higher to watch the Saxon beating a path towards Charlie already at work.

'Charlie. It's Reginald. The Saxon is coming in fast. Fall back. I repeat, fall back, Charlie.'

She didn't reply but I could see on the drone that she heard me as Jess immediately twisted and kicked out to get free. Trampling the infected down as the Saxon came in hard and slammed into the body pile.

By that time, I had altered my view and could see the higher flat roof had a couple of dozen infected attacking the skylights. They were made from thick plastic, but even I could see they were starting to crack.

'With all urgency please, Howie,' I said, and I could visibly see the reaction as Howie and the others launched themselves from the Saxon to the flat roof and set about beating the infected away. Then it was another quick trip across the lower roof to climb the ledges up to the higher roof.

However, right at the point, my focus was on the battle on the other side, which only intensified when I observed that while the rotters were not only going at the skylight, they were also forming a very fast body pile beneath the window the chap inside had shouted from. They'd spotted the opening, you see, and they were bloody well going for it.

The problem, however, was that due to the positioning of several low walls at obtuse angles the Saxon would be unable to get in flush against the building line at the back and clear that body pile.

Sergeant Blowers was already under a great deal of pressure, nor could they direct fire *at* the building for fear of rounds going through to those hiding inside. And to make it worse, Howie and his small unit were only then just getting onto the higher flat roof. And don't forget of course, that our two snipers – Roy and Joan, who would be able to kill the buggers as they reached the window, were also with Howie.

It was a pickle for sure with now three very pressing situations.

1 – the skylights.

2 – the birthing mother that was bleeding out.

3 – the first floor was very shortly going to be breached – which, as I said, would mean the building being lost within a matter of moments.

'Howie. Sorry to do this to you, but there is a body pile forming beneath the open window.'

'Tappy! Clear it!' Howie shouted, or rather he grunted it while going up the ladder.

'*Negative, Howie. The Saxon will not fit into that section,*' I said.

'Okay. Get Roy to cover it. FUCK! He's with us. Er, okay, Charlie, do what you can.'

'On it! COME ON JESS!'

I rather feared there were too many even for Charlie and Jess – and the situation then got worse because I could see another layer then formed on the body pile. One or two more and those people inside would be lost – and Charlie was still some way off.

Good grief, it was all very tense.

Then I looked back to see one of the skylights was fracturing and Howie and his unit were only just spilling over the ledge onto the roof, and trust me, that was no easy climb for them.

I then observed a fellow appear in the open window who began firing a single barrel shotgun into the infected mere feet below, but in all truth, it was too little too late. He might as well have been flicking marbles for all the good it did because by then they were within height of the window with the next lot clambering up the sides of their own kind.

'They're about to breach!' I said into the radio as Howie and his unit started running across the flat roof towards the infected attacking the skylights.

Joan was firing her sniper rifle as she walked, and the power of that thing was taking the infected of their feet. The others were all firing their pistols as they ran. Trying to draw their attention from the skylights.

But I could see that unless we did something about that window there would be no point protecting the skylights.

'MR HOWIE!' I said, and yes, I admit, there was most likely a touch of urgency about my tone, but it seemed to do the trick as I, and no doubt all of us, felt the pulse from Howie as the tension really bit. It's like a rush of raw energy going through you. That's the best way to describe it.

'FUCK!' he yelled out, running faster as a great score of infected diverted from the skylight to run at him.

'MARK THE WINDOW!' Clarence then shouted into the radio. 'MARK IT, REGGIE!'

THE UNDEAD TWENTY-FIVE. THE HEAT

For a second I had no idea what he meant. Mark it? What did that mean. Then I saw Clarence's face, and I saw the position he was adopting as he ran at the infected on that flat roof. His body was lowering. His arms were stretching out.

'Oh, good god,' I said to myself as I quickly moved the drone to hover above the flat roof and over the position of the open window. 'IT'S MARKED! IT'S MARKED!'

On my life I haven't never seen anything like it. It's seared into my memory. The sight of it.

The sight of Clarence running ahead of Howie. His arms outstretched. His face snarling with a grimace as he roared out with such noise I swear everyone else stopped and twisted to look up. Of course Howie yelled at him. Roy and Joan did the same. But Clarence, see. Clarence knew what he had to do – and so he did it.

He slammed into the infected charging at him, and he scooped the bastards up in his arms and ran on like a goliath rugby player, gathering them all up and driving them back. You've never seen such strength. You've never seen a thing like it.

Howie then detonated his hive mind and we're all fizzing with rage. I'm up and slamming my battle swatter on my battle desk as Blowers and every member of our team started to turn and run for that body pile.

But Clarence. Well. He had his way - and that great man swept the infected off their feet all the way to the edge of the roof right under the drone... And then he went down with them.

Get that sight into your mind. The man ran across the flat roof *into* the infected, gathering them up to propel backwards and used his own body weight to ensure they fell.

I can see it right now in my mind. The sight of the infected all falling backwards with Clarence on top smashing his giant fists into their faces as they dropped.

And drop they did. Right down from the roof into the body pile that started collapsing from the dozens of infected all raining down. Clarence amongst them. Lost from view within the seething mass.

A second to see it. A second for the notion of what Clarence just did to settle in the mind and that rage inside made Blowers and Cookey and all of the others turn and sprint for the building.

That was the body pile taken out, and we had no way of knowing if Clarence was hurt, or even alive, or capable of defending himself – and, of course, the skylights were still being attacked by those infected left on the roof.

'THEY'RE INSIDE!' Roy shouted, seeing several drop through one of the broken skylights, and Howie who was still running after Clarence veered off and dove headfirst through that same skylight.

It was all so quick. So incredibly fast.

My own instincts were pulsing too, and so I took that drone in through the open window and across the room into a corridor filled with people crying out in fear from the infected dropping down from the roof.

But Howie was amongst them. His face a picture of utter rage as he stabbed into the bodies and grabbed ankles to rip them off their feet to stop them running off.

Then Dave dropped down as another skylight smashed through with more infected falling down inside.

'NEXT SKYLIGHT, HOWIE!' I said into the radio and saw as he jerked his head up and screamed out with fury as he got to his feet and ran hard into the ones falling down.

Gunshots rang out and I turned the drone back to see Dave firing his pistol with lightning speed. Dropping them as quickly as he could as Roy's med bag dropped down behind him, followed by Roy himself.

'WHERE?' Roy shouted, shouting at the people running off in fear before he saw the drone hovering in the air. 'REGGIE! WHERE?'

He meant the birthing mother of course, so I quickly set off towards one end of the corridor, but it was no good. I flew back the other way but again it was all offices and rooms given over as sleeping quarters.

I found the stairwell and flew down then along to see everyone gathered screaming and crying in the café on the ground floor.

'*Café, Roy. Ground floor!*' I said into the radio and flew back upstairs to see Joan was now with them with Howie and Dave taking on the infected that got inside. *'Follow me!'* I said and led them down the stairs.

Paula

I felt sick with fear, and I will never forget the sight of Clarence going over the edge of that building with the infected falling ahead of him. Nor will I ever forget the sight of him landing on the body pile, and the whole thing giving way, collapsing down into one enormous heap of thrashing bodies with Clarence on his own. Buried alive.

We all reacted. Oh my god, we reacted. And we ran with our hearts in our mouths. Every single one of us just ran to get there. Danny was fastest, and bless him, he just dove into the mess. Stabbing at infected as he pulled them away. Then Mo got there, Blowers, Cookey, Nick, Maddox and Booker. Then Jess is steaming in with Charlie sliding off the saddle to help. Even Tappy was out of the Saxon, running in with Meredith. Marcy was there. We all were. Clarence was buried beneath dozens of bodies. The man can fight, but even his body needed air to breath. He'd be crushed or suffocated.

We tore at them. We screamed out like wild beasts with Jess rearing up to crush them and Meredith ragging bodies. It was frenzied.

Then it erupted.

Oh. My. God. It erupted – and I don't mean figuratively. I mean literally because that seething pile of bodies seemed to shift and move like the tectonic plates were shifting beneath them. And in a way that's what was happening, except it wasn't tectonic plates, it was one seriously large man having one seriously bad day.

Now we've all seen Clarence when he goes berserk. But this was off the scale because that mass of bodies just seemed to slide away from this rising bulk in the middle with even us falling back and crying out until there was just this Viking warlord roaring out as he fought free while using a human leg as a club. God knows where he got the leg from. He just had it in his hand as he screamed and killed anything within range.

Reginald

I flew back to the café on the ground floor. A large open plan area filled with people in varying states of silent terror or whimpering in fear while others openly sobbed. Children were clinging to adults. Men and women were holding paltry weapons. Sticks and knives but they were shaking from head to toe, and there, in the middle, was a young woman flat on her back with her legs spread. People at her sides in obvious states of panic at the large pool of blood spreading out from between the woman's legs. Her belly swollen with child, but even I could see there was too much blood.

I saw it all within a glimpse as Roy and Joan strode into the room while rubbing liberal amounts of anti-bac gel into their hands and arms, and my gosh, the sight of them striding in sent a ripple of electricity through that room. They were both armed, of course, but it was more than that. They looked like paramedics turning up to a scene of carnage with that aura of absolute calm control.

'Move aside please,' Joan said curtly, but not harsh. She wasn't rude at all, and the people did just as she said with all of them wilting back as Roy moved in to grasp the birthing mother's hand.

'You're going to be okay. My name is Roy. We're going to help you.'

The poor woman burst into tears, staring up at him as Joan gently opened her legs and got down low to start examining her.

'Roy?' Howie shouted from outside the café.

'In here!' Roy called as Howie and Dave ran down the stairs.

'Do not come inside,' Joan ordered without glancing back as Howie came to a sudden stop and looked down at his bloodied clothing. Dave didn't have a drop on him of course, but they both stopped at the threshold.

'How is she?' Howie asked.

'How long has she been in labour?' Joan asked. 'Someone, answer me!'

'Hours,' someone blurted.

'Has she been pushing?' Roy asked.

'I keep pushing,' the woman sobbed.

'It's trapped then,' Joan said. 'Right. Let's get to it. Roy, you watch her vitals, I'll get a hand inside and see what's what.'

Paula

To be fair, the rest of us could have gone for a cup of tea and left Clarence to it. And in a way, I think he kind of needed it.

But we all got stuck in, and a couple of minutes, later we'd killed them all. Helped enormously by Bashir getting on the gimpy – then once more that strange silence came as we stood in a sea of death and broken human forms. All of us sucking air in, and Clarence in the middle, holding someone's arm in his hand. His bald head dripping with blood. His top torn and ripped away. The parachute regiment tattoo visible on his shoulder.

Honestly. I would have humped his leg right then if I could have, but instead, I just looked at him. We all did. What he'd just done was something else.

'Airborne,' Frank then said, making Clarence look over to him.

'Airborne,' Clarence said. Frank nodded once. They didn't say anything else.

Then we heard some bangs sounding out and the noise of boards being prised open. A few seconds later, and a door opened at the back of the building as the same man from the window stepped out, then balked at the sight of us and the carnage around our feet.

'How is she?' Clarence asked.

The man tried to reply but vomited instead. Then, he waved an arm at the door, urging us to go inside.

'Blowers, get sorted here,' I said as Blowers nodded. I went first through the door, with Clarence and Marcy, then Henry, and his team behind us.

We transitioned from bright light to a gloomy interior. The windows boarded up with thick planks, and we went past doors leading into the supermarket interior. The shelving moved against the plate glass windows. Defined sections clear with walls made from blankets hanging from string. Lanes and alleys running between them. A stench inside. Body odour and people, but at least they had food and the ability to clean themselves.

WE COULD HEAR it before we reached the open doors leading into the café. A grunt sounding ahead. Someone gasping quickly.

Howie and Dave were standing by the café doors staring inside to a woman on her back, grunting and panting in agony. People were gathered at the sides looking terrified.

'I've got to push,' the pregnant woman said through gritted teeth.

'Joan?' I said.

'Do not come in if you've got blood on you,' Joan said without looking back as I spotted Roy at the woman's side, pressing a stethoscope to her stomach.

'I've got to push!' the woman said again.

'Do not push!' Joan said.

That's when I saw the blood on the floor that Joan was lying in. Thick red blood that had come from the mother spread out across the floor. There was too much. We could all see that, and she looked so pale too.

But the horrific thing was the sight of Joan straining to get her hand inside the woman, pushing harder as the woman cried out with silent screams.

'Roy, look for me. I can't get an angle,' Joan said as Roy shifted position to get in low beside her. His own body lying in the woman's blood. He shone a powerful hand torch inside of her and craned to see while all the time the woman screamed.

'I've gotta push... I've gotta push.'

'No,' Joan said, calm, but full of authority while I poured anti-bac all over my arms and hands and started rubbing it in. Then Marcy grabbed a spray bottle and set out about covering me from head to toe.

'Bit more, Joan. Just a bit more,' Roy said as Joan grunted and focused while clearly trying to turn the baby inside.

'I need to push!' the woman cried out.

'No!' Joan ordered.

'We'll have to cut it out,' Roy whispered.

'We are not cutting anyone,' Joan said. 'Not today.'

Another grunt as Joan pushed her hand further inside the woman who screamed out from the agony of it with fresh spurts of blood coming out between her legs.

'I'm coming in,' I said. 'I'm anti-bacced,' I added as Joan shot me a look.

'Head to toe,' Marcy said as Joan nodded. I ran inside to the woman's side to take her hand.

'Hey, I'm Paula. You're going to be okay. What's your name?'

'Donna,' she said as I heard Howie telling the others what's happened.

'It's stuck,' Howie whispered. 'She was pushing but it won't come out.'

'The cord?' Henry asked.

'I think so,' Joan said. 'And the baby is twisted inside.'

'She's lost a lot of blood,' Henry said.

'If you've nothing useful to say, Henry,' Joan said while trying to get at the cord without forceps or tools or anything other than her hands. And all the time that blood kept coming out and the woman screamed in pure agony.

'Carmen, get some plasma in our medkit,' Henry ordered while striding in and rubbing anti-bac into his hands and arms. 'You need to turn her. Let gravity aid you.'

'She'll bleed out,' Roy said.

'She's already bleeding out,' Henry said, dropping to the woman's side next to me. 'You and you,' Henry ordered, nodding at people nearby. 'Don't just stand there. Get in here. We're going to turn her. Which way, Joan?'

'This way,' Joan said, motioning the direction as Donna wept and gasped. 'Now,' Joan said. Nodding at us to gently ease her over onto her side as the woman screamed with a sound of pure agony. Making people cry out and turn away. 'Bit more,' Joan said as the blood came out thick and fast, and while she delved her hand deeper into the birthing canal. 'Hold her there!' Joan said. 'I've got the cord. Hold her… Okay, yes, it's free, let me… It's moving! I can move it.'

'That's it, Joan! I can see the head,' Roy said. 'It's clear.'

'Now push,' Joan hissed. 'PUSH DAMN YOU!'

An animalistic roar as Donna finally gave in to the urge to push with every muscle locking out. The veins pushing proud through her skin.

'Crowning!' Roy called as the blood sprayed from the skin tearing. A sudden release and it slid free in a rush of liquid into Roy's hands.

A tiny baby covered in gore and blood. A perfectly formed human child that Joan took to rub as every person in that room held their breath.

'Is it?' Donna asked, her voice barely a whisper. 'Please… is it…'

Joan took a breath, turned the baby, and slapped its tiny bum, making it cough and clear the airways with a gasp and a cry. 'He's fine,' she said as the little lungs gave their first noise in this brave new world.

'Listen to him!' Howie said from the doorway with tears rolling down his cheeks.

'He's beautiful,' I said.

'A boy?' Donna asked, her eyes filled with tears. Her voice wavering.

'A boy,' I said with my own tears flowing. 'A beautiful boy.'

'Is he okay?' Donna asked.

'Don't sit up!' Roy said, pressing something below to stem the bleeding.

'He's perfect,' Joan said, shuffling on her knees to press the baby into her arms.

'My boy,' Donna whispered, holding him close and feeling her baby in her arms for the first time. Seeing his face. His nose and ears. The strands of dark wet hair on his head. The tiny arms and tiny legs.

'We have to cut the cord,' Joan said as the woman nodded. Her mind solely on the child. The tears still falling. The blood still coming as Carmen ran back in with a med bag. Dropping at her side and working fast to get a line into her arm from a bag of plasma while Joan and Roy clamped and cut the cord.

The gasps and sobs of relief sounding out from all around.

'Have they gone?' someone asked as Henry looked at the woman and her child then over to the man asking the question. To everyone listening. Dozens of people. Men, women and children. The young and the old. The weak and the terrified.

Henry nodded. 'They're gone,' he said. Glancing back to Howie in the door. Dave at his side and Clarence at his back, towering over him. His top still ripped into shreds. His great head still pouring with sweat and blood.

'Coming in!' Reginald called, threading a careful route inside to pick the drone up from a nearby table before peering down at the baby. 'Ooh. Well done you, and don't worry, I think all babies are wrinkly to start off with. Anyway! Can someone tell me how long they were here for. The infected people I mean.'

'They been going through for a few days,' one of the men replied, looking to the others for confirmation. 'Like going past. Then they started trying to get in.'

'Same as Petworth,' Howie said.

'But they were going past *before* they started to try and break into here. Is that correct?' Reginald asked as they all nodded.

'Same up the road,' another man said, moving forward to be seen. 'I saw them going past for a while.'

'Where up the road?' Howie asked.

'Ashington,' the man said. 'I came down a few days back. Like. I was going for the fort then stopped here and got stuck.'

'Jordan's from the community centre in Ashington,' The first man said. The one that was leaning out of the window then puked when he came outside. 'He was meant to be scouting for a way to the fort.'

'Yeah,' Jordan said. 'Listen, if you're going that way can you check on them?' he asked. 'Only they've got a few kiddies there and the food was running low.'

'We cannot rescue everyone,' Henry said.

'Well. We do need to go that way, Henry,' Reginald said.

'He's so beautiful,' Donna said from the floor. Her baby cradled in her arms. 'Thank you,' she said to Joan and Roy. The tears still flowing.

'You need to thank Mr Howie and those two men,' Joan said, nodding at Howie, Dave, and Clarence standing in the doorway as the woman turned to look at Howie.

'Howie,' she said with a soft smile as Howie frowned in panic.

'Oh god, no, don't call him Howie.'

'Eh? I wasn't going to,' Donna said. 'Oh god! Did you want me to call him Howie?'

'What? Oh shit. No! Sorry. I thought cos Joan said then you said and... Right. But no. Sorry. My mistake. I er...'

'Cos I was thinking about David actually.'

'Aw, that's lovely,' I said with a smile at Dave.

'After David Beckham,' Donna added. 'Sex on legs,' she said with her own legs still spread open while Roy stitched away with a strange look of happiness on his face. 'Don't suppose you've found him, have you?'

'David Beckham?' I asked. 'Er, no. We haven't.'

'Aw. Hey! I could give him a middle name though. David Dave Davidson! Oh my god. That's so cool.'

'Right. On that note! Shall we?' Henry asked, looking at the others.

'Eh? Hang on,' Howie asked, staring longingly towards the coffee shop counter.

'Mr Howie, we cannot keep stopping,' Henry said.

'Fuck's sake. Fine,' Howie said with a sigh. 'We'll get takeout then. Right. Who's serving? We need twenty lattes, one carton of oatmilk for a horse, and one cup of Darjeeling to go please.'

30

D iary of Charlotte Doyle

THEN ONCE WE'D ANTI-BACCED, checked weapons and hydrated we were back into the Saxon, or, as we came to call it, back to being hot bodies in a hot tin can.

'Woohoo! The Saxon on the blacktop, speeding through the backdrop,' Tappy called as she started the engine.

The energy was high too and everyone was buzzing about the battle and how Clarence threw himself off a building to demolish a body pile single handed. Good gosh it was incredible. Then we heard how Howie dove headfirst through a skylight and landed on the infected inside and he and Dave kept them busy while Reginald used the drone to lead Roy and Joan to the woman in labour – and then how Henry came in and saved her life by turning her onto her side.

All in all, it was a brilliant team effort all around, and so yes, the energy was high. We'd just saved a mother and child and more survivors. Plus, we were allowed to go inside and look at the baby as long as we didn't touch anything or go too close.

He was so beautiful! Well. Actually. If I am being completely honest, he was a rather ugly wrinkly thing, but super cute in a tiny defenceless way, and we stood there in silent awe for a moment – I say silent, Henry and Howie were bickering about coffee. Henry didn't want to stop. Howie said we'll get take out. Henry called him an idiot. Howie called Henry a twat then Joan cleared her throat and gave them a Paula look and they stopped – but we did get coffee. Paula said we deserved it after that, and she was the XO and was allowed to make that decision. Frank then said he concurred with a cheeky grin at Henry who clearly saw he was outnumbered and conceded with a graceful nod.

So, yes. We then got our hot bodies back into our hot tin can where we drank strong, caffeinated, hot drinks. Which Maddox said was a really stupid thing to do, then he went all odd for a second and announced that he too would like a coffee.

And then, we all settled in to continue our merry journey.

'Fuck just happened?' Howie asked – while once more cramped in the back of the Saxon.

'We made a baby!' Paula said.

'Well. We didn't make a baby,' Clarence said. 'I think that young lady made the baby.'

'You know what I mean. Oh, but his little arms and legs and his dark hair. Literally the cutest thing ever,' Paula said.

'Wow. Never took you for the broody type,' Marcy said.

'Yeah, me neither,' Paula said with a sudden frown. 'But did you see his little nose!'

'Ooh, she is,' Marcy said while nodding at Clarence. 'She's broody.'

'Why are you nodding at me?' Clarence asked, sipping from his takeout latte on the bench seat. Paula wedged in next to him. Marcy opposite winking and nodding while Howie sat on her other side. Quietly enjoying his coffee and the rising caffeine levels while again pondering why the shit they didn't get into the van. I know that because he was muttering it. (He mutters a lot)

'I was just thinking that,' Marcy said. 'Why aren't we in the van?'

'Fuck's sake,' Howie grumbled.

'You said it out loud,' she said.

'I didn't!'

'You did,' Clarence said before sipping his coffee as Marcy went back to nodding and winking at him. 'Stop doing that.'

'Stop what?' Paula asked. 'Shit name though. Poor kid.'

'What would you call your baby?' Marcy asked her.

'Oh god, no idea.'

'Something beginning with C maybe?' Marcy asked with another wink at Clarence.

'Seriously. Why are you doing that?' Clarence asked as Paula sighed at his side again. Her body pressing into his. But then there wasn't not much choice really. Not with Clarence taking the space of three normal sized people and everyone else crammed in like sardines.

It was so packed that I could barely lift my arm to drink my coffee, which only got worse the first time Tappy used the brakes and we all slid a bit. 'I'm getting crushed,' I said with a yelp while wedged between Danny and Booker. 'Someone pull me out.' I stretched my arms and felt Blowers and Cookey grab my wrists to pop me out like a cork from a bottle – and I don't know why, but I just did it. I saw the opening and I took it. You have to remember that I was the captain for the under 21's England hockey team and played league polo. I'm super competitive and able to seize a chance when I see it. And so yes. I saw a chance right there with Cookey right next me and with nowhere else to go I plopped down on his lap with a big grin.

He of course went all wide-eyed as everyone else cheered and made noises- because as I said, the energy was high. The mood was good. 'Oh my gosh,' I announced while stretching my legs out. 'That's so much better. Do say if I'm squashing you though.'

'Yeah. Get off fatty,' Cookey said with a laugh as I pushed down harder and wriggled about to a few more laughs.

'Fatty is not on the safe word list!' Tappy called from the front.

'You're fine. Paula's dreaming of babies,' Marcy said with another wink and nod at Clarence. 'Have you ever thought about kids, Clarence? You'd make such an awesome dad.'

'You sure I'm not too hot?' I asked after twisting around to look at Cookey and motioning that I will rise and leave him alone. But he shook his head while sipping from his coffee and pulled me back down. I smiled at his blue eyes and reached out to push his hair back. Wincing comically at the sodden sweat. But then we were all dripping with sweat so it was nothing new – but there it was again, that sudden closeness between us while everyone else chattered on about babies and Dave's mum and this and that.

'You ever thought about kids?' I asked Cookey. 'You'd make an awesome dad.'

'You'd be an awesome mum,' he said. 'You could teach them horse-riding and languages and all that smart stuff.'

'You can teach them the new sock dance,' I said, making him laugh with delight as I slipped further along his thighs to settle into him a bit more.

It was strange really. I mean, the heat was nothing short of brutal, but it was a golden moment and one I shall never forget. The way everyone was chatting all around us. The laughs and the jokes. The vibration coming up through the wheels. The Saxon had become a home from home for us. A place of safety. It was incredibly uncomfortable and induced motion sickness all the time. It stank to high heaven and was far too hot and rattly, but we'd all been wrenched from our lives and families, and that was all we had. The Saxon and each other.

And there I was. On Cookey's lap with my body pressing into his. There was something between us. An energy or perhaps a yearning. It was so clear from the way he looked at me – and yet he suddenly shifted with a look of discomfort.

'Am I too heavy?' I asked.

'No! It's fine,' he said but he wouldn't meet my eyes.

'Cookey, what's wrong?' I asked quietly. Then a second later I felt it. His erection pushing into my backside. Honestly. It was the last thing I expected and I'll admit I gasped with surprise and I've no doubt my eyes widened. Then he looked at me with deep worry in his eyes and shame burning his cheeks. I immediately thought I should get off and spare his blushes and not mention it, or perhaps pretend I hadn't noticed and make some small conversation about something else.

And perhaps I should have done those things, but I was flushed with high energy and a good mood, and I was horny. Good god I was horny, and so I felt a rush of mischievous delight.

'I'm so sorry,' he whispered.

'Don't be,' I said and gave him a slow smile while shifting a little to push into him. That made his eyes go wider, that's for sure, and so I did it again. I pushed down a little bit more before turning to face front. Smiling and laughing at whatever jokes and banter were going on while pushing down into his hardness. Then I quickly looked back to make sure he was okay and saw him give me a nervous smile. I winked and faced front again.

There was a delicious naughtiness about it, and just doing that tiny, almost insignificant act gave me a deep sense of joy. It was escape from the horrors of what we do, and it heightened the intimacy between us, which only then I realised I had been craving a great deal more since Blinky died.

'Honestly though! Who calls a kid David Dave Davidson?' Paula asked as the chuckles and laughs rolled about while I ever so slowly pushed down into his lap.

But then it got even better because I felt my top being tugged out from my trousers then a sensation on my naked back from his fingertips finding my skin. Drawing small circles and sending shivers up my spine. I turned to smile at him. To show him that it was okay. That he could touch me and that this was safe.

A few miles later and we were on the London Road heading out of Storrington and still heading north east. Barrelling into the green and lush countryside. We then happened upon Squire's Garden Centre and observed the large car park bordering the warehouse buildings were filled with infected. A moment later and the air split apart from the sound of gunfire.

A few moments given. A few words shared.

'We can't stop. Head to the fort. Don't touch the bodies.'

Then we were back into the Saxon. Back to being hot bodies in a hot tin can.

The energy high. The day growing hotter. We were cracking skulls and saving lives with heroic deeds and courageous acts.

Cookey took his seat, and without saying anything again, I took his lap. But it was cool. A few people smiled but it was so packed I think everyone was glad of the extra few inches of space they'd gained. And then, once we got going, I felt it again beneath my bottom then his fingers were inside my shirt, gently tracing patterns over my skin. It was divine. I was in heaven. That's my happy place now. When it got dark, which it did later, that's where I went.

We reached Ashington. The infected spotted on the road here and there. Heading in the same direction. Others seen crossing the fields to the side. Giving indication they were heading towards something. Or after something.

We headed for the community centre as I understand a young man called Jordan said there were survivors with children hiding at that location, and they were low on food, but also that they wanted to make a break for the fort. I gather our intention was to help them get on their way and render what aid we could, while of course, still searching for the CP that Henry wanted to see.

We found it easy enough. **Ashington Community Centre**. Low buildings nestled between lush green sports fields, and there was a gorgeous school across the road with a lovely playground outside that any parent would feel blessed to send their child.

It was a tranquil place. A place of wonder and beauty.

But it was also a place of horror and death.

We parked the Saxon in the car park. The van behind it. The SUV alongside. Then we got out to stare at the smashed in windows and doors of the community centre. The pools of blood and the flies feasting upon the bodies.

We were too late.

The infected had got inside.

We could see the hole in the windows where the boards were not strong enough and how the people inside tried to fight back. The sticks and knives they used. The shotguns dropped on the ground. The spent cartridges amongst the bodies of the ones they killed before they were overwhelmed and taken.

And there. Seen through the ripped out windows and doors lay the bodies of those that took their own lives rather than face the horror coming for them.

Men, women and children lying in dried pools of blood with their throats cut, and to the last we could only imagine the absolute horror of what they faced and the pain of killing their own children.

Reginald

It was a truly awful sight. Tragic in a way that rendered us all to complete silence, and especially after the battle of Storrington.

But there we stood, in that great silence broken only by the swarms of flies buzzing between the rotting corpses.

But that view juxtaposed the serenity of an otherwise perfect place. The fields were still green. The playpark was still shining in bright colours. The sun was still climbing the sky. The air was still thick and shimmering.

I stood back from the others to keep an overview of the whole thing, and although this sounds so very wrong, I was glad Henry had seen it. Henry *needed* to see it and be exposed to the true scale of the event and that it wasn't something just happening to faceless victims.

That real people were suffering in the very worst ways imaginable. That is exactly what Henry needed, and truth be told, I couldn't have asked for a better sequence of events.

A child being born followed by the sight of people we *didn't* save.

'When did this happen?' Howie then asked as Frank walked inside the community centre and through to the back where the bodies lay dead with their throats cut.

'Overnight probably,' he said, looking around at the corpses. 'Heat makes it hard to be precise, but they've all pissed themselves.'

'What does that mean?' Marcy asked.

'Means their bladders were full from sleeping,' Carmen said. 'They probably woke up to the things breaking in.'

'That nipper was right,' Frank added while holding a single tin of baked beans up. 'That's all they had left. Poor sods.'

A grunt from Howie. From others too. All of them feeling it. Seeing it. Smelling it.

'Where's closest to here?' Carmen asked, looking back to me then over to Henry.

'Either Billingshurst or Southwater,' I said. 'They're roughly equal distance.'

'And this CP were looking for did this?' Carmen asked as Henry turned away with a dark look on his face. 'Billingshurst is larger. I suggest we start there,' he said.

We loaded up without needing orders to do so – because the chase was underway, and we had our foe formed in the shape of the elusive CP we were now tracking.

A thing now defined as monstrous from the horrors we'd just saw.

It was taking time, but the pieces on the board were moving into place, and Henry was slowly being drawn into the game.

31

D iary of Maddox Doku

WHY THE FUCK *would you volunteer for this?* Nick asked me while shaking his head. *You had actual air-con. Our vents don't even work.*

I gave him a smile as the sweat poured down my face. *Beats listening to Roy talking about bows,* I said.

The battle of Agincourt, Cookey said.

The V's! I said and stuck two fingers up and did my Roy impression of a flat nerd voice. *Did you know that's why we give people the V's, Maddox?* It was cool. It got some laughs.

I wondered why you ran over to cover me, Booker said from next to me. *I was like what the fuck is he doing?*

Nah bro. I saw you struggling, I said with a quick grin as the rest jeered while Booker gave me the middle finger. *Cheers for covering me though,* he said.

Then I was like *anytime* and playing it cool and doing that thing Frank said about not wanting anything.

I saw the chance when we stopped in Ashington and saw the dead bodies in the community centre. Everyone was really down, especially after Storrington. So then I was like, *take the van and cool off* to Paula. I said I'd jump in the Saxon. *Bless you,* she said, even Howie and Clarence said cheers and Marcy gave me her nice big smile.

It felt good too. I liked the tactic Frank had suggested about being nice and playing the long game.

Actually, I said a second later. *It fucking stinks in here. Can I change my mind?*

Ha! Too late you cheeky cunt, Booker said with a laugh. But he wasn't laughing at me this time. It was just normal banter. But man, that heat was something else. Even with the back doors open.

You've got your seat back, Cookey then said with a smile at Charlie.

Aw, you missing me? she asked. *I could always come back over.*

Jesus. Get a room, Nick said as Charlie winked and Cookey shifted in his seat then laughed it off, but then I saw Charlie looking confused and wondered what the dynamics were. I figured they were going to hook up, but then I realised I'd been thinking that for ages, and it had never happened. Not that it was my business. My focus was on Booker and getting into his life.

Paula

What a relief it was to be in the van! Bless Maddox for thinking of it.

Mind you. Although we had more room, it was still bloody baking. 'Is that air-con on?' I asked as I heard Roy talking to Clarence up front.

'I felt it when we were up on that flat roof,' Roy said as Clarence grunted in the front passenger seat. 'Just a niggle in my left side, like down my arm and I thought to myself, Roy, this is it old chum, you're having a stroke.'

'Why is it so bloody hot in here? Is the air-con on?' I asked, leaning through the hatch to see Roy smelling the air. 'What are you doing?'

'He's sniffing for toast,' Clarence said, giving me a sideways look.

'Oh god. I can. I can smell toast.'

'That's cow shit you idiot,' I said, pointing to a farm alongside before heading back into the rear and Marcy talking to Howie.

'I'm just saying he was really good with that woman,' Marcy said as Howie grumbled and shook his head. 'Nobody else thought to turn her over.'

'Roy would have thought of it,' Howie said.

'I probably wouldn't,' Roy called. 'Not with my current medical condition.'

'He thinks he's having a stroke,' I said to the blank looks.

'And he got Carmen to give her plasma,' Marcy added.

'What about in the department store?' Howie asked. 'All that shit he said about us.'

'Yeah but…' Marcy started to say but fell silent.

'What?' I asked her.

'I mean. Some of what he said kind of makes sense,' Marcy said carefully. 'Oh god, don't start frothing at the mouth again, Howie. I'm on your side. Yes, he was out of order and you're awesome and he's a prick and blah blah, but, you know, to him I guess we do look like a bag of shit. *And* I did just sneeze on that man.'

'So what? We just let Henry take charge then?' Howie asked.

'I'm not saying that,' Marcy said. 'I don't know what I'm saying. I just mean one minute he's a complete twat then he's cool as anything...'

'What?' Howie asked at the way she trailed off. Reginald and I stayed silent, having already figured her point. Then a second later Howie figured it out too. 'You can all fuck off,' he said. 'I'm nothing like Henry! What the actual fuck! Reggie, tell them I'm nothing like Henry.'

'You're nothing like Henry.'

'See!'

'Henry's bald,' Reginald added to a deep braying laugh coming from the front.

Carmen

So then we're back in the vehicles and driving on with Henry having a rant at Frank.

'They're nothing like us, that's for damn sure. They're winging their way through the whole thing.'

'My point is they are coping,' Frank said. 'And we've winged it enough times, Henry. Falklands? Bosnia? Kuwait? Northern Ireland? Africa? Want me to keep going?'

Henry didn't reply but did that thing and snorted air from his nose while tapping the air-con controls with a grimace at the warm air coming from the vents.

'And when we met her in the back. Remember that? The Russian guys?' Frank asked.

'The Russian guys you shot you mean,' Henry said.

'Oi! Her in the back has a name,' I said.

'My point is, we've done our fair share of winging it,' Frank said. 'In fact, you always said we train so hard so that we *can* wing it.'

'But we had training, Frank.'

'Clarence was a Para,' Frank said, shooting him a look. '*We* were Paras, Henry. Look what he did back there. And Blowers was a Marine, and they've had Dave with them. Do you remember Milo?'

'Yes. I remember Milo,' Henry said heavily.

'Who was Milo? I asked.

'Before your time,' Frank said, glancing in the rear-view. 'Lad in Bosnia. He was a pig farmer and didn't know one end of a gun from the other.'

'Stavi?' I asked. 'Is that his first name? He's amazing.'

'Stavi?' Bashir asked, hearing the name.

'Exactly,' Frank said. 'Even Bash has heard of Stavi.'

'Stavi,' Bashir said with a nod before reeling something off in his language.

'Bash said Stavi was one of the best he worked with,' Henry relayed.

'I am assuming you trained this Milo Stavi?' Joan asked as Henry turned to nod.

THE UNDEAD TWENTY-FIVE. THE HEAT

'Pig farmer,' Frank said at Henry rolling his eyes as we drove on through the deep countryside.

It went silent for a moment and I stared up through the window to the sun still climbing high. A day of days already. Not a breeze in the air. Not a cloud in the sky. I was choosing my moment, and it felt right to ask what was on my mind. 'This isn't revenge for us is it, Henry?' I asked.

'Of course not,' Henry said while looking out of the window to his side.

'Because I'm fine if it is,' I said as Frank shot Henry another look and the silence once more came back as we followed the van onto Harbolets Road and through Broadford Bridge. A small hamlet of houses opposite a farm. Infected seen in the fields heading northeast.

The Saxon in the lead. Tappy holding the road squat and centre. Leading the charge as we went through Adversane. A country pub on the main road. A few infected outside. A couple of moments spared. A few words given.

We can't stay. Head for the fort. Don't touch the bodies.

Then we were back onto the road driving on. A mile or two and we saw thick smoke in the air ahead of us. Plumes of it coiling up into the sky from a lumber yard stacked with wood. The houses and buildings burning with it. But it was old. Not new. Maybe a day ago. The walls and structures had already crumbled in.

Of any survivors there was no sign, and we drove on with each vehicle slowing to look and ponder the fate of the people that lived there.

We hit the first roundabout at the edge of the town and once more proceeded without a briefing – much to Henry's irritation.

But we did see more infected on the road, and more in the fields all roughly heading in the same direction. Tappy was killing the ones she could drive over, and I smiled with a grimace at the thought of her and Nick having to pick body parts and scalps out of the vents and pipes again. 'Dick on a stick,' I muttered with a laugh.

'Pardon?' Joan asked me.

I said it was just something one of the lads said as we went past some multi-purpose sports fields next to a set of larger buildings. A leisure centre and school side by side, and we could see tendrils of smoke coming from the buildings, plus the outer perimeter chain-link fence had been busted down in a few places.

'We'll go in and check,' Howie ordered over the radio as Henry tutted again, but we followed the vehicles in and came to a stop on the concrete tennis courts. The fences ripped down. The nets hanging and broken.

The buildings looked silent, dark, and empty. The windows smashed. The doors broken, but it was recent. We could see that. Wet blood was on the walls and we could smell burning in the air and see smoke, but there were no obvious signs of fire.

'Is that toast?' Roy whispered, earning a sharp look from Henry once we'd all gathered together. 'My arm was tingling.'

'It's from the medical bag you had on your back. The straps were too thin,' Henry said, and I could see he was biting the frustration down. 'Mr Howie?' he prompted. Meaning *can we go?*

Howie nodded. 'We'll be quick. Tappy, drive around the outside. Paula, you and Marcy stay here with Reggie. Everyone else get ready to go inside and check.'

'What for!?' Henry asked. 'The CP clearly isn't here. You have to cease these constant stops. It's bloody infuriating.' He turned to sweep his eyes over the building line as Dave ordered Mo up front and everyone else started getting ready.

'Wait!' Henry said as the others paused and watched him pulling his rifle strap over his head and making ready as he tutted and huffed then walked out to address them all. 'Right, listen in. The mission objective is to clear those buildings. Time is a factor so we will do a fast sweep through to search for survivors. There are three sets of buildings. The school. The leisure centre and those council offices. Frank, take Bash and clear the council offices. I will take the leisure centre with Carmen. Dave will take the school with Mohammed. Mr Howie. I propose you hold in readiness to give support in the event of a contact.'

THE UNDEAD TWENTY-FIVE. THE HEAT

'Yeah. Sure,' Howie said. 'But er, I can go in though if you need more people. I mean. We've done this a lot now.'

'This isn't the time for another pissing contest, Mr Howie.'

'Fuck's sake. I didn't mean that, Henry! I was just saying-.'

'It's hot as fuck!' Paula said, glaring at both of them.

'Make ready,' Henry ordered with all of my team activating the red laser sights on our rifles.

'Yo, Dave. Why's don't we have those?' Mo asked, looking over at us..

'Because we can aim properly,' Dave said as we all blinked in surprise.

'Did Dave just make a joke?' Frank asked.

'I think he did,' I said, staring at Dave's expressionless face while getting the impression he was smiling on the inside.

'Move out!' Henry ordered.

We started forward with Henry and I going for the leisure centre while Henry grumbled about Howie needing to check every bloody house in every bloody street and that at this rate we'll never bloody well get anywhere. But, by the time we were nearing the first point of entry, he'd stopped moaning and was lowering into a combat sweep stance with his rifle up in the aim position.

I could sense him focussing too, and it was weird because it had been a long time since I'd done any kind of active role with Henry. His reputation in our world was unmatched, but then I wondered if he'd got rusty. It was also good that he split the teams up otherwise it would always be me and Frank doubling up and Henry and Bash. Henry never liked that. He liked to keep the teams mixing so we integrated. He said it prevented cliques forming.

We reached the first set of doors into the building and we both stacked up outside. Listening and letting our senses adjust to the specifics of this defined area.

'I think Frank will like working with Bash,' Henry whispered. 'US special forces trained him, and guess who one of his instructors was?'

'Stavi?'

Henry nodded, and I knew what he meant. It meant Bash was

taught properly. Which is because Stavi was taught properly. Which is because he was taught by Henry. 'Bloody pig farmer,' he muttered before motioning that he will go first. I took his back and gave him the tap then we swept inside to a long entry corridor.

Squash courts to the left and a junction ahead that opened out to a reception area. Chairs overturned. Blood smeared over the walls.

A set of double doors. Henry went first. I paused for a second then followed suit. Aiming left while Henry aimed right. A modern gymnasium. Treadmills and rowers. Cycles and resistance training machines.

Sweat and detergent in the air. We clocked the bottles of cleaner used to wipe the machines down and figured people were still using the gym.

Out the doors. Back to reception and into the female changing rooms. A body on the floor. An infected with a knife handle jutting out of one eye. Blood on the floor from a fight. Another body in the shower amidst a large pool of blood. A woman in exercise gear with slit wrists. A dropped razor at her side. A bite mark on her arm. A nod from Henry to me. Both of us grasping the events. The woman used the gym then came for a shower when the infected got inside. She was bit and took her own life.

We swept through the offices moving low and fast and using hand signals at points of danger and I could feel that Henry was enjoying it. Being back in the field and on the ground. His senses primed. His breathing controlled. He'd spent too many years in an office. Too many years in London. Too many years of traffic fumes and grey skies.

But it was all gone, and he was back on the ground once again. Rifle in hand and sweeping through a building looking for the enemy. Like I said. I got the feeling this mission was revenge for us, but I also meant it when I said I was cool with it if it was a revenge job.

Either way. It was good to see Henry back to doing proper craft, but then our foe was formed. We were hunting a monster. A killer of babies and women. The elusive CP that was somewhere ahead of us.

I could see it in his eyes. Reginald's plan was working, and he was getting drawn into the game.

THE UNDEAD TWENTY-FIVE. THE HEAT

Charlotte

And so Henry took off to clear the buildings, which was a weird dynamic as Mr Howie was going to do it, then he got moaned at by Henry for another delay then watched Henry go and do the thing he was going to do. Yep. It was all a bit weird, so the rest of us pretended not to notice and waited outside on the tennis courts.

'We would have done it by now,' Howie muttered.

'Let them get hot and sweaty for a change,' Clarence said.

'Talking of hot,' Tappy said, trying to change the subject. 'Bash, Henry and Frank. Snog, marry, sex.'

'Urgh, Tappy!' Cookey said.

'Ooh,' Marcy said, waggling her fingers in delight at the question. 'Okay, so… Er… snog Frank, sex with Henry, marry Bash.'

'Jesus, Marcy, you didn't even hesitate,' Howie said.

'It's too hot for stupid games,' Paula said.

'Charlie?' Tappy asked.

'But if I had to choose,' Paula said. 'Snog Bash, sex Henry and marry Frank.'

'Wow, really?' Marcy asked.

'Yeah. Bash is too young for me. I want a proper man,' Paula said as Clarence blushed.

'So why not sex Frank then?' Tappy asked.

'Duh. I will have sex with Frank when we get married. Like literally all the time. It's only once with Henry.'

'Oh okay. I can see that logic. Right. I need to change my answer,' Marcy said.

'No takey backeys,' Tappy said. 'Charlie?'

'No! hang on,' Marcy said. 'Snog Bash, sex with Frank then marry Henry.'

'Henry?' Paula asked, giving her a look.

'I like alpha males,' Marcy said with a shrug. 'Charlie? Your turn.'

'Er. Well. Two are slightly too old for me,' I said.

'Stop being diplomatic,' Marcy said. 'You were snogging Tappy this morning.'

'It was the dog!' I said.

'It bloody wasn't,' Tappy said. 'Anyway. Come on. Snog, marry, sex.'

'I don't know! Er, snog Henry, sex with Bash and marry Frank,' I said.

'Frank!?' Marcy asked.

'He's funny! I really like funny guys,' I said with a glance to Cookey. 'And he's got blue eyes and that thick hair.'

'Do you know what. I can see that actually,' Tappy said.

'What would yours be?' I asked Tappy.

'Er, so,' Tappy said, giving it some thought. 'Snog Henry, sex with Frank cos he is funny, and marry Bash.'

'This is so sexist,' Cookey said. 'Men aren't pieces of meat to be ogled you know.'

'Shush. Just stand there and look pretty,' I said, making the others laugh. 'Actually. Are there any bike sheds around here?' I asked him with a wink.

'Oh my god!' Marcy said at my brazen flirting. 'Cookey! Are you blushing?'

'He is. He's actually blushing,' Blowers said.

'Fuck you! I'm not blushing. It's like fifty degrees.'

'Cookey, go and cool off behind some bike sheds,' Marcy said as the laughs kept going. 'Charlie will help,' she added as I smiled and winked at him again, and the blush spread in his cheeks.

'What the actual fuck! I've never seen you blush before,' Nick said. 'Best day ever.'

'I'm not blushing!'

'You are so red,' Blowers said.

'Ah fuck off. Whatever. Anyway, Charlie's too posh for bike sheds,' Cookey said.

'Don't try and joke your way out of it,' Blowers said.

'He's probably right though,' Nick said. 'Did you have bike sheds at school, Charlie?'

'Of course not. We had pony stables,' I said, enjoying the jokes while clocking the obvious discomfort in Cookey. But then he flirted with me all the time and again I just didn't get the confusing signals.

'Hang on. Why isn't Paula telling you off for being un PC?' Cookey asked, looking from Tappy to Paula. 'What about if we did that?'

'What? You mean if you'd snog, marry or have sex with Carmen?' Tappy asked. 'Which I would totally do by the way, if I was gay like Nick's demon ex-girlfriend.'

'Or like Charlie,' Marcy said.

'It was the dog!' I said.

'And er, I have already snogged Carmen,' Marcy said.

'Alright then. Not about Carmen,' Cookey said.

'Then you'd have to ask about us,' Tappy said. 'And just try it and see what happens.'

'That's not fair!' Cookey said.

'You can do it when we're not listening,' Tappy said as Marcy glared at Howie.

'What!' Howie asked.

'You'd better pick me for all three,' Marcy said. 'Actually, you're not allowed to play at all. Urgh! But now I really want to know who you'd pick. Right, Howie. Snog, marry, sex me Paula, Charlie and Tappy.'

'Oh god no!' Paula said to more groans and face pulling from the others. 'He's like my brother! Howie, you're banned from playing. And Clarence. And Roy. Just the lads, otherwise it's gross. And take me out of it. I'm not an option.'

'Yeah, this is getting weird now,' Marcy said. 'Jesus, Cookey.'

'I didn't start it!'

'Cookey,' Tappy said, giving him a filthy look as Frank and Bash headed back over.

'What's the faces for?' Frank asked.

'Cookey's being disgusting,' Tappy said. 'And Charlie's on heat,' she added as I winked at Cookey again.

'This is sexual harassment,' Cookey said.

'Really? Can I get harassed?' Frank asked.

'You just did,' Marcy said. 'We'd all either have sex or marry you.'

'Can't say I blame you,' he said, striking a manly pose before farting.

'You dirty shit,' Carmen called, walking back with Henry, Mo and Dave.

'That was good, Mo. Dave's trained you well,' Henry was saying. 'Just watch you don't overextend when Dave is advancing. Stay in a position of cover in case the person on point gets attacked because if you're both exposed, then you both get taken out.'

'Okay, boss. Yeah, that makes sense,' Mo said.

'Yes, not yeah,' Henry said mildly, clapping him on the shoulder. 'Re-join your unit, but good work. All clear, Mr Howie. Several deceased within the two complexes we searched. No signs of the enemy. Recent action estimated to be within the last 12 hours. Frank?'

'Same,' Frank said. 'Two bodies in the offices. One infected that went through an internal window and severed its own jugular. The other just outside at the back. Looks like she got on the roof and fell off. Broken neck.'

'Ouch,' Paula said with a wince.

'No, it's good,' Carmen said. 'Instant death normally. Good way to go.'

'Beats bleeding out,' Frank said to a few murmurs.

'That, however, was the good news,' Henry continued. 'The bad news is we estimate the school was housing in excess of seventy people.'

'All gone?' Howie asked.

'I'm afraid so,' Henry said with a dark look to the grimaces and tuts sounding from the others. 'It appears we've now got a sizable force ahead of us.'

'We need to push on then,' Howie said.

'Indeed. Yes, that is exactly what we should be doing,' Henry said. 'Right, load up. We're moving out.'

'Is everyone taking a turn to say that today?' Howie asked and looked like he immediately wishes he hadn't.

'My apologies, Mr Howie. Please give your orders to your team,' Henry said. 'My unit, move out.'

THE UNDEAD TWENTY-FIVE. THE HEAT

'It's fine. Just move out,' Howie said, aiming for the Saxon.

'You not coming in the van?' Paula asked.

'Not if we're going into a town,' Howie called. 'You and Marcy stay with Reggie. We'll keep Mads with us.'

'If you're expecting a significant contact then hold a briefing,' Henry called with one foot in the SUV as we all stopped. 'Or at least launch the drone.'

'You said you wanted to us to keep moving,' Howie called back. 'Which is it, Henry? Stop and plan, or keep going?'

'That is not what I meant!' Henry said. 'I mean greater planning can only aid our efforts.'

'Planning for what?! Fine. Let's stop for another fucking coffee then and have a chat and look at some maps.'

'We don't need a coffee every time we hold a quick briefing. Forget it. Just move out.'

'Don't tell me to move out!'

'Move out!' Henry shouted, dropping into the SUV and slamming the door.

'Howie!' Paula shouted as Howie looking ready to reply. 'It's way too hot for this shit. Just move out!'

'Stop telling me to move out!'

'I will bloody say it, and I'll call it in a minute if this doesn't stop between you two. Henry! Do you hear me? One more fucking argument and I'm ending today. It's too hot.'

'Do not talk to me like that!' Henry snapped, pushing his door open to get out and argue as Frank leant over to snag his tac-vest and pull him back in.

'Close your damn door, Henry,' Joan said.

'Howie. Get in the Saxon,' Paula ordered, pushing him into the Saxon with Marcy.

So... Back into the vehicles we went. Hot bodies in the hot tin can.

'Woohoo! The Saxon on the blacktop speeding through the backdrop,' Tappy said as she started the engine.

The heat still rising. The weather only getting worse – but person-

351

ally I was quite happy at having the elders back in the Saxon as it meant I could get back on Cookey's lap.

Thinking back now, I was becoming rather forthright with him, but well, he was dithering about and as Joan always says, nobody likes a ditherer.

And so while I continued my flirting with Cookey, Howie, Marcy, Paula and Clarence all shuffled up to behind the front seats. Meredith was still in the front wagging her tail at them while also half grumbling and half growling with a confusing show of signals that suggested they don't try and take her seat because she wasn't entirely sure how it would end.

To be fair though, Howie was pretty much the same as the dog. Half grumbling and half growling.

'Sorry about all the shit with Henry, guys,' he said. 'He just really grips my fucking goat.'

Carmen

And Henry was clearly fuming with himself for losing his temper to the extent Frank had to drag him back into the car.

'It's the heat,' Joan said from the back. A voice of calm and reason with an aura of authority that even Henry respected.

'My apologies,' Henry said. 'I shall adjust my manner. But he's just such an impudent little shit. The sooner we can separate the better. Then he can go house to house saving every budgie he can find.'

'We need Howie to get into London,' Frank said.

'We didn't have Howie when we set out,' Henry replied. 'We can damn well get it done without him.'

'Sure,' Frank said with a mild tut. 'Bloody pig-farmers eh?'

Charlotte

'We'll get this done then split up,' Howie said. 'Then he can fuck off and sneak around as much as he wants.'

'Henry knows where the Panacea is,' Marcy said.

'Fuck Henry. Reginald can find it,' Howie replied.

'Sure,' Marcy said with a mild tut. 'Or maybe, you know, just be less of a twat?'

It wasn't just hot bodies in a hot tin can. It was hot tempers in hot heads.

Carmen

We drove on in relative silence and soon got into the town of Billingshurst.

Small gardens and small houses. White UPVC windows and white UPVC doors. Suburbia in all its sterile glory.

A mini roundabout ahead. Gouge marks on the tarmac from a goods vehicle that took the corner too fast and flipped over before careering off into the side of a small church.

I figured it would stay there forever until it rotted and rusted and became nothing more than a pile of slag as the walls and roof slowly crumbled in.

We carried on into the High Street proper. The energy still high but mixed and weird. A bizarre combination of making progress and enjoying the hunt while feeling the angst of Howie and Henry tearing chunks out of each other.

That heat too. That awful crushing heat. It was like breathing the fumes from an oven and even my face was glistening with sweat. Frank was the same. Even Bashir could feel it and he's from a country that swelters in the summer, but this was different. The humidity was the crushing thing.

It struck me about what Paula said. That she would call it if Howie and Henry didn't stop. Then I was wondering why she didn't call it anyway. She was the XO and more than anyone else she could do that. Everybody respected her. Then I realised that <u>none</u> of us were recruits. We were all there voluntarily. We were doing it of our own free will.

Which meant we could stop if we wanted. We could simply say *hey, it's too hot for this shit* and go and find cool shade, or do what Paula suggested and find freezer trucks to sit in.

But we didn't, and I wondered why. But then I looked out the window and saw the infected moving in the same direction, and I knew the sense of responsibility that Howie and his team felt kept them going. But then why was I going? I wasn't being paid any more. There was no contract. No rules. Howie was right. The old world was gone. This was the new world.

I don't know. Something about that concept got my mind stirring as we got closer to the town centre.

Charlotte

It got worse by the second. The feel of it. The pressure growing. The Saxon became silent. The chat and banter now gone. The thumps and bangs coming one after the other as Tappy ran them down.

Meredith was growling. Her hackles were up, and her teeth were showing. Her front paws planted on the front. Giving voice to the things outside. Giving fair warning.

We all felt the surge of energy coming from Howie. His eyes were growing dark as the air filled with the sounds of everyone making ready.

The clunks and clinks of magazines being taken out and tapped to rid the grit. A thing not needed but still done. A ritual as it were. A way to steady hands and get the body in the right groove.

Through the open back doors I could see Carmen and Bash in the SUV doing the same thing. Checking their weapons and making ready. Henry did his rifle then checked Frank's while Frank was driving and checking his pistol.

And on we went. Further into the town with the numbers of infected increasing by the second. It felt like we were transitioning from peace to war as we delved into the midst of the enemy we were hunting.

'*There must be a concentration here,*' Reginald said over the radio. '*There are too many in the street to be simply passing through.*'

'Seen that boss?' Tappy asked, pointing ahead to a thick nucleus of infected blocking the road.

'*Roy, Frank. It's Howie. Road ahead is blocked. We'll speed up and punch into them. You two slow down but keep moving.*'

That was it.

It was game on and we braced as the engine in the Saxon roared out and we all felt that surge of power. Then Howie was cursing because he couldn't see properly and vaulted the seats into the front and pushed the dog over to get space. But his energy was such that the dog paid him no heed. She just carried on barking at the window.

'BRACE!' Tappy yelled as we all locked arms and legs. I was still on Cookey's lap as there was simply nowhere else to go (especially as Mads had somehow ended up with us) and I felt Cookey's arm wrap about my stomach, holding me tight as the Saxon went deep. Rocking and jolting with bodies flung this way and that. Smashed and pulverised from the impact before Tappy stamped on the brake and spun her around to get that big end into the horde. Tappy is an incredible driver, believe me when I say that, but good lord. It was like being in a blender.

Anyway. We soon gained sight of a road to the left leading to a row of flat-roofed buildings. Grey and ugly with two storey flats over the shops at ground level. There was another row of ugly buildings coming out at a right angle at the far end forming a plaza.

That, however, was not what caught our attention. It was the hundreds of infected within that plaza moving with speed and purpose towards the buildings. Literally pouring across the ground from the street as they flung themselves at the steel shutters covering the store windows and doors.

'Up there!' Tappy said, pointing to faces in the windows of the flats over the shops.

'Survivors!' Howie said into the radio. *'Shops ahead of us. Two rows joined together. People in the top. WE'RE GOING IN!'*

'Reggie doesn't have a guard,' Roy called. *'Pull back so I can get him in the Saxon with Tappy.'*

'Do it,' Howie ordered as Tappy selected reverse and started driving backwards from the junction as Roy sped up to meet us. Honestly. I thought we were going to collide and I wasn't the only one as a few of us called out in alarm, but Tappy had it covered and angled at the last second as she came to a stop so the open back doors of the Saxon were alongside the sliding door of the van - which was my cue to get out and mount Jess, but before I left, and I'm not sure if he even noticed such was the energy of the moment, but I planted a quick kiss on Cookey's head then jumped out.

Reginald

It was rather like ballet if I'm honest. The way Tappy and Roy drove at each other then swerved at the last second. Then, while I was pulling my sliding door open I saw Charlie jumping out of the Saxon and Frank already out of his SUV kicking the bolts out to let Jess get out. I must say, it was all very well timed, and for a ragtag bunch of misfits we certainly looked quite professional for a good thirty seconds.

I even launched the drone from the back of the van. I was getting rather good at flying it and simply started her up and flew her out instead of anyone needing to stand and launch her.

However, our appearance of sublime professionalism was not to last because while I was quite adept at popping out of my van launching drones, I was not adept at getting myself into the Saxon. The back is rather high, and my legs are not long, nor am I an athletic type able to run and vault things. The mere thought of which gives me palpitations.

Not that I had to worry as the lads were very accommodating and grabbed my wrists to pull me up while I felt some hands about my waist giving me a boost from behind. I wondered who it was and caught a glimpse of Carmen giving me a smile.

'Need a firing point, Reggie!' Roy said while tugging bags of arrows and his bow across his back and gathering his rifle.

'That one there,' I said and pointed out of the Saxon to a three-storey building on the left side. 'It overlooks the plaza,' I said.

'On it!' Roy shouted and he was off and running as Henry snapped his head up. Seeing the same thing. A perfect OP.

'With me,' Henry ordered his team as they set off after Roy – but I then lost sight as I tried to fight through the Saxon to get to the front while all the time flying the drone and watching the small screen on the handset and cursing that I couldn't stay in my van at my battle desk, but at least I had my battle swatter with me.

The Saxon then set off into the charge while we all bounced around while stuck like proverbial sardines. But I kept the drone on Roy and saw him reach the door to the opticians on the High Street and give it a good kick.

Then Frank said something behind him and stepped past with a small black object in his hand. A glass shattering device that he used to make the glass all fall out, then they were inside and so I started to lift the drone up past the first and second floor windows, catching sight of Henry and Co inside running up the stairs.

Then I zoomed up high over the rooftops to gain view of the field of battle and could see we needed to take a smaller road off the High Street into the plaza that was bordered on two sides by blocks of those ugly cheap shops developers crammed in anywhere. You know the sort. Small units on the ground floor with flats over the top of them. But what was also very noticeable was the size of the horde. It was by far the biggest one so far that day – and far more than I think they were expecting.

That said – we were in it so to speak and so we had to crack on and get the job done, besides, we'd seen the survivors in the flats over the stores and the infected throwing themselves at the metal shutters covering the shop windows. (You know you're in a rough area when the shops have roll down metal shutters.)

A moment later, and just as the Saxon turned into the side road, I saw Henry, Frank, Bashir, Carmen, Roy and Joan all spilling out onto the flat roof. It looked rather nice actually with potted bushes and some nice rattan seating – if not sadly let down by those awful cheap multicoloured solar lights strung up everywhere.

I could see they were all sweating, which is fair enough seeing as they'd run up three flights of stairs in that awful heat, but I also saw as they ran across the roof to gain view of the plaza below just as Tappy shouted *brace* and we ploughed into the rotters.

It was rather strange actually. Feeling it within the Saxon, while also seeing it via the drone and the bloodied wake of broken bodies we left behind.

We went deep too, but then we had to make an entrance to get the buggers attention away from trying to get into the buildings. Booker was up top strafing them with the machine gun and taking care not to hit the building line -while I observed Roy setting his bags of arrows at his feet and pulling his bow forward while Joan looped the strap of her sniper rifle about her arm and rested the barrel on the ledge while getting into position to aim down.

Then of course came the inevitable stop and debuss with Tappy slewing the Saxon around to carve a nice clear spot for Howie and the others to charge out all heroic and yelling Rarrrr or whatever it is that hero types yell.

It was impressive though. I'll say that, and the best sight was seeing Dave drop out first from the back doors to stare at an infected charging at him who was then taken off his feet with an arrow through his head.

'*Overwatch on,*' Roy said into the radio. Then I heard the deeper percussive shot of the sniper rifle and saw another infected ripped off her feet while launching itself at Jess who was battering the line away to make room for Howie and Co to debuss the Saxon.

At which point three more rifles then opened up with Carmen, Bashir and Frank firing single shot into the crowds below them – and with that underway, Howie then banged on the Saxon and told Tappy to get to work – while I, ever the graceful one, was nearly upside down trying to get over the seat into the front. Ably assisted by Tappy heaving me over while the dog gave me a pitying look.

But I must say - I rather liked it. It was a nice adventure to be out of my van and in the actual thick of it while feeling very protected by Meredith and Tappy, who, I might add, is an excellent driver.

I then went back to my drone screen and observed Henry peering most intently into the plaza, no doubt trying to find the CP we were hunting. Of course, I knew the CP wasn't there, but Henry didn't, and so he was peering this way and that and watching the infected hammering their heads and throwing themselves at the doors and windows of the storefronts.

What I then saw, for the first time that day, was a large portion of the horde suddenly turn and make aim for the team in the middle. That was interesting because it was the first time I'd seen that horde react *collectively*. I mean in the sense that they had been attacking us in the previous battles, but only as if we were hosts to be taken. As in the closest infected were going at us while the others still went for their primary target – which previously was either the people in Petworth or Storrington.

But now was different, and it was the first show that the CP was even aware of us as an entity as it sent a dedicated number of infected to finish us off.

Howie saw it too of course. Everyone did. 'INCOMING!' Dave then shouted as they instantly compressed and fell back into a much smaller fighting unit. 'HAND WEAPONS!' Dave then ordered and the rifles were slung with axes and machetes and blades being readied. A second later and the proper battle commenced with that sound of meat on meat with the grunts and shouts.

Arrows were flying in. Taking infected out while Joan kept watch on Charlie, keeping Jess's rear end clear and safe.

'Building line. Far right,' Carmen then transmitted into the radio. I immediately rotated my lens on the drone and flew closer with a jolt at seeing the infected pouring into a shop at ground level. The window smashed. The boards inside snapping away. A second later and I was muttering a curse at seeing the flats over that shop had balconies on the third level. Which gave a perfect way for the infected to flow from one flat to the next and the people hiding in terror inside them.

'*Howie, they're in the buildings on the far right,*' I transmitted while knowing Howie couldn't even do a damn thing. They were so busy they couldn't even transmit back.

That only left Charlie on Jess, and the Saxon, which I was inside of driving circles around Howie to try and ease the compression – with Charlie pretty much doing the same thing. A few minutes more and we would be able to free Dave and Howie up to give assistance, but once again we didn't have minutes.

Darn it. The joys of battle eh?

But of course, we did have another resource. '*Roy,*' I transmitted. '*Bit of a pickle old chap, but Howie can't break away and we've got infected breaching the building line.*'

'*Yep, no probs,*' he said calmly. (Roy is a wonderfully eccentric fellow. Put him in a fight to the death and he doesn't bat an eye but give him a twinge in his side and the man goes to pieces.)

Carmen

Then, Roy, who for a few moments looked close to tears while sniffing for toast and telling everyone he'd had a stroke, was ditching his bow and asking Joan to cover him.

'What are you doing?' Henry asked.

'We don't leave people, Henry. It's not our way,' Roy said while drawing his sword (love his sword BTW. I actually want one) as Henry blinked at the gentle but wholly unexpected rebuke.

'I'll go with him,' I said.

'Stand down, Carmen,' Henry ordered.

'I'm immune, Henry.' I said with an edge to my voice from the way he spoke to me. 'Carmen! CARMEN!' he yelled when I set off with Roy. 'This isn't our mission. I said wait!'

'Wait for what!' I demanded, coming to a stop to glare at him. 'I am immune, Henry. I am not standing by and letting people die. You made me take an oath for that shit. Remember?'

I set off again. Furious to the core and feeling that thing inside that was flaring up earlier. That different mindset, I guess.

'Bloody idiots!' Henry shouted, but there was a tone in his voice that made us stop once more and look back to him shaking his head. 'Roy. Stay here with Joan, we'll go over the side.'

'Eh?' I asked.

'Come on then! Don't bloody stand there,' he said, and with that, he was off and running to vault over the side of the roof. We all cried out, thinking he'd done a Clarence and ran over expecting to see him dead on the street below only to see him on another flat roof one level below. 'I said move!' he shouted as Roy gave me a smile and rushed back to his position with Joan while Bash, Frank, and I went over the side and dropped to the roof below.

A quick run across. Another roof below that one. From high to low and finally to the street. Frank was leading the way by then. By far our most experienced combatant and we swept along the edge of the building line with rifles up and ready.

'Howie! If you can hear me, Henry is going for the survivors,' I heard Reginald transmit as Frank held a clenched fist up to make us hold position.

'Tappy. Be a love and come and clear a path for me would you, angel.' Frank transmitted.

'On my way, Frank!' Tappy said.

A second later and we heard it coming, and bloody hell, what a sight that is. Seeing the Saxon ramming a path through human forms with the big front end splatting them apart while the big wheels broke bones and popped skulls with Tappy grinning and waving behind the wheel the whole time. Frank gave her a smile and nod and she drove straight at us before twisting the wheel to face out.

Then we were out and running behind the Saxon as it carved a path through the horde to the building line. Steering off at the last second to give us access to a street level door. Frank snapped the lock while Henry wrapped some C4 around the padlocked chains. We took cover, blew it open then swept inside to a communal concrete staircase then up and out into a long access corridor running the length of the block at the back of the flats.

'Bash, hold the stairs,' Henry ordered. Giving him the hand signal 'Frank. Get them into the end flat. Carmen, with me.'

We rushed on as Frank started booting at doors and telling people to get out. The corridor filling fast with survivors screaming in panic. Getting grabbed and moved while Henry and I work to the far end. To the far flat. Booting the door open and sweeping inside to a family huddled together in absolute terror.

'Get to the end flat now!' Henry ordered.

'Go!' I urged them, motioning for them to move as Henry and I found the stairs up to the third floor and the balcony overlooking the plaza. Patio doors leading out. Feeble flimsy things that we wrenched open and stepped out into the noise and carnage of a battle underway.

Joan's rifle firing deep shots. The Saxon roaring past underneath. The howls of the infected and the shouts coming from Howie and his team right in the middle. And fuck me, they were surrounded. Jesus.

'Damn it!' Henry shouted as I looked over to the other building line jutting out at a right angle. Stores on the ground floor. Flats over the top with balconies on the top level. An exact replica of this block, but the infected had breached and were already inside. We could see them flowing in through the ground floor at the far end, then we could see them through the windows on the first floor and we both tensed as they came out onto the balcony on the third floor.

I hunkered down onto a knee and took aim to get fire into them. But the distance was too great for an assault rifle, especially as I didn't have a scope. I was scoring hits, but they were body shots and not kill shots.

'*Roy. Balcony,*' I transmitted quickly and took another shot as one of the infected on the balcony flew back from an arrow hitting his head.

Henry then joined in and for a few seconds we kept it clear and hoped that would do until another option presented. Unfortunately, though, the infected were too fast and driving too hard and that balcony started flooding with them pouring out of the patio doors. Then a second after that they were going over the thin wall separating the balconies and smashing through the patio doors into the next flat, and once they'd found the way they started flowing even faster.

We searched for a way into that block, but there were too many infected on the ground between us, and the gap between the blocks, although leapable by an infected, was way too much for a person.

The only real option we had was to stem the flow before the infected reached the end flat and made the leap over to this row of balconies otherwise we'd lose both blocks.

'Enemy!' Bashir transmitted as we heard firing coming from the other end of our block.

'Joan! Get fire into that doorway,' Henry ordered as we saw Joan switch her aim to try and slow the infected pouring in through the door at street level.

'UPDATE?' Howie then shouted with a backdrop of pure carnage coming through the radios.

'Two fronts again, Howie,' Reginald said. *'They're already in one block. We're defending the block closest to you, but they are breaching the door in.'*

'Okay. Charlie, clear a path from us to the door. We'll get Paula and Marcy over there. WATCH HIM, DANNY!'

He clicked off as we saw another frantic push from the infected and Howie back to battering them down with his axe as Charlie and Jess fought through then angled out to start fighting towards the street door. *'Can anyone get into that end block?'* Howie asked between cutting them down.

'It's lost, Howie,' Henry said

'GET INTO IT AND HELP THEM!'

'I said it's bloody lost! All we can do is protect this one.'

Reginald

'FUCK!' Howie then shouted, and I could completely understand his frustration, but the battle was intense and right then, there was nothing anyone could do for that other block. Plus, there were more infected running into the plaza from the road. Not vast swathes, I grant you, but there was enough backfill going on to hamper our efforts to make progress.

Then of course, came the thing we all dreaded seeing.

There were eight flats in that other block. The infected already had four of them and were about to go over the balcony wall onto the fifth when the patio doors opened from inside and a family ran out screaming and crying. A man and a woman with a child held in the woman's arms. The man had a bat that he was using to swipe at the infected pushing him out through the doors – which is when we realised the infected were not just going balcony to balcony, but they were also using the rear access corridor to force their way into the flats.

'JOAN!' Carmen shouted into the radio, and from my position above the field I saw Roy and Joan both divert their fire onto that balcony. I have never seen Roy fire so fast as right then. He had four or five arrows in flight at the same time and they were landing too. That family were pressed up against the far wall while Roy took them out coming over the other wall and Joan shot them back through the patio doors.

My god I had never seen anything like it. The precision of those two made the hairs on the back of my neck prickle and once again, the ebb and flow of battle made me think we'd save them, but a second later and the infected were just too many, and even the combined firing rate of Joan and Roy wasn't enough.

The man went down first. Bravely too. He did what he could to protect his family, but against such a foe there was no hope. That also meant the woman holding the child had to see him get taken down as two more shots rang out.

Two fast clear shots.

One through the woman's head.

One through the child's.

'May god have mercy,' Joan said into the radio as Carmen screamed out. I could see her on the balcony of the other block leaning over the railings with the veins pushing through her head and neck. Then a second later she ditched her rifle and was up onto the safety railings then up onto the roof and running back the other way while Henry was shouting at her to get down.

She stopped, paused for a second then ran full pelt along that roof top then launched herself over that gap to the other block. It was a distance too. Let me tell you that, and she barely made it. She just about gripped the guttering with her hands then started scrabbling up to grip the actual roof as the guttering broke away and dropped into the hordes below.

Then she was up on the roof and running before sliding down the slope to grip the edge and swing onto the third from end balcony. Landing on her feet then she was up and throwing a potted plant through the patio door and going inside. I flew the drone in with her. Doing what I could as she raced down the stairs to a living room already full of infected biting down into a woman on the floor. Carmen screamed and went at them. Clearly intending to kill the lot.

'No, Carmen!' I shouted into the radio. *'The next flat. Get to the next flat!'*

She must have heard me as she stabbed one through the neck then leapt over the others and ran out into the access corridor into more infected pouring along. She was fast though, and whipped her pistol out to get close quarters aimed shots into heads. Blowing brains out all over the show.

'Behind you!' I transmitted and watched as she turned and moved back to avoid the ones at her rear and shot them both dead. *'That's it. You're clear. Next flat, Carmen. Hurry, they're coming through.'*

She turned and ran, pausing only to boot the door open into the next flat. 'Reggie, check upstairs!' she shouted out as she started clearing the first floor while I went up to the second.

'Up here, Carmen. End bedroom. Mother and child.'

She raced up and grabbed them and shouted at them to move but I had flown down into the first floor and could see the rear door into the access corridor was breached.

'Balcony, Carmen. The door is gone,' I said into the radio as Carmen

dragged the woman and carried the child out onto the balcony while I flew out and up to see them coming over the next balcony. *'At speed please, Miss Eze.'*

She pretty much manhandled the woman over the wall then clambered over with the child and dragged them through the patio doors into the last flat. I flew in ahead and down to see one other woman with a young boy hiding underneath a wooden table. I directed Carmen to them then quickly flew out and over to look for an exfil option.

But Howie was still seriously pinned. Frank and Bash were protecting the last flat in the other block and the dozens of survivors they'd secured, and Marcy and Paula were busy holding the stairs.

I thought to get Charlie in. At least she could carry the children away, but she was on the far side of the plaza. That only left Tappy in the Saxon.

I rather gather that Henry was also running the tactical options through his mind because he then called out through the radio. *'Tappy. Get inside and get them out.'*

And I'm wondering what the bloody hell he meant. Tappy is an excellent driver, and she's good in a scrap, but she wasn't Dave. There was no way Tappy could single handed fight through a horde that size to save Carmen and the survivors.

But of course, Henry didn't mean Tappy. He meant the Saxon.

'The walls, Tappy. Thin walls! Get in there!' Henry shouted.

'What?' Tappy asked, frowning up at him on the balcony with her hands held up and watching as he swooshed a flat bladed hand out towards the last block and curved it off to the side.

'Thin walls, Tappy,' he said.

'Oh, you bloody genius!' she said with a sudden grin

'Why is he a genius?' I asked. 'Tappy? Why is Henry a genius?'

'Thin walls,' Tappy said with a yell as she started driving at speed towards the last unit in that block. Aiming directly at the plate glass window of the hairdressers within.

'TAPPY!' I yelled while scrunching back into my seat and grabbing the dog for dear life, who, it seemed, appeared to be having a grand old time.

'BRACE!' Tappy then yelled and darn it if she didn't drive the bloody Saxon straight into the bloody hairdressers window. Not just into it, but through it and deep inside where we pinged metal swivel chairs off their stalks and sent them flying off into wall mirrors while plaster and bricks rained down. *'You're right, Henry. It's got thin walls,'* Tappy transmitted.

'Well done, Tappy! Now draw back. Carmen! Get out the window. The Saxon is below you.'

'I bloody felt it,' Carmen said as I looked down at the screen to see her dragging and shouting at the survivors to get them across the living room to the window and the Saxon jutting out below. *'Tappy! I bloody love you,'* she transmitted before climbing out and dropping the few feet to land on the Saxon roof. 'KIDS! QUICKLY!' she yelled as Henry, Roy and Joan got fire into the infected aiming for the Saxon now jutting out of the shop.

The first child was dropped and caught by Carmen then dropped down through the hole into the Saxon with Tappy in the back, grabbing it to put to one side. Then the other one came down followed by the two mothers, who, despite being shocked, were admirable in their presence of mind. Then a moment later Carmen dropped in and Tappy got back into the driver's seat.

'We're in!' Carmen relayed.

'Take the walls out,' Henry ordered.

'Roger that, Mr Henry!' Tappy said. 'Come on baby. Give me some power!' she shouted at the Saxon as we backed out of the building with Carmen getting the survivors to hunker down low in the middle before she came up front to lean over the seat and my shoulder to look at the screen on my controller. She was rather close too. I mean, I could feel the heat from her head, and she was breathing very hard.

'Well done,' I said to her. 'That was very brave of you.'

'Thanks for your help,' she said with that nice smile she gave me earlier. Then she stayed looking at me for a long second with a funny expression, but I went back to my screen and clutched the seat in blind terror as Tappy sped up and once again drove the bloody Saxon straight into a bloody building. Only this time she went into the shop next door with enough power to demolish the insides and knock interior walls down.

The next few minutes were a blur if I am honest. We just seemed to go out and in, and by in I mean into the buildings where Tappy had wonderful fun driving through the walls inside the block. Battering her way from one end to the other.

I could see, however, that the infected were now pouring over the balcony towards the last flat where they would make the leap to the block holding the survivors.

'Anyone for wine?' Tappy then asked, making Carmen laugh as I looked up to see us battering into a wine shop with bottles of Merlot and Sauvignon Blanc exploding in a chorus of colours. Then we went straight through the far wall with another huge bang and more bricks and god only knows what else coming down on top of us.

'That's it. Now get out, Tappy!' Henry ordered as Tappy got the Saxon into reverse and pulled us out into the plaza.

By then I could both hear and feel the building around us groaning and shaking. The supporting walls all along the front side were now gone and cracks were forming in back walls and spreading out like spider webs.

I could see Henry watching from his block. His fist clenched as though urging it to happen, but I gather one of the internal walls was still too intact. The one between a café and the wine shop.

Henry then suddenly ran off and was gone for a moment then came up clutching a grenade, by that time the infected had got onto the last balcony and started flowing over to make the leap. Henry though. He was calm as anything and popped the pin out then lobbed it inside the unit he wanted.

One thousand.

Two thousand.

Three thousand.

I heard the dull whump and saw fragments and bricks blowing out and Henry cursing that it wasn't enough. The building was still upright and the infected were now on the roof and running to make the leap as the ground beneath them simply dropped away.

Good grief. It was a thing to see. The whole block just simply collapsed in on itself with scores of infected disappearing into the dust and rubble.

'Yes!' Henry said, punching the air as Tappy and Carmen whooped inside the Saxon – at which point Carmen planted a big kiss on my cheek. Why do women keep kissing my cheeks? I am beginning to think I have highly desirable cheeks or something.

'*Well done*,' Joan said into the radio before firing once more into the door leading to the stairs of the first row. Carmen and I then focussed on the screen and watched the battle as Tappy drove about killing things.

We could see Howie below the drone still cleaving them down. Jess thundering past. Charlie breaking skulls. Henry, Bashir and Frank firing over the balcony while Marcy and Paula were now at the street door, shooting out into the horde.

The gaps were showing. The horde was thinning out. A few moments later and once more the ground lay thick with bodies. The hand weapons dropped as assault rifles were used to kill the last ones.

Then it was done.

Another battle. Another victory.

The Battle of Billinghurst, and Howie once more stood in the middle. Covered in blood and gore and surrounded by death on all sides. His team with him. The sweat pouring down. Chests heaving. Hands and arms sticky and wet with blood. Clothes sodden. Hair stuck to scalps. The rage still showing. The flush of battle.

The Saxon came to a stop. The door to the stairs opened with Henry leading the others out as Howie seemed to notice the buildings at the far end had come down. 'Who did that?' he asked.

'Tappy,' Henry said.

'Wasn't my idea though,' Tappy shouted, jumping out from the Saxon with a big grin as she rushed over to Henry for a hug. 'You bloody genius! Honestly, Mr Henry. That was so cool.'

A glimpse of mild surprise in Henry's face at the contact, but he took it in good grace. Smiling at the energy in Tappy and the sense of victory.

'Seriously,' Tappy said, turning back to run over to the lads. 'Mr Henry was like, *Tappy! Drive into those thin walls.* And I was like, *are you fucking joking!* But did you see it come down?'

'That was very good, Henry,' Roy said, picking his way over with Joan. 'Brilliant fight. Best one in days.'

'Jesus, boss,' Tappy said, turning back to see the sea of death surrounding Howie and his team. 'Holy fuck. We are on a roll today.'

Then Carmen and I got out of the Saxon with Carmen rushing ahead. 'Joan,' she said. 'Are you okay?'

'I'm fine,' Joan said curtly. 'It had to be done.'

'What had to be done?' Howie asked as everyone else fell silent.

'I can tell them,' Carmen said while looking at Joan.

'No. I said I am fine. I killed a mother and child,' she said with her head held high, but the strain was there in her eyes. 'They were about to be taken.'

'Jesus, Joan,' Paula said, moving towards her.

'No fuss please. We do what we must,' Joan said, making Paula stop as everyone else just looked at the older woman standing in quiet dignity.

'If it ever comes to it, you do me like that,' Carmen said. 'You have my permission, Joan.'

'You couldn't get to them?' Howie asked as everyone looked from Joan to Howie staring at Henry. 'Why couldn't you get to them?'

'We tried, Howie,' Carmen said. 'And I did. I went over the top and-.'

'You do not need to explain yourself, Carmen,' Henry said with a furious look. 'Do not question my team, Howie. Do not ever question my team.'

'Henry, it's fine,' Carmen said. 'Howie can ask. He didn't see it.'

'Roy,' Howie said without taking his eyes from Henry.

'There was nothing we could do,' Roy said. 'You were hemmed in. Charlie was at a distance and even if Tappy got in close she couldn't get through that building.'

'Concurred, Howie,' I said. 'Joan taking those shots were the best option.'

Howie nodded, appearing to accept our words before frowning. 'If Carmen got over, why didn't she go sooner?'

'Howie,' Paula said, her voice was soft but urging. 'We just saved nearly seventy people.'

'And Carmen did get two families out from that block,' Roy said.

'I'm sorry,' Carmen said.

'Do not apologise!' Henry snapped.

'No, he's right,' Carmen said. 'I should have gone sooner. I didn't think I could make the gap… I… I'm sorry, Howie.'

'Carmen!' Henry snapped, clearly furious at her apologising to Howie not for the act of it but because it meant she was starting to accept Howie's leadership.

'We have to be able to say these things,' Howie said. 'We did well. All of you did, especially you Tappy. But if we see a chance to help survivors then we take it. We are immune. We are armed, and we are capable. That means we have a responsibility. We have to do the right thing for the right reasons. Do you understand?'

'Yes, boss,' the words rolled around as they nodded while Henry looked ready to explode.

'But it was good work. I'm proud of you,' Howie added, nodding around at them, and again, I could see Henry struggling at how they said *cheers* and *thanks, boss*. Henry just couldn't see what everyone else saw in Howie. Or he could see it but just simply refused to accept it.

'Right. Well. We *have* saved a few dozen,' I said before anything else could start between Howie and Henry. 'Teamwork makes the dream work. Isn't that what they say. Eh, Danny?' I asked, giving him a wink as I started handing out the post battle bottles of Lucozade. 'Marvellous stuff! I'd say this CP better watch out, eh? Nasty brute killing all those kiddies. We're on it now though, lads. We're chasing it down. What do you say, Nick?'

'Evil cunt,' Nick muttered before swigging from his own bottle of Lucozade.

'My sentiments exactly,' I said. 'And the only thing needed for evil to triumph is for good people to do nothing. And we're not doing nothing! No sir! We're running it down. They don't like it up 'em, do they?!'

A few grins. A few smiles.

'They don't like it up 'em,' Clarence said, one bottle already guzzled down.

'We'll push on then. We're having this prick,' Howie said to the lads murmuring in agreement. 'Is everyone okay? Anyone hurt?'

'I broke a nail,' Marcy said, holding a finger up. 'I chipped it while changing magazine.'

'You need some tac gloves,' Carmen said, holding her gloved hands up. 'Protects your nails. And you look badass.'

'I need those!' Marcy said with a laugh as Henry tutted and shot Carmen a hard look.

'Hang on' Paula shouted as the lads start heading towards the Saxon. 'You're not getting in like that. We need to hose off and clean up.'

Maddox

We then walked back up to the High Street and waited while Tappy got on the gimpy to shoot a few more infected down.

Once that was done, we pulled a hose out from a garden and got to work cleaning up.

Jess and Meredith were washed and cooled off while Snack bars were scoffed.

I grabbed another Lucozade from Roy's van and headed back to Booker. *Got you another one,* I said and chucked it over.

Cheers, Booker said, giving me a grin and a sudden laugh. *That dude with the huge knob though. What the fuck!*

I know! I said with a laugh.

Fucking thing, Booker said as the others looked over. *It was like down here,* he added, waving his arm in front of his groin. *This old guy was like about 90 but with this massive schlong and it's going like bang bang*

bang against his leg while he's running at Mads, and then Mads is just staring it like what the fuck! Funniest thing I ever saw!

Was it bigger than Danny's? Cookey asked.

Nah bro, don't be stupid. He'd be tripping over it, I said as Booker burst out laughing and we got on with cleaning up. *So where you from then anyway?* I asked.

Who me? Booker asked. *Bit of everything. Grandad was Nigerian. Mum was half Arabic. I think my other Grandad was Irish or something though.*

Mongrel then yeah? I asked, giving him a wink as he threw the Lucozade at me with a laugh.

I'd stayed at his side the whole battle. It was cool actually. Like, we covered each other's flanks and when we needed to change mag and stuff. He can fight too. Holy hell he can fight. And I could feel his distrust of me was easing off too.

Carmen

'That's nice to see,' Paula said as we stood off to one side behind the van with Marcy and Charlie to scrub down and get changed. 'It's about time Mads made some friends.'

'I'll tell you what isn't fun,' Marcy said, holding her broken nail up. 'And neither is listening to Howie and Henry going at each other.'

'Got that right,' I said quietly.

'Yo, Carmen,' Mo called with an excited wave. 'We's seen a bird innit.'

'Is it a seagull?' I asked.

'The ones that eat the pigeons,' Danny said.

'Really?' I asked and rushed off to join them further along the road. 'Where? Oh wow. It is. That's a sparrowhawk. Well done!'

'Danny spotted it,' Mo said, fist-bumping Danny.

'What's the Latin name?' Danny asked.

'Accipter nisus. You need to see the yellow eyes. Hang on, Joan. Can I borrow your rifle?'

'You's gonna shoot it?' Mo asked.

'No! For the scope,' I said, running over to take Joan's rifle to take sight on the bird of prey standing on top of chimney. 'He's so beautiful! And look at him just standing there in broad daylight. It's amazing how quickly creatures adapt. We're down here killing each other and he's up there just living his life. Do you want to see?'

'Please,' Danny said as we used Mo's shoulder to lean on and I showed him how to look through the scope.

'Okay. I think we're done,' Howie called out, stubbing a smoke out as Paula waved at him to hold on for a second with a nod to me and the lads. Howie just looked over then up to the sparrowhawk and said *take your time.*

'We ready?' Henry called. I thought he was looking at maps with Reggie, but he dropped out of the van and clearly wanted to get on.

'Yeah, just give them a minute, Henry,' Paula said.

'I'd rather we moved out,' Henry said. 'Carmen?'

'Hang on, Mo hasn't had a look,' I said as the lads swapped over so we could use Danny's shoulder to rest the rifle on.

'We are moving out, Miss Eze!' Henry said sharply. And Jesus Christ it brought a stink to my cheeks being spoken to like that.

'And I said they could take a minute,' Howie said from across the junction with everyone once more growing still at the next stand-off. 'Mo, it's cool. Take a look.'

I faltered for a second before thinking *fuck it* and handed the rifle to Mo for a look.

'Oh man, the eyes! Yeah, yellow innit, and his feet things.'

'Talons,' I said, but inside I was growing bloody furious.

'But there's a pigeon!' Mo said. 'On that next chimney. Why isn't the sparrowhawk taking it out? That's his lunch right there!'

'They don't always recognise static birds as food,' I said as everyone else listened in. 'He hunts birds in flight. The pigeon isn't flying.'

'No way!' Danny said. 'So if the pigeon flies then the sparrowhawk might take it?'

'Yep.'

'Oh man, don't fly now little pigeon,' Mo said. 'Dude no!' he called as everyone looked up to the pigeon flapping his wings to take off from his perch and a second later the bird of prey took it out. Snagging it from above with the pigeon flapping like mad to get free. The two birds dropping fast and looking ready to fly into a building before the hawk gained height and took his prey off. 'Did you see that!' Mo said.

'That was nuts,' Danny said

'If we are finished now, Miss Eze?' Henry said and fuck me. That was my limit right there. I took the rifle from Mo to give back to Joan then strode at Henry with a look of thunder on my face while Howie gave the order to load up.

'Word please, Henry,' I said.

'We'll speak in the car.'

'In private,' I said before striding off to one side. 'I am not a teenage squaddie.' I said when he came over. I kept my voice low, but there is no doubt he saw the anger in my eyes. 'Do not *Miss Eze* me in front of people ever again, and do not order me like a soldier. I'm an operative, Henry. I ran my own missions for years.'

'Carmen.'

'No, Henry! Your issue with Howie is your issue. Do not take it out on us. We're not being paid anymore, Henry. Your leadership is by consent.'

It was a harsh rebuke that showed in his features, but it needed to be said. I hadn't finished there either. 'And I asked you if this mission was revenge,' I said.

'And I answered you,' he replied, we stayed staring at each other for a long second. There was a lot I could have said, but that was enough.

'Do not call me out in front of people again,' I said and started grabbing my kit and rifle.'

'Where are you going?' he asked as I walked off.

'I'll jump in with Reggie,' I said over my shoulder. I think he called my name but I was still bloody angry with him, so I ignored it and smiled into the van and Reggie at his desk.

'Room for another one?' I asked.

'Of course!' Reginald said as I chucked my kit bag in then spotted Howie walking to the front of the Saxon to open the passenger door before stepping back sharply from the low growl sounding out inside.

'Oh fuck off!' he said at the dog wagging her tail while showing teeth while trying *not* to show teeth. 'You were fine a minute ago. Whatever,' he said, slamming the door closed and walking to the back with a glance at Henry. 'I said the dog should stay in the front. It's cooler.'

'Of course you did,' Henry muttered, giving me a last look before moving back to the SUV.

I got inside the van and slumped down on the cases and stretched my legs out.

Hot bodies in a hot tin can. Hot tempers in hot heads.

The engine fired up and a minute later we were pulling away as the only slightly cooler air started flowing.

A day of days already, and it wasn't over. Not by a long shot. We'd won the Battle of Billingshurst, but we hadn't found CP, and there was still a hell of a ride left ahead of us.

It was cool though. And in a way I felt better. I'd told Henry what needed to be said and I'd gained a sense freedom. That's how it felt to me anyway. That I'd stepped away and gained a sense of privacy, or dignity. I don't know. It just felt better. I love Henry. I adore Frank, but I'm not a kid squaddie. I don't need ordering.

Besides. There might have been another reason lurking in the back of my mind for deciding to get out of the SUV for a while, and there he was, looking all dapper and lovely in his shirt and tie while surrounded by his books and maps.

Like I said. I was thirty years old, and I was definitely getting a crush on Reggie.

32

Diary of Reginald

WITH THE BATTLE of Billingshurst over, we once more set off in our vehicles, or, as Charlie would say, hot bodies in hot tin cans, which was rather apt given the blistering heat.

Of course, the big difference this time was that Carmen was in the van with me and Roy. Which was fine. It just meant I had to be a bit more careful with my maps, so she didn't see I already knew the route we needed, but then I am always very careful.

It was also interesting that she had stepped away from Henry – but again that was not a surprise. Not with Henry addressing her like she was a teenage recruit instead of an extremely capable operative working within the British Security Services.

Of course, that wasn't the only factor, but I did wonder, now that Henry and his team were out on the road and no longer hunkering down, how long it would take for them to question his leadership and seek to understand his true motivations. To be blunt, they were no longer being paid, so staying the course with Henry meant they had to be absolutely committed to the cause, and I rather believe Howie hit the nail on the head when he told Henry this was revenge for him.

So, with all said and done, I felt it was a good thing for Carmen to get some distance from Henry. If nothing else than to make him check his abuse of authority and the assumption that he, because of his former role, should take overall charge.

'I thought you'd have a hot water caddy in here,' Carmen then said as I glanced back to see her looking around the inside of the van.

'We keep meaning to get one,' Roy said from the front. 'Mind you, Howie does like regular breaks so it's not too bad. Correction. Howie likes regular breaks when he's *not* on a killing rampage, which he now is. So, we probably won't get another break today unless Paula steps in.'

'Reminds me of someone,' she muttered. 'Anyway. Where's next?' she asked while looking over my shoulder at the maps on my desk. 'They're still moving north east, aren't they?'

'Indeed. That is the question, but I rather thought we'd try Southwater,' I said while tapping the map to keep her focussed on that spot. 'But I say, is everything okay with you and Henry?' I asked with a look of concern.

'We're fine. But thank you for asking.'

'I wasn't trying to pry.'

'Two bloody great big egos. That's what that is,' Roy called from the front, making her smile and thankfully turn away from my desk as I quickly dragged some books over the other maps. 'They're both alpha types that need to be in charge,' Roy said.

Carmen snorted a laugh then once more sat down, thereby showing that while she agreed, she was not going to be drawn into gossip or tittle-tattle.

We then drove on in relative silence while I resumed my discreet study. However, after a moment or two, I began to get that feeling of being watched. You know the feeling, and so I turned with a polite smile and observed her taking in my books and desk.

Carmen

Reginald then must have felt me staring at him because he turned and gave me a polite smile while I quickly looked from him to the books stacked up on his desk. More on the floor beneath it. More on a shelf above him. Sciences and medicine. Economics. Geography. History and more. Bookmarks poking out, indicating they've all been read. Maps spread on his desk and the monitor at his side showing the feeds from the cameras at the front and back. 'You've read all of them?' I asked.

'Mostly,' he said. 'An eclectic mix, that's for sure.'

I really liked his voice. It's cultured and full of nuance and lilt and meaning, and it made me think of that morning when he was reading the diaries in the café.

It was bizarre though, because it both took me back to that time in the facility *and* transported me to another place where I wasn't the person in the story.

I found myself lost in his voice. Like I was drinking coffee in a café, listening to an audio book and the world wasn't over.

Then it got to the end and the bit about the sex and the blowjob, and I felt degraded and somewhat humiliated. That was weird, because I'd had never felt that way before. Not when I was an escort, and not since.

I'd killed many times over. Jesus. I've had knife fights with Taliban warriors and pressed the button to detonate explosives with the full knowledge that bystanders would be killed, and yeah, now and then, when it was needed, I used seduction to do what was needed. Not frequently, but only if I liked the man, and never with six-pack soldiers with bulging muscles and square jaws. They were ten-a-penny and held no attraction at all. They still don't.

But it was strange, because right there, in that café, I didn't want Reginald to think badly of me.

'Everything okay?' he asked with the enquiring smile of an educated man capable of using tone and facial expressions to convey meaning.

I nodded while leaning forward to call through the hatch. 'Roy, would you mind giving me a five minute warning before we reach Southwater.'

'I can do it. I'm monitoring our position,' Reginald said. 'You'll have plenty of time to lick and lock or whatever you hardy robust people do.'

'Lick and lock?' I asked with a chuckle.

He shrugged with a comical expression and turned back to his desk as I spotted Neal's diary open over the map and felt a pang inside at what he must have thought of me. 'Neal was nice,' I said before I could stop the words coming out.

'Indeed. He was a very nice man,' Reginald said.

'I mean I didn't use him,' I added as he smiled politely. 'Not like that anyway. You know. Like how it came across in the diaries. I mean I wasn't in love with him. But... I don't know. I don't know what I mean.'

'Sometimes things have no meaning,' he said kindly.

'Everything has a meaning,' I replied as he slowly nodded and turned in his chair to face me.

'Yes. You are right. Everything has a meaning. My point is that the meaning itself might not be worth examining.'

I frowned to show I didn't understand.

'May I offer my thoughts?' he asked as I nodded while held rapt in his gaze and the van trundled on, and however strange it may sound, I became very aware of the sweat gliding down my face and felt an urge to wipe it away and check my reflection.

'Perhaps you were attracted to Neal on a physical and emotional level,' he said in that way of his. His voice so full of nuance and tilt and tone. 'And perhaps his obvious intelligence coupled with his inability to protect himself compelled a protective nature within you, and so you decided, from *all* of those reasons, to form a physical connection with him. And yes. Perhaps you did manipulate him. But you did what you needed to do. What I am trying to say is this. You were, to a certain extent, driven by hormonal impulses of a physical nature, while also becoming emotionally attached, *at the same time* as doing your job with the knowledge that more than seven billion souls were at stake.'

He paused to roll his eyes.

'This is the point where Mr Howie would ask Charlie to translate,' he said, making me smile. 'To which, she would say, *it happened, move on. Don't beat yourself up.* And, if she were being particularly astute, she might add *there are bigger things at play here.* The old world is gone, Carmen. Don't carry that baggage around with you. The new world doesn't care what happened. It doesn't care if Howie worked in a supermarket, or if Marcy was a waitress. The rules have been reset.' He offered a smile that reached his soft brown eyes.

'Good gosh! That was a monologue, wasn't it. I do apologise, but one more nugget of advice. If you nudge over a few inches, you'll get the down blast from that vent.'

I glanced up while feeling like I was outside of my own body looking down at a point in my life that was marked and different. Like something just happened without me knowing entirely what it was.

Only that his words sank deep and were already taking root as our small fleet left Billingshurst and took the road east into the rolling fields and meadows with another transition from hell to paradise.

Charlotte

With Billingshurst complete, we once more became hot bodies in a hot tin and set off on more of our adventures.

'Woohoo! The Saxon on the blacktop speeding through the backdrop,' Tappy called from the front as we got going.

'Why does she keep saying that?' Cookey asked.

'Why do you keep breathing?' Blowers asked him, earning a middle finger in response as Nick frowned.

'Paula?' he asked.

'Yes, Nick?' she said. Glancing over to him on the bench seat opposite. 'I'm hungry.'

'We'll grab something soon,' she said and turned back to her conversation with Marcy, Clarence and Howie.

'Paula?' Nick said

'Yes, Nick?' she asked, trying to look irritated but smiling at his tone.

'I'm still hungry.'

'I promise we'll get something. Okay?'

'Okay,' Nick said and waited for her to turn back to her conversation. 'Paula?'

'Yes, Nick!' she asked, still trying to be cross but unable to stop the laugh coming out as Marcy and the others smiled.

'I'm really hungry.'

'What do you want me to do?' she asked as he pulled a face with big sad doe eyes. 'Nick! Pack it in,' she said, turning away.

'Is he doing the face?' Tappy asked from the front.

'Yes!' Marcy said with a laugh at Nick's pining hungry face.

'Paula?' he said. 'Please, Paula... I'm ever so hungry, Paula.'

'Jesus Christ,' she said, grabbing her bag for a snack bar to throw at him.

'Yes!' he said, squishing against the others to lean across and hug her.

'Get off! You're all sweaty,' she said, patting his back before pushing him off.

'You jammy shit,' Blowers said, looking from Nick to Paula's bag. 'Do you have any more?'

'No!'

'But, Paula?' Cookey asked.

'Paula?' Blowers said.

'Please, Paula?' Booker said.

'We're ever so hungry,' Blowers said, trying to pull a sad face with one eye, which just looked weird.

'Dude. You just look weird,' Cookey told him.

'I'm trying to look cute. Don't I look cute?' he asked, pulling a more exaggerated cute face.

'Fuck no! You look messed up,' Cookey said as Blowers leant into him. 'Get off you fucking weirdo. Seriously!' Cookey said, leaning away into Booker who squashed up into Maddox with all of them laughing. 'Charlie, quick,' Cookey called and grabbed my wrists to pull me onto his lap to block Blowers.

'That's cheating,' Blowers says as Cookey reached his arms in-between mine to give him a double middle finger. It was funny, and especially when I tucked my arms in and he carried on pretending his arms were mine and started miming actions. Putting one hand to my chin while pressing a finger to my cheek as I struck a thoughtful expression, and it was nice to see Howie and Clarence even breaking off from deep and serious discussions to chuckle along. Then I said, *Hark yonder, what is that in the distance,* and Cookey immediately shielded my eyes from the sun while I pretended to look at something far away.

It was a lovely moment to see everyone laughing. Even Dave had a glint in his eye, then a second later Meredith erupted. Going from passive and panting to full on hackles up and exploding at the windscreen with her paws planted on the front. Good lord. It certainly sent a jolt through everybody. Especially when Tappy yelled 'CONTACT!'

The jokes cut off instantly and Howie was over the seats into the front. 'Two of them ran through that hedge on the left,' Tappy said urgently.

'Mate, they're all around this area,' Howie said.

'No! They were running. Like chasing something.'

'Okay. Go through. *Roy, Frank. We've got two infected chasing something through a hedge. We're going in.*'

Reginald

At that point, and while we were just starting to enjoy a fractional reduction in air temperature, Howie began shouting through the radio that they were going after two infected chasing someone through a hedge.

'Quickly!' I said and unplugged the drone to thrust it at Carmen. 'Open the door and launch it.'

She responded instantly as I grabbed the controller and got the blades going while she yanked the door open and leant out to hold it aloft, then a second or two later she's at my desk staring at the live feed on the monitor watching as the Saxon swan necked out then turned sharply towards the hedge to batter through the brambles.

It was fast too, and I was still giving lift to the drone as we saw a very steep grassed bank on the other side, and both heard and saw the Saxon's engine as Tappy powered up the side of it. But at that stage we could not see any infected, nor indeed anything beyond that hillside.

'Reggie? Are we going in?' Roy called.

'Hang fire,' I said as we felt the van slow and heard Henry asking for an update – at which point the drone gained sufficient height for us to see the land beyond the hillside, and what a shock that was.

There was a very large oval shaped lake at the base of the hill with wooden buildings off to one side. One of which had a striped café awning canopy outside and signs advertising food and drink. Tables and chairs were outside on decking bordering the edge of the lake, all of which was overlooking a tree lined island in the middle of the waters.

It was a beautiful view, complimented by willow trees and tasteful bushes and reeds growing here and there, and no doubt, when the world was still functioning, the café would have been a very welcome spot for a pot of tea with some clotted cream scones.

However, the world was not still functioning and what we saw was a horde of infected racing down the bank towards the lake with more of them running in through the gaps in the buildings chasing people that had obviously been hiding out in the café, all of whom were now running for their lives.

It was sight to see. Let me tell you that, and within a split second we saw the people were running for the lake as though they had a pre-arranged escape plan to make for the island in the event of a breach. Indeed. Some were already splashing into the shallows and diving out to swim for it, while others were holding babies aloft while small children clung to backs. But those were the ones in the lead, and there were plenty still on the bank and running out from the café.

One of them was a big old chap with silver hair swinging a bloody great sword at the rotters. He got a couple of them down too and bought time for his kin to get away before the infected swarmed him.

'Roy! Get in,' Carmen said as we felt the thrust of the van driving in behind the Saxon to power up the bank with the SUV hot on our heels.

It was fast too. I mean in the sense of the it wasn't a planned battle we were going into. We were responding to an event in progress so to speak with a massive adrenalin dump, and of course, Carmen and I gained an earlier view through the drone, earlier even than Howie in the Saxon who only then breached the top and saw what we could see.

'SHIT!' Howie yelled out with his hand still pushing the radio button down, which was at the same time as the passenger door flew open (while the bloody Saxon was still moving) and he was leaping out with Meredith. Both of them running hard with Meredith going from static to full on sprinting in an instant.

Tappy must have then connected that for once, this was *not* a job for the Saxon. It was too big and there was no way she could run the infected down for fear of hitting survivors. She then slewed the brakes on and was out and running a second after Howie with everyone else piling out the back doors with Danny easily outstripping the lot of them just as our van and the SUV reached the crest.

'Bugger,' Roy said, and he grabbed his bag of arrows and bow and was out of his door, dumping the bag and nocking an arrow as fast as anything while Carmen leapt out and started running. Joan was fast too. She was out of her door like a shot and dropping into the prone position to sight down her scope while Bash ran off behind Carmen and everyone else ran hell for leather down that steep bank.

'Right side, Roy.' I called through the radio. '*Woman in a red top.*'

'Got her,' Roy shouted from outside as he turned and loosed and I watched the infected running the woman down then fly off his feet from the arrow hitting his spine.

'*Left side. Yellow hat!*' I called. Seeing a woman with a child in her arms wearing a yellow sun hat mere inches in front of an infected woman readying for the lunge. A loud crack from Joan's rifle and she went down with a pink mist hanging in the air.

Good grief it was tense with the screams of the survivors so clear in the air. Crying out as they ran into the waters, and with such panic and haste they were tripping over and falling with bodies splashing all over the show and adults grabbing kids to try and get them to safety. Plus there were still more on land being chased down.

Very front! I called out on seeing a big meaty adult male infected running at a woman carrying a little boy. The child screaming in fear as he looked over his mummy's shoulder to the beast with wild red eyes gaining with every step. The bloodied saliva drooling from his mouth. The hands clawed into talons. The face twisted with hate and hunger. The small boy screamed louder. His little heart filled with terror. A sound heard by Meredith and by god that dog streaked through the lot of them. Low and sleek and fast as the wind, and we all felt it too. That pulse of pure energy. A rush as it were. A voice unheard but felt. Just an instinct pushing into all of us.

Little ones.

The whole team gave a surge of speed as the infected male gained and the little boy screamed as the mum ran too fast into the shallows and went down as the big male made his lunge. Diving through the air only to be ripped off his feet with an angry German Shepherd attached to his throat.

'GET THAT ONE!' I yelled out, slamming my battle swatter on my battle desk and watching as an infected female ran in to replace the big male taken down by Meredith. The dog ragging him through the shallows with water spraying high and that woman still trying to get to her feet with the boy in her arms.

I could see Howie sprinting with everything he had with his eyes fixed on the rangy female infected and I swear the arrow must have touched his ear as it went past and took her off her feet. And so close was Howie that he caught that female infected in the air and took her down hard no more than a foot away from the woman and child.

But it wasn't over there. Good god no. A third infected took her place. Then a fourth and a fifth and more of them all flowing like the beasts they were. Never tiring. Never slowing, and they hit the water as one with plumes of water splashing into the air.

The boy was still screaming. That poor mite was simply terrified. His mum was too. Coughing and retching water that had got into her mouth and lungs, but she was still trying to get away with the kid held aloft.

A surge of water then erupted as both Howie and the dog surfaced from their kills with both of them diving out into the horde going for the woman and child, and I doubt either were aware of the streak of motion going past as Danny sprinted by and ripped the child from the woman's hand then grabbed her wrist and dragged her through the water. Taking them both away as yet more infected slammed into the shallows.

Howie had taken several down with his arms outstretched. The dog had one down and was going for another, but there were still plenty up and moving as Tappy ran into the fray and snagged another couple off their feet. Taking them down into the water.

'BLOWERS! TO YOUR RIGHT!' I called and watched as Simon veered off to take two out chasing a woman into the water. Slamming them down with vicious punches as they all became lost within the waves and splashes.

And, as he took his quarry out, so Cookey and Charlie went past his back into another group. The two of them working tandem and going into another small horde running into the shallows. Diving into them to rip them off their feet.

It wasn't just them either. The whole team were running in. Nick, Paula, Marcy, Clarence, and Carmen all of them sprinting into the shallows. Ripping infected from their feet. Bashir too. Splashing into the lake with a knife in his hand as he leapt onto the back of a huge male aiming for two children. Stabbing down into the neck again and again as he wrenched back to take him down into the waters.

Arrows were flying in and the sniper rifle was booming, while Henry and Frank strode down the bank taking what shots they could with their assault rifles.

However, I did see Dave during that melee, and what I saw was him at the edge of the lake with a very rare look of worry. Howie was in the water you see, and Dave hates the water. In fact, I'd go so far as to say is clearly phobic of open water, and so he couldn't get to Howie. Instead, his pistol was out, and he was taking what shots he could. But it wasn't enough and twice I saw him start to go in then quickly back up with a fresh look of terror, and he still didn't go in when Frank strode in past him to grab bodies in knee depth water and drag them up to shoot through the head.

By which time the water in the shallows was positively red with blood, and the first lot of survivors, the strongest swimmers, were reaching the island and dragging themselves onto the bank while yet more were still trying to get across.

A moment later and the mad thrashing waters started to ease as the fighting subsided, and as those waters grew calmer, so I could see a great many corpses floating face down.

Then the shots were ringing out as the team drew pistols to shoot through heads to ensure death was given. All of them drenched and heaving for air. Wading and tripping and gasping as they tried to get balance.

'Bashir!' Henry called, wading into the lake. 'BASHIR!' he yelled again as everyone started looking around.

'BASH!' Frank shouted as the call was taken up with the team grabbing at bodies to turn them while shouting his name as another great surge of water shot up from Bashir breaking the surface with his knife in one hand and the decapitated head of his foe in the other.

'SOULJA!' he yelled out, holding the head aloft. 'SOULJA!'

Charlotte

It was all so fast. One moment we were in the Saxon with Cookey pretending to be my arms, the next we were racing down a steep bank and running into a lake to kill infected. What a bizarre day it was, and it wasn't over by a long shot. In fact, I'd go as far as to say it just got weirder as it went on.

But right at that point Cookey and I were still trying to get to our feet in the shallows, and it may sound refreshing that we were able to get into the water on such a hot day, but trust me, it was disgusting. That water was filthy, and by then it was covered in bodies with gore and entrails floating about – and we were still heaving for air when Bashir popped up with a human head.

'What's he saying?' Cookey asked as we used each other to get upright.

'I think he's saying soldier,' I said with the two of us using each other as leverage to stay on our feet.

Both of us were drenched, and we were both breathing heavily, and the moment just caught me out. The way his blonde hair was slicked down and the way the water was pouring over his jaw, and how his shirt was clinging to his frame. Mine was the same and with our chests heaving and touching. I don't know. There was just a moment between us, and everyone else was watching Bashir. Plus, our bodies were flooded with adrenalin and our hormones were running wild. Life and death situations do that to you.

But yes. There was a closeness that had been forming throughout the day with our secret touches and right then there was a chance to take. Everyone else was distracted, and I felt this very great surge of courage while figuring that we could die at any time, and Mr Howie said we had to be fast to exploit the chances we were given and this new world rewarded the brave and the bold.

And so, with all of those things in my head, and while Cookey turned to fix those blue eyes on me and we became still and silent and the world existed only for us, I did it. I moved in to kiss his mouth - then immediately blinked when he turned away and felt the instant harsh sting of rejection. Then a second later I was questioning if Cookey had even noticed anything.

'We need to get these bodies out,' Clarence said as my mind came back to the present and I saw him grabbing a corpse in each hand to drag towards the bank.

Cookey ducked down to snag a body by the ankle while I searched his face and waited for him to look at me. But he didn't. He heaved back instead and stumbled, and only then, did he glance at me, that thing in his eyes again. That fleeting look of discomfort.

'What's wrong?' I asked and I swear it looked like he was about to say something before we all turned to Howie yelling over at Dave at the edge of the lake.

'Dave! What the fuck,' Howie said, wading through the water with a body held by the ankle while Dave remained dry as a bone on the bank.

'I don't like water, Mr Howie,' Dave said with a rare look of angst that none of us had ever really seen before.

'We were only knee deep. Mate, you need to get over this fear of water.'

'I really don't, Mr Howie.'

'You really bloody do! What if we needed you?'

'I shot one from the bank.'

'Was that you?! Fuck, Dave. His brains went in my mouth!'

'What is with you and eating people, Howie?' Marcy asked

'It was Dave!' Howie said. 'Right. We're going to teach you how to swim,' he added as Dave stepped back in alarm. 'I didn't mean now,' Howie said before turning to see Bashir grinning at him.

'Soulja,' Bashir said proudly, holding the head up as Meredith splashed around Bashir's legs slapping his knees with a severed hand hanging from her mouth.

'Jesus,' Howie said. 'Soul mate more like,' he added as Carmen snorted a laugh a full second later.

'I only just got it. Sorry,' she said with a grin. 'That was a good plan though. The people swimming to the island.'

'It was,' Paula said as I walked down the bank to collect the drone. 'Hey! I'm Paula,' she called over to the island. 'That was a good idea to swim over there!'

'It's deep,' one of them called back. 'And we didn't know if zombies can swim.'

'Not zombies,' Reginald said as he walked down the bank. 'And probably not judging by the state of evolution within these, but others might be able to.'

'Depending on the CP you mean?' Henry asked.

'That and other factors,' Reginald said. 'Such as if the CP can allow their hosts to retain any form of their own minds. But it would largely depend on the genetic mutation within the control point. As for those people, if they stay out of the water for a few hours it should be safe for them to swim back.'

'It's not contaminated?' Carmen asked as everyone else showed surprise.

'It is right now, yes. But the virus does not survive outside of the host for very long, and this is a large body of water in comparison to the infected fluids leaked into it, and despite us all moaning about it, this heat and sunshine will help.'

'The Spanish flu,' Howie said, glancing up at the sun.

'What the hell does the flu have to do with it?' Marcy asked.

'Not *the* flu. The Spanish flu,' Reginald said. '1918 to 1920. It killed millions, but they nurses worked out that putting patients out in strong sunlight helped them recover because the sun's UV rays killed the virus off. That's what it will do here in the lake if they wait a while.'

'Ooh clever, but hold on,' Marcy said. 'How did you know about the Spanish Flu?' she asked Howie as Clarence laughed.

'I saw that episode too,' Clarence said.

'What episode?' Marcy asked.

'It was on QI,' Howie said.

'Love Stephen Fry,' Paula said. 'I hope he made it.'

'We should look for him,' Cookey said. 'Could you imagine Stephen Fry and Reggie working together? The zombies wouldn't stand a chance.'

'And again, they're not zombies,' Reginald said.

'Definitely zombies,' Howie said. 'Anyway. Right. I say we grab a coffee, get changed *again*, and get back on it. Everyone happy? Oh, and where's Danny? Did you see him run and grab that kid? Jesus, Danny. That was impressive. I'll even make you one of my lovely coffees.'

'Do you have to?' Danny asked, risking a cheeky quip.

'You're getting cheeky like Mo,' Howie said.

'Fact, bro!' Mo said, fist-bumping Danny as they waded out of the shallows.

'Er! So. Hi?' someone calls from the island.

'Ooh shit. Forget about them,' Howie says with a wince. 'Er. We'll get some boats to you. Have they got boats here? Where? Oh yeah. Okay. Stay there. We'll come and get you while we borrow your coffee machine. Dave? They need someone to take the boats over,' Howie added as Dave about turned and rushed off up the hill. 'I was joking!'

33

Diary of Paula

ONCE THE BATTLE HAD FINISHED, we had to get sorted and back on the road, and okay, yes, perhaps I went into overdrive, and yes, maybe I did clap my hands a lot but see it from my point of view – my entire team (except Dave and Reginald) had just run into a stinking filthy lake, and then immediately after had to drag the infected dead bodies from that sinking filthy lake and stack them up to one side. Which was also a stinking filthy job.

And that was while most of them were wearing their last full set of clean and dry kit, which we'd only just got changed into just before we left Billingshurst, which was literally about one mile down the sodding road.

Cookey didn't have any clean trousers – I told him to borrow a pair from Roy because they're the same leg and waist size. Then Nick had run out of tops, but the only other male of the same size is Maddox. Luckily Mads had a spare top but no boxers. Booker gave him boxers but needed socks. Clarence thought he had spare socks but no tops, and nobody else in the entire country had tops that could fit Clarence. Thankfully Joan took his, scrubbed it, wrung it, spun it, and handed it back while he, Clarence that is, went on the scout for more socks after realising he'd given his last pair to Booker, meanwhile Roy was getting pissy because Cookey wanted his last pair of clean trousers.

'What if I need them?' Roy asked.

'Jesus, you okay, Roy?' Cookey asked him while leaning in. 'What's that lump on your head?'

Cue Roy going into a meltdown while Cookey snaffled his trousers, meanwhile Joan and I had to instantly check Roy's new lump, which was an insect bite, and then the rest of him just in case it was an outbreak of fucking bubonic plague or whatever.

But then Clarence – still on the scout for socks – saw a pair on the ground, which Roy had placed there prior to trying to call for an ambulance, and according to the grand old military tradition of *if it ain't nailed then then it's fair game,* Clarence promptly snaffled the socks, which caused a big hoo-ha with Roy saying they were stealing the kit from a dying man.

Now add that to Dave also ordering them to strip and clean weapons because they'd been submerged in the lake and trying to dry boots, (we don't carry spare boots as they take up too much space) and Dave (and me) making sure they were all hydrated while raiding the café for food *and* Marcy offering to deal with the survivors.

'Don't sneeze on anyone,' Frank said. I don't know if he meant it as a joke or if it was a genuine warning, but Marcy called him a cock and walked off, but then stopped, and walked back to wrap a silk scarf over her mouth and nose before sticking a middle finger up at him.

Then, add a sprinkling of *something going on between Charlie and Cookey. Something going on with Mads. Something going on with Carmen and Henry* and *something going on with just about every sodding one of them while it was fifty fucking degrees,* and you might come close to the level of chaos we had achieved.

And don't even mention the evil tie wearing genius working away in his van.

Oh. And that was still the warm-up because things really got weird after that.

34

Diary of Reginald

IT WAS ALL RATHER frantic by then, but then the day was upon us and we were deep within the game.

I was checking my route and deciding where to steer the ship next when Henry presented himself at the sliding door to my van. 'Henry! How goes it?' I enquired.

'Frustrating. But seeing as we've got a moment perhaps we should launch the drone and look for this CP rather than relying on guesswork.'

He was feeling the pressure too. I could see it in his manner and hear it in his voice. He was getting drawn in, but I also had to tread carefully.

I did think to try and bluff him and say the drone needed charging, but Henry was too sharp, and I doubt that would have worked. So instead, I said of course we could do that, and in actual fact, I was just about to do that very thing myself. 'Would you mind holding it aloft for me?' I asked as I passed the drone outside and waited for Henry to step away so I could cover the maps on my desk. 'Right. Launching it now, Henry.'

'What's going on?' Howie then asked, no doubt having spotted Henry at my van.

'I am suggesting we gain intelligence by using aerial reconnaissance,' Henry said. Which he didn't need to say as it was plainly bloody obvious we were putting the drone up.

'You looking for the CP then?' Howie asked.

'That's what I just said,' Henry replied.

'Really?' Howie asked him. 'Cos it sounded like you'd just invented something awesome rather than using the exact same method we've been using all day.'

'No, Howie. You have been using the drone to give aid to survivors. I am suggesting we use the drone to look for the CP.'

'Er. No, Henry. We've been looking for the CP *and then* finding the bloody survivors,' Howie said.

'Let's just get it done,' Henry ordered. 'Reginald, I suggest we go high and follow the infected in a north-east direction.'

That was concerning as the last thing I wanted at that point was for Henry to see what was ahead of us. Not yet anyway.

Fortunately, however, I had prepared for the eventuality and had a fall-back plan of sorts, but it wasn't great and would not withstand scrutiny, and so I mentally prepared while flying the drone very high and very fast until I gained sight of a thick line of infected running across a field. I then took a breath and injected some drama into my voice.

'We've got something!' I said, cutting them off mid-argument as they crowded in to see my monitor. 'Infected. Right there. See?'

I went low to keep focus while also making a show of pulling maps out to make it look like I was trying to work out where they were going.

'Is that still north-east?' Henry asked. 'And that's just a small group. Go higher, Reginald. Get an overview.'

'Hang on, they're running at something,' Howie said.

'Howie! We have to find the Control Point. Reginald. Go higher,'

Henry ordered as I fumbled a little at the controls and apologised as he tutted.

'My hands are sweating,' I said.

'Let me do it then,' Henry said.

'Hang on. What's that?' Howie asked urgently as some outbuildings came into view on the monitor. 'Where is that?

'I er, hang on a jiffy,' I said as though I didn't know and pretended to make use of my maps to trace the route. 'Ah yes. Some kind of learning establishment I gather.'

'You mean a school?' Howie asked. 'Is that a school?'

'What school?' Clarence asked from outside as he crammed in with Frank and Carmen.

'I'm checking,' I said while flicking through a local guidebook. 'Ah yes. Here it is. Christ's Hospital.'

'A hospital?' Howie asked. 'You said a school.'

'Not a hospital. A school,' I said.

'Eh?' Howie asked.

'It's a boarding school,' Henry said.

'He just said it was a hospital,' Howie said.

'It's called Christ's Hospital, but it's a very well known school,' Henry said with forced patience.

'It's a school?' Clarence asked. 'Are there kids there?'

'Kids?' Carmen asked.

'Kiddies?' I said in alarm, driving the drone in low and fast to gain view of the infected charging across the fields towards the backs of the outbuildings bordering the school grounds.

'Kiddies?' Paula asked, hand clapping her way past the door but stopping to rush in. 'What kiddies?'

'They're in a school,' Clarence said. 'An old boarding school.'

'A boarding school?' Paula asked.

'Oh god. Are there kids in a boarding school?' Marcy then asked, trying to lean in and see the monitor. 'Where is it?'

'Near some hospital,' Howie said.

'It's not near a hospital! It's called Christ's Hospital,' Henry said.

'Why didn't they call it Christ's School?' Howie asked.

'Christ's Hospital?' Joan asked from the van door. 'That's a school, but they do have a hospital.'

'I'll bloody need one in a minute cos my head is about to explode,' Howie said.

'But what about the school?' Paula asked.

'Are there kids in it?' Marcy asked.

'Henry said it's a boarding school,' Clarence said.

'Oh god. There will be then. They'll have kids in it,' Paula said. 'Is that where the infected are going?'

'I don't bloody know. It's flying too low,' Henry snapped. 'Go higher, Reginald!'

'I am,' I said and flew it up enough to gain a glimpse of the quadrant of mansion style red brick buildings overlooking an ornate square, which was rather fortunately full of children being rushed inside. 'Kiddies, Mr Howie!' I shouted in alarm while turning the drone at speed to see the infected pouring across the adjoining fields.

'Fuck!' Howie said. 'LOAD UP!'

'We need the damned CP!' Henry said.

'Kiddies, Henry!' I said.

'Jesus, Henry. It's kids,' Paula said.

'When isn't it bloody kids?' Henry muttered, dropping out after the others to run for his vehicle as Carmen jumped back in and Roy slammed his door closed.

A moment or two later and we were back on the road building speed to get through Barns Green village on the way to save the little kiddies. Those being the kiddies safely within the quadrant of the highly fortified school buildings that the infected stood no chance of getting into.

But, you see, I couldn't tell them that because otherwise they'd get the drone up high and start ranging out to find our blasted CP. Which wouldn't do at all. For a start the CP wasn't anywhere near us, and there was no way I was going to show them where it was.

'*Cock it!*' Howie said through the radio as we sped through the tiny village. '*We've got infected outside the Post Office. Dave's going to gimpy them. Just hang fire a sec.*'

We both looked ahead to see Dave popping up through the roof of the Saxon to fire the GPMG into the horde.

'*Sorry guys. We can't stop!*' Tappy's voice came through the loudspeaker when Dave finished. '*Don't touch the bodies. Head for fort on the south coast.*'

With that we were off, and I turned back to my desk to see Carmen examining the maps in close detail. 'Hang on a second,' she said, shooting me a look.

Oh, crikey, I thought. *She's rumbled me.*

Then she grabbed her radio with a steely determined look in her eye, which most certainly put the willies up me.

'Howie,' she said. '*It's Carmen. I'm in with Reggie. I've just looked at the maps.*'

I was desperately trying to think of a diversion, and the only thing that came to mind was Roy thinking he'd had a stroke. 'Oh god,' I said with a grunt and clutched my chest, then remembered that a stroke was more in the arm and left side of the body, whereas a heart-attack was in the chest. So being the idiot that I was I tried to do both and slouch my left side while thumping my breast.

'*Howie. The maps show the access road goes for a few miles around the grounds. But listen, you can go off road as the crow flies and get there within a much quicker...*'

She then broke off and glanced up in alarm at the way I was lurching over and flapping my left arm while thumping my chest. 'Jesus! Are you okay?' she asked.

'Sorry what? Fine! Er, just indigestion! Too much Darjeeling. But I say. What a marvellous idea! Going off road.'

'*What direction?*' Howie asked.

'*Use the drone,*' Frank then piped in.

'Has it got enough juice?' Carmen asked me.

'Well. We should most certainly try and find out,' I said, now fully recovered from my heart attack and stroke while leaping into my battle chair at my battle desk to turn the drone and alter course back towards Barns Green.

'Okay, Howie. We're flying the drone back to you,' Carmen said. 'Hang on. *We're going higher. The view's opening out. Got you now. Confirm we have visual on the Saxon.*

'We can't see you,' Howie said. '*You're too small. Ah hang on, we got you. Er, confirm sighting visual on the drone.*'

'*Copy that,*' Carmen said with a smile. '*Just follow the bird.*'

'*What bird? Do you mean the drone?*'

'*Yes, Howie. Follow the drone,*' Carmen said as I pictured Marcy in the Saxon calling Howie a twat.

'*Fuck yes. Off road baby!*' We heard Tappy shout then watched as the Saxon went through a hedge into a field and sped up across a wide dry field. But, most surprisingly, we then heard the SUV overtake us to follow the Saxon.

'*Go on, Frank!*' Carmen said into the radio.

'*They're not having all the fun,*' he replied.

'*Radio discipline,*' Henry then said.

'He's got a stick up his arse today, that's for sure,' Carmen said with an eye-roll. 'And you did not hear me say that,' she told me with a mock stern look.

'*STOP!*' Howie then shouted. '*Roy. Get Jess out. Charlie will ride her in.*'

'*Wilco!*' Roy said, braking hard as Carmen shouted that she was on it and flew out of the sliding door and a moment later I heard the clang and saw Jess galloping through the hedge to the sound of Charlie calling her.

'We can go off road now too,' Roy said as Carmen got back in.

'What was that?' she asked.

'I said we're going off road,' Roy said. 'We don't have to worry about Jess being bounced around,' he added as he set off.

'What about me?' I called. 'I don't want to be bounced around.'

'You're funny,' Carmen said, giving me a grin, but buggered if I knew what she was smiling at.

Anyway. So we set off into the field, which, granted, was very dry and so traction was not an issue, but as predicted, I was shaken about all over the place, and at one point I almost slid off my chair and had to be held down by Carmen clamping her hands on my shoulders.

'You're very knotted,' she said as her hands started kneading my poor muscles. 'I'll try and loosen you up.'

I tried to say I'd rather not be loosened up if it was all the same but ended up yelping from her thumb jabbing into the back of my neck.

'What was that?' Roy asked with another glance back. 'Oh, are you good at massages, Carmen? Only I've got this twinge.'

Good lord it was most surreal. And while that was going on, I was watching Jess galloping along while still flying the drone to lead Howie to the school that we didn't need to save. Which was all because I didn't want Henry, or Howie for that matter, looking too far ahead until I was ready to show them.

We'd only have one chance you see. They had to be mentally ready, and they weren't there yet.

'Reggie. We've got the buildings in sight. Get the drone ahead and scout it,' Howie ordered into the radio. His voice all full of energy and passion to save the poor kiddies. Not that I could do anything while Roy was driving like a maniac and Carmen was digging her fingers into my poor neck after I pretended to have a heart attack.

Paula

'I don't get it. So, is it a school or a hospital?' Cookey asked again.

'School!' several people replied as we bounced about in the back of the Saxon.

'Duh. Then why's it called a hospital?' Cookey asked.

'Exactly!' Howie said from the front. *'Reggie! Get the drone ahead. Is he there? Roy? Can you hear me?'*

'He's fine. He's getting a massage,' Roy said.

'What the fuck!' Howie said.

'I'm not getting a massage! I'm being held down, so I don't bounce around like a blasted pinball.'

'Is Carmen giving him a massage?' I asked, looking at Marcy.

'Reggie! You smooth shit. She's only been in the van for ten minutes,' Marcy said.

'Radio discipline!' Henry then snapped into the radio.

'Oh, sod off, Henry,' Marcy said. 'Reggie's getting his groove on.'

'I am not getting anything on other than my bottom on this chair!' Reginald squawked.

'Watch out for his mayonnaise, Carmen,' Cookey said to a chorus of laughs and cheers.

'Very quick,' Carmen said.

'What me or him?' Cookey asked, earning more laughs as we went past the outbuildings and through the last hedge bordering the school.

'FUCK!' Tappy then yelled as we all held on for dear life while sliding and falling about from Tappy swerving hard at the same time as Frank yelled *fence!* Into the radio.

Reginald

Then Frank yelled a warning through the radio just as we went through the hedge in time to see the Saxon and the SUV steering hard over to avoid the huge metal fence in front of them.

'HOLD ON!' Roy shouted, twisting the wheel while braking hard and trying to account for the weight and motion of the horse trailer.

Carmen was still trying to keep me firmly within my seat, but the harsh braking and turning were simply too great and so the poor woman went over the back of my chair and face first into my lap just before we both flew off onto the floor in a tangle of limbs – which was really most undignified.

'Who put that sodding fence there!?' Roy said as I popped my head up to see an infected lady running face first into it before flying back several feet in a shower of sparks.

'It's electric! Tell Charlie not to touch it,' Carmen shouted from somewhere beneath me as Roy swerved harder to give it a wide berth and I tumbled back down and inadvertently grabbed one of her bosoms.

'Oh my good god. I am so terribly sorry.'

'It's fine. But maybe buy me a drink first?' she said as Howie yelled through the radio. *'Charlie! Don't touch the fence. Holy fuck did you see that?'*

'That must be some serious power to generate that kind of reaction,' Roy said as I then saw rows of heads popping up over the crenelated edge of the roof. Small ones and big ones. Which was bizarre enough in itself given the position I was in, but then it got even more bizarre when I saw them all bringing rifles up to aim down towards the ground.

'GUNS ON THE ROOF!' Carmen yelled into the radio as they opened up with Dave returning fire a second later. Strafing the roof with the gimpy.

'Tell him to stop!' I called in alarm as both Roy and Carmen tried to transmit.

'NO, DAVE!' Charlie shouted through the radio. *'CEASE FIRE! CEASE FIRE! They're shooting the infected.'*

'Infected!' Roy was trying to say at the same time. *'They're shooting the infected.'*

'Get on the loudspeaker. Tell them we're friendlies,' Henry then ordered as Howie's amplified voice boomed out a second later.

'DON'T SHOOT US! WE ARE HERE TO HELP!'

'THEN GET OUT OF THE BLOODY WAY!' An amplified female voice replied.

'We'll lead out,' Henry said with Frank powering on to get in front and driving along the fortified fence line.

That fence was very well put together too. I caught sight of the big linking stems buried deep into the earth connecting the thick chain-link fence panels topped with razor wire with sandbags stacked up on the inside giving it weight and strength, and of course the massive current running through it from the generators connected by thick wires did the rest.

Indeed. All along that fence line we saw the bodies of the infected. Either zapped then shot or shot dead before they even touched the fence.

It was big too and looped around four large buildings all framing what looked to be a big open square in the middle.

We followed the fence line, listening to the shots coming from the rooftops and finally found a road running along the front.

By that time, I figured I could finally give them some aerial assistance and respond as though we had just 'stumbled across' the place. Which, to all intents and purposes, we had just done.

And so, I managed to get myself untangled from Carmen, who was being very decent about the whole breast touching thing, and quickly recover my controller before getting back to my battle desk and monitor. Which was lucky as the drone was slowly dropping out of control.

A jiffy later, and I had it up with a commanding view of the four large red brick mansion buildings set in a quadrant with a large open area in the middle.

However, one of those buildings was set back a little, which allowed the road to run past the front of it and give access to that large inner square, and it was upon that road and towards that square the infected were running towards.

Dozens of them in fact, and in actuality I then surmised that perhaps it was good fortune we had 'stumbled' across them because the attack they were under was rather large, and I rather feared the infected would either short their fence out, or simply knock it over with enough bodies thrown at it.

Carmen, however, also saw the same as I, and was very quick to assess the situation.

'Howie, get on the loudspeaker,' she said through the radio. '*Tell them we'll take these out if they focus their fire on the rear and sides.*'

Howie didn't question her but relayed the instructions as the SUV slowed for the Saxon to take the lead and batter through the backs of the attacking horde with the SUV and the van running close on its heels.

The fact that re-adjustment of tactical positioning was done without the need for communication was the first real show of collective teamwork. Albeit it was Frank driving the SUV and not Henry. But it was an important step, and one that I did not miss.

Nor did I miss it when the Saxon led the charge and gave room for the SUV and the van to get into a line behind her, with all of the vehicles presenting side on to the attacking force.

A second later and the teams were out and firing into the infected. Knowing there was no risk of rounds going into the buildings behind them. Carmen was out too. Standing just outside the sliding door and firing her assault rifle.

'Where's Charlie?' Howie shouted into the radio.

'She's safe. She's in the field at the side chasing them down,' I relayed, seeing Jess galloping along like the wind with Charlie up in the saddle, swinging her bloody great big axe down on skulls.

And of course, those *poor little kiddies* were still on the roof shooting the infected at the rear.

I then switched the view back to our line and saw the infected, although now vastly reduced in number, were closing in with alarming speed. Which duly prompted Dave to give the order.

'HANDWEAPONS!' he shouted, and my word, what a voice he has. Then Howie and the others were slinging rifles and once more the axes, blades and machetes were being gripped and made ready.

'INTO THEM!' Howie gave the yell as Carmen slung her rifle, drew a knife from her belt and gave a big yell as she too set off. Interestingly, I also saw Bashir leap over the front of the SUV with his knife in his hand and set off too, while Henry, Frank and Joan remained in position firing single shot. Then Charlie and Jess came a-galloping around the corner, and it got all very intense with limbs and heads being lopped off all over the show.

'Alright then Randy Reg,' Marcy then said with a big smile as she leant in through the still open side door. 'Did you get a happy ending?'

'What?' I asked her as she mimicked masturbation with a closed fist.

'Marcy!' I said with much disgust.

'Don't Marcy me you mucky little man. She is hot though.'

'Good lord! Close the blasted door and go and help the others.'

'I'm guarding you,' she said with a wink. 'And I'm still injured,' she added, showing me her chipped fingernail. 'I made Roy write a note and gave it to Paula.'

'For a nail?'

'I'm joking, Reggie. No, I mean I did make him write a note but for a laugh. Sheesh. You get one handjob and you're all up your own arse.'

'Marcy, please!'

'I'm teasing you! Anyway, what are you up to?'

'I'm not up to anything, other than becoming highly irritated.'

'You are. You're up to something. I know you, Reggie.'

'Marcy.'

'Relax! It's fine. Howie trusts you so whatever. Just do what you need to do. How big is it anyway?'

'How big is what?' I asked her.

'Your willy,' she said with a mock serious look as I rolled my eyes and huffed. 'The horde we're following,' she said in a quieter voice as I reminded myself of just how bloody astute she could be. 'Okay,' she said when I didn't answer. 'Just be careful. Don't bite off more than we can chew. Unlike your new girlfriend.'

'Marcy!'

She burst out laughing and poked her tongue at me before turning to look out. 'I think we're done.'

I brought the drone in to land and popped it back on charge before stepping out to see Howie and the team once more surrounded by a sea of death and Jess popping skulls.

'Bloody hell,' Roy said. 'You seen this?'

Of course we all looked over to him, then to what he was looking at. Which was the world beyond the fence, and specifically, the inside of the square between those four buildings – and I'll admit, that while I knew the school was fortified from scouting the area in advance, I hadn't scrutinised it for specific details.

What I had seen, by flying at a very high height and zooming in close, which that drone was able to do very well, was a fortified area defended by people with rifles.

That was all I needed to know, and so when Roy drew our collective attention I duly showed as much surprise as everyone else. Well, maybe slightly less, but I made up for it with some good facial expressions and suitable utterances.

Three of the school buildings were off to our left side. All framed around that central square complete with statues and green areas with the outer electrified fence encircling the whole area.

The road we were on then ran into that central square, with the last big red brick building on the right. It was all very stately, and clearly very old, but those buildings were also very imposing with thick walls and tall narrow windows.

But that wasn't the surprising bit. That came from the incredible array of defences they had in place with a high wall running from building to building forming a perfect defensive line. And better yet was that the wall had a walkway upon the top meaning defenders could look down and out over the attacking forces.

We then also saw two sandbag sentry points on ground level forming a road checkpoint just inside the electric fence.

They had the same configuration on the far side of the road leading out of the square, and we could see other sandbag walls constructed at key locations to be used as firing points for a fighting retreat back to the largest main building.

And of those buildings we observed that anything low and scalable had been removed so the infected couldn't climb up, and the ground floor windows had been boarded up, but with firing holes left in them.

Now that was all very interesting, but two other things also stood out. One was that the whole area looked like something from World War Two, and the other were the firing lines of students all wearing what looked like uniformed P.E kit of shorts and polo t-shirts with NATO helmets and body armour on while clutching assault rifles. With adults at the ends also in uniformed sports kit and wearing NATO helmets and body armour and clutching assault rifles.

Honestly. It was like Hogwarts were going to war with St Trinians.

'Unit! Unit stand fast,' a female voice then said in a curt clear tone from within. 'You sirs! State your business,' she called to us.

'We kill zombies,' Howie shouted as Paula, Marcy and several others including Henry all groaned.

'Not zombies,' I said, not that anyone ever listened to me.

'Zombies,' Howie said again as Henry stepped out from behind his SUV at the same point as Paula waved at the woman inside.

'Hello! I'm Paula!'

'Name, rank and unit please,' the woman shouted as Henry waved a discreet hand at everyone to stay quiet.

'The name's Bond. James bond,' Cookey whispered in a Scottish accent to a few low laughs, Frank included.

'Good morning, ma'am. My name is Major Henry Campbell-Dillington, formerly of the Royal Parachute Regiment, the Special Air Service, and commissioned agent within Her Majesties Security Services.'

'Ding dong, hello sailor,' Marcy said, fanning her face. 'Look who's back to being Mr Hot.'

'Ahem,' Howie said.

'Shush. I've told you, you're not the jealous type,' Marcy said. 'And you seriously need to start introducing yourself like that.'

'Fair enough. Hey! I'm Howie. I worked at Tesco,' Howie said as Marcy called him a twat.

'I've heard of you,' the woman inside the square said.

'Woohoo. I'm famous,' Howie said with a wan smile.

'Not you,' the woman said abruptly. 'You,' she added. Pointing at Henry.

'Burn,' Marcy whispered at Howie.

'Major Dillington. You served with Mikey Chavers,' the woman said.

'I did not,' Henry replied immediately. 'I served *under* the command of Colonel *Sir Mickey* Chavers.'

'Cheeky Mickey Chavers?' Frank called as the woman cocked her head over then burst out laughing.

'Units stand at ease,' she said, striding out with a grin. 'Frank? That you?'

'Might be. Depends who's asking,' Frank said. 'Watcha, Tilda. When did you get out of prison?'

'Shut up, Frank! He's joking,' the woman called to the kids and adults behind her. 'Open the gate up, Corporal,' she ordered.

'You heard the Major!' A spotty teenage boy squawked as a unit of P.E kit wearing pupils in NATO helmets and body armour ran out from behind one of the sandbag checkpoints. Some of them double timing it to the closest generator to kill the feed as more of them removed sandbags before grabbing and pivoting one of the heavy metal fence panels to open the gate.

'You a Major now?' Frank asked with a smile at the woman marching towards them.

'I am. Where's my salute, private,' Tilda said sternly.

'You leave my privates alone,' Frank said, slapping his forehead with the back of his hand in mimic of a salute while the P.E kit kiddie soldiers all gawped at us after hearing Henry say he was in the Paras and the SAS, which by proxy meant they assumed the rest of us must be.

'Frank. My god it's good to see you,' Tilda said, rushing forward to hug him.

'Tilda? Introductions please,' a man said from behind her. Tall with a domed bald head and bushy brown hair at the sides. He marched over with an assault rifle while dressed in the same weird fashion of school sports kit with a helmet, body armour and combat boots on.

'Mr Leeson, this is Frank McGill. Ex-Para and SAS, and his CO Major Henry Campbell-Dillington, whom I have heard of and can vouch for.'

'Gentlemen,' Mr Leeson said, coming forward to shake their hands. 'Gerry Leeson. Headteacher of Christ's Hospital. What's the play then, Major? Is it over?'

'Afraid not, Mr Leeson,' Henry said. 'What do you know?'

'Virus. Pandemic. Worldwide. Highly contagious. Turns people into those things,' Mr Leeson said with a nod at the dead bodies.

'That's confirmed,' Henry said.

'Damn it. I'd rather hoped it would be gripped,' Mr Leeson said.

THE UNDEAD TWENTY-FIVE. THE HEAT

'Afraid not,' Henry said again.

'Right. Government down then, is it? Yes? Damn. We thought as much. And confirmed on the whole world, is it?'

'Comms are mostly down, but from what we can tell I'd say affirmative,' Henry replied.

'Right. Well. There we are. Better to know what we're dealing with,' Mr Leeson said. 'So what's your intent, Major? What's the to do? You're welcome to hunker in with us, of course.'

'Very kind, Mr Leeson, but we are otherwise committed.'

'Committed? What with?' Mr Leeson asked.

'Major Dillington means they have a mission, Mr Leeson,' Tilda said.

'Ah! Understood,' Mr Leeson said with a nod at Henry. 'Well. I'm sure we shan't ask any more questions. Hush hush no doubt. But good on you though chaps. Eh, I said good on you chaps,' he added with a thumbs up to everyone else. 'Doing God's work, eh?'

'God's work?' Howie asked. 'This isn't God's work.'

'We're all of God's creation my good man,' Mr Leeson said.

'You're saying God did this?' Howie asked.

'The Lord works in mysterious ways. We are all within His plan.'

'Indeed! But my word,' Henry said before Howie could reply, and after seeing that dark look in his eyes, which also suggested Henry was starting to read Howie, which was also a good sign. 'What's all this?' Henry asked, nodding to the checkpoints then beyond to the militarised square within the fence line.

'You found a time machine or something?' Frank asked. 'Why's it all look so old.'

'Ah, now that was our stroke of luck,' Mr Leeson said.

'You won't believe it,' Tilda said with a smirk at Frank.

'Go on. Impress me,' Frank said.

'Ah. It's a movie set!' Henry said before she could speak, which in turn prompted Mr Leeson to grin with a look of delight. 'Yes,' Henry continued as he looked this way and that. 'Those white trucks over there have got production company logos on the side. And those lighting sets aren't security lighting. I'd suggest someone was filming a war time movie. Most likely world war two judging by the style of things. Ah. Yes. That would account for the electric fences. Movie sets need generators and wiring, and they use metal security fencing. Put them together and you've got instant security.'

'Good show, Major!' Mr Leeson said, pumping his hand with another shake. 'Eh kids. Did you see that? Observation and deduction. A good lesson for us all. And yes, Major. You are absolutely right.'

'Big set though,' Henry remarked as everyone else looked around in surprise.

'Netflix money,' Tilda said. 'Huge budget! They were producing an alternative history piece on the German's invading England after Dunkirk. Hence the heavy fortifications.'

'What about the guns?' Howie asked with a nod at the child soldiers. 'They didn't use SA80's in the 1940's.'

'No. But our military cadets did,' Tilda replied.

'The school is connected to the military, Howie,' Henry said. 'Navy and air force mainly I believe, but I gather they would have had a firing range and cadet college on campus.'

'Affirmative,' Tilda said. 'I was head instructor. Tilda Tanners. Captain. RLC.'

'Now Major Tanners of Christ's Hospital defence force,' Mr Leeson added.

'And now I'm feeling like a fraud in front of a real SAS Major,' Tilda said.

Now I don't know why, but something about it all irritated me slightly, and there was no way I was going to let Henry soak all the glory up.

'A pleasure to meet you, Major Tanners. Mr Leeson. My name is Reginald. I serve under Mr Howie who has been leading the fight back since the outbreak started, and who also set the fort up. Do you know it? Fort Spitbank. It's on the coast. We've got a thousand plus refugees in there now.'

'Good gosh!' Mr Leeson said with a fresh look at Howie.

'Ah yes. We've been very hard at work,' I continued while shaking hands with Major Tanners. 'We've cleared that area and we're now moving out to gain a greater view, and we are most fortunate that Major Dillington has joined us after a strategic period of non-combative observation.'

'Under a table,' someone muttered to a few laughs.

'Ah! The banter of the troops, eh Major,' Mr Leeson said with a hearty nod at Henry. 'My lot are cheeky too. Eh, Rogers? Cheeky wotsit, aren't you.' He said to the spotty corporal in his P.E kit standing to attention. 'But still. Good to see you out and doing God's work.'

'Indeed!' I said loudly before Howie could erupt at the mention of religion. 'Whatever our motivations are, I am sure we are all working to the same objective. Which is to keep people safe,' I added with a look at Howie.

'How many are here?' Paula asked.

'Nearly one hundred and fifty children between eight and eighteen,' Tilda replied. 'Plus, staff and some locals who got inside when it started. All in all, we're just over two hundred. That's not counting the old chaps though.'

'Old chaps?' Henry asked.

'For the Netflix thing,' Tilda said. 'They brought in a load of former second world war soldiers and airmen to advise the actors and crew. And I think they were doing a behind the scenes documentary and interviewing the soldiers that served and fought.'

'And they're here?' Paula asked.

Tilda nodded as Mr Leeson grimaced. 'Nearly fifty of them,' Mr Leeson said quietly.

'Fifty?!' Clarence asked. 'How old are they?'

'Most of them are pushing a hundred,' Tilda replied.

'They were only meant to be here for the weekend,' Mr Leeson said.

'What could we do?' Tilda asked.

'And we've already lost a good twenty in the last month,' Mr Leeson added.

'Fuck!' Howie said.

'Language!' Mr Leeson said.

'That's so sad,' Paula said.

'Most of them were on meds,' Tilda said. 'They had enough for a day or two, but...' she trailed off. Not needing to finish the sentence. 'It's hard on the kids seeing them dying. And we have to take them out to bury them.'

'Plus the food,' Mr Leeson said. 'We're okay on supplies, but the extra mouths and dietary needs are hard work. And some have got very confused in the last month. You know. Dementia and what not.'

'I am so sorry,' Paula said. 'But thank you for looking after them.'

'It's God's work,' Mr Leeson said.

'Not a word,' Paula said, holding a hand up to Howie without looking at him.

'But at least they had that last day,' Tilda said. 'The Friday when it happened, I mean. The old boys got to see the Spitfire and Hurricane and the tanks, and that old bomber. They loved it. Especially the live firing. Should have seen them. And the kids loved it!'

'Whoa. Stop,' Nick said, starting forward with Roy and Tappy. 'Spitfires? You've got Spitfires?'

'What tank is it?' Tappy asked.

'Live firing?' Roy asked.

'Chaps. We need to push on,' Henry said.

'Mr Henry! Spitfires,' Nick said, doing his doe-eyed thing that he normally reserved for Paula when he was hungry.

'And a tank, boss,' Tappy said.

It should have been awkward with Nick and Tappy deferring to Henry as an authoritative decision-maker as that was Mr Howie, Clarence, and Paula's role. But strangely, it wasn't. And again, I noted the organic shift of the dynamic flow between them all. Which were all very good signs.

'Henry, come on,' Paula said. 'Jesus. Nick's dribbling. Have you really got a Spitfire?'

'They're right over there,' Tilda said, nodding towards the grounds beyond the road on the other side of some more buildings.

'Paula. We really cannot keep stopping,' Henry said, but the vehemence wasn't there this time, or the brutal goading tone he used with Howie.

'Ten minutes, Henry!' Paula said. 'Give them ten minutes. You've seen what they have to do. Actually. Stuff this. I'm pulling XO rank. Can my lot have a quick look? Not a word, Henry,' she added, giving him the same hand she'd given Howie.

'I'd love to see a Spitfire,' Clarence said.

'And me,' Frank added with a nod to Henry.

'Fine. Ten minutes max then we're moving out,' Henry said. 'Oh, and don't touch the bodies. Use a digger or something to pile them up and burn them. And I would say head for the fort but perhaps you're doing okay where you are.'

'The words eggs and basket spring to mind, Henry,' I said.

'Concurred,' he said. 'Right. Load up. Let's see this Spitfire.'

35

Diary of Charlotte Doyle

I MANAGED to get Jess hosed off again before popping her back into the air-conditioned trailer, because by then the heat was just incredible.

She was coping with it very well though. Horses can often wilt when the temperature goes too high. The same with dogs, but both Jess and Meredith, although very obviously hot, seemed to be okay. That said – we were watering them constantly and doing what we could to cool them down.

I saw it in the children at Christ's Hospital too. How hot they were. Which is why they were all in their P.E kit and looking all sweaty with rosy cheeks. I didn't say anything at the time, but it reminded me of my own boarding school.

Interestingly, I did wonder why Reginald hadn't observed the location was so well fortified *before* we rushed to give aid. That is most unlike Reginald. But then again, one cannot express enough just how unbearable that heat was, and I guess it was affecting us all in different ways.

I for one was certainly becoming most pre-occupied with Cookey, and in a way, the point of needing to know had been reached for me. We were either going to connect, or we were not, and I wanted to know.

I do accept that sounds pushy, and if a man were to demand attention from a woman he had been trying to court in such a fashion it could be perceived as predatory, but it wasn't like that, and time is different now. Things seem to move faster, and the constant fear of death changes how you think. It makes you take chances you might not otherwise take. It makes you want to live and feel and - forgive me being blunt - but it makes you want to fuck before it's too late.

That is a recognised thing. People within war-torn countries have accounted for that same desperate desire to connect physically, as though their days are numbered and they are trying to cram as much into whatever time they have left.

As it was, we gained a short respite with a rather interesting interlude, and after a quick scrub down, while taking into account none of us had any spare kit, we followed Major Tilda Tanners and Mr Leeson through the square and out the other side onto a road known as The Avenue.

From there we cut between some buildings onto what was formerly a car park leading onto playing fields, but now the whole area had been taken over and adapted for the Netflix production, and my word, what an experience it was.

It was like we'd walked through a time machine and had been transported into the 1940's with military checkpoints, sentry huts, swinging road barriers and sandbag machine gun posts all over the place.

Then of course, we stepped out onto the airfield and good gosh. I think we were all astonished, but Nick, Tappy and Roy showed absolute delight at the machinery in front of us.

There were two aircraft parked close. Low and sleek with beautiful symmetry. To me, and I think to most, they looked identical, but they were not. One was a Spitfire. The other was a Hurricane. Both of which were iconic fighter aircraft used to defend the skies during the Blitz and the Battle of Britain.

'I thought this was meant to be just after Dunkirk,' Roy said as we all walked around the Spitfire. 'This is the Mark 5 which didn't really come into mass production until 1941.'

'And?' Paula asked.

'The Dunkirk evacuation was in 1940,' Roy said with a tut. 'Typical bloody Hollywood. They spend all that money then get a key detail like that wrong. Might as well have Mel Gibson painting his face and shouting *freedom bonza*.'

'Who gives a shit. It's a Spitfire!' Nick said.

'I give a shit. Details matter,' Roy said. 'You'll be telling me they've got a Churchill tank here next, and they definitely weren't in service until 1941.'

'You'd best not turn around then,' Tappy said from behind him before running off as Roy duly turned and groaned.

'I take it that's a Churchill tank then?' Paula asked as Tappy clambered over the top to peer inside the turret.

'It's not even a Mark 1,' Roy said. 'What is it? Mark 6? That wasn't developed until 1944.'

'It's bloody gorgeous though,' Tappy said, her voice muffled from leaning head first into the tank.

'The old boys told them the same thing,' Tilda said. 'About the wrong details here and there. But the production crew said they were lucky to get what they could seeing as it was over seventy years ago and re-building the original chassis' on the tank and the fighters to get them running cost millions.'

'They're not just props?' Nick asked.

'Nope. They filmed the three aircraft flying and the tank running on the Friday morning when it happened,' Tilda said.

'They were readying for the live fire scenes on Saturday,' Mr Leeson said. 'Which sadly never happened.'

'You said that before,' Henry said. 'Live fire? Surely not with live rounds.'

'Live rounds,' Tilda said. 'They wanted authenticity.'

'Fuck. No way,' Howie said.

'Language!' Mr Leeson said.

'No. I refuse to accept any governing body would give consent for two fighter jets to fire live ammunition over such populated areas,' Henry said. 'You must mean blank firing for the effect of it.'

'That's what we thought when they approached the school to book the location,' Mr Leeson said. 'The EP was a Head Girl here. But no. They were going to use live rounds. But not in the air. Only on the ground. The Germans were attacking the base and the scene called for the two aircraft and the tank to fire in a line at the advancing soldiers. See the big earth banks down the end of the landing strip they made? They were built to take the rounds.'

'It was very clever really,' Tilda then said. 'They'd already filmed the Germans attacking the day before. We had hundreds of extras running towards us all getting shot down. Then they were going to film the living firing and merge the footage.'

'So, let me get this right,' Roy said. 'They were going to all the trouble of authenticity of firing guns but in the wrong planes and on the wrong tank. Brilliant. Absolutely brilliant.

'Stop being so bloody pedantic, Roy!' Paula said.

'I'm just saying,' Roy said.

'Which is the most passive aggressive comment ever used,' Paula snapped. *'I'm just saying,'* she said, mimicking in a whiny voice. *'I'm just saying they got everything wrong. I'm just saying I know better than everyone else. You're a bloody troll, Roy.'*

'I never said that,' Roy said. 'I just like things being correct.'

'Just shut up! How about being nice instead of moaning that something isn't good enough, or, get this, shut the fuck up and fuck off and shut up! Fuck me this fucking heat! Not a word!' she snapped at Mr Leeson, giving him the hand. 'I'm going into the van to cool off. Hurry up and wank over the things that are wrong, Roy.'

'Paula!' Roy called as she stormed off. 'I was only saying,' he told everyone else.

'Yeah, that phrase is *really* annoying,' Marcy said. 'Anyway. Awesome. Nice tank and nice planes. Can we go now?'

'Jesus, Marcy. Give me a minute,' Nick said. 'It's a Spitfire. And that's a Hurricane!'

'Honestly. I love this tank!' Tappy's muffled voice floated from the big gun.

'So?' Marcy asked. 'We've seen them. Let's go.'

'What's up with you?' Howie asked.

'I'm hot, Howie, and I don't want to stand in the heat praying to a thing that was used to kill people. Fuck me! We're doing that ourselves every bloody two minutes. Why don't we pray to our gimpy, or our rifles? How about Dave's knives?'

'I think Dave does that already,' Howie said.

'It's not about what they did. It's about what they represent,' Clarence said.

'They're still guns, Clarence. Guns on a plane. Guns on a tank. We use guns to kill people. They're just tools. No, I get it. Don't all start moaning at me. I said I get it. They dug us out of the shit when the Germans were winning or bombing us or whatever. But don't honour them. Fuck me. Honour the people that used them. Whatever. I'm going into the van.'

'We did honour the people that used them,' Henry said as she walked off.

'How?' she called back without looking. 'By stuffing them in care homes? My fucking grandfather fought in that war,' she added, turning back to point at him. 'He came back with one arm and couldn't work cos of his injuries and my mum grew up in poverty, and my dad's grandad came back and hung himself which meant *his* family almost starved too. How is that honouring them? How did that feed their children? Howie was right. That's the old world where men glorified war and taught their kids to hate.'

'No,' Nick said simply, making her cut off and look at him. 'It's about the engineering, Marcy. The Spitfire was an incredible machine. It's got an elliptical wing design with sunken rivets to give it the thinnest cross section possible. Which meant it was faster and more agile than anything else. These things went toe to toe with Messerschmitt's, Marcy, and Germany had fucking thousands of them. It's like… It's like us taking on the infection. We're tiny. It's huge. We're the Spitfire. The infection is Nazi Germany.'

'They killed people, Nick.'

'They defended us against a bigger force, Marcy,' Nick replied. 'They started it. Hitler fucking started it. And those planes and that tank said fuck you.'

'Nick, the people said fuck you. Not the tools they used.'

'Where are the people, Marcy? They're all dead or getting dementia. They're all gone.'

'Exactly!'

'No! You don't get it. We're not honouring the machines for the death they caused. We're honouring the people for the sacrifices they made by using them. We don't kill zombies cos we want to. We do it because we have to, and when we're all chomped up some fucking cunts will look at the Saxon and be like, *oh wow, they did it in that? Just them? Just those few.* And they can see the link to history so they don't forget what we did. It matters, Marcy. You don't get it then whatever but don't fucking piss on my parade because I do. How is that different to Roy?'

'I was just saying,' Roy said.

'Fuck off, Roy!' Nick said. 'Jesus. I just wanted to see a fucking Spitfire. You lot can be fucking cunts sometimes. Fuck this. Let's just go then.'

'Nick,' Marcy called as he walked off. 'Nick! I'm sorry. Okay? Just bloody hang on. I said I was sorry,' she said as she ran after him to grab his wrist. 'I didn't see it that way.'

'We don't all see shit the same way,' Nick said.

'I know. I'm sorry. I apologise, Nick. I see what you mean now.'

'Don't mug me off, Marcy.'

'I'm not! I get it. I'm sorry. Okay?'

'Whatever. It's fine,' Nick said.

'So, tell me about it,' Marcy said.

'Marcy, come on,' Nick said.

'I'm serious. What does elliptical mean? And the shrunken rivets.'

'Sunken,' Tappy called from on top of the tank as she jumped down and ran over to kiss Nick's cheek. 'It's just the heat. Chill out. Sooooo! Sunken rivets mean less friction and drag which means the plane can go faster.'

'And turn quicker,' Nick added.

'Which made it more agile, which is how it kicked Hitler's arse,' Tappy said.

'Which is why they used it for dog fights with other fighters,' Nick said. 'And used the Hurricane to take out the bombers. Cos it had a better view from the cockpit.'

'Not all though,' Tappy said. 'The Hurricane actually got more kills than the Spitfire.'

'Only because more were built,' Nick said. 'And because the Hurricane took less than ten minutes to refuel and rearm.'

'Whereas the Spitfire took nearly half an hour,' Tappy said. 'And it had way less range than the Hurricane.'

'I still can't believe they've got them geared up to fire,' Nick said.

'That's why're up this end closest to the school,' Tilda said. 'We can't fly them, but we can turn and shoot them.'

'You know they've only got sixteen seconds, right?' Nick said as everyone looked at him.

'Sixteen seconds of what?' Howie asked.

'Of firing. That's all they had. Sixteen seconds before they ran out of rounds.'

'Jesus. Sixteen seconds?' Cookey asked. 'So they couldn't afford to miss then.'

'Eight guns mounted on the wings. Some are .303 rifle rounds, then they had the 20mm cannons added in. But yeah, sixteen seconds. That was it,' Nick said.

'Can't we use them?' Cookey asked. 'I mean. That's a tank. We need a tank.'

'Nah. It's too old and too slow, nipper,' Frank said, but not unkindly. 'A thing like that drinks more fuel than we can carry, and they're good when they work but when they break they can be buggers. And we're definitely not towing a couple of fighter planes for sixteen seconds worth of shooting zombies.'

'Not zombies,' Reginald said.

'Anyway. I'm with Busty McGoo. We've seen 'em now and it's too hot to stand around. You happy now, lad?' Frank asked with a look to Nick.

'Yeah, I'm good. Cheers, Frank. Sorry, Marcy.'

'Come here,' Marcy said, giving him a hug.

'Come here,' Frank said, holding his arms out to Nick while puckering up.

'Fuck off!' Nick said as we all laughed.

'I didn't mean you. I meant Busty McGoo. Eh? Mr Howie. Good job you're not the jealous type with her slipping the tongue in this morning.'

'I didn't!' Marcy said. 'And stop calling me Busty McGoo,' she added with a slap at Frank's arm.

'Just tell him he's old and stinks of piss,' Carmen said.

'Eh. What's this about massages?' Frank asked as Carmen gave him a look.

'Mayonnaise,' Cookey coughed into his hand.

'Mayonnaise?' Tilda asked.

'Long story,' Carmen said as we took a final moment to stare at the planes and the tank. I could see what Cookey meant too, because those machines could have helped us, except firstly we couldn't use them, and second, we couldn't either maintain, rearm or keep refuelling them. Especially the tank. It was incredibly frustrating, but again it spoke of the dedication of the people that used them. The training they went through while knowing there was a very high chance of death.

'Major Tanners, Mr Leeson, thank you,' Henry then said, offering his hand once more. 'And we shall certainly keep you in mind if we return this way.'

'Yes, do, Major,' Mr Leeson said. 'We shall give prayers for your safety.'

'Did you go to a school like this?' Cookey asked me, making me turn and smile as the others shook hands with Paula having cooled down enough to come out and say goodbye.

'Similar,' I said.

'Were you a head girl too? I bet you were.'

'I may have been,' I said with a smile.

'Knew it. You're so posh. Did your house have servants?'

'No!' I said with an eye roll. 'We had housekeepers instead… And a nanny,' I added as he laughed at my delivery.

'I had a nanny,' he told me. 'She used to give me a quid to buy a can of Dr Pepper on a Saturday. Jesus. Different worlds or what.'

I shrugged and frowned at him. 'It *was* different worlds, but not now. Do you fancy me, Cookey?'

'Eh?' he blurted with a sudden blink at the direct question. 'What the fuck.'

'It's a straight question. Do you find me attractive?'

'Charlie.'

'Because I'm getting mixed signals and it's confusing me.'

'No. I mean. Yeah, I…'

'Okay! Load up. We're moving out,' Howie called.

'Alex?' I asked.

'Reggie? We got a route yet?' Howie shiouted from the Saxon to the van.

'Let's talk later,' Cookey said.

'When? We're always busy. I just need to know!'

'I do have a route, Mr Howie,' Reginald called. 'I shall update you when we're on the move.'

'That's intel military speak for it's secret,' Tilda explained to Mr Leeson.

'Cookey! Charlie! You two can flirt later. We're going,' Paula said with a hand clap as I looked at Cookey, hoping he'd just say yes that he did find me attractive, or that he'd do or say something. But again, he seemed to panic and turned away as I exhaled and headed after him back into the Saxon.

Back to being hot bodies in a hot tin can.

Back to being confused in a day of days that was only getting weirder by the moment.

36

Diary of Reginald

THAT BRIEF SOJOURN marked a significant turning point for me, because while neither the Spitfire nor the Hurricane or the tank held any real interest for me – the reactions of everyone else did.

I must admit I was rather in the same camp as Marcy in that I held no interest in honouring the tools of war. However, from a historical point of view, I absolutely understood the significance of them, and Nick was entirely right in that the honour was meant *not* for the tool, but for the people that used them.

It was very eloquently put to. Nick has dyslexia and swears profusely, but I have observed that he swears more when he feels either judged, or under pressure from his peers. In this instance, he did swear, but only when he became frustrated at feeling he wasn't expressing himself.

I have a lot of time for Nick. We all do. He, like Blowers, Cookey and the others, have all experienced very turbulent and often highly unpleasant lives before now, and in many ways, the familial unit

THE UNDEAD TWENTY-FIVE. THE HEAT

established by Howie and Paula are their first real experiences of what a functioning family looks like.

As it was, I thought that brief stop was most interesting on several levels.

What it demonstrated was not only a heightened (and essential) level of unity within our team, but also that Henry did not intervene. He didn't try and tell Nick to be quiet or tell Marcy that she was wrong. Instead, I observed him listening to both sides with keen interest, and of course, he then saw as they resolved the dispute.

At which point, Frank expressed concern for Nick and asked him first if he was okay, then made a joke, which again served to break the tension.

I also noted that neither Henry nor Howie went at each other during that time. Indeed. Howie seemed to accept Henry taking the lead in speaking with Mr Leeson and Tilda Tanners.

And more importantly, Henry did not try and put Howie down in front of Mr Leeson or Major Tanners. Nor did Henry show irritation when Howie reacted to the mention of religion.

It may seem I was over scrutinising the entire episode, but in short, and as Charlie would translate, I had them in the right mood for what needed to come next.

However, I had a decision to make.

We either changed direction and turned back. Or we proceeded. But if we were to proceed then there would be no guarantee of survival.

I knew the question of direction would come up within a moment or two and I very quickly studied my maps to make sure I knew what I was doing, and more so, that I was prepared to accept the consequences of failing.

'Reggie. It's Howie. Where are we going?' Howie asked through the radio as I felt a last-minute stab of nerves and a bead of sweat roll down my cheek which served to remind me of that incredible heat. And that alone was a very desperate concern.

Was it too hot? Should I call it off?

'*He's not replying,*' Frank's voice then transmitted.

'*Mucky sod's probably getting another massage,*' Marcy said.

'*She's best be careful. Mayo's got a lot of calories,*' Frank added as Carmen snorted a laugh.

'He's such an idiot. Just ignore him,' she said, reaching for her radio as Henry piped in.

'*Ah. Now I see why Carmen wanted to ride in the van.*'

Carmen and Roy both laughed, and through the radio I could hear chuckles coming from the Saxon, and right then, from Henry finally cracking a joke, I knew we were as ready as we could be.

'*You are all very witty,*' I finally transmitted to a chorus of cheers. '*But yes. I do have a route in mind. Let's get onto the A24 and head down to Southwater.*'

'*Reggie. Henry here. I thought we established the CP is north east. Southwater is south of here. From memory we should be heading towards Horsham I believe.*'

'*Yes, we are going north-east, but the local guidebooks indicate Southwater has a fuel station, which I believe we need?*'

'*We need fuel!*' Tappy cut in.

'*Yeah, we're on less than half a tank now,*' Roy said from the front.

'*Understood,*' Henry then added through the radio. '*Fuel stop then we'll continue north-east.*'

I felt bad for lying, and I felt worse for knowing what I was taking them into

But that was the game, and that was the hunt.

Paula

It was afternoon by then, and it had already been a very hard day, and to be honest I was thinking of calling it.

That awful heat was crushing us. There was no escape from it either and I knew both the SUV and the van were pumping out hot air as their AC units just couldn't cope. Plus, it kinda felt like we'd lost a bit of traction after stopping at that school.

There was also something going on between Charlie and Cookey.

She refused to sit on his lap when we set off and instead went up through the hole in the roof.

I shared a look with Marcy, but there was nothing we could do. There just wasn't time to stop and ask Charlie what was up, but I did manage to get Cookey's eye for a second.

You okay? I mouthed. He nodded and offered a smile, but he seemed troubled. Then a second later he turned away to Blowers saying something as the lads all burst out laughing.

Then I saw Mads and Booker sitting next to each other and thought it was nice to see Maddox relax and just be a lad.

But that heat. I could see it in all of them. We were wilting - which is why I was thinking of calling it.

But then it all changed because we reached Southwater.

Charlotte

I went up top to ride the gimpy because I needed some time alone.

I also thought the breeze would be nice. But it wasn't. It was hot and awful and did nothing to cool me down, although perhaps it did dry the sweat a little.

I was miffed about Cookey. About our conversation, or lack thereof. I was sore at him and at myself for pushing the conversation and feeling rejected.

I ran my hand over my head to feel the stubble and regretted ever cutting my hair. I felt the scar on my cheek and the missing chunk of ear and questioned my appearance. I felt lonely, dejected, and ugly, and I felt confused.

Please don't misunderstand me. I am not a girl that crumples into a heap because of a guy. But right then, I felt crushed and low. I was desperate for human intimacy, and I was desperate for something to replace the pain of losing Blinky, and as we went south through fields and meadows, I stared out at nothing and hoped Paula would call it because I wanted nothing more than the day to end.

Then we hit Southwater.

Carmen

The A/C in the van had pretty much given up. But at least it wasn't as bad as the Saxon. It was better than the SUV too.

That said. I was ready for the day to be over, and I know I wasn't the only one.

'Maybe we should call it,' Roy said from the front. 'This heat. Reggie? You listening?'

'I'm listening,' Reginald said.

'Well? What do you think?' Roy asked. 'It's been a long day already.'

'I don't think it's my decision,' Reginald said while studying his maps and books.

Roy seemed to think for a moment. 'I'll mention it when we stop for fuel. Bloody hell. The tarmac is starting to go. Seen that?'

I went forward to see big black patches of bubbling tarmac. 'You know it's hot when the road melts,' I said. 'Maybe we should stop for the day. I'll speak to Henry when we stop.'

'You back on speaking terms then?' Roy asked me, but he went silent in such a way it made me turn and look out the front, and in fairness, all thoughts left my head too.

Because we'd just hit Southwater.

Charlotte

I could smell it before I saw it. The stench of death and fire. It made me blink and jolt my mind out of the self-pity I had lapsed into.

We were on a country road passing a cemetery on the right and just as that smell reached me, I saw a house burnt to the ground. The roof had crumbled in, and the heat was still pouring from the blackened timbers.

There was a cricket club after that, also burnt out and still smouldering with bodies in the playing fields alongside and blood smeared over the grass.

Then we hit the first proper housing estate. Rows of redbrick standard houses with fenced in front gardens. All of them blackened and burnt.

It was like driving into hell.

Not one house we passed remained intact, and the further into the town we went, the worse it got.

Paula

We reached the end of Church Lane as Charlie readied the gimpy for firing, which prompted everyone else to check magazines and make ready, which only added to the ominous feeling as Tappy came to a stop in the middle of the junction.

There were two shops across the road. A convenience store and a food take-away place, and on the other side a pub called *The Cock Inn*, but not one of us made a joke about the name. Not even Cookey.

All of them were destroyed with the roofs fallen in from fire and the windows smashed. The doors ripped off, and the walls that weren't blackened by fire were red with blood. It was still giving off heat too. Which meant it was recent.

Howie told Tappy to keep going and stay on the main road as the big wheels crunched over the debris and through the sticky patches of melting tarmac.

Maddox

We could smell it in the back of the Saxon. Burnt out houses and dead people. It was grim AF.

Me and Booker were in the cheap seats staring out the back to Roy and Carmen in the van behind us. I could see past them to Reginald staring down at his desk and figured he'd seen this town already because Reggie used that drone a lot more than the others realised.

Then we went past another building. A doctors surgery and a

pharmacy. It had been on fire too with smoke pouring out of the windows with a few bodies outside. Some charred up from the fire. Others just dead and mangled. But then me and Booker shared a look because it kind of looked how we leave bodies after a battle.

Same over there, we heard Howie say from the front and me and Booker were trying to see ahead, but Charlie was up top, and her legs were in the way. We stuck with staring out the back doors and clocked what Howie must have meant when we turned and saw the building opposite was burnt out too with more bodies outside, then more along the road as Tappy drove slowly into a car park with all these stores around the edges and flats over the top of them.

We heard the front doors open then Blowers gave the nod for us to pile out and we're dropping into the sun and squinting from the light while looking at the warzone around us.

There were bodies everywhere. All mangled and cut or shot or run over. Cars were ditched in walls. Nearly all of the buildings had been burnt out. Whole rows of them crumbled in with smoke and heat hazes still coming out. A few were still on fire with flames still eating whatever fuel they had left inside. Wooden beams or furniture.

What's that smell? Howie asked as he inhaled then coughed at the stench.

Petrol, I told him. He looked at me as I went closer to one of the shops and inhaled. *Yeah. They used petrol to burn them out.*

Who did? Paula asked.

Whoever did this, I said. *I reckon they threw Molotov's in.*

Nipper's right, Frank said, shoeing a chunk of burnt glass on the ground. He picked it up and sniffed it. *Milk bottle filled with petrol.*

Someone fought back then? Booker said as I noticed he was staying close to my side.

Yeah. I said and nodded to a body. *See. Cut in the neck. And that one got shot in the head by a shotgun.*

Spent cartridges, Frank said, picking one up off the ground.

5.56 here, Carmen said as we walked over to see brass shells on the ground near her feet. We followed the trail to a body dressed in black lying dead over the top of a police issue assault rifle surrounded by dozens of spent rounds and a couple of empty mags.

He took a few down, Frank said.

She, Carmen said as we all looked down to see a face so chewed up it was impossible to see gender. But then we clocked the bulges of her breasts and her wider hips as Booker started coughing and turned away.

You okay, bro? I asked.

Yeah. Fly went in my mouth, he said.

Close your mouth then bellend, Blowers said.

This looks recent, Paula then said.

Few hours I'd say, Frank said as Henry and Carmen and a few others nodded and said they agree. *Looks like they went that way,* Frank added.

I could see he was right. There was a flow going from one side of the area to the other then we all looked through the treeline at the end to a big building set in big playing fields behind it.

Leisure centre, Paula said, seeing a sign telling visitors how to get to it.

They had fences up, Joan then said, looking at the leisure centre through her scope. *Windows were boarded but have been ripped out, and it was on fire.*

Commune? Howie asked.

Looks that way, Joan said. *And there's a lot of bodies across the fields into this car park.*

She lowered the scope to use her naked eye to track from the edge of the car park across the area we were all standing to the direction Frank said the fight went in.

Then we heard the gunshots.

Carmen

An assault rifle then opened up somewhere nearby. It was hard to tell instant distance and specific direction as gunshots bounce and roll off buildings.

We set off north and ran through a small precinct feeling the heat and coughing from the smoke. More bodies marked the route, and we spotted a crawler dragging itself along with flies feasting on the ruined stumps of her legs. A quick shot from Dave put it down.

I heard the Saxon firing up and knew Tappy was going on the road while we went through the narrower alleys.

We got through the shopping area into a residential road and grimaced at the houses all burnt down with some still on fire. The air was filthy and hotter than hell.

Everywhere we saw was the same. Fires and death and destruction. It was like an army had gone through with a scorched earth policy of leaving nothing behind, and the further we got into that town, the worst it got.

'Horde ahead!' Tappy said into the radio. 'They're by the garage… no, hang on. School! They're going for a school!'

That did it and we all sped up with a burst of energy. Me and Danny and some of the faster ones striding out.

'I've found the school!' Charlie transmitted. 'People inside!'

'Run, Carmen!' Henry shouted as I started sprinting with Danny and Mo. I figured Dave could leave me standing if he wanted, but then Dave refused to leave Howie.

We got onto the last road to a row of houses on fire ahead of us, but I could see the top of the school building beyond and figured to go through the gardens as the crow flies.

'Stay behind me,' I shouted to Danny and Mo. They were good lads and if it was just infected, we were going into then I would have let them go for it. But it wasn't. Someone was firing a weapon, which added a greater risk, plus we had to navigate the burning houses.

I went wide around the last one to avoid the wall of heat coming from the flames. The back garden was on fire too, but we dodged and weaved the flaming shed to vault the last fence over into the shrubbery bordering the school building - a long low structure with the sound of gunfire coming from inside with shouts and yells.

Then we saw the Saxon on the entry road. Running the infected down.

'BREACH! THEY'VE BREACHED!' Charlie shouted into the radio.

I set off to see her and Jess wading into a thick crowd of infected pouring in through the ripped down boards on a window at the back of the school as the gunfire inside intensified.

'Help Charlie!' I told Danny and Mo and went with them as they ran in to attack the horde, diverting some of their attention from the breach point. I stayed low to get through the broken window. Dropping into a bathroom with the flimsy interior stalls already busted down. Blood on the floor and walls and a young man was on his side hugging his belly with fresh bite marks on his arms and legs.

I didn't hesitate and put a round through his head as more gunfire erupted further within. I went into the corridor. Ducking low and seeing infected with gunshot wounds. Some still alive and crawling. Snapping their jaws at me and reaching out with clawed hands. I fired a few more times. Putting them down and moving as fast as I could.

There was a corner ahead. The walls made of painted concrete blocks. Coat hooks here and there alongside small lockers. A primary school for tiny kids. The desks and chairs inside the classrooms so small and tiny. The brightly coloured storage boxes on the walls. The art on the walls. The low benches and the small paintbrushes in their small cups.

The sight of it spurred me on as I ran along the corridor, leaping crawlers and shooting infected coming at me from open doors. The gunfire still ahead. Deep within the centre of the school. Shouts and yells sounded out. Screams of fear and anguish. Screams of pain.

'NO!' A deep male voice yelled. The terror obvious. I ran faster and turned a corner into the back of a horde to see infected ahead battering through a set of doors leading into the main assembly hall. The people inside screaming out. Men and women rushing to brace and try and hold them while a woman in black police clothes fired an assault rifle through the gaps. She got shots into the infected, but she was panicking and getting body shots, which had no real effect.

'HEAD!' I yelled out, ducking back from a round whizzing past me. 'AIM FOR THE HEAD!'

She couldn't hear me. The noise was too great. The infected were screeching and howling and the people inside were screaming. It was chaos. Pure chaos, and I could see that barricade sliding in as the infected forced the doors open. The people holding it were giving it everything they had. Fighting for their lives and to save the children inside. I was firing as fast as I could, and when my rifle emptied, I slung it and drew my sidearm for CQB and put rounds in. I thought between us we could hold them off until the others arrived. I honestly believed that Frank and Dave would be at my back any second. Howie and Clarence. Blowers and Cookey. Somebody. Anybody.

Then the police officer's rifle clicked empty, and the look on her face will haunt me forever.

It was like shock and horror and disbelief. That this wasn't really happening. That this *couldn't* be happening. She had nothing left to give. No more magazines. No more bullets.

Then the doors went in and I caught sight of the survivors inside all staring out. Dozens of them. Men and women and children. All of them frozen in that split second forever in my mind as they looked up to see the infected beasts pouring into the hall.

Some of them closed their eyes and held their children. Some of them found last surges of pure wild bravery and rose up to fight, and my god they fought. They fought with nails and teeth, but it was over the second the doors went in.

I went in with them. Fighting and shooting and screaming out with this great well of fear and rage inside. Not for my own safety, but fear of what I was about to witness.

Every second of that attack is now scored into my head. The way a big male lunged into a woman shielding her two children and bit into her face while she screamed and other infected went for her kids.

I reacted without realising and killed the kids. I did that. I ran towards them and got rounds into their heads while the infected pounced. Then I turned and shot a man pinned down with infected ripping his intestines out. Then a woman beating at an old lady biting into her arms. It was just me. In the middle. Turning and firing. Turning and firing. I don't know how many rounds I put in, or how many people I killed. I know I changed magazine in my pistol more than twice because of having to replace them later. But right then. It was a fucking blur of murder and blood and fear.

Then I felt this impact from behind and was lifted off my feet and thrown into the tables set up to hold the rations the people were using. I went down hard but managed to turn and see a big female infected screeching as she ran at me. Her chin coated in blood. More infected at her back and sides. All of them now fixed on me. I fired fast. Getting rounds into heads and dropping them but more joined in.

I got up and fired as I retreated then my pistol clicked empty. I had no time to change it and grabbed a chair to throw at them. Then another and another as they came in fast. Sweeping me backwards. I drew my knife and got one through the neck as I was taken off my feet and rammed into a wall.

I felt teeth on my right bicep and left forearm while nails raked down my neck. Teeth came for my face. I bucked and heaved and headbutted and bit someone's nose off and spat it away while wishing I'd kept one round in my pistol to shoot myself with because in my mind it was over.

They were pressing into my neck. I couldn't breathe. I was started to black out. Then a gnarly old bastard called Frank McGill was in amongst them. Slicing throats and snapping necks. Stamping on knees. Cutting arteries. Frank McGill. The man that saved me from the Russians. The man that had watched over me ever since.

Frank McGill. The most dangerous man I ever met other than Dave.

The infected didn't know what hit them. Frank took them all out until he finally grabbed the big female by of her hair and stabbed his blade into her neck as he twisted to throw her over his hip.

I dropped. Unable to hold my own weight but Frank caught me on the way down.

'I gotchu. Just breathe.'

I was coughing and retching. Clawing for air. He pushed my hands down and looked at me.

'I said breathe.'

His voice slowed the panic. I started to breathe and ease my terror. He nodded. Seeing the sense coming back into my eyes.

'I fucking killed them,' I tried to tell him. 'The kids. I fucking killed them.'

He just looked at me through eyes that have seen more war than anyone else alive, and all he could do was swallow and nod.

'We're going to find who started this, Frank. And we're going to kill them.'

'Love.'

'Listen to me! I said we're going to find them,' I spoke through gritted teeth. On my backside on the bloodied and corpse covered assembly hall of a primary school, and I meant every word of it, because right there I'd seen the world through Howie's eyes. I'd seen what he saw, and I was in it to the end.

The others swept in. Henry. Howie. Clarence. Dave. I don't know. I sucked air in and had water poured over my face, but I had to get out. I had to be away from the children I'd killed. I pulled free of whoever was holding me and went out through corridors that were too long and too confusing. When I finally got outside, I walked over to some grass and sat down with my head low.

'Here,' Reginald said and pressed a bottle of Lucozade into my hand. I wanted to tell him to fuck off. I'd killed kids. I'd shot children in the head and watched others die. What the fuck did he think Lucozade would do. He just nodded and told me to drink it.

I drank the Lucozade.

And while I did that. Reginald peered at the bite marks on my arms as Roy dumped his medical bag by my feet.

'Okay. Let's have a look,' Roy said as he got in front of me.

I didn't say anything. I drank the Lucozade and looked at Reginald.

'Not too deep,' Roy said. 'This might smart a bit. Need to clean them out.'

He poured something on them. Something anti-bacterial that

wouldn't cause damage to an open wound. It should have hurt like a motherfucker, but it didn't, nor was there as much blood as there should have been.

I looked at Reginald standing over me as the others came out of the school.

'How is she?' Henry asked.

'She's fine. Superficial wounds,' Roy said. 'I've taped them up for now and we'll keep an eye for signs of infection.'

I realised that I wouldn't get an infection because I already had one.

'You alright, bird?' Frank asked.

I nodded and held my hand out for him to pull me up.

'I'm good,' I said as Henry and the others came closer.

'Get it out of your head and move on,' Frank said quietly. 'You tried. Okay? Don't let it fester.'

'Copy that,' I said.

'Boss,' Blowers called, jogging down the entry road as we all turned to face him. 'The garage had survivors too. Out the back,' he said then shook his head. 'Nick found them while he was getting the pumps working. All dead.'

'Fuck,' Howie said.

'Suicide,' Blowers added. 'They all drank some fucking liquid or something. Load of kids and adults. One of the windows was busted in. Charlie said the infected were probably breaching when they took themselves out.'

'How many?' Howie asked.

'Nick reckons about twenty.'

Howie didn't reply but looked at the school then back to the houses still burning between us and the shopping area.

I could see the darkness in his eyes, and for the first time since meeting him, I truly understood why he was like the way he was.

I knew something else too.

I knew we had to find that CP and kill it, no matter what.

37

Diary of Reginald

WE WALKED UP to the main road to the garage where Nick and Tappy were getting fuel into the vehicles – during which time Nick had discovered another group of survivors had very recently died by way of suicide.

The mood was already dark, and it was getting darker with every passing moment.

If that wasn't bad enough, Charlie then found the second school.

'Next to the garage!' she called through the radio. 'I think it's been breached.'

Dave and Mo took point with Frank close behind. But it was obvious we were too late. The windows were broken, and the boards were pulled off with bloodied smear marks all over the walls and ground.

Howie then came out shaking his head. Carmen looked darker than ever and even Henry was showing the strain of it.

There were no survivors.

THE UNDEAD TWENTY-FIVE. THE HEAT

Once more we went back onto the main road as Joan and Roy drove the SUV and the van up to join us. Our small fleet now refuelled, and while that was being sorted, we watched the coils of smoke rising from the housing estate opposite.

More rows of houses blackened and burnt. Smouldering. Some aflame. Some in ruins. Everywhere we turned was the same.

In every view of every direction, we saw the same thing. Smoke and fire. Bodies and death and that awful heat bore down upon us all. A most crushing heat beneath a sky of such dark blue I had never seen before. It didn't look real. It was like a child had painted it with cheap watercolours.

But it wasn't over. Southwater had more to offer, and as the team gathered to drink water and compose themselves, so the next explosion came from further up the road. A deep loud bang followed by a fireball rolling up into the sky.

We piled into the vehicles with everyone grabbing whatever seat they could. Henry and Bash ended up in the Saxon while Frank drove the SUV with Howie, Dave and Clarence, while Joan and Carmen got into the van with me and Roy.

We set off at speed with the SUV powering ahead. Overtaking the Saxon to get there first as we heard another explosion and looked out to see another fireball rolling into the sky.

'DIVERT!' Clarence then ordered via the radio. 'Go wide. Go wide. Gas cannisters.'

Tappy duly swerved hard and drove into a field with Roy hot on her heels as we once more started bouncing over rougher ground. Charlie was still on Jess. Galloping alongside the Saxon as we heard another bang followed by a flaming missile going over our heads.

'It's a caravan park,' Clarence transmitted as we caught glimpse of static holiday homes all set in a row. Each one fed by reusable gas bottles that were now exploding due to the fires sweeping through.

We bounced back onto the road further along just in time to see a flaming gas bottle strike the end of a row of cottages, smashing through bricks with an explosion that tore out the front wall and set fire to the rooms within.

'Someone's inside!' Tappy shouted, braking hard as we all rushed to see someone on fire with flames licking up over their head. They screamed and floundered then fell through the broken wall to land hard on the ground as Henry took aim and shot the person dead.

Another human life snuffed out. An unknown survivor that had stayed silent and alive, but who was now lying charred and burnt with their brains sinking into the melting tarmac.

It was beyond grim. It was truly awful and there was simply no end to the suffering they were being exposed to, but then I'd already seen how bad Southwater had been hit.

Which is why I had taken them there.

This was the plan and it had to happen this way.

But still it wasn't over and as we stared at the melting body lying upon the melting tarmac, we heard the next lot of gunshots.

'Load up!' Howie shouted as he jumped into the SUV with Clarence, Dave and Frank. Henry was close to the van by then and got into the front with Roy.

'Go on!' he ordered at Roy taking too long.

We pulled away with the Saxon already ahead and the SUV going wide around us to overtake. Joan and Carmen were in the back with me. All of us could feel the thrum of the game with adrenalin coursing through our bodies.

'Go on, Roy!' Henry urged, motioning with his hand to speed up. I saw Roy drop down a gear and felt the thrust as Carmen clamped a hand on my shoulder to stop me sliding off my chair.

Charlie was already ahead of us all. Having spurred Jess on the second we heard the shots. *'Horde ahead!'* her voice crackled into the radio. *'Round that last corner, Tappy! Drive straight into them. I'm going for the front.'*

My word it was very tense. We rounded the last corner with Tappy holding a central line and the van close in behind while the SUV went out wider. Then a second later the SUV was braking hard and tucking in to avoid the infected in the road ahead. Roy slammed the brakes on too. Giving the SUV room to get between us and the Saxon just as

Tappy ploughed into the back of the horde. Popping bodies apart and sending limbs and gore spraying out to the sides.

'Jesus,' Roy said with a flinch as a bunch of wet innards splatted into the windscreen. Henry didn't blink. He just stared ahead and cursed softly when Roy used the windscreen wipers to smear the blood over the glass.

But we could hear the gunshots coming fast and frantic. Loud deep shotguns and fast sharp rifles and pistols, and I realised even I had become conversant enough to discern the different sounds.

'GOT THEM!' Charlie said. *'Through the trees. Small track. Industrial estate. I can see the survivors... they're cops or soldiers by the looks of it.* THEY'RE GETTING OVERWHELMED!'

'I've got the track,' Tappy said, veering off into the treeline into the backs of the infected. The SUV close behind and the van doing the same as we gripped on in the back while Henry told Roy to speed the hell up.

'URGENT ASSISTANCE!' Charlie yelled to a backdrop of firing as our hearts pounded.

'I'M IN!' Tappy shouted, braking hard to slew the end of the Saxon around, coming to a stop with the rest in the back debussing a split-second later. Pouring out with axes up as we saw Charlie in amongst the horde. Swinging her axe down left and right.

Howie was out a second later. Running hard with Dave, Clarence, Frank and Bash. Joan and Carmen went out the sliding door with Roy grabbing his bow and arrows and vaulting to get on the van roof, pausing only to grip Joan's wrist and pull her up behind.

I couldn't see a damn thing so I yanked the charge cable out from the drone and had it flying out of the sliding door a few seconds later as the monitor blinked with the live feed, but the view was not good.

The horde was big, and the defenders - men and women of either police or military bearing firing whatever collection of weapons they had. Old shotguns. Rifles and handguns - had a score of survivors behind them pinned against a wall to one of the industrial units, and there was no place else to go.

They were hemmed in and doing what they could while that

relentless horde kept coming. Impervious to pain and ignorant of that heat, whereas I could see the exhaustion on those survivors faces. They must have been running and fighting all night and all day. Burning the town as they fell back to try and kill the infected behind them, but against such numbers they never stood a chance.

Roy and Joan did what they could as the survivors clocked the arrows coming in and gained a burst of hope.

But the horde rallied and surged in. Taking a woman down. Then a man. The defenders compressed again. Shooting their own mates as they screamed in agony from the bites and cuts.

Back they went. Compressing tighter as they fired while Joan and Roy gave what cover they could. Tappy couldn't use the Saxon for fear of driving the horde harder into the defenders. Nor could our team lay down sustained fire as the rounds would whip through and hit the defenders.

Instead, Howie, Dave and Clarence carved a path through the ranks. Slicing them down to try and reach the front while Charlie hacked at the compression going against Blowers and the others.

Good god it was frantic, and I willed Howie to get there. I willed it with every ounce of my being, but another defender went down. Then another until only four were left. Four people protecting a dozen. That's all they had, and they knew it was over. I could see it in their faces as the horde howled and gave that final push just as Howie broke out and turned to slam back into the front line. Dave beside him. Then Clarence. Then Blowers and Cookey and Nick. Danny and Mo. Mads and Booker. Tappy and Paula and Marcy. Carmen and Bashir too. All of them absorbing the weight and fighting out with axes, blades and machetes.

The dog in amongst them. Tearing infected off their feet. Henry at the back, firing single shot into heads with Frank. Joan and Roy on the van, then Charlie broke through with Jess rearing up on her back legs and that huge beast dominated that tiny stretch of ground between the infected and the survivors. She whinnied loud and long while Charlie screamed her war cry because the infected just lost. They just picked a fight with the wrong people and out they went. The whole team fighting charging with Jess thundering back into the ranks. Decimating them to create gaps for people like Dave and Mo and Clarence to exploit. Giving them room to work.

A few moments and it was done.

Another sea of bodies. Another scene of death, but at least we'd saved a few, and what's more, it had given us another valuable boost of energy.

'Hey! look at me,' Howie called to the survivors all weeping with the four armed people now slumped back in silent shock that it was finally over. 'I said look at me!' Howie shouted, striding towards them. His face pouring with blood and sweat. His arms and hands dripping with it. 'Did you come through this estate?'

'What?' a woman asked. Dressed in worn and torn camouflage soldier clothes with the bearing of a squaddie. Her face gaunt. Her eyes nearly glazed over.

'The estate!' Howie said. His tone harsh and demanding.

'Howie, ease up,' Paula said.

'We don't have time to ease up,' Howie snapped, turning on the survivors. 'Did you come through this industrial estate. Yes or no?'

'We did,' one of armed men croaked.

'Okay. Fan out,' Howie called to his team. 'We need to check for survivors. Paula, get some water into these people.'

'Stop!' Henry shouted as Blowers and his team started to move out while I brought the drone back into the van. 'Howie, what are you doing?'

'Survivors, Henry!'

'What about them?!' Henry snapped, striding over the bodies towards Howie. 'They're right there. We can see them,' he added, pointing at the people behind Howie.

'In there!' Howie said, pointing into the estate. 'There might be more infected and more people hiding.'

'So what!?'

'We don't leave people, Henry!' Howie shouted back as the row erupted from nowhere. The heat. The running. The adrenalin. The pressure and the whole of it giving them fuel to go at one another again as everyone else braced. 'I said fan out!' Howie added.

'And I said stop,' Henry shouted over him.

'Henry. I am not fucking doing this with you again. We do not leave people! End of.'

'Then more people will die you idiot!' Henry roared at him. 'If we go back to look we will let that CP get further ahead. We have to go after it.'

My word. I was not expecting that, and I looked out from my van door to see Henry's face etched with passion because the game had finally hooked him.

'*They* can look,' Henry said, pronouncing every word with grim deliberate care while pointing at the survivors huddled behind Howie. 'While we track and negate the CP before it takes another school. Just bloody listen for once in your life you stubborn idiot. I am not working against you here.'

'Howie,' Carmen then said as everyone looked at her. 'Henry's right. We need to push on right now.'

'Speak to your XO,' Henry said, looking at Paula.

'I'm not tactical. That's Reggie's bag,' Paula said as they all turned to me while I thought this whole gruelling bastard of a day had been a walk in the park compared to what was to come.

But that was the game, and that was the hunt, and so I glanced up to that cheap painted sky and looked out to that sea of bodies and nodded at Howie.

'We need to push on,' I said, and for all his faults, for all of his stubborn pride and his rage, Howie trusted me and so he took a breath and nodded at Henry.

'Fine. Load up. We're moving out. And Henry? That town we just went through. That's what the world looks like if we lose.'

38

D iary of Charlotte

Mr Howie then told Henry that Southwater was how the world looked if we lost. I think it was flippant comment made in the heat of the moment, but it was also very profound, and it made us all stop and think because what we'd seen so far was that the towns and villages were mostly unscathed.

For instance. When thirsty we could simply get into the nearest dwelling and take water from the tap. Or find tinned food in the cupboards and we could use those buildings for shelter, or to find fuel to make a fire. The roads were still full of vehicles, from which parts could be taken and used.

But in Southwater we'd seen a different future of a broken and charred landscape where there was nothing left to use.

Granted, it appeared that the survivors had burnt the town out as they fell back, and they'd done a remarkable job. I wish we could have stopped and spoken with them. Or given them time to recover and taken the remaining soldiers into our team. But we did not have the time, and likewise, it didn't matter *who* or *how* Southwater got destroyed. Only that it was.

The other very important factor was that the infection was still evolving. What was to stop it using such tactics to eradicate humans?

As profound as it was, we still had work to do and so we rushed to scrub the filth off as best as we could. Our clothes were soaked and coated in gore, but we couldn't do anything about them. We had no spares.

We couldn't even find a hose for Jess and Meredith and had to use large bottles of water to cool and scrub them down before we got the horse back into her air-conditioned trailer.

A few minutes later, and once Paula and Blowers had given the survivors some ammunition and supplies and told them to head for the fort, we once more became hot bodies in hot tins cans.

'Yay,' Tappy said weakly from the front with sweat pouring from her nose. 'The Saxon on the blacktop speeding through the backdrop.'

We all felt the same, but as exhausted and as hot as we'd become, we were all still very committed because Henry was right. We needed to find that CP and kill it because the horde it controlled was decimating that area.

One positive was that the elders had finally opted to travel in the van with Reginald, which meant more space in the Saxon, which in turn meant I could return to my seat and avoid any jokey expectations of sitting on Cookey's lap.

I did catch him shooting glances at me, but I found myself avoiding his gaze. It was becoming obvious he did not find me attractive or see me as a potential partner and that I had massively misjudged his signals. That was fine. Well, no. It wasn't fine, but of course I had to respect his choice and so I withdrew into myself a little to recover my energy, and in a way, although I still longed for the day to be over, I was also glad it had become so frantic because at least it left no room to dwell.

THE UNDEAD TWENTY-FIVE. THE HEAT

Carmen

I was back in the SUV. But only because Henry wanted to jump in the van with Reginald, which was what Howie, Dave, Clarence, Paula and Marcy also did, which meant there was no space left.

I guess I could have crammed into the back and nobody would have said anything, but to keep life easier I jumped back into the SUV with Frank, Bash and Joan.

'Don't even think about trying to massage me,' Frank said as I got in the front.

'Ew,' I said, thinking it would be like massaging your own dad. But then I had no clue who my real dad was. *Hashtagbrokenhomeusualstorywhogivesafuck.*

'What a day,' I said with a sigh as I felt a hand on my shoulder and turned to see Joan leaning forward with a look on her face. She smiled grimly. I offered one back and covered her hand with mine. We didn't need to speak. She'd killed survivors in one of the other towns, and I'd just done the same.

Bashir said something then frowned before tutting and grabbing his radio as we heard Mo's voice coming back.

'*Carmen? It's Mo Mo innit. Bash said that was fucked up, you get me. What you had to do in that school. He said he did it before his family left for the fort. He was out getting supplies and a lady got bit then some of the blood went in her kid's mouth. Bash took 'em both out with his knife cos he couldn't risk the gunshot being heard. He said it hurts his heart, but he said it had to be done and it's why you were put there in that school cos otherwise those people that got bit would kill more.*'

I listened intently. We all did. Even Frank stayed silent, and I stared at Bash as Mo relayed the message and looked into his soft brown eyes and the creases in the corners. I looked at his moustache and his wispy beard and the gaps between his teeth when he smiled. And, as much as it horrifies me to admit it, I finally looked past his ethnicity of an Afghani to a young soldier feeling a need to share his experience.

I reached out to touch his arm.

'Soldier,' I said.

'Soulja,' he said.

'Thank you.'

'Welcome,' he said in heavy broken English. Which is when Frank farted. I tutted and smacked his arm as Bash burst out laughing while Joan leaned away and wound her window down.

'You're disgusting,' I said as the vehicles set off.

'Guess what?' Frank asked, leaning over to do another one.

'Frank! Jesus. I wish I'd gone in the van now.'

Paula

It was odd because the second we set off I kind of wished I'd stayed in the Saxon.

I think maybe the whole H & H thing had jaded me a lot. It had been a brutal day already and I was fed up trying to play referee between their egos.

Don't get me wrong. Everything Henry said back in that department store was out of order. But Marcy was right, because to Henry we probably did look like crappy amateurs. But Howie was also firing up and inflaming the tension.

They just had that thing between them like two wolves prowling around each other to see who was going to be top dog, and in truth, if I had Clarence's strength, I would have picked them both up and banged their bloody heads together. But by then even Clarence had seemed to withdraw from the H & H thing and was instead focussing on the job at hand. That showed just how bloody professional Clarence really is, albeit a very red-faced sweaty one. But then we all were, and the guys didn't have breasts and if you've never had under-boob sweat then you've no right to moan about being hot.

'Right. Let's consolidate our intel,' Henry said as we set off. 'What do we know?'

I braced and shot a look to Marcy who rolled her eyes with both of us expecting Howie to get sparked up over Henry's choice of words.

'Okay. We've got a big horde moving north east,' Howie then said without any trace of sarcasm as Marcy and I shared another surprised look.

'That's good, Howie. Can we determine numbers from what you've seen so far?'

'Er. Okay, I mean, Southwater was a big town, and it looks like they took the whole thing in one sweep through. Does that make sense? Like they hit it as one unit but left smaller units or whatever to deal with the survivors they found. Like the leisure centre and the schools. I don't know. What do we think? Clarence?'

'I'd agree,' Clarence said twisting his bulk to look through the hatch as I clocked even Reginald looked a bit surprised.

'Excellent. Well done. That's good,' Henry said, jabbing a hand towards Howie as he spoke. 'In summary then. Big horde capable of breaking into smaller teams to deal with survivors. Sound about right?'

'Yeah. I reckon,' Howie said as Clarence nodded and shifted a bit more to get into the conference.

'Numbers then?' Henry asked.

'Fuck. Er, I'd say a lot,' Howie said. 'But it's hard to be accurate.'

'I absolutely understand,' Henry said.

'But at a push. I'd say the biggest one yet.'

'Definitely,' Clarence said.

'More than Hinchley Point?' Henry asked. 'What was that? twenty k?'

'Yeah, that was about twenty,' Howie said. 'But this is more. It feels like more. But I can't quantify that.'

'Trust your gut, Howie. You've been doing this non-stop for a month. Your brain is absorbing data you can't quite express so instead it's translating it into instinct.'

'Yeah. Shit. That makes sense,' Howie said.

'But that means they're going somewhere,' Clarence said. 'If it's one big horde moving along with smaller teams breaking off then it suggests they're heading towards a destination.'

'Outstanding observation,' Henry said, at which point Marcy and I were pretty much open mouthed at how they were all cooperating.

'Okay. More than twenty k, but how many we can't tell. We have a direction of north-east, but no known final destination. Right chaps. Makes sense to me that we get the drone up.'

'Definitely,' Howie said as Clarence nodded, and we all looked at Reginald.

'It's charging,' he said.

'It's been bloody charging all day,' Howie said.

'No. It's been flying over your head all day,' Reginald said.

'Reggie. We need aerial reconnaissance,' Henry said.

'Indeed. And if we had another drone then I would give it to you. But we don't. We have that one and it needs charging. Howie!' Reginald said sharply as Howie started poking at it.

'Reginald, we need to see where the CP is,' Henry said.

'Okay chaps. Fine. Go ahead. Put the drone up. Roy, pull over please we're launching the drone, and then when it crashes and you're screaming out that you need help mid-battle and I can't send Charlie or get Tappy to you because Howie's gone too deep, or direct Carmen to survivors because Henry is still on the edge, or ask Roy and Joan to get fire into a specific point then don't bloody moan. Yes, we need to know where the CP is, but right now, that drone is our single biggest asset when we fight, and I will not risk losing it. We will find the CP. Roy! I was being sarcastic. Don't pull over.'

'Righto,' Roy said, speeding back up.

'Right,' Henry said. 'So you're saying you won't launch the drone. Is that right?'

'Fuck me. Did you zone out or something?' Howie asked him. 'He just said it needs to charge.'

'I heard that, Howie. I was confirming it,' Henry said. 'Never mind. In the absence of aerial reconnaissance, I suggest we head north-east and try and find it on the ground.'

'Why do you do that?' Howie asked.

'What?'

'That! making it sound like you just came up with a brilliant plan on your own.'

'Good god man. Stop biting so easily, and Reginald is right. You do go too deep.'

'Fuck you! At least I don't hide at the edge, but you're good at hiding, aren't you.'

'How dare you!'

'Ah well,' I said with a sigh as Clarence turned away to face front and Marcy pulled a nail file out to work on her chipped fingernail.

Reginald

It was a shame to get Howie and Henry going at each other again, but it needed to be done. The silly idiots started cooperating to form a plan. But I already had a plan, and my plan was working, whereas whatever plan they came up with would be stupid.

That sounds mean, but I was hot and irritated that they were all in my van being hot and noisy and thinking they had any say in what we do.

The other reason was that I couldn't bloody well show them the CP because while I had no clue where it was, I knew where it would be, but I still didn't want them looking too far ahead.

And so, to keep them busy for a moment I made some goading comments and fired them up while I told Tappy to come off the A24 and take the smaller road straight through Horsham.

'What. Wait. Horsham?' Marcy asked because she has the hearing of a bat.

'Horsham is big,' Paula then said. 'Howie. HOWIE!'

'What!' Howie said, breaking off from arguing with Henry.

'Reggie's taking us to Horsham,' Paula said.

'And?'

'Horsham is north east of Southwater,' Henry said.

It wasn't. Horsham was north of Southwater. Well, maybe a chunk of Horsham was slightly north east, but it was where we needed to go next.

'Horsham is big,' Paula said.

'It's not that big,' Howie said.

'Howie, Horsham is a big town,' Paula said while I really wished she'd sod off back to the Saxon and stop interfering.

'What do you want me to do?' Howie asked her. 'If that's where the CP is then it's where we're going.'

'I've got some on the road,' Tappy transmitted as we looked ahead to the Saxon swerving over to mow an infected down. Then another a few seconds after that as we started passing more of them heading in the same direction.

'Okay. We *really* need to put the drone up,' Paula said.

'There's more than I can run down,' Tappy then said.

'Reggie!' Paula snapped. 'I will pull rank and throw that fucking drone out the door if I have to. Get it up. Now!'

Damn it. You try and argue with Paula when she's like that. I had no choice and so I unplugged the damned thing and told Howie to open the door.

'Don't we need to pull over?' Howie asked.

'Just open the damned door,' I said as he yanked it back and I flew the drone out.

'When did you learn how to do that?' Howie asked.

'While you and Major Dillington were comparing willy sizes,' I retorted as Marcy said *Ha!* And carried on filing her nail.

Darn it. I needed the drone completely charged for what was to come later, but at that stage I still couldn't tell them that. There was still a risk they'd call it off.

And the other reason was because I knew there was no point in putting the drone up over Horsham, even though Paula was right, and Horsham was a big town. In fact, I'd suggest it was over four times the size of Southwater.

But the point was that I knew that Horsham was already gone.

39

Diary of Carmen Eze

HORSHAM WAS GONE.

We went in on the Worthing Road where the London bound train-line acted as a natural border between the countryside and the urban town, and the second we crossed the bridge over those lines we knew the horde had been through it.

It was the same thing as before. An idyllic home counties market town filled with idyllic homes where people existed while trapped in cycles of life that never changed. Waiting to live and waiting to die and then regretting it all when the end came.

And the end did come.

It came on that Friday night when the outbreak started, and then again when the horde swept through during the last few hours.

Smashing windows. Battering doors in. Using their body weight to force through barricades. Using their heads to break boards. Sniffing the survivors out. Hearing them. Chasing them. Hunting them down street by street and house by house.

There was one difference between Southwater and Horsham, and that's the fact that Southwater had an organised defence force that fought a disciplined tactical retreat where they made use of fire and whatever they had to slow their attackers.

Horsham didn't have that, and so the houses were not burnt out, which perhaps made it look less destroyed, but to our eyes it was really just the same.

It was just death and carnage and suffering on an epic scale. We saw crawlers and killed them.

We saw slow movers and killed them too. Stragglers and late comers. Anything with red eyes we killed to the best of our abilities. Either by Tappy running them over, or by the SUV slowing so we could lean out and put rounds into them. (Because only a complete twat fires a gun inside a car.) We even saw a few of the lads riding the top of the Saxon and putting rounds in.

Charlotte

I wanted to go up top after we'd been driving for a few moments. The thing with Cookey was still bugging me, but as I stood to go up Nick did the same.

'You going up?' he asked. 'I was gonna have a quick smoke.'

'You go,' I said.

'I know. We'll both go,' he said with a wink and wriggled up and out as I frowned and peered up to see him climbing fully onto the roof. 'There you go,' he called down.

'Is it cooler up there?' Blowers asked.

'Nah. But the breeze is drying the sweat a bit.'

Cue a mass exodus of people wriggling up to ride the roof. One of whom was me. It was quite funny actually watching the lads' bottoms wriggle up. Cookey went just before me and called down to give him a push.

I forgot that we had an issue and promptly started shoving at his backside.

'My bum not my balls!' he yelled in pain as I burst out laughing and climbed up after him to see his blue eyes all twinkling and the others chuckling while finding places to sit.

'You okay?' he asked me.

'I would be if you'd talk to me,' I said, but again the Gods appeared to not want that conversation to ever take place as Tappy duly reported seeing infected on the road and began running them over.

That meant we had to focus and get our rifles ready as we crossed a bridge and started pushing into Horsham.

We soon started seeing more infected, more than Tappy could take down, and so we started firing as we went by. Shooting them dead with our rifles. All of us on the roof, apart from Mads and Booker. They were still below, and from glancing down, I could see them taking advantage of the space and sprawling out on the bench seats with their heads hanging out of the open back doors.

Maddox

This is fucked up, Booker said as I burst out laughing again. I couldn't help it. We were lying flat out on the bench seats with everyone else up on the roof, but we had our heads hanging off the edge of the seats out the back door watching the world going by upside down. Something about it. I don't know. The heat, or the tension, whatever. It was funny. Then Booker started chuckling which got me going and for no reason we were laughing as we bounced along and watched infected getting shot down.

It wasn't the loss of life or any shit like that. It was the angle of it. And cos we'd been cramped up all day and now we could lie down and be stupid for a minute.

I thought you were a right cunt when we first met, Booker said as he glanced over.

I am, I said which made him laugh again.

Fact, bro.

You get me, I said in street slang.

You get me, he tried to mimic it, all deep and street but it was strangled and fucked up, especially with us hanging upside down.

Then he grabbed a bottle of Lucozade and started taking the cap off.

No way, I said as he got the opening to his mouth and tried tilting the bottle while his head was upside down. It went up his nose and he coughed then gagged and had to roll over and fell off the bench seat.

Man. I know I was meant to be faking it and getting in to be a spy and shit, but it was funny AF. I was gone. I was just gone. I've not laughed like that since Darius and me were in a police cell and he took a shit that blocked the toilet up. It was disgusting, but funny. You know when you just get going with a mate. It was like that and Booker was on the Saxon floor still coughing with Lucozade pouring out of his nose while everyone else was shooting zombies.

Horsham though.

Yeah. That was rough. Big town too. Bigger than Southwater.

But for once my mind wasn't on the end goal of whatever we were doing. I was actually having fun and just going along with whatever happened.

But then I didn't know what was to come later.

Paula

It was so weird. We were going through a town probably five times bigger than Southwater and seeing awful signs of devastation and suffering, but the lads were all on the Saxon roof smiling and joking as they took shots at the infected we were passing. Cheering at headshots and jeering at misses.

And what was even weirder was the sight of Maddox and Booker on either side of the bench seats in the back of the Saxon with their heads hanging out. The pair of them laughing before Booker tried to take a drink and nearly puked before falling off, which made me realise I'd never actually seen Maddox laugh before. I'd seen him smile and chuckle, but not a full on belly laugh.

'It's a good sign,' Clarence said as I stood in the hatch and stared out the front of the van. I looked at him as he smiled at me. 'Squaddies doing that is a good sign. Means they're comfortable.'

'Even with all this shit going on?' I asked, nodding behind me to H & H.

Clarence just shrugged as I patted his shoulder and left my hand there. We didn't say anything. He didn't even look at me, or at my hand, but I did see him smile.

Reginald

'Fuck me,' Howie said, shaking his head at the monitor as we watched Horsham below the drone and our small fleet driving along. 'They must have ploughed through here.'

'No fires though,' Henry said. 'And no horde either.'

'They're still moving north-east though,' Howie said. 'We'll go through the town centre and see what that's like.'

'Do we need to?' Henry asked. 'The horde isn't here. We can see that.'

'I know Horsham a bit,' Howie said. 'The main road runs through the centre. It's on the way out.'

'Ah yes. You are right. Okay, we'll do that and head through the town centre, and before you erupt that I just stole your plan I am merely confirming it back to avoid confusion. It's what we do in leadership, Howie. Tell you what, when we get ten minutes, I'll tell you what happened in the Crimean War at the Battle of Balaclava.'

'The charge of the light brigade?' Howie asked as both Henry and I shot him a look, and I'll say it again but it's easy to forget Howie has a very sharp mind. 'Didn't some orders go wrong?'

'Which is why we take great pains to be clear about plans,' Henry said.

'Aw, you two,' Marcy said, stepping between them with a look only Marcy can give. 'You boys, carry on playing nicely, and I'll give you both something to suck.'

Henry then spat the water he'd been drinking over his feet while Howie's mouth just dropped open as Marcy beamed a smile at them both and produced a small lollipop in each hand. 'Filthy sods. What did you think I meant? Anyway. Let Reggie bring his drone back cos we do not want to be stuck in some shitty scrap without our specky little angel watching over us. God. You know what? I really need a cool title like Paula has when she does that XO thing. Maybe I could be the SO. Like the Sassy Officer. Yeah? We all voting for that? Motion passed. I'm the new SO. Reggie! Bring that bird home.'

'Don't look at me,' Howie said when Henry shot him a look. 'You bloody argue with her.'

'Howie doesn't like arguing with me,' Marcy said to Henry. 'Cos I've got these,' she added while using the lollipops to point at her boobs as Henry muttered something and turned away.

I however, gave Marcy a nod of thanks while I duly flew the drone back and in through the sliding door.

'You are sneaky little shit though,' she said when it landed on the charging station. 'How much have you flown that drone to get so good at it?'

I didn't tell her how much. They didn't need to know.

And besides. We were almost at the town centre, which is when we stopped to talk to the Train Guy.

Charlotte

Mo was winning the shooting competition until he got disqualified for having the unfair advantage of being Dave Trained. Blowers then told everyone to shut up cos he was going to win. But, as it turns out, only having one eye does impact on the ability to aim at a moving target while on another moving object.

'Fuck!' he said when he missed again.

'Blind fuck,' Cookey said. 'Meredith could have hit that one. Danny, your side. Red top.'

'I got it,' Danny said, aiming his rifle.

'No pressure, Danny,' Cookey said before he started chanting his name. 'Danny! Danny! Danny!'

We all joined in as Danny finally burst out laughing and took his shot.

'You wanker!' Nick shouted as the head blew apart. 'Shot mate.'

'Skills!' Mo said, leaning over to fist bump his mate.

'Charles! Your side,' Cookey then said. 'Naked man. Shoot his willy.'

I snorted a laugh and brought my rifle up to aim while remembering that Blinky always used to call me Charles. The pain hit again. The loss and grief and that need to replace it with something else, then the hurt of rejection.

'Shoot it then!' Nick said as I took my shot and shot the infected in the back.

'Miss!' they shouted and opened up to shoot it dead as Cookey gave me a worried look.

You okay? He mouthed.

I nodded and looked away, which is when I saw Horsham train station and the office block next to it. And specifically, the thing poking out of the side.

'Holy shit,' Nick then said as he saw it and the others all turned to exclaim. 'Tappy! You seeing that?'

'I'm seeing it,' she shouted, easing the speed off as the Saxon coasted into the train station car park then came to a stop. The van on one side. The SUV on the other, and all of us just staring in silence.

I heard the sliding door and glanced back to see Henry and Howie dropping out and blinked at the surreal sight of them both sucking on lollipops, but they too just stared up.

So did Reginald and Clarence and the others.

It was hard not to, because I don't think any of us had ever seen a train carriage poking out the side of a building before.

Carmen

Honestly. I've been to a lot of places and seen a lot of things, but I have never seen a train carriage stuck out the side of an office block before.

It was surreal. Like a CGI thing in a movie. But it was real.

An office block maybe fifteen or twenty levels high with a stonking great full length blue and white train carriage poking out of the middle. Just one carriage embedded into the side. Big enough for a huge chunk to be poking out, but wedged enough so it didn't topple back out. It was still right side up too with the wheels facing down. And of course, it had clearly made a very big hole in the block when it hit and somehow got wedged because we could see into the building and the desks and chairs.

But that wasn't the oddest thing.

The oddest thing was a couple of levels below the train at the edge of the broken building. A man in a big comfy swing back office chair with his trouser legs rolled up and his feet on a desk.

He was just there. On his chair. A big fat guy with hair on the sides but not on his head. Like Friar Tuck in the Robin Hood stories. But he had potted plants all around him and was holding a mug in his hand and just staring down at us while we're staring up at him.

'Hot day,' he said after a moment.

'Very hot,' Howie said. 'Er. Did you know you had a train stuck in your building?' he asked as the guy looked up at it for a second.

'I did. I was on it.'

'What the what now?' Howie asked as the man nodded towards the train station and we all looked over to see another carriage end poking up into the sky, and another row of carriages crashed through the terminal. But it was so silent and serene and the colours were all so muted that none of us had clocked it.

'There's two sets,' Nick said. 'See the red carriages?'

'Oh yeah,' Tappy said. 'Oh shit. They proper collided then.'

'Signal failure I think,' the Train Guy said and we all looked back up at him as he took a sip from his mug with his office trousers rolled up around his calves, and his office shirt open to show the vest underneath. His potted plants all moved to the edge near the hole in the wall and the office laid out behind him.

'Oh,' Howie said, I guess not knowing what else to say.

'You were on it?' Nick asked.

'I was. From Waterloo. I was going home to Portsmouth,' he stopped talking then seemed to realise we all wanted more. 'And it crashed.'

'Oh,' Howie said, I guess still not knowing what else to say.

'Head on,' Train Guy added. 'Right there in the station. Mine was the blue one,' he said with a nod to the carriage poking out of his building.

'How the hell did you survive that?' Paula asked.

'I have no idea,' he said simply. 'I was passed out drunk before we even left Waterloo. Next thing I woke up and the carriage was stuck up here.'

'No fucking way!' Howie said as Train Guy just shrugged and took another sip.

'Why are you still here?' I asked him.

He looked at me again and smiled gently. 'I just stayed,' he said. There was something compelling about him. Something very centred and real.

'No family then?' someone asked.

'I had family. Wife and two daughters,' he paused while the question hung in the air. 'They hated me. I hated them,' he shrugged again. Matter of fact. Simple. Calm. Centred. 'I was a banker. I had a Porsche,' he added with a smile and a wink that made us all smile back at him. 'Now I have these plants and this view.' He looked out and I saw a man at peace and could only imagine what he went through to get there. 'But on the plus side. I've lost two stone in weight, and I haven't had a drink since it happened. This is a new world. The air. It's so clean now. And silent. Have you seen the stars at night? There's no light pollution. And you see that red carriage? The end one poking out of the station. A fox just had her cubs in it. Three of them. Gorgeous things. They come over to where you're standing and I throw food down for them. I shouldn't really. They need to hunt. But there's plenty of rats out now. And Badgers too. I saw two of them in the station a few days ago. I think they found a way into the café. I'm assuming you're Mr Howie then.'

I saw Howie blink in surprise then nod. 'Yeah. I am.'

Train Guy nodded. 'People pass through. It's nice really. They stop and talk and share what they know. People didn't do that before. They said you're fighting back.'

'We're trying,' Howie said, as mesmerised as the rest of us.

'To you then, Mr Howie,' Train Guy said and raised his mug. 'It's just tea, but it's nice tea. Convenience store wholesalers on the ground floor,' he added as we all dropped our heads to look at the signs advertising convenience store supply chains next to the main doors, and right then, right there, I wanted what he had.

Not the tea. I mean the calmness. The acceptance of what was and the truthfulness of what he said about his family. *They hated me. I hated them.* A few short words, but they summed up the toxicity of the lives we had.

'Anyway. They went that way,' Train Guy said, pointing north east as we all turned to look that way then back at him. 'They went through here last night and this morning. There's a lot though. Is it just you?'

'Just us,' Howie said.

'Well. From all accounts you're very capable,' he said as he started looking at Howie's team one by one. 'You must be Dave. You're obviously Clarence. Paula. Blowers with the eye-patch. Roy the archer. Ah, smiling blonde Cookey and handsome Nick, and you must be Charlie. Which means that young man is Mo Mo?'

'Is Mo Mo, innit,' Mo said.

'They said you were cheeky,' Train Guy said with a smile. 'So, you must be Marcy,' he said with a nod to her then looked at the last two. 'And of course Danny and Tappy.'

'Yes! Get in!' Tappy said. High-fiving Danny. 'They've heard of us.'

'And Reginald the brains,' he added as we all turned to smile at Reginald.

'Pleasure,' Reginald said. 'And you are?'

'I haven't decided yet,' Train Guy replied with what must be the coolest reply ever given. I wanted to be him. I wanted to be somewhere with that level of peace talking to people travelling by and saying I hadn't yet chosen a name. 'You have more people with you,' he then added with a look to my team. 'I'm sure they'll talk about you too soon enough.' He smiled again and sat back in his chair as we all stared up.

'Er. Do you need anything?' Howie asked.

'I'm fine, Mr Howie. Just fine.'

'Right. We'd best get on then,' Howie said. 'It was nice meeting you.'

'And you. Good luck! Stop by on your way back. Let me know it's cleared, and I'll pass the word.'

'When what's cleared?' Howie asked.

'Crawley, Mr Howie. They're all going to Crawley.'

40

Diary of Charlotte Doyle

Mr Howie didn't say a word. Neither did Mr Henry, but they both just looked at Reggie when Train Guy said the infected were in Crawley.

'Not here. Load up,' Paula said. She didn't need to explain what she meant either and so we all piled back into the vehicles and drove up the road looking at the carnage until we hit the edge of Horsham. 'Here,' Paula said from the back of the Saxon as Tappy pulled over.

I caught Maddox's eye as we dropped out, but we didn't need to say anything. Nobody did. Because we all heard Train Guy, and we all realised right then that Reginald was taking us to Crawley, and Crawley wasn't just more than twice the size of Horsham.

Crawley was a city.

'Crawley?' Paula asked as she marched towards Reginald coming out of his van. 'Bloody Crawley?'

'No, hang on,' Reginald said.

'*The* Crawley. The massive town right next to Gatwick airport which just happens to be the busiest single runway airport in the entire fucking world! That Crawley?'

'Did you know that was our destination, Reginald?' Henry asked as we all converged next to a large roundabout connecting several main roads.

'Of course, he bloody knew,' Howie said, pointing at the huge signboard at the side of the road. 'Gatwick and Crawley. We've been seeing signs for it all bloody day. I should have realised.'

'Now now, chaps. It's just a town,' Reginald said.

'Reginald, Crawley is a city,' Henry said.

'Ah. Now. You're wrong there, Henry. Crawley is not a designated city according to-'

'It's a fucking city!' Paula snapped over him.

'Reggie. Crawley is too big for us,' Howie said.

'CHILDREN, MR HOWIE!'

'What the fuck! What children?' Howie asked.

'It's a bloody city. Of course there will be children,' Reginald said.

'Reggie. This is too much for us,' Paula said.

'Poppycock! This isn't too much at all.'

'We need to stand this down,' Henry said.

'No! We'll be fine,' Reginald said.

'Howie, I suggest we find an alternative plan to negate the CP from a distance,' Henry said as he turned to Howie.

'Henry, I said we'll be fine!' Reginald said.

'No. Absolutely not. Crawley is too densely populated. We'll get flanked instantly from all sides with no escape route.'

'Tosh!' Reginald said, trying to sound bright and cheery. 'Hinchley Point was built up and we survived that.'

'Hinchley Point was bordered on one side by the sea, and you also had mortars and a heavy machine gun firing from a position of height which was after Carmen blew the town on fall back. You don't have those tactical options this time,' Henry said. His cultured voice carrying clear as we listened on. 'This is inner city warfare against an enemy thousands of times your size.'

'We'll be fine,' Reginald said again.

'Reggie,' Howie said.

'CHILDREN, MR HOWIE.'

'Stop saying that! I am not getting everyone killed. It's too big. Crawley is too big.'

'It's not too big! It's a damned town the same as every other damned town we've done.'

'We've been avoiding places like that exactly for this reason,' Howie said.

'Until I thought we were good enough,' Reginald fired back. His voice louder and starting to carry. 'But now we are good enough.'

'Reggie, it's not about being good,' Howie said. 'It's simple size.'

'Reggie,' Clarence said deeply from his other side. 'We're standing this down.'

'We are not standing down!'

'Enough, Reggie!' Clarence says.

'NOT ENOUGH, CLARENCE. I say when it's enough and don't for one second let Henry's words get into your head. We're taking Crawley.'

I saw Howie tense as he looked to that big sign and the words emblazoned across the middle: **CRAWLEY AND GATWICK.** We all looked at it and the long road stretching off into the distance that we knew would take us there. And that heat bore down upon us all. Making us sweat while merely standing still. Making us gasp and see the shimmers hanging above the road.

'It's too much,' Clarence said after a moment. 'We're biting off more than we can chew. Henry's right. Stand it down.'

'No! *They'll* bite off more than they can chew. Not us. Especially when they get a face full of the Saxon driving into 'em,' Reginald added with his whole face and manner coming alive with passion as his voice grew louder. 'We'll give 'em more than they can chew, the damned rotters.'

'Reggie,' Paula said, but her voice was soft and pleading, which made Reggie seem awkward and desperate. 'It's too much.'

'It's not too much. Eh, chaps? Blasted infected. What! Charging about the place eating little kiddies. Children, Mr Howie. CHIL-

DREN! We won't have that. We shan't have that. Not on our watch. That's what I say. Crawley might be a city. She might be a big town. So what? To hell with it.'

'Jesus,' Howie said closing his eyes for a second to rub his nose while shaking his head.

'Don't you dare!' Reginald shouted at him. 'Don't you bloody dare give up, Howie.'

'Reggie. It's done. I'm calling it.'

'It's the right thing to do,' Henry said.

'Damn it all! It's not the right thing to do. We're taking Crawley. Come on now! We're the living army. We've got the unkillable Sergeant Blowers. We've got Dave and Clarence and Meredith and Charlie on Jess. We'll have Tappy driving the Saxon and Mr Howie full of fury and wrath. Crawley is too big? What is that? Who said that? Too big for who? For us? NEVER! This isn't our war. It never was, but I'll be damned if we didn't stand up and give it back to them. Eh, Clarence? They don't like it up 'em, do they?'

Clarence snorted a polite laugh at Reginald passion, but still shook his head.

'They don't like it up 'em! Eh, Cookey. What do you say?' Reginald asked, striding about in the middle of us all.

'They don't like it up 'em, Reggie,' Cookey said quietly. The humour and energy now gone.

'That's right. What do you reckon, Sergeant Blowers? Fancy losing another body part?'

Blowers offered a smile, but it seemed to be half in humour and half in pity for the desperation in Reginald's voice.

'Come on now, chaps. I can see defeat in your faces. And I know what Henry said makes sense. The man is a highly respected professional. But it doesn't mean every word is right. Not at all. We've saved thousands of people and we've given hope to countless more *because* we fought back. And yes, we've made mistakes. Good gosh. A blasted Tesco shelf-stacker? An accountant? What right have we got to even try? But we bloody did, and do you know what? We got good at it too. Every day of it has taught us how to be stronger and get better.

Sergeant Blowers held the line against twenty thousand infected with a tiny team. He did that! And do you know what else? Every battle we have taken on we have won. Every fight we have been victorious. We've had losses but look at what we have achieved. We have cleared a whole geographical area. Even Lilly recognises that!'

We listened to the passion in his voice and watched as he looked at each of us in turn. Gesturing and jabbing his hands. That small man in his shirt and tie.

'I won't sugar coat it, chaps. Crawley is bigger than we've done. And what we have before us is an ordeal of the most grievous kind.'

'That's Churchill,' Frank said, giving him a look as Reginald winked at him.

'Many long months of struggle and suffering face us,' Reginald continued. 'And Henry demands to know what is our policy? Well. Our policy is to wage war with all our might and with all the strength that God can give us; to wage war against a monstrous tyranny that must be stopped in its tracks.'

'He bloody is. He's doing Churchill,' Frank said with a smile touching the corners of his mouth. But the strangest thing is that it was working. I could feel it. We all could. That energy coming from Reginald. Like Howie does when he fires up. It was like that and so we all started lifting our heads to look at him as he carried on.

'So, if our policy is war, then what is our aim? I can answer in one word. Victory! It is victory at all costs. Victory *in spite of* terror. However long and hard the road may be. We're all that remains of hope. It's just us now. Just us few. We're the only thing to give survivors a fighting chance at life. So yes! We're going into Crawley,' he said while pointing to that long straight road.

'A big town. A huge town! And it's full too. My god, she's packed to the brim with infected. But if we don't cull those numbers the evolution will grow faster than we can control, and they will win, and everything we have done so far would have been for nothing. *Do not fixate solely on the Panacea. Getting it out will not stop our enemy from growing. We have to cull their numbers. We have to do this.'*

'Reggie,' Henry said.

'Shut up damn you!' Reginald roared at him. 'Releasing that Panacea right now means we still lose! The enemy is too big. We have to reduce the numbers before we release it, because each person we save means greater strength when we do release the Panacea. Don't you see that? You have to see that. We need survivors to give the Panacea to. That's why Lilly is building her wall. That's why I chose this route and that's why I took us through those villages and those towns. We saved one hundred people in Petworth. Thirty-six in Pulborough Garden Centre.'

'Reginald,' Henry said.

'TWENTY-FIVE in the village shop. Seventy-five in Storrington! Twenty-four in Squires. Five in Adversane. Seventy in Billingshurst. Thirty at the Lakeside Café and another forty in Southwater. That's three hundred and sixty five people now heading to the fort where they can be trained and kept safe. That's why we took that route today. To save those people so you would see it, Henry. And yes, I know the horde are in Crawley. Of course I bloody know! We've been aiming at it all day. How did you not notice, Major Dillington? Where did you think we were going? And don't look at Howie. He didn't know either, but the difference is Howie trusts me to do my job. I pick the fights, Henry. Then Howie wins them, and I would not risk my team if I did not think they could handle it. So you listen to me, Major. All of you listen to me. The infected in this town are not the infected we've been playing with. They are not as evolved as Cassie's infected. They're slower to respond. That gives us an edge. It means we can get in and cull them while we find and kill the CP. And yes! There's a lot of them. But what of it? We're still going in and we'll still fight them. By God we'll drive in and fight them. We'll fight them on the beaches if we have to! We'll fight them on the landing grounds, we'll fight them in the fields and in the streets, and we'll fight them in Crawley; we shall never surrender! Now stand up straight and get your boot laces tied because FUCK 'EM. WE'LL WIN!'

We all said it. It was impossible not to say it. That rush inside. That surge of energy was too strong to resist.

'FUCK 'EM!' I shouted out.

'That's it, Charlie!' Reginald said before spinning away to face the others. 'Eh? They don't like it up 'em!'

I saw Clarence lift his chin and saw the violence shining in his eyes. 'They don't like it up 'em,' he said while looking at Howie. To the Tesco shelf-stacker that we all followed. 'We doing this, boss?'

'I dunno. What do you think?' Howie asked looking up at him. 'You got any other plans?'

'Not really.'

'Best get in there then,' Howie said. 'Paula and Marcy in the van with Reggie. Get the drone up. Mads, you're in with us. Load up!'

We started to move. All of us grinning like maniacs.

'This is ridiculous,' Henry called out.

'I will fucking stab you,' Marcy said as she turned on Henry in an instant. She meant it too. It was there in her eyes. You don't mess with Marcy when she's like that. That's the old Marcy. The bad Marcy. The killer Marcy.

Even Henry seemed stunned at her ferocity, if only for a split-second. But it was there alright. That flinch of uncertainty.

Then we were once more loading up.

Hot bodies in a hot tin can and heading to war in a city against a countless number of infected.

41

Diary of Carmen Eze

THAT SPEECH! It shouldn't have worked. I mean, come on? Really? It was the most awful load of garbage I've ever heard BUT OH MY GOD!

If I had a crush on Reggie before, I was falling in love with the weird little nerd by the end of it.

He was right too. And it was so simple. We had to cull the numbers *before* we release the Panacea.

That's what the whole thing had been about, and while Howie and Henry were comparing dick sizes, Reggie was thunking his mammoth dong on his battle desk, because he'd already planned it.

He knew the route we were on and he knew where the horde would be the whole time, except he didn't tell anyone because he'd knew they'd chicken out and he wanted Henry to see it in stages.

Genius!

But anyway. It worked and then Howie was reeling off orders and Marcy told Henry to shut up or she'd stab him. Then they were all running off. I was close to the van and hopped inside, and the next thing Paula and Marcy were bundling Reggie in and just about to slam the door closed when Henry ran over to join us.

We set off with Reginald getting the drone out of the door and up into the air while I glanced ahead to see everyone gearing up in the Saxon. Tapping magazines on the sides to rid grit. Checking pouches and bags, or lick and locking as Reggie calls it.

We did the same with me, Paula and Marcy checking rifles. I did Roy's while he drove then a moment or two later Reginald had the drone over Crawley. It wasn't that far from Horsham at all. Less than a few miles.

'Okay, what have we got,' Paula said, looking at the screen showing the drone feed. *'Howie, it's Paula. I've got eyes on the town.'*

'What's it looking like?' Howie asked.

'Imagine Black Friday but swap shoppers for zombies.'

'Too many?' Howie asked, and there it was. The million-dollar question, because from all of them if Paula said it was a no go, then it really was a no go. She was the XO. She had that power. And she looked at that screen as Reginald took the drone in lower so they could see Crawley High Street packed from wall to wall with the infected looking like a crowd at a festival.

'Paula?' Howie asked. *'We good to go?'*

I could see Henry was waiting for Paula to stand them down now that she'd seen just how many there were. I even expected it myself, and I suspect Reginald might have been a bit worried too.

'Nah, it's fine. You're good to go,' Paula said as Marcy nodded at her side. I could feel the energy between them. It was like an electrical current. 'Where's the map,' Paula asked, taking it from Reginald. 'Where are we? Okay. Yep, got it. *Howie. We're not far off. Slow down and give me a minute to plot the best route in with Reggie and Marcy.'*

'I know Crawley a bit,' Howie said. *'Where are they?'*

'In the High Street. Town centre,' Paula replied. *'But we're coming in on the Horsham Road which is off to the west.'*

'I know Crawley,' Frank cut in. *'Let me take point. I'll lead in and get them on the Brighton Road.'*

'Brighton Road?' Paula asked as Reginald found it on his smaller scale map.

'It runs straight into the High Street,' Reginald said, tracing his finger along.

'Tappy can get a good run into them,' Marcy said.

'Good call. *Frank, It's Paula. Yes please. Lead us in. Tappy, Frank will get to the front. I'll tell you where to start the run up from in a minute.*'

'*Understood,*' Howie replied. '*Listen. We need to take the control point out. Same as yesterday at Hinchley Point. We take that out and cull the rest. Paula, I want you, Marcy and Reggie on that drone looking for it. Get Roy and Joanie on overwatch ready to take it out. Joanie, it's Howie. Are you working with us?*'

'*Not if you call me Joanie I won't be,*' Joan said into the radio.

'Fucking love her,' Marcy said as Paula nodded.

'*Count me in, Howie. You find me that CP and I'll drop it,*' Joan added as Henry tutted.

'You need to grow a pair,' Marcy told him with a withering look. 'A seventy year old woman just shamed you.'

'Okay,' Paula said as we felt the van veer and slow to come off the motorway behind the Saxon. 'We need a high point for overwatch. Somewhere central. I'd say we use the Saxon to punch a hole. Then get the van in behind it and get Roy and Joanie into one of these buildings in the middle.'

'You'll need room clearance if we're going inside any buildings in that area,' Marcy said.

'We'll have to do it,' Paula replied.

'One of us needs to guard Reggie. Mads is in the Saxon and we can't take Dave or Mo away from that. And are we taking all three vehicles in behind the Saxon or just the van. Or are we keeping the van out of it?'

'Paula, we're not far off,' Roy called from the front.

'Okay. Working on it,' Paula called. 'Right. We'll stop and get Joanie in with us then we follow the Saxon and punch into the middle. I mean, it'll be hard, but the lads can debuss and put some fire down to buy us some space. Roy can fire a rifle. So can Joan. They can clear as they go.'

'They're not trained for that,' Henry said. 'And you can't expect Joan to carry an assault rifle in addition to her sniper rifle.'

'None of us are trained,' Paula snapped. *'Howie, it's Paula. We've got a rough plan. We'll stop and grab Joan and let Henry get back in his car. Then we need you to punch into the High Street and we'll get Roy and Joanie in for overwatch. Either me or Marcy will help with room clearance.'*

'No, hang on. I'll do it,' I said as Henry shot me a look.

'I don't want my team involved,' Henry said.

'Roy and Joan need a guard,' I said. 'Snipers have guards, Henry. That's SOP. Do you want this CP or not?'

I saw him glance back to the monitor and the sheer numbers of infected all facing up the High Street and no doubt more infected pouring in from all sides. It was a suicide mission to go anywhere near that place. But then the same could be said for every town we'd been through and I knew Reginald's speech was still ringing my ears.

'The only thing needed for evil to triumph is for good men to do nothing,' Reginald said.

'Shut up,' Henry snapped at him as he leaned past to take control of the drone. Making it fly back towards the start of the High Street. Taking it lower and studying the building lines on one side. His eyes taking in the structures. The sizes of them. The windows and the way each building connected to the next. The construction materials. The rooftops.

'What are you doing?' Paula asked.

'Looking for somewhere to hide probably,' Marcy muttered. 'Roy, we'll need to stop and get Joanie in with us. *Howie, pull over. We need to get Joan in here.*'

'Henry?' Reginald enquired, but I could hear the prompt in his voice and figured Henry just got played again because there was a gleam in his eyes at the lure of it all. I could feel it. And if I felt it, Henry definitely could. But there was something else too, because Henry can't be passive. It's not in his nature. The man *has* to lead, and so I couldn't help but smile when he spoke into the radio and told them all to pull over.

They did as he asked, but then they had to for the swap over, and the second we stopped, we all jumped out with Henry striding over to the SUV and popping the back open to heave his big black tac bag out.

'You bailing then?' Howie asked him and earnt a vicious look in response as Henry dumped his bag on the ground and bent down to yank the zip open.

I shared a look with Frank because we both knew what it meant, and without Henry needing to say a word Frank and Bash grabbed their bags from the SUV and I took mine out from the van.

'Oh shit. Are you all bailing?' Howie asked. 'Carmen, I thought you'd be coming in.'

'You said you'd guard Joan and Roy,' Paula said as I dumped my bag and dropped to open the zipper.

'Right. Well. Unexpected but whatever,' Howie said. 'Cheers for today though, guys. I mean, Frank and Carmen. I appreciate it.'

'Twat,' Henry muttered.

'What the fuck? Did you just call me a twat?' Howie asked as mouths dropped open not only at what Henry said but from him standing up to take his checked shirt off.

'Hello! Mr Hot is back,' Marcy said at the muscle definition on Henry's lean frame.

Henry ignored her and pulled a tight black top on over his head before getting into his tac-vest. Frank and Bash were doing the same with Bash using spare kit we'd all donated

Henry then started shoving magazines into the pouches of his tac-vest and checked his combat knife, then his pistol. It was all fast and efficient too. All of us were, but then we'd kitted up at speed for hot missions hundreds of times. We pulled the rifle straps over our heads then fitted the suppressors to the ends of our M4 assault rifles. Then finally, we pulled the knee pads on and stood up straight to tug short-peaked black baseball caps on to soak the sweat and shield our eyes from the glare of the sun.

The transformation showed in everyone else as they stared to the four normal looking people that were suddenly dressed like the Special Forces trained operatives we were.

'Right,' Henry said. 'Before I go any further, I want it noted that I oppose this mission and do not see any tactical or strategic advantage to a frontal charge. But, if it's going to happen, then let's do it properly. Listen in, this is the briefing…'

42

Diary of Reginald

It had been a day of days already. Gruelling and weird. Often tragic, and nearly always brutal.

Infected tigers. Incest. Safari parks. That poor wolf. The things Heather said. The manipulation by Lilly. The undermining by Henry. The battles. Executing survivors. Childbirth. Sustained action. Sustained arguments. Sustained conflict and, of course, that constant sustained heat.

The team were exhausted and filthy. They had no spare kit and in truth, it was a stupid idea to attack them.

But we still did it.

Those hot bodies in that hot tin can still did it, and why?

Because it was the right thing to do. That's why.

I watched it from above. From the drone. The Saxon on the black-top, speeding through the backdrop.

And before it arrived, Crawley High Street was a juxtaposition of near serene quietness contrasting starkly against the thousands of hosts packed in with only the shuffling of feet and bodies and the buzzing of flies to be heard. It was also incredibly hot. So hot that a great shimmer of heat hung over them.

Then I saw it. In the distance on the Brighton Road. That squat army vehicle holding the centre line. The engine roaring out as the power built with Tappy's face etched with determination as she sat behind the wheel.

We had a plan, you see.

A plan briefed by Henry.

All we needed to do was make it happen, except of course, I still hadn't been entirely truthful, but that was the game, and that was the hunt.

And the game was just beginning.

Maddox

Man. That heat. And it was only getting hotter, but it was weird cos we had energy and we were up for it. Even I was. Reggie's speech did that, and then Henry giving us his plan.

And watching them kit up with all the proper gear got me hooked. I want to be on that team wearing a tac-vest and using an M4 with a sound suppressor and a red dot laser sight. Man. I will do anything to be on that team.

But yeah. A few minutes later and we were back to being hot bodies in a hot tin can.

Woohoo! The Saxon on the blacktop, speeding through the backdrop! Tappy shouted as she pushed her foot down and we felt the surge as the Saxon shot off like a rocket. *Barriers ahead!* Tappy called a few seconds later as I caught sight of the level crossing in front of us. We held on to what we could in the back. Breathing hot air and bracing as we hit the barriers. We all jolted and swayed. Cursing and muttering and pissing sweat over each other.

We passed Charlie holding position on Jess then I saw the crossroads ahead and the High Street beyond it. A central reservation between us. A small island filled with signs and bollards and traffic lights and railings.

Thousands of infected beyond it in the main street. Nearly all of them facing away and with more pouring in from the sides.

Tell them we're here, Tappy! Howie shouted as Tappy jabbed at her music player and the outside speakers crackled to life with the music kicking in. *Hypnotise* by *The White Stripes*. A fast-grungy rock guitar opening filling the air.

BRACEBRACEBRACE! Tappy yelled and took the Saxon straight through that central reservation. Pinging the traffic lights from their stems and launching railings and bollards like they were missiles.

It seemed to a take a lifetime to cross that final road. A lifetime in which Tappy stared ahead while us in the back held on for dear life. Hearing the noises from the street furniture being slammed away and feeling the bounce and clangs on the outside.

Paula

It felt like a lifetime watching the Saxon as it shot across that central reservation snapping all the railings and traffic lights away. My heart quickened in my chest and every nerve seemed to come alive. The last millisecond before impact. The last millisecond before the all-out carnage and chaos truly began. The last millisecond of pure life.

Then it was done, and the battle started as the Saxon ploughed into the horde. Skulls exploded. Bones snapped, and bodies burst apart as Tappy stamped on the brake and turned the wheel to fishtail the Saxon. Using the weight and bulk and the juicy popped bodies to slide wide.

'Fuck me she can drive that thing,' Marcy said as Tappy made the Saxon seem like it was alive. The great beast killing anything in her path. The wheels crushing bodies. The solid metal front smashing infected away. The music blaring out. That balls-out aggression showing true from the very first second.

Maddox

Then we're in it and swaying about in the back as Tappy fishtailed the Saxon to slam it side on into the horde. Cutting a whole big chunk of them down while we listened to the music and tried not to fall over.

We're in! Tappy yelled.

Dave, up top, Howie ordered as Dave squeezed through the tight space to get up through the hole and onto the GPMG. The gun coming to life a bare second later. Strafing the hordes with that rat-a-tat-tat joining the noise of the engine while we all clung on as Tappy kept driving into the horde.

Shit! Howie shouted as a hot gimpy casing went down his back.

Move out of the bloody way then, Clarence told him.

Where to? Howie asked before he yelled from another one just as Cookey shouted from one going down his front.

Blowers called him a twat then started dancing when one hit his neck and slid inside his top. *Fuck! That's on my nipple! IT'S ON MY NIPPLE!*

MOTHERFUCKER Nick said next, jiggling on the spot as the shells fell down in different trajectories from the Saxon veering and bashing into things. *It's in my pants,* Nick shouted with sudden wide eyes. *MY WILLY! IT'S BURNING MY WILLY!*

I started laughing with Booker until one hit my cheek with a pain like a bee sting as I slapped it away and Booker snorted then got one on his neck until we were all dancing and jigging and crying out with Howie yelling at Tappy to stop the Saxon.

Paula

Then the Saxon just stopped. But it was too soon. Tappy was meant to get in deeper and cut more of them down, but it just suddenly stopped.

'Why's it stopped?' I asked as the back doors flew open with the lads all pouring out. All of them tugging at clothing and jumping and twisting on the spot.

'What the hell are they doing?' Marcy asked.

'Bloody idiots,' Henry said, rubbing his nose. 'Hot shells.'

'Hot shells?' Paula I asked.

Maddox

Hot shells! Howie yelled out as we all danced and tried to get the casings out from our kit. *Ow ow ow!*

My nips! Blowers said, rubbing at his chest.

My willy, Nick said, clutching his groin, and I swear I saw Dave smile while he carried on strafing the infected with the gimpy. Gently gliding it about in a long curve with minute adjustments to guide the rounds into skulls. Popping craniums like melons. Pop. Pop. Pop. One after the other in an almost synchronised motion. Pink mists simply blowing up to hang in the super-charged air as the bodies fell like dominoes.

Then, a few seconds later, the gimpy either ran out of ammo or got too hot and Dave pulled himself up through the hole to stand on the roof and stare out to the thousands of infected who were only just then starting to react.

They started shifting and growling and moving out to encircle us while Dave held his ground. Standing motionless on the top with his hands at his sides.

Come on you fucking cunts, Howie said, but quietly, like to himself and I looked over to see him snarling with that look in his eyes. *Come on... Fuck you... FUCK YOU!*

You's all fucked, Mo then shouted. Then, we're all there, gesturing and calling them names and pumping ourselves up until this voice just sails out and silences us all.

I am Dave. I will kill you all.

I can't describe what's it like hearing Dave do that. Then I glanced back to Jess trotting towards us with Charlie up in the saddle spinning the axe over in her hand with this wild look on her face. She looked hot. (Cookey seriously needs to get his game on before someone else does because a woman like that is rare.)

But then I'm looking back to our lot and seeing the infected creeping around us and the tension is going up. Like it becomes this invisible force binding us to the battle that we know is coming and that detonation of violence.

Then it all happened at once as Dave turned and jumped from the back of the Saxon as Jess reared up and the infected screeched. Then Clarence stepped out to start spinning his chain and Dave is landing next to Howie and the horse is making her noises. Charlie was shouting out and the infected are bunching up and ready for it.

Then bang motherfucker!

It just went. You know. It just fucking went and they're charging as Dave drew his knives and spun the blades while Howie ran out to take a head off as Clarence's chain ripped three more of their feet and Jess slammed into them, which is all at the same time as the Saxon fired up with Tappy driving out to carve a whole big bunch more of them down.

Then it was game on and I lost all sight of the bigger picture cos it was just me and Booker side by side working in tandem to cut the fuckers down.

Carmen

'Now!' Henry shouted the second it kicked off in the High Street.

We all gripped on as the van pulled away as Marcy built the speed up and took the van straight over the already busted central reservation. She hit a few infected too. But there were so many she couldn't help it.

I tried to glimpse through the hatch but could only see a great press of infected pushing in to where I knew Howie was.

'That one,' Henry said as Marcy got into the High Street and steered over to get flush alongside the doors to a big office block on the corner. 'Go go go,' Henry said, giving the order and tapping my shoulder as I tapped Frank's who slid the door back and swept out with his rifle up and braced.

Frank went left. I went right with both of us firing the second we got out. Cutting the closest infected down as we secured the gaps at the sides while Henry strode between us with the glass breaker in his hand. A second later I heard the shattering of glass as Henry stepped back to let Frank take point to breach the offices.

I went in on Frank's six as Bashir led Joan and Roy from the van into the foyer behind us.

'Good luck,' Paula shouted before slamming the sliding door as Marcy pulled the van away. Then Frank and I dropped to a knee to change mag as Joan aimed her sniper rifle over our heads towards the stairs ahead of us.

'Rear,' Bash said in heavy English before hosing an infected down trying to come in through the street door. He had an M4 with a suppressor too. It was still loud, but not enough to stand out massively with the noise in the street and luckily it didn't draw more attention.

A second or two later and Frank started up the stairs on point. We reached the top floor and checked the open plan offices. Henry put thick cable ties around the inner handles of the doors while we pushed some desks over to make a barrier.

'We're in,' Henry said into his radio. *'We'll get eyes on the street. Stand by.'*

'Standing by,' Paula replied as we got to work and used rifle buts to smash through the windows to the astonishing sight of Howie's team in a wide circle fighting out against the infected.

'Overwatch on,' Roy said into his radio then a split second later I saw Maddox snap his head up with a grin as an arrow flew past his ear. Then Joan fired and Howie gave a quick thumbs up at seeing us all staring down from the top floor. Then we all started firing. Bash, Frank, Henry and me. Four more rifles adding to the battle as the bodies dropped thick and fast.

'DRAW BACK!' Howie shouted. 'FORM A LINE!'

We watched Charlie work with them to get the team into a line before she too dropped from the saddle to bring her rifle forward. All of them taking a knee with bags at feet, already opened so they can grab magazines. Then Tappy skidded wide past the end, braking hard before she got up into the hole to change the belt feed on the gimpy as the others let rip with their rifles.

A few seconds later Tappy joined in and the firing line worked in earnest with us putting rounds in from a height.

Paula

It was a thrill to see – and the whole thing was a glimpse of how much better we could be if Howie and Henry found a way to cooperate.

'Find the CP,' Henry then said through the radio as Reginald guided the drone over the horde. Marcy parked up and the three of us stayed glued to the monitor with sweat beading over our faces. I felt bad too, because everyone else was fighting and we were just staring at a screen. But finding the CP *was* the most important task.

The only problem was that we couldn't find it, or, if it was there, we couldn't see it. Not in the *first zone* anyway. That being the first section we were ordered to focus on by Henry. Which was also the effective firing range for Roy and Joan. Well, no, that's not true. They can both shoot very big distances, but the High Street curved which reduced their line of sight.

'Anything?' Henry asked a moment later.

'Nope. It's not there,' I replied. 'Howie. Can you hear me? You need to move up to section two. Repeat. Go for zone two!' Which is when I said the really stupid thing. I only meant it as a comment, but yeah. Oops. 'Okay guys. First one to the next junction wins the prize.'

You should have seen their faces. But it got them shifting with the pair of them bursting away at the same time.

'What the fuck are they doing?' Marcy asked as we saw Howie yell at his team. Then a second later Howie's tiny line were slinging their rifles and charging back into the infected while Howie risked a glance up to see Henry already gone from the window.

We took the drone down and watched as Henry ran to the end of the offices, past the windows the others were using and trying to get sight of Howie down below.

Then he reached the end wall and dropped his bag from his back to take a shaped charge out while shooting glances to the end broken window as though trying to see where Howie was.

Henry and the others got behind desks just before the C4 detonated. Sending bricks and plaster through the windows.

Then Howie was shouting for his lot to fight harder, but by that time, Henry was already through the hole in the wall into a living room above an estate agent's office with his team rushing in behind him. Smashing the windows out to get fire into the street as Henry got to a window and cursed at seeing Howie was ahead of him. *Little shit* he mouthed then he turned and ran for the next wall to start setting the next charge.

'Fucking idiots,' Marcy said, shaking her head. 'Honestly. I just want to blend them together and create the perfect man. Actually, that's really hot. God. I've made myself all fruity.'

'Marcy!' Reginald said.

'Oh, shut up. You've already had a handjob today.'

'You never,' I said to him.

'Of course I bloody didn't!'

He did Marcy mouthed while masturbating the air next to her head.

'Oops, there's the next one,' Reginald said as we looked back to see the next interior wall blowing out with another loud whump with more bricks and debris sailing down into the street. Which is right at the point Howie chopped a head off and got a face full of blood and stepped back as Henry peered down with a face full of brick dust.

Fuck you! Howie mouthed.

Fuck you! Henry mouthed at the same time, and once again they both turned to keep going with Henry dropping through a partially ruined ceiling into a small bathroom. The toilet blown from its fittings with water spraying out.

Reginald, being as caught up as Marcy and I, then flew the drone *into* the building to follow Henry splashing out of the bathroom into another set of offices and then to the end wall. Solid brick. No way through. Another building on the other side.

'Why are you in here?' Roy asked into the radio as Reggie turned the drone to see Henry's team rushing into the room to smash windows and get fire support into the street below. '*The CP's not in here, is it.*' Roy added while kicking a window out before firing his bow at an infected trying to get on top of the Saxon.

'What does this button do?' Marcy then asked, peering at the controller in Reggie's hand.

'Just leave it alone,' Reginald said, pulling away from her trying to press buttons. 'Marcy! I said leave it,' he shouted as she jabbed at the button and Reggie flew the drone into the back of Henry's head.

'What the bloody hell are you doing?' Henry yelled, turning to glare.

'*Sorry!*' Reggie said through the radio.

'Get out and find the CP!'

'Oh wow,' Marcy said. 'We can hear him.'

'Eh?' I asked.

'Marcy?' Roy said as Reggie turned the drone to look at Roy staring at the camera.

'Can you hear me?' Marcy asked.

'I can hear you!' Roy said.

'We can hear you too!' Marcy said.

'Great. Now get back to shooting the bleeding zombies,' Frank said.

'Er, not zombies, Frank. They're not technically dead,' Reginald said, earning a look from Frank as Henry shouted *MAKE READY* and everyone in the room, and I'll admit, us three in the van all ducked as the next charge went off.

The force of which sent the drone flying out the window to drop down just in time to see Howie staring up at the new explosion. 'WANKER! HE'S GETTING AHEAD.'

'COME ON!' Clarence roared out while whipping his chain into the next load of infected. Good god he was going for it. They all were. The whole lot of them on the ground were fighting like utter bastards to beat Henry and his team working through the building.

'GO ON, HOWIE! BLOW JOB IF YOU WIN!' Marcy then shouted as Reggie ducked from her voice shouting right next to his ear. 'Get back up, I wanna see what Henry's doing.'

'You not going to offer him a blowjob as well then?' I asked.

'You know. Howie's not a jealous man but...' Marcy said with a *what can you do* expression.

'Hang on. This is the double wall isn't it? Reggie. Is this the double wall?' Henry asked with a glance to the drone.

'I'm impartial to this competition, Henry,' Reginald replied.

'Answer the bloody question you idiot!'

'Yes! It's a double wall,' Reginald blurted. 'Oh crikey. Don't tell Howie I helped Henry.'

'Damn it,' Henry said as he sped up to place the charge then darted away for cover as it went off.

We flew outside for fear of the backdraft to see Howie looking up at the explosion before shouting to Clarence. 'Double wall! It'll take him longer.'

'Ha!' Clarence said. 'COME ON LADS!'

By which time we were back into the office watching Henry stretch across the gap to place charges on the next wall. It blew out a moment later as Henry grabbed and heaved a desk to make a bridge then got through into the next building.

By that time. Howie was further ahead and making use of the Saxon to make big advances. But Henry only had two buildings left to go. That meant two more walls to blow out and he'd secure the last building and reach the next junction first.

Honestly. It sounds so stupid now. But fuck the CP. We were hooked on the competition and we went back into the building to watch Henry working away on the last wall. Placing the charge as the others fired down into the street. We half expected Henry to tell them to stop helping Howie, but thankfully even he didn't do that.

Instead, he blew the charge and got through the cloud of dust into a bedroom on the other side with a curse at seeing the bodies of an old couple lying entwined on the bed. 'My apologies,' Henry told them softly, earning an *aww* from Marcy.

He then turned away and opened the bedroom door to a corridor full of infected before slamming it closed with a second's worth of pause. 'Frank!'

'What?' Frank shouted from the last building.

'Hold there for a moment please.'

'Will do, Henry. Need a hand?'

'No. I'll be fine,' Henry said as we watched on at him slinging his rifle and drawing his knife.

'He's not,' Marcy said.

'I rather think he is,' Reginald said with us three leaning closer to the monitor as Henry opened the door and stepped out to jam the end of his knife into the throat of an infected male. He yanked it free then grabbed the hair of a female and ripped her off her feet while stabbing into the neck as she dropped. Then he was up and turning to draw his blade across another neck before going low to slice an artery open in a groin at the same time as drawing his pistol and firing rounds into the head.

By then he'd reached the living room door and an infected coming out, charging into him. But Henry just took the momentum and flipped the guy over his hip before he shot him in the head. A step into the living room and more infected all coming at him. He feinted one way and went the other over a sofa to make them trip while grabbing a shaped charge from his pocket to slap onto the wall before firing his pistol at the ones getting over the sofa.

They dropped, but more came into the room as Henry jabbed the det cord into the C4 then holstered his pistol and stepped into the attack with his knife stabbing at chest and eyes and necks in an absolute frenzy.

'Jesus. He's a bloody animal,' Marcy said at the savagery of the man. It was like watching Howie. That level of rage. Then he grabbed a heavy female and took her down with her on top and him underneath as he triggered the C4. Which promptly blew the shit out of all the other infected while Henry casually shot the heavy female on top of him and rolled her off.

'Fuck!' Marcy said as he got up, went to the bedroom and called the others through. 'Okay. If me and Howie ever split up, I've got dibs on Henry.'

'Charmed. I'm sure,' Henry said while arching an eyebrow at the drone. 'Do I get a say in this?'

'Oh shit. He heard me,' Marcy said. 'Reggie, you twat!'

'You turned the audio on you blasted idiot!'

'Been busy then,' Frank said mildly as they got into the flat to see Henry kicking the bricks away to get into the last building. We went with him as he rushed to find the door out then the stairs down and another door that he booted open in frustration before sweeping into stock room of the boutique fashion store on the ground level. Then into the retail area and over to the plate glass window. Firing a single shot into the corner to make the glass crumble as he stepped out to see a grinning Howie and his team in a line at the junction letting rip with their rifles.

'What kept you?' Howie asked as Henry grunted and tried to hide the look of disappointment.

'*Update on the CP,*' he ordered instead. '*Reggie!*' he snapped, looking up at the drone.

'Oh god, he means us,' Reginald said. '*Righto, Henry. Er. Well done, chaps. The next section goes up to a small junction on the right. Get to that, and we'll try and find it.*'

I thought maybe Henry and Howie would tell Reggie to get stuffed, but nope, the toxic masculinity between them was way too far gone for things like common sense to take over. Henry clearly wanted to get a point back, and Howie clearly wanted to go two nil up, so it was wash, rinse, repeat and boom. The pair of them went straight back at it.

'Right. We need this CP. Lift the view up so we can see more of them,' I said as I leant in closer to the monitor right at the same second that Reginald cleared his throat.

I never had a chance to address it at the time because of what happened after, but it stuck in my mind. Thinking back now, I'm convinced Reginald knew what we were about to find. I think he knew, and I think that throat clearing was a tell.

Jesus. I think back now to how I felt at that point of the day, and how tired and hot I was but I had no idea just how bad it was going to get. Maybe Reginald planned for that too. I wouldn't be surprised. His intelligence is on a level most of us cannot even comprehend, and yeah, if Reginald had told us what we were about to face then we'd never have done it.

Anyway. Let me paint this picture for you. Let me *try* and describe what I saw, and I say try because there are not words to give that will come close to describing what we saw.

The infected were all in Crawley town centre. We never questioned that. We just knew that's where they were.

And specifically, they were in the High Street, which was the main road running south to north through the middle of Crawley. And it was on that road that Howie was attacking them while Henry was using the buildings in the High Street to get height to try and find the CP.

And remember – we were doing that so Henry could witness and observe the CP *before* he went into London to find and release the Panacea. Howie, however, was in a difficult spot. He wanted to help Henry, but Howie couldn't turn away from helping survivors in need. Which is where most of the issues had come from.

So we went into Crawley to find the CP, and Howie and Henry were working along the High Street section by section to do just that.

But what we hadn't done. What none of us had done, Henry included, and because of the way Reginald kept the pressure on and kept us distracted, was look ahead.

We hadn't done that.

Which is what I did then.

I looked ahead.

THE UNDEAD TWENTY-FIVE. THE HEAT

I told Reginald to fly the drone higher with a sudden impulse to get a grasp of the size and numbers we had to work through to get at the CP.

Except there was no sign of the CP, and there was no end to the infected wedged onto that main road running north out of Crawley – and the higher we went, the more we saw of them.

We went up to 120 metres and still increasing as we started seeing rooftops and alleys and the curve of the High Street. By 200 metres up the next junction was clear in view. But all we could see were infected rammed into that road.

'That's a lot,' Marcy said quietly, and that stuck in my mind too because there was no sarcasm or sassiness to her right then. Just a raw understatement at what was unfolding on that monitor and the growing unease we were both feeling, and the higher we went, the more we saw. Stretching away like a thick snake running through Crawley and out into the countryside.

I've never seen anything like it. Well, no, that's not true. I have seen things like it on the news when you'd see those countries in crisis with miles of refugees trying to escape whatever was going on. It was like that; except they weren't refugees. They were all infected, and the gasp came when we finally reached the head of the snake and the view from the drone changed significantly.

We'd been following the main road that once, many years ago, would have run directly north into London. It was even called The London Road. However, it no longer ran directly north due to a massive airport someone had built – that being Gatwick international airport. The busiest single runway airport in the world.

Yeah.

That airport.

Which we then flew into and watched as the view below changed from fields to a vast open area so very different in size and shape to anything else. And of course the perfectly straight lines of the two-mile-long runway slap bang in the middle of it.

That, however, wasn't the thing that made us gasp.

The gasp came from the sight of the narrow road disgorging the infected into the airport.

Hundreds of them.

Thousands of them.

Tens of thousands.

And if that wasn't enough – we then found the CP.

Only it wasn't just one CP.

43

Miriam Longfield used to run a second-hand bookshop in Brighton. She had a cat called Oscar and liked folk music. Life was good and Miriam was happy.

Then the end came. She saw it unfolding on the news. She hunkered down and stayed hidden for ten long days until they found her.

She died violently. Screaming out in fear. Pain in her stomach. Pain everywhere. Nothing but fear and pain before the blackness of death.

She came back, and there was no longer any pain, and the things that had killed her were no longer fearsome. She felt their hunger. Their need. She felt the thing inside. It seemed to speak to her. She retained some of her own mind and became a manifestation point within which the virus could burrow deep and gain the spark of sentient life – just as Reginald had calculated it was doing in many places all over the world.

Brighton was taken within a week, then Miriam started north. Taking the villages and towns on the way. Hassocks. Hurstpierpoint. Burgess Hill and Haywards Heath. She headed east and took Southwater and Horsham and built enough numbers to enter Crawley from the south.

Crawley, however, had already been taken. That confused Miriam as she assumed she was the one true race. She worked through the town and stayed on the London Road heading north until she reached Gatwick International Airport, which is where she found Jeremy Butterworth and his horde.

'I am the one true race,' Miriam said as her horde came to stop while disgorging from the narrow mouth of the London Road

'I am the one true race,' Jeremy said while his horde also came to stop after swarming into the airport from the east after taking Crawley, East Grinstead, Horley and the surrounding towns.

Then it got a bit awkward as the very notion of existence seemed to be called into question as the infection within both Miriam and Jeremy, while completely separate to the other, considered the possibility that it wasn't, as previously thought, one single entity.

'Can we merge?' Miriam asked.

'I don't know,' Jeremy said.

'We should try,' Miriam said.

'Okay,' Jeremy said.

Then it carried on being a bit awkward as they tried to merge, by way of staring at each other as though some magical connection would form. Which it didn't.

'We should touch,' Miriam said and poked Jeremy in the belly. Unfortunately, however, the poking did not cause the merging they so desired.

'Maybe we need to share our DNA,' Miriam said and spat in Jeremy's face, but that didn't work either. 'Maybe it's not enough. Touch my tongue.'

'Okay,' Jeremy said and moved close to poke his tongue in Miriam's mouth. But still it had no effect and they remained, individually, the one true race.

'Maybe we need to copulate,' Miriam said. 'Humans copulate to form connections.'

'Okay,' Jeremy said.

Miriam took her clothes off and laid down. Jeremy stared at her.

'You need to put your penis in me,' Miriam said.

'Okay,' Jeremy said. He didn't need to take his clothes off as he was already naked. He got down on his knees and stared at his penis.

'I think it needs to be erect,' Miriam said, also looking at his penis.

'Okay,' Jeremy said. 'How do I make it erect?'

THE UNDEAD TWENTY-FIVE. THE HEAT

'I don't know. I don't have one. What did you do when you copulated before?'

'I didn't copulate before.'

'You didn't copulate before? How old are you?'

'Forty-two.'

'You're forty-two and you didn't copulate before?'

'No.'

'Did you have a job?'

'No. I trolled people on the internet.'

'Oh,' Miriam said as though that explained it all. Which it mostly did. *'Did you masturbate?'*

'Yes. Frequently.'

'Just do that then.'

'Okay,' Jeremy said and started rubbing his penis.

'Is that working?' Miriam asked.

'No.'

'Why not?'

'I don't know. I used to watch pornography.'

'We don't have any pornography,' Miriam said before the thing inside of her accessed the vast hive-mind collective knowledge and proceeded to adjust her body's internal system to produce pheromones. *'I'm making pheromones.'*

'Okay,' Jeremy said, as the thing inside of him also accessed the vast hive-mind collective knowledge and proceeded to flood him with certain chemicals. *'Okay, it's hard now.'*

'Put it in.'

'Okay.'

'Move it in and out.'

'Okay.'

'Touch tongues again,' Miriam said, thinking to maximise the exchange of bodily fluids. Jeremy did as told and licked her tongue as he lost his virginity at the age of forty-two while being watched by several thousand hosts and one drone flying above them.

Unfortunately, however, it had no effect and they remained, individually, the one true race.

'Touch my breasts,' Miriam said, as the thing inside grappled with the confusing array of sexual knowledge contained within the hive mind. Jeremy touched her breasts, but still they didn't merge. 'Some humans say bad things to make copulation a greater experience,' Miriam added. 'Say something bad to me.'

'You're a twat.'

'Tell me I'm dirty.'

'You need to wash.'

'Tell me I'm a bad girl.'

'How old are you?'

'Eighty-six.'

'You're not a girl. Should I ejaculate?'

'I don't know. Try it and see.'

'Okay,' Jeremy and promptly ejaculated. Which still did not create the merge they both desired, and there passed another awkward moment while the infections within them tried to understand the vast complexities of existence, and the notion of cohabitation and mutually aided endeavours – while still coupled in the middle of the runway.

44

Diary of Reginald

'Seriously! That's disgusting,' Marcy said as we stared at the monitor and the runway below us. 'She's like ninety years old and he's licking her tongue. Oh god, I can't even look. She's opening her legs. I'm actually going to puke.' She added at the sight of the guy on his knees rubbing his willy. 'Oh no, he's not.'

'Yep. He is,' Paula said as Marcy turned away to gag then spotted me staring intently at the screen. 'Oh my god. Have you got a fetish for old ladies? I thought you were A-sexual you little perv.'

'No, I do not you blasted idiot! And they're not having sex for pleasure. They're trying to merge.'

'Eh?' Paula asked.

'It's two control points,' I explained. 'She's one and he's the other. And they both have very large numbers too. Certainly the biggest yet. There's got to be thirty thousand.' I knew it was more like forty to fifty thousand, but I was still trying to play it down while avoiding the look of stunned horror on Paula's face.

'Have they finished shagging yet?' Marcy asked.

'No. He's licking her boobs,' Paula said.

'Urgh! No! Stop it. Lower that drone. Lower that fucking drone. *Oi you filthy shit. She's old! Leave her alone,*' she shouted into the controller.

'Reginald. Thirty thousand is definitely too many for us,' Paula said. 'We need to pull them out.'

'No, hang on,' I said while moving the radio on the desk out of her reach.

'Reggie. It's too many. Give me that radio,' Paula said. 'You are not sending Howie into that lot. Pull them out!'

'He needs to bloody pull out,' Marcy said with a nod at the screen. 'Dirty shit.'

'Reggie! Give me that radio.'

'It's only thirty thousand!' I said. 'We'll be fine.'

'Don't you bloody dare!' Paula said, lunging for it at the same time as Marcy, while I, however, being much smarter, went for my battle swatter.

'Ow! You shit,' Marcy said, ripping her hand away from being swatted, thereby prompting a squabble of hands with us all slapping and swatting at each other to get at the radio.

'He's got it!' Marcy yelled as I snatched the radio free.

'Mr Howie!' I shouted as Marcy jumped on my back and got a hand over my mouth.

'Reggie?' Howie called back.

'He's fine!' Marcy yelled, pushing her thumb over mine to transmit on the radio while muffling my voice. *'We're all fine.'*

Carmen

Jesus it was frantic. But it was also good fun and I think we all got drawn into it with our team trying to beat Howie's to the next junction.

We also kept hearing broken transmissions coming from the van.

THE UNDEAD TWENTY-FIVE. THE HEAT

'Thirty thousand!' we heard someone shout, then Marcy said they were still all fine and to keep going.

Not that either Henry or Howie paid it much attention. Howie was OCD on going two nil up and Henry was OCD on not losing another point and levelling against Howie.

Then we breached the last wall and I saw Howie glance up to see we were about to get into the last building. But it was a big one with eight windows with eight interior walls dividing them into offices.

We were all hooked into it. Bash was loving it and I even saw Joan share a quick grin and a wink at young Danny down below in the street. I guess in our minds the day was almost over. We knew the CP had to be somewhere close and this was the last blowout before Paula called an End-Ex and we bugged out for refs.

I remember looking down and smiling as Howie urged his side on while Henry battered the first door down in the last buildings then blew the windows out.

I was still leaning out of one of the other windows, tracking their progress and seeing Howie and Clarence make a last ditch balls out crazed charge as the windows in that last building blew out one after the other.

At which point the ground floor door opened with Henry strolling out ahead of them. Casual as anything and smiling at Howie and his team all gasping for air and still swinging axes.

'What kept you?' Henry asked as I burst out laughing and Frank walked out behind Henry with a wink at the lads. 'I do believe that is one all, Mr Howie,' Henry said with a big cheese eating grin. '*Zone two is secure. Repeat, zone two is secure. Update on the CP please?*'

'Henry,' Howie then said as Henry smiled over to see Howie facing away up the High Street in such a way that made the rest of us do it too.

Then it got weird because we realised the infected had stopping attacking.

Honestly. It was like a switch had been flicked and only then did I notice how quiet it had gone. All the howling and screeching had stopped. All the violence and noise of CQB had ended. No gunfire. No grunts.

Just the sound of fires and flames from the charges we'd set.

Just the sound of us all breathing hard and the grit beneath our boots as we shifted position to look at the now silent and static infected.

'What is that?' Henry asked, striding out further into the street. 'Have we killed the CP? Is this the lull?'

'I don't know,' Howie said as he grabbed his radio. *'Reggie. Did we drop it? Reggie!'*

'Howie! Listen to me.'

'Paula? What's happening? Why have they stopped attacking?'

'Cos they're too busy shagging that's why!'

'Marcy, shush! Howie, listen to me. You need to draw back right now.'

'Why? Did we kill the CP?'

'Negative. The CP is nowhere near you. They're two miles away in Gatwick airport.'

'They?' Henry cut in.

'There's two of them. Two CP's,' Paula transmitted.

'Put Reggie on,' Howie ordered.

'No! You need to draw back. Howie, there are too many. Ex-fil now.'

'Why? What for?' Howie asked, which showed his lack of experience because when your XO tells you to ex-fil you don't ask why. You just do it.

I didn't wait for the order but got Bash, Joan and Roy down into the street to see the lads clambering on or jumping in the Saxon while Charlie was covering our six on Jess.

'We're in. Let's move!' Henry shouted, jumping up to ride the front step next to Tappy while I got in the front passenger seat and budged the dog over.

'We should be cutting them down,' Howie said as he got onto the step next to me and held the door open with his body.

'Howie, Trust your XO,' I said quietly, making him pause mid-transition with a nod at me.

'Fair one. Yeah, sorry. *Paula, we're coming to you. Standby.*'

THE UNDEAD TWENTY-FIVE. THE HEAT

A minute or two later and we found the van parked up just beyond the train line and pulled over as Paula and Marcy came out of the sliding door while the rest of us spilled out from the Saxon.

'This isn't a coffee break!' Dave shouted. 'Weapons check. Refill mags. Hydrate. Tuck your shirt in, Mr Booker.'

'What the fuck is going on?' Howie asked as we converged in the road.

'Right. That horde,' Paula said. 'Stretches from here to Gatwick airport which is two and half miles away.'

'Fuck me,' Howie said.

'And there are over thirty thousand of them with two CP's. One male and one female,' Paula said as Marcy stood behind her nodding earnestly while shoving her finger into a closed fist.

'One of them's like ninety,' Marcy said. 'Honestly. Just disgusting.'

'They're having sex?' Howie asked.

'They were. They've stopped,' Paula said.

'Hang on. What?' Howie said.

'Stop interrupting, Howie. Reggie? Report please,' Henry said.

'It's really rather fascinating. I would suspect the CP's are currently occupied with an existential crisis while attempting to determine how the one true race can be within two manifestation points simultaneously while both holding the same instinctual urge to dominate and control to become the apex species.'

At which point every person there, including Henry, all turned to look at Charlie pouring a big bottle of water over Jess's back.

'Two zombie grand masters are busy figuring out which is the big boss,' she said without even looking over.

'There they are,' Marcy said as Reginald twisted the monitor so we could see a very old woman stood opposite a paunchy middle-aged guy with greasy hair. Both naked, and both very still. So were the infected around them. 'Go up a bit,' Marcy said as Reginald gave lift to the drone, and we watched the view open up to see dozens, then hundreds, and then thousands of infected staring at the two CP's.

'See,' Paula said. 'And before anyone says anything stupid let me make it clear right now that only an absolute moron would pick a fight with thirty thousand zombies.'

'Got a map there, Reggie?' Henry asked, taking one to spread out over the van step. 'So, we have two distinct groups coming together at Gatwick. Tell me again what happens if we take the CP's out.'

'My theory is the infection will find another suitable host,' Reginald said. 'During which time the horde becomes sluggish and unfocussed. As they did at Hinchley Point yesterday.'

While he was talking, I got inside the van to grab a bottle of water and some shade while Henry studied the maps, and the rest did the same as me and took fluids onboard.

'Okay, Howie,' Henry said as though he'd decided something. 'We need to first establish our objective, then we look to the best strategy to determine the right tactical response in order to achieve that objective. Now, let's say our objective was to negate the CP's. The first obvious asset on the ground is the air traffic control tower, which would make an ideal sniping position. The boarding gates are also high off the ground. However, that would require the shooter getting into those buildings then working through to one of those vantage points. You said the hordes go sluggish for a couple of minutes while they search for the new CP. That might give time for the shooting team to ex-fil, but it certainly places them at extreme risk of being stranded once the enemy mobilise again.

'The other option would be to find a firing point from the building line on the southern edge of the airport within the bordering industrial estates. That takes the distance down to three to four hundred metres *and* it buys time and allows for a route for the shooter to get out.'

He broke off as Roy stepped in closer. 'At that distance I can have two arrows in flight at the same time and take them both. It'll be silent too,' he added as the others stirred from a plan starting to form. 'They're a bit bunched up though. Howie, you'll need to make some gaps.'

'I can bait them,' Howie said as Clarence nodded at his side and the lads murmured. 'Yeah, I like it. We go in. Make a fuss and keep them busy then Roy takes them out. That could work. I like it. Henry, I know we don't get on, but mate, that's brilliant.'

'I'm glad you agree, Howie. But what happens after we kill those two? The hordes go sluggish and unfocussed, and we've got, what? A few minutes to kill thirty thousand of them. What do we kill them with? We don't have thirty thousand rounds. And that is without factoring for Reginald's assumption that the virus will immediately seek a new CP. What if that new CP is at the far end of the runway and out of range? Assuming of course that we can even find it, which is while that CP is sending thirty thousand infected against you. And for what? What is our objective here? For those two hordes to be that size then they must have taken all of the surrounding towns and villages. Which begs the question who are we protecting? And if we're not seeking to save anyone then our objective cannot be to attack those CP's because we simply don't have the means to achieve it.'

'We just leaving them then?' Blowers asked.

'What choice have we got?' Henry asked.

Blowers shook his head and thought for a second. 'What about another stash point?' he asked with a look to me then at Henry. 'We'll drop mortars and get a fifty cal going.'

'We don't have a stash point here,' Henry said.

'But we can't just fucking leave them there,' Blowers said.

'Sergeant. I respect your passion, and I'll give leeway to your tone, but again, what choice do we have?'

I can't quantify how that moment touched me. I don't have the words to use. Maybe it was the heat or the fact I'd taken a step away from Henry and I wasn't a core member of Howie's team and therefore I was something more akin to Reginald, but I was looking at everyone the way Reginald did. Staring outside the van to everyone captured within the square frame of the doorway.

Paula. Marcy. Clarence. Frank. Roy. Bash. The lads. Charlie, Tappy, and Joan. All of them covered either in brick dust or blood and gore and all of them drinking water or Lucozade.

And there. Right at the front standing side by side were Howie and Henry. Two leaders. Two egos. Two sets of pride – but truthfully? In all the years I had known Henry, I'd never seen him more alive than at that moment. He just had this aura of energy about him. Standing there in full tac-rig with his gloved hand clutching a bottle of water with his rifle hanging to the front.

There was this energy in the air too. Like it was crackling and fizzing, but you couldn't see it. You could only feel it.

Then I looked at Reginald and felt the hairs on the back of my neck stand up from the way he was studying them. I'd never seen someone so poised. Jesus. You've heard of apex predators, right? The beasts that sit on the top of the food chain. We were all apex predators. But Reginald? He was on another level. He was what sits *above* an apex predator. They don't even have a name for that. He was the fucking alpha, and he was just waiting to make his next move – which duly came when Howie frowned and reached the conclusion that Reginald obviously wanted someone to reach.

'Then why are they there?' Frank asked as Howie opened his mouth and blinked in surprise at someone else beating him to it. We all glanced at Frank as he bit into a melted Snickers and started chewing. 'They ain't there for their health, are they?' he said between munches while everyone else looked at him and I looked at Reginald and saw the gleam in his eye.

'But people don't live at airports,' someone said. I don't know who. I was too focussed on Reginald.

'Have you checked it?' I heard Howie ask.

'For what?' Paula asked. 'Marcy just said people don't live at airports.'

'What about the terminals?' Charlie asked. 'They would have been packed.'

Cue every head snapping back over to Reginald as he showed an outward expression of *well I didn't think of that!*

'Check them now,' Howie said as Henry nodded and then everyone else all moved in a step closer to see the screen as the drone started moving over the heads of the infected.

'Shit!' Howie said as the jet airline came into view. The front end buried in the broken remains of the boarding gate stem. The drone

THE UNDEAD TWENTY-FIVE. THE HEAT

went lower. Giving us a view of the blood stains inside the cockpit windows. 'An infected got into the cabin,' he added quietly.

'Must have been one of the crew,' Henry said as we all figured the captain would only have opened the cabin door for an injured colleague. Especially as they were still on the ground. Whatever happened – it caused the jet to taxi into the boarding gates and rip a wing off before making the propped-up gates all fall down, which in turn made a handy slope for the infected to get up.

Which they did, and recently too by the looks of it because Reginald flew the drone in closer for us to see the people in the south terminal had made a barricade from the long heavy metal bench seats and whatever else they could find. Big travel bags and suitcases. Lockers and desks. All of them jammed in to seal the boarding gate off, and all of them now ripped away from the infected breaching the barricade and getting inside.

Reggie went in only for a few seconds, but it was enough to see people had been living there and the blood and carnage as they met their end. It was fresh too. The blood on the floor and walls was still wet, and the infected inside had fresh wet injuries.

But they too were as still and silent as all the other thousands of infected. All of them staring towards those two CP's in the middle of the runway.

'Seen enough?' Henry asked with a glance at Howie.

Howie nodded, giving his own heavy sigh as the energy seemed to vanish from them all. I saw it happen. I saw the slump of shoulders and the grim looks steal across all their faces.

Which is when Reginald made his move and quickly flew the drone out of the south terminal into another position.

'Oh shit,' I whispered as he shot me a look that urged me to silence.

'This has to be done right,' he whispered as I looked out to see everyone turning away.

I looked back at the screen and felt my heart thudding. I went to speak. To say something. To voice what I had seen, but again, Reginald just lifted a finger. Telling me to be silent. I shouldn't have done what he wanted. I was an agent for the British Secret Service. I had no loyalty to Reginald, but yet I stayed silent and watched on. Mesmerised at the way it was happening and how Reginald was waiting for the perfect time, because the second Howie and Henry turned away is when he uttered three quiet words. 'Children, Mr Howie.'

Jesus H Christ.

You should have felt the electricity spark as the whole lot of them stopped and looked back to see the monitor giving view to the interior of the north terminal. A glimpse to a world within. A world now filled with hundreds of people.

People who worked there. People who were waiting for flights. People who managed to get off incoming flights but never left the airport. People in crazed panic, herding kids together. People breaking down and weeping. Mothers clutching babies.

'That's why they are still there,' Reginald said. 'And that is where they will attack when they re-animate.'

'Reggie. We cannot kill thirty thousand infected,' Henry started to say but Reginald cut him off. Speaking oh so very gently.

'We don't have to. You said it, Henry. Howie can bait them and soak the damage up while you and Paula go wide and come in from the north to get those people out. Roy takes the south side for overwatch, and I'll keep the drone up. We've established the objective and now we have a tactical response, Henry. And we have the means, *and* the capability to achieve it.'

'Reggie,' Henry said quietly.

'There is nobody else, Henry,' Reginald said, cutting over him. Not shouting. Not using force because all the force had been used to get to this point. 'There's just us. We are all that is left. Major Dillington, You need to do your duty.'

Reginald fell silent as every single one of us looked at Henry.

'Mr Henry?' a voice asked from behind as Henry turned to see Tappy looking at him. At everyone looking at him. All of them, including his own team.

'Boss?' Mo asked as Henry half smiled and shook his head in defeat as the rest started to grin. 'One condition,' Henry said firmly. 'We do this. Then we go for the Panacea. No arguments. No distractions. No more anything. Howie, I want your word.'

Howie looked at him. The leaders. Two sets of egos. Two alpha wolves not paying the least bit of attention to the wolf in the van hiding his enormous teeth. 'I'll give you my word, Henry,' Howie said.

'Okay. Listen in,' Henry called. 'This is going to be a hot brief…Mo, translate please. I'll take Paula and Marcy with me in the SUV. We'll go wide and get into the north terminal from the eastern side. Roy, take the van with Reggie to the south side of the airfield. Find a high point and get overwatch on. Reggie, keep the drone up and keep us informed. Howie, you hit the airfield at the southwest corner which is the furthest point from the north terminal. Go in hard and make some noise. You *must* draw their attention. We'll find a high point for Joan from our side and start working to get the people out. Questions?'

'I'll leave Jess in the trailer,' Charlie said. 'It's so hot and if we're doing hit and run then I'll jump in the Saxon.'

'Good point. Concurred,' Henry said.

'Reggie needs a guard,' Howie said.

'I don't mind going with Reginald,' I said as Frank and Cookey coughed the word mayonnaise into their hands as everyone else laughed. 'Jesus. You two are like father and son.'

'Oh god. I can't unsee that now,' Paula said, giving them both a look while they grinned toothy grins.

'I'll go with Reggie,' Marcy then said. 'He needs a guard and I've already chipped one nail today. I'm joking! Besides, we won't all fit in the SUV.'

'Right then. We have our teams,' Henry said. 'Tappy? I'm serious. I want to hear you from the north terminal. And Howie? Don't go too deep.'

'He likes it deep,' Marcy said with a wink before poking her tongue out with a funny cross-eyed look. 'Sorry. That was my Cookey moment.'

'Howie, seriously though, don't go too deep,' Paula said as she moved off towards the SUV.

'I don't go too deep!' Howie said as he opened the front passenger door of the Saxon and got a face full of Meredith telling him to fuck off. 'That bloody dog!'

'It's those biscuits,' Charlie said, leading Jess into the trailer.

'Biscuits don't make dogs aggressive,' Clarence said.

'Gateway drug!' Marcy sang before slamming the sliding door closed and then opening it again. 'Oh, and good luck everyone! And Howie?'

'Don't say it!'

'Don't go too deep, honey.'

'Boom!' Cookey said as the laughs rolled around and Clarence slapped Howie on the back.

'Oops, sorry, boss,' he said, picking him back up. 'I've got to stop doing that.'

'Yeah, you bloody do,' Howie said, clambering into the Saxon before getting an idea and leaning back out. 'Yeah well, don't hide too much, Henry!' he called with a grin and a wink as the tumbleweed blew past and Marcy winced before slamming the van door closed again.

'Howie,' I said, giving him a look while I shook my head.

'What?' he said. 'It was funny! It was! Danny laughed. Danny, am I funny? Whatever. Right. Let me choose the music.'

We set off with all three vehicles pulling out to take different roads.

As far as we were concerned it would be a hit and run. Make some noise. Get the survivors out and end the day on a high.

What could possibly go wrong?

THE BATTLE FOR GATWICK

45

Diary of Reginald

We reached our position first with Roy driving the van through side roads to get into the industrial estate bordering the southern side of the airport.

Thankfully the whole area seemed deserted and so once Roy parked the van behind some industrial units and gathered his bags of arrows and bow up, he quietly slipped out of the van.

Which, of course, left Marcy and I alone with her perched on some crates filing her nail while I contacted the other two teams for location updates.

'*We're in position and ready*' Tappy said.

'*ETA five minutes,*' Frank relayed.

I could feel the tension climbing in the same way I could feel Marcy's eyes boring a hole into the back of my skull. I even turned to see her staring at me. She didn't blink. She didn't move a muscle. Nor did she smile or show any humour at all.

'It'll be fine,' I said and turned away. She didn't reply.

THE UNDEAD TWENTY-FIVE. THE HEAT

'*SUV to the van. We're approaching position now,*' Henry transmitted. '*This side of the target location is clear so far. Repeat. This side is clear so far. Update on the Saxon.*'

'*We're ready,*' Howie said as I felt that tension climb another notch.

'*Give me a minute,*' Roy transmitted, his voice a little breathless from climbing or running.

'*Standing by,*' Howie said.

'*We'll get in closer and start on foot. Essential comms only from this point. No chat. And no names. Henry out... And yes, I know I just said my name. I'll do brew duty tonight as punishment.*'

I couldn't help but turn to share a smile with Marcy, but she was still glaring at me and showed such little trace of humour I cleared my throat and turned back to my desk.

Charlotte

We did laugh at Henry's transmission, but it did nothing to break the tension that was mounting by the second.

Our route in had been easy. But then going anywhere in the Saxon is easy. Especially with Tappy driving, and by that point, we were tucked up in the large long-stay parking area bordering the south-wester fringes of the airfield.

I'd got onto a bench seat next to Maddox. The heat was intense, and we were all dripping sweat. I certainly was and I ran a hand over my head and felt the stubble of my hair and then fingered my scarred ear again while thinking how unattractive I must be. That made me think of Jess and how beautiful her ears were, and I don't know why but I suddenly missed her terribly. It brought a lump to my throat, and I thought I might cry. I wasn't scared of the fight we were going into. Not at all. But my emotions were yoyoing all over the place. Then the next thing I knew I was thinking about Blinky and how she would have loved going in to fight so many infected, and that gave me another great surge of pain.

I even had to keep my head down and blink the tears away. Which is when I felt a hand on my leg and looked up expecting to see Cookey staring with concern, but it was Maddox leaning in to ask if I was okay.

I said I was. 'I'm just missing Blinky… And Jess,' I said quietly.

'You'll see Jess again,' he told me and patted my leg again. But not in a groping way. Maddox isn't like that at all. 'You got this, Charlie. You're strong. You're going to be okay.'

His kindness almost made me cry again but I managed to swallow it down and pat his shoulder and say thank you.

'You sure you're good?' he asked me. 'You want me to speak to Howie? You can go with Paula or jump in with Reggie. You don't have to be here.'

'I'm fine,' I told him and thanked him for his concern.

He nodded but kept looking at me for a while like he could see the pain inside. Then he glanced at Cookey, and his features hardened. I thought he might say something, but instead, he turned back to me. 'Hey so Books and me are gonna get a freezer truck later. You know. Couple of bowls of cold water for our feet and some wet towels on our heads with a few beers. Fancy it?'

'I'd love that. Thank you, Maddox.'

'What's that?' Booker asked as he leant over Mads to hear our chat.

'I invited Charlie into our freezer truck,' Maddox said.

'Yeah? Cool,' Booker said as he gave me a big smile and held his fist out to bump, which, I noted was something he'd started doing since hanging out with Maddox.

It was nice of them to look out for me like that. I appreciated it. I did catch Cookey glancing over with a funny expression, but what could I do? I'd made my intentions clear, and he didn't want to know.

'I'm almost there,' Roy then transmitted as that tension rose even higher.

Carmen

We heard Roy transmit that he was nearly in position and got the nod from Henry to debus the SUV. Paula was loving it. Especially now that she had our spare carbine with a suppressor and some scrounged knee and elbow pads, then she tied a bandana around her forehead to keep the sweat from her eyes and looked full on badass.

'Cor. If I was younger,' Frank whispered, giving her a wink. 'And if your boyfriend wasn't a seven foot tall ex-para.'

She smiled at the joke as I motioned for her to slip in behind me while we positioned with Frank on point and Bash on our six and the SUV parked up beneath an underpass. We couldn't risk the engine being heard, so we were on foot for the final approach.

But it was cool. This was urban warfare which is where people like us excel.

A moment later we breached the edge of a car park bordering one of the airport hotels and used the abandoned minivans and cars as cover to filter our way to the building line.

We saw that the hotel had been hit as soon as we approached it. We didn't go inside but we did see old bodies as we skirted the outside. They looked decayed and eaten by rats and covered in litter swept up by rains and storms.

And by then I knew another storm was coming because the air pressure had changed. It was crushing us. We could hardly breathe.

Anyway. We got across the next road and over the wall then into the ground floor of the multi-story car park which we knew connected to the north terminal. All we had to do was follow the ramps up and find a way in.

'We're on the final approach,' Henry transmitted.

Charlotte

'Beyonce? Actual fucking Beyonce?' Nick said.

'Strong independent woman with the best arse ever who can sing like Whitney. What's not to like?' Tappy said.

'She has got the best bum ever,' Cookey said.

'Fact,' Blowers said.

'I'm not disagreeing about her bum,' Nick said. 'My point is we can't attack thirty thousand zombies while listening to Beyonce.'

'It's a classic!' Tappy said. '*All the single ladies* has an awesome beat.'

'Not a fucking chance,' Nick said. 'Seriously. I'll hotwire a Micra and fight them on my own before I attack a horde listening to Beyonce.'

'What do you want then?' Tappy asked him. 'Some shitty rock thing like Status Quo or Queen, or some grungy shit like Nirvana.'

'Whoa! Nobody dis's the Quo,' Clarence said.

'Whoa. Nobody dis's Nirvana,' Nick said.

'And what's wrong with Queen?' Howie asked.

'I mean, they made good tunes, but they're not battle anthemic,' Tappy said as we all agreed that indeed, they were not battle anthemic.

There followed a brief and rather silent pause as we all gave weighty consideration to the most appropriate tune to use when attacking a horde of such a size.

'I know,' Blowers said with a sudden grin. 'Bruce Springsteen.'

'Jesus, Grandad,' Cookey said. 'Go back to counting your nine fingers.'

Reginald

'Come on,' I said to myself while drumming my fingers on the desk and waiting for the update from Henry and Roy. 'They must be close,' I added while checking the monitor and the two CP's still static upon the runway. But they had been so for over ten minutes, and I knew that status would not remain so for much longer.

'*Guys, it's me,*' Roy's transmitted somewhat breathlessly. '*I've got one escape ladder left to go up then I'll be in situ.*'

That was Roy nearly in place too. Which only left Henry and so I drummed my fingers while in the reflection of the screen I could see Marcy behind me. Her face half in shadow, half in light.

One half an angel.

One half a demon.

THE UNDEAD TWENTY-FIVE. THE HEAT

Carmen

I found out later that Paula took a whole town out before she fell in with Howie's team. She'd prepped it using razor wire and fuel bombs and gas cannisters to whittle the numbers down as she drew them on.

It struck me as strange that a woman that capable would take on the role of a mother-hen to a group of young soldiers. And Paula was *very* capable. Even then as we worked up the vehicle ramps, she showed a highly developed aptitude. She would have made an excellent operative. But war does that, and history is full of civilians that would otherwise lead calm and peaceful lives suddenly adapt to become great leaders.

She did something else that stuck in my mind.

We'd worked through the ground floor of the car park and out onto the road running in front of the north terminal. There were actually two multi-story car parks constructed either side of a giant vestibule jutting out from the north terminal.

Both of those car parks were six-levels high, and each level connected to a stairwell and lifts that gave access to that vestibule, which in turn, fed into the north terminal proper.

We were on the road running in front of the car parks trying to see if there was a way in, but we soon discovered that the whole area had been prepped for defence.

It was well put together too. The vestibule had lifts and long disabled access ramps running up from the ground level. All of which were blocked off by hundreds of luggage carts stacked high and rammed full of suitcases.

They'd also driven vans, taxis, and buses into the barricade. The end result was the ground floor effectively had an impenetrable wall sealing the north terminal off.

That meant we couldn't get in, which in turn meant running back into the car parks and working up each level with the hope that the defenders had left themselves an exit option.

We were just about to go back when we noticed a few infected gathered on the road. Only four or five of them all groaning softly while shuffling on the spot.

Paula stared at them until Henry whispered that we needed to go back into the parking area and find a way in.

'They're not part of the hordes in the airfield,' Paula whispered. 'They don't have a CP. I bet they were bitten on the first day and never got caught up into a horde,' she added as she looked at Henry and saw he wasn't getting it. 'Just stay here a second.'

'Paula!' Henry whispered as she slung her rifle and ran out from our position of cover to jog across the road while pulling her machete overhead from the sheath on her back. We all aimed and got cover on then watched as Paula gave a low whistle which made the small group turn towards her. But they were slow and ungainly and like the zombies from old movies. Drooling and twitching with limp arms and stiff legs. A second later and Paula took the first head off then set about dispatching them one at a time with brutal ease.

Then she ran back, breathing hard from the heat and the exertion. 'See? That's what they'll be like if we take the CP's out. And it also means there will be more like them that got turned on the first day and never found a horde. I don't know, but maybe if we get enough shufflers, we can use them as camouflage in London. We'll tell Reggie and see what he thinks. Anyway. Let's get on. We need to get inside.'

Like I said.

Paula was badass.

Charlotte

'I'm not saying it's not good,' Tappy said from the front. 'But Gloria Gaynor's *I Will Survive* is not battle anthemic.'

'It so is!' Cookey said.

'*Ace of Spades*. Motorhead,' Blowers said.

'No! Too cliched, they'll be expecting it,' Tappy said.

'Who will?' Blowers asked.

THE UNDEAD TWENTY-FIVE. THE HEAT

'Duh. The zombies,' Tappy said.

'What the fuck,' Blowers muttered, sharing looks and shrugs with the others.

'Okay okay. We get one suggestion each then we vote on it. Boss?' Tappy said.

'Oh fuck,' Howie said. 'Wow. Pressure. Er... Oh I know!'

'Don't,' Clarence said with a groan.

'I have to,' Howie said as Clarence shook his head. 'It's my favourite song.'

'What is?' Tappy asked.

'Tiffany. *I think we're alone now*. Don't all bloody groan. It's Tiffany! You lot have no taste. I bet young Danny likes it. Eh, Danny? Tiffany? See, Danny's up for it.'

'Clarence?' Tappy said while shaking her head.

'Ride of the Valkyries,' Clarence said.

'Now that's clichéd,' Blowers said.

'Is it now?' Clarence asked him. 'And what do the Marines use? Yellow Submarine?'

'Yellow submarine for Sergeant Blowers,' Tappy said. 'Cookey?'

'That wasn't my suggestion!' Blowers said as everyone jeered him down. 'Fuck's sake. I had a really good one.'

'Was it Bruce Springsteen again?' Cookey asked him.

'No,' Blowers said unconvincingly. 'It was the er, the... The other one. Bon Jovi.'

'You fucking dick!' Nick said as we all burst out laughing.

'Oh my god. I fucking love you,' Cookey said while laughing at Blowers. 'Tommy used to work on the docks yeah?'

'Fuck off!'

'But he's down on his luck cos it's tough... like soooo tough.'

'Fuck you!'

'Hey, but Gina words the diner all day,' Tappy said from the front. 'Working for her man she brings home the pay.'

'For love?' Nick asked.

'For love,' Tappy said.

'Twats!'

Reginald

My word, it was tense, and the sweat beaded down over my forehead as I stared into the monitor, willing the CP's to keep talking and not reactivate. What the deuce was taking so long I had no idea, and I could only imagine the heightened levels of tension they must have been experiencing in the Saxon. Those poor sods sitting in a hot tin can waiting to charge into an airfield chock full of infected.

Charlotte

'It's okay, Blowers. We'll give it a shot,' Cookey said as the whole Saxon went totally silent.

'Don't. Please just don't,' Blowers said as we all let rip.

'WHOAAAH, WE'RE HALFWAY THERE... WHOAAAH WE'RE LIVIN' ON A PRAYER!'

'Fuck you,' Blowers said, sticking middle fingers up at the rest of us singing Bon Jovi at him.

Carmen

We ran off the first ramp over to the bridge connecting to the north terminal entry vestibule, but that was also barricaded.

'Second level,' Henry ordered as we about-turned and set back off. *'North side checking in, control. Slight delay. Looking for ingress. Standby.'*

To which there was no response.

'Control means you in the van,' Henry then added.

'Ah I thought you meant me! I was about to answer,' Reginald said. 'Er but roger roger. Copy that. Er, control to the er... the... um... Ooh I know. Control to Robin Hood?'

'I'm still bloody climbing.'

'Roger that, Robin Hood. Er, control to the Saxon, over?'

THE UNDEAD TWENTY-FIVE. THE HEAT

'TAKE MY HAND, WE'LL MAKE IT I SWEAR... WHOAH, LIVIN' ON A PRAYER.'

We all froze mid run to quickly turn the volume down in our earpieces and I couldn't help but snort a laugh and clocked Frank grinning while Paula smiled and shook her head, which is while we all waited for Henry to start bawling them out.

Except he didn't. He just tutted mildly and nodded for us to keep going.

'They grow on you,' Paula said to him.

'So does fungus,' he muttered, but I saw his lips twitch.

By the second level we were breathing hard with sweat pouring down our faces, but again, the connecting bridge was blocked off with luggage trolleys and vehicles. That left four levels to go, and we figured with our luck the only way in would be on the top sixth level.

We started running back to the ramp when I caught scent of cigarette smoke. The car park had open sided walls, but with the low ceiling the smell lingered. It made me stop and go back and sweep along the barricade until I found a small pile of cigarette butts on the ground outside of the back doors to a big van parked nose into the barricade.

I motioned to Bash then at the van as he gave cover for me to ease one of the door handles down.

It gave instantly and swung open as I smiled at how they'd ripped out the front passenger seat to create an open path from the back doors to the front, which were poking out the inside of the barricade.

'North side to control. We've located an ingress. We're going in. Standby for confirmation.'

Frank took point and got through the van to the front to check it out before giving a nod to proceed.

It was cleverly done too. I think we were all impressed.

The doors to the north terminal were opposite. We started jogging over, seeing that they'd also barricaded those but left single entry points within the barrier to create tactical pinch points.

That's when we finally made contact as a guy stepped out with a police issue rifle slung at the front and started to light a smoke.

'Fuck!' he said, spitting the cigarette out as he grabbed his rifle. 'CONTACT!'

'Friendlies you numpty!' Frank said. 'Get your CO. We're getting you out.'

'Out? We're not going out. Have you seen the other side? It's crawling with them.'

'Control. It's the north side. We're going inside. Are the Saxon and Robin Hood in position?' Henry asked he walked towards the guard. 'Get your CO. Come on man! Look lively!'

'Control to north side. Yes. We're ready and standing by,' Reginald said as Henry ushered the guard inside with us following through into the vestibule which we realised was the monorail train station that connected the north terminal to the south via a raised railway line.

'Sir, it's Colin. We've got some guys here to get us out,' the guard said into his radio as someone transmitted back into his earpiece. 'I didn't let them in! They found the van. I don't know but they're tooled up. Fuck's sake. Hang on then,' Colin said as he came to a stop. 'My boss wants to know who you are.'

'Give me that radio,' Henry said.

'You're not having my radio,' Colin said before stiffening from Frank pressing the pistol barrel pressing into his temple. He gave Henry the radio.

'My name is Major Henry Dillington. I need your CO immediately. We're in the train station coming into the north terminal.'

We ran through through a doorway and out to the top of static escalators running down to the ground floor and saw the airport had been transformed into a mini-city with sectioned off areas for living filled with wires and hanging sheets and cardboard walls.

Stairs and more unmoving escalators led up to defined eating areas and more living quarters with bedding on the floor. People had taken over the duty-free shops and the kiosks had been stripped of food and drink that was now stacked inside the main refs area to be rationed out.

There were also people everywhere. And far more of them then we'd realised.

I could feel the fear in the air. I'd felt it before in cities at war in the middle east and Africa. That same barely suppressed panic caused by people not knowing what's going on and hearing only whispered rumours.

'Who the hell are you?' a man called out from the ground level, older with grey hair. An air of authority. Underlings and assistants at his sides. All of them armed and all of them with the same deeply worried expressions.

'Major Henry Dillington. Special Air Service and sanctioned CO within the British Security Services,' Henry said as we rushed down the escalators. 'And you?' he asked, striding forward with his hand held out.

'Chief Inspector Michael Dawson,' the man said, clasping Henry's hand. 'Sussex police. I'm the CO for airport security.'

'James Dramford,' another man said as he shook Henry's hand. 'Senior logistics manager.'

'Hi! Sally Burfoot. Senior duty manager.' Another woman said as more lined up to shake Henry's hand.

'We do not have time for this,' Paula cut in with a hard tone. 'Get everyone ready to go right now. No, stop. Stop talking. Stop talking! You have thirty thousand infected out there about to attack this building. You will not stop them, and they *will* get inside. No! Listen to me. There is no time for discussion. Do you understand me? If you stay here, these people will die.'

'Just hang on,' Dawson said.

'Major Dillington will not hesitate to assume command,' Paula said, cutting over him and everyone else. 'And the rest of our team are out there right now ready to distract those things to buy you time to get out. You need to listen, and you need to take this in. You will all die if you stay here. Do you understand?'

'We've got nearly seven hundred people here,' James Dramford said into the hard silence that followed.

'Where do we take them?' Sally Burfoot asked. 'They can't just walk out.'

'Okay, listen in,' Henry said with a quick sweeping look while urging the guards and workers in closer. 'This is a hot briefing, leave questions to the end. I need you to get everyone into this area facing the train station. They are not to carry anything except small children that cannot run. You will keep them as silent as possible. No noise. No shouting. No screaming. You and you,' he said, pointing a bladed hand at the two managers. 'Will stay here while I take every armed person with me. When we give the order, you lead the people into the train station and out along the monorail platform to the coach yard. Do not interrupt! Find a way down. Find the keys from the kiosk and get those coaches away as fast as you can. Head south to the coast. Find Fort Spitbank. Do you understand? Yes or no! Do you understand the instructions?'

They both looked terrified, but they both nodded.

'What if they won't go?' one of the airport guards asked.

'Tell them they will be shot by the rear guard,' Henry said to a chorus of gasps. 'Because if they stay here they will get turned and they will be coming after us.'

That hit it home. Jesus.

'I'm sorry,' Paula said in a softer tone. 'You have to trust us. We've been doing this since the start. Get them stacked up here ready to go.'

A second for them all to absorb it. A second and no more.

'That's understood,' Chief Inspector Dawson finally said in a weak voice as he looked to his teams. 'Do as the Major says. Get everyone here.'

'Double time!' Frank snapped, sending them running off as the panic started to increase. But that was normal and there was no way of making seven hundred terrified people do anything *without* creating panic. All we could do was try and control it.

'Okay. Now we need to see the defences,' Paula said as most of the guards ran off.

'This way,' Chief Inspector Dawson said, striding off deeper into the airport.

'North side to control. We're inside. Repeat. We're inside and preparing for evacuation,' Henry transmitted.

'Understood. Robin Hood and the Saxon are ready to go.'

THE UNDEAD TWENTY-FIVE. THE HEAT

'*Standby,*' Henry transmitted as we jogged through the airport behind Dawson and his assistants as they led us through the rising panic of the people living inside. And the sight of us certainly didn't make it any better.

'Hey! What's happening?' someone demanded, stepping in front only to get pushed away by Frank as we ran on. 'They're not telling us anything!' the man shouted as we jogged on through the check in gates to the security gates beyond. Passing survivors and refugees from all over the world. Africans. Indians. Europeans. Asians. I remembered reading that Gatwick was a major transport hub with over sixty thousand people a day passing through.

'When did the South Terminal fall?' Paula asked as we ran on.

'Only a few hours ago,' Dawson replied. 'But a jet took their boarding gates down on the night it happened and made an entry point. Ours are intact. We're safe here.'

'Trust me. They will swarm and find a way in,' Paula said as she pointed up to a series of skylights overhead. 'How many people were there?'

Dawson shot her a look as a dark shadow crossed his features. 'Over a thousand. It was so quick. The airfield just flooded with them all running in.'

'We've got almost seven hundred in here,' Sally added. 'But we had over three thousand the night it happened. A lot left. English people mainly. You know, those going on holiday that thought they'd try and get home. Then more left and a few died.'

'Died?' Paula asked.

'Heart attacks. A few suicides. Oh, and the police shot two after that murder we had.'

'You had a murder?' I asked. But then I don't know why I was surprised. People are people. Put them anywhere for any reason and they'll rape, steal, murder and lie the same as they always did.

We hit a set of stairs and started rising until we reached another hastily formed barrier made from trolleys, disabled person carriages, bench seats, luggage and furniture. A single entry point in the middle with an armed guard looking stricken to the core.

Dawson took us straight through to a secure area used as a junction leading to the three sets of boarding gates.

One set was ahead of us giving a view over the eastern side of the airfield.

The second set of boarding gates were off to our left giving us a short view of the southern side between the north and south terminals, and the enormous concrete forecourts and taxying areas.

The third set of boarding gates were accessed via a corridor leading to a bridge high enough for commercial jets to drive underneath - and it was that bridge we aimed for. Being the highest point with the best view of the airfield. It took valuable minutes to reach it because of the size of the place, but we eventually we got up to see paned glass windows either side.

There we stopped to draw air. All of us sweating hard. But then everyone in the airport was. That heat was brutal, and inside those metal buildings without the air-conditioning running it was beyond hellish.

Paula looked around at the armed guards. Henry, Frank and I did the same. Counting bodies. Counting guns.

A handful appeared to be police while the rest looked like either current or ex-military, and while we were looking for defence points, Joan went forward to stare out of the window to the air traffic control tower five hundred metres away in the centre of the airfield.

A few seconds for us to take it all in.

A few seconds and no more, that's all we had because right at that second, every infected in the airfield suddenly turned to face the north terminal.

'Hold your position!' Paula shouted at the soldiers and cops starting to panic and draw back.

'We need to seal this off!' Dawson shouted.

'I said wait!' Paula said, turning back to the window as she grabbed her radio. *'Control, this is north side. They're coming back to life. Go for the Saxon. Repeat. Go for the Saxon... And Tappy? Make some noise, honey.'*

Reginald

I'd checked Roy's position on the drone then looked back down to the runway just in time to see the two CP's both turning towards the direction of the north terminal. The old lady seemed to say something, to which the younger man replied as they both lifted their arms to point, and a split second later every infected in the airfield turned to face the north terminal.

'Darn it!' I said as I grabbed my radio, but Paula beat me to it.

'Control, this is north side. They're coming back to life. Go for the Saxon. Repeat. Go for the Saxon... And Tappy? Make some noise, honey.'

'North side. This is Control. You are correct. They're about to charge. Go for the Saxon!'

46

Diary of Charlotte Doyle

HOT BODIES in a hot tin can.

'Control, this is north side. They're back to life. Go for the Saxon. Repeat. Go for the Saxon... And Tappy? Make some noise, honey.'

'North side. This is Control. You are correct. They're about to charge. Go for the Saxon!'

'Roger that,' Tappy said as she faced forward and cricked her neck while we all waited for her to say it, and we smiled when she did. 'The Saxon on the blacktop, speeding through the backdrop.'

She gunned the engine as we all looked at Blowers while he, in turn, sat there with a *fuck the lot of you* expression.

Then we were off and all leaning from the shift in momentum as the speakers outside hissed and crackled with the tuneful melody starting to rise.

'BRACE!' Tappy yelled as the Saxon battered through the fence. A clunk and a bang. We all tensed. We all braced, and we all sang the song as the Saxon powered into the airfield towards thirty thousand infected with *Jon Bon Jovi Livin' On A Prayer* blasting from the speakers.

I'll never forget that moment. It's seared into my mind. The distortion of the music from the awful speakers. Our voices all cracking and out of tune. Shouting more than singing. That heat. That awful heat. But despite the exhaustion, the fear, the dread, the frayed nerves and our heads thumping from the pressure in the air, we still did it.

We still went in.

I'll always take pride in the fact that we did that.

Reginald

Good gosh it was thrilling to see. But perhaps not thrilling in an entirely pleasant way, because there was also dread and fear and worry, and the air pressure had become so intense my head was hurting.

I took the drone high and watched until the Saxon drove through the fence. Only then did the scale truly hit me because the Saxon, which in my mind was always so big, suddenly looked very tiny.

For a moment I was flooded with doubt, and I had to fight the urge to tell them to stand down and go back. I couldn't bear it. I couldn't do it. It was a mistake. I'd made a mistake.

'Haha! I can hear them!' Roy transmitted. 'I can bloody hear them! GO ON TAPPY! GET IN THERE. PRESS THE RADIO DOWN. LET US HEAR IT'

'SHE SAYS, WE'VE GOT TO HOLD ON TO WHAT WE'VE GOT... IT DOESN'T MAKE A DIFFERENCE IF WE MAKE IT OR NOT...'

Carmen

Fuck me! Hearing them singing with the actual track playing in the background amidst the roar of the engine sent a jolt through all of us. It was like someone touched spark plugs to my heart. I even ran to the window and grabbed a pair of binos from the side to try and see the Saxon.

'What the hell is that?' one of the guards asked as the other armed men and women shared looks at the awful sound of singing and music coming through our radios.

'That's your rescue,' Paula said.

'Got it,' I said. Seeing a blob in the distance at the far southwestern edge. 'Jesus. It looks tiny.'

'That's what she said,' Frank muttered as I rolled my eyes while Henry got to work bossing everyone around.

'I can make that tower,' Joan then said as we all turned to look at her. 'It's only five hundred metres away.'

'The tower's cut off, Joan,' Henry said.

'I don't have clear line of sight from here,' Joan said. 'You heard Reggie, Henry. We slow the CP's, we slow the horde. I need a door out,' she said to the closest soldier. 'Stop dithering! I can't abide it. Quickly now.'

A nod from Henry to Dawson. A nod from Dawson to the soldier and he rushed off, leading Joan away as we turned back to the airfield and that terrible sight of thousands of infected staring at us with drool pouring from their mouths.

Reginald

The Saxon was still coming in from the southwest and only just hitting the runway as I saw the distance it had to travel to the CP's. Which of course, the Saxon couldn't see due to the sheer number of bodies in front of them.

'I can't see the CP's,' Roy transmitted, and I watched with dread in my heart as the naked man and woman seemed to reach an agreement with both of them nodding as they started lifting their arms as though to give the *go* order to their hordes.

I was about to transmit to Tappy to guide her to the CP's when Marcy took the controller from my hands, and with a level of skill I was not expecting guided the drone over the top of the male and female.

'Roy, it's Marcy. Can you see the drone?'

'My call sign is Robin Hood, but yes, I can see it.'

'Ten inches left and right directly below.'

'Roger that. Overwatch on...'

She tilted the lens just in time to see Roy nock, draw and lean back. He fired one then the other as the two CP's dropped their arms and the infected screeched as one. Tens of thousands of them all giving voice and bursting to motion as they started charging towards the north terminal with numbers that were so thick it looked like the entire ground was suddenly alive and rippling.

My heart quickened. My chest felt tight. I couldn't breathe. I couldn't move. I'd got it wrong. So terribly, horribly wrong.

And right at that point, when my fear was almost taking over, the arrows dropped and hit dead centre, which was the exact same second Marcy slapped the back of my hand with my battle swatter.

'What the buggering hell was that for?' I cried out, snatching a look up at her towering over me with my swatter held in her hand.

'That was for earlier you little shit. Now get your head in the game. They need you. Do you want me to hit you again?'

'No!'

'I will hit you again.'

'Don't hit me again!' I said as she gave me an arched eyebrow and grabbed her radio.

'This is Marcy. The CP things are dead. Get the people out while Reggie looks for the next one.'

She glowered down at me as I shot a look at the screen to see the infected all slowing as one to become sluggish and ungainly.

'Joanie, go!' Paula transmitted.

'Find us the next CP,' Howie said.

'This is the north side. We're commencing e-vac. Repeat. We are commencing e-vac.'

I heard all of those transmissions and I knew time was vital and that I had to start searching, but for the life of me I could not take my eyes off Marcy looming over me with my swatter held in her hand. She didn't do anything. She just breathed in and out without saying a word and yet, the strangest thing happened because I felt the panic fade away. Not all the way. Dear me. The fear never truly leaves, but it went back enough for my intellect to resume control.

'Good,' she said after a second. 'Now stay calm and find the next CP.'

'Where are you going?' I asked as she moved to the door and slid it open.

'I'm just getting some air. Find the next CP.'

'Marcy!' I said, intending to say she should help me look but she slammed the door closed, sealing me in as I tutted at another bizarre event and ignored what I thought it meant and instead focused on the monitor.

Carmen

That moment was off the chart for tension, but in a weird way, we were also very calm. We were committed to the plan, and it would either work or it wouldn't.

Then the hordes came to life, and we heard tens of thousands of them screeching as one as they started charging towards us. Fuck me. That was a sight.

'Wait for it,' Paula said, holding a hand out as though to keep us all still. 'Just watch...'

'Got 'em,' Roy said.

'Yes!' Paula shouted, making more than a few people flinch as the screeching cut out and the entire horde slowed to a shuffle with heads lolling about and feet scuffing the ground. 'GO ON, ROY!' Paula said, grabbing me to hug before she leant over to kiss Bash's cheek. 'Look at that! Just look at that!'

'Incredible,' Henry said with a nod at her.

'*Joanie, go!*' Paula said into her radio.

'*Find us the next CP*,' Howie transmitted as Henry waited for him to finish talking before he cut in.

'*This is the north side. We're commencing e-vac. Repeat. We are commencing e-vac.* Chief Inspector. Get them moving. Tell them to go and to keep going. They must not stop no matter what happens.'

'*Go on old girl*,' Frank then said into the radio as I turned to see Joan running through the shufflers with her guard still at her side.

'*Less of the old*,' she said without any show in her voice that she was running.

'So. I mean. Just how sure are we that she's *not* Dave's mum again?' I asked as Henry shrugged and Frank tilted his hand side to side. 'I mean. She's the right age. We need to DNA them. Speaking of which. I'm assuming that's Dave on the gimpy we can hear?'

Charlotte

It was all very exciting. We'd gone in making lots of noise just as the two hordes snapped back to life and all turned and then started running off towards the north terminal. Fortunately, however, that's when Roy dropped two nice arrows on their heads, and they went back to being slow and dribbly.

'Tappy, stop,' Howie ordered. 'Everyone out. we'll start reducing the numbers but headshots only! Preserve your ammo.'

We shuffled out and set to work, and after the bloody awful day we'd had with every zombie and his aunty trying to eat us that lot were a walk in the park. All of them drooling and unable to control themselves beyond basic motor functions.

'Don't cross fire. Everyone aims in front of them. Dave will focus on the front of the Saxon,' Clarence yelled as we selected single shot and started shooting them down with the louder GPMG strafing the front of the Saxon.

Reginald

I think the size of the endeavour and the build-up throughout that awful hot day had got to me. Which is why I had that brief panic-attack, but after a moment I was back to being in control and realising that our plan was working.

We'd taken out two CP's and bought time for the evac to start, which, by all accounts was underway.

All we had to do was repeat the same thing.

But the only way to do that was to wait until they all came back to life – because it would be the ones *not* in motion that were the new CP's.

I was already studying the screen and flying the drone northwards towards the buildings when I saw Joan with an armed man getting inside the base of the air traffic control tower.

'WE'VE GOT MOVEMENT!' Howie then shouted into his radio as I turned the drone and gave it height to see the whole southern and Eastern side of the airfield come to life with one horde re-animating as they started charging north.

Charlotte

It was fast.

One second we were shooting stationary human beings, and the next the whole lot of them came to life and started charging as we compressed towards the back of the Saxon with the belief they were about to engulf us.

Except they didn't go for us. They were all heading north.

Carmen

We could see motion in the distance, and from that and the radio bursts we knew the horde closest to Howie was heading our way.

Which is when the horde closest to us all came back to life with their own screeching howl, making us all flinch and tense as we prepared for a mass assault.

Except they didn't go for us. They all set off south towards Howie.

Which is something we did *not* plan for.

Reginald

What a sight that was, especially when they started colliding. At any other time, it would have been farcical, but in reality, it meant the whole airfield was filled with too many bodies moving in too many different directions.

'Damn it,' I said as I grabbed the radio with a grimace. *'North side. This is control. My apologies but you must prepare for incoming. Repeat. Prepare for imminent attack.'*

Carmen

'Okay! Listen in,' Henry called when Reggie gave us the good news. 'We've got incoming. Stand fast and make ready. Do not waste your ammunition. Paula? Where is the most likely point of breach?'

'End of this bridge on the southern side,' she said without hesitation.

'Understood. Frank, get a firing team at the far end to try and stem the flow. Do not draw back until you are instructed. Carmen, place charges on the bridge please. Paula, stay close to me. I need your expertise. Chief Inspector Dawson, make sure that last barricade is as strong as you can make it and get some firing points on the other side for when they breach. Has the evac started yet?'

'We're finding out now,' he relayed between shouting into his own radio.

'North side to control. Are the survivors leaving yet?' Henry asked into the radio.

'Negative. No survivors coming out yet.'

'Chief inspector. It appears your survivors are not yet vacating.'

'There's some confusion,' Dawson said, looking more stricken by the minute.

'There really shouldn't be,' Henry said calmly. 'Carmen. I'll take over the charges. Please take Bash and encourage the survivors to start moving.'

'On it,' I said with a nod at Bash as we set off at a run back long the bridge and through the duty free stores and bars and areas still full of people trying to pack bags and gather belongings.

Bash said something and made me look over to the side. I nodded fast and he rushed over to slam his elbow into fire panel to break the glass and activate the fire alarm.

Red lights instantly started to flash as sirens screamed out.

It's human instinct to fear fire. It's built into us, and it was needed to create the panic those people needed to get going. They'd trample and stampede. I knew that. And I winced at seeing it start to happen. Some wouldn't make it, but enough would. Darwin's theory of evolution. Survival of the fittest.

We ran on through the crowds while shouting the word *fire* until we heard it being repeated. A moment later we reached the gallery overlooking the main check-in area leading to the train station to see everyone screaming and panicking but still not running out.

The people at the front were too scared to leave and the organisers and workers were too fucking stupid to follow orders, and so with a surge of irritation I ran off into the food area and booted things around until I found a bottle of vodka. I screwed the top off and got some over a hanging sheet used as a makeshift wall as Bash got his lighter out and set it on fire then used other rags to fan the smoke out into the air above the people all gathered below.

I then fired a shot into a bookcase to get attention. It worked a treat with people turning to see and scream out at the thick black smoke. A second or two later and the whole lot of them were finally surging for the train station as we got the fire extinguisher and put the flames out while shaking our heads at the immense stupidity people have when they get into a large group with a herd instinct.

And a few moments after that, and after wading *back* through the screaming, wailing, panicking people finally fleeing for their lives, we re-joined the unit on the bridge while gasping for air. 'All done.'

'Thank you, Miss Eze,' Henry said with a simple nod. 'Continue with the charges please.'

A roll of my eyes. A gasp of air and I went back to what I was doing as the first shots rang out from the end of the bridge.

'HOLD YOUR FIRE!' Frank yelled as we started running towards them, thinking the swarm to have started already. But it was just a terrified young cop letting a few rounds off in panic. I stopped to suck air and stared down the escalators connecting the bridge to the lower boarding gates.

'Why aren't these blown?' I asked Frank. 'Have you prepped them?'

'Do you want me to shit in your tea cup?' he asked me with a look. 'Now bugger off and leave me alone. It's bad enough with those bloody fire alarms. What idiot set them off?'

I went to reply then shrugged and went back onto the bridge.

'Carmen! The charges aren't set,' Henry said, also giving me a look.

'I'm doing it!' I muttered while wishing I was in the van playing nerds and nurses with Reginald.

Reginald

I was starting to wish I was anywhere else by that point, because for the life of me I couldn't see the new CP's. Not with the whole thing in motion the way it was.

Which then gave me a rather splendid idea. *'Tappy. Get everyone inside and drive along the runway.'*

I glanced back via the drone to see the Saxon moving off.

'You bloody genius!' Roy then said with a laugh as I smiled at the effect the Saxon was having by making one of the hordes veer direction to try and go after it. Which in turn meant greater confusion as the infected ran into each other and got in each other's way.

It didn't do a lot. But it slowed the whole thing down.

'Keep doing that, Tappy,' I requested and sat back with a sigh then felt a lurch when I saw a small group of infected standing still next to a white building halfway between the runway and the bridge.

I guided the drone over, hardly believing my luck and there it was. An entirely average male infected with short greying hair and a bite wound on his abdomen standing in the middle of a circle of other infected, and I realised he must be the CP going for Howie.

'Joan. Are you in position?' I asked.

'Ready and waiting,' she replied immediately.

'Approximately four hundred metres west of the tower. White building on the northern side. Group of six. The male in the middle. Naked torso. Grey hair.'

'Got him. Do I have a greenlight?'

'You have the greenlight,' I said and like magic his head blew out in a cloud of pink mist as he slumped backwards.

'CP down,' Joan said calmly and a second later the horde going for Howie slowed once again.

'Go on, Joanie!' Cookey said into the radio.

My word what a sight it was and again I felt the trill of a cohesive working together to a plan, but it still left the horde going for the north terminal, and with the other horde now static they were able to move faster.

'Tower to control. I've got sight on a static group just inside the eastern edge of the south terminal boarding gate. I can only see two of the outer ring. Not the CP. North side should have a clear line of sight.'

'I'll get the drone in,' I transmitted as I started flying towards the wreckage of the south terminal's boarding gate. Most of it now crumpled and broken to the ground amidst the nose of the jet airliner that ploughed into it.

Carmen

'We need a DMR,' Henry called out. 'Mr Dawson?'

THE UNDEAD TWENTY-FIVE. THE HEAT

'A what?' the Chief Inspector asked, blinking rapidly with a show of stress.

'Designated Marksman Rifle. Where's your sniper?' Henry asked him.

'We've got an LMT back at the barricade,' the guard who'd shown us in said while already running off.

I jogged back to Frank with a set of binoculars and dropped into the prone to get a stable viewing platform by resting the lenses on my kit bag. Frank nestled in at my side while I slowed my breathing and gained sight of the wreckage of the boarding gate on the south terminal then started working in over the heads of the shuffling infected, while yet more angry infected ran through them.

'I have them,' Reginald said in the radio as I heard Colin the guard running up behind me.

'Give it here, lad,' Frank said.

'Control. This is north side. We're setting up for a view. Where are we looking, please?' I asked.

'Er, so, from your point of view you need to find the nose of the crashed jet then work right. Can you see the remains of the HSBC logo on that downed section of wall? The static group are behind that logo. The CP is looking through a window to the north terminal.'

'FUCK THEY'RE GETTING IN!' someone screamed out.

'Calm it down, nipper. They're not inside yet,' Frank said as I felt and heard him setting the rifle up. 'Right. What we got?'

The binos gave me a more powerful, cleaner view of the target than the scope so I acted as spotter and guided Frank to the target.

'Which side of the window?' I asked.

'Your left,' Reginald replied. 'An inch right of the frame. Twenty inches up from the base.'

'Twenty inches up. One inch in,' Frank said as he sighted down the scope. 'Go?'

'Go,' I said.

He took the shot. Sending the 7.62 high velocity round through the plate glass window and across four hundred metres through another window and into the skull of an adult female.

'CP down. Good shot,' Reginald said as the entire horde outside suddenly stopped screeching and running to slow to a shuffle.

'Shot, Frankie,' Joan said.

'Yeah, not bad for an old man,' I said giving Frank a smile. 'Frankie.'

'Piss off and make me a cuppa,' he said as the screeching came back outside from the other horde coming back to life. The ones that had been going for Howie. Except they didn't go for Howie.

They started coming for us.

Reginald

The best laid schemes of mice and men is a line adapted from a piece by Robert Burns. I couldn't rightly speak on behalf of the rodent species, but I think I was confident in saying it was certainly true of the hominoid species, and specifically the sub-group known as the Great Apes, that being the one which the human species belong to.

Either way, our plan was now beginning to unfold, and once that tiny corner of the plan started to fray it wasn't long before the whole bloody thing went to shit.

And, as per the law of sod, it was only a matter of time before the other horde also re-animated and they too decided to join their brethren in attacking the north terminal.

'You're losing your touch, nipper,' Frank said into the radio with a jokey comment aimed at Howie and his troupe currently sat in the Saxon wondering why the buggering hell none of the infected were going for them.

'Honestly. I'm actually feeling rejected right now,' Howie replied.

'Then I suggest, Mr Howie, that you come and join our party as it appears we are about to be swarmed,' Henry transmitted.

'Quickly lads! They're coming in fast,' Paula also said, which did the trick and no sooner than anything the lads had once more piled into the Saxon with Tappy setting a course for the north terminal.

'They're body piling the pier,' Joan then transmitted.

THE UNDEAD TWENTY-FIVE. THE HEAT

'What pier? I thought we were in an airport,' Howie said.

'The long stems holding the boarding gates are called piers,' Joan explained as I think a great many people all thought, *oh, I didn't know that*. I, of course, did know that, and indeed, Joanie was quite right because the darned infected were, indeed, body piling the bloody pier.

'Howie! Focus on the body pile. Joanie, can you search west of the tower. Roy, you look along the southern fringes. I'll do the western side,' I said into the radio as I continued my search, and in so doing I caught sight of the survivors starting to pour out of the train station from the north terminal on that raised monorail.

And it was at that point that line by Robert Burns came to mind, because I then saw a rather large horde coming out of the south terminal train station on the same raised monorail that our survivors were trying to flee on.

Which, as Howie would say, was a bit shit.

'Howie, it's Reginald. We have an issue. There's infected on the monorail coming from the south terminal.'

'Oh. That's a bit shit then. Right. Er. No worries. Leave it with me.'

'Oh, and Howie?'

'Yes, Reginald.'

'They're running rather fast, old chap.'

'Righto!'

Maddox

Righto, Howie said into the radio. *Well. It was all going a bit too well really*, he added as Clarence and Blowers both nodded.

Every half hour, Clarence said.

Every half hour, Blowers and Howie said as Howie bit his bottom lip before shifting to look out the front window to the thousands of infected running in the same direction we were driving.

Henry. We need some C4, Howie transmitted. Henry replied and said *understood* and told Howie to drive under the bridge.

Okay, Mads, I need you with me and Dave. You can hotwire cars. Clarence, you keep them here clearing the north terminal.

I can hotwire, Books said. *I'll jump in, boss, and give you cover.*

Fair one, Howie said as me and Books shared a quick fist bump at getting a mission on our own. *Tappy, get us under that bridge. We'll grab the C4 then bug out. Lads, get ready. Dave, you good?*

Good at what, Mr Howie?

I mean are you good to go? Fuck's sake. I meant are you ready, Dave?

Yes, Mr Howie.

Great.

I think Dave does it on purpose sometimes to wind Howie up. Which is quite funny when we're not driving into a shitstorm of hell.

Then a minute later we were in that shitstorm of hell.

We're coming under the bridge! Tappy shouted.

Carmen

So then the guards are using a metal bench to batter through one of the extra toughened panes of glass on the bridge while Henry was on a knee getting det-cord, detonators and C4 into a bag while Frank was shouting at the guards not to fire.

'We need to fucking kill them!' one them yelled.

'Yeah? and what happens if we start shooting?' Frank asked him. 'We break the glass they're smashing their heads into, and we end up letting them in. Everyone hold. Do not fire.'

I knew the guards were panicking. Jesus. Who wouldn't be in that situation, and it was counter-intuitive *not* to start firing down the escalators and through the windows. But even if we fired every bullet we had and got a kill with each shot, there would still be thousands of infected left, and the fact was that we weren't there to get kills.

We were there to buy time.

Which, from all accounts, was about to go bent after Reggie said the infected were on the monorail. Which is also why Howie was asking for C4, which by then Henry was about to throw out of the window to the Saxon below.

'Midway between the pylons,' Henry shouted down.

'Are you seriously telling me how to blow things up?' Howie shouted from the roof of the Saxon. 'We've got Dave.'

Henry went to reply but thought better of it. I mean. What can you say to that? Dave blew a cow up. *And* he was the guy that blew the refinery up that was seen by astronauts on the space station.

Either way. Howie had the right person with him to blow the monorail out.

Dave

My name is Dave. I am writing a diary because Paula said it is important to tell people what we did.

We were in Gatwick airport. It was very hot. We were meant to be making the infected attack us so Mr Henry could get survivors out of the north terminal. But the infected were not attacking us. Frank said Mr Howie had lost his touch. Things like that confuse me as I don't know if it meant Mr Howie had lost the sensation of touch from his fingers, or if it was said as a saying which meant he could not do what he could do before. I did watch Mr Howie touch his radio and his face, and it appeared his sense of touch was okay.

Then Reginald said the infected were on the monorail and Mr Howie said that was a bit sh*t. I thought it would be a lot sh*t.

Then Mr Howie told Maddox and Alan to come with us because they knew how to steal cars. I thought we were meant to be stopping the infected from body piling and not stealing cars. Then Mr Howie asked Mr Henry for some C4. I don't know why because I had some C4 in my cubby hole in the Saxon, but I thought maybe Mr Howie wanted to use Mr Henry's C4.

Mr Henry then gave Mr Howie some C4 by throwing it out of a window and he told Mr Howie 'midway between the pylons.'

Mr Howie then said he had Dave. Which meant me. Mr Henry

didn't say anything else, and we carried on driving.

'Right, Dave. You got this?' Mr Howie then asked me.

'Have I got what, Mr Howie?'

'This! We're blowing the monorail up.'

'Okay.'

'Okay what?'

'Okay, Mr Howie.'

'Eh?! What the f*ck. No, right, listen. We're going to go and blow the monorail up. Okay?'

'Yes, Mr Howie.'

I don't know why he told me twice. I heard him the first time.

'Right. So you ready?'

I wasn't sure what he meant because he'd already asked me and I'd said yes. 'Ready for what, Mr Howie?'

'OH MY FUCKING GOD! Where's Marcy when you need her.'

'She's with Reginald,' I said to Mr Howie.

'No! I know. I meant. Okay. No. Sorry. We'll start over. We need to go and blow the monorail up, got it?'

'Got what?'

'The boss means do you understand?' Clarence asked me.

'Understand what?'

'He's doing it on purpose,' Clarence said. 'You're doing it on purpose.'

I waited for a second and looked from Mr Howie to Clarence. Then I didn't speak because I didn't know what to say.

'Er, may I?' Charlotte then asked as Mr Howie wiped some froth from his mouth. 'Dave? Mr Howie is asking if you are ready to assist them in destroying the monorail.'

I said I was ready. Which I had already said when Mr Howie asked me.

'And you have the C4?' Charlotte asked while holding a hand up to stop Mr Howie from speaking.

'I have my own C4,' I said.

'Then why the f*ckity f*ck did we stop for Henry's C4?' Mr Howie asked.

'You didn't ask for my C4,' I said.

'And Mr Howie understands that now,' Charlotte said.

'I'm driving round in f*cking circles. Where are we going?' Tappy then asked while driving the Saxon. But we were not driving in circles. We were driving in a straight line.

'We just need a car or something,' Mr Howie said. 'Look for something big we can use. Like a van or a lorry.'

'North side to the Saxon. Will you be assisting with removing our body pile anytime today?' Mr Henry then asked.

'Monorail, Howie! They're running,' Reginald then said.

'Sh*tting f*cking *rsing C*UNT!' Mr Howie then said, which I think made him feel a bit better as he sighed after. 'Tappy. We need something big so we can reach the monorail from underneath.'

'Stairs!' she then shouted as I looked out the window to see a set of set on wheels that airports use to attach to the side of aircraft. 'Perfect.'

'We're not driving some mobile stairs across an entire airport!' Mr Howie said. 'They go at like two miles an hour. That! Over there. That police van. See it.'

I said no.

'Eh?' Mr Howie said as he and everyone else looked at me.

'No,' I said.

'No what?' Mr Howie asked.

'No, Mr Howie.'

'F*ck! I meant what are you saying no to?'

'There's a catering truck!' Tappy then shouted. 'That's bigger.'

I said no.

'What the f*ck! What do you keep saying no?' Mr Howie asked me.

'Dave, what are you saying?' Charlotte asked.

I said I was saying no.

'No to what?' Mr Howie asked with that weird look he gets in his eyes sometimes. 'No to the van? No to the catering truck?'

'Yes.'

'Oh my f*cking god. What's wrong with the van and the truck? What do you want?'

'That,' I said and pointed out the window as Mr Howie looked back at me. 'I f*cking love you, Dave,' he said with a nod. 'Mads, Can you steal that?'

'It'll have an autostart,' Tappy said. 'It's not a road going vehicle, so it doesn't need keys. Hang on. You ready? I'll swing my fat ass around for you.'

I wondered why Tappy was going to swing her bottom at us, but instead the Saxon span around and everyone inside swayed before Maddox and Alan Booker jumped out and ran over to the vehicle.

Mr Howie and I went after them as they got into the cabin while Mr Howie and I kept them covered with our rifles, but the infected were not attacking us. They were running past towards the north terminal.

'We'll get into that body pile,' Clarence shouted from the back doors of the Saxon as it pulled away.

'Look at that sky,' Mr Howie said as I looked up. 'Bloody colour of it. That's a storm. Can you feel it? Oh god, no forget I asked. We'll be here for half an hour trying to explain what I meant.

I looked at him. He looked at me.

'I can feel the storm is coming,' I said.

He narrowed his eyes and pulled a face. 'I bloody knew you did it on purpose.'

'Do what, Mr Howie?'

'Don't you bloody *do what, Mr Howie*, me, Dave.'

'Boom!' Alan then shouted when the engine started.

'To be continued,' Mr Howie told me.

'What is, Mr Howie?' I asked but he winked and said he wasn't falling for it. 'Right. Let's go,' he said as we climbed up the ladder on the back to get on the top. 'Mads, go for it!'

The vehicle got moving with Maddox driving it back under the bridge.

'Do not drive that sodding thing under here!' Frank said in his radio as we went underneath it with Paula and Carmen waving through the window.

'With haste please, Mr Doku,' Reginald said into the radio. 'They are on the monorail and moving at speed.'

'Where am I going?'

'I'll guide you. Aim for the south terminal.'

Maddox was driving fast, but Reginald wanted him to go faster. I cannot drive, but I think Maddox was struggling because the gears were making crunching noises, and the truck was jolting. We also kept hitting infected which made Mr Howie pull faces as though we shouldn't be doing that.

'Jesus, Mads!' he shouted from the roof.

'What do you want me to do?!' Maddox shouted. I thought he already knew what he had to do. He had to drive the truck.

'Oh god. This is going to go pop,' Mr Howie then said as Maddox swerved to avoid a thick crowd of infected and hit the tail end of the jet that had crashed into the south terminal.

'Now straight ahead! Fast as you can.'

I felt the truck speed up then Mr Howie, and Alan, and Maddox, all screamed when we went around a corner and drove into the back of another truck that was the same as the one we were on.

'My f*cking heart,' Mr Howie said as Maddox pulled back and got us going again.

'And er, watch out for other vehicles,' Reginald said in a strange tone of voice.

Then we were out of the airfield and away from the infected. We could see the monorail ahead of us. It was raised up on high pylons. I could also see a lot of infected were on the top of the monorail platform running towards the north terminal.

'Where?' Maddox shouted.

I understood what he meant now as I could grasp the context, and I knew what we needed to do. I told him to aim for the curve as that would be weakest. He drove fast through some more bushes while I studied the structure overhead.

'Go back out and get under the next one,' I said.

'Fuck, Dave!' Mr Howie said. 'They're right there. Jesus. Mads, do it. Go back out and in again.'

Maddox reversed as the infected got closer to the point of passing overhead with more of them coming out of the south terminal train station. Then he veered off and went back in.

'This is Dave. Tell them to lie down,' I said into the radio.

'Dave?' Reginald asked. 'Tell who to lie down?'

'The people on the monorail. They must lie down.'

'Dave! It's Carmen. I'll pass it on, but don't wait. Blow it.'

'They must lie down.'

'Dave, It's Henry. Blow it now!'

'You are not my CO, Mr Henry. Mr Howie is. You made me stop working for you and told me to work for Tesco.'

I don't know why I said that.

'I liked my old job, Mr Henry.'

I don't know why I said that either.

'I was lonely. Mr Howie was my friend. He spoke to me. I liked my old job, Mr Henry. I was good at it, and I liked working with Carmen and Frank.'

'Chaps! I'm sure this is important, and everyone's feeling are valid but blow the bloody monorail up!' Reginald said.

'You made me lie to Mr Howie.'

'Dave. I am sorry,' Henry said. 'Listen. We'll sit down and talk about it when this is over, okay?'

I said I didn't need to talk about it. 'I've said what I had to say,' I told Mr Henry as Maddox, Alan and Mr Howie all stared at me.

'Dave, we need to set the C4,' Mr Howie said, but his voice wasn't shouting or angry. He was quiet.

'We don't need C4,' I said and took a grenade from my pocket and pulled the pin.

'Fuck, Dave!' Mr Howie said as he and the other two moved back several steps.

'Run,' I told them, because it is important to give clear instructions when handling explosives. But I didn't need to say it as Mr Howie and Alan and Maddox were already running.

I ran too then stopped to throw the grenade so that it landed underneath the fuselage containing the jet fuel carried on the back of the truck. I then counted in my head until it detonated.

THE UNDEAD TWENTY-FIVE. THE HEAT

The fuel ignited and blew out with the force of the blast funnelled up by the solid concrete pylons either side. That meant the monorail platform took the brunt of the pressure wave and broke it with a fireball that went very high into the air.

I like explosions.

I like the colours and the noise, and I like the chemical changes that take place that make it happen. It's not confusing or difficult like people are. You put things together and make them into something else.

I watched cooking television shows when I was not working at Tesco. It was the same thing. You put ingredients together to make something else.

I was lonely at Tesco.

I was angry that Mr Howard and Mr Henry made me leave my job. But I didn't know I had that feeling inside.

'We're getting engulfed!' Clarence said into the radio.

'Howie. It's Reginald! I've just found a CP at the far western end of the runway in a fire training area, but the Saxon is getting swamped.'

I like it when Mr Howie is under pressure. He never panics.

'Mads, Books, can you two take the CP out? We'll help the Saxon.'

Charlotte

We'd gained a false sense of security while we were on the runway.

But just in the first few seconds of being closer to the north terminal we saw the difference because that immediate area was fast becoming the epicentre for both hordes, and without buildings or streets or structures it meant they were coming in from all sides.

In fact, they were coming in so fast that as soon as Tappy drove along the length of the pier clearing them away more were pouring in behind us climbing over the broken bodies we'd just run down – and to make it worse, there were four physical boarding gates jutting out from the pier that created recesses between them which the Saxon couldn't get into.

And so, with no other choice, Clarence ordered us to debus and get rapid fire into the attacking horde.

It was brutal from the second we alighted. The heat was bouncing off the tarmac and because of the numbers we were firing *as we got out*. There were seven of us and I know we each emptied a full magazine in one go. That's over two hundred rounds fired within a couple of seconds, and I guarantee that every single round struck an infected. That's how densely packed they were, and they just kept coming.

'LEGS!' Clarence then shouted as I caught a glance of him strafing the legs of the attacking horde.

We all did the same to break shin and thigh bones and blow knee joints out. It sounds gruesome, and it is, but it normally slows a horde down as the ones coming after have to go over the ones in front.

But that didn't work either. Not this time. The numbers were just too great.

'BODY PILE!' Blowers shouted as we all turned to see them behind us stacking up in the middle by a curved section of the pier. 'TAPPY! GET INTO IT!'

We star burst to the side as Tappy drove in hard. Ramming the body pile aside to make the people fall and scatter as we put rounds in.

I then heard an almighty bang, and we all snapped our heads over to see an enormous fireball rolling up into the sky just outside the airfield.

Tappy then pulled out and drove on as we changed magazines and aimed into the infected charging towards us. But we just didn't have enough guns, and the size of the area we were trying to defend was too great.

'We're getting engulfed!' Clarence said into the radio.

'Howie. It's Reginald! I've just found a CP at the far western end of the runway in a fire training area, but the Saxon is getting swamped.'

'They're on the top of your pier,' Joan then transmitted. I glanced back and up to see the infected were already clambering up over some smaller outbuildings attached to the eastern end of the pier.

And a second later we felt and saw the whole horde suddenly veer and shift direction to aim for that eastern edge.

We all ran for it. We ran firing and yelling with Clarence sprinting *at the same time* as firing the gimpy. The Saxon shot past us and rammed through the pile – which gave us all a fright as even the Saxon found the sheer numbers of bodies harder to get through. She still did it. My god that Saxon did it, but it faltered for a split second which made us realise how hopelessly outnumbered we were.

That's when we heard another engine and turned to see Maddox and Booker driving by in an armoured police van with the two of them wearing police hats. They swept by within a few feet of us. Gaining kills and giving what aid they could as they built speed up and drove off.

'GET FIRE INTO THEM!' Clarence ordered and we did what we could.

But it wasn't enough.

It wasn't anywhere near enough.

Carmen

It went south fast. In fact, it got so bad so quickly I was having flashbacks to Mogadishu.

By then all the guards and Dawson, along with Henry and me, and Bash and Paula were all at the end of the bridge staring out to the absolute carnage the Saxon was in the middle of.

I thought Hinchley Point was bad, but they came in waves whereas the Gatwick hordes were coming all at once and from every direction with a relentless surge.

Then the infected started to body pile by the middle bulging out section of the pier below us. We could see it happening through the plate glass window, but the glass was strong and withstanding the pressure.

'Fuck this!' one of the cops shouted and started firing his rifle down the escalator into the windows. We all shouted at him to stop as Bash knocked the lad out clean with a vicious punch to the side of his head while his mates all gasped and looked on in horror.

'No fire!' Bash shouted while pointing outside. 'No fire. No fire.'

'Hold your fire!' Henry ordered as we all turned back to see the bullet holes in the window as the spider web cracks started spreading out.

That's when we heard and saw the fireball go up from the monorail. It was huge and I think it really added to the nerves and fear the soldiers and cops were feeling. Then, a second or so later, Reggie started transmitting that he'd found another CP, but it was at the far end of the runway.

'I'll go for it,' I said, spotting vehicles outside that I could use. Henry nodded to give his consent as Mads and Books called up to say they were on it.

'Mads'll sort it,' Paula started to say but she cut off as we heard the sound of glass cracking and looked down to see more cracks spreading through the window the idiot cop had shot. Then we heard more creaks and bangs and realised the infected were now body piling over the smaller outbuildings attached to the eastern edge of the pier.

I've never seen anything like it.

It was like a shadow spreading from window to window as the pier started falling to darkness from the daylight being blotted out.

'Hold,' Frank said when one of the other guards looked ready to either fire or flee. 'Everyone hold.'

'They're on the top of your pier,' Joan said into the radio as we started hearing thuds and bangs coming from the roof and looked out the through the bridge side windows to see them on the pier roof and growing in number as that shadow grew and spread out. The gunfire outside was intense and fast, and we saw bodies flying off from being hit.

Which is when the window the idiot cop had shot finally gave out and fell in with a crash and dozens of infected falling through into the pier.

'Now we can bloody fire,' Frank said as we finally opened up and started putting rounds in.

But it wasn't enough.

It wasn't anywhere near enough.

Which is when Howie piped up over the radio.

'Clarence! Clear them out. Clear them out. Paula, get away from that pier thing.'

'Control to north side! Clear that bridge!'

Paula didn't hesitate. 'MOVE BACK! THE SHOW IS STARTING!'

I thought the show had already started.

But it hadn't.

My god it hadn't.

Reginald

We were about to lose the north terminal. There were just too many of them swarming in and using each other to clamber over. Two hordes. Tens of thousands of them and the whole airfield was still thick with them running across, all of them aiming for that one spot. For that small pier of four boarding gates.

I was glued to my screen with the van starting to rock from Jess moving about in her trailer attached the back. I could hear her snorting and making noises, but I had no time to check on her because Maddox and Booker were in a police van racing for the far end. I could see the flashing blue lights, and I tried to find the other CP, but my eyes kept going back to the sight of that pier and the sheer number of human forms spreading across it. They were blocking the windows, and already on the roof.

Then I risked a glance to the monorail and saw the survivors were still bunched up by the train station and not going out. I could only assume the fireball they'd seen had made them stop, but we just didn't have the means or the numbers to get them going.

And to make it more fun, it was right at that moment that one of the main windows on the pier went in with dozens of infected falling inside. Then, a second or so *after* that and more were veering for the breach while yet hundreds more were already on the roof and climbing onto the bridge.

Damn it all to hell! I thought we'd lost the game right there. Let me tell you that, but see, I'd discounted Howie and Dave. And one should never do that.

'Clarence! Clear them out. Clear them out. Paula, get away from that pier thing,' Howie said into the radio as I turned the drone with an outward cry of surprise.

'*Control to north side! Clear that bridge!*' I shouted into the radio while watching Howie driving the fuel truck that Maddox had crashed into with Dave on the top holding a hose that was spraying fuel over the infected as Howie ploughed through them.

Good god! One spark. Just one bloody spark. It was all I could do to watch as Charlie and Clarence and the others all ran for their lives.

The driver's door then flew open, and Howie leapt out while the truck rolled on and Dave ran down the end to leap free of the rear as they both sprinted away as fast as they could while the infected were already swarming up over the outside of the bridge, and yet hundreds more were pouring in through the broken window.

'*BLOW THE PIER!*' Howie shouted in his radio while running.

'*PAULA, HENRY. BLOW THE BRIDGE,*' I called into mine then I watched for what seemed like an eternity. By then the whole pier was thick with infected and they were already on the bridge and running across the roof.

Then finally, I saw an orange flash. Then another and another and the bridge windows blew out in a series of charges going off that rolled down towards the pier until the last one seemed to ignite the fuel sprayed over the infected.

The flames roared in an instant. Engulfing the infected in fire, but they just kept going. Heedless to the pain and their flesh melting away until the last charges detonated, and that pier seemed to lurch a foot into the air with a loud crack, which of course helped ignite the rest of the fuel that danced back all the way to the hose on the ground, followed swiftly by the fuel truck exploding.

It was like a mini nuke with a huge bang and a mushroom shaped fireball killing every single living thing on that pier. Then the bridge blew apart and snapped off to drop to the ground, killing more infected as the heat and flames and the pressure wave went out, knocking hundreds more off their feet in all directions.

Maddox

Man, it was insane! Me and Books were in this police van with me driving and Books pressing buttons to make the lights flash and get the siren going. He even found a cop's hat to put on.

Ello ello ello, he said as I burst out laughing. Then he found another one and got it on my head while I ran more infected over. And it wasn't like I was even trying to run them over. It was impossible *not* to run them over. *Drive by the pier,* Books then said. *We'll give them a hand on the way.*

I steered over as we both saw thousands of infected all swarming up over the end of the pier. It was like watching a frenzied ant nest. It was so fast. We got a few down and saw Charlie glance at us, but we couldn't stop and help. We had to kill the CP.

I tried to speed up, but it was hard going because of the amount of bodies we were hitting. The Saxon was strong enough to take that sort of punishment, and the cop van was armoured, but it wasn't anything like the Saxon.

Bro. This is fucking relentless, Booker said with his cop's hat still on his head. I nodded at him and tried to steer around a big fat guy, but it was too late, and he slammed into the bonnet and buckled the grill. The windscreen cracked and I could feel the steering came loose and figured he'd done some damage, but we were still moving.

Then we heard the panicked shouts in the radio. I don't mean panicked like people screaming. Not like that. I mean fast and loud to express urgency. They were doing that as we hit the runway. But the engine was making noises and I saw steam coming from the front and the temperature gauge on the dash was in the red.

Just up there! Books said while pointing ahead. We booted it towards a row of hedges, and I could see a big airplane behind it. But it was an old one all covered in smoke stains and scorch marks. I saw the wings had been chopped off halfway along. I figured that's where the airport fire services practised putting airplane fires out, or emergency drills or whatever.

I'll ask Reg where the CP is, Books said.

Nah, leave it. I said. *He's busy. We'll find it.*

Booker nodded as I burst out laughing at the police hat wobbling on his head. *You look like a right cunt.*

And you don't? He asked, flicking me the bird as the front of the police van went bang and the engine seized up. *Fuck it. Come on fatty.* He shouted as he grabbed his rifle and kicked his door open to jump out.

I went after him with the two of us running the last hundred yards through the bushes into the fire training area to a whole load of infected all turning to face us. Seriously. There were dozens of them and there was this split-second when me and Books stopped, and they all stopped, and we were all staring at each other.

Then I glanced right and caught sight of an infected female standing in the middle of a few more next to some old shipping containers. She was different to the others. I could see it in her eyes. That spark of intelligence. She was definitely the CP.

Books! Take her. I'll keep these off.

He set off as I emptied my magazine at the bigger horde just as they started charging at me. I got a few down then slung my rifle and pulled my machete out to go hands on. Slicing into necks and legs with a glance back to Booker slamming into the bodyguards protecting the CP.

It got intense AF. One of them bit my arm and another got into my shoulder. It hurt like hell, but I got them off and stamped on a head then cut into another neck just as I saw Booker lunging at the CP, but they went out of sight around the end of a container.

That's when I heard the explosion coming from the pier and saw the mushroom cloud fireball rolling up.

Then maybe a few seconds after that the infected all went slow and I killed the rest then staggered back to gasp air for a few seconds before I ran over towards the containers.

BOOKS? I yelled out. I heard him saying something and got round the container to see him rolling onto his back away from the decapitated CP next to him on the grass. She was young too. Like twenty or something. It was fucking grim. Especially with her clothes all ripped off and her breasts and vagina all exposed. It made me feel wrong to see it. Like she was human again or something.

Fucking bitch bit my shoulder, Books said, rubbing at a bite near his neck but then Reginald was calling up for more help.

Chaps! I've got the second CP in sight. It's behind a large hanger just north of the control tower.

I'll get it! Tappy said into the radio as we set off running and I glanced to the decapitated head of the CP and saw the fresh blood on her mouth where she'd bitten Books.

Charlotte

The fireball that went up from the pier and the fuel truck was something else. I was hugging the tarmac and truly thinking I was about to die.

Then I cried out at someone stamping on my hand and flipped over to see the pier engulfed in flames and the bridge now collapsed with thick black smoke pouring into the air. We must have killed thousands. But it didn't slow the horde.

It was hopeless. Utterly hopeless, until Mads or Books must have finally got their kill as suddenly all around me infected stopped charging and became instantly slow. It was astonishing and for a second, I thought to cheer until I realised it was only one of the hordes. The other one was still going for the north terminal.

That's when I started to rise and got slammed into by a big male that took my off my feet face down into the road. I felt the tarmac graze my face and arms and flipped over to get my knife into his neck.

But he was very thickset, and I had to stab him several times until I finally got the artery and a face full of blood. I got out from underneath him as another one ran into me. A scrawny woman that I managed to flip over, but then another hit me from behind and I went sprawling again. It was awful. They weren't attacking, but just running and I was in the way, and with the smoke and the heat hazes it was hard to see.

That's when I realised I was on my own.

'Chaps! I've got the second CP in sight. It's behind a large hanger just north of the control tower,' Reginald said

'I'll get it!' Tappy said as I spun around and tried to see Clarence or Nick, or Cookey and Blowers. I shouted out for them, but the noise was still so bad I couldn't hear if they shouted back.

Reginald

We'd killed at least three or four thousand in that explosion. Maybe more. But against forty thousand? It wasn't anywhere near enough.

Then I spotted another cluster of stationary infected on the far side of a set of hangars out of sight of Joan.

I called it in while unable to see any of the team on the ground because of the smoke and the heat hazes.

I'll get it! Tappy then said into the radio as I spotted the Saxon already driving that way.

'Control to north side. The survivors are not moving. They have to evacuate.'

'North side. We'll see to it,' Henry responded as I felt the van sway and tilt and heard the bangs increasing as Jess kicked at the doors. She sounded angry, but to me she was always angry, and very fearsome too.

'Marcy! Check the horse' I called. I waited for her to reply and was about to open the door when Tappy transmitted.

'I can see them! Give me two minutes.'

I saw her driving into the gap between the buildings but because of the smoke I couldn't follow her progress and lost sight of the Saxon. I called up and urged Tappy to find and kill the CP, then a moment later the other horde ceased their charge and I sat back with a blast of air.

We'd gained a moment of respite. Enough for me to check on the blasted horse as the kicks were becoming harder and the van was rocking rather violently.

However, the second I stood up to open the door, the first horde re-animated and re-commenced their charge. But they didn't charge for the north terminal.

They went for the team on the ground.

Diary of Natasha Drinkwater

Yeah. Right. So er, not my thing doing diary stuff. I'm not a girlie girl like that. I mean it's cool if anyone else wants to do one, but I'd rather change an oil filter than write my emotions down. That's how I cope.

But Paula said we should record it if weird shit happens. Like if it's something totally different.

Anyway. So during the battle, Reggie shouted up that he had the next CP behind some hangers and I called up and said I'll go get it.

It wasn't that far and when we started getting closer, I spotted this thick cluster of infected in this narrow area between the hangars and this long warehouse style building. And there's a lot of them, right. I mean infected. I knew Mads and Books had taken one of the CP's out, which made half of the zomboids go still, and so I figured some of the ones at the back of that hanger were all sluggish and dribbly.

Anywho. So we drove in and I'm giving the Saxon a nice burst of speed then stomping on the brake for a hard turn slide. The old shake'n'bake with that big old ass slapping them down. And it's working, right? We get a whole load of them down, but that smoke was coming across and I couldn't see where the CP was.

'*Is it dead yet?*' I asked over the radio. But Reggie said not yet, and he was like *Hurry up, Tappy. Get on and kill it.* Or you know, however he says it with his posh voice.

And I'm like, 'Fuck it,' cos honestly, I just couldn't see. Plus, the windscreen was all caked in dead flies and bugs, and bits of dead people too.

So I told Meredith we had to find it and we stopped and got out and I'm walking along shooting zombies in the head and trying not to cough from the smoke.

Meredith is out too, and I could hear her snarling and biting things and I got about halfway along when I spotted this group of bodies off to the side. Half of them were still alive, but with broken legs or whatever. I went over and shot a couple of them then I saw another one looking at me. And honestly. It gave me the willies. It was so different. Zomboids aren't people. They don't have intelligence, but this one did, and it looked right into my eyes.

'*One race,*' it said.

'Fair one,' I said and shot it in the head, then literally a second later *all of the zomboids* were sluggish and slow and I was like, 'Fuck yes. Winner winner chicken dinner.'

But that's when the other horde came back to life and man, they were ramped up to shit. I don't know what had changed, but I turned around and saw them charging in and they were fast and mean and snarling. I shot a few, then, this big female took me off my feet and slammed me into the back of the hanger so hard it broke my nose. There was blood spraying out everywhere, and I could feel teeth on my back, and nails raking down my cheeks.

But my rifle was tangled up on the sling and there were too many infected piling into me. Like bang bang bang. All of them coming in. And I could hear Meredith snarling but I'm going down, and it was like the night when it first happened, and I was at home with my mum and dad and my brothers and my sister. I was asleep and they all got turned and attacked me. I ended up knifing them all to death when the rage was triggered inside.

I did it then and went batshit crazy and had my knife out stabbing anything I could reach, and all the blood and gore were going in my eyes and in my mouth and I knew I was fucked.

Dave

I was running with Mr Howie to get away from the smoke and heat coming from the pier. We'd killed thousands, but many more were running back towards the north terminal.

I could not see the Saxon or any of the team. Mr Howie was shouting for them. I shouted too. I have a very loud voice, but they did not hear me.

Then we heard Tappy say she was going to kill the next CP and Mr Howie stopped and grabbed my arm.

'We have to keep them focussed on us,' Mr Howie said. 'How do we do that?'

'We're not a big enough threat, Mr Howie.'

Mr Howie looked at me with a strange expression. 'How many did we just kill? Roughly, Dave. Roughly how many?'

I said it could be between three and five thousand.

'F*ck,' Mr Howie said. 'Okay. We need to go bigger.'

I understood this. Mr Howie wanted to blow more things up so the infected would focus on us instead of the survivors.

'Big, Dave. It has to be big. As big as you can.'

'Yes, Mr Howie.'

'Which way?' he asked me. I pointed and we started running but the infected were running against us. I shot many of them in the head as I could see in my mind which ones were going to be in my way.

Then they all stopped.

'Tappy's done it!' Mr Howie shouted. We ran faster for a few seconds but then the other horde found a new CP and they all started charging again. But I think Mr Howie had now got their attention because they didn't charge for the north terminal. They charged at us.

Carmen

We'd killed thousands, but it didn't make a blind bit of difference, because when the smoke cleared enough, we could still see tens of thousands of them pouring across the airfield towards us.

The bridge had snapped off leaving a small chunk jutting out. But that meant the hordes would then go for the next piers, and those didn't have a nice bridge to blow up.

Those piers were connected to the north terminal.

On top of that. The smoke and heat and chemical fumes were pouring in through the broken bridge and making us all cough as we fell back towards the last barricade.

I think we all lost track for a moment in that chaos, but then we saw half of the infected go still and figured Mads and Books had dropped the CP.

I knew Tappy was going for the other one. But we were still coughing and clearing our eyes and picking ourselves up from the mini nuke that Dave set off when he blew the fuel truck.

Then a moment or two later the other horde went still.

'Well done, Tappy,' Paula croaked as we shared a look for a second.

A second and no more, because that's when the first horde found a new CP and started charging again. Except they didn't go for us. They went for Howie and his team.

Reginald

It appeared that Howie had now triggered the fury of the second horde, because they came back and started charging at him. Which also meant they charged at Charlie, and Danny and Mo, and Blowers, Cookey and Nick, and Clarence.

I had to get them all together. It was the only hope they had and so while Jess was getting increasingly angry and kicking so hard I had to hold onto my desk I tried to form a plan.

'Joan,' I said into the radio. 'Guide them together. Tappy, you need to pick them up. TAPPY! DO YOU READ ME?'

THE UNDEAD TWENTY-FIVE. THE HEAT

Natasha

So I'm thrashing and bucking and I can hear Reggie going nuts on the radio and everyone is shouting but the smoke is still pouring across and I'm buried under the bodies. It was too hot. I couldn't breathe. I was still stabbing them, but my arm was getting wedged down and I couldn't get the knife up anymore. Then I dropped it and I'm trying to bite at the fuckers, but the only one I could reach with my mouth was already dead and all I was doing was biting a dead guy.

Charlotte

They turned on me the second they came back. I'd just got back to my feet and was picking the grit from my face and calling for the others when the first horde howled and charged. Then I was running backwards and dragging my axe overhead from my bag and taking a head off. But more were coming in. More than I could fight. I took a few down. A male then a female. Then a teenager and a kid, but it was relentless.

I span around and caught sight of the tower as a big female lunged at me then flew back off her feet with her head blowing out as I gasped and offered a fast prayer to Joanie on overwatch.

'Charlie. Fifty yards to your right. Danny and Mo,' Joan said.

I set off through the chaos and it felt like I was back on the hockey pitch. Dodging and weaving on a run for the goal. Then I saw the Danny and Mo back-to-back.

'YOU TWO! WITH ME NOW!' I shouted out as I ran in and clubbed a female down going for Danny as Joan shot another one to my right. 'Stay at my back. *Joanie, where's Blowers?*'

'Go left. No, the other left. That's it. Run that way. Sergeant Blowers. You have Charlie, Danny and Mo coming in on your six.'

'Roger that.'

I set off with Danny and Mo at my back. It was hard going though.

Especially with so many coming at us, and I could still hear Reginald shouting for Tappy who wasn't responding.

Reginald

The damned van was rocking so violently I couldn't risk standing up. The monitor was shaking and the thuds coming from Jess kicking her doors was deafening. But I had to keep looking for the CP's and do what I could to guide them out of danger, and I was desperately worried about Tappy, because the Saxon was our greatest asset on the ground.

If we lost that we'd lose the battle.

Natasha

Honestly. I was about to die. I couldn't get air in. I couldn't move.

I think I kind of accepted it because I started to wish I'd told Nick that I loved him. I wished we could have grown old together and have babies. I wished we'd had time for me to ask Charlie what was wrong cos she'd been upset all day. I wished so many things and all of them were quick. Like these images flashing in my mind, but the most powerful one was my dad. Tappy Drinkwater. The greatest man I ever knew. I wished I could see him again. It made me angry, but I couldn't do anything. I couldn't get free, and all this blood was going down my throat and I was drowning while being crushed.

Charlotte

'Not far, Charlie. Just a bit more.' Joan said as we fought on, but the compression increased and the infected coming against us got worse until all we could do was fight and walk instead of run and gain ground.

It was all so fast, and I was also worried because Tappy was still not responding and there was no word from Mr Howie, or Dave, and I couldn't see Clarence. Then I swung out to take a female down. I got her in the neck and as she went down her hand slapped me across the face with her ring cutting my cheek down to the bone, and in that second's worth of distraction I was taken down.

Reginald

Charlie went down and I felt the whole van lift on one side from Jess slamming her body side to side into the trailer. I fell over my desk and sent all my books and maps across the floor. Then the other side lifted and again I was thrown. I feared she would tip us over or kill herself and I had no doubt she could sense the danger and fear Charlie was in.

I had no other choice and so I threw myself at the sliding door and got it open enough to fall out and run to the back of the trailer. Good lord I was terrified. Jess scared the hell out of me. But I darted forward and kicked at one of the bolts then shouted out from the pain in my toe, but the bolt held firm and so I had to go back and prise it open then run around and do the other one.

At which point the ramp pretty much flew off the hinges and a very wild eyed and mouth-frothing Jess came out. Clearly furious that she'd been held inside for so long. She even came at me. I swear that she did. She used her head to knock me down at the same time as she kicked both of her back legs into the side of my van. Then she was off. Galloping away and I scampered back into the safety of my van.

Which was no longer safe as Jess had buckled the sliding door. I pushed it to then checked the monitor and nearly wept at the awful sight of Danny and Mo now down on the ground with Charlie. All of them getting swamped. Blowers, Cookey and Nick were trying to reach them, but the onslaught they faced was just too great. There really was no other choice and so I grabbed the radio.

'Howie! Detonate! You have to detonate!'

Natasha

I knew I was dying when I heard *Karma Chameleon* by *Culture Club* playing in my head.

Dad loved it. He'd sing it all the time. I grew up learning how to take engines apart while singing that song.

I heard it then. The jaunty harmonica intro and Boy George's awesome voice. I couldn't breathe. I couldn't move. I was drowning in blood and being crushed to death at the same time, but at least I was going out listening to my dad's favourite song.

Reginald

'Charlie is down! Danny and Mo are down! Howie. You have to detonate! THEY NEED THE HIVE MIND!'

I broke off as I saw Nick, Cookey and Blowers give a surge of furious energy and break through the final few lines to reach Charlie, Danny and Mo.

Oh my gosh it gave me a surge of hope that those three lads were still up and fighting. The unkillable Sergeant Blowers. The forever smiling Cookey, and Nick with his dashing looks and strong arms. It was going to be okay. They would save the day, and all would be well.

Then the second horde reanimated, and they too charged for the team, and I knew in my heart it was all over, and I watched those three brave young men as they swung their axes and fell back over the bodies of their fallen comrades.

Then I stopped and frowned because I could hear music coming through the radio. Something jaunty and fun. An old pop song from decades ago. But if Tappy was down then who was playing it?

Dave

THE UNDEAD TWENTY-FIVE. THE HEAT

We had to run fast, but it was very hot, and the smoke was coming into us from the fire on the pier. That meant the wind had changed because smoke only drifts in a breeze.

'The wind has changed,' I told Mr Howie because I knew that people like to make conversation about the weather.

'Storm,' Mr Howie said. I thought that was a very short conversation about the weather. Then I realised Mr Howie was struggling to get enough air. We were running very fast, and I was shooting infected to keep them out of our way.

But they were coming in faster, and Mr Howie had to draw his axe and I had to draw my knives so we could fight through them.

We then heard that Tappy was not responding.

We then heard Joan directing Charlie to get to Danny and Mo.

Those things happened very quickly. But things happen very quickly in a battle.

The infected then attacked us with greater aggression and we could not make much progress to where we needed to be.

Then Reginald was shouting into the radio. *'Charlie is down! Danny and Mo are down! Howie. You have to detonate! THEY NEED THE HIVE MIND!'*

'Dave! You have to go,' Mr Howie then shouted at me. I did not know if he wanted me to go back and help the team, or finish what we were doing.

'Go where, Mr Howie?'

'JESUS FUCKING CHRIST NOT NOW, DAVE.'

'I don't know what you mean, Mr Howie.'

He chopped a head off and looked at me. 'I'm so sorry, Dave. Please go and blow something up.'

'I can't leave you, Mr Howie. There are too many.'

'Dave, go!'

'I won't leave you, Mr Howie.'

'I SAID FUCKING GO!' he said, and I saw that thing in his eyes. I can't read people or their expressions, but it's different when Mr Howie does that. His eyes get darker. His whole face gets darker and his energy changes. 'Make it big, Dave. It has to be big. The biggest you've ever done. Go!'

He turned away. Then I turned and ran too because the I could feel the thing inside when we all connect. I could feel the energy coming from Mr Howie.

I could feel his rage.

Carmen

It all happened so fast. One minute we were telling the cops and soldiers where to position and fire from when the final breach came. Then the radio traffic was going nuts with Reginald trying to raise Tappy who wasn't responding, and Joan telling Charlie how to find Danny and Mo.

Paula looked stricken. 'I have to get out there,' she said. I held her arm and said we had to stay where we were. 'My team need me!'

'Seven hundred survivors, Paula,' Henry said. 'This is the plan. We hold our ground.'

But I knew what Paula meant because it didn't feel right. I could see it in Frank's face, and I think even Bash looked worried. The comms were getting worse by the second with a rising panic in Reginald's voice.

'I need a door out,' Paula said.

'Paula, please. I need you here,' Henry said.

'They're my team, Henry!'

Then the transmission came.

'Charlie is down! Danny and Mo are down! Howie. You have to detonate! THEY NEED THE HIVE MIND!'

Then two things happened at once.

The first was that we heard *Karma Chameleon* coming through the radios. And the second was that I could feel this rush of energy inside bringing forth a rage unlike anything I have ever felt before.

THE UNDEAD TWENTY-FIVE. THE HEAT

Natasha

I thought I felt the hive mind. I don't know. I was dying. But hearing that song gave me peace in a weird way. Like this sense of calm, but I couldn't understand why the music was getting louder.

Reginald

I felt the hive mind which told me Howie was alive, but the smoke was billowing across that airfield blocking my view. I couldn't see Charlie or the lads. I couldn't see anything and all I could do was beat my swatter at my desk in pure frustration.

I'd taken my team in and got them hurt, possibly killed. I'd done that. My folly and pride had done that. What a ruinous awful human being I was to do such a thing. To have such arrogance to take a small team and pit them against an enemy so many times our number. I thought of the Churchill quote I used earlier in the day and felt like I had abased the memory of the true and valiant.

The truth was that Mr Howie's hive mind could not save us this time. It was a matter of science. We were simply too few. And to make matters worse, those survivors had not left. They were still clustered near the train station on the monorail.

The team would fall. The north terminal would be taken, and it would all have been for nothing.

I sat down. Slumped and defeated and lowered my head in shame.

Natasha

I was at the brink of death. I knew that. My heart had slowed. I couldn't breathe or move or do anything other than listen to Boy George singing *Karma Chameleon*.

But then it got louder. Like it was coming closer, and I felt the world tremble a little. Then a bit more until the bodies on top of me started to shift and move. Then the big twat that was squashing me shifted enough so I could turn my head and cough the blood from my throat. But that tremble kept coming. Like the mound of bodies above me was shifting and I could feel the pressure of the bodies on top of me was reducing, then all of a sudden, I could see daylight the bodies slid away as though something was pushing them from the side.

And honestly. Seriously. I'm not lying but that whole mound seemed to slide off me until I was lying on a bed of gore and bodies with the Saxon creeping forward pushing them all away. Then it stopped and I'm lying between the two front wheels listening to *Karma Chameleon* through the speakers. And I don't know why I thought it, but Paula said we had to write down any weird stuff, but I'm lying there and all I could think of was this is what my dad would do. He was big and strong and if I was down like that, he'd stand over me with a fucking big wrench in his hand until I was safe. That thought was just there in my head while I was still puking and coughing and trying to breathe. That it was my dad that moved the Saxon over me. It had to be.

Then someone grabbed me, and I started fighting because no fucking way was I going to get crushed again. But they were strong, and they dragged me out. I got a headbutt into one of them then felt hands on my body as I was lifted off the ground.

'I've got her. Behind you, Mads!'

I came awake enough to feel Booker holding me from behind as he carried me away while Maddox fired his rifle at the infected coming round the corner. Then Books was dragging me into the Saxon and Mads was in the front. I tried to get free, but Booker was holding me too tight.

'Get off!' I shouted and he finally let go, but I was angry and scared and full of that rage Mr Howie has when he goes nuts and I'm crawling over the back seats and telling Mads to let me drive.

'Fuck off, Tappy. Just rest.'

'Let me fucking drive!' I yelled and started heaving him out of the seat. He called me a twat, but he got out and I got behind the wheel spitting blood and still heaving for air.

'Your nose is broken you crazy bitch,' Maddox yelled.

'Yeah, said the cunt in the police hat,' I said as Meredith jumped back in and politely requested Maddox to move out of her seat.

'Just get to the others,' Maddox said as Meredith bit his arse.

I turned to look at him and Booker both wearing police flat caps and shook my head while still thinking maybe I did die and that was some weird fucked up afterlife.

It got crazy mental after that, and a few minutes later I really did think I was in the afterlife cos the world went white.

Charlotte

I was down and getting swamped, and every time I fought to get free, someone else hit me from behind or from the side, and I went down again, but the worse thing was seeing Danny and Mo getting ripped off their feet. Especially Mo. He's one of our best fighters and if even he was going down then I knew it was bad.

But we weren't finished yet and we fought like filthy dirty bastards. Oh my good lord, we bit and gouged and we clawed and hacked and stabbed eyes out and heaved our way over the bodies to stay on top. It was the most violent thing I'd ever done. I bit into flesh and opened arteries with my teeth. I pushed my thumbs into eyes and felt teeth on my skull while I bit fingers off.

I watched as an infected spat Danny's fingers back at him, and I saw Mo pull his head back from a female with her teeth on his ear lobe, biting it clean away.

Then Blowers, Nick and Cookey were in amongst us and for a second, I felt hope that we'd get free, but the infected charged even harder and I saw Nick go down with a male biting into his face while he clubbed at the head until he got the thing off, but his face was pouring with blood.

We felt the rage coming from Mr Howie, but it wasn't enough. We fought harder and nastier, but the numbers coming against us were too many.

Then Cookey landed next to me with one biting into his arm and another slashing at his face with sharp nails. Scoring cuts over his eyes. I got over the top of him and took the pain in my back like he'd done for me in the golf hotel. And during that I saw Blowers was the last one on his feet. His axe was lost. He had no weapons other than his fists that were clenched and up as he boxed and punched them down one after the other. They couldn't touch him. He was too fast and too strong.

Then one jumped on his back and bit into his neck, and I saw Mo leaping up to take that infected down into the heap. Then another female went in on top of Mo. Then more swarmed over Blowers as more and more infected came charging in.

My apologies for cursing. But we were fucked. There was no hope of fighting free. I couldn't breathe. I couldn't move. None of us could, but in that moment, right at the brink of death I felt the greatest surge of energy I had ever experienced.

It was stronger than anything we had felt before and it was growing stronger by the second. I struggle to describe it. But it was like this wave of pure strength was coming at us. And it wasn't from one source. It was from lots of different sources all at once.

That's what the hive mind is. That's what happens when we feel each other. When we truly open our minds and let it happen and within that crushing darkness, I felt only light and hope with an instinct pushing into my mind.

Hold on.

Hold on.

Pack are coming.

Pack fight.

And they were coming. I felt them all one after the other like different wavelengths of energy. Each of them unique and individual. I could feel another one of them too. Not human. Not Meredith. An energy of a different sort that ran like the wind with muscles that dwarfed Clarence's. An energy within a beast that hated people and loved biscuits and oat milk and snorting lines of chocolate powder. A strong willed, grumpy, violent, angry creature filled with rage as she ran across that airfield slamming them aside. Faster than they were.

THE UNDEAD TWENTY-FIVE. THE HEAT

Bigger and stronger. I felt her coming. I felt her energy as I screamed out and started to push and fight to get free and as my head finally got clear I saw her leap over the mound and slam into the horde coming at us.

Then another force of energy hit us as Clarence steamed in and started grabbing at bodies to fling them aside as he went into full berserker rage. The strength of him was astonishing as he picked large adults up to fling away like they were made of nothing. I wriggled and pushed to get clear of the bodies, but the infected were still writhing and biting, and hands were clawing at my body, pulling me back down.

That's when a large female jumped on Clarence's back. He reached back to grab her hair, but she bit down hard into his shoulder. He roared in anger and twisted on the spot as another one jumped onto his body from the side, then another from the other side, and another on the front. They were so fast and just kept coming. I tried to shout and scream. I tried to get free, but my legs were trapped. Clarence stayed on his feet and flung one away, but two more slammed into him. He took the impact and wrapped his arms around two males and squeezed so hard I heard the bones snapping from metres away. But still they bit into him. Then more were on his back, and more were going into his legs. How he stayed up is testament to his raw strength, but against so many even he buckled and fell to a knee. The infected immediately howled even louder as though sensing victory from one who had killed so many of them, and my god they swarmed into him. One after the other after the other. I was screaming. I saw Nick trying to get free. His face drenched in blood. I couldn't see Cookey or Blowers or anyone else, and when I looked back Clarence was toppling over. I heard him roar. I heard the huge bellow coming from him then his right arm shot out and started grabbing at bodies to fling away. I felt a surge and knew he'd rise. Nothing could defeat him. He was too strong and too big, but a rangy male with big buck teeth dove in and clamped his jaws on Clarence's wrist. Blood sprayed out thick and fast then another did the same and bit deep through the flesh. Severing tendons and tearing at the sinew and muscle like starving hyenas on a flailing wildebeest. The whole mound seemed to heave and still I screamed at him to rise, but he couldn't, because even he, our strongest by far couldn't fight against so many, and that blood poured from his wrist, opening it deeper and deeper.

Then with a flash Jess was there rearing up to slam her front legs down into the lot of them. I don't know if she knew Clarence was there, but she did it twice then a third time until they were falling away, broken and ruined then she turned like a whip and backkicked the lot with her hind legs and sent human beings flying off into the ranks.

I knew Clarence was there and, in that instant, I feared Meredith would kill him. It was all so fast. Like a blur of motion then I bucked and thrashed to try and get free and when I focussed again, I saw the Saxon flying by, scooping dozens of infected away and Mads and Booker pushing at Jess to get her away before they heaved at the bodies on top of Clarence.

Then Paula was there, diving in with a scream as she leapt into the mound, tearing at limbs and heads to heave them aside with a strength drawn from her gut.

Carmen was at her side. Then Bashir. All of them working with Mads and Booker as I caught sight of Frank behind them, keeping them clear with a machete in his hands. An older man that moved like Dave with simple steps and sweeping strikes and everything he touched seemed to drop and die.

I felt air part past my head and saw an arrow sticking out of an eye then I twisted to see Roy striding through the smoke firing arrows faster than I could see. They were flying past me and each one was a kill. Each one was slamming into a head, through an eye, into a neck.

When I looked around I wilted back and thrashed from a female charging in with her red bloodshot eyes fixed solely on me. Her lips back showing me her teeth as she screeched. I couldn't get free. I couldn't do a thing and at the last second as I roared with defiance and prepared for the impact she was taken off her feet by Mr Henry stepping in front and flipping her over his hip. Then he simply lowered to drive the point of his knife into her neck while firing his sidearm at another infected. Two in the head and it dropped. Another one behind. One through the eye. More shots fired until the magazine clicked empty and he started to rise to fight with his knife as Mr Howie swept in front of him. Taking two down with his axe then booting one back before lashing out to take more off their feet.

I felt the force of him. That primeval dark energy that flows when this happens. When we get cornered and trapped and we start getting hurt, and by far this was the worst we've ever known. The onslaught was unceasing. They just kept coming, but Mr Howie. I don't know. It's hard to describe what he does in a fight like that. But his aura projects out. Now we know more I'd say he is the CP, and we are the horde. That's how we connect. That's how we can feel each other, and I think we all felt him then. That absolute fury, but it was different because it wasn't just coming from Mr Howie.

It was coming from Mr Henry too. It was that same energy, less powerful perhaps, less raw, more refined and directed maybe. Different but the same. It was only there for a flash, but it was there and it seemed to give us enough to fight and scream and withstand the pain long enough for Clarence to finally surge up as the thunder rolled overhead. Deep and booming and the bolts of lightning razed the sky. Crackling with electricity as Clarence fought to rid the infected still clawing at his body.

Pulling them back with his left hand to slam his forehead into skulls. Killing then outright while the bone poked through the flesh of his right wrist. The hand limp and ruined and only held on by a few thick ligaments and tendons.

It didn't stop him. He didn't even seem to notice, and the second he was up, he grabbed a thick leg from the ground with his left hand and used it to beat the infected away while the blood sprayed from his right.

I saw Nick pulling Cookey out of the mound and watched as he slapped Cookey in the face to rouse him while shouting. 'GET UP! GET UP!'

Cookey shook his head and staggered back then caught sight of me and lurched over to grab at bodies. Pulling them away as I fought clear while others got Danny and Mo out, but Danny was out of it. Not responding. Mo was struggling to breathe and hurt bad as Mads and Booker fended the infected off while Paula slapped at his cheeks.

I got free and tried to rise and fight but I stumbled and fell to my knee. I tried again while sucking air in as I saw Howie grab Henry's arm and shout something. Then they both turned and shouted together and the next thing I know we were being grabbed and heaved and told to move, but the infected were still charging in so we had to run and fight.

That's all we could do. We fended off and we staggered, and we fell. We went down and we picked each other up while Frank worked our rear and Jess ran around us while the Saxon did what it could.

The next bit is a blur. I saw a building ahead. Concrete and white. We aimed for it, but I didn't know why. All I know is we went around the corner to the other side and I stumbled again and went down hard, and when I tried to rise I saw Howie running in behind me carrying Danny over his shoulder while shouting *now, Dave* into his radio.

Then the world went white.

Reginald

It was like a flash at first. A single solitary flash that made me look to the northern edge of the airfield to a place known as *the fuel farm*. Where five large silos fed the fuel trucks, pipes, tanks that all supplied the commercial aircraft with highly combustible aviation fuel.

That's where the first flash came from. Followed a whole series of flashes as the C4 detonated almost faster than the eye could see, which were all placed to transfer energy, heat and fire into the pressurised fuel storage system.

All of which then went bang.

I saw it first on the drone as the fireball went up and the noise rolled out. Then a fraction of a second later I heard it with my own ears as the ground started to shake and tremble. Rocking the van on the chassis as the pressure wave blew the hangars and warehouses apart and smashed every single plate glass window in the airfield, and not just there because I could hear glass smashing and structures breaking apart in the buildings around me with debris and bricks slamming into the van. Cracking the windscreen and denting the panels. The broken sliding door flew back from the pressure wave and through the open side I saw the fireball going up over Gatwick. Hundreds of metres high and wide enough to scorch the aircraft sat on the tarmac still waiting for passengers a month after the pandemic. With each one exploding as more fireballs rolled up into the air, and each one of those explosions sent countless shards of metal and flaming material out across the airfield in all directions.

I looked back to the monitor and fought to control the drone as it spun crazily from the blast, and when I got it back on line I saw the boarding gates on the piers attached to the north terminal were buckled and coming away and tearing chunks out of the piers, leaving gaping holes and entry points. One of the piers crumpled and broke while other parts melted and every window in the north terminal blew out as most of the roof structures of the closest buildings were ripped off.

It made the sky go dark. It turned day into night and cast a shadow over the land.

It made me feel small and puny. It made the whole battle feel small and puny, and something Howie said came to my mind, that all we ever needed to win was Dave.

For all of my genius. For all of Howie's bravery. For all of Henry's training and experience.

All we ever needed was Dave.

I lowered the view on the drone while in my heart I knew we'd won. We had to have won. But I couldn't see the ground. I couldn't see anything through the smoke and heat hazes. Chunks of debris on fire here and there. Whole parts of aircraft now scattered across the airfield. Vehicles blown apart.

I looked harder and cried out when through the gaps and rolling clouds I saw the bodies littered across the grounds. Bodies that were sitting up. Bodies that were getting up.

Bodies that were still charging.

Carmen

The ground was heaving so much it took most of us off our feet, and the noise was like something from another world. Impossibly loud and deep and going on forever.

But that was just the initial bang, and the pressure wave hit us a split-second later as the air roared past. Super-charged and super-hot. I saw bodies flying by on fire as though they were twigs. Chunks of buildings and vehicles went overhead. A huge section of a boarding gate. The wing of a jet aircraft. All of it on fire and pouring with smoke. An aircraft tow truck went past with the tyres on fire, cutting through swathes of infected in the way.

A set of motorised stairs on its side spinning around and around as it gouged across the tarmac onto the runway.

Something hit our building on the other side and sent a chunk of bricks flying out that rained down on us. Hitting Clarence on the head. Striking down into Henry and Frank. Then I heard a scream and saw Bash dropping to the ground with his legs on fire as Tappy jumped on him to smother the flames with her own body.

'RIGHT SIDE!' Dave then shouted. I don't know where he came from, but only that he was there without a mark on him. His eyes seemed so alive and his whole face was bathed in the light of the fires he'd made. He was still up and still firing, and I realised that even in the midst of that hell, they were still trying to get at us. I went for my rifle and got rounds in. Frank did the same. Then Bash was up and firing on one knee with his clothes still smouldering.

'LEFT SIDE!' Clarence shouted as I turned to see him resting the barrel of the gimpy over his ruined right arm while firing it with his left. But they were still coming. Some of them on fire. Running while engulfed in flames and leaping into our midst.

'NO!' Howie yelled as he grabbed the dog to stop her trying to attack a body on fire. I spun around and fired into the head.

Then, the fire and smoke started spreading out into the sky, and it got dark quick, with bits of flaming debris raining down all over the place. Chunks of aircraft were landing on the runway killing scores more infected. Walls and buildings. Bricks. Windows. Wheels.

I felt a stinging pain to my arm and looked down to see a chunk of glass sticking out. I yanked it free with a spurt of blood coming out as Danny dropped at my side with an infected going for him while he was trying to club it in the head. I jumped in and rolled it off before drawing my pistol to get a round in the head. Then I was up and pulling Danny to his feet and pushing my knife into his good right hand. Two fingers gone from his left.

Mo's neck was covered in blood from his ear ripped off. Cookey had an eye taken and a chunk of flesh bitten out of his arm. Nick's face was ripped open. Charlie was cut deep. Tappy's nose was broken. Bashir had glass shards poking out of his neck and cheeks.

We were broken and ruined. We were bleeding and dying, and that heat. I cannot begin to describe it. It was just heat.

Pure unforgiving heat.

I couldn't swallow. My mouth was bone dry. My throat the same. We were breathing fumes and that fireball was stretching up into the sky, dwarfing our plight with smoke overhead, blotting the light out.

And still they came.

They came running and howling and screeching through the smoke. Wild and pumped with rage and hunger.

'Behind you, Carmen!' I heard someone shout and turned to get the last few rounds of my mag into a female. Body shots on the move. Centre of mass but it took her off her feet then Jess stamped down and finished her off as I looked up to see the drone in amongst us with Reginald giving what aid he could.

Reginald

It was a relentless onslaught with no respite, and even with the airfield engulfed in smoke with the top quarter on fire it made no difference and I cursed at the sight of the infected running through the smoke and fires. Trampling over corpses and tripping over the debris. And that debris still came down as more fuel tanks went up, and more infected were killed. Dozens at a time. But it wasn't enough.

It wasn't anywhere near enough.

Then, through the smoke and haze, I caught sight of a horde not running towards Howie. They were running south towards me.

Charlotte

We couldn't move or run. There was nowhere to go, and it was too chaotic and too fast.

Even the Saxon couldn't be used because the smoke was so thick Tappy wouldn't be able to see. Plus the whole airfield was littered with chunks of aircraft on fire. Whole wheels and wings and nose cones. Sets of seats smouldering and adding fumes to the already choking air.

For a few minutes we poured what rounds we had left into them until one by one we ran out of rounds.

'I'm out,' Cookey shouted as he cast his rifle aside.

'Same,' Nick said as the same words rolled around from one to the next.

'Handweapons!' Dave then shouted.

'Got any spares?' Frank asked as Dave jumped into the Saxon and started passing out machetes and axes while Clarence dragged the thick chain with his left hand. His face a mask of pure rage and filth, and gore and pouring with blood. The same for all of us, and all around the infected poured in while we compressed.

I mounted Jess, but my hand was broken. I couldn't hold the reins, so I wrapped them over my wrist and gripped my axe in my good hand as Jess turned a circle while snorting and flicking her head up.

THE UNDEAD TWENTY-FIVE. THE HEAT

Reginald

I looked at the horde coming south. There weren't that many of them. Forty to fifty perhaps. And I could only assume that the CP controlling them had intelligence enough to work out that someone must be flying the drone. And the only viable place to be flying the drone from was my location.

Whatever the reasons, they were coming for me, but I could not, and I would not leave my post. Howie was in it to the end. And that meant I was too. I wasn't a brave man. Not by any degree, but that pledge meant something. We were brothers in arms. We were a unit. We were a pack. Such things once made me cringe and repost with witty or cutting cynicism, but I understood what they meant by then.

I was just sad we'd failed.

We'd won many battles, but sadly, the war was not ours to win, because they had nothing left to give, and the horde were still going for them.

Then, a gust of a breeze cleared some of the smoke, and I felt my heart quicken, and I looked back to see Paula grabbing at Howie. She gripped his hand in hers and held it aloft, and for a moment, he seemed confused until he realised what she was doing, and together they waved the invisible magic fuckstick.

Then, a split second later, the horde in Gatwick erupted, and the air filled with a thunderous roar of howls as they commenced their charge.

It was the final stand. The last few seconds of life. The last defiant act of a species that refused to surrender. We'd won every battle and we'd given back against an enemy so much bigger than us, but the war was not ours, and that horde poured into the team as they cried out and brandished their weapons, and outside I heard the sound of feet drumming towards the van. I heard the growls and the screeches as they got my in their sights, and in those last few seconds of life I thought to hell with it because this was the game and this was the hunt, and we were all in it.

Carmen

We were fucked. Exhausted. Drained. Hurt and surrounded by thousands of infected that wouldn't stop until we were all dead, and they charged towards us on all sides at the same time.

And in those last few seconds of life I looked over to Paula holding Howie's hand in hers and waving it in the air like they were conducting an invisible orchestra. I had no idea what it was or what they were doing but they stopped and stared up with the strangest expressions I have ever seen on either of them.

Which is when I heard the sound of something different in the air. Something growing closer with a noise we all knew so well, and as the infected charged we all snapped our heads up to the sky to see the smoke swirling and parting.

Jess reared as Charlie let rip with a battle cry and as one we gave voice to scream and cheer at the sound of the Rolls Royce Merlin engines coming in fast as the Spitfire roared into view with those beautiful wings creating twirls within the smoke.

Then we saw the Hurricane right behind it and we threw our arms into the air as the infected charged at us and the two fighters lowered to start a shallow dive, sailing over our heads a split second before their wing mounted machine guns opened up to strafe the infected.

Reginald

I was on my feet once again slamming my battle swatter into my desk at the sight of the Spitfire and the Hurricane. I knew what it meant. I knew what she'd done. I knew why she'd gone out to get some air.

And Marcy didn't just come back on her own.

She bought an army with her.

Carmen

It was on.

Holy fuck it was on.

'INTO THEM!' came the order, but it wasn't from Howie. That one came from Henry. I kid you not. Henry led the charge next to Howie with the two of them going at the infected with Dave and Frank striding in after them. Both of them with blades slicing throats while the rest of us charged our lines and hacked and bludgeoned and killed whatever was in front of us.

'GO ON, JESS!' Charlie screamed as she went in with Jess battering the infected down.

Seeing the Spitfire and the Hurricane galvanised us. It gave us the energy we needed to hold on and fight and as we slammed into the lines. And those two fighters completed their turns and came back in low and fast, and the air filled with the sound of their machine guns strafing the dense crowds once again and I snapped my head over to see a one-hundred-year-old man at the controls. Worn and weathered. Lined and wrinkled, but upright and more alive than he had been for decades.

They scored kills and made gaps and I fought on with Bash at my side swinging out with an axe. Taking heads off. Taking limbs off.

Howie was in deep, and that hive mind happened again. I felt it and knew I had to be part of whatever Howie was. That meant I was infected too. It raised instant questions, but right then was not the time.

I could feel the others though, and I could feel Henry. It wasn't like I could see their thoughts or anything that powerful. Just the essence of them. Their energy, I guess. And as I opened my mind up to it, so it became more fluid and organic, and I started to sense urges and notions.

Pack fight together. Stronger together. As one.

It was incredible to experience what the infected had. That the very thing driving them to kill us was being used in a mutated version by Howie to will us on. I could feel his energy pouring into us, and I could sense Meredith's instincts driving us to accept the energy and be as one with the pack.

The next thing I was within that flow, and I knew without looking where the others were and the whole of us sped up and flowed around each other, and in the backdrop the fighters flew overhead strafing the crowd with live ammunition intended to be used to make a movie.

Reginald

My word what a sight it was. To see two such aircraft flying low through the smoke was stirring and it gave them all a boost of hope.

I willed them on and felt that crushing heat bearing down under that sky made dark from the smoke, until I realised it wasn't just smoke filling the sky. It was clouds too. Low dense clouds full of anger and rage were rolling in as the heat seemed to drive up and peak.

And outside I heard the screeches as the infected charged at my van and at the last second. I gripped my door and held it closed with all of my might as they impacted on the front and quickly clambered over the roof.

I had no escape. There was no way out. And all I could was hold on while watching the monitor as the first drops of rain fell from the sky.

Carmen

The thunder rumbled overhead as we held onto that surge of energy, and the flames were still burning from Dave's explosions. Jesus. It was incredible, and that heat got worse until I thought I would pass out. I could hardly move. The hive mind was wearing off as I guessed Howie and the others were feeling the same.

We kept going, but what choice did we have? It was either that or die.

Then the fighters went overhead again and put more rounds into the crowd. Scoring kills and making gaps, but they were filled instantly.

'Marcy! Get them firing into fuel trucks and planes!' Howie shouted into the radio as the two fighters cut off firing and instantly flared up to fly high and loop over before diving in fast. Both of them opening up with fresh bursts at something near the south terminal, and a second later the fireball went up from a fuel truck igniting.

It was a good idea, and no doubt it got more kills, but it was just too little too late and that hope we all felt started to fade once more.

Reginald

Good lord I was in a right pickle with infected hammering at the van and I knew it was only a matter of time before one of them saw the door was broken and threw themselves against it.

I couldn't very well keep holding it, but then the second I released it the buggers would be inside.

Or perhaps it would take longer than a second. Perhaps I could grab the controller and get myself locked in the cabin *before* they got through the door.

Mind you, it wasn't like I had any other options, and so I looked back to my desk and worked out what I needed to do.

1. Grab the controller.
2. Turn and run through the hatch.
3. Seal the hatch.

That was it. I could do it. I had to be brave and take decisive action.

I was ready.

Maddox

We were getting beaten back. There was nothing we could do. I was shoulder to shoulder with Books and trust me, that guy can fight. He's savage and fast, but against that many? We didn't stand a chance. It was over.

We were done.

Charlotte

I thought when the planes went overhead that we could hold on. I assumed help was coming. But we just couldn't sustain the punishment.

We had nothing left to give. I wanted to tell Jess to get away, but I knew she wouldn't leave me. I felt angry again and a rush of rage that I'd read it so wrong with Cookey. Why didn't he want me? What was wrong with me? It's absurd but that's what was in my mind. But a battle does that to you. It strips away all the fake emotions and leaves the raw truth exposed in your mind.

And in that moment, as they all fell back once more, I caught sight of him looking at me and felt deep sorrow that one of his beautiful blue eyes was gone.

Then he too was gone from view as the infected drove in and I screamed out as Jess reared and I lost my grip on the reins from my broken fingers and I fell from her back to land within the ranks of infected.

Reginald

'Grab the controller. Turn and run through the hatch. Seal the hatch.'

I repeated it a few times as I plucked the courage to go for it, then, right when one of them threw itself against my sliding door, I finally went for it.

I grabbed the controller.

THE UNDEAD TWENTY-FIVE. THE HEAT

I turned and started running for the hatch.

I tripped over my feet and went down as the door slid open a few inches. I cried out and got onto my back with my battle swatter ready as the door slammed open to a sea of hate filled faces all staring at me.

'One race?' I asked. 'It will be once race. My race. MY RACE. FUCK YOU! I said as the door slammed closed. I blinked and wondered what had happened then glanced at my monitor with a cry of alarm at the sight that greeted me.

Carmen

The fighters went overhead again as Jess reared and Charlie went down. I tried to run for her, but I couldn't get anywhere. Then our line broke and the infected were in amongst us. Cookey went down. Others too, but it was too fast to see properly.

Then four things happened at the same time.

The first was that it started to rain.

The second was that I heard a loud engine and looked over to see Marcy poking up out of the top turret of a Churchill tank carving a path through the infected.

The third was a 130-kilo infected male that *must* have been a bouncer came charging at me and got taken off his feet from an uppercut delivered by a ninety-year-old man wearing a beret and a chest full of medals as more old men swarmed in from all around us.

Old men that woke up that morning with stooped backs and ruined bodies. Old men that couldn't see or hear properly. Old men full of age and illness. Old men that once held the line against Nazi Germany.

Old men that were slowly dying when a beautiful young women walked into their midst and offered each of them a kiss.

And a few minutes later that beautiful young woman walked back out of their building with those old men striding out behind her. No longer blind of deaf. No longer stooped or slowly dying.

The kiss fixed all of that. The thing given to them cured all their illnesses. They became instantly strong once more, heedless to pain and fearless to boot.

And the price?

The price was their minds and the ability to have free thought. But as the beautiful young woman said, *you've already lived. Help me save the world again.*

I don't know if she said that. Jesus. For all I know Marcy spat in their faces. But I doubt it. She's way too stylish for that.

All I know is that about thirty old commandos that looked ready to keel over with heart attacks ran in and put us to shame. They were like animals. They swarmed into the infected and started kicking knees out and snapping necks and using old daggers to slice jugulars.

Then the fourth thing happened because the rain cleared some of the smoke and I cried out at the sight before me.

Charlotte

I landed hard and banged my head and for a second, I was seeing stars and half aware of Jess kicking and bucking at infected over the top of me. Then I wasn't seeing stars. I was looking up at an infected female screeching at me as she lunged in for the kill.

Except she didn't quite make it because a very old man kicked her away and stepped over me to stab a few more infected down before he turned and grabbed my hand.

He had to be over one hundred years old. There was no doubt about it, but he lifted me with ease and turned away to keep fighting. He moved like Mo or Dave. He had that fluidity about him, but that wasn't right because he was so old.

Then I looked over and saw Marcy going past in a tank and I thought why wouldn't I see Marcy going past in a tank? It's Marcy. If anyone was going to use a tank Marcy definitely would.

I got back on Jess, but I had to take two attempts because I was so drained. Then I felt a few drops of rain on my head and the smoke began to clear and I screamed out from what I saw.

THE UNDEAD TWENTY-FIVE. THE HEAT

Reginald

I forgot about the infected outside my van. I forgot about whomever was killing them, or whatever was going on, because all I could see was the airfield slowly clearing as the rain fell and the breeze took the smoke away.

What I saw was a broken and ruined world.

What I saw was that Dave had killed far more than I realised, but there were still plenty left alive.

Except they weren't all charging at Howie.

They were going for the tower.

Carmen

The rain fell and the smoke cleared, and I could see the airfield was littered with corpses. We'd done well. We'd killed thousands and I staggered back and turned then cried out at the sight that greeted me.

The air traffic control was nearly gone from view because of the infected bodies piling to reach the top. They were on all sides, with hundreds of them being used as a platform for more to climb over as they worked toward the top and that silver haired woman who hadn't uttered a word.

I cried out at the sight of it and watched as Joan aimed and fired a round from the balcony at the top and a few feet away an infected went down that had lunged at Bashir.

She was still covering us. She was still there but that horde were only inches away. Then the Spitfire and the Hurricane went overhead firing their guns, but the rounds didn't come anymore. They were all used up. They were all gone.

'Joan,' I whispered.

'Tappy! Get the Saxon,' Howie yelled, but Tappy couldn't get the Saxon. Nobody could get the Saxon. There were too many infected. It was too far away, and even if we did, we couldn't use it to remove a body pile that size.

'Marcy. It's Joan. You know what to do.'

'Fuck no,' I said. 'NO!'

'Joanie, I'll come for you,' Frank said into his radio as he set off.

'Marcy! Do it now! For the love of God, please do it now, Marcy.'

'Joanie,' Marcy said.

'I killed children today. I'm okay with this. Come on now. Needs must.'

I felt sick as I heard the Spitfire and the hurricane start to turn back.

'Joan,' I said into the radio as the fighters started lowering.

'Carmen. It's okay. It's my time,' Joan said as she paused to shoot her rifle into an infected grabbing the edge of the balcony. Then she turned the rifle and used it to club another one away before drawing her pistol to shoot two more. 'Howie, You listen to Henry. Let him guide you. And Henry?' She paused again to fire a few more rounds into the horde as the fighters levelled out. 'Howie is not a threat to you. He's young. Guide him.' A few more shouts as the fighter engines increased in pitch and we all stared up while knowing what was about to happen. 'Here we are then,' she said as she emptied her magazine and dropped the pistol. 'Gentlemen. Ladies. It's been an honour.'

She snapped a salute right there on the balcony staring down at us all. I saw Blowers salute back. Then Cookey and Nick. I did it. Henry and Frank. Clarence and Bash. All of us saluted. Not just for Joanie, but for the pilots in those fighters for what they were about to do. For what they had already done.

For the greatest generation this planet ever saw.

I wanted to close my eyes. I wanted to turn away and scream, but I held on, and I held my salute as I stared at Joanie as the Hurricane hit it at full speed. Exploding instantly with a wall of flame that blew the tower out and Joanie was gone from view.

Then the Spitfire dropped low to score along the length of the airfield with a stunning display of precision as the front prop eviscerated human forms in one long brutal bloody wake while the wings tore bodies in half. The plane rocked and tilted but held the course until it suddenly dropped and scored along the ground. Killing hundreds more before it exploded into flames that took swathes out.

The whole thing left us speechless, and it was only then that we realised the infected had all gone still and that either the Spitfire or the Hurricane had killed the CP.

Then another noise came up from behind and we all turned, feeling drunk and ruined, to see a fifty-cal burst firing from the back of a pick-up leading the way for a white school bus decked out with protective metal grills welded over the windows and wheels. I blinked at the arrowhead inverted snow-plough scoop fitted to the front that was pushing through the infected with ease while assault rifles fired out of window slots.

I JUST STARED AT IT. I couldn't move and the rain came down harder. Rinsing the blood from my face as I glanced back to see the tower was half gone. Torn off from the middle. I wanted to cry, but I had no moisture to give. I had nothing left to give.

The school bus stopped, and I saw the words **Christ's Hospital** written on the side. The doors opened, and several dozen kids came running out in PE kit and body armour and formed into firing lines before they began shooting controlled bursts into the infected as the pick-up drove closer, and Major Tilda Tanners stopped firing the fifty-cal.

'We've got the survivors, Marcy,' she called. 'Leave it with us. We'll take some and get the rest to the fort.'

'Thank you,' Marcy said as she dropped from the tank and stood amidst the ruins of another broken landscape. Fires and smoke. Bodies and spent rounds. Limbs torn off and the air thick with chemicals.

'And thank you for them,' Marcy said as she nodded at the old soldiers still snapping necks and stabbing throats.

'They weren't mine to give,' Tilda said. 'You asked and they accepted. Right. I suggest you fall back. We'll draw off and shoot the rest down.'

That was it.

It was over.

But it didn't feel right. It didn't feel right at all, and I looked around at the tens of thousands of dead bodies and turned with a wince to stare at the ruins of the north terminal then over to the broken tower, and none of it seemed real.

Reginald

It was done. It was over, and I lay in my van on the floor staring up at the monitor on my desk at the ruins of Gatwick, and I didn't know what to feel.

I'd seen Joan die and I didn't know how to feel.

Something Howie said came to my mind, that all we ever needed to win was Dave.

For all of my genius. For all of Howie's bravery. For all of Henry's training and experience.

All we ever needed was Dave and I looked upon the ruins of Gatwick and could see he'd killed tens of thousands in an instant. We didn't win that battle. Dave did.

I got up and opened my sliding door and stared out to see the horde that had attacked my van were all dead. Then I frowned and realised that Major Tanners had gone to help the survivors at the northeast point. And the old commandos had come in from the western end. Whereas I was on the southern edge.

So if it wasn't Major Tanners, and it wasn't Marcy, then who killed the infected outside of my van? I couldn't see sign of anyone. But I did see the cut marks on the bodies that indicated a sharp blade. But Dave and Mo were both with Howie.

It was a mystery, but right then I had no energy to give it greater thought.

We'd played the game and won, but Joan was dead and everyone else was hurt.

It was a victory, but it didn't feel like it.

4 7

Diary of Carmen Eze

IT WAS A MESS.

We were a mess, and I thought back to Hinchley Point. A place once famous for its Mediterranean architecture and white-washed walls.

It wasn't anymore.

It was another place of ruin and death in this brave new world.

Then I looked around at Gatwick. A place once famous as the busiest single runway airport in the world.

But that too was another place of ruin and death in this brave new world, and I stared up for few seconds and let the rain land on my face. Rain that came gently at first. Just a few spots. A light drizzle. But then it came down properly and within a few seconds I had my mouth open to let the pure clean waters pour in.

We all did the same. We all stood there and did nothing because we had *nothing* to give. No words. No energy. No thoughts even, and while the pick-up drove off, and the trained army cadets cut the rest of the horde down, we stood and let the rain soak our faces and bodies.

But time rolls on. I guess it always will, and after a while I lowered my head to see the terrible state we were in.

Danny's fingers. Mo's ear. Cookey's eye and the top of his arm. Nick's face. Blowers had deep bites over his neck and shoulders and cuts down his face. Howie was cut and bit. Paula was cut and bit. We were *all* cut and bit. Tappy's nose was bent, and her eyes were already going purple with bruises. Then I looked at Charlie. Her cheek was flayed open down to the bone and she was covered in lacerations and grazes with grit and glass sticking out of her arms and neck and just about everywhere. But she was still upright, and she looked regal and majestic with her head high and her back straight. Hurt, but not broken. Damaged, but not defeated.

Then I heard an intake of breath and turned to see Howie staring at Clarence's hand as more of us did the same and sucked air in at the sight of it.

'Mate,' Howie said, looking from the hand to Clarence.

'It'll be fine,' Clarence said. Hurt, but not broken. Damaged, but not defeated.

'Yeah, so I'm not a doctor,' Howie said with a grimace. 'But er...' he trailed off to look at Roy

'Yeah. I'm not a doctor either,' Roy said. 'But that needs to come off.'

'It's not coming off,' Clarence said.

'Mate. It needs to come off,' Howie said. 'It's literally hanging by a few tendons.'

'Just gaffer tape it. Dave, give me that tape.'

'You can't gaffer tape it! Dave, finish taping Danny's fingers. Clarence, seriously. Just cut it off,' Howie said.

'I'm not cutting my hand off.'

'Clarence. It has to come off,' Paula said.

'But I'm right-handed,' Clarence said.

'You *were* right-handed,' Frank said.

'I *am* right handed. Pass me the bloody gaffer tape.'

'How are you going to unwind it?' Howie asked. 'You've only got one hand. It needs to come off. Dave?'

'Don't you dare,' Clarence said as he spun away only to find Dave in front of him whipping out with his blade through the tendon as the hand dropped to the ground. 'You cut my hand off,' Clarence said in disbelief.

'Fuck, Dave! I meant pass the tape,' Howie said.

'You cut my hand off,' Clarence said again. 'You actually cut my hand off! I'M GONNA BLOODY KILL YOU!'

Clarence then went for Dave who stepped back and threw the tape at Clarence's head. 'There you go.'

'I'LL FUCKING KILL HIM!'

'Stop the dog!' Marcy then yelled as we all span back to see Meredith snaffling Clarence's hand up then pulling back with a low growl at us all looking at her.

'Nick! Get my hand out of your dog's mouth!'

'She's not my bloody dog!'

'Sod the hand, that needs cauterizing,' Roy said as the blood spurted from Clarence's stump.

'But we've got the virus thing. It'll scab over.'

'You're losing too much blood,' Henry said. 'Roy's right. It needs to be cauterized. There's enough fire here. Someone, grab something hot.'

'It has to be red hot,' Roy said as Mads and Booker ran off to drag a chunk of aircraft over the ground. One half of it burning with flame, and the metal glowing red.

'Right. Grab him,' Henry said. 'Come on, lads. Get in here.'

'He doesn't need to be grabbed,' Paula said as she walked over to stand in front of Clarence. 'It needs to be done. Okay?'

He nodded as she reached up to loop a hand around his neck and guided him down onto his knees as she did the same and pressed her forehead to his while she held his forearm out. 'We'll get a freezer truck,' she said softly as Henry and Roy dragged the flaming debris closer. 'Just you and me,' Paula said as Clarence closed his eyes and nodded gently. 'We'll sit and shiver all night. Just you and me. It's going to be okay. I've got you.'

He tensed when they pressed the stump into the flames near the glowing edge of the metal and the air filled with the stench and sizzle of burning meat, but Clarence didn't say a word. He didn't scream or cry out. He couldn't. His lips were pressed to Paula's.

And that kiss kept going when they let his arm go and so we stood in that place of ruin and death where Joan gave her life for ours. Where we gave everything we could to protect the lives of people we never knew. People that were too stupid to flee and run when they were told.

But they were our species, and in order for the Panacea to stand a chance against the virus enough people had to survive to receive it.

That's why we were there. Because that was the game, and that was the hunt, and as much as we moaned and bickered and suffered the heat and hurt, we were all in it.

By fuck we were in it.

All the way to the bitter end.

48

A small town with a single road running through the centre. An old pub with a thatched roof to one side. A small supermarket opposite. The windows broken.

Rows of thatched cottages stretch off along leafy lanes on one side while on the other the newer properties stand in all their ubiquitous glory. Small gardens and small houses. White UPVC windows and white UPVC doors.

Suburbia in all its sterile glory.

An idyllic home counties market town filled with idyllic homes where people existed while trapped in cycles of life that never changed. Waiting to live and waiting to die and then regretting it all when the end came.

And the end did come.

It came twenty nine days ago when the world fell to a pandemic and society ceased to exist, and with it the loss of law and order and the ability to get medicine.

That was the problem for Edith. She ran out of medicine a few days ago. The government used to let patients with chronic illnesses build stockpiles in case of supply problems, but new laws and new regulations put a stop to that.

And so, a few days ago, she had no more medicine to take, and her heart grew weak. But then she was old. She'd reached ninety-five. She'd lived through the Second World War.

So did Bert. He'd fought in the war. He lied about his age and enlisted. But then he was always big and strong for his age. Even now at the age of ninety-nine he still has enough strength to push the wheeled bed out through the front door.

Edith always said she liked the rain.

'Bert. When I go. I want to be out there in the rain. I want to feel it on my skin.'

It was raining as he grunted and struggled to get the heavy bed down the garden path and over the weeds that were already growing thick and fast.

It was hard work, but then his own body was dying too. From the pills he took washed down with brandy. The nice one from the liquor cupboard.

'You and that brandy,' Edith always said. 'That's your thing, Bert. Mine is the rain. I want to go out under the rain, but you can drink that bloody horrible stuff when you go.'

Bert thought that was a good idea at the time, but he did wish he'd waited until *after* he'd got the bloody bed out of the bloody house and down the bloody garden.

But then his plan came unstuck, because the wheeled bed the hospice had provided, wouldn't fit through the garden gate. It was too wide, and that made Bert sad because the big willows and oaks he'd nurtured for the last fifty years had grown so big and spread so far they were blotting the rain out.

'Bugger,' he said as he sagged on the spot and looked down at the beautiful face of his wife of more nearly seventy years, and a great sadness came over Bert that Edith would never get to feel the rain as she slipped away.

Then he heard a noise. An engine. Low and throaty, but not sounding so clean. Bert worked with engines all his life, and that one had clogged filters no doubt.

It got closer, but the night had come, and the low cloud made it dark and so he couldn't quite see it until it came into view a good twenty metres away. Driving slow and chugging. A squat military vehicle covered in dead bugs and maybe dead other things.

Bert frowned at it as the vehicle stopped and he heard the sound of doors opening and boots crunching on the road, and he stood and waited until two men came forward close enough to see.

One older and lean and with a bald head. Cuts on his face. Bruises and marks. An assault rifle strapped to his chest.

One younger with curly dark hair and a face covered in scars and cuts, but he looked kind.

They both did.

'Are you okay?' the older one asked.

Bert nodded then looked at Edith then back to the two soldiers.

'It's raining,' the younger one said.

Bert nodded again while from somewhere nearby they heard a howl and a screech. The things were close. Bert had heard them for the last few days.

The two men looked out as Bert heard more boots crunching and more men and women with guns came forward into the light. All of them cut and bit. All of them hurt, but not broken.

'My Edith,' Bert said as the older man with the bald head spotted the medals on Bert's old tunic and the stitched stripes on his arm. 'She liked the rain. But I can't get her out. The gate, see. It's too narrow.'

The two men looked at the gate then at Edith as a giant of a man loomed over them. His right wrist wrapped tight in gaffer tape.

The younger man nodded. He understood. 'We can carry the bed out.'

Bert nodded and the young man motioned with his head for others to come into the garden. A lad with blond hair smiled at Bert. His eye was swollen. Another one with an eye-patch. A black lad. One of them mixed race. A young woman with a shaved head. More of them. The big man too. They all came inside, and they all took hold of the wheeled bed to lift it over the gate and out into the road so the rain could fall on Edith's face.

Bert went after her as a beautiful young woman took his arm and smiled as she helped him over to the bed.

Bert hesitated and looked at them all as the drugs and the booze sank into his system and made his eyes grow heavy and his legs grow weak.

'Do you want to go inside?' the beautiful woman asked.

'Edith,' Bert said. 'I'll stay with my Edith.'

He tried to get on the bed, but his legs were too weak, and his body was too frail. He started to slip but hands caught him and helped him up.

Another woman pulled the blanket from Edith as Bert cuddled into her side the way they'd done every night for over seventy years, and he felt it when the blanket was pulled back up.

Then the things howled again. They screeched out and Bert lifted his head with a look of worry in his drowsy eyes.

'You sleep, sergeant,' the older man with the bald head said. 'We'll stand watch.'

Bert wanted to tell them not to fuss and that they must be busy, but he was suddenly too tired and anyway. That rain was nice after the last few weeks of that unbearable heat.

He cuddled into Edith and kissed her cheek and inhaled the scent of the woman he'd loved for his whole life, and as the rain fell and the soldiers moved out to stand in a circle around his bed there in the street of that quiet little town, he closed his eyes and slipped away from this brave new world.

THEY STAYED FOR A LONG TIME. Those soldiers in that street of that quiet little town. Bruised. Cut. Bit and hurt.

But not broken.

They kept watch because it was the right thing to do. Because there was nobody else to do it.

Just them.

Just those few.

THE UNDEAD TWENTY-FIVE. THE HEAT

And a small man with glasses stood his corner with his swatter in his hand and he felt the rain pattering down on his head and he stared out into the darkness while knowing that was the game, and by then, they were all in.

By fuck they were in it.

All the way to the bitter end.

49

Day Twenty-nine

IT WAS a distance for Heather and Paco to walk in that heat, and they couldn't go back through the safari park, so that meant walking all the way around to reach their SUV.

'Those poor wolves,' Heather said as she came to a stop after a good ten minutes of fast walking to burn the rage away. The rage inside that made her shout at Howie, but she needed to vent and express what was inside, and perhaps, on some level, Howie needed to hear it.

Heather wasn't sure about that. But that rage eased back enough for rational thought to creep back in, and with it a surge of guilt that they'd left one of the wolves on its own.

Which is why she stopped to look at Paco and without a word being said they both sighed and turned to go back.

But the wolf wasn't there. Only the dead tigers, and the other two dead wolves. Only blood and gore and more carnage for the flies and rats to feast on. Nor was there any sign of Howie and the others.

She tried to radio them to ask if they'd taken the wolf, and, you know, to say *hey* after the things that were said. But the radio wouldn't work. The filthy waters from the lake maybe. The heat or the radio being dropped and bashed around in the stampede and the attack after.

'Whatever,' she said with another sigh as they once more turned and walked that long hot route back to their SUV, and so it was with some great relief that they slumped into the seats, started the engine, and then sat in silence for several minutes as the air-conditioning slowly reduced the temperature within the car.

They'd left the windows open to try and avoid it becoming like an oven, but it was still oppressively hot. Hotter than either of them had ever known.

'Zade?' Paco said, holding a bottle out. She grunted and took it to drink, and the car filled with the sound of them both guzzling down the sugary contents until Heather lowered the bottle with a belch. Then Paco did the same. Belching from the gas. Both of them drenched in sweat. Battered and bruised. Filthy and torn. There in the SUV in that oppressive heat.

Which is when the third belch came from the back, followed by the sound of rummaging and motion, and something moving. Something that was in the car waiting for them to return.

They moved fast with both drawing pistols to aim at the red macaw on the back seat preening an outstretched wing for several long seconds before it turned to look at the two filthy faces glaring at it. 'Who threw that?' it asked in perfect mimicry of Heather as the two pistols lowered and the two faces turned to look at each other.

They didn't need to say anything. Heather drove while Paco split a bottle to make a well of water for the bird to drink from as the car left Stickleton and got back out into the countryside. Away from the death and carnage and once more back to their barn on the hill.

They washed under the hose and scrubbed down with anti-bac. They drank water and cleaned their weapons in the shade while the bird explored the barn and flew up into the rafters. But Heather noticed it never strayed far for long. It flew outside at one point and went high into the air on the thermals. They stood in the grass shielding their eyes while thinking it would fly off and never return.

But it was back within minutes. Back to mimicking Heather and eating nuts and fruit.

Who threw that?

They need food!

'Jesus. Does it ever stop talking?'

Fuck off!

They didn't leave the barn again because the heat got so bad that simply existing became hard work. It was like the air had become charged and the pressure in the sky was crushing them. Even the bird fell silent. They all did.

Heather felt the tension inside too. That thing that told her the others were in trouble. But without the radio working she had no idea where they were.

Eventually the sky grew heavy and dark, and the thunder started tumbling deep and long, and the sky flashed with arcs of light. They heard a distant explosion at one point, but from where or by what she did not know.

Then finally the rain came, and the heat eased enough for them to settle in and grow drowsy. Paco drew the barn door closed and with only a small fire to give light they lay back on beds of straw covered with blankets and listened to the thunder rolling overhead while the parrot murmured quiet words as Paco gently rubbed its head.

Then the night came. The night proper, and the rain fell upon the barn roof. Giving a song of sorts that helped them drift into sleep until they heard a single word whispered by the macaw.

'Bear.'

A word that had them both up on their feet reaching for assault rifles with hearts thumping in chests. The fire burning low. The noise of the rain still falling on the roof.

Heather glanced to the bird. 'Don't fuck about,' she whispered as it hopped from foot to foot and swung its head side to side.

'Bear,' the parrot said again. Low and quiet. A whisper and nothing more. A breath of air but a word they'd already come to know.

The things had found them. The infected were outside.

A silent nod shared. Paco heaved the door open as Heather aimed into the pitch-dark night and the rain still coming down. Waiting for the charge. Waiting for the howls and screeches.

A pair of eyes glimpsed in the darkness from the light of the fire. The glowing eyes of a creature that tracked them for a long distance.

A creature that had no place else to go.

They didn't say anything. They just stared at the wolf sitting outside in the rain. Alone for the first time in life. Alone and lonely. His head low. His soul crushed.

They still didn't say anything, but instead they retreated to their blankets to lay down to rest and listen to the rain falling upon the barn roof. Giving a song of sorts that helped them drift into sleep until they heard a single low word almost whispered by the macaw.

'Bear.'

And in the faint light of that barn, Heather caught glimpse of the wolf curled up next to the fire with its tail over its nose and those glowing yellow eyes staring fixed at her.

Glowing yellow eyes that didn't blink as hers grew heavy and outside, the rain fell in the pitch-dark night of a brave new world.

50

Day Twenty-nine

'Thank you! Settle down please. I've just got a quick update for everyone then you can get back to your evening.'

The conference room fell to silence as Alistair Appleton, the honourable Member of Parliament for Westminster called out. But then he was the Head Chair and so it was only right the others should go quiet when he asked.

'Right. Well. We are here because today marks the end of day twenty-nine, which, I am sure we all know, means we have successfully reached the completion of the first month in our brave new world. Eh? Round of applause I'd say. That's right. End of the first month,' he said as the people gathered about the table clapped while those on the screen did the same. Some of which, Alistair noted, were doing so with decidedly less energy than the others. But that was to be expected. Especially given the circumstances of how it all came about. Not that Alistair cared one bit that it was early, and if anything, he was glad the release date was brought forward as it saved him from some embarrassing, and potentially career ending, questions concerning his finances, and specifically, his sudden wealth. Oh, and that thing with his daughter being kidnapped too. But the greedy slut probably arranged that herself.

'Yes, well done, all,' he said to quieten the applause. 'Let's get this over then we can go for a drink. Sound good? Eh? Right. The outward laying stations have sent their boys and girls out to poke about. Sorry. I should use the correct terms. The *forward operating bases* have deployed their initial reconnaissance patrols, that the correct wording, Colonel?' he asked with a glance to one of the screens showing Colonel 'Mary' Poppins staring out into the conference room.

'I'm sure we all know what you mean, Minister,' she said without expression.

'Thank you. Anyway. As I was saying. The first patrols have had a look around, and I think it is safe to say the results are what we expected with a ninety nine percent rate of infection. That's right. Yes,' he added to a few murmurs. 'Tragic stuff but there we go, and it *was* what we were expecting. There are pockets of survivors. As we predicted there would be. Mostly in fortified locations. I believe our North-East FOB observed a high-security prison in good use, and North-West FOB have reported Chester Castle is being put to use by some locals, and SEFOB have reported that Spitbank fort is in use. That one came through you didn't it, Colonel?'

'It did,' Mary said as she detected those in the room wanted more information. 'SEFOB had a brief OP set up in a neighbouring boatyard overlooking the area and observed a concerted effort being made to fortify the location using shipping containers.'

'I think somewhere else saw shipping containers being used,' Alistair said. 'Scotland maybe? Or was it in France? Damned if I can remember. But yes. I should image we may find more fortified places in time, and of course, we may discover those fortified places have become overrun as this whole thing plays out. But that does lead me onto the weather. I'm sure you're all aware of the storms. They've had a significant impact on the geographical landscape with substantial damage reported from all areas. Every town and city has been affected. Fire damage is significant, as is structural damage. Flooding too, but we knew the weather patterns would be altered, and the prediction is the weather patterns will continue to be significantly different going forward. But at least it hasn't prompted an ice age. Eh? Imagine that. Blizzards everywhere in August.'

'Er, just to jump in here,' someone said from the side of the table. 'We don't actually know what impact the cessation of humanity will have on the weather, so we can't actually an ice age *won't* happen. Even a small one.'

'Right,' Alistair said. 'Never make a weather joke with a meteorologist in the room. Anyway. I wanted to give you all the idea of the bigger picture. We're almost one month in now, and I think, unless command heads have any different input, that we're largely on track for what we expected. That brings us to the next stage, which is intel gathering and getting the boys and girls out from our FOB's to see what's what and help us build a bigger picture going forward.'

'We need to start gathering the immunes, Alistair.'

Alistair cut off to smile and nod at Gudipta Patel. The honourable Member of Parliament for Islington. An Indian woman of stern countenance and a high-ranking shadow cabinet member for the Labour Party who sat on the same select committees as Alistair did in his role of Conservative Party minister for the Treasury Department.

'That was on the original manifesto was it not?' Gudipta asked. 'We hunker down for the first month to let the initial devastation play out, and then we start gathering immunes.'

'No. That's not technically correct, Gudipta. We said once the first month was passed we would *assess* the suitability of starting to gather the immunes. Which is exactly what we are doing,' Alistair replied.

'We need to ensure we adhere to the timetable as prescribed,' Gudipta cut in. 'We've all put our lives on hold for this.'

'We've done more than put them on bloody hold,' someone else muttered.

'And I am sure we will,' Alistair said with a nod to Gudipta while thinking he might snort some coke off her back when he bends her over later. Alistair did have a thing for young men for a long time. But there's something about Gudipta. The whole *opposing political parties feuding enemies* thing makes it all very sordid and sexy.

'Anyway. Sorry. Where was I? Er, right. Well, I think that'll do for now. Go and enjoy your evening. We'll keep you in the loop with events, it's not like we've got anywhere else to go, is it? Yes. Bad joke. My apologies. Thank you all. Bye then!'

A moment or two passed for the others to file out, apart from one man holding back in his seat while on the screens only Colonel Poppy remained while Alistair sealed the door and returned to his own seat with a heavy sigh.

'Right. Go on then. Spit it out,' he ordered while glancing through the glass door of the ultra-modern underground complex to the backside of Gudipta Singh walking away.

Colonel Poppins cleared her throat with a glance to the other man.

'Oh god, she's clearing her throat,' Alistair said with an eye-roll. 'Is it that bad?'

'As the report details, Minister,' Mary said. 'SEFOB sent a patrol out. They were checking a weapons cache on the coast.'

'Where?'

'Hinchley Point. It's in the report.'

'That's the old Italian town, isn't it?'

'It was,' Mary says.

'What do you mean it *was*? Have the storms destroyed it?'

Mary paused, knowing full well that he hadn't read the report. But then ministers never do read the reports. They expect minions to do that for them and feed them the key points. 'SEFOB sent a patrol out yesterday, Minister. They were tasked to conduct reconnaissance, in addition to checking a few key sites. One of which was…'

'Get to the point, Mary!'

'One of which was to check a weapons cache, where they fired upon by an unknown group.'

'This is the woman. Right?' Alistair asked, pointing from Mary to the other man in the room. 'And what's that got to do with Hinchley Point being totalled by a storm?'

Ministers do that too. They get details wrong on purpose to keep people jarred and uncomfortable.

'The SEFOB patrol left the area, Minister,' Mary said. 'Their orders being not to engage. However, they did return early this morning and have reported the town of Hinchley Point has been destroyed.'

'It's like pulling teeth,' Alistair muttered while rubbing his face. 'By what? By a storm? By a whale leaping from the Ocean? Aliens? Avalanche? By what method was this town destroyed?'

'By war, Minister,' the other man in the room said.

'Good god. That's rather dramatic,' Alistair said, giving him a look. 'What kind of war? General warfare, or perhaps the war on drugs?'

'Minister,' Mary cut in. 'That is how the report details the findings. They said the town looked like a warzone with evidence of mortars and the use of a heavy machine gun in addition to multiple small arms. The team leader stated it appeared a concerted, trained, and disciplined stand had been made against a very sizable attack from infected hosts numbering in excess of twenty thousand. That, in itself, is of note. But added to the contact the patrol had earlier in the day from-.'

'Hang on. The woman. What was her name again?'

'Carmen Eze,' the other man said.

'That was it,' Alistair said while clicking his fingers. 'She's highly-trained, then is she?'

'Carmen is one of the most effective agents this country has ever had,' the other man said.

'I see. Or rather, I don't see. What's all the concern for? One woman chopping down a few infected doesn't prompt a secret meeting like this, especially when I've got Gudipta scrutinising every move I make. Chances are that this Carmen has rallied a few young squaddies and got them fighting back, or are you worried about who she might be with? Yes? You're worried she's with her old team. See. You lot think we never read our reports. Ah, I won't lie. I never read it. Somebody told me the key points. Anyway. Tell me again. But quickly.'

'If she's with Henry,' the man said

THE UNDEAD TWENTY-FIVE. THE HEAT

'Major Henry Campbell-Dillington,' Alistair said as he reminded both of them that a sharp mind lay beneath the bluster and bluff. 'Formerly of the Parachute Regiment, The Special Air Service and latterly CO of a clandestine deniable ops unit hiding within the department of fiscal studies. That Henry? Is that the one? Or are you worried about his right hand man, George? Or Frank McGill? Or perhaps this Carmen Eze running around with some squaddies. That right, is it? Four people? You're worried about four people in the midst of this shit. Whom, I might add, are probably all dead. Did you even have confirmation it was Carmen Eze?' he snapped the question out when the man and Colonel Poppins both tried to cut in. 'Did you get a picture? No? A black woman then. A black woman shot at one of your soldiers. Oh, and this being the highly-trained unit that lost the fucking scientist! The one that ran off with our fucking list.'

'Alistair,' the man said.

'Head Chair!' Alistair snapped at him.

'We just thought you should know,' Mary cut in.

'Great! Do I need to know if the fucking toilets block up? We're in a highly fortified secret underground bunker in the centre of London. What the hell is this Henry going to do? Sneak in and tell us off? The games of old spies are gone.'

'Minister-.'

'What part of saying Head Chair is difficult for you? Okay. Listen. Let's wind this down. I get it. You're bored. You need to prove you still have relevancy. No! Don't speak over me. You've played your part. And for that we are thankful, and you have your place. You don't need to invent dangers to prove you are needed. And I get it. I do! I know you lost your children, but I lost mine too. My darling Cassie was the love of my life, but we must push on and strive to be a better society. And I know you need to feel involved, and you will be once we get going. But right now, there isn't anything happening. So sit back and enjoy the time off. Eh? Right. Good work. Now. I must get on. I have a country to run. Albeit one with a much smaller population than a month ago. Ah, apologies. Bad joke given the chat about our dead children. Yes. Poor taste. Stay sane and keep your eyes on the prize. That's what I always say.'

They watched him go and sat in silence as the glass door to ultra-modern underground bunker sealed shut behind him.

'Are you worried?' Mary eventually asked the other man while staring at his dark eyes through the screen on her desk.

'No. No I think it will be alright. But keep me in the loop would you, Mary? I don't think the PM will.'

'Of course. Speak soon,' Mary said while reaching out to cut the feed, but she paused to think for a second. 'And he's not the PM, Howard. He's Head Chair. Didn't you get the memo? This is the new world order.'

She blinked out leaving Howard alone in the conference room with his dark, brooding eyes staring at nothing while inside the worry gnawed at his gut because you don't leave someone like Henry to chance.

Not in any world, even if it is a brave new one.

ALSO BY RR HAYWOOD

A Town Called Discovery

The #1 Amazon Time Travel Thriller

A man falls from the sky. He has no memory.

What lies ahead are a series of tests. Each more brutal than the last, and if he gets through them all, he might just reach A Town Called Discovery.

EXTRACTED SERIES

EXTRACTED

EXECUTED

EXTINCT

Blockbuster Time-Travel

#1 Amazon US

#1 Amazon UK

#1 Audible US & UK

Washington Post & WSJ Best-seller

In 2061, a young scientist invents a time machine to fix a tragedy in his past. But his good intentions turn catastrophic when an early test reveals something unexpected: the end of the world.

A desperate plan is formed. Recruit three heroes, ordinary humans capable of extraordinary things, and change the future.

Safa Patel is an elite police officer, on duty when Downing Street comes under terrorist attack. As armed men storm through the breach, she dispatches them all.

'Mad' Harry Madden is a legend of the Second World War. Not only did he complete

an impossible mission—to plant charges on a heavily defended submarine base—but he also escaped with his life.

Ben Ryder is just an insurance investigator. But as a young man he witnessed a gang assaulting a woman and her child. He went to their rescue, and killed all five.

Can these three heroes, extracted from their timelines at the point of death, save the world?

THE CODE SERIES

The Worldship Humility

The Elfor Drop

#1 Audible bestselling smash hit narrated by Colin Morgan, star of Merlin & Humans.

#1 Amazon bestselling Science-Fiction

"A rollicking, action packed space adventure…"

"Best read of the year!"

"An original and exceptionally entertaining book."

"A beautifully written and humorous adventure."

Sam, an airlock operative, is bored. Living in space should be full of adventure, except it isn't, and he fills his time hacking 3-D movie posters.

Petty thief Yasmine Dufont grew up in the lawless lower levels of the ship, surrounded by violence and squalor, and now she wants out. She wants to escape to the luxury of the Ab-Spa, where they eat real food instead of rats and synth cubes.

Meanwhile, the sleek-hulled, unmanned Gagarin has come back from the ever-continuing search for a new home. Nearly all hope is lost that a new planet will ever be found, until the Gagarin returns with a code of information that suggests a habitable planet has been found. This news should be shared with the whole fleet, but a few rogue captains want to colonise it for themselves.

When Yasmine inadvertently steals the code, she and Sam become caught up in a dangerous game of murder, corruption, political wrangling and...porridge, with sex-addicted Detective Zhang Woo hot on their heels, his own life at risk if he fails to get the code back.

THE UNDEAD SERIES

THE UK's #1 HORROR SERIES

AVAILABLE ON AMAZON & AUDIBLE

"The Best Series Ever..."

The Undead. The First Seven Days
The Undead. The Second Week.
The Undead Day Fifteen.
The Undead Day Sixteen.
The Undead Day Seventeen
The Undead Day Eighteen
The Undead Day Nineteen
The Undead Day Twenty
The Undead Day Twenty-One
The Undead Twenty-Two
The Undead Twenty-Three: The Fort
The Undead Twenty-Four: Equilibrium
The Undead Twenty-Five: The Heat

Blood on the Floor
An Undead novel

Blood at the Premiere

An Undead novel

The Camping Shop

An Undead novella

THE FOUR WORLDS OF BERTIE CAVENDISH

A rip-roaring multiverse time-travel crossover starring:

The Undead

Extracted.

A Town Called Discovery

and featuring

The Worldship Humility

---

www.rrhaywood.com

Find me on Facebook:

https://www.facebook.com/RRHaywood/

Find me on Twitter:

https://twitter.com/RRHaywood

Printed in Great Britain
by Amazon